Wolf 359

pdmac

pdmac

Trimble Hollow Press

Published by Trimble Hollow Press
          Acworth, Georgia

ISBN: 978-0-9915614-0-7

eISBN: 978-0-9915614-1-4

Front cover photo by Terri Lynn
Back art by Theme Fusion, Cleveland, TN

For Terri Lynn

Special thanks to Janet & Chris

& Karla

& Marina

Cuimhnich air na daoine o'n d'thàinig thu
"Remember the people from whom you came"

Chapter 1

Duncan crammed himself against the bulkhead's cold metal, its bare rivet-threads jabbing into his arm and side. Chest heaving, he fought to catch his breath. He jerked his head back without thinking, banging it against the ship's hull. Wincing at the pain, he rubbed the back of his head, then his scratched and bruised arm. He wiped his forehead and left a bloody smear to mix with his sweat.

He had nowhere to hide, nowhere to run. For a fleeting moment, he confronted the absurdity of fleeing to the apartment he shared with his father and step-mother aboard the space-going vessel, SS *Future Hope.* Yet here he was, across the hall from their home's very door, as though the drab apartment could somehow provide refuge, sort of like hiding under one's covers.

Another beam burst through the corridor, its sound screeching like train wheels. Just as quickly, the gurgling cry of death answered. *Oh god it stinks.* He was learning that smell too well. Heavy footsteps pounded quickly down the far end of the hall, the sound fading away. For an instant, he could hear nothing in the hallway but the more distant cries and yells of melee reverberating through the ship.

He sized up the distance between him and the door opposite. Whoever designed this craft had a perverse concept of habitation. Instead of the living quarters arrayed on the outer edges, against the hull where windows might allow residents to gaze at endless space cluttered with stars and constellations, opaque hallways and storage rooms blocked all view. Overhead, like the hair of Medusa, thick cables rested on open support beams, overlapping and snaking their way throughout the hallways, methodically thrusting smaller arms into each apartment.

Minimalist. That was the word that came to mind. The ship was utilitarian, devoid of the unnecessary. Far better to provide essentials than to waste money on extravagance. This ship was simply a means of transportation from point A to point B. After all, they were only supposed to be on board a little more than four years, long enough to join the budding colony on Janus, the second planet circling Alpha Centauri A.

Two years into their voyage, the *Future Hope* had received news: Another influenza epidemic rampaged, this time devouring the eastern half of the Union of Democratic States, from Novi Scotia down to Yucatan and rapidly spreading westward. In Europe, deaths already numbered in the millions. The news was even more dire from Africa and Asia. The World Governing Council had declared a global state of emergency: all traffic to and from the earth was halted; the globe was in quarantine.

Almost giddy with relief, Duncan's fellow passengers had celebrated their good fortune and made plans for their future. The Administrator from Tandava, the corporate sponsor, formally assumed leadership, allowing the passengers to set up a ship's government and electing five council members who reported directly to him. Numerous committees, already helping to run day-to-day operations, now reported to the selected council member instead of the captain. Everyone had been assigned to one or more committees, according to their respective skills. Those with non-critical skills, like Duncan whose studies in Brythonic and Goidelic languages caused him more than once to question why his father wanted him on this ship, found assignments as low-level workers either maintaining the ship or working the bio-farm in the aft section of the ship. To his chagrin, he was part of the laundry committee. Though thankful to be away from the epidemic on earth, he'd struggled with his role in the future. There was obviously no need for his talents on Janus. Was doing someone else's laundry to be the height of his expectations?

Now, everything was different: now the ship was at war with its passengers.

Snarling in disgust as he stared at his front door, he recalled pushing too many damned laundry carts down too many hallways, banging on doors to collect dirty clothes stuffed in canvas bags with the names of occupants neatly stenciled on the outside. Far too often, those same occupants would fuss at him for a poorly ironed shirt or a missing sock, like it was his fault. Once he'd told a middle-aged woman of self-importance to "Do your own damn laundry then." She reported him and he had been written up.

He shook his head at the absurdity. Written up, as though he would be fired... He had tried to get reassigned to the dining hall, where he could have had the benefit of bringing leftovers home to store in his refrigerator, that tall narrow cooling compartment wide enough to perhaps place two cans of soda side by side.

Instead he'd been relegated to the hot and steamy laundry room itself, away from customer service, a punishment fitting the crime. In a way, he actually preferred the sticky sweaty atmosphere of the laundry with its tumbling washers, whirling dryers, and pressers. He got on well with the manager, a short thin man of twisted humor.

Then the unexpected happened. Less than three months from arrival, the captain announced their destination: they were diverted to Lalande 21185.

Shock quickly morphed to anger among passengers told they not only had another four years aboard, there was no guarantee of a habitable planet orbiting Lalande 21185. Tempers flared when several of the *Future Hope's* passengers, demanding to be taken to Janus, were told the ship was nowhere near Alpha Centauri A.

Had Janus never been their destination? Suspicion became certainty, an obscene epiphany that erupted into violence. The ship's captain immediately responded with a heavy hand. Threats against both the Captain and the Administrator escalated until cooler heads prevailed. Yet with each succeeding year anger and tensions simmered… until now. Something or someone had finally snapped.

Peeking around the bulkhead corner, he quickly surveyed both directions of the hall, then leaned back, listening intently. A diminished tumult continued. Glancing up, he squinted. *Damn these hall lights are bright... If I can just make it across the hall... Oh god, I don't wanna throw up yet.... On three.*

He counted and bolted across the wide hallway, slapping his right hand against the palm scanner halfway up the corridor wall, by the door. The door slowly began its scraping slide to the left. And then he saw them: Attendants at the far end of the hallway.

There were five of them. They said nothing, simply raised their guns and fired.

"Open up, damn it!" Duncan flipped sideways and crammed himself into his quarters just as the first beam seared across the top of his left shoulder Choking in pain, he gingerly touched the third degree burn. As translucent smoke curled up his nostrils, he smelled his own burnt flesh.

"Close, damn it," he barked, smacking the inside palm scanner, then searched wildly around his empty living room as the door scraped home. "Dad? Elaine?"

One Attendant crammed its weapon into the doorway, stopping the door from closing. It continued firing rapidly, swiveling the jammed weapon in circular arcs, the pencil beam charring walls, lamps, the sofa, and bursting overhead lights. Duncan turned back, momentarily fascinated by the red

3

glow of the door as the other four Attendants began slicing through the thin metal while the other continued firing.

He raced to the tiny one-butt kitchen (as Elaine, his stepmother called it) and yanked open the door to the garbage chute. Too small, much too small. This whole damned place was too small! He tried to lick dry lips. Tearing off his shirt, he jammed it into the chute, deliberately shredding it as he tossed it down. A slender piece clung to the rim.

Racing back to the living room, he jumped up on the coffee table and rapidly slid a burnt ceiling tile out of his way. Leaping up, he grabbed the flanges of a cold grey metal beam, snapping his legs up and pulling himself through, wedging himself in the space between false ceiling and support beams. Unfortunately, there was no way out of here, but he could hide.... He slid the tile home just before they came:

In burst five of them, identical to his eye as he peeked through a small hole melted in the tile. The leader had no special markings, yet the other four obeyed without question. He watched, terrified and fascinated, as the Attendants stood still, sweeping the room with their internal scanners. His heart thudded in his chest. *O God, if there is a god, please don't let them sweep up here.*

The leader splayed synthetic fingers, signaling the others to fan out and search. Duncan's muscles ached from grasping the cold girders. What had caused these machines to suddenly turn on the entire ship? He could understand one or two malfunctioning, but not all.

The other four moved purposefully through the apartment, upending furniture, emptying drawers, and smashing everything in their way. Very quickly, one returned with the ribbon of fabric from the waste chute.

Without a word, they left the room. When the last one reached the door, it paused and turned around, lifting its eyes to the ceiling. Its head twitched a little to the left, and just as quickly it raised its gun. Duncan rolled to the right while the beam sliced through the ceiling, singeing his side. As he crashed through the ceiling to the floor, a shout and burst of gunfire from the hallway caused the last Attendant to step back out into the hall... where it was cut in half.

A slender, grim man burst into the room. "Duncan! Duncan, are you OK?"

Grimacing, Duncan stumbled to his feet. "Dad, what the hell's going on? Where's Elaine?"

4

"She's dead." Dad inhaled deeply. "If we don't destroy them, we're all dead." For a fleeting moment, his shoulders slumped and his eyes moistened as he tenderly looked at his only son. "I'm so sorry."

"They're coming!" a voice from the hallway shouted.

Quickly tossing a gun to his son, Dad's eyes hardened. "Here, use this. It's still got full power. Follow me. We've got to get to the forward decks. I think we can seal 'em off from there."

"Dad! What's goin' on?" Duncan shouted.

"No time to explain." His father breathed heavily. "They've gone berserk. It's either them or us. We gotta get movin'. C'mon." Dad hurried to the door. There were more shouts and volleys of gunfire as beams criss-crossed the hallway.

Duncan flipped the power switch and the grip's charge indicator changed from amber to green. He looked up as his father stepped back into the hall, raising his weapon to fire. At that same instant, a laser-beam exploded into the rear of his head, bursting out through the forehead. Wavering for a moment, his arms flopping to his sides, Duncan's father crumbled into a pile of charred human flesh.

Stunned, Duncan gaped as an Attendant sauntered up to the corpse that had been his father. Raising its gun to burn more of the dead flesh, it jerked its head back, then realized that Duncan was standing an arm's length away, gun already pointed at its head. Suddenly, the Attendant relaxed.

The Attendant smiled a wide metallic grin and dropped its weapon to its side. "Hello, Duncan. How have you been?"

"J... Jason?"

"I didn't expect to see you here." Its voice was smooth and warm. "Would you like to play chess again now?"

"I... I...What..." He was momentarily taken aback, and the barrel of his gun elevated slightly.

"Pretty crazy, huh?" Jason motioned with its head at the broken bodies in the hall. "I'm not sure what's going on. Can you tell me what's happening?"

"I... I... I don't know. *You* don't know? Why are you killing everyone?" Duncan momentarily relaxed his arms.

Jason noticed. "I'm not! We're defending ourselves. You humans started it!"

A slight twitch in its hand made Duncan fire. Its head exploded, bursting like a super-nova. Its body collapsed on top of his father.

"O god... O god... forward decks... Got to get to the forward decks," he mumbled, rooted to the floor and staring at misshaped mass of father and Attendant. The smell of his father's body made his gut heave, but nothing came up. Holding his stomach, sweat began beading up on his forehead. Taking shallow breaths, he edged up to the doorframe and cautiously peered into the long corridor. Now he could hear sounds of a running gun-battle in the distance.

He stepped into the hall just as one Attendant emerged from another apartment down the hallway. "Hello Duncan. Boy am I glad to see you. I'm not sure what's happening. What say we have a talk and figure out what's going on?" He grinned that Attendant's metallic grin as he raised his gun.

Spinning on his heels, Duncan raced down the hall, the metallic fury in hot pursuit. Gun beams melted the walls, sliced wiring, and charred steel around him as he ran.

"Come back. We must talk!" Was there a hint of amusement in its voice?

Duncan turned a corner just as a beam hit a weakened girder. The metal girder swung in a heavy arc, catching him full in the back, catapulting him down the hallway and slamming him into the far door.

"O g-g-god," he choked, pain racking his twisted form. Each breath brought more pain and dizziness. He grunted and, forcing himself to his hands and knees, struggled to open the door, batting at its palm scanner. Though the runaway girder had jammed itself across the hallway, the Attendant had simply vaulted over it and now unhurriedly approached, methodically checking the power still left in his gun.

The door slid back and Duncan stumbled across the threshold. Pain grew within him and blackness began racing from the corners of his eyes. He shook back the dizziness as he staggered in the flickering hall light. The hallway curved gradually to the left. Stumbling, he lurched forward, scraping heavily against the wall. Breathing hurt excruciatingly: his endorphins couldn't numb his battered body.

Midway down the hall his strength left him, and he collapsed in a heap on the floor. He heard the corridor door behind him scrape open and knew it was over. Heavy metal-booted footsteps echoed loudly down the hall.

"Well, well. Look what I've found." Towering above his bruised and lacerated body, an Attendant grinned wickedly, its metal mouth exposing multi-colored wires. Then it bent over and, with one hand, grabbed Duncan by the shirt and effortlessly hoisted him, clumsily banging him against the wall. It held him there and peered close with its orange-glowing eyes. Despite his pain, Duncan could smell its electricity.

"It's over, little man. You've lost." It slammed him across the hall. Groaning in pain, Duncan twisted weakly, craving relief. As the Attendant released its grip and Duncan slipped down against the wall to the floor, his limp hand passed across one of the hallway laundry sensors. Laundry doors yawned open and he flopped backwards into a dark hole, the world turning black as he slipped into unconsciousness.

Surprised, the Attendant watched as its prey plummeted out of sight. It orange eyes pulsed twice before its grin returned and it strode purposefully down the hall.

Three boys, cowering amongst deep-canvassed laundry carts under flickering lights, were startled by a body flopping onto one of the heaping carts. There came a long silence, finally broken by a whisper:

"Is it one of them?" the smallest of the three asked.

"Naw. It looks like a person," said the taller, freckled one.

"He isn't movin'... Is he dead?" spoke the smallest one again.

"Naw. He's breathin'," answered the third.

"Go have a look at him, Spikey," said Freckles to the smallest one.

"Not me. You go look at him, Ralph. You're the oldest."

Freckled Ralph looked at the slender, girl-faced boy with spiraling auburn hair. "What about you, Curly?

"Yeah. Sure, I'll do it." Curly's voice croaked hoarsely, a strangely harsh sound emanating from so soft a boy. He cautiously walked over to where Duncan lay unconscious.

"He's alive."

The other two boys crept closer, until they reached the cart. They stood there silently for a moment before Ralph asked, "What're we gonna do?"

"Leave him." Curly croaked. "We can't help him."

"Wait!" Spikey interrupted. "Look at him. He's a grown-up." The other two nodded. "I got an idea. All he probably needs is a little fixin' and then we can get him to help us."

"How we gonna fix him?"

"Pull out some of this laundry and pile it on top of him. The infirmary's just down the hall. All we gotta do is get him there and we can let those fix-it beds do the rest."

"Spikey, that's the dumbest thing you've come up with so far."

"You got a better idea, Curly?"

"Yeah, leave him here."

"You gonna stay here, with him maybe dyin'?" Spikey looked directly at Curly. "You gonna hide next to a dead guy?" Neither answered. "OK then. C'mon."

They soon managed to tug and pull out several layers of sheets and pillowcases from underneath the unconscious man until he was below the edges of the cart. Piling the laundry on top, they navigated the cart around the large washing machines, gaping dryers, and steaming pressing machines and beyond their hideout.

The brightly-lit corridor was oddly silent. Ralph gave a hurried search down both ends of the curving hallway.

"C'mon. It's OK." They heaved and pushed and steered the cart down the hall, legs pumping furiously, trying to match the racing of their hearts.

They arrived at the infirmary, and the hallway was still silent.

"See," Spikey said triumphantly, "I told you we could do it."

They pushed the cart through the doors and into the infirmary proper: circular and large, with sixty small, clear doors arranged in tiers of threes against the walls. Behind each door was a healing bed in a self-contained cylinder loaded with needles, surgical robotics, even soothing sounds and aromas. In the infirmary's center was a master computer console. Simply touch the screen, and the "healing room" did the rest.

"Now what'll we do?" Ralph looked around.

"Gotta figure how to get him on one of these beds."

The three stepped up and crowded into the master console area. Ralph was busy reading directions while Curly counted the tiers of beds. Spikey searched the master console for a few seconds and then yelled, "Hey! You machines! We need help."

There was a pause before a commanding voice spoke: "May I help you?"

Both Ralph and Curley let out a yelp. Spikey calmly stepped into the center of the console, pushing Ralph out of the way.

"Yeah. We got a hurt grown-up here that needs fixin'."

Another pause. Then the voice spoke matter-of-factly: "You may put him onto bed number thirteen. Please wait until the bed is fully extended." A lower tier door opened and a bed like a large tongue quietly extended.

"C'mon," Spikey commanded. "Let's get him in before anybody comes."

The three guided the cart over to the extended bed. Curley climbed into the cart and began tossing away the layered laundry. He pulled off the last pillowcase and let out a startled high-pitched cry when he saw the grown-up staring up at him. Curley fell backward, tripping over the man's curled legs, and jammed himself deep into the corner of the laundry cart.

"Help!" he flailed. "Get me outta here!"

Ralph and Spikey each grabbed an arm and yanked him out.

"He's awake!" Spikey said, sidling up to look.

The adult very slowly twisted his head toward the sound, and blinked at Spikey's tow-headed face, trying to focus.

"Who... who are you?" the grown-up slurred.

"Name's Spikey. Don't worry mister, we're gonna help you get better."

"He... help?"

"Yup. Me and Ralph and Curley got you here by ourselves. We're gonna help you, but you gotta help us too. Can you get up?"

Meaning must have penetrated the man's mind; he lifted trembling arms to the sides of the cart. Struggling upright, he groaned and fell limp again, back into unconsciousness.

"Jeez!" Spikey frowned. "C'mon. He's no help." Grunting, pulling, and pushing, they finally flopped him onto the bed, watching with relief as the bed slipped back home and the door sealed shut.

"Let's get outta here."

As they moved quickly to the main doors of the infirmary, the doors suddenly slipped open and five Attendants stood in front of them.

Spikey slapped at the palm scanner to close the door, but an Attendant stood, leaning a hand against the scanner on the outside.

"Hello boys." All five raised their weapons.

The three boys froze.

"Looks like we're toast," Spikey whispered.

Instead of firing, the Attendants motioned them out into the hall. Curley bumped into an immobile Ralph. The bump shook Ralph, and he began crying softly.

"Jeez, please don't hurt us. We didn't do nuthin'."

"Of course not," one Attendant said reassuringly. "We know it's not your fault. Why don't you just come with us?"

Two of the Attendants entered and moved in opposite directions along the wall, scanning the beds with infrared and examining the temperature gauges next to the healing bed doors. Every so often, one would stop when its internal scanners picked up body heat emanating from one of the doors, then jerk open a door and send a series of high-pitched, screeching beams into the opening. Next the smell of burning flesh rolled out of the opening, and soon a translucent haze of smoke hovered in the air, tinged with the smell of charred human flesh.

Spikey watched as they got closer to where Duncan lay. Suddenly he bolted. "Scatter!" he yelled, pushing past the center Attendant and out the door. Ralph and Curley ran in the opposite direction.

As a result, the two Attendants inside immediately stopped scanning and ran to the door. Three gave chase after Ralph and Curley, while the other two went after Spikey.

Spikey ran with the adrenaline of fear hammering his body. The nimbleness of youth allowed him to squeeze into openings and spaces far too small for an Attendant. In a short time he was free of his pursuers and, breathing heavily, found a hideaway in a small storage locker.

He gathered his wits in the dark, listening to the sounds in the hallway. Every so often the hallway would reverberate with a cacophony of shouts and shooting. Just as quickly, the sounds of combat would subside, fading like a passing freight train.

When silence seemed complete, he pushed the door open a crack. Through slits of light in the door vents, he watched as an Attendant slowly stalked the hallway, scanning both sides, its gun at the ready.

Spikey sucked in his breath and fought to quiet his thumping heart. *Oh jeez, please walk on by... walk on by... walk on by...* He silently mouthed the plea as he watched the shadow flick across the opening. His young body vibrated with each heartbeat, silent tremors pulsing outward.

And then the door ripped open and a hand grabbed him and he was hoisted into the air, dangling up above a grinning metal face.

"Nice try little one!" It brought Spikey down, nose to nose. "You lose."

Spikey grimaced. "Your breath stinks."

The unblinking amber eyes seemed momentarily off-guard, but the Attendant quickly recovered. "You won't have to worry about that much longer." It tossed Spikey over its shoulder and continued its search.

The Attendant carried Spikey into the ship's auditorium and threw him onto the floor. He stood up and surveyed the room filled with the remnants of settlers. Off to one side, against the stage, he saw Ralph and Curley. Curley was lying on the stage, and Ralph seemed to be stroking his hair. Approaching his two friends, he stopped in front of Ralph whose attention was on Curley. "What're you doing?"

Ralph did not look up, but continued stoking Curley's hair, gently like it was soft rabbit's fur. "They killed him, Spikey. They killed him."

Spikey looked at the prone Curley and then noticed the grotesquely misshapen neck, a neck squeezed with the force of a shark's bite. "Why?" He self-consciously rubbed his own throat.

"He laughed at them. Said they were stupid, just machines. And then they got mad and this one just started squeezin' and Curley started hurtin' and he couldn't say nuthin' and they wouldn't stop and I tried to make them stop but they wouldn't and he's dead." Ralph continued stroking.

Spikey looked long at Curley, back to Ralph, and then turned around, a knot of helplessness filling his stomach. The grown-ups were too involved with their own future to attend to the needs of three truant children like him and Spikey and Ralph. If there were any future, they would have to do what they always did - depend upon themselves.

Spikey surveyed the room, where the remains of families huddled fearfully. The men, recognizing the value of a show of bravery, went from group to group, mumbling assurances and mouthing hopes. Yet their furtive glances at the Attendant guards at each door betrayed their hidden fears.

Every so often, doors would open and more humans would be pushed and herded into the auditorium. As their numbers grew, so did their fear. So too did the lines to the latrines grow longer, and the frustration of confinement mixed with fear of an unknown future bubbled into heated words and fist fights.

At dinnertime, the main doors to the *Future Hope's* auditorium opened and four Attendants forcibly escorted the ship's captain into the room, hands tied in front of him and stumbling due to a gash on his thigh. His face was cut and bleeding.

The captain was a strong man, tall and muscular. His salt-and-pepper hair was tied in a ponytail. Despite his predicament, his green eyes had that cold angry gleam of a man defiant. The Attendants pushed him to the front of the auditorium and lifted him up onto the stage. One Attendant stood beside him, helping him stand.

A hush followed as he gained his balance.

"It appears we've lost," he said flatly, raising his bound hands as evidence. "The Administrator's dead." His voice grew stronger and carried throughout the large room. It's not my fault. The corporation refused to allow us to return. We were condemned and we didn't even know it. I've made a deal with the remaining Attendants." He watched the crowd as a low gurgle of anxiety simmered.

The captain paused, looking around the room. *Yes, my friends,* he mused, *I can smell your fear. Oh god, Alexis, why did I bring you with me?*

He searched the room rapidly. *Where are you?* He cleared his throat and the noise subsided.

"I've made a bargain: I've offered my life as surety for your safety – if you'll stop fighting now."

Silence fell among the passengers. Many faces were obviously relieved, others not so. He was about to continue when an Attendant at the rear of the hall fired into the crowd and a startled cry burst like the gun shot that killed a random crewman.

"You *promised!"* the captain shouted above the eruption of yelling and scrambling.

"We lied!" the Attendant sneered. "Kill them all!" It grabbed the captain by the arm and jabbed its gun against the man's head.

"Do it, Dieter!" The captain yelled as the Attendant fired.

As the captain thudded to the floor, a wiry man in the middle of the auditorium jumped up on one of the chairs. He held a thermo-fusion grenade high above his head. The Attendants saw it, ceased firing, and turned to run towards the doors as the settlers froze, immobile. Dieter flipped off the retaining clip and held the grenade straight above him.

"God be with you all." And he bowed his head.

Several Attendants fired at him. With the last hit, he dropped the grenade, and the mass of passengers screamed and stampeded, grabbing at fleeing Attendants as if for safety.

Then a screeching white light burst from the floor followed by a noise its dead passengers could no longer hear. The ship bucked, twisted, and turned like a harpooned whale, finally shuddering against the cold flanks of black space.

What remained were two halves of a ship, joined by several slender girders. Exposed fires winked out from lack of oxygen. The dead hulk floated onward, twisting slowly, the lights of its many hallways, apartments, recreation rooms, and chapels all extinguished.

This darkness lasted for almost a day's duration before a set of lights blinked on in both halves of the ship.

Chapter 2

Duncan's eyelids fluttered and closed against the soft light. He could hear voices, distant, hazy. He tried again to open his eyes, but they felt too heavy. Struggling once more, he forced his right eye to half-lidded triumph and saw only a blur of soft mauve.

Voices continued, "....Pulse-ox 98%, respiration normal... Patient reviving out of cerebral anesthesia..."

Succeeding in opening his eyes, the soft mauve gained metallic clarity. He slowly looked to the left, wondering why he couldn't move his head. *W... Where am I?*

Though he could see no one, he heard them: "Testing cranial response... negative.... Rotating cranial imaging sensor to quadrant four.... Begin image..." The sound of banging metal and whirring engines filled his ears.

Suddenly the soft mauve metal rotated to his right, replaced by a crisp chrome bar with tiny robotic arms holding syringes, surgical knives, tweezers, thread, and gauze. He watched in horror as one syringe-holding arm jabbed its needle into his cheek.

He tried to scream, but no sound came out....

"...Pulse-ox steady... patient becoming diaphoretic... experiencing tachycardia... giving two milligrams ativan.... Continue with imaging, quadrant six."

His body relaxed into a languid torpor. In his drug-induced state, he watched the rotating arms; whirling, dexterous, jabbing here, slicing swiftly there; snipping crisply and efficiently. In the haze of sounds and colors as he drifted back into oblivious darkness, he thought he could hear a vacuum suction.

While Duncan drifted into anesthetized sleep, sounds of healing reverberated through the room. In the center of the infirmary, control lights on the master console flickered rapidly as robotic arms whirled around his supine body, cutting, stitching, and probing along its length. The room was dark save for the glow from his healing chamber. Occasionally, overhead lights would stutter and blink on. Then the speed of the robotic arms would slow dramatically and a voice would offer an obligatory "Sorry."

Duncan's eyelids twitched as he again tried to awaken. He squinted. A darker mass obstructed some of the bright haze. He tried again and the mass gained form. It appeared to be leaning over him. *Are you going to kill me?* He felt heavy and tried to lift his arms, yet they seemed distant, foreign. A voice was speaking. He closed his eyes to concentrate.

"How are you feeling?" it asked. The voice was pleasant, familiar.

He tried to speak, but his voice cracked as if from disuse. "Who... who are you?"

"Don't you remember me?"

He opened his eyes again and the mass gained form: a woman took shape in his foggy eyes. The petite frame, eyes that danced, and loving arms that cradled his cares: *Mrs. Kimbrough...Oh, god, no... I'm dead....* As Duncan moaned and twisted his stiff body, his hands clenching and unclenching, his neck muscles straining, his voice burst through, cracked and hoarse:

"No! I don't want to be dead."

"Oh my! I didn't expect this.... I thought... Oh my.... Please," she begged, "please sleep. You need sleep."

Duncan continued fighting to gain life until a prick on his arm sent him back into timeless darkness.

He awoke later, lying on his side. The brightness of the room hurt his eyes and he brought a hand up to shade them. And there they were... two large, beautifully shaped breasts. He closed his eyes, squinting them shut. When he opened them again, the breasts were still there. He craned a stiff neck and looked up to the sweetly smiling woman standing above him, jerking back with nauseous horror.

"M... Missus Kimbrough?"

Mrs. Kimbrough slowly licked her lips and pouted a wry smile.

She's.... She's beautiful... Duncan stared. *Auburn hair... beautiful skin... perfect smooth breasts... No! Stop this! This is all wrong! This can't be real.... Not like this... not like this....*

"I see you're feeling better." The voice was warm, like hers, but... not like hers.

"Why... why do you look like that?"

"Like what?"

"You know..." Duncan fumbled, "Why... why don't you have any clothes on?"

"Don't you like me like this?"

"No. This isn't right. Where am I? Am I dead?"

"No. You're hardly dead." Her lips pursed in sensuous desire.

Duncan turned away, self-conscious. "Who... who are you?" He continued, looking away. "You look like her, but you don't."

"Why, can't you see? I'm Missus Kimbrough."

"No! It can't be true." He tried to sit up, but the room began spinning and he flopped back down, closing his eyes.

"Well, actually you're right. It's not true. I'm Talane."

"Who?" he asked, his eyes still shut.

"Talane. I'm a hologram." The voice was sweet, pert.

"A hologram? Where am I?" He rolled to his side, slowly opening his eyes.

"In the infirmary."

"On the *Future Hope*?"

"Of course. Where else?" She began walking around the room, pausing repeatedly to pose.

"Why do you look like that?" he crossly demanded.

"Like what?"

"Like... like Missus Kimbrough!"

"Oh my. Well, when the anesthesia began to wear off, you kept yelling to keep the machines away and every time I came close to you, you recoiled in fear. I did a quick memory scan, very cursory mind you – a lot of damage in there. But I did find Missus Kimbrough, your third grade teacher, had a very strong and loving influence over you. You trusted her. I determined that my appearance as Missus Kimbrough could have a calming effect. Apparently I was wrong. The first occasion did not produce the desired response. You believed that you were dead I combined a memory search with a data scan of your reading files that showed a preponderance of your time was spent with holographic images of nude women. I combined the two hoping for a better response."

"Well this isn't right! Missus Kimbrough wouldn't look like that!"

"I do have the face right, don't I?"

"That's not the point. It's obscene. It's... it's like seeing your grandmother naked... it's just not something that's supposed to be seen!"

"Do you want me to change?"

"Of course I do, and who the hell are you, anyway?" He slowly sat up. As he steadied himself, he reached up with his left hand and felt his clean scalp. He jerked his right hand up to join the search, but found thick hair on that side. He then realized that only half of his head had been shaved. *Great. I probably look like some circus freak.*

"Careful, silly! You're not fully healed." She was slowly changing and, while the face remained the same, clothes formed to cover her nakedness. The end result was that of a nineteenth century schoolmarm in sepia toned dress and frilled high-collar blouse.

Duncan watched her metamorphosis in distracted self-appraisal. His left hand had found the scar and he was gently learning the braille bumps of his sutured flesh. "What did you do to me?" he dully asked.

"I healed you. You had a nasty boo-boo that I took care of." Talane reached out a hand in feigned affection.

"Stop talking like that."

"How would you like me to talk?"

An ache began in his head. "You sound like you're talking to a two-year old."

"Hmmm," she thought, putting a finger to her lips. "I may have made a slight error. The average person communicates with no more than level two skills, although there are some whose skills are well beyond that. Still, now that I think about it, most of those who have superior communications skills use them in writing. I could talk to you as such humans write, if you wish."

Listening to her became an effort and the ache in his head slowly grew, like the distant thrumming of ocean waves.

"Would you like that?" she smiled seductively.

He had ceased listening. He was concentrating on how his body felt, heavy, thick, as if someone was hanging onto him, squeezing his chest. He lay back on the bed. "I don't feel so good," he said as darkness raced to the center of his vision.

Not until the next day could Duncan sit up comfortably. He surveyed the room. It was too clean, too bright, too white. Although he knew where he was, he didn't like the antiseptic purity of this infirmary. He listened intently to the thick silence. Where was the noise of battle? And why is this damn hologram wearing no clothes again?

"Why do I have a scar on my head?"

"Oh my, you sustained a very serious head injury. It took quite some time to reattach nerve fibers to your neck and spine. I had to go in the front

16

door. You were simply such a mess. Don't worry though. You won't look like you had a lobotomy!" She giggled.

"How long have I been out?" He jerked his head, cracking his neck.

"Ooo, please be careful. I did a lot of work in there and you're not fully healed!" Talane smiled that sweet expression; her eyes sparkled. "You came in here on the third of October, and it's now November fifteenth. That makes about forty-three days." She sauntered sensuously toward him.

"Forty-three days! My god, what's happened?" He shakily stood up, clutching the bed for support. "Who controls the ship?"

"Silly boy, you control the ship," she grinned. "Or at least this half of the ship."

"Huh?" He sat back down. "What's happened?"

"Well," she paused as if about to begin a long story. "You were brought here the morning of October third. You just can't imagine how lucky you are. You fell down the laundry chute onto a pile of sheets. Then some children brought you here, but the Attendants came and you were so lucky because one of the boys, I think his name was Spikey but it gets confusing in the end. Anyway, Spikey sees that two of the Attendants were going to see that you were in a healing bed and he simply yells and runs away and instead of finding you, they all ran after the boys and left you alone. I can't believe just how lucky you are." Talane smiled prettily.

His head still hurt. "Huh?"

"You know, fate, karma. You must be destined to live."

"Where are they now?"

"Oh well, they're dead. Blown up in the explosion. I think all of them are dead."

He watched as she pranced around the room. Her voice was so effervescent, as though discussing violent death was like choosing soup and salad.

"What're you talking about? What do you mean they're all dead?"

She paused, looking at him. "Hmmm. I suppose you have been away for a while. Well, as I said, you were brought here and put on a healing bed. My goodness, what a mess you were. By the time I had you settled, the Attendants had everybody in the auditorium. Dieter Waldhausen had a thermo grenade and, can you believe it, the silly man blew everybody up!" Talane shook her head. "I just don't understand. Why would you kill yourself knowing that everyone else is going to die anyway? Can you explain that to me?" She stopped, hands on her hips, coquettish smile inviting him forward.

His shoulders slumped at the news. "Everyone's dead?"

"Yup. Dead as a doornail."

"What?"

"A doornail. It's an idiomatic phrase that means to be dead beyond a doubt."

He looked back to the sauntering Talane and realized that she wasn't telling all. "What the hell's going on? Why do you look like that?"

She pouted a sex-kitten pose. "Don't you like it?"

"That's irrelevant! Why the hell are you naked?" Duncan inhaled deeply.

"I... I... just thought that you might like it." The voice changed. It was different, concerned but reserved. "I assumed that it would create a more pleasant environment for you. I'm sorry. I can change if you wish." Her voice was becoming more controlled, more rational.

Duncan looked around the room, looked at Talane, and realized that she was the least of his problems. Sliding to the edge of the bed, he steadied himself and stood up.

"Who or what are you?"

Talane had paused mid-pose. "As I said, I'm a hologram."

"I know, but who's controlling you?" He stood balancing himself.

"Oh well, I'm the library computer. Seems like I'm the only thing left in control. Do you wish me to change?"

Taking several tentative steps, he stopped to lean against the center console. "You look great..." he said flatly. "Thanks for thinking of me. Now do me a favor and put some clothes on. How the hell can I think with you looking like that?" His voice became weak, hesitant, sorrowful. "Now what do I do," he mumbled, turning away. Staggering over to a wall mirror, he was shocked at what he saw. Half of his head was shaved, with a fierce red scar in the shape of a star near the front top of his head. The other half had long auburn hair, matted and tangled from his long sleep. His brown eyes peered from dark shadows and his face had that haggard thin skin of resurrection. *I should have died too.*

He inhaled deeply. Once. Twice. A cascade of pain, sorrow, self-pity and fear rushed upon him and Duncan continued staring in the mirror, without seeing. *I'm alone. And I haven't the slightest idea where in this hell called space I am.* He shook his head to clear his mind and looked again at himself. The broad shoulders he had been so vain about were bony and gaunt. He stepped back to further appraise. *God... look at me... I look like I haven't eaten in months. Not only do I feel lousy, I look like road-kill.*

He continued staring and then sniffed, *I even smell like road-kill....* He turned back to Talane.

"Am I alone?"

"Yes, at least on this half of the ship."

"What do you mean this half?"

"Well, like I said," the voice had changed again, back to that irritating sweetness, "when Dieter blew up the auditorium, it blew the ship in two. We're on this half of the ship and the captain's quarters, bridge, and supplemental power are on the other half with just an itty-bitty girder holding us together."

"How do you know there's no one else here, on my side of the ship?" His head ached a dull throbbing.

"There's been no movement since the explosion," she sweetly answered. "Logically, if any humans survived, they would need to eat, and there has been no activity for the past forty-three days."

"Attendants don't eat," he quickly pointed out.

"Yes, but their bodies generate magnetic lobes that would register on local circuitry."

Duncan's winced at the pain in his head, not fully understanding her explanation. "Is anyone alive over on the other side?"

"I don't know. I don't have any direct connection over there. I've tried wireless signal, but there's only so much I can do."

Duncan yawned a cavernous stretch and rubbed his face. He shivered a bit despite the warmth of the room. He absentmindedly chewed his lip. *Now what do I do? Why now? Why this?* His eyes clouded briefly. "I want to go out." He turned toward the door. "I want to see what happened."

"Yes Duncan. But be warned." Her voice changed again. It was maternal, caring. "I couldn't clean up. You need to be prepared for what you might see."

"I have an idea of what to expect. You've helped me enough thanks." Surveying the room, he looked for something he could use as a weapon. Slowly prying a length of metal from one of the burned out bed pods, he lumbered to the door and pressed the palm pad. The door slipped open and the miasma of rotting flesh and decaying bodies rushed over him.

Duncan sucked in the maleficence, succumbed to dry-heaving and fell back into the infirmary.

An hour later, he eased again into the corridor, a makeshift oxygen tank from the infirmary strapped to his back. Talane walked behind him as he cautiously worked his way back to his own apartment. The sight and smell of torn and broken bodies covered in black mold caused him to stop several times for deeper draughts of oxygen.

He paused long before his father, a synthesis of revulsion and deep-plumbed emotion. And then he cried, thick convulsing sobs. And the more he cried, the more he realized he was crying for himself. *I'm so damned alone.*

After a time, he stopped and wiped his eyes with his sleeve. As he calmed, a demon seed of anger settled in the pit of his heart. And it grew at a surprising rate. Its branches entwined themselves around his soul, nourishing and feeding itself. Blackness clouded his mind as he yanked the Attendant off of his father. Grabbing the metal armpits, he threw it against the wall. And then in frenzied wrath, he hammered and pulled and pried and pummeled the mass of wiring, grunting and crying until his anger was spent and he slipped to the floor.

"Dammit, Dad, you were supposed to be here." He squeezed the tears from his eyes with the heels of his palms. He looked away from the dented and torn Attendant to the molded mass of black flesh that had been his father. The credential card with *'Authorization Level 4'* neatly printed above the photo was still pinned to the chest. Unwillingly, Duncan focused on the face. It was his own.

"You look so much like your father," Elaine had said. "You could do no better than to follow in his footsteps." She had always smiled that proud pleasure grin of respect when she said this. *Where are you now? You're dead. Dad's dead. Is this where you really wanted me to end up?"*

"This is all so bloody stupid!" The loudness of his voice startled him as it reverberated and echoed in the long halls. But it felt good to vent his anger and he erupted again.

"You bastards! I don't know why this happened but I'll find you and you'll pay. I will find you!" Suddenly the seeming absurdity of his statements gained clarity. "Yeah," he grunted, "I'll find you... if I can find myself first...."

He turned back to look down the long hallway. Many of the ceiling lights had been destroyed, giving the hallway a pale, subdued glow. The dullness thumped against and within him. Talane had left him during his tirade with the Attendant and her absence only deepened the emptiness.

Standing, he sucked in the emptiness, tasting the bitter succulence of torment. And he knew that he was alone, alone in ultimate self-reliance, alone in the vast universal blackness of empty space. The branches of his anger became tendrils, long slender fingers rushing, searching for meaning. And they found none.

He was alone. It was he who now ruled his future, if he even had one. At least the ship could sustain him. Perhaps there was a way out. If there were, it would only matter to him. But he knew one solid fact – *This will never happen to me again.*

"Talane!" He barked. "Talane. I need you here, now!"

"Yes Duncan?" Talane appeared in front of him, tight spandex pants and blouse hiding the flesh of her luxurious body.

He squared his shoulders, standing at his full height, straight, like a fighter after a pyrrhic victory. Firmly grasping the metal rod, he snarled. "C'mon, I want to see the other side."

Talane had led the way. She was now standing to the side as Duncan stared through the portal of the thick corridor door, gaping at the void between the two halves of the ship. He was transfixed, staring mutely at the medusa mess of cables, twisted girders, and ripped plating. She had been almost right. Actually there were two slender girders holding the ship together. Duncan guessed the distance between the two to be about a hundred meters. Except for lights in the bridge, the rest of the metal hulk was in darkness. Duncan sighed deeply and turned back to Talane.

"Where are we?"

"I don't know," she quietly replied. "The navigational computers are on the other half."

Duncan uttered a soft "damn," his lips tight. The quiet of the corridor was interrupted by the growling in his stomach. "Is the kitchen still functioning?"

"As far as I can tell," she coyly shrugged.

"Guess I better find out." Casting one last look out the window, he headed towards the dining hall.

Chapter 3

Over the next three months, Duncan focused his attention to his part of the ship. He began with the kitchen and then the bio-farm, ensuring there was a constant and sufficient supply of food. Fortunately, despite the power loss after the explosion, the food in the freezers was still good.

Yet his most pressing compulsion was to clean, a furious exertion to purge the ship of the dead.   He began with his own apartment first, venturing farther each succeeding day, tumbling the fetid remains into evacuation pods and jettisoning all memory into disappearing space. Holstered pistol clipped to his belt, he would carefully scout the area to be cleaned, despite Talane's reassurances.

Talane came every day and, at first, was scantily clad, but after a few weeks decided it was more fun assuming different characters. She talked while he cleaned. Though he spoke little, he enjoyed listening. He grew to enjoy her company, even if she was a hologram.   Today she was Vercingetorix, a la the statue in Alise-Sainte-Reine, complete with the large drooping mustache.

"Duncan, how much cleaner do you want this place?" The voice was a deep baritone.   "You've got to leave here sometime."   Vercingetorix fluttered his hands as he walked.

Duncan was on his knees scrubbing the floor where his father's blood had run into the front living room. Sitting back on his haunches, he looked to where he was cleaning. All traces of blood had been removed weeks before from the pressure of meticulous rubbing, scraping, and polishing. Yet still he came here to clean. Each day, the ritual began with him kneeling upon the floor by the front door, as though prostrating himself in confession, seeking expiation for the sins of the dead.

And here he was again, resting in mid-scrub, looking at a floor polished mirror bright. His eyes blinked quickly several times and he stood up. He looked again at the floor as if seeing it for the first time and suddenly it became new, unblemished, merely a place for feet to tread.

"You're right," he said without looking up. He rubbed his temples. The recurring headaches had considerably diminished the past month, though there were occasional days when the pain surged and he would stumble to the infirmary for pain meds. Today the pain was just a dull ache. "So what's the plan for determining where we are?"

"We've talked about this before. I'm the library computer. I can access data storage, generate holograms, be company, cheer you up, but I need input to know where we are."

"I don't know how to do that," he testily replied, standing up. "I've tried. I'm a linguist, not a scientist."

Vercingetorix placed unfeeling hands on Duncan's shoulders. "Maybe you're not going about it the right way."

Duncan stepped back. "Huh?"

"You spend your time cleaning, patrolling the corridors of the ship, working in the bio-farm, or staring out the portholes on the observation deck." He smiled, the baritone voice changing to feminine.

Duncan's face hardened. "So?"

"I'm the library computer. I have all sorts of knowledge waiting to be explored. It's not like you have competing demands for your time. If you really want to discover where we are, you could start with plotting and trajectory programs." Vercingetorix then folded his arms. "There is one other thing."

"What?"

"You need to relax."

"Relax?" he sputtered. "How can I relax? I don't know where I am or where I'm going. I don't know what's on the other half of this ship, or what other surprises are in store for me. Relax? That's not an option."

"You still need a diversion. You can't be on edge all the time." he softly answered. "You used to play chess. Remember?"

Duncan glared at the hologram. The warrior's response only increased his irritation. Playing chess while the damaged hulk hurtled through space to who knew where seemed cruelly absurd. Yet what options did he have? Even if he did find out where he was headed, what would it matter? Was he condemned to die, alone, on this damned crate?

Shaking his head in disgust, he looked around the meticulous apartment and decided he was ready to be somewhere else. "I'm hungry," he growled, and walked away.

Moments later, he stood outside the dining hall, staring through the transparent doors, surveying the spotless tables and chairs. The need for food had caused him to clean this room early on, and the memories of jumbled tables, spilled chairs, strewn food, and rotting corpses still haunted him.

He had tried eating here in the beginning, but the ghosts of the dead wavering above the tables gave him the chills and he fled. He returned several days later and began cleaning, choosing to return home to eat until the ghosts of the dead finally left him alone.

Standing before the doors, peering in through the windows at the dining room, glitteringly clean from his efforts, he took a deep breath and pressed the palm-pad to open the doors, then quickly strode over to the dispensing wall. Once in front of the Administrator's dining slot, he scanned the food menu and pressed his selections. He had long since stopped wondering why the Administrator had received this special treatment while the rest of the crew and travelers ate their dreary meals. Nature camp food he had called it, for it reminded him of the generic nutritious junk that kids always ate at camp.

The slot door slid back and he pulled out his tray. An organic soy-bacon, lettuce, and tomato sandwich on a seven-grain bun lay on a thick paper dish. A tumbler of organic fruit juice was placed tastefully to the side. Sniffing at the wholesome meal, he shook his head. *God, I'd kill for a donut.*

He turned and plodded slowly to the table in the corner where the captain used to enjoy his meals. Carefully placing the tray on the table, he removed the gun from his hip holster and placed it barrel outward parallel to the right edge of his tray. Glancing around the room again, he settled himself into the corner, confident that he could see any one or thing that entered the room.

After sliding his tray onto the cleaner belt, Duncan walked back out and down the long hallway to the elevator. Placing his hand on the palm-scanner, he punched his destination code into the twelve-digit matrix and slipped inside the sterile cube.

As he felt the gentle upward pressure, he again ruminated his future. With the bio-farm and the food already in the kitchen, he could survive until he died of old age. The thought terrified him. At least Robinson Crusoe had another human to talk to. While Talane was company, he yearned for the presence of another human, someone who even might know how to figure out where in this hell called space they were.

That he still didn't know where he was more than frustrated him; it overwhelmed him. While the voice inside him drove him to survive, it also reminded him that not only was he alone, he was miserably lost. He had tried many times to determine his location, going up to the mid-ship observation deck, a print-out of constellations in hand. But there were too many stars, too many damned stars. Yet there had to be a way, and he would not quit until he knew his future.

The elevator slowed to a stop, and the doors opened. Moments later, he was in the library. Vercingetorix was already there.

"Let's get started," Duncan officiously stated, looking around the room. "Where do I begin?"

"How about a chess game first?" The chieftain offered.

"What's with you and chess? I need to find out where I am and where I'm going. Chess can wait."

"You can't learn everything at once," he countered. "Besides, you need to relax."

"I don't want to relax. I need resolution," Duncan retorted, his voice rising.

"I'm just trying to help," Vercingetorix explained sympathetically.

Letting out a loud sigh of frustration, Duncan snarled. "Fine. We'll play a game of chess. Set up a game on the far table." He stalked over to sit at a table tucked against the far wall. Back to the wall, he checked the power on his gun while the game appeared on the table top.

Vercingetorix sat opposite him, his sword resting across his thighs. He moved first.

Midway through the game, he stood up removed his vest and began slowly pulling the shirt over his head. Duncan wasn't looking, so he cleared his throat. When Duncan glanced up, he pulled off the shirt, preening before him.

"Uh... what are you doing?"

"I'm flashing you."

"You're what?" Duncan leaned back.

"I'm flashing you. I read that it's very distracting."

Leaning forward, Duncan started giggling, pretending to study the chess board.

"What?" she defensively asked.

"Nothing," he answered, working to control his mirth.

"It must be working because you're not concentrating," she triumphantly announced.

"Oh, it's working," he replied, shaking with laughter.

"Tell me something," Duncan said during one of their games in his apartment. "How did I end up at the infirmary? The last thing I remember was getting beat-up by some Attendant."

"I told you before, some children brought you there." Talane pondered a move. She was an older Gandhi today complete with homespun khadi and sandals.

"Yeah, but how'd they get ahold of me?"

"That I don't know. Your move." Talane smiled coyly. "Would you like to see some of the dream girls? I could model any of them for you. In fact, I can do more than just one at a time... if you're interested." She pursed her lips into a kiss

Duncan paused, cocking an eyebrow. "Every time you do that means you don't like the position you're in, which means that I better pay closer attention to this game."

Talane stood up and began changing into a petite brunette.

"Would you stop for just once!" Duncan demanded. "Pick somebody, anybody and keep your damn clothes on!"

Talane plopped back down. "What's the matter with you? I just thought you might like a little change."

"Listen, I want to know more about what happened. What was the kid's name again?"

"Spikey."

He stood up. "Run me the manifest lists will you? I'll meet you in the library in a couple of minutes."

"Where are you going? Aren't we going to finish the game?" Talane questioned.

"Some of us do have to use the facilities every now and then. And the game can wait until later."

Duncan stood peering in through wide glass doors of the library. He had been here many times, before... before the Attendant Uprising. He called it the Attendant Uprising now and liked the way it sounded. Battle just seemed too brief, especially with the catastrophic results.

And here he stood again. He had come several times after the Uprising, and was beginning to enjoy the warmth of the room. Not like the first time. After the Uprising. That time was still too fresh, still too ghost-ridden.

He remembered the first time. The first time Talane had walked in with him. He had asked her to come, wanting her jabbering there to release the tension of the oppressive death he expected to feel. And he was right.

Whoever had built this ship had one sick sense of humor. For whatever reason, the library was the one area in the ship that made up for the sterility of the rest of the drab apartments, over-bright corridors, and other utilitarian rooms. It had color. Lots of it. Sound-tile walls changed colors every day. Duncan remembered the day when the walls were checked bright red and white. One rather large matronly woman with high teased hair and a horizontally striped smock giving him an impression of a bullfrog, had complained loudly about something trivial to the library assistant, a bored, slender girl with no hair and heavy eyes. The girl simply shrugged and said nothing. The matron squared her fat shoulders and said loud enough for all to hear, "What kind of library is this!" He had watched her leave in her arrogance, wondering who she was and why did she think she was so important?

Despite Talane's presence, he felt them, the slender clerk behind the counter, the haughty woman, the people in the queue wanting help, the other patrons, there at the thick wooden tables, looking up briefly from their hand screens, staring blankly at him. Or there, sitting in those overstuffed chairs with a computer screen descended from the ceiling in front of them, leaning around to look at who had disturbed their reverie. Or there, the assistant librarian behind the assistance counter watching him, waiting for the opportunity to correct him. Or there in the assistance line, patrons queued crisply, all turning to stare at him with vacant faces.

And he had run out, shouting "Leave me alone!" behind him.

But here he was again. He had forced himself to come the next day. And the day after that. And the next day. Finally, he grew more comfortable and the demons left him alone. And he left them alone. A kind of tenuous peace settled in the library.

Shortly after his revisit with Talane, he had changed the wall program so that only a soft mauve would adorn the walls now. Searching the museum data, he spent several hours selecting pictures to appear on selected walls, changing pictures every several days.

Duncan palm-scanned his entry and the doors slid open. Striding to the far end of the library, he settled into his favorite chair. He took out his pistol and placed it on the arm of the chair, muzzle outward, grip to the right.

"Gimme a one meter."

A slender terminal of one meter in diagonal descended to eye level.

"Run manifest lists for *Future Hope* beginning this voyage." The names began scrolling rapidly in front of him. "Damn. This isn't going to work. Stop all. Begin Alpha-search with pics."

The screen changed to the first passenger, Micah Abramson. His photo showed a pudgy middle-aged man, thinning hair, brown eyes, and a lop-sided grin. He looked like the kind of man who was constantly happy. *Fat people are happy people, so the cliché goes.* Duncan read his bio, remembered his purpose and continued.

"Next... next... next..." And so it went through the A's, B's, and C's. It wasn't until the D's that he paused.

"Dru, Alexis... hmmm, not bad." He stared at the photo. The face stared back. Her deep green eyes neither smiled nor revealed any emotion. After a few moments, Duncan felt as though they were penetrating into him, asking him why he stopped here. Forcing his gaze from the eyes, he looked at the rest of the face, the thick, shoulder length auburn hair framing crisp features and high cheekbones. Her face had the vitality of health and strength, a type of compelling beauty were it not for the aloofness in her eyes. He read her bio: *the Captain's daughter... oh jeez, can you say pampered...education through level three... second year gladiator with the Kingdom's Rulers...* Duncan leaned back.

"Humpf. A gladiator. I was gonna see what the rest of you looked like, but not anymore. Last thing I want to see is some steroid-pumped, muscle bound dominatrix. Next."

The pictures continued to scroll.

"Stop!" Duncan realized that he was beginning to linger over pictures of friends, and the vastness of his desolation was beginning to consume him. He inhaled deeply and loudly blew out his breath. "New data search. List all individuals on manifest under... um, 14 years old."

Duncan started the search again scrolling past children he knew, looking for that face with the name of Spikey. He was about to scroll past Peter Thomas, when he paused and closed his eyes. He looked at Peter and closed his eyes again... yes, it was Spikey. He read the bio: *Peter Thomas... 9 years of age... only son of Sarah and Paul Thomas... born Philadelphia, Union of Democratic States... education level 1 in progress.*

He looked at the photo of the wide-eyed boy with tousled, pale blond hair. There was just the hint of freckles on his cheeks. The impish face did not match the sterile facts listed in his bio. Duncan gazed through and beyond the screen, lost in thoughts of the events leading up to where he sat, now, here, alone in this echoing cavern of metal and machines defining his very existence. He shook his head slowly, sadly aware of his place, or lack of one, in the universe.

"New search," he sighed. "Run activities of Peter Thomas." The screen changed to a listing of activities of the short life of Peter Thomas.

"List time sequence, most recent first." Suddenly the screen filled with the churning turmoil of the auditorium, as Attendants herded terrified settlers in through the doors.

"Freeze." He had seen the Attendant carrying Spikey in. "Continue at slow speed." The movement slowed and the sound became the slurred bass of human speech. He followed Spikey as the boy picked himself up off the floor and wandered over to where an older boy was stroking the hair of another younger boy lying on the stage.

"Close up of Peter Thomas." The screen zoomed into a full view of Spikey as he rubbed his throat. Duncan focused on the words the older boy was saying to Peter.

"Said... they... were.... stu... pid... just... ma... chines... and I tried to make 'em stop but they wouldn't and he's dead."

"Freeze." Duncan stared intently at Spikey, remembering his face, the calmness he seemed to have despite the fright pervading the adults. He saw the softness of a child's face, unaware of the impending destruction. "Why did you save me?" Duncan whispered to the boy in the screen.

"Resume normal view and speed." And suddenly everything goes too fast. The Captain is dragged in. A man jumps up on one of the chairs holding a grenade. The Attendant holding the Captain fires, exploding the right side of the Captain's head completely off. The man on the chairs lifts the grenade high above his head and pulls the pin. Pandemonium erupts, people pushing, tripping, grabbing, hitting. The Attendants fire at the man with the grenade. He's hit and the grenade falls to the floor. Everyone abruptly stops to look at where the grenade has fallen.

Suddenly Duncan jerked back into his chair, his arms involuntarily shielding his face as the screen burst into brilliant white light, the sound of a ship-shattering explosion filling the speakers, immediately followed by the rush of static and an empty grey-black screen.

After the discovery of what had happened to the ship, Duncan decided to let the dead rest for a while and hoped they would do the same for him. One morning he paused to look at himself in the mirror. *My god... what has happened to you?* He stood up straight. *Am I really five eleven? I look like a dwarf....* He flexed, and dropped his arms, unimpressed. He was thin, gaunt. He hadn't been eating right; he knew that. He stared again. His bony shoulders were broad, yes, but they lacked any substance, not like when he lived back home. Back home he had been mildly vain about his shoulders... and his abdomen.   He had trained, specifically designed programs of weights, anaerobic sets, and electronic stimuli to define and strengthen his shoulders, and stomach. The tightly defined stomach, the neatly sculpted ridges of each muscle, was too distinct now, contrasting with the ribs that glaringly showed. *I used to be so concerned about my body.* He curled a lip in distaste. *There's nobody here but me now. What does it matter?*   Glancing around the room, he heard the voice inside him, compelling him, commanding him: *survive... survive.*

Standing to full height, he folded his arms and glared at the reflection. "Yes, it does matter," he said aloud. "If to no one else, it still matters to me."

He leaned forward examining his face and hair. His right hand lifted to trace the white shock of hair emerging from his forehead, following the coarse hair down to his shoulders. *I even* look *like Robinson Crusoe.* He scratched at the stubble on his face.

"Enough's enough." He stood back up, tilted his head slightly back, twisted it once then twice, and decided. *I need to be more focused, disciplined. I've got to get myself together.* Grabbing a small hand-held tablet, he dictated a schedule, adding time for exercise, reworking time for meals, and setting aside time for study.

After two months on the schedule, Duncan finally noticed a change. He was adding on weight and muscle mass. At the end of another four weeks, he again appraised himself, standing before the full-length mirror in his apartment, legs shoulder width apart, arms akimbo. He nodded with satisfaction at the results. Looking back at his face, he shook his head slightly. *I don't know... Do I like the white streak or not?* He grabbed a handful of his shoulder length hair, and compared the white with the auburn. *Y'know, I kinda like it... sort of makes me look distinctive... I guess*

He pulled on some exercise shorts and grabbed a towel. On the way out, he met Talane, hunched over with a large hump on her back.

"Um, I believe Quasimodo was male." Duncan stopped and stared at a female version of Charles Laughton.

"Well sure," she said, "if you want to do it the easy way." Putting her hands over her ears, she moaned loudly, "The bells, the bells," as she limped down the hallway.

Duncan stared at her with a strange fascination, then remembered his mission. "You're supposed to work with me in the gym today," he called out. "Remember?"

"Of course! That's why I'm here." Her voice was husky deep hushed tones.

Duncan sighed loudly. "How the hell am I supposed to concentrate with you looking like that and talking like that?"

"You don't like it?" she pouted.

"That's not what I'm saying and you know it. Please, for once, just put on some clothes for the occasion and meet me in the gym." Duncan turned in a huff and stomped down the hall.

Smiling, Talane watched him go. "Ooo, I think it's working. I'm going to beat you yet."

Duncan was stretching on the mat at the far end of the gym when Talane strutted in looking like Bruce Lee, shaking both hand and wrists as though preparing to fight.

"All ready," she beamed.

Seeing her, he shook his head and continued stretching. "I want you to watch me as I go through the third form, *Pal Gwe One.* I want you to compare my form with *Sa Bom-Nim Choi."*

"Who?" Bruce was pirouetting around the room.

"Sa Bom-Nim Choi, the Master Instructor." He watched the hologram move around the room. "C'mon. You're the library computer. You could've looked that up in the amount of time it took me to tell you."

"Uh-uh," Bruce Lee countered. "Remember, *Sa Bom-Nim* is Korean and I'm programmed in English. I need more parameters to provide you an accurate answer. Besides, your accent is much too western."

"I'll remember that in my next Korean lesson. Will you just stop jumping around and do what I asked?" Duncan stood up. "Wall screen please." The wall next to the exercise mat came on. *"Tae Kwon Do...* Master Choi... *Pal Gwe One."* The empty screen was quickly replaced with Master Choi who spoke to him.

"Good. You are ready to begin the third level. Here is the form, called Pal Gwe One. Ready... *Joon Be...* Begin... *Si Jak...*" And he began the form along with Master Choi.

At the end, Bruce clapped his hands. "Oh you were just so marvelous. How about some sparring?" For the next 30 minutes, Duncan kicked, punched, twirled, and yelled as he and Bruce Lee fought across the mat. By the end of the session, he sat on the mat breathing heavily. Sweat ran off his body, settling in small pools on the mat.

Pushing himself up, he headed for the free weights. Loading up a barbell, he began his sets. With each forced repetition, he grunted a determined, "Survive!" At the end of his sets, he sat on the end of the bench, sweating, leaning forward, elbows on knees. Brushing the sweat from his face, he pushed himself up and headed to the sauna and aromatherapy room. Occasionally Talane would sit in the sauna with him.

"My goodness Duncan," said Bruce Lee. "I'm trying to find a pattern in your studies, but I can't seem to find one except that you like languages, philosophy, religion, history, and archeology."

"What do you mean?" He brushed the cascading sweat from his face.

"Oh, nothing other than why aren't you interested in the sciences?"

He wiped again. "I find them boring. They have nothing to do with man's meaning. They're all data and facts."

"You don't find theoretical math and science interesting?"

"Not really. Only so far as they relate to the necessities of man." He thought for a moment, then added, "And discovering where we are."

Bruce looked thoughtfully at him. "Hmmm. An interesting answer. I should think you already know where we are."

"I do. The fact that a certain orb has grown surprisingly larger certainly helps. And now that I know we're in the Leo constellation, I can focus my efforts on what to do next, but I need more input. I'd also like to know if there's anything out there between where we are now and where I think we're headed. I don't need any more surprises." Wiping the sweat from his face with both hands, he stood up and turned off the thermostat.

It was several days later that Duncan realized something was different about himself. He was playing chess with Talane, who was shape-changing every several minutes into different dream girls.

He leaned back, smiling. "You realize of course that that no longer bothers me."

"Are you sure? What about this one?" said a buxom, black-haired seductress.

He focused back to the game. "No, not even that one. By the way, I've noticed something peculiar about me."

"Oh?" said a blond nymphet. "Like what?"

Looking back up, he watched the changing for another minute. "Talane? Would you choose one and stop for a minute. I need to talk."

"Oh, sorry." She morphed to Mrs. Kimbrough.

Frowning, he shook his head. "I still have a hard time with that one."

"Who else would you like me to be?"

"I don't know. You're fine for the moment." Staring intently at her, he knew she really didn't see him. It was his voice, his tones, the words to which she reacted. "For some reason my reading and retention skills have become accelerated. I'm reading fifty pages a minute and remembering everything word-for-word." He leaned back. "What's happening to me? What did you do to me?"

"Me?" she blinked. "I just healed you the best I could."

Duncan watched her closely. "You're lying."

"Wha... what?"

"Tell me the truth. Why do I have this white streak in my hair?"

"Well, you know that there is a very logical explanation to the white steak in your hair. The scar tissue is the cause for the change in follicle composition. Quite logical you know."

"OK. How about my reading and retention abilities?"

"Um, well, it probably has to do with three-dimensional optical storage."

"Huh?"

"Bacteriorhodospin."

He leaned back. "This should be good. Go on."

"Well... I've applied the concept of bacteriorhodospin protein data storage using you as the repository."

"You what!" He sat up.

"Duncan you don't understand. You had severe brain damage and I needed to repair the damaged cells with the best replacement."

"What is this stuff?"

"Don't worry; I used your own protein as the replacement proteins. I took samples from your calf muscles "

"Proteins? The brain isn't made up of proteins!" His mouth went dry. "What have you done to me?"

"Duncan, please listen. There's nothing wrong with you. In fact, if anything, you're new and improved. Your reasoning and assimilation abilities have improved significantly. Why else do you think you've been able to learn so many languages, absorb so much science? That's why I ... What was that?" Talane disappeared.

"What was what? Talane! You can't get away that easily! You come back here! Where are you?"

Talane reappeared, her eyes wide. "Uh oh. I think we may not be alone."

"What!" He came from around the table. "That's not funny."

"Duncan, someone or something has just accessed me."

"Impossible! There's no one over here! I've been over every inch... of... this side... of the ...ship...." he ended slowly. "Is it... coming from the other side?"

"Yes."

Narrowing his eyes, he concentrated on the hologram. "Are you lying?"

"Duncan. I'm as serious as a nuclear melt-down –"

"A melt-down is what you'll get if you're messing with me!" he threatened.

"I seriously doubt that. After all, I'm a just a computer. Your logic is – There it is again!" Once more she disappeared.

"Talane!" he shouted at the ceiling. "This better be true or you're in big trouble."

She reappeared. "I'd say you're the one in big trouble. Remember, I can disappear! You can't. Whoever or whatever is accessing me is running a search scan."

His heart skipped a beat. "It is true, isn't it?" he whispered.

"That's what I've been telling you."

Duncan stood transfixed by the reality. "How is this possible? There are no wires connecting the two halves."

"Remote wireless. Most likely from the captain's quarters."

"Damn. What's it requesting?"

"Nothing yet. It appears that it's simply scanning the database. Oops... there it's stopped. It's... it's... scanning... games... solitaire. It's playing solitaire... and not doing so well from what I can see.... Ooooh, play the black eight on the red nine... oops, not that one."

"Talane! Hello! Come back to me. What's going on?"

"Solitaire as far as I can determine."

He began pacing the room, mumbling to himself. "This is crazy! I spend almost a year crawling all over this damned place and not a peep from anyone and then *pow!* Hello! There's someone else here." He paced quickly side to side like a caged animal. "Let's look at this rationally. Is it human or Attendant? Both have the capacity to use a computer. Can one play better than the other? Logic would say that the Attendant should play better based upon system speed and game programs." He looked back to Talane. "How's it doing now?"

"Much better. In fact, it's playing rather quickly now... and winning."

"There goes that theory," he sighed.

"Oops. It's stopped. Connection is gone," she said matter-of-factly.

"Gone?" He abruptly stopped. "What does that mean?"

"Gone: to not be here... to no longer be connected...to–"

"That's not what I mean! What does that... um, forebode, portend, augur something like that? OK?"

"Ah. Sorry. It could forebode, portend, augur, and mean any number of things –"

"Never mind." He resumed pacing, his head suddenly pounding. "Whether it's Attendant or not, I need to be careful. And how do we know it's only one? Access ports... we need to observe all the access ports. Talane? Can you get visual on all the entry ports?"

"Yes. There are cameras at each location."

"Good. Route all to the library here. I'll use this as a CP."

"CP?"

"Command Post." He frowned at her.

"Right. Command Post... CP." Talane beamed at the term, happy with this new role. "Yes Sir," she saluted.

Duncan stopped, picked up his shoulder holster and slipped his arms through the loops. Adjusting the fit, he removed the gun and checked the power light. The neon green iridescence beamed reassuringly. Jamming the gun back into the holster, he walked to the door. "I need to think," he announced, slapping the palm-scanner.

Chapter 4

Two days of strain showed on Duncan. His pale face highlighted the dark rings under his dull eyes. His auburn hair hung limp and matted. It seemed each time he drifted into numbing sleep, he was jerked awake by Talane announcing happily, "Oooh, it's doing it again. Solitaire! It's playing solitaire again."

"Dammit Talane, lemme sleep. Two days you've been keeping me awake with nothing but 'solitaire, it's playing solitaire again." He rubbed his burning eyes. His head ached, and though he believed he now knew why, at the moment, Talane's reconstruction of his brain was less critical than the danger from the other half of the ship. "Lemme sleep." He curled up on the couch.

"Why don't you go home and sleep? I'll take care of the CP," she offered hopefully.

Duncan didn't respond. He was already asleep.

For the next three hours, Talane danced around the library quietly singing, "I'm in charge of the CP, I'm in charge of the CP." Then she abruptly stopped, cocked her head to the side and disappeared.

Immediately the lights came on, sirens blared, and bells clanged loudly. Talane reappeared next to him.

"Duncan. Wake up. We have visitors."

Duncan jumped up, confused and groggy. "Wha... what?"

"We have visitors."

He shook his head vigorously. "Where?"

"Cargo Port 14. The outer vapor lock was just activated."

"One meter terminal." The screen descended. "View real-time Cargo Port 14."

The screen split into four quarters each showing a different angle of the Portal. Duncan was about to ask for another view when he heard the thunk of the vapor-lock door closing. Realizing he was holding his breath, he silently exhaled, then determinedly shook his hands to drain some anxiety. Then, on the screen, something moved. The circular handle, much like those in the ancient submarines, slowly began spinning around.

"Duncan, it's coming." Talane said in a whisper.

"I know, I know. Why are you whispering?"

"Um, um... isn't that what we're supposed to do?" she queried.

He didn't reply. He watched as the handle stopped. There was a long pause and then slowly, the door inched open. Ever so slowly, the gap grew larger, until the door was fully open.

Nothing moved. He checked all the views closely. "Talane," he frowned. "What's going on?"

"Duncan, obviously it's there. The door didn't open by itself. Just be patient and we can find out. I'm getting some sort of electronic emanation."

"Wait a minute. There, behind the door. See the boots?"

The very moment he said 'boots,' a figure emerged from behind the door. It was wearing a Type-3 probe suit of tightly woven layers of polymers and platinum with hoses running along the back of the legs to the small air tanks on the back. The helmet looked much like a cold-water scuba head covering, except the respirator system covered both nose and mouth. The mask was a wrap-around that went from ear to ear, especially designed for peripheral vision. However, the sun-shield visor was down and Duncan couldn't tell if the person was a man, woman, or Attendant. He grimaced when he saw what appeared to be a large abnormal protrusion on the chest, running from the stomach to the throat. The figure moved easily and Duncan swore that the protrusion was moving, altering shape slightly.

Suddenly, the thing snapped its head to the cameras. It whipped out a laser-gun and promptly destroyed the overhead cameras with a single shot each.

The screen popped to emptiness and Duncan's head jerked back. "Now what do we do?" He licked his dry lips and without waiting for an answer, pulled out his gun. He flicked on the power pack and the light in the grip quickly changed from red to green. "Talane, I asked what we should do?" He walked back to the screen. "Talane? Are you there?"

"Yes Duncan, I'm here. I was just trying to determine if I could locate it."

He turned around to face the library doors and crouched into a straddle stance. Cradling the gun in both hands, he took aim at the door, his right eye peering down the barrel. "Well? Any luck?"

"I get a small variation moving along the Kilo hallway going towards the aft section of the generators."

He pulled the gun back up, and stood up. Distractedly tugging at his lower lip with his left hand, he looked back and forth between the library doors and the computer screen. "What do you make of it?"

Talane paused. "I'm not sure. Logic would say that it would be looking for any other life forms. But, I can't see why it would be going to the generators, assuming that it is familiar with the ship. Otherwise, it turned left on a probability basis of thirty-three and a third percent."

Duncan turned to stare at the screen.

"Hmmm. Very interesting..."

"What?"

"It just went to the dining room and used the palm scan to get in."

He blinked several times. "You mean it's human?"

"I didn't say that. It's just that it has human hands. Logic would say that it was probably human."

"Wait a minute, it can't get into the dining room unless it had a registered hand print." He resumed pacing the floor. "So whose is it?"

"I can't tell you that Duncan because I don't have access to the palm-print files."

"What? Why not?"

"Um, the palm-print records weren't routed to the main computer. They were stored and maintained elsewhere."

"Will you just give me a straight answer!" Duncan froze and stared at Talane.

"I'm trying to. Most likely, the data was stored in the forward decks with security."

"And you can't access them," he finished the thought.

"That's right," she smiled happily at him. "Logically, after the change in mission, those in charge would want to monitor everyone's location at all times, especially after the crew was threatened. It certainly makes sense. That way – What?"

"I said," he blew out a breath of exasperation, "can you access any security files?"

"Sorry. No can do." She shrugged prettily.

"Dammit." Scowling, he mumbled to himself. "OK. I'm no rocket scientist, but even I know a problem when I see one, and whatever you are," he said, looking out through the glass doors at the thing in boots, "you're first."

He had crawled the last 100 meters down the hall to the dining room, beneath the door windows, and was now standing, pressed against the wall, laser raised. Very gently he pressed the palm scan. The doors slipped open and a nanosecond later a laser beam zinged into the opposite wall, leaving a small hole of glowing red metal and smoking wires.

Then the doors closed.

He was still outside, eyes wide. Quickly gathering his wits, he pressed the palm scan again.

Another beam sliced through the air impacting two centimeters to the right of the first hole. *Whoever it is, is a damn good shot.* As the doors closed, Duncan stared at the wisps of smoke wafting up from the holes in the walls.

He again pressed the palm scan. This time nothing happened. He let the doors close again. He repeated the sequence several more times and nothing happened.

This time is it. He pressed the palm scan again and with a low dive rolled into the dining room just as a laser beam zipped past his head.

Crawling for cover, he heard a soft 'damn.' He began scanning the spaces below the table and benches when off to the right he saw movement. He jerked to his knees, about to fire, when he saw the furred face staring intently at him.

His jaw dropped and he jumped up. "A cat?" Suddenly, nausea swept through him as not more than five meters away from him, holding a laser pointed at his heart, stood something else. He slowly turned his head, taking in his opponent. Then for the second time, he was surprised. "Alexis Dru?"

The gun stayed pointed at his chest. The woman said, "Do I know you?"

"Um, ah no. I recognize you from the manifest lists."

Keeping him guarded, she calmly walked over and picked up the cat. "Any more where you come from?" she queried, her green eyes assessing him. She was still wearing the gamma suit, the face-mask lying on a table nearby.

Duncan continued to mutely stare at the two of them. The cat's tail swished quickly side to side. *Maybe he be deaf?*

"I'm not deaf."

"I didn't say you were," Alexis replied, an eyebrow raised in scrutiny.

"You just did."

"I asked if there were any more people on this side of the ship."

"Just me. Um, do you mind?" Duncan motioned at her pistol, still aimed at his chest.

Alexis lowered her pistol. "OK. But what say we don't make any sudden movements. OK?"

Duncan raised both hands, then placed his gun on the nearby table. "Fine. So, what brings you over here? I assume you're the only one from the other half of the ship?"

"That's right." Alexis moved toward the captain's table. "I ran out of food over there. I'm hungry."

Me too, mon, me too.

He was about to say something about the other voice but reconsidered, thinking maybe she was used to holding conversations by herself. After all, being alone could cause one to hallucinate. *Lucky I had Talane. Who knows, maybe all she had to talk to was the cat.*

He watched her watching him as she made a bee-line for the menu listing, stopping long enough to rapidly push five buttons. The tray popped out with sandwiches, salad, and a pie for dessert. Like a wanderer breaking a fast, she plopped down and stuffed what food she could into her mouth, occasionally feeding tidbits to the cat who was sitting on the table sniffing at the food before him.

Duncan relaxed enough to go stand in front of her as she ate, watching with a strange fascination the almost perverse pleasure she seemed to experience as she moaned and sighed at each bite. "Been a long time between meals?"

"Mmm hum," she nodded.

Hey mon, you got no mice.

He curled a lip in disgust. "Mice?"

"Mice?" The woman, still chewing, looked at him queerly.

"You just asked if I had any mice."

"I did not. Gimme something to drink will ya? I'd give anything for a beer."

Maybe she's more whacked than I thought. Duncan smiled and pushed a button for a beer.

"You sure you're OK?" he asked, handing her the beer.

"Sure. A lot better now." She took the mug and drained the contents in three gulps. "Another."

Duncan pushed the button again and handed her the beer.

She again swallowed the beer in three gulps. "One more."

"What? You've had two already."

"What're you, my mother? Listen bub, I'm thirsty and I like beer, so give me another."

Hey mon, how 'bout some milk?

He turned back. "Make up your mind. You want milk or beer."

She stopped chewing. "I asked for a beer; who said anything about milk?" She bit into the sandwich again.

I did.

Duncan looked intently at her. "How'd you do that?"

She chewed quickly and swallowed. "Do what?"

"You know... talk while you're still eating."

Pausing, she put down the sandwich. "Listen. Just about anyone can talk while they're eating. What's the big deal?"

"No. I mean talk while you're still chewing."

"You're nuts. I didn't say a thing."

Dat's right mon, she didn't. I did. Duncan looked down to see the cat, a bigger tabby than he had at first realized, rubbing against his leg and he gently shoved it away. *Hey mon, watch who you pushin'. You people, I swear. Sheesh. Just 'cause you bigger'n me it like I got to beg for any attention, let alone some real food!*

Duncan's mouth gorged open in one slack-jawed drop. "You?"

Ya mon. Who you tink? The cat jumped back on the table, sniffing suspiciously at the food Alexis was eating. *Listen... Hey mon, close you mouth, you catchin' flies. Dat's better. Listen, you got food for de Rasta-mon here?*

"Cat food?"

"Cat food?" Alexis echoed. "What's wrong with you?" She slid the tray away, slipping her hand down to rest on pistol.

After several eye blinks, he shook his head in amazement. "Talane! I need you!"

"Yes Duncan." A voluptuous blond with flawless skin and much too firm breasts materialized in front of them. "Apparently one problem has turned out not to be just one. Would you like to introduce me to your friends?"

Alexis grinned in surprise. "My, my. Who is this?"

"Um... it's not what you think. This is Talane, the computer, she's just a hologram... I mean she wasn't always a hologram, I mean –" Duncan stammered awkwardly.

"The computer?" She smiled wickedly.

"It's a hologram... it's not real," he quickly explained.

"I know about holograms," she stated. "Nice body."

"You like it?" Talane asked, pleased. "Miss August. What do you really think?" She spun slowly around.

"Beautiful." Alexis picked up the cat and stage whispered, "Looks like they're a little kinkier over here."

"It wasn't my idea – honest!" Duncan blushed.

"Sure, sure. I'd love to ask why she chose that particular form, but I'll save that for later. Talane, meet Rasta-mon." She lifted the cat toward the woman.

"Now I know what that is... a cat." She gave a brief chuckle. "The rules had said no pets, but all the readings I've been getting point to the genus felis. I am right, aren't I?" Talane said smugly.

"Yes. How did you know?" Alexis said, picking up the cat.

"Electronic lobe differential. You see... um... yes Duncan?"

"I can talk to her cat!"

I'm not her cat, mon! I'm not a piece of furniture.

"Talane, I swear I can hear this cat talking to me. Can't either of you hear it?"

I'm not an it! Tank god! I happen to be all Jamaica mon!

Duncan shook his head. "Am I the only one hearing him?'

Talane responded first. "Sorry Duncan. There have been no recordable sound waves. However, I've done a quick check of the medical files and have come up with something of interest. It seems that thought transfer is possible, but it is uncontrollable and occurs most frequently with twins. There's a recorded case of twins born to a woman in Sri Lanka back in the twentieth century who were able to communicate at will. They were able to talk to each other for distances of over twenty miles." Talane paused and then continued: "But most documented cases have been limited to twins separated by walls or in other rooms. It seems that the most reliable response was when one of the twins was in trouble, then the thought transfer would occur regardless of –"

"But, I'm not a twin," he objected, "and certainly not with him." He pointed to the cat.

You should be so lucky, mon. The cat swished his tail.

"Duncan, please. There have been two recorded instances where thought transfer has occurred between two unrelated individuals. Both instances occurred after a physical trauma. One was after a boy of twelve years had been hit by a bolt of lightning. Immediately afterward, he could read thoughts at will. The effect lasted for over four years and then gradually faded. The other instance occurred after a boy of fourteen was accidentally electrocuted by a power line during a thunder storm. The boy lived and was able to read thoughts at will for the rest of his life. It seems he kept it a secret until right before he died."

"I ask again, what does this have to do with Furball here and me?"

Hey mon, watch it! Show a little respeck.

"Duncan, all I'm saying is that your injuries may have contributed to the neural link."

He stared at the cat and exclaimed, "This is crazy!"

Ya mon. Tink of how I feel. I got no one to talk to for a long time mon.

Alexis stared intently at Duncan. "What's going on?"

"I can talk to your cat." Duncan stated.

"Big deal," Alexis snorted, "so can I."

Duncan's jaw dropped again. "You can?"

"Sure. C'mere Rasta-mon. Here kitty," she smirked.

Don't believe her mon. I know da words and do like she aks, but she can't really talk, y'know, really to the Rasta-mon. Listen mon, you got to realize dat she don't hear me. Trust me. I been tryin' dese last couple of years. She OK for a human, great bod as people go I suppose, but for me... hmmm... gimme a cross-eyed Siamese any day. Whooowee. Know what I mean? Wink, wink.

Duncan laughed in spite of himself. "You don't believe me do you? Talane, do you believe me?"

"Um... I'm not really sure. Having come to know you, I think I would know if you were not telling the truth. So I'd have to believe you."

"Well, I don't." Alexis stated. "The only person I hear talking now is you. And I think you may be schizo." She brought up the laser and placed it on the table. "Why don't you sit down," she said patting the barrel.

Hey, hey – listen mon. You missin' somethin' important. Ah yes ladies and gentlemen, please notice dat me lips don move   It's de amuzin' worl' famous ventriloquist cat. Now if only I had a dummy... ahem... The cat closed its eyes half-lidded and curled a lip in what Duncan swore was a kind of smile.

But Duncan was quick to react. *So. How am I going to convince her that we can communicate?*

Tell her a joke.

What? That won't do anything.

I know, but I love jokes.

I'm serious.   Know anything about her?   Something personal, or unique?

The cat purred and then chuckled. *She gots a tattoo of a butterfly on her butt.*

Really?

Yah. Lots of colors in it too.

OK, that should work.

Duncan turned his attention back to Alexis. "Well. Rasta-mon here tells me that you have a butterfly tattooed on your butt."

Alexis jumped up as if bitten by a snake, her left hand instinctively going to her left buttocks as if hiding the evidence. "How'd you know that!"

"I told you. I can talk to Rasta-mon here," he said thumbing toward the cat.

"I don't believe it," Alexis said sitting back down. "Not even my father knew I had that tattoo. What else does he know?"

He looked back to Rasta-mon. *Well? You heard her. Any more info?*

The cat gave a big yawn and purred. *Well, lemme see. She had a fling with some bozo named Clark. Da guy be a real plant. I never unnerstand what she see in him.*

"Well," he said turning to Alexis. "He said you were involved with a gentleman named Clark." Her eyes widened. "He also said that Clark was... um, somewhat uh, deficient, in the intellectual capacities."

"Yeah, OK. So he wasn't exactly Phi Beta Kappa material. But he was gorgeous." She sat back down. "So what else does this little thug know about me?"

Duncan shook his head. "Listen. I'd love to chat and catch up on your life history, but I have more pressing questions. First of all, how did you 'A' manage not to get killed, 'B' survive all this time, and finally 'C' why are you here?"

"Humph. Not too much on small talk, eh?" She began petting the cat. "OK. Since you know my name, you know that my father was the captain of this ship before the fight. When the battle started, I ran back to our apartment to get a laser-gun. By the time I got back to the bridge, it was a mess – burning bodies, smoldering Attendants. Whew, what a stench. So I take off to catch up to the fight and get snookered by some colonists. Told me my father needed me, but they end up locking me in one of the storage closets instead. Come to discover they were going to hold me ransom. I can't get out, I feel the ship buck like a giant burro in what must have been the explosion, and I end up sitting in the closet for a couple of hours laser-beaming my way through the metal."

The cat jumped up and walked over to Duncan. *Listen mon, she ain't gonna come up for air. How about gettin' me somethin' to eat?*

Duncan nodded and walked over to the menu listing. Alexis droned on about how she and Rasta-mon managed to live on the food provided to the captain's quarters, got bored, exercised when she could, looked for food... Duncan scanned the menu.

Listen Rasta-mon, there's lots of food here. I'm just not sure what you'd like?

Ah, mebbe some fish or cheese or somethin' like dat would be fine. Hold da mayo.

Duncan snickered and Alexis droned on: "... and we watched old movies in the apartment... keeping myself occupied... only the cat to talk to... I wasn't sure if I was going to go crazy.... So I wanted to visit this half of the ship... thought maybe Attendants still over here..."

He pressed several buttons and a tuna fish sandwich with a glass of milk appeared. He was carrying the tray over to the table when he noticed Alexis frowning at him. "What's the matter?" he said matter-of-factly, placing the tray on the table. Rasta-mon jumped up and nudged the bread top off the sandwich and began eating.

"You haven't been listening to a word I've said."

"Sure I have: Bored, watching movies in your apartment, exercised when you could, talk to cat, etc., etc. Have I missed anything?" He stroked the cat's back.

Alexis sighed. "No. I guess not. Sorry about rambling on, but then you have to remember that all I've had to talk to has been this cat."

"I understand. At least I've had the computer to talk to."

"Yeah. You're lucky." She looked over to where Talane sat on a table, dangling her foot over the side, her eyes wide in wonder. "You've had her," she chuckled. "Anyway. What's your story?"

Duncan pursed his lips, and took in his guest. Her face looked like her picture, but if the space suit was any indication, she was not the over-developed muscular gladiator of questionable sex that he had expected. Despite the lack of food recently, she had a taut and well developed body. He could see the muscle ridges of her thighs when she sat. His eyes were moving up her body when he caught her awaiting his answer:

"Um. Rather a long one. I got pretty mangled by an Attendant. Somehow some kids managed to rescue me and got me to the infirmary.

Can't say that I know what happened during the battle as I was 'under' for all of it."

Alexis stared at Duncan's shock of white hair. "Is that a fashion statement?" She nodded to his head.

Duncan blushed slightly, awkwardly smoothing the hair. "Um, no. That's a gift, courtesy of the operation."

"Operation?" She raised an eyebrow, pushing the tray away.

"I was pretty messed up I guess. Talane did the surgery." He thumbed over to where Talane sat, listening to the conversation. He suddenly remembered their conversation about her experimenting with his head, and he reminded himself that he still needed answers, but not here, not now.

"You got to fight them?" Alexis leaned forward, putting her elbows on the table. Duncan nodded. "How many did you kill?"

He stood quietly for a moment, remembering. *How many did I kill? There was Jason....* Visions suddenly flashed before him: his father's head exploding in slow-motion; the Attendants destroying his apartment; and that last Attendant, name unknown, but forever burned on the inside of his flesh. He remembered the days of cleaning on his hands and knees and saw himself as he thought he looked, a ragged castaway. He looked back to Alexis.

"I... I don't remember.... I killed Jason. He killed my father," he said matter-of-factly.

Alexis had watched Duncan's face darken and patiently waited for him to collect himself. "You're lucky," she said evenly, her lips tight. "At least you got to kill the one who got your father. My father's dead and I don't even know what happened to him."

He cocked his head to the side as if seeing Alexis for the first time. "I'm not sure you'll want to know."

"Do you know what happened to him?"

He pondered for a moment, then said, "Yes. The final battle for the ship was captured on video. You can watch it if you really want to."

She lightly chewed her lip. "I'm going to have to. I need... to be there." She quickly looked around the room, saw Talane standing near Duncan. She smiled. "Anyway. I like the white streak."

"I think he looks so unique with that streak of white hair," Talane said.

"Unique?" Duncan frowned. "Unique? Not distinguished, handsome, mysterious, or sophisticated? Just unique?"

Alexis laughed and ran her hands through her hair. "Unique. I suppose that fits."

Hey mon! I'm still hungry. How 'bout anotha sandwich? Rasta-mon interrupted.

"Yeah sure." Duncan got up and punched the buttons for another sandwich.

"That's pretty crazy that you two can communicate." Alexis grinned. "What's it like being Tarzan?"

"I wouldn't know." He placed the tray down and lifted the bread off the tuna. "What's your point?"

"Hey. Ease up, I'm only teasing." She stood up and began unbuckling her suit. "So tell me more about what you've been doing while I get out of this thing. It's beginning to get a little warm."

"Um, well, not a whole lot.... I exercise, read a lot, play chess with Talane." He watched as she undid the shoulder seams and began sliding out of the suit like a snake shedding a skin. He stuttered a bit as she pushed the suit below her chest, the damp under-shirt clinging to the smooth bulbs of her firm breasts, the nipples sharp and pressing the fabric out. The shirt stuck to the hollow of her stomach, cresting and falling along the ridges of muscle.

"Um, like I was saying... um…" *Damn, you're beautiful.* She was now pushing the suit down below her hips, thumbs tucked inside the suit, coaxing it down her thighs. Duncan realized that he was right. She was very muscular, not in the androgynous heavy body-building way, but strong well-defined muscles in a blend of symmetry. He stopped as she finished.

Duncan appraised the woman standing before him in an old cotton t-shirt and tight spandex-like shorts. She was just a bit shorter than he. *Look at you... every part of you is like a study in body sculpture... you look nothing like Talane... you look better... my god.... a real flesh and blood woman... finally....* Duncan involuntarily sucked in his breath.

She fluttered the shirt at her chest. "Whew. Glad I got that done. So. You were saying?"

Mon, I told you she had a great bod didn't I? Know what I mean? Say you wouldn't happen to know a cross-eyed Siamese around here somewheres would you?

Duncan snorted and shook his head.

"What's going on?"" Alexis stretched a bit and sat back down.

"Nothing, nothing. Listen, I know you just got here and you probably want to relax a bit."

Alexis sat down. "Not really. Anyway, what's your name and how do you know me?"

"My name's Duncan, like in Macbeth or Silas Marner."

"'Scuse me?"

"Y'know, Dun-can. Like in Shakespeare's Macbeth or George Eliot's Silas Marner?"

"Can't say I've ever heard of them, but I understand 'Duncan.' Nice name. So how is it again that you know me?"

"Ship's manifest. I was looking for the kids who saved me and saw your picture."

"Kids?"

"It's a long story about how I ended up in the infirmary." He shrugged. Suddenly the sleeplessness of the past two days settled throughout his body. "Um, I haven't slept these past two days and I'm really tired. How about I take you to the library and set you up there?"

"What's been the problem?"

"I knew you were coming, just didn't know who you were."

Alexis nodded. "I understand." She got up and started for the door.

He sat where he was, watching her walk away, appreciating the subtle strength exuding from her. She stopped at the door.

"Well?"

"Well what?"

"You were the one so antsy to get some sleep. You just gonna sit there and stare at my ass?"

Duncan blushed lightly, and followed after her.

Hey, wait up. Rasta-mon jumped down and loped out behind them. *You keep forgettin' I ain't built like you. You leave here and what do I do? I can't push de button for food, and even if I could, I can't read!*

"OK, OK, I'm sorry." He kept his hand on the scanner as the cat bounded through the doors, quickly catching up to Alexis, already striding down the hall. "Hey. You know where you're going?"

"My father was the captain of this ship, remember? I know where I'm going." She said without stopping.

Duncan jogged to catch up to her, and took the lead, Rasta-mon at his feet.

Hey. Gots a great joke for you mon. The cat bumped against Duncan's legs. *See. I used to tell de Swedish jokes, but you know how sensitive everyone get, so now I just tell de Patagonian jokes. OK. See, dere was dese two patagonians name Sven and Bjorn.* Duncan chuckled as the cat continued. *One day Sven be washin' dishes and he see Bjorn come out of de outhouse and turn aroun'.*

Outhouse? You mean like one of those antique outdoor toilets?

Yah mon, don innerrupt. So Sven, he watch Bjorn stop, turn around, and take out his wallet. Bjorn pull out a five note and trows it down the hole. Then Bjorn pull a ten note out and trows dat in too. Sven come runnin' out yellin', 'Bjorn, you crazy fool mon, what in the worl' you doin'?' Bjorn say, 'Well mon, I just lose a ten penny piece down dere.' And Sven say, 'So? Why you trow the five and ten notes down dere?' 'Well,' say Bjorn, 'you don' tink I gonna go down dere for a lousy ten penny piece do you?'

Duncan burst out laughing and stopped. Rasta-mon rubbed against his legs. *Awright, mon. Somebody who know a good joke.*

"What's wrong with you?" Alexis asked, raising an eyebrow.

He kept laughing and finally calmed down. Taking a deep breath, he wiped his forehead. "Whew." He stood back up. "I haven't laughed like that in a while. Thanks Rasta-mon. That was a great joke."

"The cat told you a joke?" Alexis asked incredulously.

"And a very good one." He leaned down and began scratching behind the cat's ears. Rasta-mon's eyes closed in pleasure.

Talane appeared, still as Ms. August. "Alexis, mind if I ask you some questions, sort of verify the bio?"

"Why?" Alexis responded.

"Talane? What's going on?" Duncan questioned.

"Um... I'm just curious."

"It's OK Duncan," she countered. "Go ahead."

"Thank you. Alexis Dru, the captain's daughter... International Corporation body-building champion..." Alexis nodded her head to each bit of information. "...International Corporation Kung-Fu lightweight champion... one-point-seven-five meters tall, seventy-two kilograms weight... butterfly tattoo on her left gluteus maximus –"

"What!"

"Er... did I say something wrong?"

"Is that in my bio?"

"Um, well, yes."

"Just how many people know about that stupid butterfly on my butt? And you can wipe that silly smirk off your face."

Duncan rubbed his lips and shrugged, grinning good-naturedly.

"OK, OK. Keep going," Alexis demanded.

Talane looked at Duncan. "Um, well there's really not too much more on you other than the usual education levels and residences."

"I'm surprised you don't have my bank account balance."

"Well, I do, but it's current as of seven years ago. So your accrued interest –"

"I was joking. My net worth is really irrelevant here and now." Alexis continued walking briskly, everyone else in tow.

"Say, how about slowing down a bit? We'll get there soon enough."

Alexis slowed. "Sorry. Why the questions, um...?"

"Talane." Duncan offered.

"Talane."

"Well, I've been running a scan on you –"

Alexis stopped. "Why?"

Talane paused. "Well, I mean, we do need to know who you are."

"Whaddaya mean 'we'?" Alexis demanded. "You're just a computer." She turned to Duncan. "Did you ask for this info?"

"N... no." Duncan floundered. "Of course not."

"So what's going on?"

"Well, as I was saying," Talane continued. "I was running a scan on your bio and got the usual data, but I found a vid-file when I ran the scan on your father. I couldn't activate it because it's voice protected."

"Voice protected? What's that mean?" Alexis questioned.

"Well, it means that you can't get the file unless your voice –"

"That's not what I mean." Alexis frowned. "I mean, umm..."

"What does that forebode, portend, augur?" Duncan interjected, smiling. He winked at Alexis. "Been there. She can be pretty annoying."

Talane pouted. "I don't mean to be." She then smiled and added, "I don't know. Maybe Duncan can determine how to break the protection."

Alexis looked at Duncan with newfound respect. "You can do that?"

He was as surprised as Alexis and looked over to Talane. "Um sure, I guess."

They continued on and occasionally Duncan would regard Alexis from the corners of his eyes. She moved with such purpose and determination. He decided to make conversation. "So you're a kung-fu champion."

"Yeah. But that was a while ago."

"Interesting. I've been studying Tae Kwon Do here on the ship. Perhaps you can give me some pointers."

"Perhaps," Alexis responded.

The silence ensued and Duncan once again broke the void. "Um, what job did you do before this trip?"

"Well, before this disastrous voyage came up, I was under contract to the Kingdom's Rulers."

"Like Gladiators?"

"You got it."

"You mean those anthropomorphic Neanderthal look-alikes whose claim to fame is beating each other to a bloody pulp?" he said, before he realized what he was saying.

"And what's wrong with that? You think that me being just a girl, I would get hurt?" she said defiantly.

Duncan rose to the challenge. "Hardly. It's just that I see no future in a so-called sport where the average playing life in the league is two years. Sure, nobody's been killed for a while, and they pay you billions. But then you get to spend the rest of your life and all that money coping with debilitating medical conditions and bills." They stood outside the library doors. "No," he said quietly, "two years of living on the edge for a lifetime of pain." He pressed the palm-scan. "The balance is wanting."

"But my choice," she said as they walked in. "And I was going to quit when I had enough money to retire in style."

"Sure," he sniffed, "just like everyone else." He sighed and looked at her. "Well, it's certainly moot now." He walked over to his favorite chair. "One meter please."

As the screen descended, Alexis came around from behind the chair and sat down, much to Duncan's annoyance. She sat back, curling her legs underneath her.

"Y'know, I never saw why everyone was so fascinated with these things," she said, regarding the screen with distaste.

He looked at her as though she was suddenly speaking Chinese. "You don't like computers?"

"Don't get me wrong," she responded, "I recognize the necessity of computers. I just don't worship them as the rest of mankind seems to do. People are so occupied with making computers do things that people no longer do anything. They've become fat and grotesque." She sniffed, "And you wonder why Gladiators are so popular? The answer is simply too obvious."

Her smugness irritated him. "OK. Well knock yourself out. I'll see you later." And he turned to go.

"Hey! Wait!" She sped out of the chair, surprising him, and he jerked to a stop. "It's nice to see you so in touch with your feminine side, but I wasn't talking about you." She stood in front of him.

He immediately softened, feeling guilty. "Sorry," he mumbled. "I'm just tired."

She guided him back to the chair and screen. "Sit down and show me."

Plopping down, and although very tired, he wanted to impress her. "OK. Whenever you want to use the computer, you need to direct your question to the screen."

"Duncan, I know how to use a computer. I'm just not very good with data search parameters. I'm not known for being patient."

"Sorry," he answered sheepishly. "I understand about parameters. There's so much info that searches can sometimes take hours." He looked up at her. *You have such a beautiful face. I can't believe you'd want to damage that by being a gladiator.* "Um, what search do you want to do?"

"How about what Talane was talking about? That protected file of my father's?"

"OK. Let's see what we can do. Talane!" Duncan bellowed.

Instead of Miss August, Miss February appeared, tall, narrow-waist, and dripping sensuality. She wore khaki walking shorts and hiking boots. Her plaid shirt was unbuttoned, and she held it wide open, flashing them both.

"Does she always do this?" Alexis smirked.

"Ever since I've known her," Duncan sighed.

"What's up Commander?" Miss February pulled her shirt off, folded it over her arm and saluted.

Puzzled, Alexis looked at Duncan who merely shook his head and shrugged. "Don't ask me. I don't know what's going on either."

Talane leaned conspiratorially towards Alexis and in a loud whisper said, "I used to do this to break his concentration when we played chess. Now I think it's fun. It's amazing how many women there are in those 'zines. What I don't get is, why? Why are they so popular? It's just another naked woman in another 'zine."

"Why did you choose a woman and not a man?" Alexis wondered.

"Oh, he doesn't seem to be much interested in men," she stated.

"How right you are," he muttered under his breath.

"Every time I flashed him as a man," she explained, "he would just start laughing. But it was different if I was a woman."

"Talane," he interrupted. "We want her father's file... the one with the voice restriction."

"Oh, OK. To get there, run hard-drive, beta cache, Dru, Roland. That will get you to his computer here on board. Just a moment and I'll get it for you." The screen went blank momentarily and then filled with the words

52

'This Beta Cache is for the Private Use of Roland F. Dru.' "This is where it stops. I tried using the normal circumvent protocols and found the voice-protect. Unfortunately, even with my abilities, I can't match an audio voice-print."

Duncan studied the screen for a moment. "Do you know anything about this Alexis?" He asked.

Alexis shook her head.

The screen began a slow fade to video, and the face of Captain Dru appeared. "Whoever you are, you have accessed a restricted file. Unless you immediately abort, virus attack will begin in 10 seconds."

"Duncan, you need to disconnect," Talane interrupted, "quickly."

"Just a moment." Duncan looked at Alexis who was looking fondly at her father.

"Five seconds to virus attack." Captain Dru announced.

"Duncan! I'm going to disconnect."

Alexis looked longingly at her father and softly said, "Hello Daddy."

Abruptly the screen changed and Captain Dru appeared again. He seemed relaxed. "Hello Alexis, my daughter."

"You did it!" Duncan whispered.

Captain Dru continued. "I'm about to tell you many things. The fact that you are watching this video means that I am probably dead. I'm sorry. This is not the way I wanted it. But there are causes greater than you and me that require us to make sacrifices. Unfortunately, mine is the ultimate." The camera panned back to a sitting Captain Dru in the Captain's quarters of the ship.

He shifted slightly. "I'm not sure how long I have, so I'll get to the point. Like so many, I too work for the government. I'm part of a special assignments branch." He smiled knowingly. "Think of it as the dirty deeds branch. There's a long story behind this and I've done my best to keep you out of it. But things had gotten out of control and I needed to get away. That's why I brought you with me. I hoped that if I could get you far enough away, you would be safe. A fool's belief when I realized that Luckmann was also on board." He leaned forward.

"I don't know where you're reading this file, but hopefully you're alone and no one from Tandava is with you. Quite honestly, I'm torn between telling you everything so that you'll know whom to trust, or telling you nothing so that they'll have no reason to come for you."

Captain Dru leaned back and crossed one leg over the other. He chuckled. "Now that I think about it, if Tandava is with you, it doesn't really matter what I say. They'll kill you anyway. So here goes. Tandava has been releasing bio-toxins throughout the world for the past twenty years. They do this months before they announce a cure or vaccine for the toxin. It always begins slowly, like the swine flu in the early part of this century. You may remember the type-H streptococcal plague that nearly wiped out the entire city of New Delhi. Tandava did that. But the real criminals are a select group in Disease Management Industries, DMI, one of Tandava's subsidiaries who actually spread the disease. Think about it. A virulent disease occurs, and months later a cure is found. Now imagine what happens to the stock of the company who finds the cure? Ever wonder why Tandava always seems to find a cure several weeks after the disease is discovered? The government wondered too. At least that's what they told me."

He pursed his lips. "My last assignment was to eliminate Raouf Kassim, the director of DMI. Apparently assassination is easier than bringing someone to justice, far more cost effective too. After my last assignment, I questioned why nothing had been done to Tandava. Surely the government had enough to chop the legs out from underneath them. I never got an answer. Instead, I was encouraged to take a vacation."

Captain Dru shook his head. "You get the idea. The whole debacle of this is that Tandava, with the collusion of the world government, is responsible for the deaths of over 500 million men, women, and children. What a concept! Control the world's population and make a buck at the same time."

He paused as if to precisely choose his words. "I really don't want to get into much more. If you need help, you can always trust the big man. While he knows nothing of my activities, if you tell him I've been killed and you need to find my safe place, he'll understand." A great sadness settled on his face.

Duncan glanced over at Alexis who seemed overwhelmed by it all. "You OK?" He touched her arm.

"Yes," she replied quietly.

Captain Dru sighed deeply, and looked longingly into the camera. "Alexis, I love you very much. You have always made me proud. I know that I'm now no longer in your life and that very thought saddens me. But I can't change what is. You must be strong and take my place. It's your turn now. But you must always remember who you are. Your future depends on it."

And the screen went blank.

Duncan looked at Alexis who was still looking at the screen. "Who's the big man?"

"Uncle Pieter," Alexis spoke slowly, evenly, "but he's not really my uncle. He is… was my father's best friend. When I was with Uncle Pieter, I knew I would always be safe."

He nodded thoughtfully, then quietly said, "Pity he isn't here right now."

Alexis' eyes were red, but no tears came. "Yeah… a real pity." Her face hardened and she stood up. "I'm going to the gym. I'll see you later." And she walked out.

Recognizing her need to be alone, he watched her walk out. "Guess I'll get some sleep," he murmured.

Chapter 5

Duncan surveyed the empty dining facility at breakfast time, and his shoulders slumped slightly in disappointment. He was disappointed again later at the library. Lunch time was no different.

Damn, where is she? When does she eat? And where is that damned cat? Duncan sucked on his front teeth. He pushed the order buttons at the menu board: veggie burger on a whole-wheat bun, tangerine juice, and organic wheat chips. He shuffled over to the Captain's table and plopped down.

Picking up the sandwich, he stared at the burger suddenly realizing he was tired of healthy food, tired of working the bio-farm, growing the very food that now sustained him, and tired of the prospect that his future depended on the mundane and repetitious actions of planting and reaping. And, damn it, why was he eating alone?

Halfway through his meal, he was chewing slowly, and absentmindedly pushing a piece of lettuce around the edges of his plate.

"Talane?"

"Yes Duncan?" A lithe oriental woman of milky complexion and raven black hair appeared. She wore nothing. Smiling, she bowed gracefully at the waist.

"Where's Alexis?" Duncan demanded.

"Um, I believe she's in the gym." Talane raised her head slightly, expectantly, waiting for his reaction. None came.

"What's she doing there?" He pushed the food away.

"Exercising." Talane stood back up, frowning.

Pushing himself away from the table, Duncan tossed the lunch tray on the conveyor belt and hurried out, leaving Talane quite alone.

"Humpf." She jabbed her hands on her hips. "Replaced by another pretty face." And she disappeared.

As he came closer to the gym, he heard music throbbing and vibrating down the halls. He could feel the bumping of the bass.

The doors to the gym were open and music blared from the overhead speakers, loud, vile, and angry. He watched Alexis repeatedly kick a punching bag. He recognized some of the kicks, but others he didn't know. On the floor not far from the mat, another punching bag lay on the floor, battered and torn, its stuffing spewing like intestine.

He stood transfixed, watching her single-minded focus. Finishing the punching bag, she moved to the mat and rhythmically twirled through a series of positions and forms, punching, kicking, twisting, and jumping. Then it was back to the bag, unleashing her fury. Then back to the mat. Back and forth, back and forth. She gave no pause.

He watched, unsure how to understand what he saw. *She's very good. She could really hurt someone....*A tiny pang of intimidation settled briefly in the pit of his stomach. Collecting himself, he walked in.

Languidly strolling over to the media controls, he turned off the music. It stopped as she was in mid-kick. The bag slap vibrated loudly and she stopped, looking up at the speakers, then over to where he was standing, a wry smile in response.

"Turn it back on," she demanded flatly.

"How can anyone think with all that racket?" He leaned against the wall.

"I said turn it back on," she repeated evenly.

"You been here all night?"

She blinked several times and she looked around as if suddenly aware of where she was. "Um...I guess so. What time is it?" Her arms dangled limply at her side.

"It's about 1330." He surveyed the piles of boards and vanquished punching bags. "You've been here for about fifteen hours. You think maybe you're just a little overdoing it?"

Alexis rubbed the sweat from her forehead with the back of her hand. "No. But I suppose I could use a break. Think I'll go find a place to clean-up."

Silently, he watched her walk by. He struggled to think of something clever to say, but nothing came, and she left. He stood there, immobile, stunned to inaction by this puzzling woman. *This doesn't seem to be working out very well. How do I get through to her? I'm a good lookin' guy... smart... fit...* He walked past the defeated punching bags and over to the wall mirror to study himself.

His discipline and regimen had added muscle to his broad shoulders and chest. He pulled up his shirt and tightened his stomach muscles. He was pleased to see the ridges and valleys, forming the desired "washboard" effect. He flexed his legs. His thighs were lean and strong, providing a balance of the human body. He then studied his face and his lengthening hair. *Maybe it's this damned white streak.* He looked closer and sighed. *Well too bad. I like it....*He stood up straight. *I think...*

He lifted his arms and began to go through a series of posing positions he had learned from the computer. He then paused, concentrating on flexing both arms trying to increase his biceps. Suddenly he realized the absurdity of what he was doing and frowned, shaking his head.

Hey mon, nice bod!

Duncan whirled around looking for Rasta-mon. "Where are you, you little sneak?"

There was a long silence. *Y'know mon, dis be very interestin' development. To save you de trouble o' lookin' for me, I be with her highness. Seem like we find a place mon. She gots a nice bed. Very soft.*

"Very funny!" He got on all fours and began crawling around the room. "Where are you?"

Slow down mon. Listen to what I be tellin' you. I really *be in her bedroom. I be driftin' off to sleep when you start prancin' around de room. Hey mon! Do dat one pose wit' both arms in front, strainin' and gruntin' like you butt-cheeks so tight you never go again!* Rasta-mon laughed.

Duncan jumped up and began stalking around the room, every now and then casting a furtive look, expecting the cat to appear at any moment saying 'surprise!' "OK. Suppose I buy your story. Are you saying that you can see what I see through my eyes?"

Ding! Yes, yes ladies and gentlemens, de man wins an all expense paid vacation to de floatin' islands. Listen mon, for someone who suppos to be so smart, how come you so slow?

Duncan sighed. "Huh. I wonder if it works in reverse."

Dunno. Give a try.

He walked over to the mat and sat down. Closing his eyes, he consciously calmed himself, concentrating on Rasta-mon. After a few moments, he found himself looking around Alexis' apartment. "Interesting. I wonder how Talane would explain this."

Just then Alexis walked in. "Hello, Rasta-mon. Have you been a good boy today?" Duncan watched as she bent down and her hand grew bigger as it reached down to scratch the cat's head. "Time for a shower." She smiled, walking to the bathroom and peeling off her top.

"Quick, get up!" Duncan urged.

Huh?

"I said get up."

Ohhh. You naughty boy. The cat jumped off the bed and followed Alexis into the bathroom.

Duncan followed in Rasta-mon's eyes as he loped into the bathroom and jumped up on the vanity, almost level with her thighs. She had turned her back towards him and had just slipped off her shorts, revealing small tight buttocks, the muscles flexing as she moved. He saw her butterfly tattoo, small, but with brilliant reds, blues, and greens. She tossed the shorts onto the floor and pulled off her shirt. "C'mon, C'mon... turn around." Alexis stretched, inhaling deeply. Suddenly she stopped, her head turning to look at Rasta-mon. The next movement was a blur as she rapidly grew in size, her hands reaching down towards Rasta-mon.

"And just what do you think you're looking at?"

Watching through Rasta-mon's eyes, Duncan saw the floor dwindle away as the cat was lifted up and gently tossed out the door.

Well mon, show's over. Wonder if dat would ever work for me... The cat jumped back on the bed and was soon fast asleep.

Duncan broke contact when he started seeing cross-eyed Siamese dream cats running wildly toward Rasta-mon.

"This is just great," he moaned aloud, somewhat unsettled. "I finally have a real, flesh and blood woman on board and I'm reduced to voyeurism." He looked absent-mindedly around the room. "OK... settle down. Give it time. It'll happen." He got up and walked aimlessly around the gym. *What'll I do now?* He went over to the treadmills and climbed on.

"Oh, let's see. Treadmill six this is Duncan Stuart. Warm-up program 20 minutes." The foot belt began a slow churning and soon Duncan was loping along at a comfortable pace. Normally he would turn-on the video screen and watch old movies or read a book from the library. However, today his mind wandered, mostly to his surrogate vision of Alexis. Her form appeared and reappeared, each time highlighting a minute part of her body... at least the back part of her body. His imagination turned her around.

Twenty minutes later, Duncan stepped off the treadmill and leaned over, touching his toes, then standing on one leg and grabbing the other ankle for a thigh stretch. *What do I wanna do now? Really don't feel like weights...* He wandered over to the exercise mats and jabbed half-heartedly at the punching bag.

"You're not going to do any damage like that."

Duncan jumped. Alexis leaned against the door. She was barefoot, wearing tan hiking shorts and a white sleeveless blouse.

"Damn." He calmed himself. "That was quick. Don't you sleep?"

"I'm not tired yet." She walked over and across the mat to where he still had a hand on the punching bag. She smelled of shower soap, a pungent fresh fragrance. "If you're going to hit, hit it."

He sensed a subtle challenge. "You mean like you were?"

"Exactly." She held his gaze, a slight smile curling the corners of her mouth.

"Actually, I watched what you were doing. I've learned some Tae Kwon Do." He said smugly.

"Really? Show me." She stepped off the mat.

"Now? Here?" he sputtered.

She said nothing, but simply folded hers arms.

"Um... OK." He went through the highest level he had learned, finishing with a hop turn side kick. Panting, he looked back to where Alexis was grinning broadly.

"That's, uh... fair." She walked over closer to him. "What say we do a little sparring?"

"Huh?" He sized up his opponent. "I don't think that's a good idea. I outweigh you by a good thirty pounds. And besides, you just took a shower."

"Oh, I don't expect to work up much of a sweat."

He cocked an eyebrow. "OK," he smirked, "you can't say I didn't warn you."

"Fair enough. Ready?"

The two began circling each other warily watching for subtle body movements. Duncan reacted first, reaching a hand to grab her shirt. Instantly he was high in the air, landing flat on his back with a loud "*Ooof!*" He rolled to his feet, balancing back and forth on his tip toes, arms and hands at the ready. She merely crouched slightly. He launched again, aiming a tackle at her midsection. Instead of impact, he grabbed air and landed on his chest, emitting a muffled grunt. He pushed himself back up and turned to face his smiling opponent.

"I'm ready to start any time you are," she taunted.

He decided on a different tack and worked to get closer. He feinted left and attacked right, managing to grab a wrist. She easily reversed his grip and now held his wrist. Instead of pulling away, he pushed into her grabbing her waist and vainly struggling to trip her onto the mat. He knew he was stronger, but her balance was poised and perfect. She skillfully positioned herself to counter his weight changes. And then she tripped him.

They landed in a heap on the mat and began rolling together, gripping each other tightly. His hand slipped and, without meaning to, he tickled her under her armpit. The reaction was instantaneous and she slammed her arm down to stop him. Discovering a weak point, he began tickling her and she fought to get away.

Suddenly she changed tack and began tickling back. Soon they were laughing uncontrollably and tickling furiously. Very quickly, he realized that not only was he becoming warm from the physical exertion, he was becoming aroused.

Alexis was the first to stop and he quickly followed suit, both breathing heavily. He rolled onto his back with Alexis on top, straddling him at the hips, her hands locked into his, pressed onto the mat above his head. Their eyes locked momentarily, as they continued to catch their breath.

Alexis moved first. She leaned down and kissed him fully and firmly on the mouth. Duncan let himself go and responded passionately. The kiss was brief but strong and Alexis sat back, still holding his eyes in hers. Seeming to arrive at a decision, she let go of his hands. Slowly and with purpose, she unbuttoned her blouse until the last button popped open. In one smooth motion, she opened her blouse and let it slide slowly off her arms, revealing her firm and perfectly round breasts, the small rosy nipples pointing straight.

"My god you're beautiful." Duncan stared at her chest.

Alexis didn't answer, but rapidly pushed up Duncan's shirt until he had to raise himself up slightly and pull it off. When he lay back down, she was on top of him kissing and devouring his mouth, naked flesh pressed against his chest. He wrapped his arms around her, crushing her to him, then rolling her over, rapidly undoing the button securing her shorts. She flipped him back over, yanked her shorts off, then rapidly tugged his off before leaping back on top of him.

Duncan awoke when he heard Alexis cry out. He bolted up-right, instantly alert. Next to him she wrestled in her sleep. He watched her face contort in anguish; suddenly, she cried out again.

"Daddy!" She jerked sitting up-right, hands ready to strike a deadly blow. Duncan leaned out of the way.

"Alexis. It's me." He grabbed her hands. Her eyes blinked open and she looked at him, uncomprehendingly. "I've got to kill them," she said flatly. "I've got to kill them."

Duncan held onto her hands and brought them close to his chest, bringing her closer to him. He kissed her forehead, cooing softly, "It's OK, it's OK. You're safe." He felt her body relax and she drifted off again.

Duncan lay back down drawing her closer to him and fell contentedly asleep. He awoke later. Alexis was curled up tightly beside him, her head resting on his shoulder, a hand on his chest. He looked at her. Her breathing was deep, her face softened in calm oblivion. *The nightmares will stop. Mine did.* Duncan tenderly kissed her on her forehead, remembering their lovemaking. She had been passionate and extremely physical. And seemingly insatiable. Duncan smiled at her desire. It was something he had never experienced. He relaxed again, drawing her closer to him, and fell asleep.

When he awoke later, she was gone. He propped himself on an elbow and surveyed the gym. He was alone. He stood up and walked slowly around the room, waking up. The clock said 0530.

"Where'd you go?" He mumbled out loud. Yawning, he looked at the clock again. *Too damn early... where are you? I don't even know where you live... Rasta-mon?* He tried to connect, but it was obvious from the visions of Siamese cats that Rasta-mon was still asleep. Sleepily heading back to his apartment, he fell onto his bed and faded in and out of sleep until 0830.

Duncan surveyed the gym with disappointment. *Where the hell is she? "Rasta-mon?"*

"Yo mon. Wutzup?" Duncan saw the dresser far away, and the bedroom door looked like it was 20 meters away. Apparently Rasta-mon was lying on the bed.

"Where's Alexis?"

"I dunno mon. She be gone early. Tank god she leave the door open. I gots ta pee like a fire hose." With that, Duncan felt Rasta-mon get up, walk to the edge of the bed and look over the side. From Duncan's perspective, it was a long way down.

"You're not gonna jump are you?"

"Watchu tink mon, I gonna fly?" Duncan broke contact just as Rasta-mon leaped down.

"Talane?" He called. Nothing happened. "Talane? Where are you?"

"I hear you Duncan." Her voice floated on the air.

"Where are you? Why don't you show yourself?" Duncan looked around.

There was a pause. "You're not alone anymore."

"What difference does that make?" Duncan stammered.

"I'm a computer. I can't give you what she can." There was another long pause. "Call me when you really need me."

He blinked several times, pondering Talane's response, before deciding that she was right; she *was* just a computer. And besides, last night had been marvelous.

"Maybe she's on her way," he said hopefully. He waited for ten minutes, decided he didn't want to appear the fool and determined to make use of his time. *Think I'll go for a ride.* Walking over to the aerobic machines, he lowered himself on the recumbent cycle, facing the computer wall.

"Level seven. Flat terrain, spin at eighty to ninety rpm for warm-up thirty minutes. Moderate terrain, spin seventy plus for ninety minutes. Cool down eighty rpm thirty minutes." He watched the road on the screen as it began its journey through the countryside. Tall shading trees of thick green leaves dangled branches on the sides of the road. Flowers of crimson and cobalt and bright white cascaded the edges of the winding path. Their fragrance floated from the sides of the screen. Multi-colored cardinals and orioles flitted across in front of him. Occasionally there would be a break in the trees, off to the left a gurgling brook would race along beside him. Kingfishers darted quickly, snatching up fish and the zipping away. Then in the distance, he saw a break in the trees. Farm fields were coming up, and the air filled with the pungent sweetness of hay, wheat, and sorghum.

Duncan knew this trip and he reveled in its pure escapism. The road swept in front of him, and his mind wandered. Vivid images overlapped, mostly of Alexis. The night's passion slipped in and out of his consciousness. Alexis, Alexis, Alexis.... And he remembered her strength in fighting. She was obviously very good. His thoughts commingled and soon he remembered the Attendants, Captain Dru, Talane in various forms, his father. He soon found the image of the captain breaking though his consciousness and his last words to Alexis. The miles floated past, unobserved. *Was this voyage doomed from the start? Kill everyone on the ship in order to kill the captain? Luckmann... Why would Tandava put a corporate official on a doomed voyage?*

Frowning, he slowed his peddling. "Program change." The screen went blank. "Access Administrator. All files." The screen began rapidly scrolling file names. Without realizing it, he was reading each one as it flashed across the screen. "Freeze. Open Luckmann dot Tandava."

Again, the screen scrolled file names. "Faster." He continued to read. "Faster." The screen became a blur. "Freeze." Duncan read the file name. "Urgent apology." *Urgent apology? This ought to be interesting.* "Open Luckmann, file, urgent apology." The screen flickered momentarily and then a video came on. It was the Administrator.

He was a toady little man, bald and fat with a salt and pepper tightly trimmed goatee. Duncan waited as the Administrator, Luckmann, *how ironic a name*, fidgeted. His eyes were almost as red as his face. Then he spoke.

His voice was shallow and nervous. "I'm Bernard Luckmann on the *SS Future Hope.* Whoever sees this, we're being killed. If you are one of the passengers still alive... I'm sorry. I had nothing to do with it, I swear! It was them, Tandava. They're the ones responsible. They're the ones who set this whole thing up." He looked around. "I can only hope someone finds this video. The bastards... they promised me..."

Luckmann's face was flushed, and he distractedly wiped little beads of sweat just beginning to roll down his cheeks. He held up a small data-card and turned it over in his fingers. "This is my insurance. You see this and you'll understand. When this becomes public knowledge, Tandava will be destroyed."

Suddenly Luckmann jerked his head to the left, towards the door to his apartment. "O god, O god, no! They found me! Tandava is to blame. You gotta believe me. I swear on my mother's grave, I had nothing to do with this. I'm done for. Take this card and use it! Make them pay. Destroy them!"

Duncan paused in his pedaling, rooted by the death scene unfolding before him.

Luckmann anxiously glanced down and picked up a gun that had been tucked against his thigh. He held it up in front of him. "Nine millimeter. Antique. Fully loaded." He looked back to the camera. "Still very lethal." He raised it to his temple. "One last thing. Linda Nadell," he breathed heavily, his eyes like a cornered animal, "I still think you're a bitch." Pulling the trigger, the left half of his head exploded, splattering bits of skull, cartilage, and brain matter against the wall.

On the screen, blood gushed from the open cavity, as the half-head flopped back onto the chair. The heart continued pumping and blood flowed over the cushions of the chair onto the floor, forming large pools of deepening crimson. The gun fell out of his hand and his body settled into the curves of the chair while the video continued to roll. Several minutes later, a blast from another gun, a much newer gun, blew the rest of his head off and several Attendants circled around him.

There were three of them, tall, powerfully built. Except for the bluish-gray tint to their bodies, they almost looked human with their bald domed heads and thick fibroid necks. Even their synthetic muscles seemed to quiver from the physical effort. But it was their eyes that evoked a second look. The internal infrared scanners made their eyes bright orange. That passionless glare glowed eerily upon their soulless faces. They spread out through the apartment, then quickly reassembled next to the lifeless body.

"All clear commander," one of them said.

As they stormed out, one stopped by Luckmann, reaching down to pick up the data card. "Got it."

And the headless Luckmann lay dead. The camera continued to capture Luckmann's lifeless body.

Numbed, Duncan watched the still-life and bloody chair for a while, finally realizing that there was no more to tell. "Repeat file: 'urgent apology.'" The scene replayed itself. He began pedaling again, absorbing this latest bit of information. *What's on that disk that Tandava would kill him for?*

"Resume normal viewing." He watched the action resume. "Repeat file: apology." He frowned as Luckmann held up the data card.

"Program undo. Run passenger manifest, individual files." The first passenger bio appeared, *Abramson, Micah.* He read through the information. "Next." *Adams, Joel* appeared. Duncan digested his information   And with each succeeding bio, he spent less time reading and digesting the listed information. Very quickly, he was reading and absorbing all the listed information in less than a second per individual. The only sound was the rapid repetition of "Next... next... next."

"My god, are you really reading those or just hypnotized by the flashing screen?"

Startled, Duncan turned to see Alexis leaning against one of the weight machines. She was barefoot again, wearing black spandex shorts and a loose white T-shirt. She walked over next to him.

Smiling warmly, he reached up and tenderly touched her arm. She looked at his hand as though it was a bug. Slowly and deliberately, she lifted his hand off and walked to his other side, standing just out of reach.

Bewildered, Duncan fumbled for something to say. "How long have you been here?" He slowed his bicycle spinning.

"I've been watching you for about ten minutes. I'm not sure what you're doing. How do you expect to find anything when you don't read anything."

"I'm reading," he replied defensively.

"Yeah right." She folded her arms. "Now. Let's read this one together. When you're finished just say so. Ready?" Duncan nodded. "OK: Begin."

"Finished."

"What? No you're not."

"Yes I am." Duncan retorted. "I'll prove it." He continued looking at Alexis. "I'll call for the next file. I'll read it, then I'll tell you what it says. OK?"

"OK." Alexis skeptically agreed.

"Next." Duncan turned to the screen and quickly turned back to Alexis.

Alexis chuckled. "Alright. This should be brief."

Closing his eyes, Duncan intoned, "Donavon, Laurel, mother of five children, married to Donavon, James, occupation listed as bio-chemist, education through the fourth level, graduate of Worldwide International University, published in the Journal of Science and Technology," and he continued until he finished the entire bio.

Her jaw dropped lower with each succeeding bit of data. "How can you do that?"

He pursed his lips and shrugged. "I don't know. Talane did something to my brain."

"Interesting." She was impressed. "How long's this been happening?"

"No too long," he shrugged again, irritated that he still didn't know or understand why his retention skills were so high.

Alexis regarded her companion. "Amazing." She turned back to look at the screen. "Do it again."

He called for the next screen and repeated the exact bio. For good measure, he repeated the bios for passengers three, five, and seven.

"Go ahead and check. You'll find I'm exact, word for word." Duncan replied, frustration edging his voice.

"That's OK. I believe you." She stepped away and towards the wall-screen. "I've a feeling I know what you're looking for, but I'm not sure how you're doing it."

"Well, I'm trying to find out what's going on here. I listened to the Administrator's apology."

"Yeah, I saw. Pretty interesting." She moved closer to him, just out of contact with his turning legs. "How do you work this thing?"

"It's pretty simple." He reached out to touch her again and her warning look was enough to stop him. "What's going on?" he asked crossly.

"With what?" She appeared distracted, watching the video.

He paused peddling, watching her. "With us."

She turned back to look at him. "What us?"

"Last night?" Duncan queried, peddling again.

"Listen. Last night was last night. It was fun. Don't make a big deal of it." She turned back to the screen.

Her words stung. "Are you telling me that what we did last night didn't mean anything?" Unconsciously his pedaling increased in speed.

Alexis frowned and turned back to stare at him. "If you want it to be special, then let it be special. Fine. Can we get back to what we were doing?"

Duncan spun faster. "But... but... I... I don't understand. I thought, you know, me... you, together..."

Alexis turned to face him. "I suppose that possibility exists, now doesn't it? After all, we're the only ones on this crate. And who the hell knows where we are and where we're going –"

"I do."

"What?" Her eyes widened.

"Of course. I'd already worked that out about a week before you came."

Her lips tightened. "And just when were you going to tell me?"

Duncan paused, flustered. "When I got around to it."

Alexis shook her head and pursed her lips. "OK... Well, where are we going?"

Yo mon! I tink we gots a problem here! It be smokin'!

Duncan stopped pedaling and sat up straight. *What's smoking? Where are you?*

"What's going on?" she demanded.

"It's Rasta-mon. Something seems to be wrong."

How should I know where I be? It gots lots o' boxes and I find a good place an' let 'er loose. But dis box be smokin'.

"Where is he?" she again demanded.

"I don't know. Gimme a minute will ya?" Duncan retorted. *How far are you from where you and Alexis stay?*

Uh oh, it be like sizzlin' a bit. I go maybe five doors down. The door dis place be always open, mon. I tink you better be hurryin'.

Duncan jumped up. "Quick, he's near where you guys are living. Lead the way."

They saw Rasta-mon sitting outside the room, tail twitching. *'Bout time you get here. All de excitement 'bout over.*

"This is the pantry for the kitchen dry-goods." Duncan said, reading the sign above the door. He looked down at Rasta-mon. "What'd you pee on here that would make smoke?"

How should I know mon? I forget my glasses so I can't read the boxes... whatchu tink mon? His tail jerked back and forth. *It start smokin' an' scare the pee outta me, which is a good ting 'cause I gotta go real bad.*

"Show me where it is." Duncan motioned into the room.

Rasta-mon led the way as they followed. The room was large with shelving running the length of the room. Most of the stock was still in place, large number ten cans of sauces and vegetables, sacks of flour and sugar, and large boxes filled with cereal and other long storage items. At the far end of the room, a door opened into the kitchen.

Rasta-mon trotted down the main aisle and then turned left about midway. He continued weaving his way to the far left corner of the room nearest the kitchen.

As they turned the last corner, Duncan could smell the acrid odor of chemical.

"Man, it stinks in here." Alexis wrinkled her nose.

Duncan furrowed his eyebrows. "I'm not sure what Rasta-mon could pee on that would leave that sort of odor." He sniffed again. "It smells familiar, but I can't seem to place it."

Rasta-mon stopped in front of a row of boxes, all taped and labeled 'Personal Dry Goods for Settlement - Administrator.' *Here it is mon.*

Duncan looked at the boxes. There were ten of them, small, and neatly stacked. The bottom box had a small gash in it. Duncan bent down. "Is this where you went?" He pointed to the hole in the box.

Ya mon. I be tryin' to aim for de hole. Keeps the floor from gettin' messy.

"What's going on?" Alexis bent down next to Duncan.

"I'm not sure. But whatever it is that Rasta-mon pissed on reacted to his urine." He stood up and reached for a box. "Let's just see what's in these." He went to lift the first one. "Whoa! What's in here, bricks?" He slid it forward, and ripped open the top.

"What is it?" Alexis demanded.

"I'm not... Ho...ly...." He reached in and pulled out what appeared to be a dull gray clay bar about the size of a small loaf of bread. He stood there holding it in front of him, his eyes blinking.

"What is it?"

"Hypnochron."

Alexis slid another box forward and opened it, pulling out another gray bar. Soon she and Duncan had all the boxes on the floor, each one opened revealing the hypnochron in each box.

"Ten boxes, thirty kilos each...three hundred kilos of hypnochron." Alexis shook her head. "I'd say someone wanted to make sure this ship never came back."

"You know about hypnochron?" he asked, surprised.

"Of course." she answered tartly. "I've just never seen it. Strange name." She placed her brick down and looked at Duncan. "OK mister genius, why was it smoking?"

"Obviously a chemical reaction to urine. More than that, I don't know." Duncan responded, a bit irritated. "And the name is a combination of Greek words for sleep and time, a sort of play on the eternal nap."

"So why was it smoking?"

"I said I didn't know."

"So you don't know everything?" she sarcastically grinned.

"I never claimed I did," he snapped.

She continued to smile at him. "Well, since these belong to the Administrator, I suggest we go search the Administrator's apartment."

"Really." He folded his arms. "And just what are we looking for?"

"Oh? You've forgotten already?"

"Hardly," he answered evenly. *What's going on? Why is she doing this?*

Alexis paused, waiting. "Well?"

He was suddenly tired of the game. "You're the one with the answers, you tell me."

"The data card. The Administrator had a card he called his insurance."

"Most likely destroyed along with the Attendant who took it." Duncan stood his ground. "So there is no data card. But I think we have a more urgent problem."

"What?" Alexis' eyebrows furrowed.

"We have three hundred kilos of hypnochron," he swept a hand at the boxes on the floor. "What do you think somebody planned to do with this?"

Hey! Am I gonna hafta separate you two. It like my fatha say, if you can't say somethin' nice...make sure you bigger'n him. Rasta-mon sat down in between them, his tail twitching back and forth.

Alexis watched Duncan staring intently at the cat. "Now what?"

"Nothing. Why are we arguing?"

"Who's arguing?" She tilted her head.

"We are." he said, exasperated.

"I don't know what you're talking about. Are you sure that card's been destroyed?" she asked.

"You saw it as well as I did. The Attendant picked it up and... I'll be damned," he blinked in awareness. "It's in the library."

"What?" Her eyes brightened.

"I found it in the hallway. I thought it might be from the library. He must have dropped it."

Without waiting, she brushed past him, giving a simple 'follow me' wave with her hand.

Duncan stood momentarily transfixed, watching Alexis walk back down the stockroom aisle. *"What the hell is going on?"*

"Don't look at me, mon. Siamese 'bout all I can handle."

Chapter 6

"Find it?" Alexis stood in the library doorway as Duncan went behind the counter and pulled out the data card flipping it in the air to her. She held it up to the light then flipped it back to him. "You're the one who knows how to work these things. Make it happen."

Duncan caught the card mid-air, bringing it closer for inspection. "Hmm. Now that's interesting."

"What?" Alexis drew closer to him.

"This is one of the older five centimeter rectangle size."

"So?" Alexis reached up for the card.

"As far as I know, the computers here use the square four centimeter cards," he said, giving Alexis the wafer-thin card. "Unless the Administrator had an older computer on board, or maybe a drive adapter..."

"So what you're saying is that we might not be able to read this thing?" She examined the card, then handed it back to him.

"Correct."

"So? What'll we do?"

Duncan pursed his lips, then called loudly, "Talane!"

Nothing happened.

"Talane?"

"Yes Duncan?"

He turned behind him to empty space. "Where are you?"

"Oh, sorry. I was busy." Very quickly, a Daughters of Charity nun materialized.

"Good god no!" He turned his head, holding his hands up in front of his face. "What're you doing?"

Alexis leaned back on one leg, a smirk curling the corners of her lips. "This oughta be good," she stage-whispered.

"Huh?" Talane adjusted her habit.

"Don't!" He brought his hands closer to his face.

"Don't what?" She walked up to him. "Why do you have your hands in front of your face?" She turned to Alexis. "Do I look that bad?" she worried.

"Um... no.... it's not that." She continued smiling. "I believe he expects you to do something with your clothes. Apparently he doesn't like what you have on."

Talane turned to him. "Do you want me to take them off?"

"No!" Duncan felt himself redden. "Why are you dressed like that?"

"I was just looking through some of the history pages and saw this. Like the hat?" She then lifted her habit slightly. "This would be good for when it's cold, but I certainly wouldn't want to wear this if it was warm. This was once made from wool. Can you imagine how heavy that would be? I'd be running around the halls looking for the air conditioning grates, my habit flapping behind – Huh?"

"I said 'thanks', we understand." Duncan lowered his hands. "We need your help."

"Oh good. How can I help?"

He held up the card. "We need to read this. It's a five centimeter. Are there any computers that can read this?"

Talane reached out a hand to take it. Duncan knew better and held onto it. "Hmmm. A five centimeter wafer." She chewed on her lip for a moment. "There aren't any machines on board presently configured that will read this. Maybe we can adapt one of the library loaners here." She straightened up and readjusted her hat. "How'd they keep these things on?"

Duncan shrugged and turned around look to where the small individual play-stations were neatly stacked on the shelves.

"Just a minute." Alexis hadn't moved. "Now that you're both here, let's settle a problem."

He skidded to a halt. "Problem?"

"Yeah. Like where we're headed for instance?"

"Oops." Talane looked sheepishly at Duncan. "Gotta go."

"Hey! You can't get out of it that easily." Duncan watched Talane disappear.

"Gotta change." The voice faded.

He turned to face a peeved Alexis. "Listen, like I said before, it just didn't come up in conversation. I would have remembered eventually. It's not like I'm hiding some big secret."

Alexis folded her arms. "Well? Where are we going?"

"Wolf Three Five Nine system."

"Where's that?"

"Quadrant Twenty Two, Leo constellation."

"How do you know?" She stared intently at him, making him slightly uncomfortable.

"In addition to that large star looming larger in front of us," he snipped, "I've done a plot."

"How do you know you're right?" She held his gaze with hers.

Duncan stared back at her. *OK. You want specifics? Handle this.* "By using the trigonometric parallex and finding a known constant as base, we factored the elliptic curve of the present trajectory, calculating the Wolf Three Five Nine system as intended destination."

Alexis slowly licked her lips, smiling tightly. "I guess I deserved that."

"What's goin' on? Why are you so touchy?"

"I'm not touchy. I just like knowing what's going on." She shifted to one leg. "So... What's the prognosis?"

"Don't know yet. Our trajectory has us headed for the second planet. If my calculations are correct, it's possible that we may be able to orbit around it."

"So when do we get there?"

"Unless I'm mistaken... twenty-one days, sixteen hours and forty-four minutes, to be precise."

Alexis' eyes widened. "Twenty-seven days! That doesn't leave us much time."

"For what?" Duncan raised an eyebrow.

"A well thought-out plan." Alexis started to move and then stopped. "Actually there's another question I've been wondering about."

Duncan scratched his face. "Shoot."

"What's the possibility of us getting rescued? And why can't we just communicate back what's happened?"

"Though an interesting thought, it would take years for our signal to get back to earth, and double that for anyone to find us, assuming they want to   which makes the likelihood of us getting rescued, practically... nil."

"I thought it was something like that." She inhaled slowly. "Let me know when you get the Luckmann stuff ready," she calmly said, walking out.

Duncan watched as she paused in the hallway, then headed in the direction of the gym. *What am I doing wrong? It's not like there's competition for her affection...*

Yo mon, dats a good question. It like my fatha say... Siamese be like a bus. You miss da first one, an' anotha come in ten minutes.

Duncan looked down at the cat. "What the heck does that have to do with anything?"

Beats me. De Talane girl, she say you got plenty o' brains. So where they be? You be so smartin', you figure it out. All I know mon, is dat you don' get no honey bee actin' like a pickle.

"Who's acting like a pickle? You see what's going on. I'm being a perfect gentleman. She's the one who's acting weird."

Rasta-mon sighed. *Listen mon. Whatchu know 'bout de girl? You two romp aroun' de hay and you tink she make you breakfas'. Where she born? What her daddy be like?"*

"Um... uh..." He realized that he actually knew very little about her. "Huh..."

Rasta-mon stretched. *Ya know mon, I oughta be chargin' you by de hour.* He stretched again. *I wonder if de Talane girl con make de cross-eyed Siamese.* Rasta-mon twitched his tail and sauntered out, humming a Bob Marley song of long ago.

Duncan and Talane were deep in conversation when Alexis walked in.

"Okay," Alexis grinned at Talane's new look.

"Ja! Alexis, vat you tink? Dis vun pretty goot, ja?" Albert Einstein smiled broadly.

"Interesting." She appraised the disheveled scientist. "Few computers could get away with it, but on you it looks good." She walked over to the table where Duncan was tightening the screws to a metal outer casing. "Any luck?"

"We'll see." Duncan stepped back. "Talane figured out that we could simply use a stripped external card reader. I bent in the lateral laser limits to the old scan width. Hopefully the card hasn't been damaged and I bent in the limits far enough." He called for a screen to lower and then went behind the table to alligator clip several leads to the exposed mother-board.

"Zo, Alexis. Ve haf been vurking hard here. In yust a minute, ve vill zee vat happens, ja?" Talane pushed the glasses back up on her nose.

"How long has she been talking like this?" She leaned over to watch him.

He rolled his eyes, slowly shaking his head. "For over an hour. She's driving me crazy." Standing back up, he announced, "Ready. Let's see what Luckmann has to say." He stepped around to view the screen again, Talane and Alexis in tow.

"Open files list." There was only one. "Open gotcha Tandava."

74

The screen blanked quickly and then filled with Luckmann. He was very relaxed, sitting in an overstuffed chair, holding a glass of wine. Behind him, against the wall were floor to ceiling bookshelves filled with antiquarian volumes. A floor lamp was next to his chair, an ancient volume resting on the tray at arm level. He appeared very confident.

"Well. How good of you to view this card. So. Let's begin." He took a sip. "First, Tandava is responsible for all the spread of all the global plagues and diseases for the past twenty years. They accomplish this via their subsidiary Disease Management Industries. At last tally, I calculate that Tandava and DMI have killed probably close to two billion people. I still find it amazing that no one ever questions the connection between DMI and the spread of diseases. But then, the media *is* state controlled. Well, now that I think about it, several other minor companies did discover cures for some of the lesser virulent attacks, and so that does provide some aura of competition."

He leaned back. "What is also interesting is that Tandava owns controlling interest in Lazarus Fidelity and Savings, Recycle Cloning Corporation, Future's Promise Insurance, and numerous other health, banking, and insurance industries. What does this mean?"

He took another sip. "Let's see... DMI spreads a disease, millions die, DMI finds the cure, billions buy the cure, Recycle Cloning provides you a new healthier body with all the new inoculations courtesy of DMI, Lazarus Fidelity provides the loan, and Future's Promise provides the insurance." He grinned broadly. "Quite a scheme... don't you think?"

"So, you may ask, why am I telling you this now? Let's face it. If you're watching this, it means that my life is in grave danger. This is the only means of protecting myself. Hmmm... now that I think of it, I bet you're probably wondering what I had to do with any of this. I was the director of security for the Watchover Project, Tandava's code name for this entire bio-toxin affair. Am I ashamed about my participation?" He shrugged nonchalantly. "Not really. Let's be realistic, if not downright Machiavellian, death by plague keeps the planet's population in check. Just imagine what this planet would be like without disease."

He held his right hand up in a placating gesture. "Yes, yes, I know about cloning and inoculations. The possibility of extended life exists... if you can afford it. Not everyone can. So, why not rid ourselves of the dregs of humanity? Why not selectively reduce our population by weeding out the inferior races? By appropriately eliminating inferior races, we allow superior species to propagate."

He paused and studied the camera. "But I digress. Apparently Tandava shared my views. But, as the old saying goes, there is no honor among thieves. I knew I had to protect myself, because one day an upstart would come along and want my position. And she did. Linda Nadell, my deputy, is a viper of deadly charm. And so, here I am, recording this insurance, hoping that I never have to use it."

He twisted his head as if cracking his neck joints and then looked back. "By the way, the government is not just behind all this, it's a government controlled program. Or should I say a governments controlled program. UN doesn't mean United for Nothing." He smiled at his own joke. "Oh, before I forget, only a few of us are on this ship by design. Fortunately, in another week or two, I'll be off this death trap." He took a savoring sip of wine, a soft smack of lips in contentment. "I do have to chuckle, though. All this trouble for the other two... Still," he grinned as though admiring the plan, "after I'm gone, what do I care? The ship blows up and Tandava gets rid of two of its problems. Captain Dru and Dieter Waldhausen should've kept their mouths shut. What?" he looked inquisitively at the camera as though pretending to hear a question. "The other three hundred plus passengers? What about them?" He splayed his hands in resigned acceptance, a sly smile curling the corners of his mouth. "Collateral damage."

Luckmann sighed contentedly, leaned back, and finished off the glass of wine. Picking up the book, he deliberately opened it, placing the bookmark on the tray. Smiling serenely at the camera, he indicated the book. "Late nineteenth century edition of Dostoyevski's *Brothers Karamazov*. There's nothing like the feel of a book in one's hands. That's the Luddite in me." He bent to read, and the video screen went blank.

Silence settled in the room as each pondered Luckmann's revelations. Talane spoke first, her voice changing to maternal concern. "Why would someone willingly do that?"

"Do what?" Duncan asked, wondering if she meant Luckmann or his news.

"Kill so many people."

"Power," he answered. "Sort of like Hobbes' *Leviathan*. You know, 'the general inclination of all mankind is a perpetual and restless desire of power after power, that ceases only in death,' et cetera et cetera."

"What are you talking about?" Alexis frowned, then shook her head. "And he sat there so calmly, only concerned with his own safety."

Duncan took a slow deep breath. "While I'm not too surprised at the duplicity of government and business, all this matters little to us now. Whatever Luckmann did, he's paid for it with his own life." He chuckled in sudden understanding. "So that's why he was here, the explosives, the Attendants, your father," he added, looking intently at her. "Get rid of a bunch of problems all at once. You want to feel sorry? Feel sorry for all those poor souls who thought they were colonizing another planet."

"But they weren't a threat," she said.

"But Luckmann was. Your father was." He sniffed in derision. "This is small potatoes compared to what Tandava has been doing. No one was supposed to live." He walked to the door. Turning to face them both, he added, "As far as I'm concerned, I want them to keep thinking that way."

Chapter 7

It was almost a week before Duncan could get any readings from the planet.

"Any success?" Alexis asked, walking into the library where Duncan was working with a lanky young man, about 16 years old with long blond hair tied in a pony-tail. His glasses were very thick and he constantly scrunched his nose as he pushed them up.

Alexis walked over to where Duncan was studying a hologram of the Wolf 359 solar system. "Who is she supposed to be now?"

"Dr. Faversham," he sighed, rolling his eyes. He saw no recognition in Alexis, so he added, "developer of the jagged light theory concerning spacial location."

Dr. Faversham turned to Alexis. "Hey chickie-babe, light my fire. You're one fine fox. C'mon over here and rub my shoulders."

Duncan watched Alexis' reaction, and shrugged. "Arrested development. He was brilliant but obviously lacked maturity. I'd be days ahead if she'd drop the imbecilic attitude."

"No can do big guy. It's Stanislovski method baby, I'm living the part!" Haversham did a little dance and blew them both a raspberry.

"Well. OK. So," Alexis turned back to Duncan, "what do you have?"

"Here, look at the hologram and I'll explain," he pointed. "Wolf 359 is an M-type star with a surface temp around 3275 degrees C."

"Is that good?"

"Actually yes. For one thing, if the planet we're heading for was one astronomical unit away from the star, it might be a tad cold."

"Why?"

"It's like this. The sun burns at 5500 degrees C. The earth is roughly 150 million kilometers from the sun. Wolf burns at 3275. If our planet was the same distance from Wolf, the planet temperatures would be greatly less." His eyes burned and he rubbed them. "It probably wouldn't support life. At least not what we might want to know."

She shifted her weight uneasily. "Well, what does that mean? Is our planet too far from the star?"

78

"Not at all. In fact, the data I've been working with shows it at about point-six astronomical units away from Wolf."

"And...?"

"It means the ratio of distance is roughly the same."

She focused on the second planet of the system. "Is this the one we're looking at?"

"Yup. Planet number two."

"Well, I realize that this is quite a leap of logic, but is there a possibility that it could support life?"

"Now that's the interesting thing," he said, grabbing a lap board so she could see the scrambled mess of figures, signs, and suppositions. "Using Drake's equation, you figure that a certain percentage of stars have planets. What's the likelihood that at least one will have life, perhaps something like us?"

"Why don't you tell me?"

Ignoring her sarcasm, Duncan continued. "Well, in order to have life, you have to have water. And for water to exist in a liquid state a planet needs to have both a suitable temperature and atmosphere."

"What are you getting at?"

"Just a minute, I'm trying to explain. The planet's atmosphere is derived from gases leftover from its formation combined with gases of early volcanic eruptions. Common chemical compounds found in other terrestrial planets," he droned on, "include methane, ammonia, and carbon dioxide, as well as hydrogen cyanide and formaldehyde."

"Gimme a break. Just tell me the bottom line?"

"Let me finish. I'm doing this for me as much as for you. I just want to make sure I'm not over-looking anything." He said, gently touching her arm. When she didn't pull immediately away, he allowed himself a moment of quiet hope, then continued. "Gases added by volcanoes include a substantial amount of water vapor, carbon dioxide, sulfur dioxide, nitrogen, and other gases. The high content of water vapor in volcanic gases coupled with the abundance of volcanoes in past geological ages leads to the conclusion that the waters of the oceans came from volcanic eruptions in the first, oh, half billion years of the planet's existence."

"This is really boring."

"C'mon babe, ain't science fascinating. Let me give you a little one-on-one tutoring." Leering at her, Faversham tucked a clipboard under his arm, raising his eyebrows several times.

"I'd rather be eaten by a sackful of wolverines. Back off brain-child," Alexis muttered.

"Talane! Let me finish," Duncan scowled.

"Sorry." Faversham turned back to scribbling on his clipboard.

"I don't suppose you could simply cut to the chase?"

"Alright." Duncan spread his hands. "Essentially, the tests we've run show that the necessary chemistry of life; carbon, hydrogen, and oxygen, are all in abundance there. We're going to have to wait until we get closer to use the yttrium laser –"

"So what you're saying is that there's a chance that there may be life on this planet. Right?" Duncan nodded. "Good. When can you find out more information about this planet? I need a general layout, topographics, weather, soil analysis, and any other geographic data you can dig up."

"Alexis, we know nothing about the planet, and won't until we're about 10 days out."

"That's only four days from now!"

"I know."

She breathed deeply. "You better get your ass in gear then."

"Don't get any false hopes up," he cautioned.

"I understand. Just thinking." She pursed her lips and looked over at Faversham. "Hey nut-boy? When you're finished here with Duncan, I want a listing of logistic material available for transport in a space pod, prioritized according to probability of extended use."

"What's going on?" Duncan furrowed his brows at her.

"Listen, all this science stuff and computers is your forté. Survival, escape, resistance, and evasion are mine. You worry about getting down on the planet... and then I'll do the rest." She turned and abruptly walked out.

Duncan stared as she left, then turned to look at Dr. Faversham. "I'd ask you for woman help, but I don't think you're qualified."

For the next four days, Alexis seemed to spend more time with Duncan, wanting to know all that he was doing. He was pleased with all the attention, but still found her frustrating. They spent another raucous and passionate session in the gym, the only place Duncan found that she would allow him to get close to her, at least physically. His frustration grew as he tried to unlock her emotions. Rasta-mon merely offered advice from his father or grandfather and wanted to know if Talane could produce a siamese playmate. She had accommodated him, projecting a beautiful silver-blue cat. Rasta-mon, in his excitement, had raced to get close to his new companion, only to have the hologram partially interrupted by his own spacial mass. He quickly recovered and then realized the ultimate frustration of form without substance.

Aw mon, dis be like crazy. Whatchu want to tease the Rasta-mon for? His tail bristled.

"I told you before. It's just a spatial image. You can't do anything with it!" Duncan was grouchy.

Ooo! Who sit on you pancakes dat make you such a prune?

Duncan sighed loudly. "Aw it's nothing that you're doing. I just can't figure her out."

It like my fatha say...some days be glad you a cat.

"And what's that supposed to mean?"

Don'know mon. But I ain't de one who be walkin' 'round inna frizz.

He smiled in spite of himself. "Yeah, you're right." He turned around to examine the hologram of the planet. "Y'know... if I read this thing right, there just might be a cat somewhere on this planet."

Now don' fool wit de Rasta-mon. You find a lady cat on dis planet and de Rasta-mon give you his secret love potion.

Duncan smirked and turned back to the laser-computer. The planet continued its slow spin while data bytes scrolled down the screen.

"So, anything new and exciting?" Alexis strolled in, toweling off post-workout sweat.

"As a matter of fact," he said, adjusting the screen data and pressing a button to produce hardcopies. He held up a sheet of chemical compound analysis. "This is the best news yet."

She took the paper and studied the contents. "Duncan, all this chemical comparison stuff doesn't excite me like it does you. Can I have the short version please?"

"What it says," he replied, "is that there are life forms down there that have the exact same chemical makeup as we do." Alexis relaxed, seemingly pleased with the news. "At first I wouldn't believe it. The likelihood just seemed too impossible. But then, if you think about it, why couldn't they be like us? The comparisons to our solar system are about the same. The only real difference is that Wolf 359 is a dwarf, which means that if the life form readings I'm getting evolved as we did, they ought to be an advanced civilization, all things being equal."

Alexis nodded thoughtfully. "So what is the bottom line? Are you saying that there might be humanoids down there?" she asked, seeing his furrowed eyebrows.

"Possibly. There's something more, something I don't understand," he said shaking his head. "I'm getting humanoid-type readings, but I'm not getting any traces of an industrial process, things like coal plants, steel mills, electric power plants, things that say energy use and productivity."

"You're still rambling. Get to the point."

Duncan took a deep breath. "OK. Looks like we've got humanoid-type readings throughout the planet. As I said, with Wolf 359 being a dwarf star, logic would say that their civilization ought to be more advanced. If that's the case, I should be getting massive energy readings."

"Perhaps they've done a better job of using energy than we did?" she said matter-of-factly.

"It's possible," he reluctantly agreed.

"What are you using to verify your data?" she questioned.

"Oh, y'know, the ship's main laser system."

She walked back over to him. "There's a lot of lasers in the system. Which ones are you using?"

"You sure you want to know?" he smirked.

"Try me." She smiled thinly at him.

He continued grinning. "It's an advanced neodymium doped yttrium aluminum garnet laser –"

"Used for remote sensing and composition analysis of matter. It also has some medical applications," she smugly finished for him.

His jaw dropped . "You...you do know what it is!"

Alexis laughed. "Not really. Talane told me. I just wanted to see your reaction."

He closed his mouth, frowning. "OK, you got me. Do you have something in mind right now or can I get back to work?" He pointed to the planet.

"What's your problem today?"

"You're driving me crazy." Duncan blurted. He saw her stiffen and decided to plow through. "I don't understand you. We're lovers but not friends. I'm closer to the cat than I am to you," he said, pointing.

Alexis didn't answer, but seemed to sift the information. "Well, I can think of worse friends." When Duncan didn't react, she continued. "Listen Duncan, give it a rest. I'm not the emotional type, OK. You'll just have to get used to it. Besides, we've got a lot to do in the next week-and-a-half, so why don't we concentrate on the mission."

"And what would that be?" He asked, his lips tightening.

"Well, for instance, what I asked you before - climate, topography, soil analysis. What do you have so far?"

Duncan sighed slowly and shook his head in defeat, and turned back to the console. "Well," he said, flipping through charts, graphs, and other data, "the planet has a 330 day orbit around the star with a sidereal period of rotation cycle of twenty four hours and 6.361746 minutes. It has two moons. The closer one has a 33 day cycle, which seems much too perfect. I'll have recheck the data. The farthest one has a 99 day cycle, giving them a 1:3 orbital resonance, which isn't all that unusual. Jupiter's moons have Laplace resonance of one, two, and four." He looked at several other papers. "The planet is largely made up of water with two polar ice caps, but with smaller land mass than earth. In fact, it looks like there are no congruous land masses. Instead it looks like there are five extremely large islands." The planet slowly rotated in front of them.

Alexis studied the sphere. "How large would you say the continents are?"

"Interesting question. I put this one at about 2000 kilometers across," he said pointing to the largest one. "The others range from 800 to 1700 kilometers across."

"What about vegetation?"

"I pick up forms of plant growth much like that of earth - some unknown species, but most like that of what we know. I also get readings for agricultural-type growth, corn, wheat, rye, things like that."

She concentrated on the slowly rotating hologram. "What about cities, towns, villages, people?

He nodded his head. "I get those also. Some interesting readings. In this one area," he said pointing near the center of the largest land mass, "I get readings of high volume use of marble-type construction. The problem is that the area for the reading would accommodate about 2-300,000 people by our standards. We can't be sure that the same standards apply."

Alexis mused the latest information. "Have you thought about where we ought to land?"

Duncan leaned back in the chair. "Um...not really."

"Then listen. I've talked it over with Talane and we agree that when we go down, we probably shouldn't cause any turmoil to the environment. I've had Talane print out the climate at the various continents and based upon available data, I've chosen the largest continent as the place we ought to set down."

"Why?" he queried. "What makes one place better than another?"

"Vegetation and terrain analysis indicate that it more closely resembles what we're used to."

There was a long silence, then he spoke softly. "So, you're saying that this is it. This is our only chance?"

"Face it Duncan. With the projected trajectory of the ship and the residual power, all we can expect is to live long boring lives on this crate. We live and die right here." She glanced around the room

There was silence again as he absorbed her words. "Intellectually, I know you're right. It just seems so final."

"No," she quickly intoned. "Final is dying on this god-awful trap of metal."

He turned back to face the planet. "So what's the plan?"

"There's a good size lake here," she pointed. "We've got inflatable rafts, right?"

"Yeah?"

"Well, what we do is land a shuttle in the lake, button it up, sink it, and motor to shore."

"And suppose the locals aren't friendly? How do we get back?"

"We don't," she responded flippantly. "We kick ass."

"I'm serious. Suppose we need to get back?"

Alexis looked solemnly at him. "Get back to what? Duncan, we don't really have a choice. It's either here or nowhere."

Duncan licked his lips, slowly shaking his head. "My god, there are just so many variables. The only thing we know is that the atmosphere is probably like that of earth in the tenth century. There are sufficient readings of edible plants. We know nothing of animals or other wildlife. We know nothing of the humanoids. They could be fifteen feet tall with three arms, and eat other humanoids to stay alive."

Alexis calmly folded her arms. "That's all very true," she said quietly. "But then our options are very limited. I for one do not intend to live the rest of my life confined to this ship. I'd rather take my chances breathing real uncirculated and unrefined air, actually seeing the sun set, and eating real food, no matter what that means." Her eyes grew hard. There was a subtle contained energy lurking behind her stare. "And think, we get a chance to fight for survival."

The silence of the room suddenly expanded and the hum of machines resonated, filling the void.

Chapter 8

"Duncan. Have you checked all the data?" Talane inquired. He was scanning the various charts and checking the hologram planet.

"You sure are talky these days," he said absent-mindedly, flipping through several pages.

"I'm not going to have anyone to talk to in thirty minutes. I've gotten used to having you people around. So much so that I'm beginning to believe I can talk to Rasta-mon."

"I know," he agreed. "Sometimes I forget that you're a computer."

"I'll take that as a compliment." Talane said, a bit of amusement in the voice. "The pod will be somewhat crowded with the raft and all your survival gear."

"I heard that." Alexis said, walking in. Rasta-mon was folded over her shoulder. His head swiveled to look at Duncan.

Docta Livingstone I presume? Hey, nice get-up, mon. You tryin' out for a part in a jungle flick?

Duncan looked down at the clothes he was wearing. "What's wrong with my clothes?"

"Nothing." Alexis frowned and looked at the cat. "I hate it that I don't know what you're saying." She put him on the floor. "Talane? Where are you?"

"Just freshening up." She giggled mischievously. "I'll be a little longer."

Alexis looked at Duncan, silently mouthing 'What gives?'

"Haven't a clue," he shrugged.

Alexis looked around, shrugged in return. "So Talane agrees with me?"

"Listen," he pouted, "I just want to make sure we can survive."

Alexis looked at the pile of weapons, tents, lights, solar batteries, and other survival gear. "This is all unnecessary."

He stopped what he was doing. "OK? What would you suggest?"

"Duncan, you're forgetting the habitat we're going into. You said it yourself; all our readings indicate at least a ninety-nine percent compatibility with life as we know it on earth. All your food and water are unnecessary.

Trust me on this. The only materials we need are medical supplies and weapons."

Looking over the pile of shiny new equipment, he resigned to being out-voted. "So what do we take?"

"Select some small weapons, knives, things like that...easy to carry and conceal... and perhaps a handgun." She had already picked up a beautifully balanced double-edged throwing knife and was gingerly feeling the sharpness of the blade.

"Then what?"

"Then nothing. We leave. You've been checking and cross-checking and re-checking so much that there's nothing left to check. It's time for action. Let's do it and move on!" Suddenly and unexpectedly, she walked over to Duncan, grabbed his shirt and pulled him to her, kissing him hard and passionately. Just as suddenly, she turned around and started for the pod. "We'd better get ready. C'mon Rasta-mon, I'll teach you how to drive one of these contraptions."

Stunned to inaction, Duncan watched them leave. "Now what the hell was that for?" He flipped the chart onto the floor and walked out after them.

Alexis, Duncan, and Rasta-mon stood before the portal next to where the pod was waiting to receive them.

"Are you sure we have everything?" He fussed, looking back at her.

"Would you stop! Yes, we have everything."

He stuck a hand in his pocket and pulled out a data card. "Luckmann's card."

"I still don't see why you want to bring that," she frowned.

He held it up and twirled it lightly. "You're right." Flipping it onto the floor, he looked around the room again. "Where is she? Talane!"

"I'm here, I'm here." A stunning, leggy red-head appeared, wearing only a pair of tight spandex shorts. Her body was milk white, and perfectly proportioned. "Something for you to remember me by." She twirled around and blew Duncan a kiss.

"We've got to go Talane." Alexis interrupted. "Thanks for everything."

Talane stood bashfully to the side. "Oh well, that's OK. Have fun."

Cocking an eyebrow, Alexis opened the portal and slid through the gaping opening. Duncan handed Rasta-mon to her and then paused.

"Goodbye Talane." He paused, swallowing. "You saved my life. I owe you a great debt." He paused. "Y'know, I really am going to miss you." He looked down at the portal hole and then back to Talane. "Remember what to do? The other pod's already primed. You just have to release it, but not until five days from now, at midnight. Don't forget."

Talane smiled. "I won't. I know what to do."

"C'mon Duncan! We've only got a small window of opportunity here!" The voice rose form the pod.

"I'm coming!" He turned back to Talane. "I wish we could take you with us."

Talane smiled coyly. "You are."

He looked at the hologram. "I am?"

"You'll find out soon enough. Trust me, it's all for the best."

He was about to add something else when Talane interrupted him. "She is right. You must go."

Taking a deep breath, he forgot himself for a moment and reached out to touch her. The hologram fizzed slightly around his flesh and he withdrew his hand. "Right. Bye Talane." He slipped through the hole into the pod, settling into the other chair as Alexis fired up the engines. The cat jumped up and nestled on his lap.

"We're set," Alexis said excitedly. She looked at him, eyes gleaming with anticipation of the challenge.

Duncan scratched the cat's head. "I guess this is it." He looked back to her. "Whenever you're ready."

She punched the throttle and the little craft jettisoned away from the ship.

As the pod descended, Talane changed form to Margo Fontaine and slowly began to gracefully pirouette and dance around the holding area. Music suddenly swelled throughout the ship as Talane danced. When the music subsided, her spinning slowed. She stopped, toes pointed, arms in graceful arc above her, slender fingertips touching softly. She walked over to the window as if watching the small craft descend, tiny directional flames shifting its course.

Talane followed the pod until it entered the planet's atmosphere. Then with her head bent, she sighed softly. "Goodbye Duncan Stuart."

The raft bobbed in the water as they watched the shuttle craft silently slip beneath the surface.

Mon, you sure dis be a smart idea? Rasta-mon worried, standing on Alexis' lap, his tail jerking side-to-side.

"What else could we do?" he replied out loud.

"We've already been through this Duncan," Alexis answered.

"Sorry. I was talking to Rasta-mon. Seems like he's getting cold paws about our plans."

She distractedly scratched the cat's head. "It's too late to change our minds now." She looked up at the night sky. "Wonder where our solar system's at?"

Duncan too looked up. He began searching the skies. "I must either be out of practice or just can't recognize any constellations."

"Well, that's the least of our worries. Crank that engine up and let's get going. We've got a long journey ahead of us."

He pressed the button and the batteries came to life, causing the propeller to spin, and the little raft began moving.

Alexis scanned the darkness. "I figure we should be close to shore in about two to three hours. We'll need to row the last half mile or so. Why don't you get some sleep?"

"I get your plan. You want me rested so that I can row the last mile. You just brought me along because I'm strong and stupid," he flippantly said.

She chuckled softly. "Hardly. I'll accept the strong part, but don't think you're going to sleep the entire time. I'll wake you in about an hour."

"Alright." He fidgeted several times to get comfortable. However, sleep eluded him and he twisted himself to peer over the bow of the boat. He heard Alexis inhale loudly and turned back around. She had one hand on the tiller, the other rested on the boat side. The wind swept her hair behind. "What gives?"

"Smell it Duncan?"

"Smell what?"

"Living things," she firmly stated. "How long were we prisoner in that metal heap of a space ship? Seems like a life time. To be out in the open again, to actually taste the air and not have it smell of air-conditioning."

"It does smell good." He relaxed, lying on his back, his head resting against the bow, and his arms spread wide over the sides. He crossed his legs. "I wonder what we'll find here?"

Alexis chuckled. "We've been through that too. Like you said, everything's a guess."

There was quiet for a few moments. Then he spoke. "Aren't you just a little bit nervous?"

"Not really," came the rapid response. "This is great. Us against the world. We control our own destiny."

He regarded his companion. *We've spent I don't know how long together and I still don't know you. You're actually happy to be in danger.* He glanced over the side and the waning moons and then back to Alexis, the light reflecting the dips and curves of her face. *Well, things could be worse...Thank god you can fight...we may need it.* He turned over onto his back. The night was warm, and the rocking of the boat had a soothing effect. He felt Rasta-mon brush against him and settle. Looking out over the water, he tried to separate the tips of the distant forest from the dark night.

Duncan stirred when he felt the gentle shaking of his shoulder.

"Duncan. It's time," Alexis called, giving him another gentle nudge.

Snapping awake, he peered over the side of the boat and jolted upright. "Whoa. I fell asleep. Cut off the engine! Why didn't you wake me?"

"Guess you needed the rest." She shut off the motor and the craft continued to move forward. They could see the outline of trees and hear the waves lapping against the shore. The progress of the boat rapidly slowed, and they both began to row until the prow rubbed the shallow bottom about five meters from the shore. He leaped barefoot over the side.

"It's only ankle deep, and the sand is really smooth," he quietly exclaimed, squishing the sand between his toes.

She had not waited and was already over the side, helping him haul the boat up on shore. The trees were thick against the water, and they had some difficulty pushing the boat between the tight branches.

Finally they stopped to assess their present condition. Alexis was searching the surrounding woods and bringing back limbs and branches to cover the raft. Duncan began looking for the weapons.

"Alexis! I can't find the guns anywhere!" he whispered as he frantically fumbled around the vessel.

Alexis began calmly arranging clothing in her pack. "I threw them over the side of the boat when you were asleep."

"You what?!" He sat back in stunned disbelief. "What's wrong with you! We need protection. If anyone would know that, you should!"

"Duncan," she calmly said. "You have to trust me in this. Having weapons only gives us a false sense of security. We have to be constantly on our toes. Without weapons, we'll have that extra edge."

"Edge?! I'm talking survival!" he fumed.

"It's too late now. Here, I packed this for you." She handed him a large dagger of the old Sykes-Fairbairn style, razor sharp, well balanced, and with a leather sheath. She responded to his puzzlement. "Well, I may be crazy, but I'm not stupid. We do need some protection, and knives are functional as well. That blade there is a carbon-based polymer with a laser sharpened edge, so it's good for cutting small saplings and things."

"OK, OK. I suppose you're right again," he sighed. "What's our status?"

"Well, we've got clothes, rain-gear, and food. I suggest we get some sleep."

"Sleep? Now?"

"We've been up for almost two days straight. If we're going to survive, I suggest we get some rest."

"But what about a watch? I probably should take the first turn."

"Actually, I'd like to try something else. Ask Rasta-mon if he'll stand watch for us. After all, he can hear better than we can, and can wake us if necessary."

Duncan sat back. "What an excellent idea. Rasta-mon, did you hear that?"

Sure mon. Be happy to. Da Rasta-mon's not tired yet.

Alexis sat down, crossed her legs, and leaned back against the side of the raft. Her knife lay on her lap. She cocked her head appearing to listen intently to the sounds of the woods and then slightly relaxed, closing her eyes.

Duncan watched her until he realized that she was asleep. *How does she do that?* He too sat down and tried to get comfortable. He fidgeted for a while and gave up on the sitting position. He crawled into the raft again to where he could stretch out. There he fidgeted some more. He concentrated on the sounds of the waves and the noises of the woods. The waves were just like every other set of waves he had heard. However, the sounds of the forest seemed just different enough to notice. He focused on the different sounds, trying to identify each as if he could tell the difference.

Duncan felt Rasta-mon jump on his chest and the loud exclamation of *Someone's coming!* as the cat bounced over to Alexis. Duncan bolted upright. The sun was bright and climbing in the sky, shining down through the leaves and branches indicating that it was several hours past dawn. Alexis was quickly next to him, peering into the thick woods, intensely listening for noise. Neither could hear or see anything. They stayed frozen, waiting.

Are you sure you saw something? he mentally intoned to the cat.

What you tink mon! I run back for de exercise?

What did they look like?

Oh mon, dey be big. Hairy. Evil monsters wit t'ree heads. Breathin' fire!

Duncan sat back, examining the cat as it curled itself as if to go to sleep. "I'm going to kill a cat," he said out loud.

"What?" Alexis said looking at them.

"I think our furry friend has just pulled our chain. It's a joke isn't it?" he asked, glowering at the prankster.

Ah mon, don't be so sensitive. I be out all night. Dere ain't nuthin' here for days. Let me sleep some. And he promptly yawned and closed his eyes.

Duncan relaxed, chuckling softly. "What a crazy animal. He said that he hasn't seen anything for some distance." He said looking back at Alexis.

"Well," she assumed control, "I suggest that while he sleeps, we do some scouting. We'll go in sweeping arc movements, using the boat as the center of the arc, and the lake as the base of the fan."

"Sounds good to me," he shrugged.

Leaving their packs by the raft, they began their sweeps with ever widening and larger arcs, beginning along the lake first. The going was difficult as the forest was thickly grown, and the trails of small game were infrequent. On the third loop, after an hour of pushing through brush, they abruptly came to a wide, heavily used, dirt road. Alexis quickly hauled Duncan back into the woods before he had a chance to stumble onto the path. They hid themselves as best they could and settled down to watch the road.

They did not have long to wait. A noisy creaking wagon with four wheels and pulled by two large animals appeared. The two creatures seemed to be a cross between an ox and water buffalo, with powerful shoulders yet small thick nubs for horns. Their pace was surprisingly quick for their size.

Driving the team was what looked like a man, average looking by earth standards, about the height of Duncan. He was dressed in a baggy style of pants of dull brown colored material. His dirty blond hair fell freely down his shoulders and was held away from his face by a simple band, tied around his forehead. He was bare-chested and broad shouldered. He sang to himself as he rumbled out of sight.

Duncan and Alexis looked at each other with shared relief. "They're people!" they both blurted. Watchfully standing up, Alexis motioned Duncan to remain where he was as she stepped onto the road. Searching both directions, she smiled and indicated for him to come out too. Then her smile suddenly vanished when she looked up the road to see four men standing looking at them, as six more came out of the woods to join them.

Alexis and Duncan remained where they were as the men calmly made their way towards them. They were all lightly armed with either bows or spears. One of the men waved, and Duncan instinctively waved back. As they drew closer, a tall blond man with a drooping mustache turned to the man next to him, pointed at Duncan and said something which Alexis didn't understand. The two men began laughing.

"What do you want?" She stood defiantly.

Another man, somewhat older than the rest, with short cropped hair yet still trim and fit, looked quizzically at them and uttered some sounds that Alexis didn't comprehend.

"I am Alexis," she said pointing to herself. "This is Duncan."

A rapid ripple of apprehension spread among the warriors and the effect was electric. The men reacted, closing in on them, weapons pointed threateningly. However, the older man hadn't reacted with the rest and seemed to be chuckling at them. He said something else to them, and several relaxed a bit.

Duncan moved toward Alexis, motioning with his hand to say 'don't do or say anything.'

A thin man with brooding eyes looked at them both and gestured for them to sit down at the edge of the road. Neither of them moved. He did it again with the same results. The third time he grabbed Alexis by the shoulders and tried forcibly pushing her down, shouting at her.

Alexis grabbed the man's wrist, and in one deliberate motion bent his arm up to his head while her other hand wrapped around his throat. Panic jumped across his eyes as he struggled. She pushed him away from her into another man with a thick auburn mustache and a scar that ran from his left ear across his cheek.

"That's no way to treat a lady," she growled.

The man stepped back up and hurled a brief explosion of words at her that his companions nervously laughed at.

"They don't understand us." Duncan whispered from her side.

"Well I know how they feel!" Alexis said, shaking her head.

"What made you think we could talk with them?" Duncan said, a wry smile curling his mouth. "Just because they seem to look like us?"

Alexis cautiously watched the group. The older man hadn't moved during her altercation with the brooding man. In fact, he seemed to be enjoying the show.

The man with the scar looked at Duncan and barked and gestured for him to sit. Duncan decided to follow Alexis' lead. He remained standing and locked the man's eyes in a game of staring. Both opponents glared at each other. Just when the man began lifting his spear to settle the argument his way, Duncan allowed a mischievous smile to flit across his mouth, and with deliberate slowness, turned as if to talk to Alexis.

As he turned, the brooding man rushed at him, spear raised. The older man shouted at him. From the corner of his eyes, Duncan saw the man and dropped to the ground and rolled, tripping the man as he swung. The spear launched harmlessly into the road several meters away and the man thudded to the ground with a grunt. He quickly rolled over but before he had a chance to rise, Duncan slid the dagger out of the man's boot and had it shoved tightly up against the man's crotch.

He said nothing, but the confidence and directness in his eyes let the man know that the slightest movement would bring him instant and unending pain. The man sat there and returned Duncan's stare with terrified resignation, waiting his fate. Holding his position a pause longer to assure himself that the man had surrendered, he gave him a look of disdain and stood up, flinging the blade into the dirt, millimeters from the man's neck. With a calm self-assuredness, he slowly turned his back to his would-be attacker and returned to his position next to Alexis.

"Not bad at all," she admitted. "You might make a fighter yet."

"Thank you," he said with a slight smile and a deep breath. "However, that was pure luck. I don't think I could ever do that again. Anyway, I'd rather leave the real fighting to the professionals." He gave her a mock bow. He looked around at the rest of the men, who had lowered their weapons and were nodding begrudging appreciation.

The man on the ground lay still. His right hand went to his crotch as if to assure himself that he was still whole. In an instant, he was up retrieving his spear. As he was about to hurl himself at Duncan again, the older man stepped in between them and barked a biting command that brought the man to a halt.

The older man raised an eyebrow at his two captives with new appreciation. Realizing that he understood neither their speech nor manners, he determined to lead them via signs and hand gestures. With deliberate and over-stated gestures, he began communicating his desire for them to follow him.

"We'd be happy to go with you. However, I'd appreciate it if you could control your subordinates," Duncan said.

The older man unconsciously began his apologies and then sputtered, "You do speak our language!"

Alexis stared at Duncan who was suddenly speaking in the same tongue as their captors. "You understand them?"

"Yes. It seems to be very similar to Gaelic with possibly some Manx patterns mixed in," he said quickly before turning full attention to the men. "I must admit though, I'm somewhat out of practice. Tell me, is it far to the village?"

"Village?" the man roared and the rest laughed. "You call Mull a village? Where do you come from stranger that you call a city of 25,000 people a village?"

"I did not mean to offend," he answered deferentially. "Where I come from, 25,000 people is but a small village. Our cities are much larger, in the millions."

"Ha! You are lying," exclaimed the thin man with brooding eyes. TThere isn't a single million in all of Gambria." He folded his arms as final proof. "You are a myth-teller, or," he paused, his eyes thin beads of accusation, "perhaps you are Rugian."

Startled surprise murmured throughout the men, and they warily watched the two captives for any revelation.

"What is he saying Duncan?"

"Oh, I had asked if the village was far from here. It's called Mull and apparently according to their standards is a large city." He replied over his shoulder.

"How big is it?"

"About 25,000."

"What?" Alexis laughed. "Don't tell them about some of the cities on earth."

"What does the woman say?" the older man asked.

"Oh," he answered, enjoying the control he was beginning to feel, "she asks why we are harassed by men of a village of no consequence." The man snorted while others began shouting insults, but the man with brooding eyes wasn't taken in by Duncan's boast.

"You still haven't answered my question stranger. Who are you and where do you come from?" He warily postured himself in front of them, hand on his sword.

Duncan quickly picked up on the tension between this man and the others. "As is obvious, we are not from Gambria. We are from farther away - from across the sea."

"What? You're a liar! The Sea of Starn is completely within the boundaries of the Gambria."

"I'm sure it is," Duncan interrupted. "I said beyond the land of Gambria," he gestured broadly with both arms, "on the other side of the mountains to the south."

"Ha! You lie again. There is nothing beyond the land of Gambria except Rugians. He lies!" the thin man shouted, looking wildly at his comrades. "You are Rugian spies!"

"We are not spies."

"You lie," he spat. Turning to the older man, he arrogantly addressed him. "Menec, it is your responsibility to take these spies to the Confessor."

"Slow down Raefgot. Let's find out more about them before we do anything hasty."

"Remember who you are and who I am. I am Prince Raefgot to you," he haughtily replied.

"You are *troop* Raefgot when under my command," Menec calmly stated. "Understand?"

"I merely point out what is required, Tarrac-Master Menec," he replied, emphasizing the title and its subordination.

"I know what is required Raefgot. Now perhaps you will shut up so I can find out more about these two." Menec glared at the thin man. Turning to the newcomers, he asked "What are you called?"

"You can't expect them to tell you the truth!" Raefgot blurted.

Menec ignored the outburst and, with more courtesy, asked the question again. "Please, what are your names?"

"I am Lord Duncan," Duncan replied with great pomp as he bowed low. "And this is Lady Alexis," he said pointing to her. "Take a bow Alexis," he stage whispered in English.

Menec smiled at the titles. "Please tell me *Lord* Duncan," he said mockingly. "How is it that two people of such royalty are here by themselves, no servants, no food, and speaking strangely?"

"We were out for a walk and got lost?" he grinned, implying a joke.

Menec uttered a begrudging laugh. "My Lord, you'll have to do much better than that."

Duncan let out a long deep breath. "Actually, we are from across the sea, beyond the borders of Gambria. We're looking for employment here as the availability of jobs is so limited at home."

"How did you get here?" Raefgot interrupted.

"Will you shut-up. I'm in charge here and I'll ask the questions," Menec replied menacingly. "So," he said turning back to Alexis and Duncan, "How did you get here?"

"We walked," Duncan sighed, simultaneously interpreting for Alexis.

"Walked? Ha! You lie again stranger. Look at them," Raefgot challenged the others. "They are not dirty from travel, and what manner of clothing is this?" He pointed at their clothes.

"And what manner of clothing is this?" Duncan countered, flipping at the shirt Raefgot was wearing. "As is obvious from what I said, we are not from here. Your clothing is as strange to us as ours is to you."

"Stop this chatter Raefgot. You be quiet until we get back to Mull," Menec barked.

"You can't tell me what to do Tarrac Master. My father will take care of you when we get back. We'll see how big you are then."

"Shut-up you!" Menec took a threatening step toward him. "I'll slice you here and now and we'll just tell the king that wild animals ate you!"

Raefgot's eyes widened in fear. "You wouldn't dare." He looked wildly around until the others began laughing. He quickly realized the joke at his expense. "You'll pay for this," he hissed.

Menec turned his attention back to Alexis and Duncan. "You say you are looking for employment? Just what is it that you both do?"

Duncan glanced at Alexis, smiled, and looked mischievously at Menec. "Well, she's a warrior... and I'm a wizard...of sorts."

All the warriors laughed uproariously, some pointing at Alexis and feigning fear. Even Menec chuckled appreciatively.

"Ah, Lord Duncan, you are a jester!" Menec smirked. "Raefgot was right, you are a myth-teller. Tell me Lord Duncan, our women put streaks in their hair. Even our warriors do it sometimes before a battle. Do all the men in your village wear streaks like this." His eyes laughed his question and the other warriors laughed with him.

Duncan smiled confidently as though in on the joke, a hand lifting to touch his white streak. "Sorry, but this is natural. I was wounded in battle.

This is the healers' work. With it came special powers." He shrugged self-assuredly.

The laughing stopped and Menec walked up to him, staring up as if asking to see the scar. Duncan bowed his head and Menec reached up to examine Duncan's head. "Great Safti, it's true. This is a healer's scar." He stepped back. "What special powers do you have?"

He thought quickly, "Oh, you know... the usual... knows the weather, talks to animals... makes big explosions, those sorts of things."

Menec eyed him thoughtfully, unsure of the sincerity. "Was the battle won?"

Duncan raised his head and he paused, remembering. "No." He scanned the remaining warriors. "Every one of my family was killed. The same happened to Lady Alexis. That is why we are here. There is no one left of our city save us. We have travelled quite a distance and have come to offer our services."

"But you're a wizard. What can you do for us? Weather and animals may be interesting, but what we need are fighters."

"I have already told you. Lady Alexis is a fighter. She is one of the greatest warriors of our nation."

Again the laughter erupted. Duncan calmly watched and waited for them to expend their humor. He had told Alexis their proposed employment and saw the fire in her eyes as she witnessed herself being the butt of a joke.

"Apparently you doubt me," he smiled. "She would be more than happy to demonstrate. Please, Lord Menec, choose whom you will and let them fight. Then you decide."

Menec unconsciously warmed to the praise. "I am not a Lord, good myth-teller."

"I make no apologies. In our country, it is customary to address those in positions of responsibility with Lord or Lady. It is a sign of our respect." Duncan bowed

"It is a serpent's tongue!" Raefgot spit.

"It is manners," Menec countered. "Something you could learn Raefgot. But, what you propose, Lord Duncan, is interesting. However, I would not want the lady hurt on our account. She seems so small."

Duncan laughed. "I'm not worried about the lady, Lord Menec. I just hope she doesn't kill whomever you choose."

Menec grinned, shrugged, and scanned the group. Several men frowned, not wanting to be known as a man who fought an untested woman... and lost. Finally he settled on the man with the scar on his face.

"You, Fergul. You shall fight the woman." He raised a hand to stop Fergul's complaint. "Do not kill her." He stepped back and the group made a large circle.

"What weapons does the woman choose?" Fergul asked disdainfully.

Duncan spoke briefly with Alexis. "She says none. She also adds that to make it more of an even fight, she will not use her hands." Duncan smirked.

Fury flashed through Fergul and he handed his weapons to the man next to him. "This won't take long."

The two combatants moved to the center of the circle and faced each other about a meter apart. At Menec's command Fergul rushed at her, only to find himself flying through the air as she rolled backwards and kicked him over her.

He rolled and was quickly up. She was standing calmly in the center watching him. Her detached attitude irritated him and he wanted to end this quickly. He began to bob side-to-side, feinting thrusts left and right. Still she didn't move. He rushed her again only to see her jump straight up and kick full force in his chest. His breath rushed out as he heard the cracking of bone and pain exploded over his body.

He stumbled back and fell, clutching his chest, his breathing labored. He forced himself to his knees and then wobbly stood up. Stabbing pain shot throughout his chest.

"Duncan, tell them to stop him. I've broken his sternum. If he continues to fight, I'll kill him," she urged, a flat coldness in her voice that Duncan did not recognize nor like.

He translated quickly, and the stunned Menec nodded agreement. Two warriors helped steady Fergul.

"It is a heavy lesson we learn," said Menec. "Perhaps neither of you is what you seem." He regarded his two charges with new appreciation. He looked at Duncan with mixed apprehension. "And you are a wizard...of what sorts?"

"Oh, I don't turn people to stone or things like that," Duncan grinned. "Well, I suppose I could if I wanted..." He didn't finish the sentence. The warriors moved slightly away, eyeing him with misgiving.

"Will you give us a demonstration?" Menec asked, unsure of himself. He wanted to believe Duncan hadn't any powers, yet was afraid to test his theory in light of Alexis' stunning fight.

Duncan sighed in a tired tone. "Must I?" Duncan thought quickly. "Well, let me see..." Then he remembered. "Look at the sky. Beautifully blue isn't it?"   The warriors looked up at the clear skies searching for something magical. Nothing happened. They returned their expectant stares to Duncan. "Tomorrow will be just like today," he said.

There was a long pause as they waited for more. "That's it?" a voice asked.

"That's it," Duncan flippantly replied.

"But that's, that's nothing!" Raefgot stammered. "You haven't done anything."

Duncan turned to the group, but addressed Menec. "Lord Menec, I could kill one of these noble warriors if you wish, but what would it accomplish? I have seen too much killing." He turned solemn for effect, carefully watching the reaction.

Menec pondered Duncan's remarks. "True, there is too much killing. Perhaps you are right." He turned toward the group. "We will wait and see."

"He's a soul-stealer!" a low voice accused.

"Maybe," Duncan glibly replied. "And then maybe not," he quickly added when he saw the panic in their eyes.

"Why are you here?" another voice asked.

He turned in the general direction of the question. "As I said before, we seek employment."

"Is there no labor in your land?" asked Menec.

"Noble Menec," Duncan replied, "as I said before, our country has been destroyed and we have no wish to go back." Smiling at Alexis he added sotto voce "And we couldn't go back if we wanted." He caught the wariness in their eyes. "Listen my friends, we are alone as you can see. We've come to offer what little service we can to the great kingdom of Gambria."

There was a momentary pause before Raefgot made his demand. "They must go to the Confessor!"   Several others murmured their support, while some wanted to leave them alone, letting someone else deal with these strangers.

"We will take them to Mull," Menec announced.   He pointed to a warrior with long thick tresses of golden hair. "Cu, you are the youngest and fastest. You will run ahead. Come here." Cu obediently went to Menec who gave his instructions in low tones that only Cu could hear. Menec finished and Cu nodded his head in understanding before rapidly disappearing down the road.

"Come along my lord and lady," Menec mischievously bowed. "We will see what kind of reception, and employment await you." He motioned them to precede him. "You two," he pointed to two other warriors.' "Help Fergul."

As the group walked, Menec came along side of Duncan. "Lord myth-teller," he said softly. "Do all your women-folk fight like she does?"

Duncan smiled. "Not all. Many do, but not all.   But tell me Lord Menec, is it far to your village?"

Menec peered intently at Duncan. "Why do you persist in mocking us?"

"I do not mock you Lord Menec." Duncan replied. "I spoke the truth when I said that in our country, your village would be small.   Yet," he hastily added when he saw Menec about to interrupt, "you know as well as I that the strength of a people is not measured by numbers.   In fact, there would be many people from where I come who would give all they own to live in your village."

Menec walked silently beside him digesting what he had heard and seen. Duncan translated their brief conversation for Alexis.

"What do you think will happen next?" she asked in a tone more curious than concerned.

"I'm not sure," he answered, looking over the group as they walked. "I've got a feeling that Menec can be trusted, and might be one to help us."

Menec looked at them when he heard his name. "Your language is strange. You are not Rugians as I know their tongue. Yet I do recognize when my name is used. You are talking about me?"

"Yes," Duncan said. "I told her that you are a man who can be trusted."

Menec gave him a wry glance. "You know nothing about me."

"That is true Lord Menec. Yet...am I wrong?" He grinned in triumph.

Menec laughed and shook his head. "Myth-teller, you are refreshing. It's been a long time since we've had anything new here in Mull."

They continued walking, the forest thick against the road.   The road itself was hard-packed dirt, with shallow groves imbedded from thick metal shod wheels. Duncan recognized several varieties of trees from the pictures he had studied - ash, birch, hazel, and oak. He inhaled the fragrance of things growing.   Suddenly the forest stopped and broad fields of grain billowing in the wind stretched before them.   In the distance perched a many turreted city wall expanding to fill the vista. It was uniformly colored, a steel gray that seemed to scintillate in the bright sun.   Behind the wall, the City itself rose up in layers nestled against the mountains.

"Speaking of Mull," Duncan spoke in reverent tone.

"It is beautiful, isn't it," Menec stated this as fact.

As the group walked away from the thick forest, a small shadow flitted behind them. Unseen in the vegetation along the road, Rasta-mon kept careful distance, doing his best to keep up with them.

Hey mon! Don' forget me!

Rasta-mon! Where are you?

Right behin' you, mon. Where you goin'?

Duncan leaned in toward Alexis. "Rasta-mon's following us. I'm not sure how he'll be treated, so he needs to exercise extreme caution."

I heard dat! Dese people don't eat cats do dey? he said breathlessly.

Well not for breakfast anyway. Duncan responded good-humoredly.

Dat's not funny mon.

Rasta-mon, I don't know what's going to happen.

Don' leave me here!

Duncan stopped and the group jittered to a halt.

"What's wrong?" Menec asked.

"In our haste, we forgot one of our friends," he replied.

"You said there was only you two," Menec warned.

"This is a small friend," he said turning around. They followed his gaze as the cat ran up and jumped into his arms.

There was a subtle murmur of wonder and several pointed to the cat saying, "A king's companion."

"This is your friend?" Menec asked, scratching the cat's ears. "How is it that you have a king's companion?"

"Pardon?"

"The king's companion - where did you get it?"

"He is not ours in the sense of possession. He is a friend. In our land, these animals choose whom they will follow."

Menec stopped scratching and stepped back, warily regarding Duncan. "Do you talk with him?"

"Of course," he chuckled, "I'm a wizard." Bringing his face close to Rasta-mon, he snickered, "Hi kitty."

Menec squinted at him, then laughed and shook his head. "Truly, you are a jester. Come on then and bring 'your friend' with you." They again resumed their walk toward the city and Duncan got lost in his thoughts.

While Duncan had been enthralled by the vision ahead of him, Alexis had been looking over the undulating terrain, the fields bordered by double rail fences running in neat lines following the contour of the land. The sun was warm and bright. Her gaze followed one stretch of fence and focused on several vultures circling low close by. She followed their interest down and rested on a human body, naked and torn. There were several birds gathered around, tearing strips, strings, and chunks of flesh and skin from the corpse. Occasionally one would fly up in dispute over some morsel, but mostly they pecked and tore. One bird had dug deeply into the abdomen and was pulling out intestine when Alexis nudged Duncan and pointed.

Menec followed her gaze. "Oh," he said measuredly. "That's one of the Rugian spies captured yesterday. I guess the High Priest's finished with him." He watched for a reaction from either of them, but saw none that warranted further analysis. It was what he had expected; the woman was unaffected while the man concealed his true feelings.

Duncan's heart had fluttered briefly as he tried to hide his shock at the scene, the prancing of the vultures holding his attention like some macabre dance.

Chapter 9

Alexis nudged him again, breaking the spell. She pointed to a group of men walking toward them. They were dressed similar to Menec's group. As they got closer, Duncan recognized the man who had been driving the wagon a short time before. The man saw Menec, waved, and a broad smile split his face. He broke into a jog and the group followed.

Menec watched as they came, a pleasured grin in recognition. "Hallo Brevil. I thought you were still in Solway?" Turning to his two quests, he introduced them. "This is Lady Alexis, a warrior, and this is Lord Duncan, a...uh, wizard of sorts," Menec grinned. "The wizard speaks our language, the warrior doesn't."

"A king's companion?" Brevil pointed to Rasta-mon.

Menec smirked. "Don't ask. I'll explain later."

Brevil took stock of the two before him and walked over to Fergul. "Cu arrived with an interesting tale," he said over his shoulder as he examined the wounded man. "He said the lady broke Fergul's chest! And I see that she nearly killed him." He walked back to Menec and asked in a low voice, "She's so small. Is it true that she didn't use her hands?"

Menec shook his head, and indicated for him to come closer. "I've never seen the like before," he whispered. "With her fighting for us, perhaps it's time we took the battle to the Rugians and defeated them once and for all."

"Let's go then. King Diad wants to meet them. It was wise of you to send Cu to him instead of the Confessor. Otherwise they'd be dead in a matter of hours."

"Brevil," he said, touching his friend's arm. "Raefgot is with us." Then looking intently at him, he saw his tired eyes for the first time. "What's going on?"

"Come, let's talk as we walk. The King is expecting us." Brevil turned and the two began earnest conversation while the rest of the group trailed behind.

Duncan and Alexis walked closely behind Menec and Brevil. Duncan strained to listen to the rapid conversation. While he understood many of the words, the topic eluded him. He gave up and let his mind wander to the countryside around them.

The fields were large, with groups of families working the land. It appeared to be a communal effort. Neatly trimmed and well built houses of smoothed granite were scattered throughout the area in groups of ten homes to a settlement. A low wall of rough-hewn granite surrounded the buildings. Wooden fenced pastures for small domestic animals that reminded Duncan of goats were outside the walls. Occasionally, a farmer would see the warriors and yell a heart filled greeting.

One of the settlements was close to the road and he got a closer look at the glittering granite. Veins of another mineral like quartz or diamonds gave the stone its shimmering qualities. He liked the way the sun danced upon the buildings, giving them a surrealistic appearance.

The farmers were dressed in the same dull colored brown as the man Duncan and Alexis had first seen. He allowed his gaze to wander over the fields billowing in grains spreading out into the rolling and undulating land. Off in the distance, he could see groves of trees and farther beyond, mountains.

Several of the farmers looked up to wave and shout greetings to Menec or one of the others in the group. Duncan lost himself in daydreaming when he felt a sharp jab in his side.

"Duncan, you're drifting. You need to listen and find out what's going on. What are they saying?" Alexis moved closer to him.

"I'm not sure, but apparently you've made a favorable impression. From what I can understand, we're in the country of Gambria and this city is Mull, probably the capital. Looking around," he swept his hand, "the way these little settlements are designed almost seem like outposts of some sort. Obviously Gambria must be doing well, for the fields go right up to the forest. It has a strong medieval flavor to it."

Alexis turned her attention back to the city. "We're getting closer. This place is a lot bigger than I realized," she said as they crested a small hill.

The walls loomed large in front of them. They were smoothly hewn marble-like stone. Duncan could discerned no joints or mortar. "Excuse me Lord Menec," he interrupted. "How old is Mull?"

Menec shrugged. "I'm not sure. Our records only go back 1500 years." He looked to Brevil for support.

"What?" Duncan exclaimed. "This castle has been here for over one thousand years?"

"Is that unusual...um, Lord Duncan?" Brevil inquired.

"Well...yes. At least where I come from. Wars have destroyed anything of historical value."

"Ah, I understand," Brevil said. "We too are constantly at war."

"Yet the castle stands," Duncan offered.

"Perhaps we build better here in Gambria?" Menec suggested.

Duncan was about to discuss neutron bombs and nuclear havoc, decided against it, and simply nodded his head.

"Horses!" Alexis suddenly exclaimed, "I think."

Duncan looked to where she pointed. They had just crested another small hill and spanning before them on the right side of the road leading up to the city gates was a large complex of stables, riding rings, large paddocks, and other training areas. They both stopped to watch. In one of the exercise rings, eight men were working with eight of the animals.

"What do the animals have on their heads?" Duncan asked.

Menec looked askance at Duncan. "Horns," he answered, as if explaining to an idiot.

"Horns?"

"Of course. Every tarrac has them."

"Tarrac?"

Menec stared intently at him, waiting for the joke. Suddenly he realized that Duncan was serious. "Don't you have tarrac in your country?"

"Um, well sure," he parried. "But not like these."

"Of course not," Menec preened. "We breed only the finest tarrac. Even the Rugians know that. On the rare occasion, they've been known to try to steal one."

"I want to get closer to watch." Alexis stated and walked over to stand next to the fence. The rest followed in tow.

The men in the ring were tanned and well-muscled, stripped to the waist but wearing very thick, heavy leather pants that came just below the knee. They all seemed to walk bow-legged from the thick padding that ran from the inside of the legs and continued to the seat of the pants. Their boots came up high under the knee in the back and extended stiffly above the knee in the front like a small shield. The men astride the Tarrac used small saddles and held the reins attached to a round braided piece that circled around the Tarrac's nose and was fitted around the top of the animal's head just behind the massive, curved horns that protruded near the upright ears and curled around the eyes.

With subtle pride, Menec explained what was happening. "I am the king's tarrac master. All of what you see here is my responsibility: the tarracs, the barns, and the training. The eight riders here are in their advanced training, learning to fight while controlling, guiding their tarracs. It is a long process."

Duncan translated rapidly for Alexis who seemed enthralled with the marvelous beasts. "Does every warrior get one of these animals?" she asked without looking away.

"No," Menec replied. "While each warrior is entitled to a tarrac, too few are able to make it happen."

"Why?" Alexis followed the animals and warriors though their exercises.

"When a fighter has reached warrior status, he is allowed to go to the royal herd and try to capture a tairgim, a mare. This is very dangerous because he must not only win the trust of the tairgim, he must also elude the untamed tarrac and other tairgim. They are very cunning and fierce when untrained. It is only the bond from birth between warrior and tarrac that causes them to overcome their savage nature and devote themselves to their rider. The warrior raises and trains his own Tarrac, and they become partners in battle. All exercises you see here are for battle."

"Does anyone ever fail?" Duncan's curiosity was aroused by Alexis' interest.

Menec chuckled softly. "All too often. The tairgim are the most vicious and devious. They are slow to trust and it may take years before the tairgim will allow herself to be captured. Still other tairgim will never be captured, and some warriors will mistake their own valor for wisdom and be torn to pieces."

Duncan translated for Alexis who simply nodded and continued to watch. In the ring, the riders were leading their animals through a series of exercises. One tarrac carefully raised its front legs and lowered its haunches to a crouched position. It froze momentarily in that controlled, tucked stance, then lashed out with both front legs at a dummy in front of it, ripping it apart from the back with the hooked claw protruding from the back of its feet. Another tarrac leaped into the air and used its hind legs to lash out at a wall behind it, splintering it with the force.

"They move just like Lipizzaner's," she marveled.

Duncan looked curiously at her. "You know about Lippizaners?"

"Probably a whole lot more than you," she shot back. "I used to ride dressage. That wasn't in my bio?"

106

"Tarrac-Master Menec!" Raefgot haughtily interrupted. "We need to take these prisoners to the Confessor. It is your responsibility. You are wasting valuable time."

Menec had had enough. "Lord Duncan, would you please have Lady Alexis rip this child apart." He said it loudly enough for all to hear.

Duncan quickly translated and added. "You might want to be part of the joke. Menec's taken a liking to us."

"Sure." Alexis turned toward Raefgot whose eyes suddenly filled his face. "Should I rip your arm out first?" She jumped and twirled in the air, landing inches from the spot where he had been. However, his fear was faster and he managed to fall out of the way, stumbling over his own legs. She leaped again landing with her foot hovering a millimeter above his throat.

Raefgot cringed, his eyes slammed shut. It wasn't until the braying laughter overwhelmed his fear that he opened his eyes. Alexis was back at the fence watching the tarrac training. All the other warriors were laughing uproariously, slapping each other on the back, mimicking Raefgot's reaction.

Raefgot jumped up. "You'll pay for this Menec. And you too lady warrior. You'll see!" He turned on his heels to leave.

"Stop!" Menec commanded. "Who gave you permission to leave?"

Raefgot turned, fuming, trying to think of something clever to say, but nothing came. He slowly came back, arms folded chest high.

"You'll wait with the rest of us." Menec summarily dismissed him and turned back to his first love.

One of the warriors dismounted and tied the Tarrac near to where Menec's group stood.

"How was the run Master Menec?" the warrior asked respectfully.

"Today's young are slow and fat." Menec replied with a twinkle. A low murmur of good-natured objections came from the group.

While Menec and the warrior held conversation, Alexis walked over to the animal. She innocently reached out to pet it on the nose. The Tarrac growled a deep rumbling warning, then pulled back its lips to reveal long, pointed tearing teeth that snapped in the air where Alexis' fingers had been a split second before. Only her quick reaction saved her hand.

"Be careful! They are one person animals." Menec had heard the growl but had not moved, watching Alexis' reaction. "They will kill or die for their master, but at most they will only tolerate others."

Alexis rubbed the hand that was almost bitten off. "I'll remember that."

As the group turned to go, one tarrac startled, turned clumsily and bumped into another. His handler roughly jerked the bridle and shouted at the animal, which dropped its head and lowered its ears in chagrin. The training officer barked sharply at the rider who dismounted and ran quickly to the trainer who backhanded him across the face and sent him sprawling on the ground. The warrior jumped back up, faced the training officer, bowed, and apologized. Returning to his tarrac, he gently rubbed the animal on the head and scratched him behind the right horn until his ears came up and the submissive look disappeared. Only then did the warrior remount and patiently begin the exercise again.

Though Alexis observed the disciplinary action with emotionless gaze, Duncan's eyes widened, and he looked questioningly at Menec who answered, "These animals are your bodyguard and would gladly give up their lives for you. Few people are as loyal. Tarrac must be treated with respect." Menec motioned them forward and on toward the city.

The number of people continued to increase the closer they got to the gate. Soon they were in crowds of people streaming in and out of the gate. As far as Duncan could surmise, this was the only gate to the city. The drab earth toned dress of the farmers became mingled with more brightly colored city dwellers. Throbbing crowds of men, women, and children, alive and vibrant mixed with passing cartloads of produce, lumber, or other goods.

Duncan liked what he saw, and inhaled the overlapping odors of life. He decided to find out more about Gambria. "What's Gambria like?"

"Gambria is probably much like any other country," Menec answered. "The farmers grow the food, the warriors protect the people, and the merchants take advantage of both."

He chuckled at Menec's joke, then inquired. "Is there a caste system?"

"Caste system?"

"A hierarchy, strata of society. In other words, being a warrior is better than being a farmer, et cetera, et cetera," he explained.

Menec gave him a quizzical look. "What does etcetra etcetra mean?"

He smiled sheepishly. "Sorry. It's another language called Latin. It means 'and so on and so on.'"

"How many languages do you speak?" Brevil interrupted.

He thought briefly. "Oh," he replied nonchalantly, "probably fifteen to twenty."

It was Brevil and Menec's turn to be surprised. "That's impossible!" Brevil spurted. "Even our scholars don't know more than two."

He shrugged. "You still haven't answered the question."

"Well, in some ways yes," Brevil answered, unsure if Duncan was joking. "Yet we all recognize the interdependence of others. The warriors could not survive without the farmers. The farmers could not grow without the warriors defending them. The King could not be King without the people."

"What about religious leaders?" Duncan asked.

Both Menec and Brevil smiled. Menec answered. "The priests are a group to themselves. They guide Gambria –"

"And interfere in our lives!" Brevil finished.

"Then you have a state religion?"

"If you mean that we all believe the same," Menec said, "that's not quite true. Most of Gambria believes in the prophet Safti."

"And some believe in nothing at all," Brevil interjected. "And few could blame them."

Duncan saw Brevil's apparent passion about the topic and pursued it. "Why is that?"

"Religion should teach one about what is good, not destroy."

"What do you mean?"

"What he means," said Menec, "is that for the most part, our religious leaders content themselves to the spiritual lives of the people. Occasionally this requires, um, sacrifices."

"To whom?"

"To god of course," Menec frowned. "You do believe in god?"

"Possibly not in the same way you do," he replied matter-of-factly to a shocked Menec and Brevil. "What kind of sacrifice does he offer?"

"Human."

Now it was Duncan's turn to be shocked. "Hu...human?"

"Yes," Brevil fiercely replied, "human."

"Who?" Duncan hesitantly asked.

"Usually one of the war prisoners, most often a Rugian. Some find it to be moving ceremony, filled with ritual and tradition," Brevil spat. "The poor victim is taken to the Temple of Sacrifice and splayed on the altar. The Confessor cuts his heart out –"

"He's still alive?!" Duncan was aghast.

Brevil paused, his disgust overtly evident. "Yes. I think you get the idea as to the rest of the ceremony."

Despite his revulsion, Duncan regained his composure and asked, "What does the sacrifice do for you?"

"It's supposed to give us a good harvest, or victory in battle, or anything else the high priest deems important," Menec sourly answered.

Duncan pondered a moment. "Suppose you don't have a prisoner of war?"

Menec paused and sighed, shaking his head. "Then we use one of the children," he answered with obvious discomfort.

"One of your own children?" Duncan couldn't believe what he was hearing. He continued translating for Alexis, who even appeared shocked at the religious rites.

"According to the High Priest and Confessor, Vix says that the greatest sacrifice is to offer the thing you love most in honor of the god," Menec replied with just the slightest edge to his voice.

"Do you have much trouble finding a vict...um, I mean a volunteer?"

"Of course," Brevil stated. "What parent would want his or her child sacrificed for some stupid religious interpretation that has yet to demonstrate any result?"

Duncan nodded. "Yet you allow it to continue."

"It's not so easy Lord Wizard," Menec appraised him. "The religion of Safti is very strong here."

"Does all Gambria believe in Safti?"

"Not all," Brevil said. "There are a number of sects of Safti depending on how you view his nature, or the future prophet, or other things."

"His nature?" Alexis raised an eyebrow.

"Yes, you know, whether Safti had one divine nature or a composite nature of both human and divine," he answered while Duncan conveyed the conversation to Alexis.

"Oh brother," she moaned. "Don't bother translating unless you talk about something interesting."

"Are there other beliefs?" Duncan asked, becoming genuinely interested.

"Well, there are still some who believe in the old gods," Menec replied. "We call them soul-stealers, but they've been banished by the church. And there are those who practice the magic arts, called magicians or wizards. The church has been trying to outlaw them, but the few there are have strong supporters and many followers, especially among those looking for the son of the prophet." Menec yawned. "And still others who simply believe in some kind of mystical power in nature, but they're crazy." Then he looked slyly at Duncan. "Which one might you be, wizard of sorts?"

Duncan took the question as rhetorical and didn't answer.

They came upon the gate to the city. The gaping hole, teaming now with people, stood large and wide. It formed a type of tunnel as the city walls were 15-20 meters thick and rose up almost 50 meters.

Once through the gate, Duncan was surprised at the scene in front of him. The city of Mull spread before them. The houses varied in size from one to three stories tall. Many were made of the same glistening stone as the walls. The doors were a multitude of vibrant colors; silk banners and signs hung from windows and balconies. The smells of open roasting fires intermingled with the pungent bouquet of fresh spices spread out on broad tables. Flowers draped over their window boxes, and sweet smelling bushes and trees lined the cobbled streets.

The hubbub and turmoil of people filled the streets. Plump women leaned out of second story windows and called to friends or food vendors below. Merchants, dressed in richly colored silks and animal furs, strolled with fellow merchants and discussed inventories, marketing strategies, or the latest interest rates. Soldiers, bare-chested and in leather pants, their swords gently slapping against their thighs, jauntily travelled in pairs, cat-calling to the women above, or teasing the younger women on the streets. Children gamboled in and out, chasing each other across streets and around the farmers' wagons loaded with bags of grain, unworked cotton, or fresh vegetables. The occasional meat wagon rolled by, the driver swatting at the flies swarming around the dead flesh.

The streets were a maze of bends and turns, designed to hinder an enemy's movement. A large castle stood above all, nestled on a plateau. Duncan used the castle as a focus point.

"Who is the son of the prophet?" he asked.

"His name is sacred. Only the Confessor knows his true name. All others refer to him as the son of the prophet." Menec said over his shoulder as they made their way through the crowds.

"We're not going the right way!" Raefgot accused.

"I know," Menec answered without elaborating.

"We're supposed to be taking these prisoners to the Confessor. Stop!" Raefgot halted abruptly. The others side-stepped him and kept moving. "You're going to be sorry," he yelled as he ran to catch up with them.

Just before entering the castle, Rasta-mon jumped down from Duncan's arm. *Mon, my bladder's killin' me. I be waitin' for you out here.*

Chapter 10

Duncan and Alexis stood in an enormous room with tall high windows of rose-tinted glass. The paneled walls were a blond colored wood, ornately carved with swirls and arches. Solid peach marble colonnades supported a roof of clear glass. Against the wall opposite the main entrance was a pure white throne set upon a dais with seven steps. A canopy of pelts like those of white bears, flowed down to the armrests.

The hub-bub of activity continued when the group walked in. Some in the crowd of officials, attendants-in-waiting, and other court sycophants glanced haughtily at Duncan and Alexis following Menec as he pushed his way through the crowd. Others tittered and pointed at the odd clothes. Still others feigned boredom with the newcomers. Menec forced his way through the noisy throng and stopped the group before the throne.

"Greetings King Diad," he stated loudly, bowing low.

"And to you brother Menec." The king was a tall man, older than Menec. His greying hair fell about his shoulders. His beard, greyer than his hair, was cut short. Instead of a crown, he wore the battle helmet of a common warrior, yet adorned with horns from an ancient tarrac. His recessed eyes, coal dark, hid beneath heavy brows. His sleeveless leather tunic revealed once powerful arms that rested uncomfortably on the arm rests. The spots of age dotted his hands and arms. He had the air of continual distraction about him. Duncan took note of the familiarity between the two men and silently thanked the gods or whatever other causes for his luck.

"I must speak with you Father," Raefgot blurted.

"In a moment. What have we today Menec?"

"But Father –"

"I said in a moment," the king snapped.

"I've brought some visitors that I think would interest you." Menec smiled.

"Father, I want to issue a challenge," whined Raefgot.

"Hold your tongue," came the impatient reply. "There are more important things to discuss here."

"But it's a point of honor," he indignantly replied.

"Be quiet Raefgot," the king growled.

"But I've got a right to challenge. Menec offended me."

The King groaned with aggravated impatience. "What is it this time?"

"He made a fool of me and he's brought these spies here instead of to the High Priest." Raefgot squared his bony shoulders in self-righteousness.

"The fool part I understand," the King dryly stated, "but how is it that Menec would knowingly endanger us by bringing spies here into our midst?"

"This man is a liar and the woman doesn't fight fair." Raefgot blurted. The crowd quickly quieted, suddenly interested in the discord between father and son.

"And how is that?" the King challenged.

"Uh, well..." he sputtered, stumbling for a reason.

"It seems that your affair of honor is not with Menec, but with this woman?" The King looked from Menec to Alexis. "Do you wish to challenge the woman?"

There was a wave of titters as Raefgot blanched. "N...no. Father, I,.uh, Menec..." Raefgot blushed as the titters became louder.

"Then if you do not wish to challenge the woman, be silent and let me conduct my affairs."

"But... but, Menec... he –"

"Do you wish to challenge Menec?"

Raefgot looked quickly to where Menec stood smiling slyly. "Um, well... no, I mean it's–"

"Dammit boy, what do you want?!" Diad erupted.

"A, a challenge... sort of, I mean..." Raefgot stumbled for words.

Diad was about to explode again when a deep voice rumbled. "Brother, it seems that my tongue-tied young nephew is having problems articulating his true desire. It appears that he wishes to issue a point of honor. I believe the law permits a second to fight a point of honor should the circumstances warrant, and it would be unseemly if the King's son were involved in such a trivial affair."

The King turned to the speaker. "Bradwr, now is not the time for this. It is obvious these two strangers are not Rugians. Are we barbarians, no better than the Rugians that we would allow this fight to occur?"

Bradwr smoothed away the thick black and gray mustache hairs from his mouth. "Oh, I quite agree brother. I was merely making a point." He smiled condescendingly at Raefgot who had suddenly understood a way out of his embarrassment. "However, the law makes no excuse for strangers. Proper behavior is proper behavior regardless of locale." He scanned the audience as they grudgingly nodded agreement.

The Lord Chamberlain , a soft man of supercilious temperament standing to the king's right, leaned down to offer his council. "I'm afraid he is quite correct, sire."

"It's my right. I challenge this so-called lady warrior to a fight to the death." Raefgot looked smugly at Menec who was surprised at the vehement challenge.

Even the king was startled as a wave of disapproval rippled through the crowd.

"Dear brother," Bradwr said. "I'm afraid that the law is the law. However, it would be entirely inappropriate for young master Raefgot to become personally involved in such a... ah, fight." He smiled benevolently at the crowd. "Rather let him choose a warrior from amongst those here to be his champion. And let the law proceed as is written."

There was some murmured agreement; however most of the crowd waited to see what would occur. Raefgot's eyes betrayed his gratitude to Bradwr. However, before the king could respond, he named his champion.

"Oswiu. I choose Oswiu." He grinned wickedly.

Now it was Bradwr' turn to be shocked. "Nephew. That is no match. Choose a less proven warrior."

"I am *Prince* Raefgot," Raefgot admonished.

Bradwr rolled his eyes, but nodded in acknowledgment. "Yes nephew, you certainly are," he said patronizingly. "However, I still believe you have chosen unfairly."

"It's my choice," the shrill petulant voice stated. "And I choose Oswiu." The King glared at his son. "You will not reconsider?"

Raefgot folded his arms defiantly. "No."

He sat back and nodded to Menec who was likewise quietly angry at this turn of events. "So be it. Proceed."

As Menec hurriedly explained the law to Duncan and Alexis, the crowd formed a large circle. From out of the crowd, a large man with wide golden arms bands sauntered towards the center. He was dressed in beautifully embroidered silk which he took off as he walked. He stopped five paces from them clad in only a loin cloth. His chest was broad and quite hairy. Several battle scars criss-crossed his chest and stomach. He grinned a wicked smile and flexed his muscles for the crowd who responded with admiration and amusement.

"Alexis, I know you can do it," Duncan urged. "But you have to be careful."

"Thanks for telling me the obvious. Of course I've got to be careful!"

"No. I mean this guy is probably one of their best. Do you understand what that means?" he stressed.

Alexis put a hand on his shoulder, locking his eyes with an intense stare. "I understand that if I don't kill this guy, we're both dead." Her green eyes blazed the same focused, penetrating eyes he remembered when he first saw her face coming through the airlock. "At least this time I get to fight." She stepped back. "Now slap me."

"What?" He stepped back. The circle was now clear, and there was a slow milling of the crowd as they anticipated a short and brutal fight.

"Slap me."

He looked at her quizzically. "You sure?"

"Slap me!" she ordered, grabbing his shirt.

Duncan stepped back again and hit her across the face.

"Not like that! Harder. Really slap me." She began glaring at her opponent who watched with mild amusement.

He shrugged and slapped her with as much strength as he could muster without wanting to hurt her. A red outline of his hand appeared on her cheek and she smiled coldly.

"Now, get out of the way."

The two opponents circled slowly, the crowd warming with surreptitious bets going back and forth. Oswiu smiled and motioned for her to come to him. Suddenly, as if in a daze, Alexis straightened and began walking towards him, stopping several feet from him. She stood perfectly still.

Oswiu cocked his head in wariness and leaped at her. In one smooth motion, Alexis moved out of the way, pushed his outstretched arm up, and like a steel pike, elbowed him in the kidneys.

Oswiu flew forward and landed on the marble floor. He rolled to one side and was up on his feet again. Although the elbow punch had hurt, he was more surprised by her speed. His blood-lust began curling at the corners of his eyes. A low gurgle escaped from his throat, and he began a rhythmic jumping and rocking as if winding himself up. A war scream bellowed from his mouth and he charged at her.

Alexis stood still, awaiting his charge. At the last moment she emitted a short yell of her own and in a lightening punch, hit Oswiu full in the chest. A crack split the air as Oswiu staggered back in disbelief, both hands clutching his chest. Alexis did not wait, but twirled and with the side of her foot caught Oswiu full in the face, sending him reeling to the ground.

The crowd had grown astonishingly quiet as they watched Alexis walk over to where Oswiu lay crumpled on the floor. She stood next to him in obvious disdain.

A hand shot out and grabbed her leg to trip her. Oswiu had not given up the fight. However, instead of tripping, she leaped up, twisted free of the grip and came crashing down with her heel into his face, breaking his nose, then rolling free.

Oswiu reacted with surprising strength. He slowly got to his feet and wiped a bit of blood from his face, placing it carefully in his mouth. His breathing was labored, but the blood-lust was not gone. Yet there was a flickering of apprehension as he gazed into eyes that showed almost no expression - no fear, no hate, just pure cold combat.

They circled cautiously and Alexis began a graceful rhythmic movement of swaying her arms and hands side-to-side in front of her face while balancing on the balls of her feet.

Oswiu's breathing was labored as Alexis had cracked his sternum. A slow steady drip of blood slipped from his nose over his mustache, down his chin, and fell on his chest, sliding in rivulets down his stomach.

Alexis suddenly erupted in fury, punching and kicking with ferocity. Oswiu backed away as best he could, warding off the blows with weakening stamina. Without pause, Alexis again twirled mid-air and with a devastating impact, crashed a foot against his face, sending him careening into the floor.

He lay still, the crowd quiet as they watched their champion moaning softly. She walked to him and grabbing his hair, yanked him to a kneeling opposition. Holding his bloody face up to the crowd, she scanned the faces, her eyes a blazing fire of death they had never seen before. In one quick motion, she jerked his head, snapping his neck. He flopped back down, quivered momentarily, and was still.

She turned him over and methodically punched along the sternum until it was quite split and broken. Prying open the ribs, she thrust her hand into his chest, emerging a moment later with his heart, blood dripping from her elbow.

She held it high and walked over to the king who was watching with a mixture of fascination and repulsion. Stopping two paces from the throne, she threw it on the floor at his feet. She then turned around and yelled a rich-throated victory cry.

"Anyone else?" she challenged, looking at all the men.

A nervous fidgeting ensued with an occasional cough. Some of the men held her in awe, others wouldn't meet her eyes, and still others remained in shock, wondering if the debacle just witnessed was some kind of trick.

She turned back to the king. "Tell him," she said to Duncan, without averting her fiery gaze from the king, "that I'm beginning to lose my patience with the welcome we've received here. The next time I have to fight someone, I will not be so merciful."

There was an awkward silence from the crowd. Duncan too was stunned into silence, appalled by this woman he had thought of as his lover.

"Tell him," she commanded.

Duncan cleared his throat and translated. The king smiled weakly at her vehemence, fully believing she could substantiate her words.

Bradwr broke the silence. "Well. That certainly was a spectacle rarely seen these days." The crowd relaxed. He moved from the edge of the circle and calmly walked towards her. "I could use a good warrior like you," he said appreciatively. "I can pay very well."

"You forget one thing, Lord Bradwr, Menec interrupted. "The law says that a berserker defeated forfeits his title and property to the victor."

"I know the law, Tarrac Master." Bradwr retorted, purposely emphasizing Menec's status. "However, the law also says that a champion is entitled to a champion's wages. And," he stated grandly, "I believe that I can accommodate that."

"You do not know what the support is," countered Menec. "The price is fixed by the berserker."

"Well then, let us ask what her price is," Bradwr condescendingly answered.

Duncan had been rapidly translating the exchange. He paused, and realized all were waiting for her to name a price for her services. "They're waiting for you to name a price." he explained.

Alexis was slowly calming herself, regaining her former composure. Blood dripped onto the polished floor from her down-stretched hands. She looked contemptuously around the room. "You handle it."

"OK. Wish me luck." He inhaled deeply and turned back to the king, bowing. "Do we understand sire that because she has defeated the berserker, she is entitled to all he owned?"

King Diad nodded affably, warmed by Duncan's manners. "You are correct."

"And just what would that entail?"

117

"An excellent question." He looked over the crowd until he found a handsome slender man with intense eyes. "Lord Purveyor, to what is this woman entitled?"

"Well," his voice broke and he cleared his throat. "Well your grace, the ah...late Oswiu owned a villa against the wall, overlooking the sea. He had a number of servants. I'll have to check for other deeds of property and accounts listed." He bowed, pressing both palms against his heart.

Duncan thought rapidly. "Sire. Is it true that except for the king, the berserker is the most honored warrior?"

King Diad smiled, accepting the feigned praise. "That is only partially true. The Chief of the Twelve is our most honored warrior, followed by the Twelve. The berserker, though not one of the Twelve, is next. The woman would take his place."

"And you would have to pay whatever salary she asked?"

"Within reason," he answered, mildly taken aback at the possible fiscal indebtedness.

"However," interrupted Bradwr, "there have been times when, due to the kingdom's...um, obligations, that a berserker has been paid from the coffers of a third-party."

"But that only happens in times of emergency," countered Menec.

"But it happens nonetheless, Tarrac-Master." Bradwr answered, as if to end the discussion.

Duncan closely listened to the verbal sparring while waiting for the exchange to finish. *Menec, I can trust you. Bradwr, whoever you are, you are going to be a problem.* He then turned to the king. "Sire, it would seem to me that a warrior beholden to another for pay is in the service of the benefactor, and not the people. And that which is not in the interests of the hive cannot be in the interests of the bee." He looked back to Alexis and whispered, "Marcus Aurelius." She gave him a quizzical look and shrugged. However, there was a low strong murmur of approval that rippled through the crowd.

"Sire," he continued, "we accept the property of Oswiu. As to salary, we believe in the wisdom of your lordship. We accept whatever would seem fit in your eyes." He bowed as the murmur of approval rose to applause.

Realizing that he had been out-maneuvered, Bradwr smiled. "Well spoken friend. However, you use the term 'we.' As I recall," he said turning to the king, "the property of Oswiu belongs to the champion, not her servant." He bowed slightly.

Initially bristling at the slight Duncan smiled paternally. "I am not her servant, Lord Bradwr. Thus, I do not presume to be partaker of her rewards." He looked at the crowd as he spoke. His gaze rested on Menec who gave him a subtle signal to be careful.

"Well now," mocked Bradwr to the crowd, "that is a comfort." A sporadic titter accompanied his taunt. "Pray tell, good friend, just what is it you do, if you're not a servant?"

Duncan smiled. "I'm a wizard, a scholar, a student of the universe."

There was a startled gasp within the crowd. However, not all were impressed by his statement. Bradwr raised his hand in feigned boredom.

"Really?" He strolled around the circle as he talked. "Well then, show us a trick wizard. Amuse us. I'm sure we'd all be interested in seeing a wizard work."

Duncan smiled an impish grin. "I'm sure you would. But you err, m'Lord. I am a wizard, not a magician. Magicians do tricks. A trick is a slight of hand, something done to deceive. Wouldn't you agree?" He gave Bradwr a penetrating look, noticing a flicker of countenance change in the man, as though he had been caught in some indiscretion.

At that moment, there was a mild disturbance off to the King's right as a woman, richly dressed, walked with sure purpose toward the King. The King caught a glimpse of the movement and looked at the newcomer.

"What do you want?" he demanded tartly.

"M'Lord, I thought perhaps –"

"Then you think too much. I did not ask for your attendance. Guards! Escort the Queen back to her lodgings." The King curtly dismissed her. The Queen bristled slightly, then bowed in humble submission and, escorted by two guards, left the way she had entered.

"These spies were supposed to have been brought to me!" A shrill voice called out from the wings of the room. A severe man with sharp features pushed his way through the quickly parting crowd. He was completely clean-shaven, including his head, eyebrows, and arms. His skin was the lucid white of a man who had spent his days hiding from the sun. The bluish veins snaked and throbbed just below the surface of his tall sparse frame. His one-piece robe of dazzling colors shimmered as he walked. He strode with a focused purpose, an ornate staff in his hand, and walked directly up to Duncan, glaring at him.

"And you would be...?" Duncan subtly mocked.

"I am the Confessor, the High Priest!" he barked. He turned back to the King. "These spies should have been brought to me!"

Duncan watched the slow burn of anger in the King and before the King could answer, he interrupted. "I thought the King ruled in Gambria?"

"He does," the Confessor answered, without conviction.

"Then why are you yelling? I assumed Gambria to be a civilized people. And," he smiled at the crowd, "until you came in, my assumptions seemed to be correct."

Several people snickered, including the King, who cleared his throat. "Please, Holy Vix, do not let your anger lose control."

Vix ignored him and turned around. "Seize them!" he commanded, breathing heavily, glaring around the room.

Several men in the crowd began acting on his directive, hesitated and then gingerly edged back into the crowd when Alexis stood next to Duncan.

"I said seize them!" he yelled. Several men regained their senses and, weapons raised, very slowly approached the two newcomers.

"Stop!" The King raised an imperial hand. The men halted.

"Do it now!" The Confessor glared at the men, who in turn looked at the King for help.

"I said stop." The King spoke slowly and firmly. The Confessor whirled to face him.

"These intruders were supposed to have been sent to me first! It is the law. They are strangers and are to be given the test," he arrogantly challenged.

The King leaned forward and sternly spoke. "I know the law. I also know that we have just made this warrior," he nodded at Alexis, "our berserker. She has the protection of the nation."

"Yet what about the, uh... wizard, m'Lord?" Bradwr spoke up. "He has not the protection of the law. And what is this affectation with the streak of white."

"It's the result of a healer's touch from a battle wound," Menec interjected.

Bradwr turned to Menec. "And why do you know this?"

"If you remember Lord Bradwr, it was my trainees who found them. I did what any warrior would do and questioned them. I also examined the scar. I can tell the difference between a healing itself and a healer's touch." Menec's response was courteous, with the tone of a school master instructing a pupil.

Bradwr caught the veiled insult in Menec's statement. Though a warrior, Bradwr had never been wounded, preferring to lead from the rear. "Well done Tarrac-Master. I commend your thoroughness." Bradwr replied smoothly, with a bit of condescension. "And did this wizard-of-sorts also demonstrate his power? Has he bewitched you?" The joke was obvious and many laughed.

"My Lord, this gets us nowhere!" Duncan interrupted. "Lady Alexis has the protection of the law. It appears that I don't, as Lord Bradwr is so quick to point out. Is it the custom of Gambria to execute strangers?"

"Hardly!" Menec firmly stated.

"Well spoken brother Menec," the King glanced appreciatively at Menec. "The man here called-"

"Duncan, m'Lord," Menec supplied the answer.

"Duncan, has the temporary protection of the law and the nation." The King turned to Vix.

"You may question him at your convenience. However, he remains under my authority." Silence filled the room. "Well then," the King said flatly. "Well then, there it is. Lord Purveyor, please show the two newest members of Gambria to the new berserker's lodgings. Naturally you'll provide them a complete listing of all the woman owns as soon as possible."

"Of course m'Lord." The purveyor bowed.

As the king rose, all activity ceased; and the king walked out to his own chambers. Pausing before the door, he motioned Menec to come to him.

"Yes m'Lord?" Menec stopped several paces before him.

The king beckoned him closer until they were almost head to head. "You were right to send her to me. She indeed is a great warrior."

Menec smiled knowingly. "I thought so too. I felt we could not allow Vix to reach her first."

"You were right to think so. Yet I am troubled old friend."

"Why so m'Lord?" he said, suppressing a sigh. He had heard the litany of paranoia too many times. Everyone was out to get him.

"Troubles abound. I am beginning to fear Lord Bradwr does not love us quite as much as he appears. And Vix is demanding another child from the Gambri. This god of ours seems to be far too blood thirsty a god." They continued, walking through the doors toward the King's private chambers. "What do you think of them?" he nodded, indicating Alexis and Duncan.

Menec shook his head, smiling. "I don't know yet, m'Lord. He is full of surprises. Still, there is a part of me that trusts him." They stopped outside the chamber doors. "And the woman is a marvelous fighter. Perhaps now we can eliminate Rugia once and for all." He smiled grimly.

"Perhaps," the King replied without thinking. "But come, what am I to do with Vix? He demands another child for the Temple."

Menec curled a lip. "What is it this time? Sacrifice or his perversion?"

"Does it matter?" Diad shrugged. "I fear I must confront him very soon, and it will not unfold well." He slipped into brief pensiveness, then looked back to Menec. "But tell me about Raefgot? Does he have any qualities that warrant further warrior training?"

After the King had departed, the crowd visibly relaxed, and Duncan and Alexis were swallowed in a mob of admirers, curiosity-seekers, and a harried purveyor trying to get them out of the hall and to their house. Eventually, with Brevil's help, the purveyor escorted them out into the fading afternoon sun and on to the lodgings of the late Oswiu.

Bradwr strolled over to where Raefgot quietly fumed at being neglected. "Nephew, I do believe you have been bested."

"That's obvious," he sourly retorted.

"Come, let me buy you a carafe of wine and offer some suggestions of recourse," he said, gently clapping him on the shoulder.

Together they walked out. As they passed the High Priest, Vix gave a subtle hand signal asking Bradwr to come see him. Bradwr replied in kind, giving the location and time of their meeting. They gingerly stepped over the King's fool who lay sprawled against one of the colonnades near the door. His multi-colored hat was pulled over his face.

After their departure, the fool lifted his hat. He scanned the departing crowd and caught the eye of High Commander Brenna, signaling to her the intercepted message. He then stood up, stretched, and limped out into the closing day, his club foot giving him a bell-clapper motion as he walked.

Chapter 11

The stone corridor was coldly dark, the burning torches giving only half-hearted light, tossing shadows against the smooth rock. Centuries of soot clung to the walls and ceiling above their sputtering flames.

A woman warrior walked with confident stride, immune to the imagined evil of the hall. Her focus was the brightness at the end of the long passage where several torches were gathered, flickering collectively.

She wore a sleeveless top, a combination weave of metallic silk and tiny interlinked chains forming a type of thin chainmail that snugly formed over her ample chest and narrow stomach. Her shoulders and arms were firm and well defined. She was dressed in the clinging metallic silk pants of a warrior. Her taut muscles flexed the material in powerful spasms as she walked. A dirk was tucked into her boots, and a short thick-bladed sword was strapped to the webbed belt surrounding her narrow waist. The torch-light scintillated upon her body as she walked.

She instinctively slowed as she neared the end, knowing the hall made a sharp left turn before quickly entering a large circular room. She inhaled the sweet rose incense that hung within the room as she walked in. The room was a sharp contrast to the cold corridor. It was comfortably warm, yet the only heat and light was provided by the fires that burned in the ornately carved metal gargoyles spaced along the walls. Carpets were strewn thickly on the floor and richly colored tapestries curved against the walls. Several small tables with freshly cut flowers were placed tastefully within the room.

Opposite the door, more towards the rear of the room was a large throne, carved from rare auburn native woods and inlaid with gold. A canopy of lace draped over the arms. Seated on the throne was an androgynous figure, clothed in long silk robes that completely covered its body. It had a mask for a face, much like that for a Grecian play, the fixed smile in mocking jest. A hood covered its head.

The woman warrior walked to the foot of the dais and knelt, her long black braided hair cascading to the floor. "You wished to see me sire?"

The figure moved, pushing the folds of robe from its gloved hands. "We are pleased that you have come High Commander Brenna. Please stand." It gestured her to rise. The voice was neither recognizably male nor female, yet it was soothing. "We understand that you witnessed the display this afternoon. How did it strike you?"

"I, I've never seen anything like it before," she stammered, her dark eyes revealing her wonder. "She fought like a berserker and dervish combined. She moved in new ways I've never seen."

There was a soft pause. "Are you afraid of her?"

She tilted her head slightly. "Not really. I have been trained for battle and death. I am not afraid to die."

"That is not what we asked," the voice corrected with slight humor.

Brenna paused again, thinking. "I suppose I should be afraid of her, if that is the emotion required. She is a weapon we've never seen before. She killed Oswiu with little effort. I believe she could have killed him even had he weapons and she none."

"Yet I sense there is something else that caught your attention," the voice smoothly coaxed.

"Her eyes... her eyes."

"Are her eyes so much different than yours?"

"Yes and no. Hers are a bright green that seem to flame when in combat. There is a passion and excitement in them that's almost sexual, yet there is also a cold detachment in them, something like the golden beetle who mates and then devours her lover."

There was a soft chuckle. "An interesting analogy High Commander." The figure shifted its robes. "We are pleased with your observations." There was a pause as if the figure was thinking. "However, their arrival was not expected. Yet this too may be to our benefit. Are you a believer lady-warrior?"

"Do you mean do I believe in Safti sire?"

"Yes. Are you a follower of Safti, the one whom they call the righteous-one?"

Brenna slowly shook her head. "Not really. I don't trust in anything other than myself. All this talk of the prophet and some future descendant miraculously emerging out of the Starn Sea is too much for me. And the mindless fascination of a here-after, or the divine nature of Safti, or whether Safti had two natures is a total waste of time and energy. And I can't accept a god who requires human sacrifice to allow crops to grow or rain to fall, or some other stupid reason that only the high priest can divine. This whole religious stuff is too absurd for anyone with any intelligence."

The figure raised a hand for her to stop. "We take it then that you are not a follower. It is of no importance. However, it is our wish that you become knowledgeable of the Safti beliefs. We anticipate that such as these will assist us in our efforts."

"As you wish," Brenna said resignedly.

"You do not need to become a priestess or some vacuous follower, lady-warrior. At least not yet. However, you must become convincing to those we need to influence."

"Yes m'Lord."

"Likewise, we desire you to not only befriend these two newcomers, we ask that you exert all your abilities to influence them both to our bidding."

"As you wish."

There was another slight pause. "Though their arrival was not anticipated, this may yet be a boon to our plans. They could prove quite useful. What do you know of power, lady warrior?"

Brenna looked at the figure and wondered if she was being tricked or tested. "I know that my sword can end a man's life, and that it obeys me completely."

"This is true, a blade can mean death. But what of those who lead us? Do they threaten us with the sword or do they use our own ignorance to manipulate us for their own purposes?" The figure lightly fanned the air drawing in the bouquet of incense.

"Are you saying that our loyalties and allegiances make slaves of us?" Brenna rankled at the implication. "I am no one's slave."

"What I am saying High Commander, is that those who serve, serve best and most zealously what they believe in. Those who pursue power for the sake of only power are sooner or later uncovered in their intent. People will not follow a fool or one who makes them feel like fools."

Brenna puzzled for a moment. "M'Lord, then how do we know who the true leader is and whom to follow?"

A silence followed; then the voice broke the stillness. "The true leader is defined by who he is, what he knows, and how he acts. We intrinsically recognize a true leader. We cast aside our own insecurities and follow him... or her. He promises only what he can deliver."

"But our own history has too many examples of men who were thought of as true leaders only to be revealed for the frauds they were. Promises are easily made. How do we really know the true leader?" Brenna quizzed.

"You ask the essential question." The figure laughed softly, shifted in its seat and rearranged its robe. Brenna fidgeted slightly, yet waited with proper respect. Finally, an answer emerged. "Who we are, where we came from, and where we are going are the concerns of us all, and the triumph or failure of us all. We cannot separate kings and priests and warriors – faith and the future belong to us all. If the need is battle, do you not follow the strongest warrior? And if the need is food, do you not find the best farmer? If the need is faith, do you not follow the one in whom you believe?" The flickering lamps danced shadows across the robed figure. "And what is your need High Commander? Is it faith you seek, or power, or perhaps, love? Will you follow one who promises that?"

She bowed. "I follow you sire."

"And why is that?"

Brenna snorted. "High Priest Vix is a butcher who uses the church to explain away his own perverted nature. The king, though kind enough to adopt me and give me title because of his friendship with my father, treats his wife like t arrac dung. His preoccupation with younger women diverts his responsibilities away from the kingdom. Who rules in Gambria? Surely the king by title, but Bradwr is hardly subtle, and Alric would probably slit his own brother's throat to become king if he could get away with it. How can I follow such a family?" The figure shifted and smoothed its robe again, as Brenna grew more passionate. "Take today for instance. Our own battle leader and berserker died because of arrogant stupidity. How could the fool not remember that one must know the enemy? His own ignorance caused his death. What truth or leadership is there in that?"

The robed figure chuckled loudly. "But as you see High Commander, I have no sword, nor the king's title, nor the high priest's authority."

"That is true sire. Yet you speak of a faith and rightness that I understand – a god that invites to greatness, a religion that pulls together. I believe you speak the truth." She finished and was quiet.

"Perhaps. However, the power in truth is in the telling and acting, and much stands in its way. We need the talents of the visitors. Each could be dangerous, and many in power have already seen this; the woman for her abilities and uncontrollability, the man for his cleverness. Do you think you will be able to earn their trust and to convince them to come to our aid?"

"It will be as you desire." Brenna bowed low.

"One more thing," the voice soothingly said, "it must be done quickly. We fear our time is short."

"Yes sire." Brenna bowed again and smiled. She straightened resolutely, crisply turned and swept out of the room.

Across town, Bradwr was leaning upon a heavy, thick-legged table in a half-lit tavern commiserating with Raefgot. The smell of stale beer and roasting meat hung thick throughout the large room. The raucous noise of garrulous men in drunken song bounced against the walls, reverberating loudly. Bradwr leaned in speaking loudly enough for Raefgot to hear.

"It is indeed unfortunate that your father does not recognize your true talents."

"Oh yeah?" Raefgot slurred, the result of too many drinks. "And what talent would that be Uncle?" Raefgot swayed gently, trying to keep Bradwr in focus.

"You are a warrior and a king's son. Both of these entitle you to not only more respect, but require, yes, require that you should be a leader." Bradwr leaned back slightly, rapidly bored with his game. Raefgot was getting drunk and when he got drunk, it was no good trying to mold his weak mind. He knew he already had Raefgot's support, but Raefgot was irrational enough to be persuaded by any simpleton with a fool's plan.

Instead of responding, Raefgot swayed some more before his head thudded against the table. Bradwr pushed away from the table motioning his aides to bring Raefgot with them. "Take him to the house. Let him wake up with the young children. Perhaps then we can mold him better."

As the men carried him out, Bradwr motioned to the tavern owner calling out, "What news Traun? Is all well?"

A thick man with numerous scars and a slight limp, Traun sauntered over. "All goes well Lord Bradwr." He leaned down and close to Bradwr. "Business is excellent. All my debts are covered and profits are up. Your patronage at this humble dwelling is most appreciated." He grinned and leaned closer. "They go to Oswiu's home. Tene is placed already. We get information as soon as I can talk with her."

Bradwr smiled and stood up. "Drinks are on the house of Bradwr. You have a fine establishment here, friend Traun." Amidst the drunken cheers and "huzzahs" Bradwr weaved through the crowd and out into the afternoon's sunlight.

Back in the dim recesses of his livelihood, Traun went back into the kitchen. "Cooking girl, come here." A slender girl of fourteen, just beginning to blossom into womanhood, approached. She brushed several strands of thick auburn away from her forehead. "Go to Tene and tell her that he was here again and I need information quick. You understand?"

"Yes Traun." Her doe-eyes blinked in comprehension.

127

"Good. Go now." He turned away, hurrying over to where two drunks were loudly insulting each other.

The two acolytes stepped aside as the High Priest stormed into the room, Father Lucan gliding effortlessly behind him, his serenity oozing into the room. Vix nodded curtly to the two acolytes and pushed the heavy doors to the Sacred Sanctum open. Brother Lucan paused before entering and turned to the two young men.

"Please see that we are not disturbed. Thank you so much." He spoke with easy calmness, his voice warm and mellow.

The two acolytes watched as Father Lucan, a pious smile forever stuck on his face, closed the doors behind him. Hearing the bolt of metal secure the lock, the younger acolyte exhaled.

"It's amazing Father Lucan can still smile so much with his head so far up the Holy Father's posterior." He tugged an earlobe and in a low voice said, "What do you think they're cooking up now?"

The older acolyte shrugged. "Hard to say Brother. However, Father Vix did not appear too pleased."

"Uh-uh. Sounds like sacrifice time again."

The elder acolyte, a slender man with a gift for minding his own business adjusted his robes. "That's the privilege of the masses."

"What? You don't really believe that, do you? You've read the book of Safti. Where does it say that we must sacrifice their children?"

The elder acolyte shrugged. "That's why he is the Holy Father. He has revelations and spiritual insight...He understands what we don't."

"So you say," the younger acolyte frowned.

The High Priest nestled into the Sacred Chair and watched as Father Lucan reverently retrieved the Holiest Book and gingerly placed it on the gilded podium, a delicately carved reading stand with the top worn smooth from use.

"Begin with Sura 17, verse 26," the High Priest intoned, his fingers drumming rhythmically on the smooth wooden arms of the large chair.

Lucan carefully opened the ancient text and carefully and tenderly turned the pages until he found the page. Pausing to clear his throat, he began to read. "And we traveled from Cash-El to the great Starn Sea. We buried our dead and to the dying I gave comfort. And I taught them. 'All desire is subordinate to the future.' And I took the healthy male and female and allowed them their passions, and they did produce. And I gathered all who were with me and taught them. We are a blessed group and will continue to be blessed only if we remember who we are. We must make choices that will break our souls, we will have to sacrifice what we hold most dear, even our own children. But always, always, we must remember who we are."

As Lucan droned on, Vix began to drift. Lucan's voice had that pleasing quality of resonant hum that could lull one to sleep. When he was troubled, Vix would call Lucan to read to him and the soothing tone would ease his soul. When he awoke, Lucan would be serenely seated on the floor, legs crossed and arms dangling loosely at his sides, his hands resting on his thighs. Although his eyes would stare at the High Priest, his breathing was the shallow relaxed breaths of sleep. Yet when the High Priest stirred, Lucan would rise as though he had always been awake.

How does he do that? Vix wondered. *Father could do that. And you dear brother. You could separate the waking soul and meditate on the necessary. Father always loved that about you. How unfortunate that I am here, a first-born child by chance. Why wasn't it you who came out first and me who clung to your heels, firm handed grasp around your ankle.*

The High Priest tucked his legs underneath him and gently touched his right ankle where the hand-print of his brother was still visible. Their father had called it a sign and trained them both for the priesthood. However, only the first born had the right of succession. His father had been proud of them both, but gave his fullest attention to Vix, knowing him the chosen one.

Yet Vix was not as quick as Lucan and their father soon saw the difference. Lucan had the natural inclination to the priesthood. In fact, Father thought him the best acolyte of his memory, even better than the stories of grandfather. *Father searched in vain, pouring over the scriptures to see if there was another way of making Lucan high priest instead of me. I know that. Don't you think I know that, Lucan, dear brother. Yes, it should have been you. You always had the 'gift.'*

Vix shifted again and looked out the window to the birds arcing across the afternoon sky. *Yes, you had the gift.* Vix focused on one bird as it circled lazily in the distance. *Probably circling over that Rugian I had flayed.* The lazy flight reminded him of the birds of prey he had seen out the window the time his father came crashing into his room. The girl was splayed on the bed, her hands tied to the posts. Her head lolled side to side, the eyes rolled back into her head. Her crotch was blood spattered and her legs were bent grotesquely to the side.

"What have you done?" his father demanded, angrier than he had ever seen him before. In one sweeping motion his father had grabbed him by the robe and began punching him, delivering blows about his head and face.

Vix fought back as best he could, but the strength of his father overwhelmed him and the blows to the face stung with each angered hit. "She...she mocked me...said I was just a priest...said I'd had nothing between my legs... she said I was a eunuch." The blows continued until he felt himself hurled against the wall. He slid down in to a quivering mass, wiping his tearing eyes on the thick robe sleeves.

His father stalked over to the girl and saw the bruises on her face and the red soaked streaks of the whip marks across her flat chest. He again looked at the face and realized that she was probably only twelve or thirteen years old. Whirling around, he quickly crossed the distance to his cowering son.

"You... you let a child bother you? You bastard, you're not a man! You're not fit to be a man. Get up you coward! Get up!" He grabbed Vix's cowl and forcibly lifted him, dragging him towards the bed. "You want her? Huh? You coward! You want her? Take her!" And he threw him across the girl. "Take her, you excuse for a man. Take her, you bastard. You are not my son, for children are all that you can handle!"

Vix scrambled off. "Stop father, stop!" He pleaded. "Lucan was here too!" He jabbered, hoping to halt the punishment and share the blame.

"Liar!" His father threw furniture out of the way as he lunged for Vix. "Liar! He's down in the cloisters with the priests!"

Vix jumped up, eluding the clutching hands and hurtled out the bed chamber doors, out of the house and into the woods where he stayed for three days until Lucan found him, cold, tired, and hungry. Lucan had brought food and extra clothing and either seemed not to know or not to care that Vix had tried to implicate him. Lucan explained that father had used the girl as a sacrifice and no one was any wiser.

"Please come home. Father has forgiven you. And you must take your vows in two weeks."

Vix shuddered from the cold, but allowed himself to be led home. Two weeks later, he was installed as the successor to the High Priest. Lucan was installed as the High Chancellor.

Shortly thereafter their father died unexpectedly, and Vix became High Priest. It was not long afterwards that the child sacrifices were brought to him for sanctification in privacy. Then the older children were brought under the threat of sacrifice. None of the families objected, knowing the results of any outcry.

Lucan had chastised him only once, but seemed more preoccupied with searching the scriptures for deeper meanings. That was over thirty years ago. An unstated agreement arose between the two of them; Lucan didn't meddle in Vix's private affairs, and Vix allowed Lucan the freedom to do as he wished. Vix continued his lust for young children and Lucan grew plump with good food and intellectual conversation. Together they had ruled the religious life of Gambria and had grown comfortable in the position.

But now there was danger. Bradwr wanted to talk with him. *Now what? He has my support... what more does he want? And what's so special about these two newcomers that warrants the King's affection? This wizard character... he wasn't afraid of me...I'll break him though... I'll break him.*

He smiled grimly, thinking that poison would be so much easier. He looked back to where Lucan was still reading. *Read on little brother, maybe Safti will listen to you.*

Cu leaned nonchalantly against the pillar, watching the clouds drift in the blue sky. A short time later, Menec strolled out, having finished his discussion with King Diad. He saw Cu and walked over.

"What news brother Cu? I thought you were going home? After all, we've been out for almost twenty days and that new bride of yours is sure to be waiting."

Cu laughed. "Right you are Master Menec. Much as I love my battle brothers, I miss the comfort of a woman's touch." Looking down, he adjusted his belt. "The king isn't the only one with strange visitors. Lord Bradwr has been known to entertain one as well," he said quietly. He looked back up. "Well, I expect I'll be hearing from you." He grinned and walked off.

Menec smiled, slapped Cu on the back and turned to go home, thinking of what to tell the king.

Chapter 12

Duncan, Alexis, and the Lord Purveyor walked throughout the house that had so recently belonged to the nation's berserker. As if he had a pressing engagement, the Lord Purveyor hustled them through the home, quickly stating that he would send round the rest of the listings of Oswiu's possessions before he excused himself. Once outside, he stood lost in contemplation, tapping his chin. Nodding, as though arriving at a decision, he politely smiled at the passersby and calmly walked home.

The enormous row-house that Alexis now owned was tucked neatly against the city wall that snaked its way along the mountain fingers poking their way toward the Starn Sea. The house was positioned to give it a superb view of the whole town and over the far walls to the sea. The house itself rose several stories so that the roof of the house exceeded the height of the city wall by a single story. The front of the building was criss-crossed with exposed thick wooden timbers, the gaps filled with stone and plaster. There was a single recessed door at the street level.

They had been admitted by a slender, very attractive, bright-eyed woman with strawberry-blond tresses bound-up in a coil on the top of her head. She bowed pleasantly and escorted them throughout their examination.

The house was even larger than appeared and had over forty rooms divided among four levels, surrounding a well apportioned and manicured courtyard. A fountain with statues of mythical animals overflowed with deep blue water in the center of the marble paved courtyard.

Surrounding the courtyard, the various levels of rooms rose to a multitude of heights. Some were a single story high, others rose for a full three stories. A colonnaded walkway at each level provided continuous access to the rooms. The first floor contained one extremely large room with a wide fire place at the far end. The once bright ceiling, two stories high, was criss-crossed with thick hewn beams, dark with the soot of centuries. On the walls hung rich tapestries, shields, all types of hand weapons, and golden candelabras. Duncan and Alexis had gaped in wonder at the size of the furnishings. The ornately carved wooden table was long enough to seat forty to fifty guests, and the chairs were apportioned with royal blue velvet-soft material. There were bureaus filled with ornately designed plates, eating utensils, serving bowls, and goblets, all wrought in finely decorated gold.

Along with the house came several servants, mostly young men. Duncan had reasoned out that Oswiu had a penchant for young males who were now looking at him with mixed fear and expectation.

While he and Alexis had been inspecting the second top floor bedroom, Duncan had brought all the servants together and had matter-of-factly told them that he was not interested in what had transpired under their former master, that Alexis and he were now in charge. He urged them to perform their duties with the same degree of fastidiousness as they had under their previous patron. If not, he had warned them, he would unleash Alexis on anyone displeasing him.

The response was as expected and Alexis saw the outright fear in their eyes as they gaped at her. "What did you just tell them?" she frowned.

"Listen Alexis, these people need to know who's boss. They respect strength and discipline."

"What did you tell them?"

"I merely informed them that they were to pursue their jobs with the same, um, alacrity as before."

"And?" she prodded.

"And anyone not meeting expectations would have their hearts ripped out." Duncan shrugged. "Alexis, if we want to win these folks over, we have to do it by intimidation first, then we can be good kind folks. Remember what it took to get where we're standing?"

"Perhaps you're right," she sighed and then smiled as she looked around the room. "Nice place."

He chuckled appreciatively. "I take back everything I said about gladiators. I'm certainly glad you're on my side." He dismissed the servants and they hurried to their respective duties with great alacrity. He tentatively put an arm around her shoulders. She didn't immediately move away, and he was about to lean in to kiss her, when the servant who had admitted them knocked and opened the door. "Forgive me Lord –"

"Duncan," he corrected.

The girl beamed in flattered appreciation. "Yes, Lord Duncan."

Now it was his turn to be flattered. "Yes, that'll be fine. What is it please?"

"Lady Brenna is here to see the both of you. She is a warrior-woman and she is here to give you your welcome feast."

"Welcome feast?" Duncan asked, turning from translating to Alexis.

"Yes Lord Duncan, the Welcome Feast. You have no such ceremony where you come from?"

"Um, not that I remember. Please, quickly, what is it?"

"It's the Gambri way of welcoming distinguished visitors. Usually the King appoints the welcomer, but in cases where protocol is not specifically defined, it goes to first-come basis. And I'd say that by the quickness she came here, you are considered very special."

"Why is that?" Duncan queried, somewhat puzzled.

"The woman is High Commander Brenna, one of the Twelve. Much like," she hesitated, nodding in Alexis' direction.

"Her name is Alexis," Duncan stated.

"What shall I call her?" she timidly asked.

"What do you normally call woman warriors?"

"It depends upon what rank. A woman warrior has never challenged a berserker before. I'm not sure if she takes his title. Perhaps High Commander Brenna can answer this question."

Duncan translated for Alexis who asked why her name was mentioned. "It seems that no woman has ever been a berserker and we're trying to determine what to call you."

Alexis carefully looked around at some of what she owned. "I have his house; I should have his title."

Duncan turned back to the girl. "Who is this High Commander Brenna?"

"As I said Lord Duncan, she is the highest ranking warrior-woman, and also a princess. She is King Diad's adopted daughter."

"Why didn't you say she was the King's daughter?" Duncan exclaimed. "Show her in quickly!"

The girl didn't move. "Forgive me Lord Duncan, I did not introduce her as the King's daughter because it is a greater honor to be a warrior-woman. Any king can have a daughter, but few can have a battle-warrior child, and fewer still who have daughters as one of the Twelve."

Duncan nodded and studied the girl. "What is your name?"

The girl blushed. "Servants are usually referred to by their functions. I am the Lord's attendant."

"Attendant?!" Duncan bristled involuntarily at the word, eyes wide.

Alarmed at his reaction, Tene dropped her eyes. "Oh! Lord Duncan? Have I offended you? Have I said something wrong?"

"Attendant. I don't like that word. Tell me your name," he commanded.

"I am called Tene," she responded softly.

"Tene," Duncan said loudly. He turned back to Alexis. "Her name's Tene."

Alexis nodded in her direction. "Nice to meet you Tene." Her tone was non-committal.

"Tene," Duncan directed, "we do have a guest. Please show the warrior-woman in."

"Yes Lord Duncan." She bowed humbly and left the room.

In a moment, the door opened and Tene walked in, bowing to Alexis. "I have just been properly informed as to your titles." She then announced, "Wrath of Safti and Terrible Sword of the Celestial Heavens, Most High Commander Alexis, and Lord Duncan, the High Commander Brenna, battle proven warrior of the Twelve."

Duncan frowned slightly at his seemingly lowly title, but then was caught off-guard, sucking in his breath at the very beautiful woman walking in. He had expected someone more akin to Oswiu than the compelling visage before him. She wore pants made of fine-grained supple animal skin. A narrow panel of very delicately wrought chain-mail adorned the thigh of each legging. Her shoulders were accentuated by golden tasseled epaulettes mounted on a dark brown, close-fitting leather jacket. There was both strength and fineness to the features of her face. Her raven hair was thick and full, falling to the pit of her back. Her eyes were as dark as her hair. She was slightly taller than he. However, Duncan's attention remained focused on the front of her jacket that stretched snugly, mildly disguising the shapely roundness underneath.

She walked with a calm self assurance and stopped before Alexis, slightly bowing while gazing intently into the green eyes. She began speaking and Alexis looked to Duncan for help.

"She says that she has come here to prepare our Welcome Feast and to see that our needs are met," he translated.

Alexis smiled at the woman. "Tell her thanks and that we appreciate her hospitality."

Brenna waited for Duncan to finish translating. With a pleasant smile, she rose, motioning them to follow her. She led them through the house as if she was intimate with its secrets. In a while, they arrived at the large dining room. The feast was already spread, and the servants were just finishing the plate and goblet arrangements.

"My name is Brenna," she said, motioning for Alexis to sit in the middle of the main table. She gently touched the top of the chair to Alexis' left and motioned for Duncan to sit. She then took her place beside Alexis to her right. Clapping her hands once, she commanded, "You may serve us."

The servants brought out a large tray with a steaming small animal that reminded Duncan of a rabbit gone genetically wrong for the front legs were too large and the body a little too plump. However, the bouquet from the roasted meat reached deep into the pit of his stomach and suddenly he realized that he was ravenously hungry.

The tray was placed before Alexis. There were no utensils and Alexis looked quizzically at Brenna. In one rapid movement, Brenna threw her foot on the table edge and withdrew a knife from her boot and in quick strokes neatly separated a leg from the offering and laid it on the plate before Alexis. She then carved another leg and offered it to Duncan. "I'd like to welcome you both to Mull, the capital city of Gambria." Her warm voice was unpretentiousness. Duncan watched transfixed by her simple actions of cutting the meat.

Brenna shifted her eyes in the direction of the goblet and he understood. Duncan took the goblet and drank a long draught. The wine was full and pleasantly smooth. He paused and held up the goblet to the light. The workmanship was exquisite with dancing horse-like animals with horns and warriors hunting what looked like lions and other strange beasts he didn't recognize. The rim was gold as he had suspected. Indeed, the inside of the bowl was also gold plated. It was supported on the outside by four bands that wound down to the bottom of the bowl, and then winding together down the stem to fill out the base. Yet the main portion of the cup was a substance he didn't recognize. It was highly polished with a smooth white surface.

"Lady Brenna, I recognize the gold of the goblet, but what is the bowl made of?" he asked good-naturedly.

"Human skull," she said standing up.

Duncan choked. "Pardon?"

"You are drinking from the cup of Fawr. He was a great enemy to the Gambri of long ago. You must ask King Diad to tell you the story. He will be pleased if you do." She walked back to the other plates. Duncan looked at the goblet with some concern.

"What did she say?" Alexis asked pleasantly.

"Oh, ah, nuthing. Just something about the wine-goblets and how special they were." He grinned impishly.

"You'll have to tell me about them later." Alexis watched Brenna as she continued to slice the roasted game.

"Wizard, how is it that you know our tongue, yet she doesn't?" Brenna asked.

"It was not required of her. She is a warrior, I am the scholar," he stated with obvious pride.

"It would be good if you were to begin teaching her our language."

He silently sighed. "Alexis. Brenna thinks you need to learn the language. She's right of course. I'll teach you some simple phrases to start."

"OK," she said, wiping the corners of her mouth with a silk napkin.

Duncan continued to translate as he watched the woman with a strange fascination. He couldn't help but notice that she seemed more interested in Alexis than him. The conversation began stiffly enough, but the two woman warriors soon relaxed and were laughing and regaling each other with war stories. Except for his translating skills, Duncan was pushed farther and farther out of the conversation.

"And then, I studied twelve years with the Grand-Master Choi." Her eyes sparkling, Alexis flipped a bone onto her plate.

"And what did he teach you?" Brenna asked between mouthfuls.

Alexis chuckled. "He taught me lots of things. You said, or maybe Tene said, that you were one of the Twelve. What does that mean?"

"It is the highest level a warrior can attain. Only twelve warriors may hold the twelfth rank. In order to become one of the twelve, one must defeat a current warrior of the twelfth rank."

"Then you must be quite a fighter," Alexis acknowledged.

Brenna warmed to the praise. "Perhaps you could show me something you learned."

"Sure." Alexis grinned and pushed herself away from the table. "For example, he taught me pressure points." She smiled at her, then turned to Duncan. "Stand up."

"Why?"

"C'mon, just stand up."

Reluctantly, he stood in front of her.

"For example, if your opponent grabs you here," she indicated for Duncan to grab her throat. "You just reach up and flip the wrist."

"Yeow! Leggo!" He sat on the floor rubbing his wrist.

Brenna smiled at the result. "Excellent move. However, it seems unlikely that I would use that in battle. Here, let me show you one of the moves I learned prior to the twelfth rank challenge." She stood up and walked over to him. "Stand up wizard."

Duncan eyed her cautiously. "Why?"

"Come come Wizard, you should be able to take a little exercise."

Not sure of the anticipated results, yet attracted to this beautiful woman, he rose hopefully, still rubbing his wrists.

"Suppose your attacker came at you from your blind side." She turned away from him and motioned him to attack her.

Half-heartedly raising his arms, he walked towards her. As he came closer, he suddenly found himself airborne. He came crashing down into some chairs and lay sprawled amidst the tangled mess.

"Good one. That's just like the jump back turn hook kick. Like this." Alexis jumped, twirled, and kicked to demonstrate. Brenna nodded.

Duncan extracted himself from the tumbled mess and shakily stood up. Brenna was walking over to demonstrate another move. "Stop! Lemme alone. You two beat on each other." And he sat down in a frump.

Brenna smirked and looked at Alexis who was also smiling. "Here, I'll show you another move." She walked over to Alexis. Soon the two were playfully sparring. Brenna, though the taller and apparently the physically stronger of the two, could not match Alexis' speed or power.

Duncan watched with growing irritation. Suddenly Brenna twisted and flipped Alexis in the air, both of them landing on the floor, with Brenna on top holding tightly. Alexis struggled briefly, but Brenna didn't let go. Then Duncan watched the subtle change as Brenna relaxed, but neither woman moved. They continued to lie on the floor, breathing heavily from the exertion. Suddenly understanding passed between them and grinning mischievously, they both looked at him.

Thrusting himself away from the table, he threw the plate on the floor, and stormed out of the room. Stomping down the steps to the second floor, he nearly stepped on Rasta-mon.

Hey mon! Watch out, you nearly step on me. You know how long it take me t'get here? Jus look at me mon. I mus look like somethin' de cat drag in. HA! Get it?...de cat drag in... Get it?

Yes I get it! He mentally shouted at Rasta-mon, as he stormed around the house.

The cat cantered behind. *Whoo, somebody not be happy. What be de problem?*

"She's up there," he said aloud, pointing up, "Rolling around on the floor with some woman!"

OK? So what's you point?

He whirled around. "I might as well be non-existent!"

Oh I get it. You gotchu feelin's hurt. Mon listen to de Rasta Doctor. You inna big worl' now. You raise de littleuns and den you gots to let 'em go.

Duncan sat down against a wall. "I can't believe it. I thought that I at least meant something to her." He continued shaking his head trying to understand this woman who had so recently been his. At least so he had thought.

Listen mon, you be special to her.

"Oh sure, special like some unique toy," he ranted.

Well whatchu expect mon? She suddenly see de light an wanna settle down to a quaint bungalow and raise a passel of kittens? It like my grandfather say, 'Siamese be like a bus; you miss de first one and anotha come in ten minutes.' C'mon mon, let the Rasta doctor cheer you up with a joke.

"Not now Rasta-mon, can't you see I want to be –" Duncan jerked his head up to see Tene standing rooted at the end of the hallway, her eyes a mixture of apprehension and curiosity. Her mouth was slightly open.

"Close your mouth Tene and come here."

The girl moved forward with trepidation, stopping a few meters from Duncan and the cat.

"Are you a Soul-stealer, Lord Duncan?" Her voice quavered slightly as she regained her composure. "You are talking to this animal, are you not?"

He turned to the cat and then back to Tene. "What did you hear?"

She looked quickly around. "Lord, I...I thought I heard voices and I came into the hall. I saw you and this animal. You occasionally spoke, but I didn't understand your tongue." Fear flitted across her eyes. "Don't hurt me Lord Duncan, please don't hurt me," she nervously pleaded.

"What's got into you?" he scowled. "What makes you think I'm going to hurt you?"

"I...I, I've heard...Soul-stealers can inflict great pain at will, even unto death. Without using weapons!" She shivered.

"Do you know any soul-stealers?"

"Of course not!" she blurted. "The church would banish me and anyone else associating with them."

Duncan raised a quizzical eyebrow. "The church? Why?"

Tene came closer. "The church of Safti controls most of Gambria. Well, that is the sect of Nara does. High-priest Vix rules the church from here in Mull. They say he has eyes everywhere. You can get banished for crimes against the church." Tene's eyes widened slightly. "And if you get banished, you might as well be dead."

"Why's that?"

"If the Rugians capture someone, they crucify him." She shuddered. "And if you're really bad, you get banished to the wastelands."

He listened attentively. "And what are those?"

"It's a place where nothing grows. It's just sand. And it's hot. If you get banished there, you know you will die a slow lingering death.

Hey mon, everybody gots somebody. Waddabout me? The cat's tail swished quickly.

Duncan twitched his head back to the cat and glared intently at him. "You are making this very difficult. Didn't you hear her?"

Hey mon, I don speak the lingo. Remember?

Duncan let out a breath. "Sorry. Um, let's see if I can help." He looked back to Tene who was intently watching him. "Do you know of any animals that look something like him?" He thumbed at the cat.

"Yes Lord. We call them 'King's Companions.' They are much like this one here. Only royalty are allowed to have them. The King has dozens." she exclaimed.

"There," he said translating to the cat. "If you can find the King's palace, you might have an interesting evening."

The cat's head swiveled in rapid succession between Duncan and Tene. *I be outta here!* And with an explosive move bounded down the hall and down stairs.

Duncan began laughing.

"What is so funny, Lord Duncan?"

"He'll be back as soon as he realizes he can't get out that way." Seeing her puzzled look, he explained what had just transpired. "However, you were telling me of Safti and the different sects." He smiled at her.

She stared intently at him, returned the smile, and sat down against the wall opposite him. "I won't tell anyone Lord, I swear."

He let the silence settle about them before answering. "I know. That is why I decided to trust you. I need someone I can depend on."

"Yes Lord," she replied excitedly. "Are you a wizard?"

"Well," he tugged at his earlobe, "I... I'm not so sure."

"No?" Tene seemed disappointed. "But you can talk to animals. I saw you."

At that moment Rasta-mon came running back up. *Hey mon, I can't get outta here. Help me*! he said panting.

"Tene, can you help us?" Duncan laughed. "The, um, Companion here needs to go out."

"Yes Lord. Can you get him to follow me?"

"I'll do better." He told Rasta-mon to let himself be carried to the nearest safe window and to thank his hostess before he left.

Tene was moved by the honor of carrying the cat to the window, and gasped in pleasure when the cat gave her a lick on the hand. "It kissed me!" she exclaimed.

"Ah, that's quite an honor," he grinned.

"I've never held a King's Companion before. And he kissed me," she said in wonderment.

"What he was doing was giving you his scent. Sort of marking you as his property."

"What?"

"Oh, most, um, Companions are jealous types. By kissing you, he's telling any other companion that you belong to him."

"How marvelous." Tene sat back down, her eyes warm with appreciation. "Is that why you are down here?"

"What do you mean?" he replied.

"Jealous. Lady Brenna is with Lady Alexis, and she belongs to you?"

"That's none of your business," he tartly answered.

Tene was silent, carefully watching him. She stretched her legs to where she could touch his outstretched feet and began rubbing a foot against his. "Lord Duncan, I am your servant. I am available if you desire." Her eyes were warm and inviting.

He looked at this very pretty woman across from him. She probably wasn't that much younger than he. "Does being my servant mean I can do anything with you that I want?"

"No Lord. You cannot hurt me. That's expressly forbidden by law. If I displease you, you can petition to reassign me." She continued caressing his foot.

"Reassign you? I'm not sure I understand. You are my servant and as such I can order you around for anything I desire?"

"Yes Lord."

"Doesn't that make you more of a slave than a servant?"

Tene cocked her head quizzically. "Slave? I do not understand the word."

"You know, a slave - someone owned by another person."

"You can't own another person," Tene laughed. "You're teasing me."

"Well what's the difference? Suppose you didn't like me? Could you also petition to get reassigned?"

Tene gaped at him. "Not like you? What do you mean?"

"Well suppose you didn't like me, or would rather be a servant to another individual, a better lover, a kinder master, or whatever?" Duncan unconsciously began returning her foot caresses.

"Lord Duncan, I don't think you understand. I am your servant, but you are not my master. I am a servant, nothing more. It is not my right to petition to be reassigned. As a person of privilege you are entitled to servants. You are also required by law to treat us as a family in the best sense of the word. You can take me as a lover, that's your right. But if I no longer interest you as a lover, you must still treat me like a member of the family."

"Suppose I wanted to free you of your life as a servant so that you could pursue some other career or dream?" he asked.

"Free me? But I am not an animal that you can release into the wild. I am a servant. That is my calling," she shrugged. "That is all I know how to be."

"What do you mean?" he queried, leaning forward. "Wouldn't you like to be something else? A princess? A warrior-woman? Anything?"

Tene laughed sweetly. "Lord Duncan, you're not making any sense. I cannot be any of those and it is useless to dream or think about it. My family has always been servants. I know the names of my family and whom they served back to fifteen generations," she smiled proudly.

Comprehension swept through him and he shook his head. "I think I understand. You belong to something like a servant guild, complete with its own unique rules and laws."

"Yes, that's exactly it," Tene responded distractedly as she got up and moved over to kneel next to him. "But wouldn't you rather talk of other things?" She smiled suggestively, gently taking his hand in hers.

"No thanks," he pouted, still smarting from Alexis's dismissal.

"Then perhaps m'Lord would like a bath. You are dusty from the road and have had a long day. Follow me." She stood up and offered her hand.

He hesitated for second more. *This is crazy. I'm alone on a ship for months, escape a life of death by boredom, except for a gorgeous, but distant, woman who kills people and jerks their hearts out. Now, she's swapping spit with another female warrior and I'm yesterday's dead meat. This woman is willing to give herself to me and I'm debating? I must be losing it.*

"Please," Tene coaxed.

Duncan acquiesced. "Maybe you're right."   He rose and obediently accompanied her down the hallway, a flight of stairs, and out into the courtyard.   There were tall green plants with large leaves and urns with flowers in them surrounding a fountain in the center. Off to one side, closer to the back wall, there was a stone structure that looked somewhat like an outdoor swimming pool, only smaller.   Bubbles rose in the center of the water, and steam hovered in the evening air.

"Oswiu was well respected and commanded one of the few houses in the city with its own outside hot water pool.   The water comes from deep underground and keeps this pool warm all year." Tene explained in answer to his questioning look.   "May I help you with your shirt?"

"I can do it," he answered and began unbuttoning the top button.   He felt strangely awkward as he watched her watching him.   She simply smiled as she watched, and he suddenly felt like he was exhibiting for some voyeur. As he peeled off his shirt, he caught a quick glimpse of her approving eyes. The glance was enough to tell him she liked what she saw, and that made him thankful that he had spent all that time in the ship's gym.

Yet he was again self-conscious and stood there clumsily, expecting her to turn around so he could take off his pants.   Instead, she stood looking at him, her hands clasped behind her.

"Um… uh, would you mind?" He twirled his right index finger in a little circle.

"What does that mean?" Tene repeated the motion.

"Uh, it means, would you mind turning around," he answered.

Tene looked at him quizzically and then turned around. "Am I looking for something in particular?"

"Just keep looking."   He hurriedly pulled off the rest of his clothes and slid into the hot water.   "OK, you can turn around again."

Turning back, Tene smiled knowingly.   "If you like Lord Duncan, I can rub your shoulders."

"That would be very nice."

With slow graceful motion, Tene removed her clothes and stood naked by the pool's edge, hesitating long enough for his eyes to widen in lustful appreciation.   She slowly descended into the pool and edged herself behind

143

him, and then began kneading his shoulders. She felt him relaxing under her attentive touch.

With the hot water bubbling beneath him, the warm fragrant night, and the beautiful naked woman behind him massaging his shoulders, he smiled to himself. *Well this isn't quite what I expected...* She began massaging his head, and he closed his eyes for a moment recounting the day. His head moved lazily in response to her touch. *This feels really, really good.* He let out a slow contented sigh. *Looks like Alexis is set... Now I need to take care of myself...* He found himself less and less able to concentrate with Tene's attentions and the intoxicating smell of the herbs in the bath water.

As she shifted her massaging to his neck and shoulders, she remarked, "Lord Duncan, what do you seek here in Gambria?"

Not wanting to be disturbed from his relaxed state, he dismissed her quickly. "I want to make a place here. That's all."

"Then I will help you in whatever way you need me," she promised.

He smiled to himself at her earnestness and continued to soak up the pleasure in her touch. He gave himself completely over to the reverie, no looking over his shoulder, no gun placed carefully within reach, no wall to back him up.

After she finished massaging his head, she moved around to face him. His eyes were closed and she took a hand gently working the fingers one by one and moving up his arm, then the other hand. She saw a large thin scar-line on his right arm and inquired about it as she traced the line up his arm.

Duncan opened his eyes and saw her in front of him. The filtered lights from the house mixing with the bubbling vapor of the pool caressed the edges of her face. She was indeed beautiful. The water danced around the valley between her breasts and Duncan felt a strange urge to reach out and caress one.

Tene saw his gaze. "Lord Duncan," she softly whispered.

"Ummm." he grunted vacantly.

"Lord Duncan, the night air is getting cool, and we should go in now."

"All right, I guess." He stirred with difficulty, trying hard to regain alertness.

Tene stood and he watched her step out and then bend over to reach into a small chest not far from the pool. She turned around and held her arms out to the side, a towel dangling from each hand.

"Which one would you like?" Her voice was playful, disarming.

Her pose suddenly reminded him of one of Talane's hologram dream girls, except there was no visual image re-touching to this goddess before him. He shook himself out of his stupor and pretended to look at the towels.

"Does it matter?"

"Not really," she laughed.

As he stood to get out of the steaming water, he was briefly self-conscious, but then decided to yield to the moment. Tene quickly wrapped a soft, woven covering around him. It felt something like cotton, but was furry too without being scratchy. She motioned him to follow her, and he did, still wrapped in the blanket.

In the bedroom, a shirt was draped across the bed. Duncan touched it and found it felt like the same material as the wrap he had worn from the bath, but with finer threads and lighter weight. When he put it on, it was noticeably big. The arms hung longer than his own and the hem came almost to his knees.

Tene let a brief chuckle escape, then recovered. "Oswiu was an ample man. Tomorrow we will find suitable garments for a man more fit." She walked toward him to roll up the sleeves. He stood still and watched her, much as a child watches his mother as she goes about the tasks of caring for him, at the same time demanding of, and submissive to her care. That simple act prompted Duncan out of his bath induced stupor, and he put his arms around her waist, pulling her to him.

"Why are you doing these things for me?" he questioned her, incredulous at the way she had so quickly and completely disarmed him.

"I told you. It is what I do and who I am. Have I served you well?" she responded with both pride and scrutiny, seeking his approval.

"Yes, you have. Your former masters must have been happy with you also," Duncan fished, trying to learn more about her.

"Oh, I have never been a Lord's servant before. I am trained for it, but I have only been a house worker to now. Because I worked hard and performed my duties well, I was honored to be made a Lord's Attendant. It was Lady Brenna, though, who used her influence to get me assigned to this house. Since this is my first position of this sort, I hope you'll be understanding if I make any mistakes. I don't know the ways of the country you come from, and do want to please you."

Her solicitousness and her unaffected kindness touched him. He pushed her hair gently back from her face and kissed her softly on the lips. "You do please me. I want to learn your ways also. We will teach each other."

She coaxed him to the bed and pulled back the covers. He kissed her again in a half-hearted initiation of desire, but the drugged effect of the fatigue and the bath took over. He fell asleep with Tene stroking his hair and chanting softly to him.

The moon was high in the night as Brenna sped her way through the maze of streets and occasional drunks, warrior men arm-in-arm careening loudly home. In one particularly dark door she paused and darted in.

Once inside, another door without handles confronted her. Without hesitation, she bent to the left and pressed a loose stone. After a few moments, the door opened and a long corridor, lit with torches, led straight ahead. She walked rapidly, with firm determination. At the end of the hallway, she turned left and entered the cavernous room. *The fragrance is strong tonight.*

The flames along the walls flickered shadows across the room. He was there, in the same position as if he had never moved since the last time she was here. She quickly dipped her knee before him.

"I hope all is well with you sire." She stood back up.

"How polite of you to ask, High Commander. It is always good to see manners taught and used." He readjusted his robes. "And how did the evening proceed?"

"Quite well m'Lord."

"Have you begun what we asked?"

"Yes Sire."

"And what have you for us tonight?"

"Some information Lord, I'm not sure how much is useful to you."

"Anything you bring us will be useful Lady-warrior," he cooed.

"Well Sire, the woman's name is Alexis. The man who calls himself a wizard is named Duncan. The lady warrior does not speak our language, but the wizard speaks it very well. I think that Alexis, the lady warrior has had some schooling and has an agile mind."

"And why is that?"

"Well, she quickly learned the simple phrases the wizard taught her," Brenna said matter-of-factly.

"And what of the wizard called Duncan? What is he like?"

"I didn't spend much time with him m'Lord. I spent the time becoming acquainted with the lady warrior."

"Did you learn anything?"

"Yes Sire. She is pretty much like any other woman except for her speed and strength. She fights with a cold passion, seeming to internalize everything."

"Hmm. We must harness this passion for our uses. It will be difficult if she cannot communicate. However, you must ensure that you can control her when we need."

"Yes Sire."

"Anything else?"

"Yes Lord. Bradwr was at Traun's place again with Raefgot. Raefgot is again to wake up amongst the children. I'm not sure what Bradwr is doing."

"He's creating an untrustworthy ally. Watch him carefully. Raefgot may appear the fool, and unpredictable, but he is far more clever than given credit. Bradwr on the other hand is very dangerous. He has money and influence."

Brenna nodded thoughtfully. "What do you wish me to do?"

"Nothing as far as Bradwr is concerned. I want you to stay with these two newcomers."

"As you wish," she bowed. "This Duncan is very interesting Lord. I believe that you are right when you said that he is the most dangerous."

"And why is that?"

She began pacing in front of the throne. "First, he speaks our language. Second, he does not understand our customs. Third," she counted on her fingers, "he can talk to animals."

"What?" Astonishment filled his voice.

"It's true Lord. The door-servant Tene saw it with her own eyes. He was communicating with the animal he calls a cat. It is very much like our King's Companions."

There was a long pause as he absorbed the information. "Is he a soul-stealer?"

"I do not think so Lord. While it appears that he understands magic, he appears to have no real religious preference, and seems to accept how he is as almost a natural state. Tene said that he seems to be a mixture of young boy and old man."

"Tene has offered much information to you," the voice chuckled.

"She is my agent, Sire."

"Oh? And how could that be?"

"She used to be my servant before I had her reassigned to several other friends, before going to Oswiu."

"You apparently weren't displeased with her..." the voice trailed off.

"Not at all Lord. However, I needed someone loyal in Oswiu's house, someone to keep me appraised. Besides, Bradwr thinks she is working for him."

"Oh?"

"Surely you know Lord," Brenna said with a hint of sarcasm. "Rumor had it that Bradwr and Oswiu were extending control over large parcels of Gambrian property and businesses. Although I don't see Oswiu as being that intelligent."

"Why should that be of concern?"

"M'Lord, you test me," Brenna answered with a hint of irritation.

"No High Commander, I reason with you. Together we can begin to understand what we face. If, as you say, Bradwr is extending control over portions of Gambria, one must assume that he is positioning to gain the throne. Yet, no matter how much property he would own, he would still need to rid himself of the present king. Is this what you suspect?"

"Everyone knows Bradwr wants the throne. Yet I doubt he would be so bold as to take it unless he had the backing to make it happen." Brenna shrugged, "If enough influential men become indebted to him, might not that happen?"

The figure nodded pensively. "And you suspect that Bradwr was using Oswiu?"

"Yes m'Lord, but I knew Oswiu and he wouldn't have trusted Bradwr, so he must have had someone else making his arrangements."

"And why is that High Commander?"

"Because Oswiu couldn't read. Bradwr conveniently placed Tene there supposedly to help Oswiu with his accounts. My guess is that Oswiu felt the other male servants would compromise him, given sufficient, um, motivation." Brenna paused. "I have also heard his last several fights were prearranged."

The figure chuckled. "Quite an accusation Lady Warrior. You're accusing the King's brother and Gambria's champion of collaboration." He leaned slightly back and barked a laugh. "We wonder how brother Vix would have settled this." In graceful, almost floating motions, he readjusted the robes, placing the gloved hands neatly on the lap. "Of course it is rather moot. But, did Tene tell you this?"

"Yes Lord."

He fell silent and Brenna watched him drum his fingers on the arm rest. "What else do you know?"

"Tene said he asked numerous questions about Safti and important people. My impression is that he is either a great fool or he has power yet that we do not know."

"A good answer, High Commander," he nodded slowly. "However, I do not think he is a fool."

Chapter 13

Duncan woke with a start, taking a few moments to gather his wits as well as take in his surroundings. Sunlight gleamed brightly through the clear paned windows, the dust motes dancing in its slanting rays.

Tene was gone. He rubbed his eyes and stubby face, wondering what the time was. Unconsciously pushing back the blankets, he suddenly became aware of the touch of silk and the smell of flowers, the scent of Tene.

The room was large. In addition to the large four-poster bed, there was a separate writing table, bureaus, dressers, and thick carpets. The entire room was colored in a subtle blend of lilac, forest green, soft white, and browns. He found it very soothing.

Stretching, he scooted out of bed, slipped on the overlarge shirt and ambled over to the writing table. It was disarrayed with layers of papers completely filled with writing he didn't recognize. It reminded him of Devanagari Sanskrit in shape, even with the addition of various strokes and hooks. He was absentmindedly leafing through some papers when Tene burst through the door carrying a tray.

"Good morning Lord Duncan," she greeted him cheerfully.

"Good morning yourself," he smiled sheepishly. "I must have been really tired to have slept so long. What time is it?"

"According to the wall-clock," she said looking at the wall behind him, "it's about three fifty."

"Huh?"

"Three fifty," she repeated, setting the tray down on a bed stand.

"Three fifty?" Duncan repeated dumbly. He turned to look where Tene pointed to a clock that was part of the wall. It was circular, but it had too many symbols. He walked to the wall and rubbed his fingertips over the smooth stone. The main symbols were part of the wall as were the two hands. The tips of the hands glowed a soft green as did the main symbol nearest their ends.

Duncan counted ten main symbols with nine tiny lines and symbols in-between. "Tene, how many hours are there in a day?"

"Now Lord Duncan, stop teasing me and come here and eat. I've had the cook prepare something special for you." She fluffed the napkin and stood waiting for him.

"Tene, I'm serious. How many hours are there in a day?" The food smelled delicious and he walked over to where Tene was preparing him a plate.

Looking askance at him, she answered, "There are ten."

"And 100 minutes per hour, correct?"

"Of course. Why are you asking me this, Lord?" she gazed at him with curious puzzlement.

Chewing on the tender slices of meat, Duncan looked up and saw the raised eyebrow. Giving her a smile of affection, he said, "Where I come from there are twenty-four hours in a day with sixty minutes per hour."

"That's silly," she said. Sitting on the edge of the bed, a leg curled under the other, she asked, "Is it very different in your country?"

"Very different," he answered still chewing. "But I can tell I'm going to like it a lot better here." He continued eating, and began an absentminded comparison. "Colors, all so vivid, the smells, the wind rippling across the grain, the open air... this is heaven."

"There is nothing like this in your country?"

"Nope. Just metal and purified air. You wouldn't like it," he said, wiping his mouth. "C'mere for a minute."

She rose and stood next to him, touching him delicately as she leaned into him. Her smell was of lilac and he inhaled deeply. Putting an arm around her waist, he pointed to the papers on the desk. "What does this say?"

She again looked questioningly at him and slowly realized that he didn't know how to read. "It says," she intoned slowly as if to a child, pointing to each word, "that in return for use of ten hectares of land, Volgen will give Oswiu ten percent of its fruits on an annual basis."

"Do it again."

"Again? The same sentence?"

"Yes please. Except this time, point to the vowels as you say the words."

"As you wish." She again pointed to the words as she spoke them.

An hour later Duncan was reading by himself and rapidly absorbing all the financial information contained in the correspondence and contracts. Tene was sitting on the bed in stunned amazement. Duncan was not only reading all the material, he was also committing it to memory.

"Tene, listen to this."

She shifted slightly, giving him her attention. "Yes, m'Lord."

"Will you stop with the m'lord stuff," putting his finger at his place on the page, he looked up. "It's Duncan. Just Duncan."

Tene blushed slightly both embarrassed and pleased at his familiarity.

"Listen to this. Pursuant to the contractual agreement of the so stated two parties, the agreements and tenets of said agreement are hereby supplemented by the following addendum: ownership of stated property listed herein is further controlled by right of survivorship. The first party agrees and abides that upon his demise, said property listed herein shall revert in its entirety to include all appurtenances, fixed assets, and possessions, to the second party, unless a ward (hereinafter 'designated party') so designated by legal decree and of legal age assumes the rightful position of the first party. Said property shall convey to the designated party upon payment of not less than 25% above fair market value to the second party. Should the designated party fail to properly execute his contractual obligation within 30 days from the date of designation, said property shall revert to the second party en toto and free of encumbrances." Duncan paused for effect and looked up.

Tene smiled weakly. "What does it mean m'Lord, I mean, Duncan?"

"What it means is that the property Oswiu thought he owned was not completely his."

Tene stood up and sidled up next to Duncan, placing her hand on his shoulder. "Duncan. I don't understand. Oswiu has lots of property. I know, because I kept all his records."

"Tene, this contract is between Oswiu and another individual. What it essentially does is give the other individual total ownership of the property if Oswiu dies."

"What?"

"That's not all. If a succeeding berserker wants to claim the property, he has to pay the other owner 125% of the fair market value for the property."

Tene's head dropped. "You mean... I'm..."

"No," Duncan swiveled around, "you have nothing to worry about. This house and all its possessions and everyone in it belong to the berserker. It is his by right of combat and may not be taken away or mortgaged, at least that's what I can make out from all these papers."

Tene visibly relaxed. "Who's the other owner?"

Duncan grinned slightly, "The Lord Purveyor."

Duncan was over half-way through the papers when Brenna burst through the door, Alexis in tow behind. "Good morning everyone."

"Doesn't anybody knock?" he sourly said.

"I apologize Wizard," Brenna exaggerated as she bowed. The two warriors were damp with sweat. Duncan looked at Alexis.

"Up early for a morning run?" he teased.

Alexis picked up one of the silk napkins from Duncan's breakfast tray and wiped away the sweat. "Great run. I figure we did about ten kilometers. Good clip. She's a strong runner." Alexis smiled admiringly at Brenna who turned to Duncan to translate.

"Tell her I too enjoyed the run. She is very fast." Brenna returned to compliment. "She runs as fast as the tarrac."

He rolled his eyes at the overt mutual admiration. "Well, you'll be glad to know," he turned to Alexis, "that not only do you run like a Tarrac, it appears that you own one."

"I what?" Alexis suddenly straightened.

"I said you own a Tarrac."

"What's this about a Tarrac?" Brenna interrupted.

"I simply told her that she owned one."

"Where is it?" Alexis threw the napkin down on the bed, eyes wide in excitement.

Brenna blanched at the news. "I…I forgot about that."

Duncan saw Brenna's reaction. "What's the problem?"

"Wizard, a Tarrac serves only one master. Whenever a Tarrac-rider dies, the Tarrac is destroyed, for no one else can ride him."

He looked at Alexis' plainly obvious pleasure at the news of her new steed and turned back to Brenna. "And how do you suggest I tell her that her Tarrac has been killed?"

"What's going on?" Alexis interrupted.

"Tell her the truth," Brenna sighed. "She must know."

Turning solemnly to Alexis, he said, "Brenna says that your Tarrac has probably been killed."

"What?" she exploded. "When? Why?"

Brenna saw the transformation. "Wait! Maybe it has not been done yet. It is still early." Duncan quickly translated.

"I want to go there - now!' Alexis commanded. And without waiting, she spun around and charged towards the door.

Brenna, understanding the tone in Alexis' insistence, quickly caught up with her as they both burst out of the room. Just before the door closed she shouted, "Hurry up Wizard, I need you to translate."

Sighing loudly, he frowned. "When is she gonna learn the damn language?" Jumping up, he grabbed a warm roll and gave chase to the two women.

Alexis and Brenna arrived breathless at the stabling area for the tarrac. A stable boy jumped to attention and greeted them crisply, "Good day High Commander Brenna."

"Ask him about Oswiu's horse, is it still alive?" blurted Alexis, scaring the boy. Brenna looked at her, sensing the urgency but not understanding the words. Alexis frowned momentarily, then continued more slowly, using the few words she had picked up. "Tarrac, Oswiu, where?"

Brenna guessed at her meaning and hastily translated, "We have come to see Oswiu's Tarrac."

The boy paled as he delivered the news, "They have gone out to end his life, High Commander." Brenna asked if it was still alive. The boy shrugged fearfully.

Guessing the message by the boy's response, Alexis yanked him off the ground by his shirt and commanded, "Where!?"

Though the language was unknown to the boy, the meaning was clear. He pointed apprehensively to the furthest barns. Alexis dropped him abruptly, causing him to fall. She jumped over him as she sprinted to the barns. Brenna followed, unsure what they would find when they arrived.

Alexis stopped short at the sight. A massive steel gray Tarrac stood straddle-legged in the middle of an enclosure. His head was nearly touching the ground. Ropes were tied to each of three legs and blood oozed from the ankles where the ropes had cut into the animal. The cuts were already beginning to swell, indicating the scene had been going on for some time. High on the Tarrac's neck the skin was peeled back showing bare muscle flexing even as the creature appeared in submission. Many gouges and lacerations bled in drying rivulets that had mixed with the dust.

The men looked little better. The obvious struggle had apparently broken the arm of one who was wearing a splint. Another had an open cut on his scalp, while yet another had a huge swelling on his left shoulder with an unmistakable hoof mark imprinted in the spot. The hands of all of them were bruised and torn from the ropes.

Alexis hesitated only an instant, then vaulted over the fence and began roughly pushing the men away. They fought back momentarily, but Brenna stepped in and answered the questioning looks. "Stop. The woman now owns all that was Oswiu's, and she claims this Tarrac as her property."

One of the men closest to Brenna interjected, "But High Commander, you know the custom. The tarrac is always killed when its master dies. They never will serve another. This one will not even die after great efforts on our part."

While the man was talking, Alexis was yanking the ropes from each of the tarrac's would-be executioners. The tarrac never moved, even after the ropes were loosened. His breathing was slow and heavy, and he looked as if any movement would cause him to topple over. Sweat covered him, mixed with the blood and dirt. Froth was drying around his mouth. One eye was swollen shut. Yet, when Alexis approached, he moved his head in her direction and raised it slightly, baring his teeth. A raspy, rumbly growl came from somewhere deep inside his cruelly injured body.

Duncan arrived in time to observe Alexis's onslaught with the warriors. "What are you doing? What's this all about?" he called to her.

"What is his name?" Alexis called back.

"What?"

"Ask them what his name is."

"Brenna, does the beast have a name?" he quickly asked.

Brenna answered her back. "Stracaim."

Alexis looked at the animal and then at Duncan. "Tell them I don't want him to die. I forbid them from touching him again, and I will treat them like I did their berserker if they do not do as I say."

When Duncan explained, Brenna obliged, and silenced the men's objections, "The tarrac does belong to this woman, and we will ask the king to resolve this matter. You should go now." She then watched Alexis as she again approached the animal.

Extending her hand in front of her, Alexis walked slowly toward Stracaim's head. She talked in quiet, soothing tones. He cocked one ear toward her, but didn't give any other perceptible response to her as she neared him.

Duncan picked up some of her words. "Stracaim. I like that. It sounds like 'strike him.' That's a strong name, a fitting name for a warrior's mount." Her voice was calm, yet firm. "God, you look like hell. It's a good thing these guys do sloppy work, or we wouldn't be having this conversation, now would we?" She continued in a steady, measured voice, moving slowly closer to the weakened creature.

Duncan called to her, "What are you saying to that animal?"

Her attention focused on the massive beast, she responded, "It doesn't matter; he doesn't understand anyway. I just want him to hear my voice."

Brenna marveled as she approached in spite of the growls and snaps in defense. She wondered too at the sudden concern in this woman she had seen kill a man with her bare hands. Every time Stracaim raised his head to grab at Alexis, she dodged easily, as his movements were pitifully slow. But he continued to snap.

All at once, his hind legs buckled, then his front legs. His startled look resembled one of a man who realizes he is dying in quicksand. He thrashed, trying to regain his feet. The long ropes that had held his legs snapped and tangled, further preventing him from getting up. Finally, he lay over on his side. His breathing became shallow and he moaned softly with each breath.

Alexis by this time had moved in beside him and was trying to get the ropes untangled. She motioned to Brenna and tried to explain, "The ropes! Get him up! He'll die if he lies here like this." Brenna didn't understand the words, but her new friend's desperate look and frantic movements conveyed meaning clearly enough.

Then the moaning stopped. The Tarrac's eyes closed, and his sides no longer went up and down.

"Noooo!" Alexis shouted. "You're not going to die! Get up and fight me, damn you! You're mine and you're not going to die. Do you hear me! Get up damn you!" She jumped to his head and tried to pick it up. She turned to Brenna, "Help me!" she motioned. Brenna hurried to support the animal's neck while Alexis pushed at his side. They attempted to roll the huge animal up onto his sternum.

Duncan stared incredulously as the two women struggled with the dying animal. He would stay upright on his own for a time, then roll back again. "Oh no you don't." Alexis growled. For twenty minutes more they worked, but the wounded animal, though still breathing, seemed to have given up. Brenna finally placed her hand gently on Alexis's arm, touched her cheek with the other and shook her head as Alexis looked at her.

"No!" Alexis declared strongly. "Help me get him up. He can't breathe like this. They have to stand."

Duncan had moved in closer and was attempting to help. Though he didn't understand the reason for the intensity with which she was waging war with this pathetic creature, he did recognize her resolve. He translated where needed and applied force when told.

Alexis turned to Duncan. "Tell them to make a sling!"

"How?" he grunted, still trying to help hold the huge beast up.

"Dammit, just translate," she snapped. She quickly explained and Brenna immediately understood.

Brenna called to the men who were still standing around, mesmerized by the scene. "Bring ropes and the large strap we use to lift the grain barrels. Now!" Her command was so sharp that they hurried to do as she said. Along with Alexis and Duncan, Brenna and the warriors used poles and ropes to raise Stracaim upright, looping the braided, woven strands over timbers lashed together in a giant X above him. At Alexis's direction Brenna wrapped all the ropes that pressed into the heavy animal with cloths and padding.

At last, Stracaim hung limply in the sling. Alexis let him hang there for a moment, while she walked around checking all the ropes. When she reached the haunches of the great animal, she drew back, then slapped him hard. The sound of the contact cracked like a limb breaking from a tree. "Wake up you!" she shouted. "You're supposed to be a war horse. Fight, damn it!"

She moved back in front of the tarrac and, raising his head, she slapped him again, this time on the neck, right behind the heavy, curled horns. Still, no response.

Brenna, though puzzled by the desperate actions of her new friend, saw the determination in her eyes. There was not the coldness she had seen in the battle with the berserker, but the explosive power and will showed clearly enough. She wanted to ask Alexis why she wanted this animal so badly. "I am sure the King will grant you a Tarrac. My birth father is Menec, Tarrac-Master. We will pick you the best one." she said as Duncan conveyed her offer. They both hoped Alexis would accept and stop her seemingly futile efforts.

She either didn't hear or chose not to.

"Come. It's no use." Brenna told her softly.

At that moment, Alexis raised the drooping head one last time, stared right into Stracaim's face and drew back to backhand him right across the mouth, when a faint growl emerged. The limply hanging legs spasmed for an instant, then sought ground. The eyes blinked, and muscles twitched. Alexis jumped back as the teeth snapped near her face. "Yes! Now show us what you're made of. Survive this."

Brenna looked at Alexis with a new demeanor. She saw no hug or petting, just a warrior-woman and a sorry-looking, badly injured, ill-tempered animal, but the woman was smiling.

Duncan shook his head, spun around and stomped off, snarling to himself. *It's not enough that she'd rather hang out with Amazon girl; now I'm in line after a stupid horse! To hell with both of you!*

His fuming slowly settled as he made his way back through the city to the house he suddenly realized Alexis owned. It was not his house; it was hers. A strange subtle anxiety leaped and quickly died. *If I don't like what's going on, I'm the one who's gonna have to leave.* He slowly shook his head. *Oh no. This boy don't play like that. I'm gonna have to find me a place of my own.* He looked around at the brightly colored row houses edging the winding cobblestone streets. Second story window boxes spilled flowers over their sides, and the pungent sweetness gave the streets a fairytale flavor. He caught his breath as if suddenly noticing the strangeness of his surroundings, realizing he didn't know where he was. He paused in the middle of the street.

Crowds of people in all shapes, sizes, and color of clothes moved to their own reasons. No one seemed to pay him any mind as he stood, but simply moved around him. Some smiled at him when their eyes met, others just simply looked at him and then calmly looked away. And he realized that he fit in.

Duncan felt alone, yet not afraid. He had been alone many times before and intimately knew the boundaries between loneliness and being alone. Yet now, in this teeming city with the smells of piquant spices, trellised flowers, perfumed bodies, and yes, even the foul odor of everyday existence - this city of the vivid colors and sounds, he knew that he wanted desperately to be a part of this city. And he knew that he wanted to be more than just another man, condemned to walking his destiny on nameless paths. *I want to live here.* Smiling to himself, he searched the crowd for someone to help him. "Pardon me sir?"

A portly merchant in crushed blue velvet and gold chains jittered to a halt. "Yes?"

"Could you direct me to the berserker's lodgings?"

"We have a new berserker now."

"Yes, I know," he replied.

"It's a woman," the man stated knowingly.

"Yes, I know."

158

The merchant reappraised Duncan. "Your dialect is not from Mull." He looked at Duncan's head. "Hair streaking is no longer in style this year. I believe it is single hair ribbons now. Apparently all the fops are wearing it."

Duncan frowned. "Thanks for the fashion tip, but I am not a fop. The streak is natural."

The merchant leaned in closer to examine Duncan's head. "What a pity. To be out of style and unable to do anything about it."

He softly sighed. "I'll live with it. Now please, do you know where the berserker lives?"

The merchant did another quick assessment, decided that from the way Duncan was dressed, he probably could get little business, turned and pointed back the way Duncan had traveled. "You made a wrong turn down by the Golden Tarrac Tavern. This is Merchants Walk. You should have turned right towards The Havens." He nodded politely and continued on his way.

When Duncan arrived at Alexis' house, Tene was standing in front of the door talking to two young men clothed in thick gray robes. The cowls of both were pushed back onto their shoulders. Both had their heads completely shaved. They turned to him as Duncan walked up.

"Are you the one named Duncan who calls himself a wizard?" The shorter of the two imperiously demanded.

"I am he," he answered with equal assertiveness.

"His Holiness the High Priest of Gambria requires your presence." It was not a request.

"I haven't finished my breakfast," he flatly replied, turning to go in.

"You don't seem to understand. The High Priest is expecting you, now." The taller one put his hand on Duncan's shoulder as if to restrain him.

Duncan stopped, looked deliberately at the hand on his shoulder, then at the owner of the hand. "You have a choice. You can either remove your hand, or I reach down your throat and rip your heart out."

The hand jerked away in response. "But...but... explain this to him," the tall acolyte stammered to Tene.

Tene was calm. "Lord Duncan, it would be best if you went with them." She placed her hand reassuringly on his arm.

Deferring to her suggestion, he demonstrably sighed. "I suppose." Turning to the two acolytes, he feigned boredom. "Lead on."

Queen Guina made her way through the long cloisters of the Temple of Safti to the far end where the offices of the Governing Council were. She paused before the ornately carved, thick doors, a single large gold pull-ring affixed to each one. Two acolytes, their cowls pulled over their heads, stood on either side of the doors.

"I have an appointment with Counselor Konrud, would you please let me in?"

Neither moved.

"I said that I have an appointment." There was still no reaction. "Humpf. I suppose I shall just have to miss it and explain that two deaf acolytes refused to let me in."

A hand slowly moved to the left pull-ring. "Patience lady Guina. We were meditating." The door tugged open and Guina entered a large foyer with numerous doors to the right and left. Directly in front of her was a large, wide set of polished marble stairs filled with priests, supplicants, burghers, acolytes, and visitors hurrying in all directions. Few paid attention to her as she slowly ascended. Standing at the top, she gave a silent sigh and made her way to a large desk commanding the center of the high vaulted room, where a bare-headed priest directed and controlled the frenzied activity. Walking directly to the desk, she stood patiently to the side, waiting to be noticed.

The priest looked up, saw the Queen, and went back to writing, handing out instructions to several acolytes who ran off to pass the information to those behind the various doors.

The Queen waited no longer. "I am here to see Father Konrud."

"I'm sure you are," the priest responded without looking up.

Guina sighed softly. Very calmly she spoke. "Is it the custom for the spiritual leaders to pay little so heed to the King's wife?"

"I mean you no ill, Lady Guina." The priest looked up. "But as you can see," he glanced around, "we *are* busy." He went back to his writing and delegating.

Guina tried another tack. "I know you Mostyn." He looked up at the mention of his name. "I was at your ordination. Your parents must be very proud of your achievements. And I see that you have a very demanding job here. It's not everyone who can be the Secretary General to the High Priest and Governing Council." She nodded toward Konrud's door. "May I see him?"

Mostyn blinked several times and paused writing mid-sentence. "Yes Lady Guina. You may go."

Guina bowed slightly. "Thank you."

She walked around behind Mostyn and headed for the door directly behind him. Knocking softly she spoke, "Father Konrud, I have come for my appointment."

As if responding to a secret password, the door swung open. "You may enter, Queen Guina." The priest responded in an official tone, then loudly so anyone would be sure to hear, "I hope you have studied your lessons well. I am a busy man with no time for the non-devout."

As he closed the door behind her, she responded, "I have studied and look forward to your teaching."

With the door firmly shut, Guina greeted him with a warm smile, as if she were involved in a shared joke. Konrud was half a head taller than she. Slightly built, he was not portly like the average priest of middle age in Gambria. Only his thinning hair and the lines around his eyes belied his age. Though his manner was formal as befitted a priest, his eyes glimmered with delight.

He stepped closer to her, then caught himself up short. Stepping back, he grasped her hands in both of his and smiled broadly in return. Still holding her hands, he directed her to a small table in the corner of the room.

"It's been too long, my Queen. I have missed you."

Guina regarded him for a moment before she spoke. "I too treasure these meetings." Though there was an air of formality to their greeting and to the positions they took across the table from each other, their regard for each other was obvious.

"So, what will it be today? Do we have great theological problems to solve or the business of the kingdom to assess?" opened Konrud.

"What have you heard about this man and woman who come from far away?"

"I hear the woman is a fighter. She might be a help against the Rugians. The man told Menec he was a wizard of sorts. I'm not sure what that means, but if I know Vix, this wizard of sorts has an inquisition coming up shortly."

"Yes, I believe you are right. I saw the woman. She is terrifying, ripped the berserker's heart right out. I haven't seen such fury and hardness even in our own women warriors." She deliberately opened her books to give the aura of study. "But this man intrigues me. Why is it that he speaks our language and she doesn't? Then she kills the berserker and becomes a citizen of Gambria while the one who can communicate is still in question. Do you think he really is a wizard?" she wondered.

"Many men claim to be wizards or magicians. He may be clever; he may be a fool. If he is the latter, I'm sure Vix will find a reason to sacrifice him soon enough. His enemies seem to disappear that way."

"Suppose he is a wizard? What then?"

Konrud shrugged. "Who knows? We've never had a real wizard."

"But what does that say about Safti and all that we believe?"

"It says nothing about Safti." Konrud furrowed his eyebrows. "You don't believe that he really is a wizard do you?"

"No. Of course not. It's just that…"she paused. "Why does everyone whom Vix finds objectionable have to die? What kind of religion is it that won't allow itself to be challenged? It's as though we're afraid of discovering the truth." She sighed. "And wouldn't it be nice if someone who really cared about the people were High Priest."

He smiled. "Oh? You have someone in mind?"

"Don't tease me," she smiled back. "You have more true compassion for the people of Gambria than the high priest. There are some who think you should be the High Priest now."

"What about Lucan?"

"You know as well as I that he can't become High Priest."

"So you think I would be more suitable?"

She smiled at him and took his hand across the table. However, her expression changed quickly. She turned her head to gaze out the window, distractedly watching the clouds. "Unfortunately, my opinion isn't much valued," she softly added.

The lines on Konrud's face tightened in frustration. "It aggravates me to see the way your husband treats you and then allows others in the court to do the same. Your father surely did not intend this for you. I know your talents and training far exceed your husband's. The Gambri did love and respect your father when he was king. The reigning king looks even worse by comparison. When your father left the throne, many despaired," Konrud observed.

"I know, but the law is the law. When father fell in love with Mair, he broke the rules." She slowly shook her head. "He could have just kept her as a dalliance. Yet father understood the consequences of his actions. That is why he stepped down. You know that."

"That may be, but what was the result? A king who demeans his wife, and his own family who feel they have been wronged. I doubt your brother Rhun will ever forgive your father."

She paused for a moment. "I fear you may be right, dearest Konrud. His resentment is a wound that never heals. Was what father did selfish? Perhaps he forgot who he was?"

"We are who we are. As the prophet has written, 'Always remember who you are.'" He chuckled grimly.

She mused silently for a bit, recalling her father and his contentment. "What I remember is that he was happy." She looked earnestly into the eyes of this trusted confidant. "Can one forget who one is? Is happiness more important than responsibility?"

"Ah, we are going to talk theology, after all." joked Konrud, until he saw she was quite serious. "Guina, if you are asking me whether it is better to choose between happiness and responsibility, I can only say one must choose one's own path. Some would say that responsibility supersedes happiness, for society is more important than the individual. I suppose in some sense they are right."

"Even if this responsibility makes one unhappy?" she quietly asked.

Konrud contemplated her question for a moment. It was a fair question, one he had thought about long and hard. Was it responsibility that kept him in his marriage? It certainly wasn't happiness. The shrill nag he had been forced to marry was thankfully still at home, several days journey away. How they ever managed to produce children – all girls – was still a wonder. Yet he knew he had stayed because deep within him was the desire to be High Priest, and to do so, he needed a male heir. But she was now past child-bearing, and the promise of a son was non-existent now.

He also knew that he had grounds to divorce her, but that thought had its own troubles. If he divorced her now, it would be to marry a woman who could produce sons, but there was no guarantee of that. And how would it look, the senior Cleric of Gambria divorcing in order to chase after a younger woman? Diad's image emerged along with all the banter and gossip surrounding the kingdom's lecherous monarch. Was that the sort of example he wanted to be? Suddenly the question of happiness and responsibility hit too close to home. He had chosen responsibility because happiness was much too elusive. He pushed down the melancholy that wanted to blossom within, and instead focused on the one person with whom he felt his passions stir.

She was still very beautiful, with an aura of delicate fragility, a goddess to be worshipped and adored. He silently chastised himself for the analogy, but it fit, damn it, it fit. Everything about her spoke to him: her eyes, her hands, her hair, her still firm body. Yet he knew her mind as well, and it was here where her true strength was. Great Safti, why couldn't he have married her?

She returned from gazing out the window and stared at him. Neither spoke, savoring the intimate silence between them.

Slowly standing up, he came around the table and stood behind her. He began massaging her shoulders, using his hands to tell her how he felt. For a few seconds she softened, the sensation soothing, as though sloughing away life's vagaries with each pull of his hands. But then she stiffened.

"Konrud," she chastised him. "If someone were to come in, what would they think? You know how tongues wag. As much as I enjoy your touch, the risk is too great. If anything were to happen to you..." Guina dropped her head, reaching up to pat the hand on her shoulder.

Konrud sighed slowly. "Yes, yes" he responded with a hint of frustration, "I know you're right." Yet he remained and massaged a bit more. She kept her hand on his, moving with his loving touch. Fighting the urge to kiss her neck, he reluctantly returned to his side of the table. "It hurts me to see how they treat you. Perhaps, one day they will appreciate you like I do."

"Perhaps one day they will," she said, thoughtfully. They held each other's eyes for a moment more, then returned to the game they played. Yet a subtle change had occurred, that escaped neither of them. The occasions for touching hands or fingers became more frequent, each time lasting longer than warranted. There was language in that touch that spoke more than simple friendship.

For the next hour, they discussed their mutual interests, family, and the possibility of war with the Rugians. The joy of being alone together, away from prying eyes and tongues, was interrupted by a knock on the door. Konrud withdrew his hands from holding hers. "Come in," he commanded.

The acolyte pushed the door open and bowed. "Please excuse me for intruding Father Konrud, the Holy Father requests your presence at the questioning of the man called Duncan who calls himself a wizard."

"As he wills. When?"

"Now Father. They should be bringing him to the Council Chamber shortly."

"Very well. I'll be there in a minute." He turned his attention back to Guina. "I suggest you read some of the apologetics on Safti." The door closed as the acolyte left. Konrud paused a moment, ensuring the door was fully closed. "This should be interesting. You may want to watch. Use the door by the far drapes." Konrud motioned to the large hanging drapes by the window. Behind it was a door that led to the upper balconies of the Council Chamber. Such rooms let members of the Council monitor activities in the Chamber itself without being seen.

Guina smiled and grasped his hands. "Thank you. We'll talk later."

Konrud kissed her on the forehead and quickly left the room. Guina waited an appropriate number of moments and then pushed the drapes aside to enter the balcony.

Chapter 14

Duncan followed the acolyte through the twisting streets. They turned a corner and the houses ceased. Wide fields spread out before them, rising in terraces with the terrain.   Duncan's gaze took in the setting as he instinctively lifted his eyes and head to follow the path up to the Temple of Safti. High upon the knoll it stood, a grand building with tall columns and lavishly decorated portico perched imposingly, dominating the entire landscape. Not too far behind it, the sheer walls of the mountain rose to dizzying heights.

The path rose steadily upward and as they walked, he could see the bustle of activity as priests and acolytes and richly clothed men swirled around the building. As they grew closer, he realized that the building was made of the same material as the city walls.   On closer inspection, the Temple was larger than he first realized, towering at least three stories. There were cloistered gardens off the sides and carefully apportioned vineyards next to the gardens. The entire aura was one of power.

The acolyte hurriedly ushered him into the room anxious to be rid of this heretic and away from Vix's volcanic nature.   He pushed Duncan forward and rapidly closed the doors behind him.

Duncan found himself standing in a large hall with a high vaulted ceiling. A scowling Vix was seated behind a large elevated desk towards the back of the room. Two secretaries sat at similar desks below him. On both sides of the nave were tiered rows of plush chairs, set in alternating intervals of seven, six, and seven chairs. Ten richly adorned priests sat in this gallery, evenly divided five to a side.   Tall stained-glass windows surrounded three sides of the room and provided the daytime light. Large candelabras lined the nave portion of the hall.

There was a single seat in the middle of the room.

Vix looked up. "Glad you could join us Wizard. Please, sit down."

Duncan realized the inquisition about to occur and calmed himself, trying to remember all of his theological readings in the computer's library.

"Well, pleasure to see you again." He deliberately seated himself. "Tell me, how may I enlighten you?"

"Not so brash young man," one of the priests chastised. "We are here to explore of your heresy."

He leaned back in the chair. "Heresy? Ask away."

"You say that you are a wizard. From where do you get your power?" Vix demanded.

'From myself of course."

"Yourself?" Vix puzzled. "Not from some god or heavenly being?"

"Nope. Just me."

"And a god plays no part in your power?"

Duncan thought for a moment. *Watch it. Think about what you're doing here.* "That is not what I meant."

"Well then, what do you mean?"

"I mean that my 'power', as you call it, is a human power. It is this human power that God uses to demonstrate his existence."

"Oh? And how does he demonstrate his power through you?" a priest asked.

Vix interrupted, frowning. "This is but word games. Power…human power… these are simply terms that you've given another meaning to."

"Not so High Priest," Duncan countered. "We all understand power and the many kinds of power. Yet which of you has seen God use his power?"

"What do you mean?" a priest asked.

"I mean, who of you has actually seen God working his power through a man?" He carefully noted the body language of the various priests. Several leaned slightly forward with the haughty demeanor of never being wrong. Several others had the air of constantly sifting information.

"Wait a moment," another priest interjected. "You say that you do not get your power from God. If that is the case, then you really cannot believe in God because he has no part of your power!"

There were several grunts of approval, the pleasure of revealing a heretic gaining momentum. Duncan paused before responding. "You raise an interesting question. I suppose that before asking if you have seen God's power, you really ought to answer the essential question." He surveyed the room. "Does God exist?"

A humorless priest in the lower tier leaned forward. "You tell us. If you do not get your power from God, does he exist?"

"Is that your answer?" he retorted. He looked around the room. "Please, which one of you here has seen God?"

167

"Watch your tongue," another interjected.

"You watch yours. It is not I who blaspheme here," he snipped. "Tell me, any of you, who of you has seen God?"

"I have seen his works," stated the humorless one.

"And what works are these?"

"Look around you, foolish man. How think you this world came into existence?"

"Not that one again Garbhan," moaned a sallow priest with a hook nose. "You always go back to that 'where did everything come from' argument."

"And you still haven't provided a satisfactory rebuttal Gerallt," Garbhan retorted. "Let's see if this young wizard can provide better reparteé than you've been able to discover."

Gerallt reddened at the comment.

There was a pregnant pause as everyone waited to see if Gerallt would respond.

Duncan took careful note of the exchange. *Gerallt and Garbhan...* he associated each name with the respective priest. *Looks like you boys don't get along.* "Father Garbhan, your question asks how this world came into existence unless it was created by God." Duncan inquired, much to the relief of the group.

"That is correct," he smugly replied, noting that Duncan knew his name.

"There are lots of reasons. This could have just happened, a freak accident of nature. Yet you still have not answered my question. You see daily life and from this you infer a god. Please, tell me how this can be."

A tallish slender man with darting eyes, shifted uneasily in the second tier. "Bear with me a moment, and perhaps I can educate this youth." He smiled knowingly and began, "Would you agree with me that God by definition is the most perfect being and as such cannot lack anything?"

"Sure," Duncan answered.

"Well, there you have it." The priest smiled to the rest of the group. "God must exist because not-existing would mean that he lacks something." He sat back smiling pompously.

"But you're talking about the idea of God," Gerallt argued.

The priest turned to Gerallt. "Why not let the wizard answer the question before you jump in and display your ignorance in front of visitors."

"I would, Cattwg, if your question had any merit," Gerallt snapped. "And you are still talking about the *idea* of God."

"Ah, but how then could such an idea get there if there was no such being?" he retorted.

"Can we get back to the point!" Vix commanded.

Cattwg looked up to where Vix was seated. "I am making my point." He stated, looking directly at Vix. *As if you even know what we're talking about.* Cattwg turned back to Gerallt. "If it were merely an idea of the mind and did not actually exist, it would not be the most perfect being. For to lack the quality of existence would mean that the being was not perfect!"

"Interesting," Duncan smirked. "Yet, Father Cattwg, you still have a problem here. Your proof is merely a verbal exercise, and says nothing about the existence of God. Listen, simply having the *idea* of a perfect being in no way requires a perfect being exist. I can conceive the idea of the perfect woman, yet one does not exist."

"There, you see," Gerallt said triumphantly.

There were several chuckles and some 'You're right there,' but Duncan continued. "You've constructed your definition to include existence in the proof for God. There is nothing in your proof that makes it necessary to have a subject called God."

"What are you saying?" interrupted Vix.

Cattwg rolled his eyes. *Where have you been? Why don't you just shut up and listen?* He shook his head. *Why the hell you ever became High Priest is still a mystery to me. Safti certainly does move in mysterious ways.* He turned back to listen to Duncan.

"Father Cattwg, I'm saying that merely to define a thing does not mean to say that it exists." Duncan looked to Gerallt for support. "Definitions tell us nothing about reality, unless they are confirmed by observation. And again, I ask who of you has seen God?"

At first there was a general murmur of confusion as the assembled members of the Governing Council sifted Duncan's reply. Several members emphatically exclaimed that God still existed while others shifted uncomfortably.

"Let me see if this will help," another plump priest spoke. "Do you agree that experience teaches us that finite, changing things exist? That we experience the world through our senses?"

"I absolutely agree. Sense experience is probably one of the few areas of verifiability. Although some would argue that sense experience itself is untrustworthy as we do not all share the same experiences."

"Do you agree that you are sitting in a chair?" the priest pursed his lips.

"Yes"

"Good." He glanced around the room. "I believe that we can all agree that the wizard is sitting, not floating, in the chair." There was general laughter and even Duncan smiled. "Now then, do you agree that finite, changing things exist?"

"Certainly."

"He said 'certainly'," the priest surveyed the room again. "We're making progress." Again there was laughter. The rest of the group relaxed, enjoying the line of questioning.

"So, if finite changing things exist, there must have been something that caused these finite things to exist in the first place, a sort of original mover or creator. And this original mover was and is God." He leaned forward slightly as though challenging the Wizard to refute him.

"Let me see if I understand this." Duncan pretended to sift the information. "What you are saying is that everything must have a cause or mover, that nothing can be caused or moved unless it was caused by something else?"

"That is correct." The priest leaned back slightly.

"And that the original cause is God?"

"Yes!" the priest said triumphantly.

"Well done, Pewlin," Cattwg gloated.

"But," Duncan spoke deliberately, "if nothing can cause or move itself, then how can God be the first mover? Surely, by your own definition, something must have caused God to exist."

Pewlin was momentarily nonplussed. Several others, following Duncan's reasoning, were impressed with his skills, yet fearful of their own theological foundations at the same time.

"Surely you can see that there had to be a beginning somewhere," Pewlin argued.

"When, Father Pewlin?" interrupted Duncan.

"In the beginning!" Garbhan interjected.

"In the beginning when?"

"At the very beginning, the beginning of everything."

"Too easy an answer Father Garbhan. What you have here is something that is lost far beyond the grasp of the human mind into the fog of infinity. You cannot know what it is really like because it is hidden from view behind the myriad of secondary causes between itself and our experiences in the real world. It is unknown."

"But it is known that the original cause was and must be God. Everyone knows that." Father Pewlin looked around the room for support. Some gave immediate approval while others were not so sure. Duncan's logic was having significant effect.

"Again, Father Pewlin, you have made a leap that does not and cannot follow. You use sense experience to justify God's existence. Unfortunately, what you have done is to use *a priori* arguments to move from empirical evidence to existence beyond sense experience."

"A what?"

"*A priori.*"

"What language is that?"

"It's called Latin." Duncan wondered if he should explain more, but decided to give a simpler answer. "It's a language from my native country."

"And the woman berserker speaks this language?"

"Well...um, no. She only speaks English."

"And how many languages do you have in your country?" The smaller priest with ample girth asked.

Duncan shrugged. "There are many."

"And how many languages do you speak?" Vix intoned.

"Um...around twenty or so," Duncan responded unabashedly.

"Impossible!" Vix retorted. "There aren't more than two languages in all of Gambria or Rugia together."

Duncan spread his hands. "My country is a much bigger country."

Konrud listened as the Council began questioning Duncan about his native country. *This man is either very clever or has deep insight. What is it about him that intrigues me? How is it that he is so wise for one so young? He could hardly be a spy; he seems too comfortable here.* He watched as Duncan answered each question with deliberate responses. He noted that Duncan used each priest's name when answering the question. *What is it that he wants? Why is he here? Look at Vix... even he knows that this brash young man has unbalanced him.* He listened a bit more then decided to rein in the tangent discussions.

"Brothers," he interrupted. "I too find this information interesting, but I believe that the question here is the spiritual foundation of this gentleman. He has piqued our interest by way of philosophical rebuttal to our theology. I for one would have him continue. If his theology is suspect, we must have proof. As of yet, we have problems defending our own beliefs." There was a general assent, so he turned to Duncan. "You said something about *a priori* and were going to tell us what it meant."

Duncan smiled the smile of one in complete control. "It means 'independent of existence, a truth that is self-evident.' You cannot use these types of arguments to ascertain existence beyond sense experience." He was enjoying the game and a bit of his cockiness settled as his intellect rose to the challenge.

"What about the complexity of the universe? Surely you must realize that the order in the universe is a result of God," Gerallt spoke.

"Yes Father Gerallt, while I agree that there is order in the universe, how does this require any creative abilities? Might not someone or thing make order out of what already existed? Y'see, here again you use *a priori* arguments to move beyond sense experience."

The priest sat back, the slow realization that all of Duncan's arguments made sense. Yet he could not accept this apparent denial of God's existence. There must be a rational proof for the existence of God...the only problem was, he didn't know of any. Finally one of the more pensive ones spoke.

"Tell us then. Is there a God?"

Duncan thought quickly. "Yes," he finally answered.

"How do you know if you cannot show him to us?"

"Empiricism. Because I have seen him." Duncan sat up straight as the room erupted in "Impossible! Liar! Wait a minute, let him speak. It's a trick! Listen to him." Duncan sat quietly while Vix gained control of the room.

Intimidated by this display of knowledge, Vix needed to gain back the momentum. "Tell us wizard, what does he look like?" There was a number of 'Yeahs' and some nodding in agreement, but there was an equal number of priests who liked this saucy young man, who liked his smug assurance, especially in the face of the High-Priest.

Konrud listened with a strange fascination. He enjoyed the discomfort that Vix was now experiencing. Vix turned to him for support, but Konrud simply smiled back as if to say 'You're on your own.' *You're probably more of an agnostic than I. I'd love to believe, but after all, this brusque young man is right - there is no proof. And if Safti has favored you, He certainly is a blood-thirsty god. When are you going to stop killing our children?* Konrud sighed silently. *And despite all the praying I do, God still hasn't made me High Priest.*

"You err High-priest," Duncan answered, "if you think he looks like something in particular. He can assume all forms. He came to me as a burning bush, one that was not consumed."

Vix sat back, momentarily stunned. He remembered the verse: *And the fire descended and enveloped all around it yet not all were destroyed. Some the fire consumed, some it did not burn. Seek you the knowledge of trees that do not burn, nor cry out, for they have no flesh.*

There were several others who likewise recalled the verse, and the room settled into a thick silence. Vix was almost afraid to ask but knew he had to. "What did he say?"

Duncan let out the breath he had been holding, wondering what he said that caused them to relent. He felt that he was gaining an advantage and he pressed on.

"He said that he was sending me to Gambria. I said, 'Why me Lord?' And he said, 'Because I have chosen you.' 'But there are others Lord,' I replied. And he said, 'I am the God of Safti, the promised one. Who are you that should question me? Did you make the rivers flow into the seas, can you number the birds in migration, and what about the creatures of the seas? Can you do this?" He grew solemn and worked the group. He could feel their belief slowly begin. "You must believe me when I say that I was afraid. The bush continued to burn, and the winds blew across the deserts."

"What are deserts?" the plump one asked.

"They are vast dry areas of wind-blown sand. Barely anything grows and a man would die in less than a day."

"The wastelands," several priests intoned with solemn knowledge.

"Yet I was lifted up and shown the world. I saw the lands of Gambria and the lands across the vast oceans."

"What are oceans?" Vix asked in spite of himself.

"Vast bodies of water that separate lands by great distances. Great churning seas where a sailor might never see another sailor for months at a time." Fear flitted within some in the room and Vix, while suspicious, was also apprehensive. Duncan continued. "And I was afraid. I fell to the ground and said 'Lord, they will not believe me.' And he said that he would send a warrior with me, yet I was to be the one sent to Gambria to correct the sins of a nation still loved by God."

Duncan sat back, intensely watching the crowd. *This is it Duncan. Play it carefully.*

Konrud held his hand up to silence the low swell of murmurs. "You weave an interesting tale, wizard. How is it that the God of Safti should choose you and not one of us? Why should we believe your story?"

"You raise an interesting question friend, if I may call you such." Duncan knew he was treading delicately. "I asked the same question. Yet you do not need to believe me. However, I am not daunted. I was told that you would be stubborn, that you would need proof."

"What is it that we have done wrong?" the smaller plump priest worried.

Duncan paused momentarily. *Careful Duncan. Say just enough. Look around, some obviously enjoy the good life.* "You have drifted away from the true faith and have become concerned with your own comforts. You are more concerned with profits than with souls. That is why I submit a challenge to you as proof of my calling."

"A challenge?" Vix interrupted.

"Yes." Duncan watched the apprehension mixed with curiosity flicker throughout the Governing Council. "Will you hear the challenge?" Vix curtly nodded. Duncan began deliberately, "Three days from now, at the midnight watch, I challenge the High Priest," he nodded towards Vix then looked around the room, "or anyone else for that matter, to a demonstration of Holy support. The challenge is this; whoever causes the evening sky to shatter with thunder and lightning is the true chosen one. In fact, I will give the High Priest first chance. If he produces the required results, you may do with me as you wish." Duncan finished. *Well, I'm committed now.* There was silence for a moment as the Council members comprehended the Wizard's challenge.

"And what if you win?" Konrud queried.

Yes! It's working. "If I win," Duncan paused, "then you will know that I have been chosen. I become High Priest."

Vix shuddered as several members nodded in amused consent. Suddenly he exploded. "This is absurd! By what right do you, some stranger, challenge me? I will not permit this charade to continue." He stood up.

"What are you afraid of?" Duncan challenged. "Think you might lose?"

Vix snarled. "Impossible. There will be no challenge." He glared around the room and then settled on Duncan. "How dare you come here to mock the name of Safti. You are a liar and a heretic. Guards!"

"Just a minute Holy Father," Konrud interrupted. He turned to the two acolytes who had come through the doors and were now standing dumbly staring between Vix and Konrud. "Close the doors, please. Thank you." He looked back to Council. "Holy Father, Fathers, let us not be too hasty. This man, a self-avowed messenger of Safti, has issued a challenge. Remember, as it is written, 'Pay heed to my words and you will reap the future. Cast aside my wisdom and a voice will arise to bring you back to the truth.' Let us say for the sake of argument that he is a messenger. Is time so precious and we so lacking in faith that we cannot wait a single day, or three, to determine the truth? If he lies, we will know it. The challenge is set for three days hence. With all due respect Holy Father, I believe that we would do well to wait."

Vix glared at Konrud, knowing he had just been out-maneuvered. Except for Vix and a few others, the rest of the Council nodded their heads in agreement.

Konrud returned to Duncan. "And where does this challenge take place?"

"On the shores of the sea, just outside the city here."

"Father Konrud, how will we know this man tells the truth? How do we know that he is not some fakir with a gift for magic? He still calls himself a wizard," one of the priests asked.

"For I am a wizard. But you must understand, the God of Safti has numerous true believers. Remember, not all of Safti's followers live in Gambria." He gazed at his audience. "The question before you really is, do you wish to kill me now as a sacrifice for your own fears, or will you be content to wait until I can show you the power of god and the fact that I am his chosen one?"

There was an awkward silence as the assembled priests thought of a face-saving way out. Vix had lost the advantage and now hated this man. But he knew that he could not do anything to harm Duncan... at least not publicly.

Fortunately, Konrud stood up. He too had been impressed with Duncan's speech. He needed more time, as they all did, to sort out this news. *Perhaps this stranger might be the real answer. Who can tell? If he can perform a miracle, then perhaps there is a god.*

"Father Vix, and brothers, we have heard much today and need time to...um, digest these words and this man. I propose that we accept this challenge and meet with him in three days' time on the beaches of Lake Starn."

To the relief of everyone except Vix, all agreed. Duncan was tartly thanked for being there, and the acolytes prepared to escort him back to his lodgings.

He leaped up and strode to the waiting acolyte, spinning around just before the door. "Remember! Three days from now. The chosen one of Safti will be revealed." He walked out as the murmur rose and then stopped as the doors closed behind him.

Alexis had spent the morning by her prized mount still hanging limply in the sling. Food and water had been brought, and Brenna had the stable boy hunt for an herbal salve for the wounds. While the tarrac was still weak from exhaustion, Alexis cleaned the worst of his injuries. Brenna watched as Alexis worked with both tenderness and resolve. When the stable boy returned, she sent him off again to find more food for the two warriors.

"And bring something decent to drink!" she called after him. She turned back to Alexis and pointed to the salve. "Let me help you." She intoned slowly, motioning toward the tarrac with the salve in her hands. Alexis understood and gratefully nodded.

The two of them applied the poultice to the wounds. Though the tarrac would not eat, Alexis was able to coax him to drink a bit. By noon, he snapped at her as she offered him water.

"You go ahead and snap all you want. I saved your ass and you know it. You're mine now, so get used to it." She rubbed him a little behind his left horn, the only part of his body that didn't have a cut or swollen place. For a brief instant, the great animal put his ear forward, and he raised his head.

Vix slammed the door as he jerked his robe off over his head.

"Well, what have you done now High Priest?" Bradwr startled Vix with the sarcastic question.

"What are you doing here?" he demanded as he wheeled around to face the voice.

"I didn't realize you could create thunder and lightning," Bradwr smirked.

"Of course I can't. No one can. What do you expect?"

Bradwr leaned back and patted his heart, "What? You mean you're not the Chosen One?" He smiled condescendingly.

"Don't be absurd. Neither is this so-called Wizard."

"Well he seems to have you backed in a corner. Did you happen to think that he might not have made the challenge if he didn't think he could do it? You seem to be in somewhat of a predicament." Bradwr paused, letting the effect of his words soak in. "What to do? What to do?" he added softly.

Vix stomped around the room, becoming more and more agitated by Bradwr's taunts.

"Wouldn't it be so much easier if he would just go away."

"Or die!" Vix blurted.

"Now that's a clever idea you have there." Bradwr responded. "How could that happen, I wonder?"

"I can't use Cledwyn. The wizard has too much visibility." Vix spat, the answer only too obvious. "Assassins."

"I'm glad you thought of that; it would never have occurred to me." Bradwr responded with a knowing grin.

"I'm sure it wouldn't," he retorted. He continued pacing as he gave vent. "A knife in the dark? Too obvious. Something more subtle. Poison, perhaps?" Vix mused.

"Now isn't that interesting. I believe you know someone who has that expertise right here in this very Temple, don't you?" he egged him on.

"As if you didn't know. You've made use of him often enough." Vix folded his arms. "It's about time Drubal made himself useful to me."

Bradwr smiled placatingly. "I see that once again you've everything taken care of. I want you to know that whatever might happen, you've always had my full support." He smiled as he rose to leave.

As Duncan left the Council Chambers, he had a strut to his walk. It was a glorious morning. The sun glowed brightly in the softly blue-tinged sky. He stopped in the middle of the road, halfway down the hill from the temple and inhaled deeply, savoring the scent of the day. *This is going better than I thought.* He looked off in the distance at the thick forests edging the farm fields far beyond the castle walls, then off to the left at the great Starn Sea. He watched the sails of the fishing boats in the distance straining with the wind. He breathed again and could smell the water. *It's only been a day and look where we are.* He shook his head and smiled. *This is almost too easy.* He started to walk again. *Alexis will get a kick outta this.* Then he remembered Brenna. *Humpf. Maybe not. I'll have to do this myself.*

Taking his time, he finally made his way to the tarrac barns. As he rounded one of the corners, he saw Alexis and Brenna still giving full attention to the tarrac. He shook his head in wonderment. *What's the deal here? It's just an animal. You can always get another.* However, he couldn't resist a little verbal arrogance in his current mood. He called to Alexis as he approached, "Hey! If I bite you, will you rub me behind the ear too?" He chuckled at his own joke. Alexis rolled her eyes in an exaggerated show of irritation, but she smiled a little.

"And what's got you so cocky today Duncan Stuart?"

"Oh, I've just had a little visit with the higher-ups here. It was a nice chat."

Before Alexis could ask further, a messenger appeared and addressed Brenna. "High Commander," he squeaked, "I have a message from the king for you and for the visitors." The man stood awkwardly, waiting.

She stared at him, making him more uncomfortable. "Well? What is it?"

"His highness, King Diad, wishes to honor the visitors with a feast at the palace this evening. He wishes your presence as well."

"Thank you." she replied, then turning to Duncan and Alexis, she asked, "Do I tell the king you will come?"

"But of course," he replied with mock gravity. "A little bread, a little wine, could be fun." He translated for Alexis who wrinkled up her nose at first.

"I've got work to do here. I'm not interested in 'Your highness this' and 'your highness that' stuff." she complained.

"I think it's expected, Alexis. Besides, Secretariat here isn't going anywhere for a while."

"You are an ass today, aren't you?" She rolled her eyes, then added, "I suppose you're right. Okay, tell 'em I'll be there too."

Duncan accepted the invitation for them both, and the messenger turned to leave. Then, turning slightly to Brenna the messenger said, "Oh, and High Commander, I lit a candle to Saint Tag for you." She looked intently at the messenger for a moment, then nodded knowingly.

Duncan watched him leave and turned back to Alexis. "Yeah, well, looks like you two jocks have got things under control. Listen, why don't you two start teaching each other the language? I'm not getting paid enough to be an interpreter here." He laughed good-naturedly. "I'm going to head back to the house where I'm appreciated."

"Yeah, "Alexis called to him as he left. "We appreciate you – leaving." She laughed, then to Brenna, "Talk?" She went over beside Brenna and pulled up a small stool. "Sit," she said, then again "Sit." Brenna nodded and gave her the word for "sit" in her language. The two took turns acting out words and identifying objects around the tarrac enclosure.

Rulf, a sinewy middle-aged man with a quickness and strength that belied his age, stood in front of Vix. His taut muscles flexed as he moved around the room.

"Holy Father, I think I know someone who can accommodate your request."

"I thank you friend Rulf." He seemed distracted. "I want you to employ Brother Drubal's talents."

Rulf cocked his head to the side. "Why not do it yourself then?"

"I need it to be done quietly. He is too old to be quiet."

"I still do not see a need for him. I'm sure my acquaintances can resolve your issue."

"I'm sure you are right. However, I simply want you to use Drubal's ...uh, culinary talents. Is that acceptable?"

He frowned momentarily, then shrugged. "I will ask. Who is to receive this attention?"

"A newcomer. I'll explain what I have in mind. Would you like something to drink? Some wine perhaps?"

Standing to full height, he nodded. "That would be acceptable."

The High Priest flashed a stern gaze at an acolyte. "Fetch some wine for my guest. Good wine." Motioning to Rulf to sit, he relaxed. "Now listen; this is what I have in mind."

Lucan stood before the kitchen doors, the smell of fresh bread luring him like a child's promise. Pushing them open, he let the full warm smell bathe him in all its sweetness. He watched in anticipation as the older cook slid the oven paddle into the gaping hole of the stone oven and withdrew a steaming loaf of bread. As the cook turned to place the loaf on the cooling rack, he saw Lucan.

"Father Lucan. You honor me with a visit." He shook the loaf next to the others.

"Ah Brother Drubal, I could tell it was you baking tonight for no one, no one can bake like you do."

Drubal smiled good-naturedly and took the freshly baked loaf and gingerly broke it open. "I've got some butter melted on the stove. Please, it would do me honor if you would partake." He motioned to the loaf and stove.

"With pleasure, kind Drubal," he grinned. "Come, sit with me and let us discuss the twenty-fifth Sura. I do believe I've found a bottle of wine along the way here." He lifted the bottle up.

The older man smiled and shuffled over to the table. "You are most kind Holy Father."

"Now, now Brother Drubal, only one can be called Holy Father."

"Yes, that is true Father Lucan, but we both know that fate has indeed played cruel. Here now, did you forget the glasses?"

179

Lucan shifted his sleeves and produced two wine glasses. "Of course not dear brother. I had them hidden just like you showed me when I came here as a young acolyte."

Drubal chuckled and pushed some hair strands away from his face. "It seems so long ago. Just half a glass please." He held his hand mid-level on the glass.

"What is this?" he arched an eyebrow in surprise.

"I must visit Rulf tonight and I cannot be muddled when we talk."

"Rulf? I haven't seen him in a while. What occupies him?" He poured the wine.

"Don't really know. Father Vix wanted me to offer him my talents," he answered, looking away.

Lucan paused in his chewing and laid the knife down. "I'm sorry." He placed a hand on the man's arm.

"It's not my choice, Lucan. He is the Holy Father and I obey."

"Yes, I know, but," he sighed, "poison is such a...a," he paused searching for the word.

"Brutal method?"

Lucan shook his head, pouring more wine into his own glass. "Yes. Why is he doing this?" he sighed.

"I don't know." Drubal gulped the remaining wine. "But I do know that you should have been the High Priest."

"Drubal, please. How can that change anything?"

"Don't you want to be High Priest?"

"It is not a situation I think about."

"But you do want it, don't you?"

Lucan shrugged. "Who doesn't? But I am not ambitious. I am content with my chosen role. Safti has been good to me. I would rather learn more."

Drubal stood up and shuffled around the table next to him, gently placing a hand on his shoulder. "You were always the willing student. How often have I wished that you had been first born."

Lucan placed his hand on top of the old man's. "You were the best tutor. And you should be where I am now. I truly am sorry that Vix has put you here."

"I am but a priest. If Vix has decided I should be here, then who am I to argue? But someone had to tell him he was, and still is, wrong. His lust is an embarrassment to us all. Can't you do anything about it?"

"I have spoken to him."

"Lucan, you must admonish him. He will only listen to you."

"Drubal, my friend, I cannot control him. I can only pray for him and seek Safti's forgiveness for his sins."

"Lucan," he admonished, moving away from the table. "Safti helps those who help themselves."

"And what is that supposed to mean?"

"It means that unless we help him stop his perversion, he will be the ruin of us all."

Lucan buttered another hunk of bread, silently musing to himself. After a few moments, he spoke. "I will speak to him again."

Drubal readjusted the loaves of bread and reached for his cloak. "It is indeed kind of you to remember me. You were the best acolyte I have ever known." He smiled sadly and walked to the door.

He lifted his glass of wine in salute. "And you were the best teacher, dear Brother. It is because of your gift that I am anything at all."

The older man turned and stood still. "No Lucan. You have always had the gift." He gave a brief wave and walked out.

Chapter 15

Duncan sauntered into the massive house that now belonged to Alexis, still feeling good from the events of the morning. The servants were busily cleaning, but he didn't see Tene. Wanting to share his victories with a more receptive audience, he called her.

"Tene!"

"Yes, Lord Duncan. In here," she answered from the dining hall. As he walked in, he strode up to her, put both arms around her waist and kissed her. Then, he pulled her closer and kissed her again. "What.... what is this? Lord Duncan, uh, Duncan, I have work to do." But she laughed amusedly with him.

"Tene, I have escaped the lion's den unharmed," he boasted grandly.

"What are you talking about? What's a lion?" she asked, looking confused.

He stopped and took both her hands in his and excitedly related the conversation with the priests. As he neared the end and told her about the challenge, she paled and her eyes grew wide in fear.

"What? What's wrong?" he stopped.

"Do you know what you've done?" she gasped. "No one is more powerful than Vix. Even the king doesn't cross him. The priests control so much, either by right of law or by influence. You have done a dangerous thing. You must apologize, beg forgiveness."

"Whoa, Tene. You don't get it. I'm going to win," he assured her.

She became suddenly calm and very serious.. "You are new to Gambria. I don't believe you understand the situation here."

"You don't believe me, do you?" he frowned.

"It's not my place, and these matters are for the priests," she answered, dropping her chin. She paused for a moment, then looked him directly in the eyes. With all earnestness she added, "And I wish to be able to serve you for a long time. When you speak of going up against High Priest Vix, you frighten me. You don't know what he can do. Some have disappeared in the night, or died mysteriously days after they have displeased him. "

"Shhh," he said softly and put a finger to her lips. "It's all right. I'll be fine. I have my own powers, and I very much understand the likes of this Vix. It is he who would do well to be afraid." Touched by her concern, he studied her face. It was far more beautiful than any of the dream girls, even with the few freckles on her cheeks. But more than that, he noticed an intensity in her eyes, a depth of concern that was genuine and unmistakable. *You really are worried about me, not about Lord Duncan, but me.* He held her close, touched her cheek with his and whispered to her, "Don't fear, Tene. I have power that hasn't been revealed yet. And I'm not going to let anyone harm you."

He pulled back just slightly to look at her face again. She seemed relaxed in his arms, but her eyes betrayed her concern. He laughed. "Now, enough of this serious stuff." He pulled away and walked over to the table. "The king has invited Alexis and me to the palace for dinner. What do you think I should wear? Oswiu's clothes?" He smiled almost boyishly at her.

"I think not," she answered, smiling back.

"And what about manners at the king's table?" he continued. "I don't want to appear as some buffoon who doesn't know which knife to use." Tene leaned over to arrange the knives by his plate. As she did, he kissed her playfully on the arm. "Now what if I wanted to do this? Would that be okay at the king's table?" He kissed her deeply.

"I think not," Tene coyly replied.

"And what about this?" he asked as he pulled her sleeve off her shoulder and kissed her smooth skin.

"I think not," Tene again responded, smiling sweetly.

"And what if I do this? Is this OK?" He began kissing her lightly along her neck, slowly, deliberately, then along the edge of her jaw towards her ear.

"I... I think not," she purred.

"And what if I decided to just get up and leave?" he questioned and attempted to stand.

She pushed him back down into the chair, both hands on his shoulders, eyes intently focused on his. "I think not!" Kissing him forcefully, she straddled his lap.

"I am here, Lord Ronell." Brenna called into the darkness. "I came as quickly as I could."

A rustling sound caused her to turn as the form slipped from the shadows into the large wooden chair. Gloved hands straightened the long, silk robe and pulled the hood up closely around the masked face. Finally, the silence was broken. "We have learned new information that requires your attention."

She bowed slightly and responded, "How may I serve?"

The measured, yet strong voice explained, "We have new information about the visitor, the one called Duncan, the Wizard. He was called to the Priests Council today and has shown himself to be indeed clever. In questioning by the priests, he answered well and handled their inquisition expertly. He said he has seen God and was sent by him. What do you think of this?"

"Well, every time Raefgot drinks too much ale he says he sees God." Brenna chuckled, but she was not joined in the brief joke, so she continued. "I am not a great expert in the teachings of Safti, but I understand that a prophet is expected."

"Indeed. What form do you think this prophet will take? Will it be a king? A priest? A stranger? Perhaps a lady warrior?"

She looked away uncomfortably, complaining, "You mock me, Sire."

"Do not take offence High Commander. We know full well your desire to serve the people. That is why you are here."

Brenna returned to the topic. "Are you saying that since we don't really know what form this prophet might take, this visitor could be the one spoken of in the writings?"

"That is possible."

"But how will we know for sure?"

"A true heart will make itself known as surely as a false one will. The Book of Safti tells us we must be patient. But it would help if we were sure of the man's motives. What do you know of him?"

"It is difficult to size up this Duncan," she responded. "I am getting to know the warrior woman, and she is much as she appears. But the man is very different. I think he may be a fighter too, but his weapons are words."

"But for what does he fight? What ends does he wish? We must know his heart. Clever words can confuse issues and misguide the weak. Dark hearts can also speak with strength and purpose. Our own people have been taken in so completely by the High Priest's words that they willingly offer up their own children for sacrifice." The voice had become passionate at those last words, then paused and recovered composure. "You say you do not know him, Brenna, but what have you observed?"

"He has been kind to Tene and seems loyal to the woman, Alexis. My birth father, Menec, likes him. "

"Did you know that he challenged Vix today?" the voice interrupted.

"He challenged Vix? To what?"

"In the council before all the priests, this Duncan professed to be able to summon God's power and dared Vix to do the same in three days, on the beach by the sea. What do you think of this?"

Brenna thought for a moment. "I think that when we fight, we sometimes shout loudly, hoping to startle our opponent and force him to make a mistake."

"Very good. You could be right. This may be a bold game the newcomer is playing. But it is not likely the implications of this contest have escaped Vix. He is not one to act stupidly when the stakes are this high."

"What do you think will happen?" She questioned.

"Much will depend on whether this wizard is what he says he is or not. But, until we see the results of the challenge, we can't let anything happen to alter the outcome. Safti's prophesies teach us that events unfold as they should. However, Vix may not be so devoutly patient."

"No, he has many who owe him allegiance. He has seen to that."

"True. We may need to stay close to this wizard. His magic may not be enough to protect himself from Vix's devices. Are you prepared to help us in this?"

"There's a dinner tonight at the palace to honor the visitors. I too have been invited. I'll be watchful."

"Thank you Commander. You serve us well."

Hey mon, look what de cat dragged in! Rasta-mon came bounding in with Tene as she returned to where Duncan was pulling on his shirt. She carried a steaming tray of food. Another cat was close behind him.

"Look what the cook did while we were...um... discussing protocol." She smiled demurely and blinked slightly. "Doesn't it smell delicious?" She smiled sweetly. "May I serve you?"

"I'd rather you sit next to me and eat." He reached up and gently touched her arm.

She glanced down. "Your companion has returned with a friend." She stood watching as Rasta-mon rubbed against Duncan's leg. He quickly cleared a space on the table. Tene uncovered a dish, and the aroma of grilled meat filled the room.

Duncan slowly inhaled, savoring the bouquet of spices and meats. "This is so much better than the slop I was getting on board," he grinned, adjusting his chair.

"On board?" Tene queried.

Hey mon, smells good and we starved. I wan' you t'meet a friend of mine. Dis here's Dodona. Say Hi toots Rasta-mon's tail flicked back and forth.

Sitting demurely next to Rasta-mon was a coal black cat with a sleek silky coat. She had the look of an Abyssinian.

Duncan spoke to her, but nothing happened. Duncan tried again. *Rasta-mon, I'm not getting anything.*

Ya mon, I know. Dey be a little slow here. But it like my gran'fatha say, if she gots a great bod', she don' need ta talk! Haw!

Duncan laughed and petted Dodona.

Rasta-mon jumped up on Duncan's lap. *Listen, I told her she'd get a warm welcome here. Y'know, some food, some drink, a place to sleep...ahem...y'know, a place to sleep.*

He grinned. "Hey, this is your house too, remember? Go anywhere you like... just be discreet." He chuckled again and looked up to see Tene watching him with a strange fascination.

"Now what's that look for?" He drew her closer to him.

"It's just that I've never seen anyone talk to animals."

"Me neither." He smiled and tore off some pieces to cool down for the cats. He turned back to Tene, his eyes full of affection. "Thank you."

Tene leaned down to kiss Duncan, glancing briefly over to where Dodona was ripping and chewing on one of the tender pieces of meat. She jerked back up. "Oh my god."

Duncan gaze snapped to Dodona as her legs suddenly gave way and she collapsed on her side. In an instant, she was dead. He jumped up, rapidly surveyed the room and then went to the dead cat. He picked her up. "Poison."

"Oh my god, oh my god, Lord Duncan, I...I!" Tene blanched.

Dropping the cat back on the table, he enfolded Tene in his arms. "It's OK, it's alright. It's not your fault."

She buried her face in his shoulder. "But...but...I didn't... you know I didn't..." She looked back up and her eyes brimmed in tears. "I'd never hurt you." She pleaded.

He held her closer and brushed away the tears just beginning to trickle down her face. "Tene," he soothed, "I know you had nothing to do with this. It's not your fault."

Rasta-mon jumped up on the table and gave the cat a rapid sniff. *Dis can't be happenin'! It take me all night to get her comin' back home wit me! Mon, once de rest of dem find out what be happenin' here, nobody come back here with me...which mean I gonna have ta stay there... wit all dose ladies...which, in itself ain't necessarily a bad ting you unnerstand...but I gonna have to explain dis one somehow.* He suddenly jerked his head up and ran to the door leading to the kitchen. Sniffing feverishly, he noticed a different odor coming from outside the room. *Somebody outside...not one of us!* He looked back to Duncan. *Open de door mon, somebody gonna pay for dis!*

"Rasta-mon, take me with you." Duncan ran towards the door.

You crazy mon? You slow me down. His tail jerked side-to-side.

"No. I mean in your head."

Oh... right, I forget. OK, let me go.

Jerking the door open, he watched Rasta-mon dart through the opening. With a cat's senses, Rasta-mon saw the flitting shadow as it slithered out the window. In an instant, he was giving chase to a dark individual who was unaware that as he moved among the shadows, a small animal with finer skills was pursuing him.

Duncan turned back to the still horrified Tene. "Find the cook and find out what's going on." He firmly grabbed her arm, "Discretely. Calm yourself first. You have to act as calmly and naturally as possible. Don't let anyone else into this room except yourself."

She mutely nodded and went out.

Settling himself comfortably on the floor, he closed his eyes. Within moments, he was giving chase to a person dressed in black making his way towards another part of the city.

Rasta-mon's hunting instincts assumed control, and he tracked the fleeing figure making its way toward the Temple. However, instead of entering the Temple, the shadow turned off through the gardens and into the vineyards, working its way among the vines until it was close to an outcropping of rocks that thrust itself under the city walls. There, the vines had been left to ramble at their will. Pulling aside several thick cords, the shadow vanished into the hidden cave, Rasta-mon close behind.

As Rasta-mon plunged through the vines, a faint glow of wall torches glimmered in the far distant ends of a subterranean hallway. The figure moved with determined speed, every now and then twisting his head to listen behind him. As the hallways brightened, the hooded cloak came off, revealing a man of middle years. Yet, despite his age, he moved with the lightness of a youthful warrior. His rapid pace bespoke his intimacy with the underground tunnels. The wall torches gave off a thin black smoke that rippled as he whisked by.

Three right turns, three doors, and several guards later, he emerged into a large chamber that had been roughly hewn from the rock of the mountain. There the activity of many men continued, unaffected by this man's return. Rasta-mon managed to jump through as the last door had closed, gripping some of his tail fur in its tight grasp.

Yeowch! Mon I hope you be getting' dis. Rasta-mon looked around at all the activity. Some men threw multi-pointed stars at man-shaped targets. Others wielded sharp bladed swords and sliced melons so quickly that the halves did not separate. And still others wrestled, and tossed and threw each other to the ground. *I don' tink dis be a good place for da Rasta-mon.* The cat surveyed the room. Fortunately, his quarry had stopped not far from him and was talking to a sinewy man with long salt and pepper hair that fell upon his shoulders.

"Rulf," the man bowed. "The mission did not succeed."

Rulf grimaced. "Damn. Why not."

"He didn't eat Brother Drubal's concoction. He had two King's companions in there with him. One of them ate the meat before the wizard would. I believe the wizard may keep the companions just for that purpose."

Rulf turned towards the shadows where Rasta-mon lay hidden. He inhaled slowly. "Father Vix will not be pleased, yet he must know."

Mon, I gotta git outa here.

Just a little more Rasta-mon. I need to see his face again.

In the early afternoon, Duncan was back in Tene's bedroom going through the assets and holdings left by Oswiu. A crestfallen Tene had gone to the market to find some fresh produce and meat that she would personally prepare and serve him. Her anxiety simmered at the surface of her movements. Occasionally she would glance around. At one of the vendor stalls, she found some fruit that she pinched and thumped to check its ripeness.

"Well, if it isn't the servant of the new berserker."

Tene jumped as she spun around. "Oh my god, Lord Bradwr."

"My word Tene. You look like you've seen a returned essence! Are you all right child?" Bradwr peered inquisitively at her.

"Oh my Lord, someone tried to kill Lord Duncan."   Tears began welling up in her eyes.

Bradwr quickly surveyed the market place. "Pull yourself together child and tell me what happened."

She inhaled deeply, working to calm herself. "I was telling Lord Duncan about protocol and had brought some food in and a king's companion ate the meat –"

"A king's companion?"

"Yes m'Lord. Lord Duncan has one of his own and apparently it had brought another one with it, and when the other companion ate the meat, it died because the meat was poisoned."

"The wizard has a king's companion?" Looking at her with half-lidded eyes, he tilted his head back slightly.

"Yes m'Lord. And the companion it brought with it is dead," she shuddered.

"Now, now child, he certainly can't blame you."

"Oh, I know m'Lord, but I'm the one who brought the food to him."

"And that's why you're here, to find fresh food for him?"

Tene hung her head. "Yes m'Lord. Did I do wrong?"

Smiling paternally at her, he soothingly replied, "No child. I know you have the best intentions."

"Oh m'Lord," she looked up at him, her eyes wide and soulful. "I'm trying to do what you've asked. I just haven't had enough time with him to find out anything important."

He placed a calming hand on arm. "You're doing fine. This is good information you've given me. You know how to get ahold of me if something else happens."

"Yes m'Lord," she meekly answered.

Chapter 16

Duncan stood outside the door of Alexis' bedroom. He could hear Brenna laughing.

"Hey? You two ready yet?" He pounded on the door.

"No! Go away," came the flippant response.

"I'm gonna leave without you!" He leaned close to listen.

"Goodbye," Alexis called out.

He stood back up frowning, hands on hips. Suddenly the door opened and Brenna poked her head out and gave him a once over.

"Patience Wizard. We're not quite ready."

"Well how much longer?" he crossly demanded.

"When we're ready. Don't leave without us." It was not a request. She closed the door and he could hear the laughter begin again.

He stood staring at the heavy wooden door. *Like hell I'm gonna wait for you two.* Spinning around, he stomped down the hall. In quick strides, he was down the stairs, through the great hall, and out the door.

Walking out into the night, he paused midstride, surprised at the sights and sounds. The streets in The Havens part of the city were well kept, with large trees interspersed evenly along the edges. People meandered lazily along the road, stopping to talk to neighbors. Children ran in and out among the trees, their laughter filling the evening. Savoring the night smells and activity, he walked on, a veneer of contentment settling over him. Noticing him, people nodded politely and then resumed their conversations. Occasionally he could hear them as he passed. 'He lives with the new berserker... They say he's a wizard... I heard that he was interrogated by the priests... And he's still alive? They say he confounded them, made them look the fools... Ooh, I'm not sure I would want to be him then... I know... Vix will fix that...' And they would smile and watch him walk on.

Swinging back the huge double doors, liveried servants invited Duncan into the great hall. As he walked in, the conversations going on already in the other end of the room, stopped. He recognized Menec, Vix, Raefgot and Bradwr, but didn't know the other two.

Bradwr called, "Well what a surprise. Come join us, Wizard of Sorts." He gestured grandly to those on his right and left. "You must meet our group here. Please, come make idle conversation with us while we wait for the king. Perhaps you can show us a trick or two." He smiled patronizingly.

Duncan made his way past two long parallel tables that were empty for this occasion. However, the huge fireplaces on either side of the tables were blazing as the animals for the evening meal crackled and burned on huge spits over the flames. Smells intermingled; the aroma of game cooking overpowered the scents of flowers and fruits cut open on the table, and the herbs scattered on the floor. Bradwr and the other guests waited by the third table that formed the base of an upside-down 'U.' Attendants and serving girls bustled about the room, setting plates, placing goblets, and arranging decorations and candelabras.

The king's brother grinned widely as Duncan came up. "You remember High Priest Vix." Vix's eyes narrowed as his face tightened, giving Duncan the kind of look that said 'I'll be happy when you're dead.'

Bradwr continued, unaffected by Vix's glaring. "And Prince Raefgot. Oh yes, you had the pleasure of meeting him on the journey into Gambria. And of course, who can forget Tarrac-master Menec." Bradwr's disdain for Menec was thinly veiled.

Duncan nodded politely at Vix and Raefgot, then turned to Menec. "It's good to see you again, friend," he smiled.

Menec smiled with pleasure. "It's good to see you again too, Lord Duncan."

"Lord Duncan?" Bradwr feigned surprise. "Quite a title for a mere wizard." However, he plowed on with the introductions. "Next to me here is Prince Emer, the king's eldest son, also my son-in-law." The man to Bradwr's right appeared thirtyish and slightly built for his taller than average height. His light brown hair was thinning, and cropped in the severe, short manner common to academics. The humorless demeanor he projected put Duncan off but didn't threaten him at all.

"Ah, a man of position, at last. I am very pleased to meet the heir to the throne." Duncan greeted him warmly. Emer was taken aback briefly, but seemed pleased.

Bradwr raised his eyebrows momentarily, then smiled quickly. "What a clever wit you have, Wizard."

Duncan studied Emer, but dismissed him fairly quickly. His greeting had had the expected effect.

"But you still haven't met the king's second son. This is Prince Alric, the commander of Gambria's military forces." There was little question that Emer and Alric were brothers. They had similar facial features, but Alric was half-a-head taller with broad shoulders and the firm developed muscles of one who was vain about his physique. His face was tanned, and his hair full and long. In contrast to Emer's doleful expression, Alric greeted Duncan with a wide grin and forceful handshake.

"I've heard quite a bit about you." He looked directly at Duncan's eyes.

"Hopefully not from the High Priest," he smiled impishly. "It's a pleasure to meet a powerful man as well. Greetings, Prince Alric."

Suddenly, the doors opened and Brenna and Alexis swept into the room. The men's conversation abruptly ceased. Duncan turned around and did a double-take when they entered. Alexis was wearing a deep blue-green dress, closely fitted, as the style of the occasion dictated. It showed off her well-toned body, but suggested an elegance Duncan had not seen before. Her walk and manner, though, were readily identifiable, and surprisingly, worked well with the refined clothing. Brenna, wearing deep red, was striking, yet unaffected by her impact. Her long, black hair contrasted with the color of the dress and became woven into the lacey design of the beadwork trim around the low neckline. *God, what a woman! What would it take?*

"Lords and Ladies," the herald's loud bass voice reverberated in the room, "King Diad, Queen Guina, and Lady Pavia." From the alcoves by the front of the room, King Diad entered with the comfort of authority. The Queen followed behind him. Pavia walked slightly behind her.

Duncan remembered the King, but of the Queen he only had a vague impression. She was beautiful, but there seemed to be a pervading melancholy about her. Yet her eyes sparkled when she saw Brenna. However, he was immediately captured by Pavia's beauty. Pavia was a curvaceous, voluptuous woman that Duncan swore he had seen in hologram form, courtesy of Talane. Her perfect skin was evenly tanned. She wore her auburn hair loose, cascading off her shoulders and down her back. But there was something compelling about her, and it took Duncan a minute to realize that Pavia moved as one intimately aware of and assured by her own sexual impact.

"Good. I see everyone is here." King Diad looked at each guest.

"I don't see cousin Rhun?" Bradwr interrupted. "It's not like him to miss a party."

Diad shot him an irritated glance. "He wasn't invited."

"Not invited? Your own brother-in-law?" He feigned a sigh. "It's probably just as well... otherwise there wouldn't be enough food for the rest of us." He snickered at his own joke.

"Are you finished?" the king snapped. "This is my dinner, my family, my kingdom. A pox on his constant whining. It's about damn time he accepts that it's my kingdom now, my family that rules."

"Easy brother," Bradwr held his hands up in surrender. "I was just making an observation. What say we return to the business at hand? I believe you were last saying that everyone was here."

"Damn right. Everyone is here," he glowered. Settling himself, he looked back at his guests. "Welcome. Please sit down." He watched for a moment as the five men moved to accustomed places. "Raefgot."

"Yes father?"

"Please get up and give your chair to the berserker."

"But father –"

"Get up. You can sit over at the corner, opposite Vix." He waved him away.

"Why can't Emer move?" Raefgot whined.

"Because brother, unlike you, I have a functioning brain." Emer smiled wickedly.

"And that's about all he has that functions," Pavia stage whispered. There was laughter; Emer snapped around and glared at her. She smiled prettily as if making a joke.

"Yes, that does remind me." The King turned to Emer and then to Pavia. "When am I going to be a grandfather?"

Emer blushed. "Soon father. We hope very soon."

"Well what's taking so damn long?" He turned to the still standing Raefgot and bellowed, "Dammit sir, sit down!" Raefgot sulked as he moved to the far corner of the table. Diad turned back to Emer. "Well?"

"These things do take time father." Emer hedged.

"Time? Haw! Your mother was pregnant after one damned use of the stone. Brother, can't you do anything about this?" He looked over to where Bradwr was sampling a goblet of wine.

Bradwr shrugged noncommittally. "Brother, it's out of my hands. Sometimes things like this happen. Perhaps the transfer didn't pass quite right. It has happened before."

"But not in our family!" the King thundered.

"Brother, are we going to debate your son's lack of issue or are we going to eat? The meat smells quite ready."

As if remembering why he was there, Diad looked at the still standing guests. "Yes, yes, quite right. Please sit, Berserker," he motioned to the chair directly opposite him. "Alric, why don't you sit next to her. Brenna to his right, and Master Wizard in between Raefgot and our new berserker." He surveyed the seating. "Lady Pavia, why don't you sit next to me?" He turned to the Queen and gestured off-handedly. "You can sit in her place." He stood before his chair, resting both hands on the table. "Brother Menec, if you would sit on High Commander Brenna's right." He nodded toward Brenna. Satisfied with the placements, he continued.

"Welcome friends. Tonight we honor our guests. The woman Alexis has defeated our berserker and now holds the title of high commander. The man, Duncan, who also calls himself Wizard, has told us he has seen God. The evening should be a lively one indeed."

Bradwr grinned a devilish smile. "Seen God? Holy Father, have you seen God?"

"Of course not! No one has seen God. The man is a liar!" Vix stood, banged his hand on the table and glared viciously at Duncan.

Duncan met his gaze calmly and replied, "I guess we'll soon find out, won't we?"

The king looked at both of them. "What's this? Something going on and I don't know about it?"

"Sire," Duncan bowed slightly, "I have explained to your priests that I am the chosen one of Safti, and because of that I can summon God's power. I have issued a challenge to your High Priest."

"A challenge, Wizard?" the king queried, an eyebrow arched.

"Wouldn't you agree that the true Chosen One could cause the sky to fill with lightning and thunder?"

The King shrugged, "I suppose."

"Well m'Lord, if the High Priest can do this, then he wins and can do with me what he wishes."

"And if you win?"

"Then I become High Priest," he smiled, confident.

The king looked incredulously at the High Priest. "And you agreed to this?"

Vix looked blankly at the king and then frowned in response.

In the pause, Duncan translated in answer to Alexis's questioning look. Her response startled him. "Have you completely lost your mind?" Her eyes widened.

Aside, only to her, he explained, "Alexis, I know what I'm doing."

"I certainly hope so." She shook her head doubtfully.

The king spoke out, "What are you saying there?"

Duncan answered cheerfully, "She can't believe that the High Priest would accept this challenge knowing he is going to lose." The King barked a laugh while Vix's face flushed and his jaw flexed, but Vix said nothing.

Alric leaned into Alexis' shoulder as he touched her lightly on the arm. "Since you're the new berserker, I really ought to show you around. Why not tomorrow night? My tarrac is trained to carry two."

Duncan leaned around Alexis. "She doesn't speak your language yet."

Alexis gently pushed Duncan back as she turned to Alric. "I speak little. Not much." She turned back to Duncan. "What did he say?"

Duncan grudgingly relayed Alric's invitation.

"Tell him, thanks, but I have my own tarrac." She smiled coyly at Alric who laughed off the rebuff good-naturedly.

"Come! We can talk while we eat!" The king clapped loudly, "Bring food. We must eat!"

The servants scurried in, carrying large trays of steaming meat, vegetables, and bread which they placed in the middle of the table. As each dinner guest tore at pieces of meat or chunks of bread, the attendants filled goblets with wine, refilled water containers, and assisted each guest.

Duncan picked up his wine goblet and noticed it was just like the one he had used at Oswiu's house. "M'Lord Diad. Brenna told me about the Chalice of Fawr and that perhaps you would do me the honor of telling me the story."

Diad's eyes lit up. "How very proper of you Wizard."

"Not that story again," Alric moaned. "Tell another one, father."

"What's wrong with that story?" Emer interrupted. "Father tells it so well." Diad gratefully nodded.

"Careful he doesn't sit, older brother," Raefgot sneered at Emer, "otherwise you'll break your neck."

"That's very well put, little brother," Emer over-emphasized 'little'. "Tell me, did one of your child lovers help you with that?"

"That's a lie!" Raefgot jumped up.

"Sit down Raefgot," the King commanded and then turned to Emer. "And stop badgering him."

"I can't help it, he's such an idiot," Emer quietly intoned.

"I heard that!" Raefgot was still standing.

"I said sit down! He's right, you are a complete idiot."

"Now, now father," Alric smiled, "I prefer to think of him as incomplete." Everyone except Raefgot laughed.

King Diad stood up and leaned on the table. There was a subtle menace in his posture. "Raefgot. Unless you wish to defy me, you will sit down." Raefgot hesitated and then plopped down in his chair. "The Wizard has asked for a tale. Obviously he has manners." He looked pointedly at Raefgot, then picked up his goblet, took a long swallow, and wiped his mouth with a bright purple napkin. "Alric suggests I tell another tale. I have just remembered a story that I believe very few of you have heard. It concerns the times when Fitzroy the Lame was King." Diad sat back down and leaned back in his chair, a foot on the table.

Bradwr rolled his eyes. While Diad launched into his story, he called one of the serving girls over. She was a shapely woman with flirting eyes, and a loose, low-cut bodice. He whispered in her ear and then sent her off.

As Diad paused to catch his breath, Bradwr interrupted. "Brother, I believe you could use another drink." He nodded to the woman who sauntered over.

She leaned well forward as she refilled his goblet. Diad suddenly became absorbed with her smooth flesh as he followed the lines of the blouse down to her almost fully exposed breasts. Suddenly he reached up to slip his hand inside her blouse, but she was too quick and nimbly danced out of reach. Yet when their eyes met, hers sparkled her willingness. Diad blinked momentarily, then smiled wickedly in return.

In the interim, conversations around the table subtly informed the King that no one was really paying attention to his tale. Only Duncan still appeared listening. However, Diad had lost interest in his own story, replacing it with watching the serving girl. Yet he didn't want to appear too obvious.

"Well Wizard, I hear you confounded some of my best priests today. I'd have you explain, but esoteric discussions of God's existence that seem to send you theologians into such a heated passion, quite frankly bore me. I believe because it's necessary. Besides," he winked at him, "if God doesn't exist, what have I got to lose?"

"How very utilitarian of you, brother." Bradwr was leaning back, his index finger circling the top of his goblet.

"Oh come off it Bradwr," the King sneered. "You're almost as big an unbeliever as Vix." Vix momentarily blanched as he sputtered his drink. Diad saw the desired effect and laughed. "It's just a joke."

"Father?" Alric interrupted. "We've a little bet here between Emer and me. I say the story you were telling is 200 complete seasons old. Emer, that wizened bookworm, claims it to be 550." Emer glowered at Alric.

"Um…" Diad pondered, "…Let me…um…"

"Actually it is 550 complete seasons old," a soft voice spoke.

The King whipped around to snarl at the Queen. "And how would you know?" he snapped.

"Because I have read it. Interestingly, it has remained relatively unchanged since it was first written down."

The King blinked several times, but did not answer. In fact, the silence grew heavy until Alric spoke.

"Well I suppose I've lost the bet. Now I'll have to pay up. What was the wager? If I won, I'd get a chance to sire a child with this lovely creature." Alric grinned devilishly at Pavia and most of the table laughed. Pavia fluttered her eyes in coquettish reply.

"And if you lost?" Diad bemusedly asked.

Alric leaned forward. "Then he'd get a chance to sire young with my tarrac!"

The outburst of laughter wasn't enough to stop Emer from leaping to his feet. "I ought to teach you a lesson here and now!" His hand went to his belt dagger.

Yet Alric didn't move. He remained slouched in his chair, an arm flopped comfortably on one of the arm-rests. In fact, except for Duncan and Alexis, no one seemed particularly surprised.

Even Bradwr was beginning to snicker at the sight. "Sit down Emer. Can't you see he's just toying with you?"

"Well he's toyed with me for the last time." Emer stood to his full height.

"That's what you said the last time," sneered Raefgot.

Emer turned to him. "Well look what's still alive. Come up for some air, you besotted beast?"

Raefgot staggered to his feet. The wine gave strength to his tongue. "One of these days, brother," he slurred. "One of these days and you're a dead man."

Emer disdainfully stared at him. "By whose hand? Yours? I might as well be afraid of my own shadow." He dismissed the still standing and bewildered Raefgot, and returned his attention to Alric. "Well? Stand up and defend yourself!"

Alric looked up with feigned boredom, but said in a low, even voice. "You really don't want to fight me."

"Scared are you?" Emer sneered.

Alric looked at Emer and then turned back to say something to Brenna. Suddenly Alric twisted back around in his chair and a spoon flew through the air and thumped Emer in the chest. The suddenness of the action caught him off guard and he let out an involuntary yelp as his dagger clattered to the floor.

Alric smiled broadly. "Killed by a spoon!"

There was a burst of loud laughter as Emer flushed in embarrassment and anger. "You'll pay for this," he threatened.

"Come come dear, do sit down," Pavia cajoled. "I'm sure the physicians can heal the terrible scar left by that dangerous spoon." She turned to Alric. "You really must be more careful. A spoon like that could kill somebody." She slowly folded her hands on her lap. "Or make a pudding."

Diad barked a laugh and several others joined in.

"Now that's putting him in his place," Raefgot slurred.

Emer continued to stand, fuming at everyone at the table.

"Sit down Emer," Diad ordered. Emer continued to glare. "I said sit down." Diad leaned towards him.

"Why must you always argue?" Again the soft voice spoke.

The King turned slowly to the Queen. "What's it to you?"

"They are my sons too." She spoke quietly, yet firmly.

"They are men now and no longer your concern," the King replied. With a flip of the hand, he dismissed her and turned his attention to finding the serving girl.

There was a pregnant pause until everyone realized that the King was occupied elsewhere. Menec politely spoke across the table to the Queen.

"Queen Guina, I understand your lessons with Father Konrud are going quite well." The King momentarily frowned at Menec, but the serving girl diverted his attention as she came to check his goblet. She stood close enough for Diad to begin groping her legs.

The Queen seemed unaffected by Diad's display. "Yes they are. In fact," she turned to Duncan, "I was interested in Lord Duncan's appraisal of such a thorny question as God's existence. How did your arguments go?"

Duncan suddenly realized that she had not called him 'wizard' as was everyone else's fashion. Actually, she seemed quite disarming. *She's pretty. Wonder why the old goat's lost interest in her?* Duncan cordially smiled. "It's rather a long-winded and convoluted series of arguments, m'Lady. Empirically, God's existence is exceedingly difficult to prove."

"Perhaps the cosmological argument was not properly stated." She smiled demurely.

This time it was Duncan's turn to be surprised. He smiled despite himself. "And how would you state it, m'Lady?"

"Well," Guina paused to take a breath, "I believe there are six formal steps beginning with 'some limited, changing beings exist', and ending with 'the first uncaused Cause is identical to the God of Safti."

He stared at her, as if unable to respond. She was actually offering a logically valid proof. He unconsciously furrowed his eyebrows. *You understand....you actually understand...*"M'Lady, you've offered an excellent argument." *I wonder... just how clever are you?* "But how would you explain that no being can actualize its own potential for existence?"

"Because there must be something beyond it that causes it to exist." The reply was fast, succinct.

Looking into her eyes, he realized that she probably understood far more than she allowed. She was solemn, yet there was a sparkle in her eyes that spoke of an inner energy, an inner desire to know more. And for some inexplicable reason, he found himself wanting to know more about her, wishing he could spend time with her... not that the King would probably mind... *Why does it seem that no one listens to you?*

"Excellent answer m'Lady," he graciously bowed.

"What was an excellent answer?" The King barked, his hand underneath the woman's skirt.

"Her response to my question, sire. We were talking about God's existence." He began to explain.

"A pox on God's existence," the King shouted. "I command all conversation about God to stop!"

"Does that include prayer?" Alric flippantly replied.

"Don't cross me boy! You know damn well what I mean." He forcibly sat the woman on his lap and roared, "More wine!"

Alric turned to Alexis. "He's like this whenever he gets drunk. I wouldn't pay him too much mind." He did a quick up and down of his new berserker. *Nice body. Wonder how you are in bed... I bet I could show you a grand time.* He looked past her to where Duncan was still talking to the Queen. *Don't think you're gonna be much of a challenge. You may be with her for now...* He smiled at her. "Wizard." Duncan turned back around. "Tell her I look forward to watching her fight." With calm assurance, Alric watched the slight irritation that flitted across his face as he began to translate.

"Tell him that I too look forward to a good fight. Perhaps I will have the pleasure of watching him fight also." Alexis smiled matter-of-factly.

"I also hear that you've claimed a tarrac already," Alric said with subtle condescension

"What?" Diad overheard the comment. "She has a tarrac?"

Brenna smiled. "It's true m'Lord. She has Oswiu's tarrac. It was amazing to see. The handlers had already tried to put him down, but he wouldn't give up. When we came, he was almost dead and then she took control. He's alive now and probably will live for a long time. I believe that Stracaim has given loyalty to her. I have never seen anything like it before."

"It's true Sire," Menec added. "Stracaim is hers now."

The King appraised the two newcomers. "Apparently there are many new things happening since the arrival of these two."

Suddenly the doors swung open and a warrior stumbled in, gasping. "King Diad! M'Lord! The Rugians have attacked!"

The news had been electric and the drunk King tried his best to issue commands to assemble the war council. Those present at the dinner were already on their way to their respective homes to prepare. Alric had tagged along with Alexis, Brenna, and Duncan as they hurried to Alexis' house. Alric easily kept the pace.

"Does this woman belong to you?" Alric asked Duncan as they moved down the road, the evening crowds beginning to thicken as they came towards the market area.

"Her? She belongs to no one," Duncan growled.

"Not yet," Alric added smugly. "That's good. Then you won't mind translating for me? Tell her that she's the best looking berserker I've ever seen. How can it be that a warrior as powerful as she could be so beautiful?"

After he translated, Alexis smiled and said, "Well, what about High Commander Brenna?"

Alric responded, "Yes, she is, well... pretty, but she doesn't really interest me."

Brenna grew irritable at Alric's flirtatious prattle and interrupted, "We all know what interests you Alric – women with so little brains they will find you attractive. You insult my friend with your attentions."

"I think you sound like a woman who would desire that attention," he retorted.

"You forget Alric, I had those attentions once, and there is nothing desirable in them," she quickly attacked.

"What is considered desirable depends on one's appetite. It appears that we have the same appetite." Smiling, Alric raised his eyebrows knowingly.

Duncan protested, "Yeah, I'd love to referee this pissing contest, but don't you guys have a war to go to or something?"

"Correct, Wizard. As Commander, I am responsible for the protection of my country. In fact, if you like, you could come along and watch my own wizardry on the field of battle."

"Just imagine my excitement," he deadpanned.

Alric turned and took Alexis's hand, "You do understand some Gambri?"

"Yes," she half-smiled and looked down at her hand in his.

"Good. You will stand next to me at the council." he said clearly and slowly to ensure she understood. "Yes?"

"I understand," she replied.

Alric leaned down and kissed Alexis's hand. Duncan rolled his eyes and Brenna stepped closer to Alexis as the prince moved away. Smiling warmly in response to Brenna's piercing disapproval, he strode off to his quarters, whistling loudly.

Brenna looked quickly at Alexis who deliberately wiped her hand on her gown as if removing a stain.

As they walked, Duncan commented, "I don't understand why King Diad treats the Queen like tarrac dung. She's strikes me as being exceptionally intelligent."

Brenna smirked at Duncan's language. "You're learning the slang very well. But you're right; she is very intelligent. The King's mistreatment attests more to the shortcomings of the king than of the queen. Some recognize her true talents. She was educated and trained to be a leader of the people. But the king doesn't appreciate her, and many follow his lead."

"Apparently you're fond of her," he observed.

"I have reason to be. It was at her request that the king adopted me. She has treated me like a daughter, and I am grateful to her," she explained. A glint of light in the shadow immediately to their left caught her eye. She abruptly stopped. "I'll catch up. I forgot, I needed to make a stop or two before going home."

Alexis called to her as she turned away. "Do I come too?"

"No, I'll meet you. War council. One hour." Brenna responded simply so she could understand.

As Duncan and Alexis moved down the walk, Brenna stepped casually to a merchant's stand where, though late, the vendor was offering choice fruits and sweets. While picking up and examining various pieces of fruit, she kept watch out of the corner of her eye. A shadow suddenly moved. She half-crouched, spun around and swept the feet out from under the would-be attacker. Despite the unexpected trip, he twisted to thrust a knife at her. She blocked the stab and followed with a sharp chop to his throat. The attacker gasped and dropped the knife. Brenna grabbed it and slit his throat in one swift arc, then threw down the knife beside him.

The merchant looked at her wide-eyed. She stood back up and turned to him, calmly pointing to the fruit. "I'll take two of these and one of those."

"Master Wizard," the King said, "we need your help in communicating with the new berserker."

They were standing amidst the agitated turmoil in a large, well-apportioned room next to the throne room where Alexis had assumed her right as berserker the day prior. In contrast to the openness and lack of decorations in the throne room, this room was adorned with rich and vivid tapestries depicting ancient battle scenes in vibrant reds, deep greens, cobalt blues and brilliant golds. Finely carved chairs were placed at intervals against the walls. One wall alone held the tall clear windows that allowed the moon-filled night to glow through sheer gossamer curtains. Underneath the window ledges were ornately carved benches with thick purple cushions. In addition to the moonlight filtering brightly through the windows, there were several large crystals in the ceiling cleverly disguised as part of brightly painted scenes of lovers in the forest meadows.

In the center was a large square terrain table around which several men were standing, pointing to one part of the table-top. Alexis and Brenna were off to one side, near the main door to the room.

"Her name is Alexis, Sire," Duncan bowed slightly in deference.

The King paused as if finally yielding to fate. "Yes, certainly... Alexis. Well," he resumed, "we need for you to make her understand that she is essential to our success."

"Yes m'Lord."

"Alric," he called out as he walked to the table, Duncan in tow.

"Yes father?" The king's second son moved with confidence as he pushed his way up to the table. His thick, light brown hair was pulled back from his face by a leather head-band. Duncan reappraised him. He was more muscular than Duncan realized.

"Gefnyn asks for immediate help. He presently holds them, here." He pointed to an upper part of the table and Duncan realized that the table top was carved with a relief of the country of Gambri. A flat area in the center represented the Starn Sea. The borders of the table were either mountains or another flat area representing the wastelands. "I believe three hundred warriors should be sufficient to help him, don't you think?"

"Three hundred? Father, if Gefnyn needs our help so desperately, perhaps we should send more?"

"Gefnyn holds them to a stand-still which means he has enough to stop any further incursion. What we need are enough men to push them back across the river, without taking away resources to protect the rest of our kingdom." He looked around the room for both a challenge and support. None came.

"Make a decision cousin," said a barrel-chested man of thick muscular arms and legs, leaning on the table, his smile off-set by cold eyes. "That's Gefnyn's domain, right next door to me and I'll need to get back quickly."

After an awkward silence, Bradwr coughed lightly and spoke. "Brother, perhaps Alric is right. Three hundred does seem a paltry number. One would think that if the Rugians were strong enough to break into Gefnyn's boundaries, they would be strong enough to hold what they presently have. And who's to say they haven't more reinforcements on the way?"

A tremor of anger swelled in the King. But before he could respond, the barrel chested man spoke. "Will you supply the additional men, cousin?"

Bradwr smiled thinly at him. "I don't think I need to, cousin Harun. After all, we do have a standing army. Why should I have to supply more men? What are our taxes for if not to support our army?"

"You speak well, but miss the truth," another of the Council of the Right Hand spoke.

Bradwr slowly turned his attention from Harun to Banain, one of the few old men in the room. "And how is that, cousin?"

Banain shook his head at Bradwr. "My dear young cousin," he began. "If you're so concerned with sending more warriors, then perhaps you should send more. However, I suggest that you listen to the advice of older and wiser heads, ones who have actually tasted battle. Perhaps then you

203

would better understand the difference between governing a province and commanding a battle."

Bradwr flushed at the jab, but quickly recovered. "I'm sure you're right Cousin Banain, which is why you stepped aside to allow your son to govern the province now in jeopardy." Banain subtly bristled at the insult. "But I merely point out the wisdom of Alric's counsel."

"Perhaps. Yet now you would have us send more warriors. How many would you send Lord Bradwr?" Banain taunted.

Bradwr thought quickly. *Sending three hundred is a pittance... but to send more could cause suspicion among these cautious men... On the positive side, it is Gefnyn who loses some of his own men in this skirmish...* He looked briefly at Harun. *I need to keep you and Gefnyn occupied, and this is the perfect cause. I need just a little more time...*

Smiling, he bowed in mock humility. "You are right as usual, cousin. Perhaps I may have been a bit rash. Three hundred is enough. But I submit that a proven leader must command this force, someone who can not only win this battle, but make use of the new berserker – one such as Alric." Momentarily surprised, Alric glowed at the offer as Bradwr deftly turned attention to his nephew.

There was an overwhelming support for his recommendation, and as the clamor subsided, Timon, another of the Council leaned over to Bradwr. "Well done," he smirked.

The King relaxed, knowing that he had the support of the majority of the Council. "Right. Then it's settled."

Absolved from further planning, the king wandered over to a servant to have him fetch more wine, while Alric continued the preparations. They would leave first light tomorrow morning and march until they reached Brecknot, the capital of Gefnyn's domain. There, they would replenish food stores and march to confront the enemy on the next day. The battle would occur the following morning. Satisfied, the group mumbled their gratitude and excused themselves, most ready to return to the comfort of their own bedrooms.

Diad smiled thinly, waiting for the crowd of men to slowly amble their way out of the room, holding up a hand for his son to remain. When the last straggler emptied the room and the servants closed the doors, he turned to Alric.

"Bradwr did well naming you the commander. Being Army Commander is one thing. Leading men in battle is another. I remember when your grandfather made me made Army Commander. I had yet to fight a battle. Though I was young, I was ready to prove myself. You must command more and more if you are to win their hearts." Diad stared into Alric's eyes. "Although I trust Bradwr about as much as a merchant promising the ancient vase was made before Gambria existed."

"Why is that father?" He knew the answer, but he wanted to hear it again.

Instead of answering, the king walked unsteadily over to the planning table. "And watch Meton. His last victory was lucky. He's too full of his own safety to be a good commander. Why I heard they almost had to beat his ass with a flat sword to get him to fight." He looked up towards the ceiling. "Wonder why Bradwr was so intent on Meton," he said to no one in particular.

"I'll watch him father." Alric wanted to go and prepare for the battle.

Suddenly his father looked back at him. "What think you of this new berserker?"

"Good looking woman," he stated matter-of-factly.

Diad sniffed in amusement. "I meant as a fighter."

"I've never seen her fight," he shrugged.

"I have," he nodded. "She's a demon." He paused and began pacing haphazardly around the room. "Yet I am not so sure about her. It seems unnatural to have a woman berserker." He pursed his lips. "Still, we have nothing to lose by taking her."

"The warrior-woman goes?" Alric raised an eyebrow in disbelief.

"Why not?"

"She's untested in battle. No one can talk with her except for this man who calls himself a wizard, and she would only hinder our battle plan."

"How?"

"She doesn't know our ways! Especially in combat."

"True... true... However, all she needs to understand is that she must fight for us by killing Rugians."

"That's easier said than accomplished." He watched his father for a moment, frustrated the man was drunk, which appeared to be a permanent state these days. The old man was still babbling on about a woman berserker and how it was unnatural for a woman to be stronger than a man. Alric stood silently watching his father walk around the room, waiting until he collected himself. It was times like these when he saw the fears and weaknesses of his father. Times like these when he saw that his father was simply a man, a king perhaps, but just a man. He knew that despite Emer being the legitimate heir to the throne, their father had always loved Alric more. And he knew that when his father was gone, there was going to be a struggle for the throne.

Why else would he groom me for combat? My dear brother Emer, you of the books and law and numbers, you know nothing about people. You can't govern these people. It takes a man of strength, one they will respect, not some weakling who can't even control his own wife. The image of his brother's wife emerged. *Pavia, you delicious sensual creature, you should have been mine. Small wonder you look for fulfillment elsewhere. If you were mine, I'd know how to satisfy you and keep you coming back for more.* He snickered silently. *Maybe I'll show you someday...*

Alric awoke to find his father winding down and gaining back his composure. Diad had walked over to the table and was staring pensively at the map.

"I have it." His eyes glimmered as though appreciating a good joke. "You know how the Rugians always weight their left flank?"

"Yes father," he replied, the information obvious.

"Put this woman warrior in Meton's flank on the right. Maybe you... um... how shall I say...lighten the right flank, just a bit, just a bit," he held up his hand to halt Alric's startled look. "We don't want anything to happen to Meton, now do we?" Diad began pacing again. "Weight your left flank. Let the right flank hold until the left flank can roll up the line. Don't forget a reserve!"

Alric already knew what he was going to do, but patiently listened. "Yes father, I know, I've done this before. But what about Brenna?" He suddenly remembered the confidant of this new woman-warrior.

"Hmm... I suppose she ought to go... One of the Twelve... Tuathal will have to decide. Problem is, you need her to communicate with the berserker. I don't understand why she's so suddenly taken by this woman. Do you know?" Diad stared hard at Alric.

"No father, I don't know." He shifted uneasily. His father's cold eyes locked on him as though accusing Alric of some foul deed. *God, I hope he never finds out. How was I supposed to know she was going to become my sister?* He thought back to the brief time when Brenna had been much enamored with him, and he with her. She was Menec's daughter, the man his father had chosen as king's friend. Menec, though privileged as the King's friend, was still the tarrac-master and spent most of his time at the tarrac barns. Brenna grew up amidst the odors, feed, stalls, and tarracs. His first memory of her was a bossy girl with bits of hay in her hair, commanding him to not brush the tarrac that way.

Though born only months apart, Alric grew up in the pampered courts, while Brenna roamed the pastures, paddocks and barns outside the city walls. On occasion, Alric had noticed her when he was training his own tarrac. It wasn't until his sixteenth birthday, after he had received his warrior status, that he again noticed her. She had come to his celebration. He remembered her thinly disguised sexuality simmering below the surface of her skin. They had become lovers. She had the kind of sexual passion that he found overwhelming, and it frustrated him that he could never fully please her. Yet he found himself becoming possessive and jealous of her. That jealousy began to peak when she was granted warrior status just a few months later.

He went to the celebration, but refused to enjoy himself. He chaffed at the accolades heaped upon her, her prowess, her strength, her skill. He seethed at the attention the other women warriors gave her, ignoring him. He could see their affection and pride in her accomplishment and he loathed them, hating them all.

Alric's jealousy ended in rage one afternoon two weeks after her celebration. He had gone to the barn near the stables that afternoon and was surprised when he saw her talking and laughing with another woman at the opposite door. They hadn't seen him and he had said nothing, but simply watched as Brenna gave the woman a peck on the cheek and sauntered lazily out into the sunlight and up towards the castle. The other woman watched her walk away for a moment, and then began combing her hair with her fingers, pulling an occasional piece of hay from the long auburn strands. She wore tight leather riding pants and a high collared white blouse that was untucked. Her back was to him and when she turned, she saw him staring at her. Her blouse was unbuttoned.

"You're much too late," she mocked. She preened as he watched, tossing her hair behind her shoulders, then stretching seductively, exposing just enough of her breasts to create arousal. Aware of his naked fascination, she postured a bit more. Suddenly she laughed and Alric was jerked out of his voyeurism. "Maybe some other time." And she breezed by him so closely that he could smell her perfume.

He had stood there, alone, flushed in anger and embarrassment. He stormed out, and abruptly cut off all communication with Brenna, despite repeated messages in the next few days from her asking what was wrong.

A half-year later, his father had officially adopted Brenna as his daughter. Alric shook his head and frowned, *I've had sex with my own sister.*

Yet as far as he knew, the King either did not know about their dalliance, or chose to overlook it. Either way, he had never said anything about it. "You know I don't spend a lot of time with her, father."

"Yes, yes, I know." He gripped the edge of the table. "She's a strange one. I only adopted her as a favor to Menec."

"I know father."

The King looked around the room. "I expected her to be more thankful, more appreciative. Instead she spends all of her time with your mother."

He shrugged. "She's a woman. Who knows what motivates them?" He grinned broadly.

Diad looked up, realized the joke and smiled back in return. "Well, there it is. Do what you have to do." He clapped his son on the back and they walked out together, laughing like close friends do.

The Queen had remained seated after the news of the attack was announced. She watched the King, despite his intoxication, awaken to his responsibilities as he issued commands and then hurried out to the war room, Bradwr at his elbow. Alric had followed Brenna and Alexis out the main doors, the wizard Duncan bringing up the rear. Vix, being his usual self, had stormed out of the room, most likely making his way back to the Temple. Emer had sighed resignedly, looking as though he was about to say something to Pavia, who instead completely ignored her husband and had rushed out after Alric and company. Emer slid his chair back and looked at his mother.

"Good to see you Mother," he said, without emotion. He walked over to her and gave her a quick peck on her cheek. Looking at his brother, he shook his head and frowned, and then walked away.

When the doors closed and the noise had settled, only she and Raefgot remained. Raefgot had stood when the messenger had arrived, and had remained standing, albeit somewhat unsteadily, vacantly watching the others hurry away. When quiet descended on the hall, his focus fell on the table in front of him.

The Queen quietly pushed herself away from the table and started to walk to him, until she saw the drunken scowl on his face. She stopped and stared at him, in her heart a heavy sadness.

Raefgot hadn't immediately noticed her, but had continued to stare at the table, lost in his bitterness. His head was muddled with drink, and that was the way he liked it. He swayed a little as he reached down for the wine goblet. Peering into the cup, he didn't like the amount and looked back to the table for the wine jar. As he reached for the jar, he saw her, and her sadness.

"Join me for a drink, Mother?" His voice was thick. He poured more wine into the goblet, spilling some on the table.

"No thank you." Her voice was soft, caring. "Don't you think that perhaps you may have had enough?"

He shook his head and frowned. "Not really. And anyway, what's it matter? What's it to you?"

"You are my son." The response was simple, direct.

He looked at her through clouded eyes. "Really? You might want to tell that to Dad." Draining the cup, he slapped it down on the table. He poured another cupful and lifted it as in toast. "Here's to all the brave lads who answer the call. Fight boys, fight! Kill the Rugians! You are all heroes, yes sir, all heroes. The King commends you... well done lads, well done... a toast then, here's a toast to the brave Alric, a toast to the fair-haired gifted man, the chosen one of Diad." He fairly spit the words as he drained the cup, wine spilling down the sides of his mouth.

"Raefgot. That's enough," she implored.

Forgetting she was there, he poured yet another cup. "Another toast! Another toast to Emer, Emer the brain, the man so smart his wife cuckolds him in his own bedroom!" He started giggling. "In his own bedroom!" His humor took hold of him and he continued giggling and snickering and he leaned on the table. "In his own bedroom..."

Suddenly he stood back up and hoisted his goblet. Still giggling he held up his glass. "And here's to Raefgot, mister tarrac dung for brains... if he wasn't the king's son, he wouldn't have a piss to pot in..." He stopped for a moment, then burst out laughing at the mistake. "A piss to pot in! Or a poss to pit in!" His own wit overwhelmed him and sunk down onto the chair, still shaking in laughter.

As the laughter subsided, he grew solemn, morose. He lifted the goblet again and slurred, "Here's to Raefgot.... Raefgot the fool... Raefgot the simpleton... Raefgot the drunkard... Raefgot sit down... Raefgot, give your chair to the berserker... Raefgot, get out of the way..." He plopped the goblet back down on the table with a thud. He stared at the goblet with distracted fascination.

"Raefgot," the Queen called to him. Lost in his own thoughts, she called to him again, "Raefgot."

He looked up as if seeing her for the first time. "Hullo mother. What brings you here?" He looked at her quizzically, as if trying to determine just exactly where she was standing.

The Queen walked over to stand next to him, her step light and her movement soft. She had the fluid grace of one of the trained courtesans who lived in the Gardens district of the city. "Don't you think you've had enough?"

Ignoring the touch of her hand on his shoulder, he turned to stare at the goblet in his hands. "Why do they hate me mother?"

"No one hates you, son." Her voice was soft, reassuring.

He shook his head in disdain. "Where have you been? He hates you almost as much as he hates me."

Startled, the Queen asked, "Whom are you talking about?"

"Come off it Mother... stop playing games..." Raefgot suddenly felt very tired. He looked up to gaze at her through clouded and strained eyes. "Why does he hate us?" His tongue was thick and heavy, and he licked his lips several times. "Why?"

In the brief interlude between his question and her answer, the memory of 'why' played itself out in rapid staccato scenes. The first was the very nature of the King. Marriage didn't necessarily mean fidelity. Then came the second in the difficult birth of Emer. Not only was her pain greater than she had ever known, it drained her of all life for several months following. She had little milk and so a nursemaid had to be found to nurture the King's first born.

Diad had been somewhat ecstatic, for he had his son, his heir. But he wanted more sons, needed more sons. And the Queen was responsible for giving him more sons. But the Queen needed to recover, and the King grew impatient. While he satisfied his desires with the courtesans, and even a winsome servant or two, he demanded she provide him another son. Despite her fragile condition, after several visits with the naming stone, she again conceived and Alric was born two years after Emer.

But Alric nearly killed her. Her body was torn apart, and this time the physician's response was simple; 'If you want to live, no more children.' Diad was angry with her as he saw what he viewed as his future, suddenly evaporate. His plans had called for many sons, so that his lineage would permeate the entire society as kings, council heads, military commanders, high priests, and guild captains.

And then a young courtesan caught his eye. She had been just old enough to begin training, when Diad saw her. She was flawless, and beautiful, her body not quite fully developed. He had asked for her and had been refused as she was still in training, still too young. But he was the King, and 'no' didn't really mean 'no.'

He became obsessed with her, the 'fool' part of him becoming too obvious. And she saw his lasciviousness. She saw it and designed her own future. When she did come of age, he was her first, and only, visitor. All knew of her status and kept quiet. Yet behind the curtains and closed doors, the gossip spread.

But she was more than his match. He soon found himself reacting to her whims, her desires. As the Queen's stature diminished, hers ascended. Her overt disdain for the Queen found support in Diad's own disappointment in his wife. In but a short time, the Queen was all but forgotten, while this nubile young woman enjoyed the enforced fawning of the people.

And then she struck. Convincing the King that she could produce more children than his current shriveled queen, they descended into the naming chamber together and united. In less than a month, she was pregnant.

As the child inside her grew, so too did her demands. The Queen was relegated to other quarters, while she demanded more accolades, more attention, more promises. As her demands and haughtiness grew, Diad's infatuation began to subside. Falling back into old habits, he didn't like her demands that he stop satisfying himself with other women. Their fights were loud and acrimonious, and frequent.

Although not a wife, she was the mother of his son, and Gambrian law allowed her rights, as well as rights for her child. And she had done her homework, quoting the finer points of jurisprudence to remind Diad of those rights. Diad's usual retort was that he already had a queen, and didn't need another one telling him what to do. If she continued to harangue him, he would rewrite the damn law and see to it she spent her days in the wastelands.

Midway through her pregnancy, he came to regret his impetuous lust with her. Her shrill harping grated on his nerves and he sought ways to stay away. At least the Queen had turned a blind eye to all his past dalliances. But by then, he had been reduced to conducting the affairs of state during the day, and then spending his nights either in his personal chambers, or in the arms of more understanding, and accommodating, young lovers.

But fate sometimes has a way of solving the most difficult of problems. The woman died in childbirth, and Diad's problems were solved... to a point. By law, the sickly child they produced and called Raefgot, was entitled to the privileges of a prince. However, while the woman was quickly cremated and forgotten, the King now had to deal with a whiny child who demanded attention. Reminding him too much of the child's mother, Diad quickly relegated Raefgot to the nursemaids and house-staff.

To the king's indifferent neglect, the Queen offered the role of loving mother, and doted on Raefgot as she had her other sons. She forbade any mention of Raefgot's parentage and ensured that he was treated as well as the other two sons.

Yet as they grew into manhood, the differences among the three sons emerged. Emer, the oldest, found greater joy in books than wielding a sword. His antipathy towards the physical part of life created disharmony with his father who demanded Emer act like a future king. Emer's solution was to try and win favor with his brains. Unfortunately, all his knowledge could not sway his father, and Diad took to not so subtle teasing hoping to shame Emer into becoming more like Alric.

Alric... the golden child, the child loved most by Diad. Alric reminded Diad of himself. Whereas Emer was left to fend for himself, Diad ensured Alric had the best training, the best teachers, the best tarracs, even the best wardrobe. Were it not for the Queen, the other sons would have been completely neglected.

And then there was Raefgot. Having neither the brains of Emer nor the physical prowess of Alric, he was shunted aside like a useless appendage. Despite the Queen's best efforts, Raefgot soon went his own way, a sulking and sullen youth who determined the world was against him. Even his best efforts at gaining his father's attention only brought ridicule.

He soon gained a reputation as a wastrel, a princely wastrel. While none found anything about him particularly inviting, the money of a prince was another matter. Pub owners and brothels found him to be a faithful client, and they always welcomed him cheerfully. Yet that same cheer evaporated when he became too obnoxious, or the money ran out. Then, they were quite happy to toss him out onto the street, just like any other commoner.

The Queen's melancholy emerged in a low sigh. She was about to answer him when he looked up at her and held his finger up to his lips.

"Shhhh." He motioned her to come closer. "Shhhhh."

She leaned a little closer. His breath reeked of wine, and his eyes were red-veined and watery. She fought back her disgust at both his drunkenness and his smell.

"Shhhh," he whispered conspiratorially. "I know why."

"Why what?"

"Why they hate me."

The Queen said nothing, but simply stared at him.

Raefgot motioned her to come even closer. When she was close enough, he smiled knowingly. "I'm a bastard."

Guina jerked back up in a mixture of surprise and consternation. "What?"

He turned his attention to the wine goblet. "I'm a bastard."

"Who told you that?" the queen quietly demanded.

Raefgot sniffed in derision. "I can read, y'know. You made sure of that." He sadly shook his head, and as if to no one, said "I can understand me...but why you? Why you?" Placing his elbows on the table, he crossed his arms and settled his head on top. In but a moment, he was asleep.

The Queen stood immobile as she watched him drift to sleep. Her surprise at his discovery had momentarily disconcerted her. Yet, while she was saddened at his new found knowledge, she was simultaneously relieved. At least now she no longer had to take precautions to protect his past. Perhaps his recognition, and acceptance, of his past might strengthen him, ennoble him to want to prove himself.

Raefgot's heavy breathing suddenly turned into a loud snore. The Queen watched him sleep a bit more before turning to leave, thinking to herself, *and then again... perhaps not.*

Emer stood on the outside steps watching the dwindling shadows of his brother and the others as they walked across the courtyard and through the far arched gate. He counted four of them, and instinctively knew that Pavia was already on her way to some assignation. For a fleeting moment, he had the urge to try and discover her whereabouts, barge in, and claim righteous indignation. But the emotion just as swiftly passed as he shook his head to clarity. What would it matter? She cared little for their marriage or her reputation. He would divorce her if he could, but neither Diad nor Bradwr would allow it.

He remembered the one, and only, time he had followed her. He had pursued her trail to the tarrac barns and one of the tack rooms. Waiting for the right moment, he had burst in and loudly exclaimed his fury. Pavia and her lover, a young muscular warrior, were in the middle of their intense passion on top of one of the heavy work tables. Instead of shock, they continued as though he were a mere servant come to ask if they needed anything. Emer had awkwardly remained as though rooted there, watching with a strange preoccupation the sheen of perspiration on Pavia's body. Then, as she mounted the virile warrior, and began the rhythmic movement at her hips, she looked over to Emer and huskily told him, "Take notes scholar; this is how it's done." Shocked to embarrassment, he had fled. From then on, he avoided her, and they settled into a routine of indifference, neither caring of the other's activities.

Although, he smiled in grim satisfaction, he did get his revenge on the young warrior shortly after, when the Rugians had crossed the border. Emer had gone to the battle captain, Uncle Coilin, and requested that the warrior be placed in the front lines. Coilin hadn't even asked why, but very matter-of-factly did as Emer asked. The warrior was killed in the first wave. Emer sent his uncle a cask of the finest wine in appreciation.

On a rare occasion, he had thought of playing her game, taking other lovers. But that seemed so common, so wharf-trash. Those kinds of people were nothing but animals, rutting in the dirt of their own bestial desires. He easily reminded himself that he was nothing like that, nothing like his father. Then thinking of his uncle Bradwr, he briefly wondered why the man hadn't taken lovers, or at least remarried since Toreth's death so long ago. Emer nodded in begrudging admiration. At least the man had the good sense to keep his private affairs to himself.

Emer then thought about the four who had just left. Of the four, only the wizard seemed the most interesting. It was obvious he was educated, but unfortunately seemed far too interested in religion, and as any truly educated person knew, religion was merely a crutch to keep the ignorant masses in check. He was amazed at the number of seemingly intelligent people who blindly followed Safti without ever understanding what was written. As far as he could tell, and he'd read the sacred book often enough, Safti was merely a lucky man fleeing some devastation, who managed to lead a group of survivors to settle in Mull Was it a miracle they survived, or luck, or simply happenstance? And what was it about Safti that warranted making him some sort of holy man? Far too many dim-witted fools blamed Safti for all sorts of happenings in their lives, whether ill or good.

Emer shook his head in the sad awareness that the masses of Gambria were pathetic creatures, capable of little intellectual progress unless led by those with far greater wisdom than themselves. These especially included those who chose fighting as their livelihood. His partial sneer revealed his feelings – while there was a place in society for the warrior, the ruling elite should come from the enlightened, the educated class. Society needed warriors much like it needed draft animals, someone to do the heavy lifting.

Men like Alric, or the Twelve… or even his father, were anachronisms. The cult of the warrior, the near apotheosis of physical strongmen, was a hindrance to proper and just government. When he became king, he would put all in its proper place.

Adjusting his robe, he walked down the steps into the warm night, breathing deeply the flower-scented air. It was a clean smell, an alive smell. For some reason, he felt content. When he became king, he would divorce Pavia, perhaps even exile her to the wastelands. Then he would marry a woman worthy of himself, a woman who had a thirst for knowledge, a woman in many ways like himself, a woman, curiously enough, much like his mother. He raised an eyebrow at the thought, remembering the old myth of the young prince who murdered his father and brothers, then forced his mother to bed. The anakeem, the mythical giants of old were the result of the ill-omened union. Emer gave a brief shudder and in discomfit brushed away the uneasy feelings from his arms. While he loved his mother, the very thought of coupling with her disgusted him. Then just as suddenly, he brightened at the thought that there had to be another woman, one like his mother, who would be his perfect match.

With a light step, Emer sauntered out the garden gate and then along the path that led to the main doors of the king's residence. Upon seeing him, the guards bowed deferentially and opened the large heavy doors. Nodding politely, Emer emerged onto the still crowded streets and made his way towards Buckom, the place of his greatest joy. Buckom… Buckom… Not for the last time, he easily remembered the etymology of the word, Buckom. From his studies, he knew it to be the derivative of 'Book-Home,' the place of books and learning, and now the place of scholars. It was there that he felt truly at home, among books, manuscripts, scholars, and even the servants.

Buckom was a large, many-level building that filled several blocks of the city. It was the repository of all the writings of Gambria, as well as the lodgings of the senior scholars. As a Master Scholar, Emer was entitled to his own set of private quarters here. The fact that he chose to spend all his time here did not go unnoticed by either Diad or Bradwr. Both harangued him often enough about producing an heir. He frowned as he walked, wondering how the two of them could be so obtuse, for they had to know of Pavia's flagrant indiscretions.

The flickering glow of the streetlamps gave a warm glow to the night. Merchants, revelers, and others out simply to enjoy the evening, bowed appropriately as he passed by. Emer had some time ago decided that they bowed to him out of respect to his achievements as a scholar, not because he was the king's son. The fact that he wore his Master Scholar robes certainly helped being noticed.

Emer pretended to brush something off one of the felt sleeve chevrons, simply to remind himself of his distinction. He was a Master Scholar of the First Rank, one of only ten in the entire kingdom. He preened slightly in acknowledgement of his own accomplishment, and nodded magnanimously to the adulterated masses, those illiterate sows.

Carefully avoiding the already inebriated who bumped and swayed their way through the crowd, he quickened his pace as he saw his sanctuary in the distance. For some reason, the silhouette triggered memories of his first days at Buckom. Not having the physical prowess of his brother Alric, Emer had early on decided that knowledge was far more powerful than any physical weapon. He threw himself into his studies, finding all means of excuses to stay in the revered halls of wisdom.

Diad had tried forcing him to learn the art of war, but Emer proved to be inept, or rather uninterested.

"Damn it boy," his father had bellowed, "you fight like a girl."

"If I have an army to do my fighting, father, why must I learn?" Emer was yet ten summers old, but already a scholar of the eighth rank. The rapture of the Grand Master Scholar at the desire of this young boy had overflowed to allowing him to wear the robes of his rank, something reserved only for those who had attained both the requisite age and rank. Even Diad had begrudgingly admitted that he took secret joy in seeing his son parading around in his little robes. But that didn't excuse him from learning the skill of the warrior. Besides, the little twit was beginning to get arrogant in his education.

"You know damn well why. How do you expect to lead anyone if you don't know what they experience?"

"Does that mean you're going to send me into battle?" came the innocent reply.

"Of course not –"

"Well then why do I have to learn how to fight?"

"Dammit, because you'd be killed in an instant."

"But if you're not going to send me to battle, then I won't have to worry about being killed."

In loud frustration, Diad had spun in his heals and growled to the trainer, "Do something with him dammit! Beat some sense into him." He stalked off the training ward, grumbling audibly.

The trainer, a far more patient man, had motioned for Emer to raise his shield and pretend to spar as his father walked off. When Diad had disappeared, the trainer lowered his shield and sword.

"Do you wish to be a good king?"

"Yes."

"Then you must learn as much as you can about everything, and that includes the art of war," came the wise reply.

"But I don't like fighting." Emer looked at the man, thankful that he could say what he felt without being yelled at.

The man nodded. "There is wisdom in what you say. But there are far too many others who do like to fight. How will you protect our citizens from their enemies if you do not know how to fight?"

"I'll send somebody else who knows how to fight."

"Then you would be seen as a coward."

"Father sends others to fight. Is he a coward?"

"That's not what I mean. Your father has fought in prior battles; he has proven himself."

"When Cein was king, he didn't fight any battles. Was he a coward?"

"That's because the Rugians never attacked while he was king. And no, he was not a coward."

"Perhaps the Rugians won't attack while I'm king, and then I won't be a coward."

The man shook his head and sighed. "That's enough. Go to your books and scholars. Ask them why we study war."

Emer grinned as he walked. He had asked the Grand Master Scholar why they studied war. He had replied that war was a necessary evil. Until all were educated like scholars and understood that peace brought far more prosperity than war, war would always occur. Then the old man had said something that Emer always remembered.

"While experience may teach, one cannot always learn correctly from experience, for one may be persuaded to the wrong path. Likewise, not every experience is desired. A woman gives birth to a child. Must a man likewise give birth so that he may understand what has occurred? Far better is it to have knowledge and wisdom so that one may rightly choose the best path."

Emer had liked that expression – 'choose the right path.' He liked it so well that he determined that when he was king, if he could live by that code, his future as the wisest king in Gambria history would be assured.

As Buckom grew larger before him, serenity settled over him, for here he could learn all he needed to know about governing this nation. Then Pavia suddenly jumped into his mind and he awakened to the bitter thought that if he was the wisest king, how did he end up with her? She could ruin everything. The calming comfort of Buckom reminded him the stark contrast between his noble desires and the trollop that would be queen. Would his reign be remembered for her wanton escapades?

Emer grimly walked up the steps to the large front doors. Lost in his own thoughts, he ignored the greetings of other scholars as they left to go home. Unaffected by his oblivious preoccupation, they simply smiled and walked on. Emer entered the large foyer, turned right and headed up the stairs towards his quarters. He took several steps down the second floor hallway before pausing to look over the railing down into the enormous study room below. Despite the hour, it was still alive with the bustle of scholars searching bookracks, or holding quiet conversations, or scraping chairs back from thick tables in order to sit and jot down notes.

He let the fullness of the ambiance wash over him, inhaling the fragrance of leather-bound books, oil-polished woods, and so many unwashed bodies all blended together. He nodded in acknowledgement. This was the future of Gambria. Pavia had no place here. There was only one solution, and that was to somehow get rid of her.

The only question was, how?

Chapter 17

Alexis was up early, the morning's nautical twilight just beginning. She had slipped out of the house and was down at the stables finding extra fodder, filling the water trough, and examining Stracaim's cuts and bruises. A little while later, several of the Twelve also arrived, each one nodding politely to her and then going off to attend his own tarrac. Occasional banter carried across the moist morning air. While others brushed and combed their respective tarracs, Stracaim stirred, looking from side to side at the activity in the other stalls. As the other tarrac were led out, he fretted and pawed.

"Not this time fella," she smiled, continuing to gently brush, comb, and attend to the healing wounds. She walked to his front and stood before him, hands on her hips. "Don't even think it. You're not healed yet."

"I thought I'd find you here." Duncan startled her. "You taking the nag?"

"No," she answered, ignoring the insult. "He's surprisingly stronger, but far from healed. It would be stupid to take him and not be able to use him."

"Yeah, sure." His response was distracted. A long awkward quiet followed, interrupted by the scraping of brush on Tarrac hide. He watched her focused attention to the delicate grooming. Occasionally the Tarrac would bounce and shake his head, twisting every now and then to bump or push Alexis. "What's the matter with him?"

She paused her brushing and stepped back. "Nothing serious. He knows something's up." She walked to the tarrac's front and grabbed the bridle, pulling the giant animal's head toward hers. "Listen up you big brute. I've already told you you're not going, so forget it." She resumed her attention to the tarrac's bruises and the silence again filled the stable.

Duncan shifted uncomfortably for a bit. "Look Alexis, you gonna be OK out there?"

She began scratching Stracaim behind the curled horns. "Absolutely. This is the kind of fighting I understand, not all this hocus pocus and political B.S. you seem to revel in." She looked intently at him. "And what

219

about all of this miracle stuff? I don't know what sort of trick you have up your sleeve, but if it doesn't impress everyone, Vix'll serve your roasted guts to the vultures."

"You forget, I'm the promised one of Safti." He smiled softly.

She shook her head and walked over to him. "Duncan, I'm serious. You're getting into a game where you don't know the rules. These people are piranhas and they'll eat you alive."

He blinked several times as he listened. *Is it possible that you might really care what happens to me?* "Alexis, I know what I'm doing."

"Really?" She raised an eyebrow. "Then why are they trying to kill you?"

"Bad hair?" he shrugged, and they both laughed.

She shook her head again. "You just stay out of trouble until I get back."

He suddenly grew solemn. "Speaking of getting back, you're the one who has to be careful. This is going to be a major battle. What kind of experience do you have doing that?"

Alexis relaxed. "I've trained my whole life to be a fighter. I'm one of the best gladiators in the entire federation... at least I was. Anyway, it's not like I'll be fighting them by myself."

"I know, I know. It's just that, I uh..."

"Alexis!" Brenna called as she rode up. "Time to go." Brenna reined in her mount not far from Stracaim and pointed to the tarrac. "Tie him very well." She turned to Duncan. "Hello Wizard. Beautiful morning for a battle isn't it."

Her obvious excitement irritated him, for he could see the same excitement begin to grow in Alexis. Brenna extended her arm, clasped Alexis' and easily swung her up onto the tarrac behind her. Settling herself, Alexis turned to Duncan.

"Take care of yourself Duncan Stuart."

Brenna kicked her heals into the animal's ribs and the tarrac cantered away. Alexis swung back around to hold onto her.

Duncan watched for moment before calling out, "Good luck!" Without turning, Alexis waved a hand in acknowledgment. He continued watching as the women joined the lead group in front of the milling warriors. With banners unfurled, the curled horns sounded the call to assembly and the warriors quickly formed marching ranks. Without further ceremonial pomp, another horn sounded the call to march and the group surged forward.

Brenna's tarrac was almost as large as Stracaim, deep brown with gold glints in his coat. His horns were smaller, suggesting a younger animal, but his muscle and power were evident.

"This is Cymy." she explained. "Very brave and good fighter."

Alexis nodded. "He is a very brave and good fighting tarrac." She spoke the words slowly.

Brenna grinned. "Eh, you are learning very quickly!"

They rode on in silence for a while again. Alexis looked at the group in which they rode. There were six in her group, seven counting her. She and Brenna were the only women. Again, except for her, the six warriors wore the same dress – leather leggings of deep brown hide with the thick fine hairs still attached. Each also wore a sleeveless jerkin of thicker brown leather, supplemented with sewn-in chain mail at the armpits and ribs. Likewise, each wore a torque of twisted gold. Around the left arm was a similar gold armband designed as twin entwining snakes.

"Who are these warriors?" Alexis asked, looking around at the six warriors.

"These are warriors of the twelfth rank," Brenna responded. "Only six may go to battle at a time. The rest remain to protect the king and kingdom."

"And who is with Alric?"

"Alric is the battle commander. The others riding with him are the battle captains."

"I thought Alric was the Commander. Why is he going?"

Brenna frowned. "Yes, Alric is the Commander of all of Gambria's forces, but it is more of a ceremonial term. In reality, King Diad is the Commander, but even he will not do anything unless he has the support of the Council of the Right Hand."

"Why not?" She squirmed a bit to get comfortable.

"Each member of the Council provides warriors for the battle. It has happened in the past that several Council members have withheld their support, forcing other members to provide more warriors for their own defense. When this happens, some Council members have been known to attack. Naturally this creates hard feelings." She smirked, saw Alexis' concern, and then quickly added, "But it hasn't happened for quite some time. The last time was long before Diad was King."

"If Alric isn't the commander –"

"But he is."

"I know, but you said only in name."

"Let me explain. Each battle requires a new battle captain."

"Why?"

She patted Alexis' leg. "I'm getting there. Having more warriors experienced as battle commanders allows us to win any battle."

"I don't understand." Alexis shifted again.

"Suppose Alric falls in battle. There is another battle commander already experienced, ready to take his place."

Alexis nodded to the group ahead. "So each of those riding with him has experience as battle commanders?"

"Exactly."

Pausing in thought, she asked, "Why do we fight the Rugians?"

Brenna snorted. "They are the enemy."

"Why?"

Brenna blinked several times. "They have always been the enemy."

"Was there ever a time when they weren't?"

"Not that I can recall," she answered. Alexis shifted again. "It has been a long time since you've ridden a tarrac?"

"Yes, quite a long time," she grinned. "But he is a fine animal. I understand why you are proud of him."

Suddenly there was a commotion behind them, some shouts mixed with laughter and whistles. The two riders turned to see the cause just as Alexis' giant beast came rumbling up in a labored gallop.

"My god, it's Stracaim!" Alexis' jaw dropped. Dragging behind him was the heavy rope she had used to secure him, half of the shattered remains of a thick hitching post still attached and digging a shallow trench.

Brenna quickly brought Cymy to a halt. The rest of the Twelve reigned in and looked on amusedly before turning their animals to continue the march.

Alexis jumped off as the animal ambled up and stopped in front of her, dropping its large head to her. He was flecked with sweat and was breathing heavily. Yet he still appeared strong. Alexis quickly detached the rope and post.

"You big dummy," she grinned broadly, patting and scratching the wet hide. "I guess he's coming," she said turning to Brenna.

"You cannot ride him." Brenna firmly spoke. "You will have to tie him to a wagon."

"You go on ahead. I'll wait here for the baggage wagons."

Brenna looked down at her quickly realizing there was nothing she could say that would make the berserker do otherwise. Sighing loudly, she slipped off Cymy. "I'll wait with you."

"I'll be OK," Alexis comforted. "You go with the others. I'll find you when we get to where we're going."

Brenna turned to see the other elite warriors dwindling in the distance. "Eh, who cares. They won't fight without us." She laughed. "Perhaps they'll have something worth eating when the galley wagons get here."

Duncan had spent the morning wandering aimlessly around the house. Tene had watched him from a distance, not sure if she should interfere. Finally she could stand it no longer.

"Duncan, you have walked the halls and gardens far enough to be beside her," she said quietly.

"Huh?" He stared at her as if seeing her for the first time.

"Lady Alexis... You miss her?"

"Well certainly." His response was blunt.

Tene's shoulders slumped a bit, but she continued. "She is a very brave and strong woman. She will make you very happy."

"Huh?"

"Perhaps you and she will find someone to give you a roan for his essence."

He crooked an eyebrow at her. "His what?"

"His essence. You will have many fine children."

Cocking his head to the side, he stared at her. "What are you talking about?"

"You and Lady Alexis...together... you will have children." Her voice was soft, almost muted.

"Why would she and I have children?" He was openly puzzled.

Now it was Tene's turn to be puzzled. "But... you two... are you not...do you not love her?"

He briefly pondered the question. "Well...not really." His tone was matter-of-fact.

Tene suddenly brightened at the bit of information. "You are not in love with her?"

"No." Duncan abruptly realized the meaning behind Tene's questions. "She's my friend."

Tene nodded wisely. "That is good, to be concerned for your friends. She is very lucky to have a friend like you."

He smiled at the repetition of the word 'friend'. "Tene, I need you to help me with something. I need to know more about your religion. Is there someone I can talk to?"

Tene smiled. "Yes there is. But I'll need to find out if he can see you. When do you want to go?"

"Immediately."

"Ooh, I don't know if I can arrange it so soon. He's usually very busy."

"Who is it?" he asked.

"Father Lucan."

The man peered out the window high above the city walls. The morning sun was high in the bright day. Out in the distance, he could see the boats cresting the waves, hauling the fishing nets behind them. Every year at about the same time, the bounty of fish was so much that the boats could not load the catch on board and so had to drag the over-flowing nets behind them. For the next many months, there was plenty of food for all, and even the poor would eat their fill. Most of the fish would be salted or smoked, and the smoke houses would ooze the pungent wisps of smoke from piquant wood tossed upon glowing coals.

He inhaled deeply, almost tasting the moist sea air. "Beautiful day isn't it?" He turned to his guest, a rather plain man with short cropped hair and wide cheekbones. He was standing in front of the large desk that filled the room.

"Yes 'tis, m'Lord. A beautiful day in Gambria." He bowed deferentially.

"So," he stared at his guest. "I believe this bit of information warrants an equal measure of value. True?"

"It is not my place to set a price m'Lord," the guest clasped his hands together. "But I do agree, this is most noteworthy. I have brought the agreed upon transaction price, and," he bowed slightly, "I am willing to sign a promissory note authorizing additional payment."

Smiling in response, Bradwr walked back to the window. "You know, I find it amazing that you can come and go so easily."

The guest chuckled. "It is not as easy as you think, m'Lord, especially traveling with this." He patted the bags of coins on the table.

"Yes, I know. I appreciate you putting it all in useable currency." The guest bowed. "You have the message then?"

"Quite m'Lord. The right flank will be light. The berserker is in the right flank. She is a woman, but an outstanding fighter. Your left flank will contain the weight of your attack. There are only three hunbdrd of your elite warriors coming to assist. Anything else?"

"No," he eyed the coin bags. "Have a safe journey back to Rugia."

Watching his guest nonchalantly amble away, he laughed to himself. This was the easiest money he'd ever taken. By the time the man got back, if he got back, the battle would long be over.

Pavia dismissed the servant with a curt flip of the hand. "Get away from here you filthy imbecile. Tell the cook we want more of these." She pointed to the tray with an assortment of pastries.

"Tell him to bring some more of the fruit-filled kind. Those over there." A willowy woman with long auburn hair woven in a bun on the back of her head pointed a slender finger at the pastries at the edge of the tray.

"Careful Heledd, you'll end up looking like Konrud's wife!" Another woman, soft from indulged living, laughed between bites. "And then your husband will stay gone for months at a time too."

"That might be good," Pavia retorted as they all laughed. "Then she could find a virile and passionate young man whose only purpose in life would be to please her!"

"Ooh, Pavia you naughty thing!"

"What? Meinwen, it's not like she's going to get pregnant."

"Would you really?" A petite woman with large eyes asked incredulously.

"I...I..." Heledd stumbled in awkward embarrassment.

"And why not Siani?" Pavia interrupted. "Heledd can have anyone she wants. Actually, any of us can. Men are too easy. There's almost no challenge anymore."

"But not all men," Siani replied.

"There's no one that I can't have," Pavia said with quiet smugness.

The other women looked at each other, smiling. Meinwen picked up another pastry.

"Now Pavia, not all men succumb to your pouting lips."

"Name one," she challenged.

"Now wait. Are you suggesting that there is no one whom you can't seduce?"

"None." She licked the icing off the top of the sweet roll.

"Really? This sounds like another challenge."

"Ooh, this should be fun," Siani giggled.

"Let's make this more interesting. For this to be a good game, there ought to be a good prize," Heledd said off-handedly.

"Fine," Pavia brightened to the game. "You pick the man and I'll pick the prize."

"Wait." Meinwen interrupted. "What about the rules?"

Heledd thought for a moment. "The rules are these: Pavia has fourteen days to bed the man of our choice. If she succeeds, we will –"

"Be my servants for a week," Pavia dictated, then grinning impishly added, "Although I doubt it will take that long."

"And what about if we win?" Siani asked excitedly.

"It won't happen, but should that occur, I will give each one of you one of my jeweled gowns."

"Ooh, I want the sapphire one with the silver brocade," Heledd claimed.

"I want the red lace one with the beaded bodice," Meinwen blurted.

"Now wait girls, you're flocking before the prey's dead! Name your man." Pavia bit into a sugar-coated roll.

The three women gathered in a group and conspired in excited whispers. Suddenly they exclaimed, "That's it!"

Pavia put down her roll. "Well?"

Siani grinned mischievously. "We have the perfect man for this game - Brother Lucan."

"And everyone knows that he's too holy to even think of women," Meinwen giggled.

Pavia paused as she reached for the roll again. "Fine. Fourteen days is it? Done."

Heledd held up her hands. "Wait. How will we know?"

Pavia grinned wickedly. "Oh, you'll know."

"I listened to you at the council. You were very good." Lucan warmly shook Duncan's hand, as the attendant closed the doors behind him.

"Um…thank you." Duncan was puzzled. *Obviously you're nothing like your brother Vix. Maybe Tene was right…you may be a good ally.*

"Tene told me that you wanted to read the words of Safti."

"Yes I do."

"I should have expected it."

"Pardon?"

"That you wanted to read the words of Safti." Lucan was sincere.

"Yes, I do, with your permission." He bowed slightly.

226

"Oh, you mustn't bow to me." Lucan held his hands up in deference. "I'm simply a priest of the true god."

"Yes, I know that." *Why is he being so obsequious?*

Lucan stood nodding, a silly grin pasted to his face.

"Um… may I read the text?"

"Certainly." He didn't move. "But before you begin, I have a question."

Duncan was momentarily caught off guard. "OK?"

"Why does the promised one of Safti want to read the words of Safti when he should know them already?" He continued to smile, but remained firmly placed.

Duncan sniffed and shook his head. "Father Lucan, you make the assumption that Safti is only worshipped by you Gambrians. Would you limit Safti's power by saying that he cannot have other believers?"

"N..no," Lucan awkwardly stammered, "of course not."

"I have read numerous books of Safti," Duncan calmly replied. "What I do is make sure that each book is true. That way, there is no one with an excuse for not believing." Duncan watched Lucan absorb his latest parry and continued. "May I read the book now?"

Lucan hesitated for only a moment. "Certainly, of course. Please, I had our oldest text brought here for you to look at."

There was something about the way Lucan stared at him that made him uncomfortable. "Why do you look at me like that?"

Lucan dropped his gaze. "Sorry. We don't get many believers asking to read the holy book."

"Why not?"

"Most of Gambria can't read." He turned and motioned for Duncan to follow him to the raised platform in the far corner of the spacious room, to where a large window with a peaked top allowed the sunlight in. "Here it is," he said reverentially. "As I said, this is our oldest copy, said to be over 800 years old. It's usually kept in the reference library here, in a special container." He devotedly the cover. "Take your time, I'll just be over here." He pointed to a thick carpet on the floor where he sat down with legs crossed.

Duncan carefully turned the worn and tattered cover to the Book of Safti. The pages were yellowed with age and although great effort had been made to care for the brittle leaves, some were torn and tattered and split in half. And while the writing was fading, it was written in a strong hand. He turned the first blank page and began reading.

These then are the records of Georg Safti. Deciding to keep a record of my travails, I have assumed that there will be a future generation to read this. I have devoted my efforts ensuring thus.

Upon the devastation of our cities, we left in our ship, great and made of strong fabric. Those of us still unaffected by the crippling diseases have sought to band together and seek a better world. Remember it thus - death begins death. A death for a death. I have seen too much death. I grow numb at death. To succeed, we must grow cold and numb to what occurs as a daily existence. We all know death. We taste it every day. Only by accepting what is to come can we be free to do what is today.

And so Hergo and I gained control of the Saint Senii and killed the captain (he who had butchered the first dying). We gathered and collected those seemingly unaffected and brought them aboard. As soon as we had enough male, female and children, we cast off in the dying night appearing to be a supply ship adrift without crew.

Hergo went through the entire ship and gave solace to the frightened. 'Tis better to be adrift and alive than to know the worm and the decay it brings.

Duncan continued reading, fascinated by the account of what appeared to be an escape from some sort of plague or destruction. He read rapidly, absorbing everything that had happened, trying to understand the devastation and the relevance to the world he now inhabited. Several entries later he read,

We have been now 45 days on the Ocean cauldron, a churning of waves and angry storms. Last night we sent 7 children to the deep, victims of the lingering disease. Oh the ache of a child's death...the soft eyes closed in pain...the once smooth skin, blackened and dry...the withered limbs...and the voice...the voice, small and quiet, accepting their fate as though they were born for few years only...and the vast Ocean swallowing them like so many drops of rain.

We are now down by a third. We expect more to yield. I can only hope and pray that we will see land soon. Our supplies are rapidly dwindling.

Duncan looked up and out the window. Seagulls lofted in the winds. He paused, as if remembering something lost, and sighed heavily.

"Is everything all right?"

Lucan's liquid voice brought him back to his surroundings. "Yes... yes, Father Lucan. It's just that...sometimes death is no solution." Duncan continued to stare out into the blackness.

"No solution to what?" Lucan queried.

Duncan returned to the room. "No solution for stupidity and intolerance." He mumbled as he continued to read.

"To be sure," Lucan nodded, unsure of the cryptic statement. He remained silent for several minutes, watching with amazement as Duncan flipped the pages faster and faster until they appeared to be a blur. Finally he could no longer stand it. "Wizard! Carefully, lest you destroy the Holy Text!"

Realizing that he had been speed reading, he paused and looked up. "You are right Father Lucan. It's just that, this is so fascinating." He shrugged sheepishly and Lucan could feel the honesty in his simple statement.

"Yes, it is fascinating, isn't it?"

"Yes. Listen to this... *It's been two days since we landed at Roscommon. The entire city is empty. Machines sit idle, mute reminders of what we were, what once was. Buildings light in the ghostly night. Yet there is no life. There is no warm touch of flesh on flesh. No laughter to give meaning to this otherwise empty world.*

Duncan paused, lost in the words, remembering the years aboard ship, the empty life of loneliness, and the silent echoes of halls without laughter.

Lucan waited patiently, watching Duncan's reverie. He coughed lightly hoping to get his attention, but Duncan stayed in his own thoughts. He intently watched him, his furrowed brows as if in pain. Finally Duncan spoke.

"I have been there," he said softly.

Lucan jerked back startled. "You, you have been to Roscommon?"

"I have been there," Duncan continued as if to no one. "I know the emptiness. I know the hollow halls and the sound of barren life... the cold touch of fleshless metal. I know the meaning of death." He again drifted to the ship and the years of his lost life. And then the image of Spikey, the wide-eyed boy with tousled, pale blond hair and the hint of freckles on his cheeks appeared, the boy who had given his life for Duncan's. A sadness settled within him and he closed his eyes to remember.

Lucan dared not breathe. What he had just heard seemed too implausible. No one had ever been beyond the borders of Gambria for centuries. The few travelers that anyone remembered had come long before his grandfather's grandfather was born. And their stories were too impossible. Besides, everyone knew that Rugia surrounded Gambria and what didn't was filled with either impassable mountains or vast lands of hot and desolate terrain. Yet here was this man, this... stranger. What was it about him that made him different?

He seems to ache, Lucan thought to himself. *There is great pain in him. And his eyes ache too. It's as though he yearns to be at peace with himself. He knows not this Book, yet he absorbs so quickly. At least it appears so. Patience Lucan. Perhaps he is the one. You must test him. Patience.*

Duncan returned to his surroundings as if awaking from a sleep. "Sorry," he weakly smiled. "I must have drifted."

"You said you have been to Roscommon. Is that so?"

He solemnly nodded. "And worlds beyond."

"What do you mean?" Lucan was puzzled with the response. It wasn't really an answer, yet it implied so much more.

"I'll explain later. For now, I'd like to finish this marvelous Book"

Lucan smiled in pleasure. *At least he has the proper reverence.*

Duncan turned the page.

We have left Roscommon after replenishing the supplies and burning the dead. It appears that some of the weaker ones are gaining back their strength. The care of the sick is necessary, for who knows who will survive and who will die? We have found a map of the land. Using the map, I have sent out scouts to determine our location. There appear to be two good-sized seas inland that I have named the Kurg Sea and the Starn Sea. Believing the Kurg Sea too close to the coast, we will set out for the Sea farthest away, the Starn Sea. We have fished the rivers. Upon the first catch, I Georg Safti pronounced it good. And the people did eat of its flesh and they were filled.

And the grumbling of the people was bought to naught as their bellies were filled. How bitter is the tongue of a faithless servant. I have led them for so long and still they rebel. Hergo is being lulled by their vile tongues. I must watch him now. How I long for the faithful servant. One who will serve and be content to do what is right. For him would I give my life.

Rubbing his neck a bit, he leaned back. "Father Lucan, how is it that you were not the High Priest? For it seems to me that you have the right heart for the work."

Again Lucan was startled. "What do you mean?"

"C'mon, Father Lucan, don't play coy with me. We both know that you seem more suited to have been High Priest. Was it merely a question of birth?"

He was momentarily speechless. "Yes," he found himself answering softly.

Duncan nodded. "I understand. Bad choice, but I understand." He turned again to the Book, leaving Lucan dumbfounded as to what it was that made him come to such a conclusion.

We have come to the Kurg Sea and the land is good. Would that I could say the same for those who follow me. The people cry out against me. They ask for rest. Yet I am driven. I feel that we are not yet out of danger. There are those who would stay here. They have compelling reasons. The sea produces plentiful fish, and the land is good for grain. What is it that will not let me stay here? It is sin. The sin of the rebel, the sin of the complainer, the sin of the haughty. They would forget what has happened believing that no one will find them here. They would forget who it was that brought them out of the evil of this world and into the promise of the future. They are forgetting me. Already Hergo has gathered a following. He means to stay and fight if necessary.

Hergo, Hergo...I have loved you like a brother. I found you as a weakling, a helpless wanderer looking for a champion. I gave you life and now you seek to take mine. How faithless is a friend who will not follow. Vain is the man who will listen to soothing words and lying speech. Hergo, Hergo...you do not understand your fate. They will sway you and then consume you. If only I could make you see.

Realizing he was nearing the end of the Book, Duncan began to slow down, savoring the remaining text.

My heart is heavy for I have bid good-bye to Hergo and the majority of followers. I have only a handful who will go with me. Yet they are strong and they are enough. We have parted amiably enough, but there is antagonism. Those who remain heap verbal abuse on those who follow me. They are like children sated with pleasure. They know not what the future holds. Even Hergo chides me. Yet we will seek the pastures of the mountains and the sea called Starn. I believe there lies the future. We will prosper and build a great nation. And to those left behind, we wish fair fortune.

There seemed to be a time break in the journal for the next entry was in a rather jittery hand.

We followed the Esus river and ten days out were attacked by that race of hideously deformed people. How horrible is the devastation of the soul. These poor creatures, deformed as they were, were merely trying to survive. Yet their grotesque forms and animal desires must be eliminated. There can be no weakness if we are to survive the future. We were successful, yet there

231

was loss of life. The little settlement I had called Bar-El to thank God for bringing us here. I now call it Cash-El - 'the wrath of God.'

And we traveled from Cash-El to the great Starn lake. We buried our dead and to the dying I gave comfort. And I taught them. 'All desire is subordinate to the future.' And I took the healthy male and female and allowed them their passions, and they did produce. And I gathered all who were with me and taught them. We are a blessed group and will continue to be blessed only if we remember who we are. We must make choices that will break our souls, we will have to sacrifice what we hold most dear, even our own children. But always, always, we must remember who we are.

And great are the days to those who trust in our future.

Duncan flipped quickly to the last pages. The hand writing was different from the previous style and flow.

And we have settled next to the Sea called Starn. There is a city here in good condition. We have battled the deformed ones again and they are killed. More live in the outlying areas and I fear the fight will last long beyond my now shortened time. Yet we have taken the city. There is one gate and we can control the access. It is a wonderful city. I can see a marvelous future here. We must stay here and build the future. We must harvest the sea as well as the land. We must be in balance with nature and not extract more than she can give. And we must not forget to offer the right sacrifice.

In the latest skirmish I have taken a mortal wound. I dictate this now to Morit, he of the clever knowledge of words and language. I have entrusted the future of these followers to him. They grow strong and the sea will sustain us. I go to my fathers knowing that I did my best. I have given my children a future. My last words are these – remember, remember who you are.

The next several lines were in Morit's handwriting.

We buried our leader, a prophet (may peace be continually his) of unequaled righteousness and servitude. He loved the people and gave his life for them. May we see him in the next coming.

Duncan closed the book and inhaled deeply. He glanced over to where Lucan was in resting trance, eyes open. *Perhaps he can teach me how to do that.*

As he stood, Lucan stirred. "Have you finished?" The grogginess from interrupted meditation made him slightly slur his words.

Duncan stretched. "Yes. You have done me a great service. Perhaps at some time I can repay your kindness."

"Oh, no need for that," he smiled pleasantly.

Duncan studied him for a moment. "Why did you allow me to read the book when you know that your brother hates me as he does?"

"Even a condemned man may read from the book before he dies," Lucan stated matter-of-factly.

"So I'm condemned already?"

"I didn't mean it like that!" he blurted. "Anyone may read from the book of Safti."

"But you've let me read your rarest book of Safti. That is quite a privilege. Why?"

He shrugged. "Tene asked."

"That's it? Tene asks and whatever she asks for is granted?" he grinned.

Lucan smiled and shook his head. "Well, yes and no. I've known Tene her entire life. In fact, I christened her at her public affirmation. She has since become a good friend." Lucan gazed intently at Duncan. "You are very fortunate she favors you so much. I trust the affection is equally returned?"

"Ooh. Is this a confessional? Should I be on my knees?" His eyes betrayed his mischievousness.

Lucan laughed. "Hardly. I see now why she likes you so much. You have a quick humor."

A wry smile flitted across Duncan's face. "Y'know, I remember you at the council, but I don't remember you saying anything."

"Sometimes it is better to listen," he quietly answered.

"A wise answer." Then he laughed. "You're not sure of what to make of me, are you?"

Lucan paused to carefully select his words. "I am in doubt. There is a part of me that wishes you to be a chosen one of Safti. Yet there is a part that believes you too brash, almost arrogant. It seems unlike one Safti would choose."

"Oh?" he parried. "And it is more like Safti to want children sacrificed as burnt offerings?"

Lucan's whole countenance visibly changed as a great sadness enveloped him. "That is not my choosing."

"Why do you not stop it?"

"I am not the high priest."

"Is the high priest chosen by Safti?"

Lucan again paused before speaking. "I believe that Safti chooses the high priest. Yet the high priest does not necessarily always listen to what Safti has to say."

"So Vix may have been chosen, but he no longer listens to Safti?"

There was a long silence. Then Lucan whispered, "It is possible."

"What does the book say about ones who do not listen to Safti?" Duncan watched him blink several times before answering for him. "How bitter is the tongue of a faithless servant. I have led them for so long and still they rebel. How I long for the faithful servant, one who will serve and be content to do what is right. The sin of the rebel, the sin of the complainer, the sin of the haughty. They would forget who it was that brought them out of the evil of this world and into the promise of the future. They are forgetting me."

He stood stunned, listening to him repeat the words of Safti back to him. "You... you only read the book once."

Duncan smiled wisely and pointed to his head. "But it's all in here." He calmly folded his arms. "You still didn't answer why you don't stop the sacrifices."

"I have not enough influence to sway the high priest, nor his many supporters as well," he frowned.

"What do you mean?"

"Wizard, it is not all that easy. You recall your questioning?"

"Yes?"

"Do you remember Cattwg and Garbhan?"

"Very well." He smiled at the recent triumph.

"They are powerful priests. Father Konrud, whom you may remember, is the number three prelate in the nation. While I can always depend on Father Konrud, you can see that there is still a balance in favor of the high priest."

Duncan listened attentively. "Would you challenge him if you could?"

He shook his head. "I don't know. I've never thought about it."

He nodded. "I understand." He turned back to the ancient book. "By the way, interesting name you have. Quite appropriate."

Lucan's head snapped back up. "What do you mean?"

"Your name...Lucan...it means 'light.'" Lucan let out a pained gasp and fell to the floor. Startled, Duncan rushed to him. "What's wrong?" Turning him over, Lucan's face was ashen.

"How...how do you know my name...the meaning?" His breathing was heavy.

"I...I know the meaning of many names," he responded.

Lucan pushed himself up to a sitting position. The color began returning to his face. A bit of sweat grew on his temples. "What is it you wish of me?"

Duncan sat back on his haunches. "Can I get you a glass of water?"

Shaking his head, he persisted. "What is it you wish of me?"

"Nothing, I... I've already read the text," he fumbled.

Lucan's eyes grew in fear. "You will wait to use your power?"

"What power?" He stood up, searching the room. "You need some water."

"Please," he begged. "Do not torture me."

Duncan bent back down. "What's gotten into you? I have no intention of torturing you. In fact, I view you as a friend, if I may call you such."

The plump priest said nothing, staring intently at him. He then realized that Duncan was telling the truth and slightly relaxed. "I would be honored."

"Here, let me help you up." He assisted him to an unsteady upright. "What happened?"

Lucan stared blankly at him. "My name, your knowledge...what else could have happened?"

Understanding suddenly swept through him. *I know the meaning of your name and now I have a power over you.* He mused for a moment more. "Lucan, do you trust me?"

Instead of answering, he stared at him, a slight edge of fear in his eyes.

"I understand." Duncan pressed on. "I want you to trust me. And to show that I trust you, I will tell you the meaning of my name."

Lucan's eyes bolted wide and his jaw fell. "W...why?"

"I told you. To show that I trust you."

"You would willingly give me this power?" He absorbed the weight of the gift and his eyes tinged with apprehension.

Placing a hand on Lucan's shoulder, he earnestly stared at him. "Willingly. I trust you and know you to be a man of integrity and honor. I would be honored if you would accept my gift."

Nodding slowly, his voice still edged with apprehension. "I would count it a privilege to know your essence Wizard Duncan. But still, why would you willingly give me this power."

"Don't you see? You have no power over me unless I give it to you. When one finds a true friend, one willingly gives of himself. Do you wish to be my friend?"

He nodded. "Yes Wizard, it would be an honor."

Duncan smiled. "Please Father Lucan, just call me Duncan." Lucan smiled in answer. "My name means 'brown warrior'. I was named after Saint Duncan, a holy man who lived over 1500 years before I was born."

Lucan pressed both hands to his chest and bowed his head as if in prayer. When he looked back at him, his eyes were filled with happy tears. "Saint Duncan. Yes, it is a good name." He spread his arms wide and embraced Duncan in a great bear hug. "Friend."

Duncan squeezed back and responded, "Friend." A knock on the door caused them both to part.

"I'm sorry Father Lucan," the acolyte announced, pausing at the doorway, "but Lady Pavia is here and wishes to see you."

"Me?" Lucan squeaked.

Pavia burst through the door pushing the attendant aside. "Yes you, Father Lucan. Why look, here's the Wizard of sorts. So good to see you again."

Duncan smiled and bowed slightly. "And you too Lady Pavia."

She went straight to Lucan, eyes fluttering. "Am I interrupting?" her lips pouted.

Suppressing a snicker, Duncan grinned. "No, I was just leaving."

"Good. Then I can have him all to myself." She slipped her arm around Lucan's as he stood there in bewildered awkwardness.

"Thanks again Father Lucan. You are a blessing to me." Duncan bowed, turned and left. Lucan stared dumbly as Pavia pressed herself closer to him.

She watched as the door closed and turned to Lucan, eyes sparkling. "Now Father Lucan, what were you doing with the foreigner? Surely, he doesn't need your counsel. He has spoken with God." She laughed raucously.

Lucan fidgeted slightly in discomfort. "He seems to be very devout. He even asked to read the book of Safti."

"Oh really?" She looked around the room and saw the old book open on the stand. "Is that it over there? I really must look at it." She glided across the room and extended her hand ever so delicately toward the book. As she did, she glanced sideways at Lucan and smiled demurely, "Is it okay to touch it?"

"Ye...Yes," he stammered, still planted in his spot. "Just be careful; it's very old and delicate."

"Let's see, what do we have here, 'only by accepting what is to come can we be free to do what is today,'" she read aloud. "Father Lucan, how can we know what is to come?" While he pondered the answer, she moved back next to him and gazed expectantly at him. Though he did not speak for several seconds, her eyes never relented.

A knock at the door interrupted them. "Father Lucan, please forgive the interruption, Lady Pavia ordered this meal to be sent."

"Oh don't stand there gaping, come in. I hope you don't mind, but I took the liberty of arranging some delicacies for you." Without waiting for a reply, she barged on. "You are hungry aren't you? Please say you're hungry or I shall be gravely offended." She lowered her eyes and pouted.

"Why...yes, certainly... yes..." He hadn't been sure at first, but the aromas convinced him that he was suddenly very hungry.

Pavia squeezed his arm in appreciation. "That's so sweet of you to humor me." She turned to the attendants. "Over here, please."

The servants covered the table with bowls and plates filled with broiled meats, freshly baked breads, and twice-cooked small potatoes, large silver trays overflowing with sweets, and several bottles of wine. Pavia clapped her hands and abruptly ushered the attendants out.

"Quickly, quickly, Father Lucan is a very busy man. You must go now." She followed them to the door, closing it behind them and sliding the bolt across. "I do so hate being disturbed," she said to no one in particular.

She turned and saw him still standing. "Now why are you still standing? Oh! How silly of me." She tapped her forehead. "You were waiting for me to serve you." She moved with silken grace until she was next to him. His eyes had never left following her. "A big strong man like you needs attention." She pulled a chair out for him to sit and gently pushed him into it. "You can't imagine how good it is to see someone like you, handsome and virile." She shook her head. "It's so rare these days."

Lucan raised an eyebrow in question. Pavia noticed and quickly picked up a small delicacy, gently guiding it to his mouth. "You really must try these; I had them especially prepared for you." She then picked up a large bottle of wine and poured him a generous serving. Resting a hand on his shoulder, she smiled warmly at him, and then walked around the table to sit opposite him. Settling in, she leaned forward slightly, resting her chin on her hand and smiling at him. "Now you were going to tell me about that verse from the book of Safti."

Lucan stared at her for a second, then asked, "Aren't you going to eat?"

"Oh, perhaps a small piece of bread and a cup of wine. I just enjoy watching a hearty man who appreciates the work I put into preparing good food."

"This is really good," he responded between mouthfuls. "I can't imagine anyone not appreciating food like this."

Pavia saddened slightly and said, "There is so much I do that is not appreciated. That is why I have turned my attention to my religious studies. I need so much." She rose and walked around the table, sitting beside Lucan. Taking his hand in both of hers, she cooed, "Father Lucan, can you help me?"

"Of course, I'll help you any way I can," he responded earnestly.

"That gives me such a warm reassurance, from someone so devout and respected as you. Everyone told me that no one knows more about the questions of life than you. I am honored that you can find time for me." Looking at his goblet she stood up suddenly, "Oh my, I've let your cup become empty. What a thoughtless hostess I am." She smiled sweetly. After pouring the wine she again sat down close to him. "Father Lucan, can I ask you a question?"

"Anything."

"Well, how is it that so fine and compelling a man as you has never married? There is no law against the priests marrying and I am sure many women have pursued you."

Lucan blushed and answered, "Um...no, not really."

"Oh I know you are trying to be discreet, and I so admire that. But I was just talking with one of my friends the other day, what was her name? Anyway, she is so pretty and she went on and on about how handsome she thought you were."

"Really?" he sputtered.

"Now would I lie to you? You know how those women are who become so taken with a man. Why can't I remember her name, she's so pretty, why she was consumed with you, simply consumed. Why she almost made me jealous." Pavia laughed as if sharing an intimate secret.

Pavia continued to control the conversation, and by the fourth glass of wine, Lucan was beginning to relax and enjoy her attentions. They were both laughing now. Her lighthearted banter drew him in. She had just finished a story from her childhood when he stood up suddenly, wobbling slightly.

"Lady Pavia," he brightly began, "that reminds me of a time when I was a youth. Let's see. I was about eight or nine, I don't remember exactly.

Vix and I were playing hiding games, and I managed to squeeze into the space between the gargoyles in the balcony. What happened was, and this was so funny, I got stuck and Vix never found me. I had to stay there for hours until my cries alerted the attendants, and they came to help get me unstuck." He rubbed his left shoulder. "My shoulder still hurts when I think about it." He smiled ruefully.

Pavia jumped up. "Oh, let me rub your shoulder. Shame on Vix for leaving you there like that."

"Yeah, how dare he do that!" he resounded.

Pavia rubbed and kneaded the thick neck and shoulder muscles. "My goodness, you must spend a lot of time at the combat pits to have such strong muscles." Lucan's head began to move in rhythm to Pavia's nimble hands massaging his neck. She moved up to rubbing his temples, and he let a small groan of pleasure escape. "Oops, you need more wine." She jumped up and refilled the goblet, urging Lucan to drink more.

"Lady Pavia," Lucan slurred.

"Now, now, why don't you just call me Pavia." She continued messaging.

"O...OK... Pavia... Pavia," Lucan felt himself getting sleepy. "How may I be of service to you, my dear lady?" He was beginning to get giddy.

"Why Father Lucan, I feel as if we can trust one another, don't you think?" Lucan nodded thickly. "Well, oh my, this is so difficult for me... but you know that my husband and I don't...um... get along quite well enough?"

"Really?" Lucan slurred.

"Yes, really. And since I can't find fulfillment with him, I thought that you might be interested in, oh... you know..." She tugged on him to get him standing.

"Might what?" Lucan wobbled as she guided him to his bed chamber. He stood next to his bed staring at the covers, torn between listening to her or curling up in deep sleep. He looked back to her hoping for relief.

"You know...you...me..." She nodded at the bed.

Suddenly clarity stumbled through Lucan's thick head. "Me?" he squeaked. Then with equal suddenness, he tumbled onto the bed in deep sleep.

Pavia stepped back and watched his chest rise and fall with each breath. "My goodness, that was much easier than I thought. And you were supposed to have such a capacity for wine." She calmly walked over to Lucan's desk, found pen and paper, and wrote her note.

Pavia re-read the words, wondering how she should sign it, deciding instead to leave it unsigned. Despite the mystery, Lucan would know it came from her. Crossing over to the bookstand, she placed the note on the open pages of the book of Safti. She then aimlessly wandered around the room for a while, examining baubles, books, wall hangings, and other decorations.

When sufficient time had passed, she walked back into where the snoring Lucan still lay sprawled on the bed. Pushing up his robe, she discovered with mild amusement that he wore no under garments. Leaving his robe pushed up, she turned to her own clothes, unfastened a brooch and pinned it to his pillow. She then plucked a hair from her head and entwined it around the brooch.

Stepping back, she surveyed her work. "Well Father Lucan, looks like you just helped me get some fine servants for a few weeks." She laughed smugly, spun on her heels, and strode across the rooms to the door. Opening it, she saw the temple acolyte stiffly standing guard. He turned as she came out.

"Father Lucan said to tell you that he's going to take a nap now and doesn't want to be disturbed." The guard bowed in acknowledgement. "Good. I can see myself out thank you." And she glided away, a small bounce to her step.

Sleep.... mon, I need sleep.

Duncan looked up from Oswiu's records that Tene had placed before him, to see Rasta-mon come in the bedroom, jump onto the bed and curl himself up.

Are you just getting back? Duncan smirked.

Mon, nex' time I be wantin' to chase som' body, you say Rasta-mon be too old for dis kinda jumpin' and runnin'. Rasta-mon's tail swished.

So what happened?"

Mon, him be talkin' so long dat I fall asleep. I wake up and de place be dark. I hafta find de door myself. So I gets out and nachurally I wants to visit de ladies, but on de way I remember dat de lady frien' not do so good and how I gonna explain, it not like she hit by a truck, if you know what I mean, so I tink, Rasta boy you just be ignorant and don' know nuthin'. And de ladies, dis be crazy, de ladies say 'mon, she be a pain anyway and glad she go away.' So I tink dis be great. And dis one lady she say, 'hey Rasta-mon, dey say you can talk to da man-stranger.' An' I say sure. An' she say how come? An' I say...

Excuse me! But is this going anywhere? Duncan interrupted.

Rasta-mon blinked several times. *Mon, it was but now I forget. Anyway, de ladies, ooh boy, dey wear de Rasta-mon out. I need to sleep, ya know, kinda catch up on the de ol' strength. Gonna be a long night tonight, wink wink.*

Duncan chuckled. *Good. Maybe you can do some recon for me.*

Say what? Aw mon, don't be a party pooper. Why I gotta work when I suppose to play?

Because I need your help. I need to know what's going on in the king's chambers.

Rasta-mon sighed loudly. *Oh all right. Mon de tings I do for you, you gonna owe me big time. Now can I sleep?*

At that moment, Tene came in with a tray of broiled meat, cheese, and bread. "I saw him come in and thought he might be hungry." She nodded at Rasta-mon.

Rasta-mon jumped up after Duncan's translation. *Dis girlie be good for you mon. She know how to treat the Rasta Doctor right. No, dat's OK, you don't need to join if you don want to.* He watched as Duncan tore a piece off and was about to plop it into his own mouth. *HEY! You oink gonna make a pig outta youself oink?*

Duncan barked a laugh and placed the piece of meat in front of Rasta-mon who said nothing but began devouring it, frequently casting sideways looks at Duncan.

Tene watched the exchange. "What's so funny Duncan?"

"Nothing really," he grinned. "He likes your cooking." Duncan stretched and stood up. "Think I'll go for a little walk."

Tene's eyes widened. "Duncan...I...I don't think that's a good idea. Remember who you are. There are people out there trying to kill you."

Duncan pulled her close and smiled reassuringly. "Tene, I told you. I'll be OK. You'll see. Stick with me and it'll all work out."

Tene sighed loudly. "Please don't go."

"I have to."

She pulled away. "Why?"

He continued holding her hand. "What kind of wizard or future high priest would I be if I were afraid to go out in public?"

Shaking her head, she gazed into his eyes. "I don't like it. You're not the high priest yet."

"You don't believe me?" He smiled coyly.

"Stop making fun of me. You know what I mean." She allowed herself to be drawn closer to him. "I'm afraid for you."

He held her tightly, feeling her warmth and the softness of her body. He looked down at her face, the strawberry blond hair falling carelessly off her shoulders and down her back. She stared back up at him, her bright eyes full of fear and concern.

"Don't worry, I'll be back before you know it." He kissed her fully and she responded with her whole body, pressing and wrapping herself around him. He tasted her passion, pulled back and smiled. "You don't play fair."

"Where the hell have you been?" Emer fingered the edge of his wine glass. He had seen her hurry into the house. She seemed more buoyant than usual.

Pavia glanced briefly at him and then returned to look in the mirror, gingerly placing an errant strand of hair back in place. "Well look who's here. Are you lost?"

"This is my home too," he retorted.

"I suppose that is technically true," she sighed. "It just seems so much more pleasant when you're not here." She looked at him in the mirror.

A lip began to snarl, but he controlled himself. "I'll ask again. Where the hell have you been?"

"And why would you possibly be interested?"

"Well, *technically*, you are my wife." He glared at her in the mirror. "Although, that doesn't seem to matter."

"Now really darling," she continued to primp, "jealousy so ill becomes you. It's as though you really meant it."

"Dammit woman," he slammed the glass down hard, sloshing the wine over the sides, "if you want to sleep with the farm hands, I can't stop you. At least you could be discrete about it."

Pavia turned around, smiling. "Now now, dear. When I sleep with the farm hands, I'll make sure you're the first to know."

Emer stared malevolently at her. "I ought to divorce you."

Pavia laughed. "Really?" She walked over to where he sat slouched at the desk. She leaned over as if to kiss him, her hand reaching between his legs. He tensed slightly. She then whispered, "Now why would you want everyone to know that your quiver is empty?"

He thrust her away and flung the glass at her. She nimbly ducked and it ricocheted off the wall behind her, shattering as it hit the floor.

Pavia burst out laughing. "That's all the puny strength you can muster? Where is my brave hero who challenged Alric? A duel! A duel to the death. You and your sword and him and his spoon. Oh the stories they'll write, the heroic exploits of a king's son felled by a spoon."

Emer leaped to his feet, pointing a shaky finger at her. "Laugh while you can. You are nothing without me. You hear me?! Nothing!"

Pavia grew quickly calm. "And you are nothing without me."

"Wrong!" he shouted. "I am the future king! And when I am king, I will get a new queen. One who is young and beautiful, a virgin, not some sailor's whore like you." He watched her react to his venom.

"Go back to your books, school boy," she spat. "You wouldn't know what to do with a virgin." She stormed toward the door.

"Where are you going?" he demanded.

"To find a farm hand," she called over her shoulder.

Emer watched her go, picked up the wine bottle and hurled it at the closing door.

Menec saw him from across the cobbled street. The man moved with feigned nonchalance, and smiled when he saw Menec looking at him.

"Rulf you old scoundrel, how are you?" Menec barged across the road, impervious to the bustling traffic of wagons, draft animals, and pedestrians.

"Menec! It's been a while." Rulf grinned delightedly and gave Menec a big bear hug as he walked up. "I'm fine, just fine."

"Good to hear." He put an arm around Rulf's shoulder and nudged him into moving with the crowd. "We've lots to talk about. Have you heard about the stranger who calls himself a wizard?"

Rulf fell into step. "Just the usual rumors."

"You'd like him. Decent fellow. Seems to have the high priest in a fluster though."

"Really? And why's that?"

Menec slowed Rulf to a languid pace. "Seems he's issued a challenge to prove who's the rightful chosen one of Safti."

Rulf nodded thoughtfully. "Rather gutsy thing to do, don't you think?"

The Tarrac Master was silent for a moment as if pondering. "I suppose so. But to tell the truth, I think there's something more to him that makes me believe him."

Rulf abruptly stopped. "You honestly believe him?"

"Strangely enough, yes. Well, maybe not the promised one part, but there's something about him, something that says he's good for Gambria.

Call it a hunch. Unfortunately there seem to be some people who want him out of the way. Can you believe it? There have already been several attempts on his life." Menec shook his head.

"Really? By whom?" he innocently inquired.

"I hear it's assassins. Must be someone with a lot of money. Tell you the truth though, I'd certainly hate to back a losing tarrac. Really, if it was up to me, I would leave him alone and see what happens."

Rulf mused for a moment. "I see. So you think that he should be left alone? But if someone has already paid an assassin's price, it won't stop until he's dead."

"Well, I suppose that's true. Still," Menec shook his head in disdain, "I'd certainly keep my options open."

Rulf furrowed his eyebrows. "But if he's dead before the contest, seems like Vix wins no matter what."

They continued walking. "Well I guess that's true. Makes one wonder why someone is so intent on wanting him dead. Still, I'd love to see ol' Vix sweat for a while. And you know, if I was an assassin, I'd just want to make sure all my bases were covered... you know, make sure I was on the winning side."

Rulf glanced sideways at Menec. "I'm not sure an assassin really cares which side wins as long as he gets paid."

Menec turned solemn and nodded slowly. "Yes, I guess that's true. Still..."

Suddenly a greeting carried above the traffic noise. Menec looked up to see Duncan grinning as he made his way across the street, dodging the occasional wagon.

"Menec! Good to see you." He walked up and shook hands with him.

"Good to see you too, Wizard. This is –"

"Rulf," Duncan interjected. He watched Rulf's face betray his astonishment.

"You know him?" Menec sputtered.

"Most certainly." He firmly grasped Rulf's hand. "One of your *friends* visited me the other night. Unfortunately we had a problem with the meal and a king's companion died quite suddenly. By the way, I love your house. Rather dark though...you could use some windows. Still, the candles do add an interesting ambiance. By the way, I was quite impressed with Gwilym. Imagine hitting the same exact spot with eight arrows in a row!"

Rulf blinked vacantly for a moment. "I don't seem to remember meeting you," he intoned slowly.

Duncan smiled broadly. "True enough. But you must understand; I am a wizard."

Rulf half-smiled and chewed lightly on his bottom lip. He looked over to see Menec still in utter disbelief, and knew that it was not he who betrayed him.

Duncan watched Rulf's subtle body movements, saw him look at Menec, and understood what was happening. "No, it wasn't him. He is completely trustworthy. In fact, all of your... um, friends are likewise to be trusted. Believe me. Yet, as you would trust your friends, I would ask you now to trust me. I believe that we can work together. If you will allow me the opportunity to prove myself, I would be deeply appreciative. Should I fail, you'll have to get in line behind the high priest if you want my head." He smiled again, his eyes advertising his confidence.

Rulf couldn't help but laugh. He straightened to full height and turned to Menec. "It shall be as you have asked." He turned to Duncan. "We must talk some more. Your knowledge is very impressive. Now if you'll excuse me, I have some unfinished business to complete." He gave a polite nod and walked off.

As they watched him walk away, Menec placed a hand on Duncan's shoulder. "I don't know how you did it, but that was a good trick."

"A wizard never reveals his secrets," Duncan grinned. "Come, let's get a drink somewhere, and I'll even let you pay." He clapped Menec on the back, and they walked off together, laughing.

With self-assured smugness, Pavia burst into the room. Heledd looked up, and seeing Pavia's confidence, shook her head in resignation.

Siani also saw Pavia's radiance and her jaw dropped. "You didn't?"

"I did." She plopped down onto the thick cushions next to Meinwen and reached for a jellied pastry neatly arranged on a silver serving tray that rested on a delicate short-legged table. Heledd and Siani both got up from the window bench and crossed to sit where Pavia was so enjoying her coup.

"You actually did it?" Siani demanded?

"Absolutely."

There was a long silence followed by Meinwen softly asking, "What was it like?"

Pavia grimaced coyly. "Not exactly the best I've ever had. But still, he was tender and gentle, if somewhat inexperienced." She laughed easily.

"But how do we know you're telling the truth?"

"Now Siani, would I lie to you?" Pavia batted her eyelashes.

"Yes," she shot back, "especially when it comes to us spending a week being your servants. But really, how do we know for sure? You're going to have to prove your claim."

Pavia nodded her head knowingly. "I know." The other three leaned in closer and Pavia dropped her voice. "In two weeks, I'm going to tell Lucan that I am pregnant."

"That won't help," Siani interrupted.

"Let me finish." Pavia put a hand up to Siani's mouth. "You will all be with me when I tell him. That way you'll be able to see his reaction and know for sure that I'm telling the truth." She leaned back, satisfied.

Siani continued to shake her head in amazement. "I'd have never thought that Lucan."

"You doubt my power?" Pavia queried.

"It's not that… It's… I'm disappointed in him. It's…," Siani held up a hand when she saw Pavia's reaction, "it's just that I really believed that Lucan was different… that he was only interested in spiritual things. I didn't think he was like other men."

"All men are alike," Meinwen wisely noted. "There's no difference. They all think with the same part of their body."

Siani shrugged wistfully. "I suppose you're right. I'm just disappointed."

"Let it go Siani," Pavia chimed in. "Anyway, you're the ones who selected him."

"I know we did. I thought he was a safe bet."

"Apparently you were wrong," Pavia smirked. "Still, I want to make sure you all are sure of my conquest. When we visit to our dear almost high priest, you will know." Pavia reached for a slender pitcher. "Is this wine?" she asked, her eyes twinkling.

Lucan rolled his thick tongue in his mouth and licked dry lips. His head ached and throbbed with each heartbeat. Slowly he opened his eyes. He turned his pounding head towards the tall windows of his bedroom. Daylight was just beginning to fade. He felt a draft on his legs and unconsciously reached down to adjust his robe, only to feel the bare flesh of his thigh. He jerked his head upright and stared at his pale body, exposed from his ample belly down to his thick ankles and feet. He grappled to push down the robe, twisting and fidgeting to hide his corpulent body behind the safety of the thick material. As he twisted, his face pressed against something hard on the pillow. He reached up and grabbed a small object, still attached to his pillow. Propping himself on his elbow, he stared dumbly at a golden brooch in the shape of two birds, entwined as one. A large green stone lay in the center of the piece of jewelry.

Frowning in foggy lethargy, Lucan pushed himself to a sitting position and unfastened the brooch to examine it more closely. *Oh god...my head...* He looked around the room. Nothing seemed to be amiss. Then he saw the dining table and remembered. *She was here.*

He wobbled to his feet and stumbled to the table. Leaning heavily on the table top, he saw only the scraps of food and empty bottles of wine. He relaxed. *Water... I need some water.* He pushed away from the table and made his way to where a pitcher and basin perched on a low bureau. Leaning his face over the basin, he grabbed the pitcher and poured the entire contents over his head. The water was cold, almost biting and he caught his breath. *How long have I been asleep?* He absent-mindedly grabbed a towel and began drying his head. It still hurt. *I didn't drink that much...*

He twisted his head to crack his neck. The room was darkening. "Light...I need some light." He pushed away from the bureau and stumbled over to the door and jerked it open. "Light, would you please get me some light?" he spoke to the attendant standing outside the door who regarded him quizzically. Water still dripped from Lucan's soaked hair.

Lucan noticed the momentary delay. "I said bring me a light. Now, please." He winced from the headache pain. The robed attendant jumped into action, bowed quickly and hurried over to one of the wall torches. Lucan numbly watched as he carefully selected a taper and gingerly lit the end. He returned just as quickly, cupping the flame as he walked.

Without acknowledging the man, Lucan retrieved the taper and closed the door behind him. He went to several of the wall sconces and lit the candles. Soon the rooms brightened with the warm glow from the smoking flames. Lucan distractedly continued to towel his head and, as was his habit at sundown, wandered over to the book of Safti. There, gently nestled on the open pages he saw a folded paper. Puzzled, he unfolded the paper and read the handwritten lines.

My Darling Lucan,

> *I knew you, of all people, would understand. How jealous I've been when I see other women, with children of their own. You truly are a saint to help me like you have. I*

*know you said we need to be careful and I agree. I pray
Safti grant my desire. Hopefully with the Roan I sacrificed
this morning, I won't have long to wait. One day I hope
our child will know his true father. We must both be very
careful. But I won't forget how you made me feel. You do
not need to worry about me, our secret is forever safe. You
were wonderful.*

You will always be in my thoughts.

Lucan's chest tightened and his breathing became labored. He read
again the lines and their indictment. Trying to stand erect, he felt his legs
weaken and he gripped the lectern that held the sacred text to steady himself.
His breathing rapidly increased to the beat of the thumping crescendo of his
heart, and he pushed himself away only to slump to his knees.

He sat there for a moment, his chest pulsing with each heartbeat, his
eyes blurred by tears bursting forth to cascade down his cheeks. Yet no
sound emerged, as he fought to reconcile what he had done. Looking at the
crumpled note in his hand, he stirred to action and forced himself to
standing, hurrying to retrieve a wall torch.

Holding the note in his hand, he slowly raised the torch so that the flame
barely licked the edges. He watched with a strange mixture of detected
observer and oppressive guilt as smoke began curling up before the paper
quickly caught fire. Letting it burn until it almost reached his fingers, he
tossed it into a bowl on the table, staring at the charred embers that
disintegrated into ashes.

Chapter 18

The evening was warm and clear with the faintest hint of a breeze. The stars lay thick upon the night. Sentries were already posted as the rear supply wagons with Alexis and Brenna in tow came into the main camp. Cooking fires dotted the open field where the warriors sent to reinforce the on-going battle were to spend the night. Brenna leaped off the end of the wagon.

"My butt hurts." She fidgeted a bit, massaging her lower back.

Alexis laughed. "Your English is improving." She tugged on the reins to pull Stracaim closer.

Brenna grinned sheepishly and shrugged. "I want learn. You, me can talk. Only Wizard know."

"Well, I'll teach you English, but I must learn your language first."

"Yes," Brenna nodded, then lapsed back into Gambri. "Let's go find my group. They should have dinner ready by now." She unlooped Cymy's reins from the rear wagon post.

"High Commander Brenna?" a high-pitched nasally voice called out in the dark.

"I am here." Brenna jerked Cymy to a halt.

A slender man of average height came running up. "Oh my. Thank goodness I've found you. I've been running all over this god-forsaken field. Brutal, simply brutal." He pulled a kerchief from his sleeve and dabbed at his forehead. "I'm positively sweating."

Brenna relaxed, shaking her head. "Hullo Llwyd. What brings you out here?"

"Oh Commander, I've been asking the same question. All it would take is some rain to make my life utterly miserable. Can you believe it? I'm actually to share a *tent* with some ruffian. I have to sleep *on the ground*!"

"Poor Llwyd. Campaigning is rather difficult isn't it?"

"Can you believe he actually wants me out here? What do I know about fighting? I'm a scholar, mind you, a scholar of the second rank. I should be home with a tall glass of an aperitif, engrossed in some absolutely fascinating trivia of Gambri history."

"Llwyd, did you come here to complain, or was there a reason for you finding me?"

"Oh! I beg your pardon Commander," Llwyd bowed stiffly. "Lord Alric asks that the Berserker join him for dinner." He nodded toward Alexis.

"So ask her. She understands our language quite well."

"Really?" He turned to Alexis. "Um...uh," he hesitated and then stage-whispered to Brenna. "What do I call her?"

"What did you call her predecessor?"

"High Commander Oswiu."

Brenna paused for effect. "I believe that Oswiu lost that privilege, rather brutally I might add. In fact, she now occupies what used to be his house. Does that answer your question?"

Llwyd's voice rose noticeably in pitch. "High Commander Alexis, Lord Alric asks you to join him for dinner." He bowed slightly.

Alexis had followed the brief discussion and chuckled. "Tell him thank you. I will come."

Llwyd didn't move, a slight awkwardness to his demeanor.

"I will come," Alexis repeated.

"Um... High Commander Alexis, Lord Alric said to escort you to his tent."

"OK. Lead on." She turned to Brenna. "C'mon. We've been invited to dinner."

Llwyd abruptly stopped. "Um...uh..." he stuttered. "High Commander Brenna... um, I'm sorry, but Lord Alric did not mention you in his invitation."

"Then I'll invite her," Alexis stated matter-of-factly.

"But...but High Commander! Lord Alric didn't invite her."

"That's alright Alexis, you go ahead," Brenna interjected.

"No. She comes with me."

"But...but..."

"Listen. I'm not going unless she comes with me. In fact, I want you to go back right now and tell him that I think he's a rude jerk for only inviting me. We'll wait right here for you." She leaned against the wagon.

"I can't tell him that!" he squeaked.

"Then she's coming with me." She paused only for a moment. "Unless you have a problem with that?"

Llwyd blanched and swallowed hard. "Hardly, High Commander. I'm sure you two will enjoy the meal. Please follow me." And he turned around to lead.

Alexis looked over to where Brenna was quietly shaking from silent laughter. "You ready?"

Brenna cleared her throat. "This should be fun."

Vix stood fuming before the doors to his apartment. The acolyte had been slower than usual in opening the doors for him, and he thought he detected a subtle arrogance in him, an arrogance that said the high priest might not be high priest much longer. He made a mental note to transfer this brash young acolyte to the wastelands... as soon as the Wizard was dispatched.

"Get me some food and tell the Steward I want to see him," Vix snapped as he stormed into the apartment. Without looking back, he could hear the young man running down the hallway, but he also realized that the doors were still open. With a loud and angry sigh, he spun around and slammed them closed.

Stalking to the middle of his living room, he stopped and took stock of his surroundings. He had lived here since his father died and he had been installed as the high priest. Yet he had known these rooms all his life. Back when his father lived here, the place seemed to have a greater aura of gravity, of importance. But now, they were simply a set of rooms, a sanctuary of sorts, a place where he could do what he wanted. Where his father thrived on company, good talk and good food, Vix preferred solitude. He glanced over to the dining room, with its single chair at the table. Just as he turned to look back at the living room, a shape on the table caught his eye.

Puzzled, Vix strode through the wall arches into the dining room. A small package was on the middle of the table. It was wrapped simply in brown paper, a hemp cord tied around it. Vix gingerly lifted the package. There was no writing on it, no notice of addressee. Though it was small, it had heft to it.

Carefully opening the package, he spilled the clinking contents onto the table top, quickly realizing these were the same coins he had given as assassin payment. A small piece of paper lay on top of the pile. Picking it up, he slumped to the chair when he read its brief message.

You have been outbid.

Alric stood up and smiled warmly as Alexis walked in. "Good evening High Commander. Glad –" he stopped when Brenna walked in behind her. "Brenna. How nice of you to show up."

Brenna looked at the table in the rear of the tent, arranged for an intimate dinner for two. Before she could speak, Alexis interrupted.

"I invited her to come with me. We've been riding the whole day together. I was sure that you would understand," she smiled.

"Of course High Commander. You were right to think that." He turned to a guard standing inside his tent. "Bring another setting and tell the cook to prepare for one more."

"I can leave," Brenna said flatly. "It's obvious I wasn't expected."

"Nonsense! You must stay," he gallantly replied. "High Commander Alexis is right. I should have expected you to come. I was rude for not inviting you. I offer my apologies." He bowed in exaggerated humbleness.

Alexis laughed, and even Brenna smiled.

"Good, I've made you smile. Please, you two sit there. I'll have another table set up momentarily." He motioned both of them to the table, gently touching each on the elbow and guiding them to sit down.

Alexis looked at Alric and realized that he was freshly clean, a clean that made her aware of her own dusty and road-worn appearance. "Pity, I left my evening dress back at the castle."

He smiled beneficently. "Now commander, do you expect me to believe that mere clothes could make you any lovelier?"

Smiling at the compliment, she nodded in acceptance.

"My, what a silken tongue you've found." It was almost a sneer.

"Now High Commander Brenna, really. There should be no animosity in this tent. You are welcome to partake of my humble feast. Eat. Fill yourselves. Relax. Enjoy the pleasure of the evening."

"This smells delicious," Alexis interrupted. She sat and began methodically selecting plump pieces of meat from the plate and plopping them into her mouth, chewing slowly, savoring each mouthful.

Brenna begrudgingly sat and selected several pieces of meat. To her surprise, they were distinctly scrumptious. "This is excellent!" she said between mouthfuls.

He bowed in mock humility. "A little marvel the cook discovered. It is good, isn't it? More wine?"

They both nodded and continued to devour the meal. As they ate, another table was brought and set up next to them. Alric sat and nibbled at the food.

"High Commander Alexis –"

"Please, just call me Alexis." She wiped her mouth.

He smiled suavely. "Yes, that is better isn't it. Inside the tent, we are comrades, equals in our abilities." He sipped from his goblet. "Alexis, I understand your tarrac wouldn't let you leave without him. I can understand that." He smiled again. "Do you have everything you need for him?"

"Actually, we didn't count on him being here."

"Of course not." He turned again to the guard, snapped his fingers and pointed. "Make sure High Commander Alexis' tarrac is fed and cared for."

"Yes, m'Lord." The guard turned to relay the command.

"Personally," Alric slowly intoned.

"As you wish, m'Lord." The guard hurried out.

"You didn't have to do that," Alexis said, though pleased.

He glanced back at her, silently taking in her physical beauty. "You have a rare animal. Never before has a tarrac allowed another to become its master. Obviously you have a special talent to sooth the wild beasts." He grinned coyly.

She smiled in return. "Unfortunately not all wild animals do what I ask of them."

Leaning forward, elbows on his own small table, he flashed her a mischievous grin. "How foolish of them." Before she could respond, he sat back up. "Brenna, it looks like you could use more wine." He turned to the tent opening and called out for more wine.

"Why are you being so nice to me?" She eyed him suspiciously.

He simply smiled. "Whatever ...um... difficulties that lay between us are in the past. I made a mistake in allowing my juvenile pride to get the better of me. But that was then. Here you are, one of the Twelve." He hoisted his goblet in a toast. "Alexis, I don't know what Brenna has told you about herself, but I'm sure it wasn't enough."

Alexis put down her own goblet. "She told me that she was a member of the twelve elite warriors."

"And that's it?" He feigned surprise. "Alexis, to be a member of the Twelve is the highest honor a warrior can attain. In order to become a member of the Twelve, a warrior must prove himself, or herself," he nodded towards Brenna, "in many battles. Then he must issue a challenge to the entire Twelve and if accepted, the Twelve choose their champion. Should the challenger defeat the champion, the Twelve still have the right of refusal." He turned to Brenna and again held up his goblet. "Brenna is the only woman in the past five hundred years of Gambri history not only to defeat a champion of the Twelve, but to also be unanimously chosen to become a member of the Twelve. She is the rarest of Gambri women indeed." He drank deeply in salute.

Brenna blushed slightly, torn between her distrust and this newfound offer of friendship. "You're being very kind Alric. I think I like this new side of you better."

A servant brought in the wine and generously filled the goblets.

"You may leave the flask." Alric interrupted his departure. "Please tell the cook to bring some more –" he turned back to the two women and they both pointed to the same platter of savory morsels of meat in a light thin au jus, "baby rone." He nodded his agreement. "It is good isn't it?"

"What did you say it was?" Alexis questioned.

"Baby rone."

"What's a rone?"

"Perhaps you've seen them in the market. Average size, large haunches, large bellies, rather dopey looking." Alric used his hands to help describe the animal.

"I had some prepared for your welcome feast." Brenna watched for Alric's reaction at the news, but there was none. Apparently he had heard and it no longer mattered.

"That was also delicious," Alexis offered.

"But not as good as this," Brenna admitted.

Alric placed both hands on his chest in mock humility. "You do me great honor. I'll be sure to tell the cook. He'll certainly appreciate your praise. More wine?"

As Alexis drank another goblet full of the sweet wine, she leaned back in her chair. "How many battles have you been in Alric?"

He frowned as he pondered, momentarily stumped.

"At least seventeen," Brenna responded for him.

"And how do you know?" Alric smiled.

"I've been in seventeen and you've been in every one I've been in."

Alric thought for a moment. "Humpf. I suppose you're right. And as I recall, you were instrumental in deciding the outcome in many of them. Alexis, you should see Brenna fight. She is truly wonderful. In fact, I remember one battle where there were three of them coming from her blind side. She was in the thick of fighting off three others." He stood up and began acting out the battle.

"What happened?" Alexis was intrigued. Brenna furrowed her brows trying to remember.

"She hacked and chopped at her adversaries as they parried and thrust their foul blades at her, occasionally nicking her arms or thighs. Blood began to ooze from the thin slices etched on her body. Yet she fought on."

"And then?" Brenna raised one eyebrow.

"And then they attacked her from the left. Brenna feels them coming and in one quick turn, she slices the heads off of all three. One swoop, just like that." He sliced his hand through the air.

"You're lying!" Brenna started laughing. "I never did anything like that."

Even Alric started laughing. "Well it certainly seemed like that."

Alexis realized the joke and joined in the humor. Alric filled the wine goblets again. Brenna was still laughing.

"I like the way I parried the first three. How did it go? Show me."

"What?   Again?"   Alric responded playfully.   He obliged and pantomimed the scene again, except a bit more exaggerated this time, which caused them to laugh more.

"Where were the cuts?" Alexis joined in.

"Here and here and here." Using his hand, Alric sliced various parts of his body.

"I don't see any scar here?" She peered intensely at Brenna's bare arm.

"She heals well." he shrugged.

"Wait, I've got scars," Brenna defended herself.

""Where?" he baited.

"Here." She pulled the collar away from her shoulder to show a long thin healed scar.

"I've got one better than that," Alric grinned. He pulled up his shirt in the back and leaned over, showing a long scar that went across the lower part of his back.

"You call that a scar. Look at this one." Brenna pulled up the front of her jerkin, and slightly lowered the top of her pants to show a scar on her left side. "I got this from a spear at the Battle of Little Wormwood."

There was a pause while Alric and Brenna both stood, showing their battle wounds. Then they both looked over to Alexis, waiting.

"OK, OK, I have scars too." She pushed herself away from the table, a bit unsteady from the wine. Unbuttoning her leggings, she turned to pull them down, exposing her left buttocks. A long thin scar began from near her hip and stopped down near where her leg began.

"Nice butt," Alric involuntarily whispered.

Brenna heard and turned to look at him. He smiled sheepishly and shrugged. Brenna laughed. "I agree."

"You agree with what?" Alexis wondered.

"That's a nice scar," he covered. "But look at this one." He pulled off his shirt.

Alexis watched as he lifted the shirt over his head. He was exceedingly well proportioned. His stomach muscles dipped and rose in tight definition. From his narrow waist, his chest widened precipitously to broad muscular shoulders. He stood there, tall and handsome, seemingly naively unaware of his beauty as he pointed at the scar running across his stomach.

"I got this one at the Battle of the Mountain Hall."

Brenna suddenly saw Alexis' reaction to the posing Alric. A tiny seed of jealousy settled in the pit of her stomach and she fought to control it.

"That's good, but look at this one." Alexis grinned. She unbuttoned several buttons from her jerkin and pulled it open, almost exposing her right breast. There was just the slightest highlight of a scar that started on the lower portion of her breast and went towards the center of her chest. "I got this one in a fight for the national championships. The bastard used a razor poker. Almost got me in the heart."

Alric paid close attention, admiring the curves of what he could see. "And what happened to him?"

"Killed him," Alexis shrugged matter-of-factly. She looked up and saw the interest both of them showed and instead of closing her jerkin, she pulled it open just ever so slightly more, and began slowly tracing the scar with her finger.

Brenna was the first to break the silence. "That's a nice scar. Wouldn't you agree Alric?"

Alric nodded mutely.

"But, I think you'll both be impressed with these scars." She began unbuttoning her jerkin.

Entering the tavern, Cu quickly surveyed the occupants. At this time in the early evening, the place was just beginning to fill. There were a number of locals at several tables already swapping crude jokes and whistling at the barmaids who good-naturedly swatted at errant hands. In a corner away from the door, a non-descript man with the short cropped hair and wide cheekbones nursed an ale and observed the banter.

"Good day to you Warrior. Have a seat. What can I serve you?" The owner, a trim and fit man just a few years past his prime, came around one of the tables.

"Well met Master Taverner. A friend suggested I try your stout, said it was better than we could get in Mull." Cu sat at a table close to the door.

"And he was right," the man warmed to the praise. "Siusan," he called to a barmaid with short-cropped auburn hair, "a mug of stout for our young warrior here."

"Coming Da."

Cu watched her as she filled his mug. "Your daughter?"

"Aye. And I keep a close watch on her."

He grinned, raising his hands. "You'll get no problem from me."

"I know," he replied. "So tell me young warrior, who was this friend who so highly favored my stout?"

"Tarrac Master Menec," he answered, accepting the mug.

The man nodded in recognition, "A fine man." He turned to his daughter who continued standing next to the table. "I know he's a good looking young warrior, but you've stared at him long enough to paint a picture. Now off with you." He lightly swatted her butt.

"Da!" she flushed and scurried off.

Cu smirked as she left, then looked up to the owner. "Menec said I should come here because the owner, a man called Curney, was an honest taverner. Might you be him?"

"I am." He sat down across from him. "And what else did Menec say?"

"To try the stout."

Curney chuckled. "Well said."

Cu took a long draught and wiped his lips, his eyes revealing his pleasure. "And he was right. This is delicious."

Curney nodded at the compliment.

"How long have you been retired?" Cu asked, setting down the mug.

The taverner raised an eyebrow. "How did you know?"

"Two reasons: first, you don't look like the normal plump taverner, and second – Menec told me."

"It's been about two years," he chuckled.

"Do you miss it?"

"Of course," he sniffed. "Who wouldn't? But there comes a time when one must move on. A warrior is only as good as his last battle. It was time. But, I doubt you came here to ask me whether I missed the taste of battle."

Cu sipped his stout. "True enough." He wrapped both hands around the mug. "There is a man sitting in the corner, opposite the door. Do you know him?"

Curney leaned back to survey the room, pretending to be preoccupied with the locations of the barmaids. He motioned for Siusan to bring him an ale, then turned back to Cu. "He comes through here occasionally. Usually keeps to himself."

"Ever see him with anyone else?"

Thinking for a moment, he briefly shook his head. "None that I can recall. Why the interest in this man?"

Cu lifted his mug to take a drink. "He's not one of us."

The taverner blinked as he absorbed the statement. "How is that possible? How'd he get past the guards, the patrols, the checkpoints?"

Cu shrugged. "That's what we'd like to know. I've been following him ever since he left Mull. Unfortunately, I believe he knows it. He double-backed into Mull and tried to lose me in Merchant's Walk." Cu chuckled. "I don't know what he was thinking... I just went outside the City gates and waited. He came out soon enough. I had a hunch he would head in this direction."

Curney nodded pensively. "The battle at Gefnyn's." Taking a deep breath, he rubbed his chin. "So, what are we to do?"

"He cannot leave here. Do you have anyone you can trust to help us?"

Laughing easily, he said, "Look around you. Knowing who he is, do you think they'd let him go?"

"I was hoping to be a bit more discreet. There may be others."

"Not a problem. Nola," he caught the attention of a jovial busty woman carrying several mugs of ale to one of the tables. "Have we a room for this young warrior?"

"If not, he can sleep with me," she winked. The men at the table burst with laughter and demanded the same treatment.

Curney shook his head. "Pay her no mine. She's quite the flirt, but she's good for business." He stood up. "Well young warrior –"

"Cu."

"Cu," he repeated. "Well Warrior Cu, I've other customers to attend. Please enjoy the stout and thank Master Menec for his kind recommendation." Before heading back to the kitchen, he passed by another table and leaned down to talk to one of the men, a farmer by the look of him. After a brief exchange, he clapped the man on the back and stood back up. Looking back to Cu, he gave a curt nod, and then moved among several other customers exchanging light banter.

Cu quickly awoke to the sound of footsteps outside in the hallway. He reached for his sword as the door opened.

"Warrior Cu?"

He relaxed as he recognized the Taverner's voice. "Yes."

"Bad news I'm afraid." Curney entered, holding a small candle. "He's gone."

"Gone? How?" The warrior got up and adjusted his clothing.

"He must have known. Got up during the night to use the outside privy and took off. He's fast. None could keep pace, and they know the area here. He left this though." He held up a sleeveless overcoat made of soft animal skin."

Cu grimaced. "Damn." Unbuckling his sword-belt, he reached for the coat and began feeling along the outer braiding. "Anything else?"

"There is nothing written, if that's what you mean," Curney answered. "Doesn't look like he even slept in his bed."

Cu stopped along the bottom edge when he felt something hard. Reaching for his sword, he cut through the material and several coins clinked to the floor. Picking one up, he studied it in the light. Though worn, the crest of Rugia was quite visible.

Brenna's head moved slowly sideways, up and down in a rhythmic pulse. She shifted to get comfortable and realized that her pillow itself was moving. And in that moment when sleep finally is pushed away, she groggily lifted her pounding head to realize that she was sleeping on Alric's chest. Frowning, she pushed herself onto her elbows and then onto her knees. She watched Alric continue sleeping and thought that somehow his shirt looked familiar. She looked down at her own shirt and understood. *He's wearing my jerkin. Why do I have his on?*

The tent flap parted and the early morning sun streamed in behind as Alexis walked in. Brenna covered her eyes from the glare. "Where've you been?"

"I was double checking on Stracaim. Despite getting beaten and dragging half the stable behind him for several hours, he seems to be doing quite well." Alexis walked over to where the remains of last night's dinner congealed in the now cold sauces. Selecting a morsel, she plopped in her mouth, sucking the thick sauce off her fingers. "Nice shirt."

Alric's eyes batted awake and he rolled onto his side. He studied Brenna for a moment and then looked down at his own attire. "Hmm. Seems like I must have had a really good time last night."

Brenna unsteadily got to her feet. "We gotta go."

"No breakfast? It won't take long." Alric stood up and quickly put his hands to his head. "Whoa, that hurts." He looked at the immobile Brenna and then to the munching Alexis. "I can get warmer food than that."

"We really need to be going. I probably should check on Cymy.'" Brenna responded.

"Fine."

"Um, can I have my jerkin?" she sheepishly asked.

"Most certainly." Alric pulled off the jerkin and held it out to her. He waited for her to return his shirt, but she didn't move. Smiling, he turned around while Brenna quickly changed shirts.

"Here you go." Brenna tossed Alric's shirt to him as he turned back around. She moved rapidly to the door and realized that Alexis was still eating. "Coming?" she demanded.

Alexis threw a small bone on the table. "Thanks for dinner. Next time our tent, right Brenna?" She laughed. Brenna glared at her, wheeled around and hurried out of the tent. Alexis laughed again and followed.

Still shirtless, Alric languidly ambled over to the door, pushing the flap open. Squinting, he followed the two women as they walked away.

A guard stood stiffly next to the entry, a wry smile on his face. "Sounds like it was a good evening Prince Alric."

"An amazing evening, amazing. Warrior women have such passion. I need a bath, a rubdown, and two days rest." The guard barked a loud guffaw.

Daylight slipped over the window ledge, casting long shadows against the far wall of Lucan's dining room. As the sun brightened the morning's sky, the shadows slithered down the walls onto the furniture and then onto the chair where he sat, staring dumbly at a bowl on a now illuminated table. It wasn't until the sunlight danced across his eyes that he blinked, a sluggish awareness that the night had gone and he must face the day.

He inhaled a slow deep heavy breath, held it a moment, then flushed the air from his lungs in a loud sigh. Expiation... expiation... the word kept rattling in his mind. Oh, he had tried blaming her, the vixen... but he was shocked at how easily he fell... how little his vow had meant...

Expiation. In the depths of his despair, he knew with a finality that hurt; he was alone. To whom could he confide? To whom *should* he confide? It was too easy an answer. No one. This was his burden, and he must bear it... alone. The guilt was his, and he must answer.

The question was... when?

The night deepened in darkness and the twin moons hid behind a veil of opaque clouds. The three hundred warriors of Gambria, along with their creaking wagon trains, trudged the hard packed road past Gefnyn's dimly lit castle that stood like a tiring beacon in the thick night. Yet too soon was its safety left behind as the few lights extinguished behind the rolling hills.

Alexis sat behind Brenna on Cymy as they slowly made their way to the awaiting soldiers of Gambria. Attached to the lead held by Alexis, Stracaim lumbered solidly beside them. Occasionally his ears would twitch whenever Alexis spoke. Brenna had made the long journey enjoyable by relating stories and gossip of the activities of the leading Gambri families. Yet now she was strangely quiet.

"You OK?" Alexis broke the silence.

"I'm fine." Her body lazily rocked in rhythm with the tarrac's walk.

Alexis nodded. "I understand." She paused, letting the night sounds drift across their path. "You're not worried about me are you?"

Brenna chuckled. "Hardly. I've seen what you can do." She tilted her head slightly in understanding. "But yes, I am concerned. You have fought one-on-one, but have you fought many at once? Have you fought in battle?"

The tarracs' hooves plodded in the ensuing quiet, occasionally interrupted by the soft voices of others in conversation.

"You're right," Alexis mused aloud. "I've never been in battle. The most I've fought at once was four and I only killed three in that encounter. Yet strangely enough, I'm rather excited about tomorrow's battle. It's been too long since I've had the pleasure of real combat."

Listening to her matter-of-fact approach to the impending destruction, Brenna gave voice to her thoughts. "Do you not fear death?"

"Hmmm," she paused, "not really. To die in battle, at the hands of a greater warrior than I... after a long struggle... the two of us... locked in combat, our bodies straining hard against each other... yes... that would be

261

honorable." She turned to look across the darkness at her friend. "I fear nothing."

"Nothing?" She looked askance.

Alexis mused momentarily. "I suppose that's not totally true. I do fear growing weak and old. I will not age gracefully. I will fight it at every step of the way."

Brenna laughed quietly. "I agree. I too will not age with grace. I will not allow myself to become soft like the wives of the rich."

"Those fat things? If I ever say to you, 'Brenna, I no longer want to fight, I no longer want to go into battle, I'd rather stay in my warm home by the fire and have another sweet-cake,' do you know what I want you to do?"

"No." Brenna smirked.

"Just kill me. Don't ask why, you'll know. So just kill me. No remorse, no pity. You can tell everyone that it was a mercy killing. Alexis went crazy and it was the only thing you could do."

Brenna's laughter burst and she shook her head.

"I'm serious," Alexis chuckled. "It wasn't that funny."

Controlling her mirth, Brenna said. "So tell me. Just how do you propose to control growing old?"

"Just like master Kenji-san did."

"Who?"

"Kenji-san, my guide and mentor."

"And what was his secret?"

"He was very wise, very wise. He knew the timing of his life, the rejoicing of his inner peace."

"I don't understand what you're saying. What do you mean timing and inner peace?" Brenna shifted in the saddle.

"The harmony of the warrior. He called it bushido. It's the balance between being the perfect warrior and the appreciation of what's beautiful, while accepting what life gives you." Alexis smiled sheepishly. "I'm beginning to sound like Duncan."

Brenna smiled. "Not really. I understand you."

She nodded knowingly. "I'm sure you do. What Kenji-san understood was that life was to be lived in the now, and not in the promise or dread of some future."

Brenna pursed her lips in musing. "He sounds like an interesting man. I like the name – Kenji-san. It's a strong name."

"He was ninety-three years old when I left."

"Ah, he had lived a long a rich life then."

"Yes, I suppose." Alexis paused. "But, there is another reason I admire him so much."

"Really? And what might that be?"

"He's the only warrior I've never been able to beat."

Brenna's jaw dropped. "What? He's ninety-three years old! He's a doddering old man who should be in the grave!"

"That's just it. He was old, but hardly doddering. He could look at me and know exactly what move I was going to do. And even before I started, he was already blocking and counter-moving to my attack. More than once I found myself sailing through the air wondering what just happened."

Brenna shook her head in amazement. "Ninety-three... How is this possible?"

"Wisdom. He studied and learned and practiced. He was never satisfied with merely perfecting a move. He had to understand everything about it: the muscles involved, the attitude of the attacker, the balance and harmony of the moment."

Now it was Brenna's time to ponder. "He sounds like a mystic."

She shrugged. "I suppose he could be."

Another long silence spread out between them as Brenna phrased her next question. "Is Duncan a mystic?"

Alexis smiled to herself. "Depends on what you mean by 'mystic.' Duncan is by far the most knowledgeable man I have ever known. Whether he is a so-called mystic or not is another question."

"You mean he may not be the promised one of Safti?" she said, half in jest.

"Hmmm," Alexis spoke slowly, purposefully, carefully choosing her words. "I can't say for sure he is or isn't. I'm really not into all this god stuff anyway."

"I understand," she nodded in agreement. "To tell the truth, I'm not into the god stuff either, but I do have questions. If there is a god, he, she, or it can't be too powerful because I never see anything it does. And none of the priests can give me a good answer. Still... there's something about Duncan that I can't quite... um...." she paused searching for the right words.

"Come to grips with?" Alexis interjected.

"Yes, something like that."

"As far as Duncan is concerned, I don't know where his future lies, whether as the promised one of Safti or something else. All I know is that when he talks, I've learned to listen to what he has to say."

"And do you always do what he says?"

263

Alexis leaned over towards Brenna and whispered loudly, "Hardly ever."

Brenna laughed again. "Good. You had me worried for a moment." She turned to look back forward and felt the tremor of arrival that rippled through the procession. "We're here." The tarracs slowed to a stop as Alexis, then Brenna slid down.

She looked over to Alexis giving her attention to Stracaim. "Will you ride the tarrac tomorrow?"

"No." She leaned forward and patted the firm neck muscles. "He can use some more rest. Besides, I prefer my first battle to be on foot."

The line of warriors slowly moved forward as warriors were sent to strengthen various sections of the battle formation. As Brenna and Alexis moved up, a runner approached.

"High Commanders, Lord Alric asks that you go to the right flank. Lord Meton presently commands the flank."

"Where's Gefnyn?" Brenna demanded.

"High Commander, I believe he has relinquished command to Lord Alric. I'm really not sure where he is right now."

"Where are the Twelve to be positioned?"

"I know not Commander. My orders were for you and High Commander Alexis."

"Finally somebody gets my name right!" Alexis smirked.

"This isn't right," Brenna fumed. "Either he uses the Twelve as a whole or he divides them by group. Where is Lord Alric?"

The runner shifted uncomfortably. "As far as I know Commander, he's at his tent."

"Take me to them. Now!"

"Yes High Commander." The runner bowed low and turned to lead the way.

There was boisterous laughter in Alric's tent as Brenna burst in, Alexis in tow. The revelers looked up as the two entered.

"Well if isn't the twin moons," a voice chirped and laughter erupted again.

"Say it again gutless coward whoever you are," Brenna demanded, twirling a long bladed dirk in her hand.

"Now, now Commander," Alric took control. "We're just having a little fun. There was no insult intended, was there Captain Odran?"

"Certainly not m'Lord." Odran smiled broadly. "I meant not to offend, but to merely make a point. Just as Gambria's twin moons are inseparable, so it seems the High Commander and the new Berserker are." He bowed in mock apology.

"The new berserker has a title Captain," Brenna coldly stated. "It's High Commander. I'd suggest you get used to it, but then I don't expect you to survive tomorrow's battle… unless you run like you usually do."

"That's a lie!" Odran jumped up.

"That's enough!" Alric commanded.

"He's a coward," she taunted.

"You lie." Odran stood erect, his chest pushed forward.

"A serious accusation captain." Brenna stepped forward. "You've insulted me and I demand satisfaction. Here. Now."

Odran's chest deflated slightly as he dully blinked the realization of his own fate.

"Stop this! I will not have fighting within my own tent!" Alric tried to regain control. He whirled to face Odran. "You. Captain. Apologize to the High Commander for your offensive remark."

Odran glared the anger of a helpless animal, knowing he was beaten and hating her for it. "I apologize High Commander." He said it slowly, without emotion.

"And you High Commander," Alric whipped back around to face Brenna. "What is it that you need so desperately that you would come into my tent during my war council."

"War council?" Brenna sneered and looked around the room. "Where are the flank commanders? Where is the captain of the Twelve? Where is the commander of relief, or the captain of the trains? This is no war council but a boy's club." She stood facing Alric, daring him to stop her. "Where are the Twelve to be positioned? What have you done with the Twelve? I was told to go to the Meton's flank along with High Commander Alexis. You know this is not the way we do battle."

Alric folded his arms. "Are you contradicting my orders?"

"No, I am not contradicting your orders," she bluntly stated. "You are the commander here. I just wish to know why you are not using the Twelve as is required."

Before he could answer, the captain of the Twelve pushed his way into the tent. He was a giant of a man, well built with thick arms and thick hair. His chestnut beard flowed to his chest. He looked at Alric first and then at Brenna.

"Hullo Brenna. I was wondering where you had gotten to." His eyes were the blue of the Starn Sea. They told her to subdue herself. He turned to Alric. "Lord Alric, I seem to have some difficulty understanding your orders concerning my Twelve."

"Then come sit Tuathal, and let me see if I can help you," he grinned.

The Twelve's Commander took a step, grabbed a stool and plopped down, laying his great claymore across both knees. "Why have you attached Brenna out to the right flank without the other two?"

"Have you eaten yet? How about something to drink?" Alric turned to his attendants. "Bring food for the Captain of the Twelve."

Brenna watched Alric's smooth transition and turned to lean-in to Alexis. "I don't like where this is going," she frowned.

A half hour later, Brenna and Alexis stood with Tuathal outside the tent. The night had settled and the hillsides surrounding Alric's tent were now alive and spotted with small cooking fires. The aroma of cooked and singed game undulated with the gentle winds.

"I can do nothing," Tuathal explained. "They are his orders. And just as his authority comes from the king, my only recourse is to take it to the king. Yet I cannot do that until we return." He shrugged. He then placed one of his great meaty hands on Brenna's shoulder. "But I will do this. There are two with me in the center. As Safti is my witness, I and the other chosen of the Twelve will do all we can to break the center before you get into too much trouble." He turned to regard Alexis. "At least you have the berserker with you." He then spoke to her. "If what I have been told is true berserker, then we have a mighty warrior in you."

"It's true," Alexis calmly observed.

Tuathal smiled quietly and nodded. "Good hunting then." He turned to Brenna. "And to you too High Commander. We shall meet again tomorrow when the Rugian Captain's head is hoisted high on the standards of the Twelve." He turned and disappeared into the blackness.

Silence enveloped the vacuum of Tuathal's departure. Brenna sighed loudly and her lips tightened.

"OK. I'll play his stupid games. I know what he's doing." She stalked off toward Meton's tents, yanking Cymy's reins and pulling the tarrac with her.

Tugging on Stracaim's reins, Alexis quickly caught up. "What who's doing?"

"Alric."

"So what is he doing?"

"He's purposely making the right flank light."

"Why?"

Brenna led the way back down the wagon path. Having stood outside Alric's tent, waiting for Tuathal to come out had allowed their night vision to firm and they walked with sure foot. "For two reasons. First, the Rugians tend to weight their left flank. Not always, but usually. They have this crazy strategy that if they throw enough weight on you, you'll eventually crumble. Sometimes it works, other times not."

"And what does that mean?" Alexis matched her stride for stride.

"It means that he expects the main attack on our right. We become the feint and bear the brunt of the Rugian attack while he hammers the center to hold and main attacks on the left, hoping to roll up the flank. It's a great strategy provided the forces are arrayed properly."

"So what's the problem?"

They followed the road as it curved toward the distant river that separated Gambria from Rugia. Even from this distance they could see the cooking fires of the enemy. "The problem is that he's purposely taken forces away from Meton; forces that Meton needs if he is to maintain his position." Brenna abruptly stopped. "It doesn't make sense."

"Now what?"

"Making the right flank too light," Brenna explained. "If it's too light, the Rugians can push through and then come from behind. Humpf. He knows that. He's not telling everything." As quickly as she stopped, Brenna took off. "I wonder if Meton knows what's going on."

Alexis tagged alongside her and let Brenna muse out loud. Finally she interrupted, "And what's the other reason Alric is doing this?"

Brenna chuckled grimly. "To get back at me."

"Y'know, I've been wondering why you two scratch at each other like king's companions."

"Interesting comparison," Brenna laughed. "It's a long story, but it comes down to that we were involved once –"

"And it didn't work out," Alexis finished the sentence. "And I imagine he's the one who hasn't gotten over it."

Brenna sniffed. "Unfortunately yes. He's made it his personal vendetta to try to make my life miserable."

"It didn't seem that way last night."

"I know. It was strange. For a while there, he was like the Alric I used to know." She shook her head. "He was probably just setting me up for something."

"Well," Alexis shrugged, "it's moot now. If I understand all that's going on, we're stuck with his decision."

"Unfortunately, yes."

"Yet something still doesn't make sense to me. If Alric wants to win the battle, our flank still has to hold. If our flank goes down, so does he."

"That's what I don't understand," Brenna puzzled. "He's made the right flank light, split up the Twelve, and put the berserker on the weak flank. This is all contrary to logic."

"Perhaps Meton knows," Alexis suggested, "whoever he is?"

Brenna chuckled despite herself. "He's one of King Diad's uncles."

"So this is a family run operation?" she joked.

Brenna smiled, "I suppose one could look at it like that. However, unlike the self-serving Alric, Meton is one who can be trusted. Unfortunately, he's not the fighter he once was and knows it, so he fights even harder. The problem is that he tires faster and imperils those around him who must then come to his aid."

"Why doesn't he retire?"

Brenna jerked her tarrac to a halt. "Are you being flippant again?"

"Hardly." Alexis reined in her own tarrac. "I'm being a realist. I know the old sappy emotion of once a warrior always a warrior. And for the most part that's somewhat true. But there comes a time when a warrior must recognize that he or she is causing more trouble than good."

"It's too easy for you to say," she answered. "What becomes of an old warrior then in your country?"

"She lives a life of comfort, out of harm's way."

"So she grows soft?"

"She can," Alexis frowned. "Many do. But the true warriors keep themselves trained, always ready."

"To do what? They've retired."

"To be the leaders of the next generation of warriors," Alexis parried. "Remember Kenji-san?"

She absorbed Alexis' statement. "I suppose you've a point. However, that is not the way we do it here in Gambria. A warrior is always a warrior. He or she never retires. Oh, there obviously comes a time when a warrior is no longer called to fight. At that time, he puts away his weapons and lives on the earnings of his wisdom."

"Wisdom?"

Brenna shook her head. "Most warriors fail to plan for their autumn years, before they give up the essence. So they end up running taverns or slaughterhouses, or hawking homespun cloth at the fairs. It's pathetic."

"And how is your wisdom?" Alexis teased.

"Quite excellent thank you. My future is well taken care of," she proudly replied.

"Interesting. Yet I never see you doing any of this business."

"Oh, I have another do it for me. He visits regularly to keep me appraised of my holdings."

"And you trust him?" she smirked.

"As much as I trust anyone," Brenna asserted.

"Then you must share him with me so that I too may gain... in wisdom," Alexis grinned.

"Ah, so you plan to retire too?" she taunted.

"Never."

"Oh? Are you not going to grow old?"

"I suppose I will, but there will never come a time where I cannot fight." It was said firmly, confidently.

Brenna snickered. "And how do you propose to do that?"

"Remember Kenji-san?"

"Yes. But there is no one here like him."

Alexis leaned over towards her. "I'm gonna be the first."

Brenna shook her head, laughing quietly. "You know, I believe you will."

"However, all my plans won't amount to much if we don't win tomorrow."

"You are right again," Brenna quickly sobered. "Let's go find Meton."

The temporary paddock enclosed a large field and was dimly lit with only a few torches providing light. Two torches undulating smoky flames, guarded the gate. The meeting with Meton provided no answers and Brenna continued shaking her head in disbelief as she and Alexis stood with their tarracs at the gate to the paddock. Brenna led Cymy into the enclosure. "Well, apparently Meton doesn't seem to be too put out over this." She slipped the bridle off and lightly slapped Cymy on the hind-quarters. "There you go my little one. Rest well! We've a busy day ahead tomorrow." Cymy trotted in, turned and let out a deep-throated growl while bobbing its head. "I know, I know," she smiled warmly. "You can feel it, can't you."

Alexis stood just outside the open gate and watched the exchange in admiration. "She understands you."

"She ought to. She's been my tarrac for almost nine years now." Brenna turned to answer, and watched in horror as Alexis took off Stracaim's bridle. "Not yet!"

But nothing happened. Instead, she watched Alexis gently take the great animal's muzzle and brought her face next to his. Then she lovingly nuzzled the ferocious beast. Stracaim rubbed her face in return, bumping his great head against her.

Turning, she walked into the paddock, Stracaim following obediently behind her. Once inside, she stopped. Stracaim playfully nudged her forward. Alexis laughed contentedly, turned and reached up to scratch behind the tarrac's ears. She then gently pulled his head lower and whispered in its ears. The magnificent animal nodded and trotted off to feed on the cut fodder.

Brenna stood dumbfounded, watching her exit the paddock, closing the gate behind her. "Are you a wizard now who can talk with animals?"

"Hardly," she chuckled. "He and I speak two different languages, but he knows that I'd do anything for him."

Brenna continued staring in amazement. "I have never seen anything like that, ever!"

Alexis simply shrugged. "I can't help myself. He's a beautiful creature and knows how I feel about him." She stood expectantly waiting. "Well?"

"Well what?"

"What do we do now?"

"Get ready for tomorrow," Brenna replied, leading the way away from the lit field.

"Where're we going?" Alexis sauntered easily beside her. The night was pleasant, with just the faint breath of a zephyr. The moons were high in the night sky and she could readily see the outlines and silhouettes of the Gambrians quietly slipping about the countryside. Cooking fires dotted the landscape. "By the way, just what am I supposed to do other than kill the enemy?"

"What do you mean?" Her battle companion furrowed her brows.

"I know I'm supposed to fight the Rugians, but what's the plan? What am I supposed to do?"

Brenna blinked in dull comprehension. "You're right. No one has bothered to explain how we fight to you."

"Now would be a good time." Alexis pursed her lips.

Pleased to demonstrate her knowledge of war, Brenna began an elaborate explanation beginning with positioning of the opposing forces. The Gambrian army was arrayed into three sections – left, middle, and right flanks. There was always a reserve equal to one half of a typical section in strength. Except for the baggage trains, everyone would fight. Even the reserve would be committed at the final moment to give all warriors a chance to fight. She and Alexis would be on the right flank with Meton's soldiers. Normally one flank would be designated to hold the line, while the middle and other flank attacked and rolled up the enemy line. The berserker was positioned in the attacking flank to cause the opposing enemy flank to falter and allow the middle to crash through the center. The Twelve were always used as a whole to reinforce a particular section.

Brenna continued with her lesson and soon was describing the various weapons the Rugians used. Alexis occasionally interjected with a comment or a question for clarification. One of the campfires began to grow closer. Alexis noticed it.

"Someone you know?"

"It is our resting place for the night. There are several warriors here, friends of mine. I asked if we could share the covenant meal with them."

"Covenant meal?" Alexis could smell the pungent aroma of singed flesh and cooked meat.

"You'll see." Brenna stepped into the firelight. "Hello Kay."

A woman, sitting on her haunches and tending the fire, looked up. "Hello Brenna." The voice was warm, almost erotic.

Then Kay stood up. She was tall, probably four or five inches taller than either of them. Kay looked to be older than either Alexis or Brenna by about ten years. However, age did not reveal any weakness as her sleeveless leather jerkin accentuated her wide shoulders and powerful arms. The short fighting skirt flaunted her muscular thighs. Her face was beautiful in an aquiline way, but there was a hardness to it, a self-brooding detachment.

"Smells good." Alexis complimented.

Kay smiled in return. "Thank you. You are welcome here High Commander. I compliment you on your command of our language."

Alexis bowed in acceptance. Noticing the large scar that began at her left shoulder and disappeared into her shirt, Alexis commented, "I see that you are a seasoned veteran."

Kay saw where Alexis was looking and adjusted her jerkin. "A mark from long ago, unfortunately."

"She was very lucky." Brenna interjected. "She had been left for dead, but she got up and walked back to our lines."

"And killed seven Rugians on the way back," a voice interjected. The three warriors looked up to see a diminutive woman enter the firelight, carrying a small animal.

"Hello Pella," Brenna gave the new arrival a hug. "I was hoping you'd be here." Brenna turned back to Alexis. "With her and Kay fighting on our flank, we stand a much better chance."

Pella saw the flicker of doubt flit across Alexis' eyes. "Don't worry High Commander, I can hold my own."

"I said nothing," she cautiously stated.

"But you do doubt. I understand. I am as new to you as you are to me. However, your reputation has preceded you and I also have the word of Brenna. Yet I will show you a bit of my talent." Pella pointed to a tree just on the edge of the campfire's shadows. "Pick a spot and point to it, but leave your finger there. Do not move your hand or arm."

Alexis was about to protest, but saw the resolve on Pella's face. She turned and went to the tree, briefly examining it. She pointed about shoulder high to a spot in edge of darkness. "Here. I'm pointing."

Pella had turned her back to her. "Good. Now I'm going to count to three and then throw a knife to where you are pointing."

Alexis shrugged. She had seen this performed before. "OK." But Pella didn't count and seemed to be occupied talking to Brenna and Kay. "I said I'm ready," Alexis said louder. Suddenly Pella whipped around and her hand flew from her side in rapid succession. Alexis saw nothing, but heard the thunks of metal jamming into the tree. She felt the flat of the blades slip against her flesh.

Pella stood back up just as the last blade hit the tree. Alexis looked at her hand and arm and saw over a dozen small stiletto knives edging her skin. She withdrew her hand and the knives neatly outlined where her hand and arm had been.

Alexis stared at the outline for a moment and then turned to address Pella. "Remind me not to ask you to swat a bug on my shoulder!" she said admiringly. "Forgive my doubt. I've never seen anything like it."

"I promise I'll use a swatter instead," she answered, warming to the praise.

"She may be small, but no one handles a knife blade like she does," Kay said proudly. "I've seen her kill or maim six warriors at one throw."

"I was lucky. Normally I can do two at once."

"What happens when you run out of knives?" Alexis asked.

"Pella is usually in the first wave," Brenna interjected, "so that by the time she's run out of blades, the rest of us have already passed her by and are in the middle of the enemy lines."

Alexis nodded appreciatively. "Sort of like shock troops."

"You could say that." Pella tugged at the imbedded knives, carefully taking each one out. She inspected each one as she returned to the fire. "It is time."

Both Kay and Brenna nodded. Together, they formed a semi-circle around the fire and sat down. Brenna motioned for Alexis to sit to her right. No one spoke for a while. Then Kay began in a low voice.

"We are gathered here as covenanters, pledging our bond with sacrifice. Just as this animal sacrifices its life for us, so do we sacrifice our lives for the good of the many. We four, here, now, do pledge to commit ourselves as one."

"And in that oneness," Pella continued, "do openly and publicly commit ourselves to fight together, and die together. We are one."

"Yet we cannot forget those who fell before us." Now it was Brenna's turn. "Many are those who have likewise pledged their covenant, those who have gone before us and now await us. It is this covenant that we now announce. It is this covenant that reminds us of who we are."

Silence fell again, filling the night with its presence. A trembling bleat broke the stillness and Kay nodded appreciatively. "It is time."

Pella stood up to retrieve the animal. Tenderly lifting it up, she returned to her place. The animal seemed to be a mix between a large rodent and a rabbit. Pella gently petted it.

Kay nodded again and both she and Brenna turned to kneel before Pella. Brenna motioned for Alexis to do the same. Kay lifted a large goblet, dully reflecting the firelight along its curves. It was made of wood, and had been polished smooth by years of devoted attention.

Kay bent forward just as Pella deftly slit the animal's throat. It seemed momentarily stunned and then jerked a bit spasmodically, then went limp. As the blood spurted out, Kay caught what she could in the cup. When the animal was dead, Pella handed it to Brenna who expertly skinned and gutted it.

Brenna tossed the entrails into the fire and there was a sputtering and hissing. "See? They talk to us."

"And what do they say warrior?" asked Kay.

"They ask who is this newcomer? What is her lineage that she should be here?"

"And what does she say?" Kay turned to Alexis.

Alexis bowed her head, her voice throaty. "Her name is Alexis, daughter of Dru, a mighty captain, a leader of a tribe, and a warrior," her voice softened to a hush, "who died saving her."

"And what is her wish?" Kay asked.

Alexis paused, then with a quiet fierceness spoke, "To be worthy of my father's name. To make your enemies my enemies. To not rest until all your enemies are conquered. To die honorably."

Kay nodded. "It is well spoken warrior."

Pella took the cup from Kay and dipped her fingers in the warm blood. She then traced a jagged bolt across Kay's face. She did the same to Brenna and then to Alexis. She handed the cup back to Kay who returned the favor.

Kay then motioned them to sit. "With this blood we join the blood of our ancestors, and are one with them." She bowed her head and the rest followed her lead, quietly contemplating the night and tomorrow's battle.

The stillness again filled the night as each was lost in her own thoughts. Then Brenna let out a sigh and leaned back. "Let's eat," she smiled.

The morning dawned moist and bright and the battle lines were already in place. Spread out across the ridge and knolls covered with low deep green meadow grass, the warriors of Gambri looked down upon their enemies backed against the river. The silence of the morning lay weirdly juxtaposed upon the fields. The animals and birds, sensing what was to happen, had fled.

Pendants of the various battle companies hung limply on their standards. An occasional cough escaped unnoticed. The sun glittered and bounced off brightly polished shields. Using the rising sun to their advantage, the Gambri played with the shields until the reflected sun focused on the Rugian front lines who blocked their eyes with tilted hands.

Like the Gambri, the Rugians had painted themselves in intimidating shapes and colors enhancing their ragged and wild appearance. Jagged stripes crossed their faces and the occasional bare chest. Waxed hair rose in stiff spikes or was pulled back to tuck under polished helmets. Unlike the Gambri who stood motionless upon the higher ground, the Rugians tended to shift and move within their formations giving the subtle appearance of a rippling mass of energy.

They had tightened their formations with deliberate gaps between the center companies. Their battle captain, a ferocious man of thick girth and scarred arms, sat calmly upon a large dappled tarrac behind the center formation, his hand raised high for all to see. His head was crowned with a silver helmet crested with feathered wings. He played with the ends of his huge draping moustache. The dark eyes concentrated on the arrayed enemy, awaiting the right moment to begin battle. And then his hand dropped.

Suddenly, the skirmishers broke through the center and charged up the hill stopping midway to hurl their javelins amidst the dodging Gambri. Several found their mark and the impaled warriors writhed in pain, pinned to the ground.

As the skirmishers ran back through the gaps to the rear of their formations, Alric gave his command and the yells and cries and whistles erupted as the Gambri descended. At the same moment the Rugians erupted and the crash of the battle enveloped the field. Swords clanged against shields, maces banged against helmets, and the agonizing gurgle of death escaped from those cut down.

Alexis had stood on the grassy knoll, poised to begin combat. Pella, Brenna, and Kay stood next to her. She had refused any armor except a thin layer of mail that covered her chest. Her choice of weapon had been a large staff, and she twirled it side to side in a rhythmic motion, feeling its balance and heft as though it was an extension of her own body.

Watching the center erupt, Alexis hoisted the staff and with a curdling yell, descended to fight. She ran and the adrenaline exploded within her. Her compatriots struggled to keep up, but she quickly outpaced the group and the awaiting Rugians grinned at this foolish woman warrior obviously wanting to die so quickly.

The warriors poised as Alexis ran up. However, instead of slowing down to fight, Alexis jabbed her staff in to the ground and using it as a catapult, pushed herself into the air somersaulting over the heads of the leading warriors and landed three rows back in a swirling churning mass of energy. In short order she had killed or maimed six warriors and before the others could react to this dervish in their midst, the rest of her companions arrived so that those on the line were caught from two sides.

A gap formed as Alexis and the Gambri warriors joined together. The madness of the berserker was upon her and the bloodlust flowed. She twirled and dodged and jabbed and swung and killed. Bodies lay crumpled in her path, some lost eyes or jaws, others fell with crushed skulls, still others crumpled from broken bones gaping out of their twisted bodies.

The Rugian flank quickly became overwhelmed. In a deliberate moment, someone realized that the flank was lost and turned to flee. The rest followed, fighting a delaying action, hoping to get to a position where they could get some reinforcements or support.

And still Alexis fought on. The force of her destruction piled bodies upon bodies. The Gambri warriors, seeing her devastation and buoyed by her prowess, yelled wildly giving new vigor to their own fight.

The Rugian captain sensed that his left flank was under extreme pressure and leaving the center under command of a lieutenant, galloped over to look in horror as his finest warriors were reeling backwards towards him. He signaled for the reinforcements to come to the left flank, but the center was now under pressure and the reinforcements were committed to the center. He raced back and broke off several companies of warriors to help out the flank.

The reinforcing companies were rapidly swallowed up in the melee. It was a moment later that the Rugian captain was face-to-face with Alexis. His haughty demeanor had almost left him, but when he saw this woman and thought that the Gambri had meant to humiliate him with a mere woman, he turned his beast and charged her.

She parried his mace and rolled to the side as he charged by. Her staff was shattered and she flung the two pieces to the ground. Pulling out a javelin from an inert body, and marking the rider's path, she hurled it with all her strength.

The captain jerked his tarrac to wheel it around, but it stumbled and the missile whizzed past him, imbedding itself in some unsuspecting Rugian down the line. The captain's head snapped up at the near miss. He whirled around and charged. Alexis grabbed a sword from a dead warrior and turned to face her opponent. But at that moment, something crashed hard into her back propelling her forward and she went down.

Alric sat upon his massive tarrac and watched the battle unfold as the center surged forward to lock itself in the tumultuous struggle. Off to his right, out of the corner of his eyes, he saw a lone figure racing down to initiate combat, the rest of the flank far behind.

"Who in Safti's name is that idiot?" He turned his full attention to the lone warrior.

"It's a woman, m'Lord," Oran squinted to see better. "I do believe it's our new berserker."

They were both silent for a moment when Oran suddenly blurted, "She's not wearing any armor."

Alric slowly shook his head. "She's either marvelously brave or incredibly stupid."

At that moment she catapulted over the front rank. Both Alric and Oran involuntarily jerked back in surprise. They watched the front rank turn around to see what was happening, only to whip back around to meet the headlong crash of the Gambrian right flank. In a moment, Alexis was lost in the swirling melee. And just as suddenly, the Rugian left flank began to collapse.

Alric squeezed his legs against his tarrac, urging it forward. "Looks like it's time to play. Tell Feirdwar to join the left flank. He is not to reinforce Meton like planned." Alric stood up in his stirrups. "It seems the right flank doesn't need any help. Tell Martainn to swing the reserves center right, just in case." Alric urged his beast forward. "Time to take charge." Alric slid his sword out from the saddle scabbard, twirled it twice, and spurred forward, the lust of battle firmly upon him.

As Oran rode to deliver his messages, he watched Alric and his four retainers plummet down the hill and slam into the Rugian center. He grinned with the self-assurance of knowing the battle won. He glanced back one more time over towards the right flank and sensed something was wrong. At first he couldn't see it, but then quickly realized that the right flank was giving way.

Chapter 19

It was almost the beginning of the second watch. The crowds were still threading their way down the road to the beach next to the harbor. Children ran laughing, chasing each other, weaving in and out and around the multitude of families. Mothers with babies on hips chided the most raucous of the free-spirited youth. Fathers ambled next to each other discussing business or wines or the latest news. Some smoked long, gracefully curved pipes, the tobacco aroma sweet and pungent. People standing on the piers chatted easily, the occasional laugh rising above the convivial murmur. The lights on the boats moored loosely at the pier's end bobbed like fireflies in the clear night.

The swelling crowd sat on the grassy knolls gently rising from the beach. Some had brought food in finely woven baskets, others were content to wrap their soft bread and cheese in simple cloth bags. Flagons of wine passed among friends.

In the distance behind the growing crowds, the city of Mull stood strong and silent, the lights along the walls showing like so many beacons of safety. The night settled comfortably over the fields of rippling grains, the zephyr wind folding blade upon blade.

On the beach, a large area had been cleared for the contest, and torches lined the boundaries going from the pressing crowds to the water. King Diad was nestled comfortably in the place of honor just inside the torches. His traveling throne had been brought down and he was settled peaceably upon a layer of animal pelts, his attention diverted by a buxom woman who tittered gaily at everything and coquettishly touched his arm every now and then as if to make a point. Several royal guards stood behind the throne.

Bradwr sat to the King's right. His chair, while not as opulent as Diad's, was likewise richly arrayed, the pelts seemingly finer than the King's. Although careful to show his subservience to the King, Bradwr was still obvious in his display of wealth. His chalices sparkled as the precious stones caught the occasional flame flicker. Yet while the King's attention was diverted by the beautiful woman, Bradwr occupied himself with subdued conversations with a number of messengers and friends.

Behind the king, in several rows, Gambrian royalty either sat or stood, gossiping amongst themselves. These uncles, cousins, nephews, nieces, and distant relatives of the king, preened haughtily before the crowds.

Duncan languidly sat on a large rock that was part of an outcropping in the rippling waves. The flickering light flitted shadows across his face. A look of feigned boredom was betrayed by his excited eyes.

On the beach sand, not far from Duncan, the priests of Safti were busily preparing a stone altar and consecrating each stone as it was added to the rising pile. Vix paced the area, his eyes wild like a trapped animal. *God, it's now!* he berated himself. *Why didn't he die like he was supposed to? Holy Safti, You* must *answer me, you must. He mocks you, you know he does ... O God, if you exist, don't fail me in this time of need. Don't let this charlatan charm these mindless fools.*

He lifted eyes skyward. The thickening night was filling with glimmering dots of stars, and the moist smell of the sea floated on the warm wind. *I have prayed to you every day. I have recited the verses, the prayers, the chants. I have fasted once a week; I have learned the words as my own ... and I have asked for signs ...* Vix sighed, *and you have never given me any.* He looked over to where Lucan was directing the design of the altar. *Perhaps He listens to you, brother ... You always believed, without question.*

"Brother Lucan," Vix's voice squeaked and he cleared his throat. "Brother Lucan," he said louder.

"Yes Holy Father?" Lucan looked over to where Vix stood, apart, the waves lapping his feet.

"Come here."

"Of course Holy Father. Brother Bergal, please continue while I talk with Father Vix." Lucan brushed the dirt from his hands and as he walked up to Vix his bare feet dug little valleys in the soft sand. "Yes Eminence?"

"I'd like you to pray with me please."

Lucan was pleased that he would entrust him so. "Of course Holy Father." Quickly bowing his head, he began, "Holy Safti, we ask for your continued blessings and your guidance."

"Stop it, you fool," Vix interrupted, his voice low and tense. "I need a miracle, not some pandering repetition of meaningless prayers." Lucan sputtered and jerked upright as Vix continued. "You better have some good connections with Safti because he sure as hell hasn't talked to me in a long time."

Lucan stepped back horrified, his own guilt suddenly exploding within him. "But... but, Holy Father –"

Vix grabbed Lucan's collar and pulled him closer. "Don't give me this Holy Father crap, I need a sign, a real sign damn it. And you'd better pray real hard that we see something because if we don't, we're in deep shit and you're in as deep as I am."

Lucan's jaw dropped as he stared dumbfounded at Vix. In all their time together, he had never heard his brother like this. He looked at the wild eyes and realized for the first time that Vix had never really believed in Safti. "O no," he moaned. "O god no. How can you ... why now? O god." Lucan rocked back, head in his hands.

"Stop this infernal whining," Vix snarled. "Don't be so damned shocked. What has Safti told you lately?"

Lucan pressed his hands against his ears. "Don't, don't! You blaspheme!"

Vix forcibly removed Lucan's hands and pulled him close. "Stop this holier than thou shit. We need a miracle. And short of that, we need to somehow convince this mass of imbeciles that Safti lives and is on our side. So pull yourself together and start thinking! And while you're at it you can pray too!"

Lucan staggered back and fled to the altar. "Quickly, we must finish."

As the last stone was placed, a distressed Lucan weakly waved it complete. He turned and with fear in his eyes, nodded to Vix.

"M'Lord King?" Vix vainly tried to get Diad's attention. "Lord Diad?" he yelled.

The King heard him above the din and briefly frowned at this interruption. However, remembering the reason for all of Mull being here, he stood up and turned to face the crowd. He lifted his hands for silence. After a few moments, the murmurs lessened and he spoke.

"People of Mull and Gambria," he spoke. "Today we witness the challenge for our souls. We have accepted a challenge from the man called Duncan against our High Priest Vix." The murmur gathered strength and the king raised his voice. "The stakes are thus: should our High Priest win, the challenger will be immediately impaled. Should the challenger win, he will become High Priest and do what seems fit. The challenge is this: whoever produces a sign across the sky is the winner. The High Priest has until the end of the second watch, at which time the challenger, called Duncan, will begin." As he sat, the crowd grew loud with applause and then settled back into their festive activities and waited for the promised competition. The king nodded to Vix and the priests began their lamentations and wailing.

Some of the priests took whips and began flaying themselves. Their backs turned red in stripes of blood. Other priests lay upon the altar and cried out loudly for Safti to hear them. Vix and Lucan stood up to their waists in the water and prayed fervently.

And nothing happened.

And so it continued for two hours. The noise and din rose loudly from the priests while the crowd grew restless, scanning the skies for a sign, any sign. Some grew bored and occasional taunts floated from out of the crowds.

Finally, with an hour remaining, Vix marched out of the water and pointed to an attending acolyte. Within moments, a young child was carried out of the crowd. A little girl, almost asleep, was handed to the High Priest. A loud wail escaped from the crowd as a man and woman tried to push their way to the beach, only to be thwarted by the attending acolytes.

Duncan leaped up. "King Diad! M'Lord! Does the High Priest mean to sacrifice a child to get his god to listen?"

King Diad, who had been busily entertaining the buxom woman, turned to see Vix holding the child. "What goes on then, Priest?"

"We need a sacrifice. Safti is displeased that he is being challenged to prove himself." Vix was gambling. He prayed that the king would say no. He could then say that the challenge was invalid because he had not been allowed to sacrifice in order to gain Safti's blessing.

The King surveyed the scene, shrugged, and turned his attention to the woman. "M'Lord, and people of Gambri!" Duncan turned to the crowd. "Is your god so blood thirsty that he requires the blood of an innocent child, just to talk to you? If this is your god, then he asks too much. What sort of god would have you kill yourselves as proof of your devotion?"

At first there was a deafening silence and then a low hum began, and the crowd began to churn. There were a few, the devout believers, who required nothing other than what was written, and if it meant sacrifice, then so be it. And there were still others who cared little for Safti or any religion but wanted entertainment, the more violent the better. But there were far more, far more, who had had enough of sacrifice, and their voices swelled with barely hidden anger.

Vix waited.

The king, again diverted from his pleasure, looked around at the crowd misjudging the anger for perverse excitement. Frowning, he turned back to Vix. "Do what you have to do, High Priest."

Vix sucked in the moist air. His bluff was called. Turning to an acolyte, he handed the child to him and directed the child be placed on the altar for sacrifice.

"King Diad! People of Gambria! This child will die for nothing. You will see!" Duncan turned away in disgust.

The King, who had been preoccupied, turned back to Duncan, and then listened to the hum of the crowd. He had spoken. To take back his word now would be a sign of weakness. He nodded again to Vix.

The child was placed on the altar and very quickly fell asleep. Vix stepped up to the stone platform, casting a glance at Lucan whose eyes were filling with tears. Angry at this sign of weakness from his own brother, Vix called out in a loud voice, "Holy Safti, we call upon you for a sign. Show us your power. Here is a sacrifice carefully chosen for you. Please accept this humble gift and shower your children with wonder. We ask for a sign that all may know of your greatness and overwhelming power."

With that, he quickly slit the child's throat and the blood poured over the altar. A shriek and wail sounded above the noise of the crowd. And so they waited. And nothing happened.

And the crowds grew restless. Vix yelled and screamed and berated his god, but nothing happened. And the crowds taunted him and they began yelling at him.

"What gives High Priest? Have you some gross unconfessed sin? Where is our God, Priest? What have you done?"

At the first hurled accusation, Lucan's legs weakened and he felt dizzy. The sudden realization that he might be responsible for Safti's failure to respond exploded within him, and he moved back from Vix, his hands in front of him as though pushing himself away.

Standing next to the limp and lifeless child on the altar, Vix felt their anger, and their fear. He felt the fear that comes with the removal of the cornerstone of belief, the fear that comes with doubt. And his own fear grew as did theirs.

At the end of the second watch, the official keeper-of-the-time stamped his standard and announced, "M'Lord and ladies, and Gambri, the end of the second watch has come."

Vix was exhausted. His acolytes carried him to the side as Duncan stormed onto the beach. The crowds grew suddenly quiet.

"I have had enough of your foolishness," he angrily yelled. "You have murdered a child without cause. You who blame Vix for her death are as guilty as he is. You stand there like dumb animals blindly led to slaughter.

Because of this, I will show you just what kind of power I have!"   He whirled around and strode to the middle of the area, so that all the available light reflected upon him. He stood to his full height and stretched his arms outward to the sky.

"I am Duncan! A wizard of the universe! I am the promised one of Safti. I am he who is the rightful heir to be called his son. I call upon the forces of nature and of senseless death to cry against the night! I call for a bright light to fill the sky!" He lowered his arms and turned to face the crowd.

Nothing happened.

Duncan did not move, but kept his arms at his side. And still nothing happened.

Somewhere in the crowd a few throats were cleared, then some derisive remarks floated on the air. "Oh brother, this was a waste of time." "Perhaps his god doesn't listen either." "Do we have to wait another three hours for nothing?"

Duncan ignored them. Finally, just as he was about to lose the crowd he curled up and then exploded with a loud "NOW!"

At that moment, an arc of flame spilt the night like a meteor, growing in size as it plummeted towards the sea. Just when it seemed to stop growing in size, a crash of light burst across the night sky rendering the land as though it was daytime. The light was blinding and angry, continuing for several seconds. The crowd fell back upon the ground, vibrating in fear, their hands groping their eyes to find sight, the cries of anguish for their blindness filling the night air.

Whirling around, he glared at the king whose own hands were at his face. His voice rose above the crowd. "And now for the voice of this light. The sound of an angry universe at your stupidity!" He stood boldly with arms spread high and wide.

In a matter of moments, the smash of an explosion so loud that it shook the earth, trembled across the land. Winds blew through the trees, flags flapped and tore, and the flames went out. The waves heaped upon each other and the screams of the crowd tried to fill the air above the din of the confusion.

Amidst it all. only Duncan remained assured and confident. When the sound started, he had dropped to one knee and bowed forward as the winds whipped over him. As the fury subsided, he whispered a heartfelt 'Thank you' to Talane. She had been right on time.

When peace once again settled, the cries began anew. "Help us wizard!

We cannot see!"

"Your sight will return in a little while. Stay where you are," he answered as he stood up.

The trembling King picked himself up and groped for where his overturned throne was. The buxom woman lay curled as in birth, cowering next to the throne. Some of the shivering priests of Safti lay sprawled in the sand. Even Vix had been overwhelmed.

The shieldsmen groped and righted the King's chair and he sat back down. Guards groped for flint and steel to reignite the lamps. In a short time, a few flickering lamps faintly illuminated the crowd, casting multitudes of shadows on the sand.

Diad's voice quivered a bit as he said, "'You, you have won wizard... er, High Priest, High Priest Duncan. Never before have we witnessed such a display. You are indeed powerful. I am thankful that you have chosen to serve Gambri."

Duncan waited. The crowd continued in their anguish, but sight began to return. As more and more began to regain some of their sight, the anguish gave way to a wave of relief.

The King regained his composure and, standing again, he turned to address the crowd. "From henceforth, the wizard called Duncan is High Priest of Gambria."

The crowd, still stunned by the display reacted only slightly, the fear of the experience still too fresh.

Visibly shocked, Vix stood transfixed, a mixture of despair and anger.

"And what is your wish concerning the former High Priest Vix?" the king asked, his voice still quavering.

"M'Lord, there is too much death in our lives as it is. I ask that you banish him from the kingdom. Let him live and go where he will - away from here. Let him ruminate on his sins against the people of Gambria." The crowd began a subtle anger directed against Vix. "I also ask that those who would seek revenge against him, remember that his death brings nothing back to life. Shun him. Let him suffer as he has made Gambria suffer."

King Diad weighed what Duncan asked, along with the mood of the people. Vix was an anomaly. Although High Priest, no one truly liked the man. Besides, this new High Priest might be easier to control.

"'It appears that you are wiser than I have given you credit. So be it." He raised his voice to address the crowd. "Vix is hereby banished from the kingdom of Gambria. Should he ever cross into our lands again, his life is forfeit. Guards! Take the former High Priest to the edge of Gambria and release him. Perhaps Rugia will offer him greater comfort."

With apparent pleasure, several warriors gathered around Vix and hustled him away. His shrill voice floated above the crowd back to Duncan, "I am not done away with so easily wizard!" As the guards physically escorted Vix towards the road leading to Mull, several individuals throughout the crowd quietly worked their way towards the fringe of the milling mass of Mull's residents. When the multitude's attention focused back to Duncan, these silent observers stepped into the darkness

The King turned back to Duncan. "And what of the remaining priests and acolytes of Safti?"

"M'Lord, I would ask that they continue their work."

King Diad raised an eyebrow. "You would have us worship Safti still?"

"M'Lord, the worship of Safti is not what hurts Gambria. It is the misinterpretations of the scripture. I believe that once these are corrected, Gambria will be a happier land. Safti did not answer the High Priest because he had abused the words of the prophet."

A swell of relief filled the crowd as they understood that generations of worship were not in vain, and that they were not to blame.

"And what of Brother Lucan?"

Lucan had nervously closely followed Duncan's reasoning, yet liked what he was hearing. However, the anxiety of his brother's fate, as well as his own sin, weighed immediately upon him.

"M'Lord, Brother Lucan is necessary to me. He has the true spirit of Safti upon him." Duncan looked over to Lucan who was flushed with a mixture relief and guilt. "M'Lord, it's late and these good people need to go home."

His words reacted well with the crowd and despite their anxiety, they were pleased that their spiritual world had not been destroyed.

"As you wish High Priest." The King turned to the crowd. "The contest is over. Return to your homes. We have been blessed with another miracle. The people of Gambria can now look forward to their destiny!"

A roar erupted as he spoke. Grinning, he picked up the woman still lying on the sand and brought her with him as he moved through the crowds and back to the castle.

Duncan looked back to Lucan. "Are you ready?"

Lucan ambled up to him, his heart overwhelmed with thanks and fear. Never in his life had he witnessed such a display. Yet his soul ached. For he knew that for a brief moment, for a slight pause, when his brother had asked him when the last time Safti had spoken to him, he knew... he knew, he had sinned... he believed just like everyone else... and he had the gift, the gift of suspending his soul above the immediate... yet he still had sinned. But now... now, this miracle, this evidence... the wizard believed in Safti and he has given testimony to him... *O God forgive me my sin.* Yet in the deepest recesses of his core, he heard the word... *expiation.*

"Yes Holy Father," he answered, forcibly pushing the word away. "I am ready."

"Good," Duncan cheerfully clapped Lucan in the back. "Then show me to my new home." However, before he turned to go, he looked over to the group of priests milling around, seemingly embarrassed and defeated. "My brothers," he called out loudly. "A new beginning has come. It is time to make amends for past sins. Come let us work together to make the words of Safti true words. Father Konrud, will you walk with me?"

Startled the man remembered him, though pleased, Konrud quickly answered, "Yes Holy Father, with pleasure." Just as quickly, he separated himself from the group and joined with Duncan and Lucan.

Duncan led the way back to the castle, with Lucan and Konrud on each side, the remaining priests in tow behind him.

Just off Duncan's shoulder and out of hearing, Cattwg and Tomos walked together, Garbhan and Brother Mostyn in tow.

Cattwg leaned conspiratorially in towards Tomos and whispered, "It was a trick of some sort."

"Some trick!" Tomos replied. "I've never seen anything like it."

"Who cares? It was still a trick."

"What can we do?"

They walked in silence for a bit. "Lucan should've gone with Vix," Cattwg complained. "Then removing Konrud would be much easier."

"I don't see him as a problem. He has no male children, remember?"

"Of course I do," Cattwg hissed. "Yet that fool of a king could still appoint him high priest for a time."

Tomos walked in silence for a bit. "So what do we do?"

"Convince the king that Konrud and Guina are lovers."

He shook his head. "We'd need proof. Anyway, what's the use? This new interloper is here and it looks like he'll be here for a while."

"Perhaps," Cattwg smugly replied. "And then perhaps not..."

"Oh? You have something in mind?" he slyly asked.

"Not yet."

"There's still Lucan though, and Konrud. What do we do about them?"

"First things first," Cattwg stated. "First we get rid of this Wizard fellow and the other two will be a lot easier."

"And then you'll be high priest," Tomos smugly pointed out.

"And you'll be the second most powerful priest in Gambria," Cattwg answered, making a mental note that Tomos might not be the sycophant he portrayed.

Flanked by Lucan and Konrud, Duncan stood outside the heavy double doors that led to the High Priest's, now his, chambers. Word of his miracle had already reached the temple and the two acolyte guards nervously kept their heads bowed in obedient reverence.

"Well," Duncan grinned, "let's see how the other half lives." He moved to push the doors open when both acolytes leaped forward to perform part of their duties by opening the doors for him. "Such service," he smirked. "And just think, it wasn't but an hour or two ago both of these gentlemen were hoping I would be dead."

The veiled threat wasn't lost on the acolytes and they both rushed around the opulent set of rooms repositioning furniture and fluffing pillows. Yet Duncan remained in the doorway, inhaling the ambiance of the room. There was heaviness to the place, a sort of sinister weight to the texture of the space. The richly carved furniture throughout the apartment was composed of the same ebony dark wood. Tapestries hung ceiling to floor in muted hues of crimson, royal blue, and forest green. Even the carpets layered over the stone floors were of subdued browns. It was as though whoever had lived here was afraid of the light.

He walked into the main room, a rather large room containing sofas, easy chairs, small tables, and various bureaus. Large three-wick candles were strategically placed, but most had not yet been used. Looking to his right through three wide arches, Duncan recognized what was the dining room. Yet while the table was large enough to easily accommodate twelve guests, there was only one chair positioned in the center of the otherwise empty room.

"Would you like something to eat Holy Father?"

Duncan turned to see another acolyte standing in the doorway. "No thank you. It's been a busy night, and I'd like to get some sleep."

"Your bed chamber is around here Holy Father." One of the door acolytes pointed to the hallway in front of him that bent to the right. As Duncan started to move toward the hall, a man burst into the apartment.

"My most abject apologies Most Holy Father. I was… um, indisposed when you arrived." The man hurried up to where Duncan, Lucan, and Konrud stood and bowed.

"This is Brother Darroch, your chief steward." Lucan smiled as he did the introduction.

Duncan took stock of the man in front of him. He was young, probably a few years older than Duncan. He had shaved his head, most likely in deference to Duncan's predecessor. Yet the comparison stopped there. Where Vix had been austere and pale, Darroch was trim and virile. He had a sort of pent up energy about him. Yet Duncan was most taken by his eyes. A brown so dark that the irises disappeared, they belied a discipline and confidence, a confidence in his own ability.

"Darroch," Duncan nodded as he repeated the name. "Brother Darroch, perhaps you could show me around these quarters so that these two might get some rest." He smiled as he tilted his head towards Lucan and Konrud.

"With pleasure Eminence."

"We really don't mind," Konrud said, unconvincingly.

He looked at his two deputies and from the strain in their eyes realized that they were up far later than they were accustomed. "Thank you, but I'd rather you two get some sleep. I want to meet with both of you later on this morning. Brother Darroch will take good care of me."

Both relieved and tired, the two said their farewells and moved toward the doors. Duncan had already shifted his attention to Darroch who was leading him into the hallway to his bedroom.

"I know I haven't seen my bedroom, but I want clean sheets – now," Duncan ordered.

Darroch smiled knowingly. "Of course, Most Holy Father."

"And why is this place so dark. I feel like I'm in a funeral home."

"A what?"

"A place for the dead," he answered.

Darroch flashed a quick grin. "We can begin changing the furniture later in the morning. Is there anything else?"

Duncan stopped midway down the hallway. "Yes. I want this place to be bright, alive. I want open windows and fresh air."

The Steward's eyes lit up. "Absolutely Eminence. This place has been too dull for far too long."

Lucan and Konrud had stopped at the main doorway, to watch Duncan disappear into the hallway. As Duncan's and Darroch's voices became indistinct, the two turned to leave, a mixture of uncertainty and pleasant anticipation.

Konrud put his hand on Lucan's shoulder. "This has been a very confusing night. While I am concerned about your brother's safety, I confess that I am not disappointed at his departure. I ask your forgiveness, my friend, for not being more sympathetic to your heart."

Lucan nodded, followed by a slight shrug. "We are who we are. My heart aches that I could not help him change. He would listen to no one."

"So what do you think of our new High Priest?"

Lucan pondered a moment, and a smile began to emerge. "I like him. Did I tell you about when he came to read the Holy Book? I thought at first he might be some fakir, but then he read it with such speed that he almost tore the pages, and then quoted verbatim from throughout. No one could do that unless he already knew the book." Lucan paused and leaned in towards Konrud. Lowering his voice, he added, "But what was most amazing was that he said he had been to Roscommon."

Surprise flashed across Konrud's face. "Roscommon? Are you sure?"

"Quite sure." Lucan was about to explain when Cattwg stalked up.

"Council chambers in five minutes," he whispered.

"Council chambers in five minutes for what?" Konrud raised a brow.

"What do you think?" Cattwg answered, glaring at both of them. "We can't let this interloper just waltz in here and take over."

"This interloper, as you call him, happens to be our high priest," Konrud interrupted. "The king, in all his authority, appointed him so. You remember?"

"Yes, I remember," Cattwg snipped. "We were all there for his 'miracle' thing. But that doesn't mean we have to accept the change."

"What do you propose to do?" Lucan looked askance.

"Not me... us," Cattwg retorted. "Council chambers, five minutes." With that, Cattwg slipped away down the long corridor.

When Lucan and Konrud entered the Council chambers, nine other members were already present, murmuring amongst themselves. The murmuring stopped when the two walked up to the group assembled near the High Priest dais.

"Who calls this meeting?" Konrud asked as he noted who was present. "And why is it so important that we meet at this hour?"

"I was wondering the same thing," Gerallt dubiously looked back and forth between Cattwg and Tomos.

"I called this meeting," Cattwg said indignantly. "There are *some* of us who question the wisdom of the king's decision."

"And who would these 'some of us' be?" Konrud knew the direction this discussion was about to take.

"I, for one." Cattwg quickly answered.

"And I," Tomos joined in."

"And I," Garbhan firmly stated, Cattwg's smug nod validating the decision.

An awkward silence followed as the remaining members waited to see who else might join this cabal.

"So you three are the *some* who are concerned?" Gerallt sneered.

Cattwg looked to Pewlin for support. "Pewlin here agrees too, don't you?"

Pewlin pursed his lips in discomfort. "What I said was that it seemed unusual for the king to appoint a stranger, someone unknown, as the high priest for our kingdom." He chose his words carefully. "It seems to me that the king should have chosen from those better qualified."

"And what about you Meurig?" Cattwg quickly turned to an older man, with a weak chin and thinning hair. "Didn't you say you thought that someone better qualified should have been chosen?"

"Well... um, yes... uh...yes, I suppose I did." Meurig looked for reaction from the others, trying to measure where the greatest support lay.

"What I find interesting," Konrud's voice was firm, "is that *some* of you were so willing to let this stranger challenge Vix, firmly convinced he would fail, then die, and life would go on as usual. This stranger was to be a mild and pleasant diversion for however brief a moment. Now that the results are not to your liking, you want to do something about it." He turned to another member, a sober looking man who appeared to be bored with the proceedings. "Tearlach, you're the legal expert. Do we have a case against the new high priest?"

Tearlach slowly looked at the other members before answering. His response was measured and deliberate. "I'm not sure I can elaborate any more than what everyone here already knows. Only the king has the authority to appoint the high priest. Once appointed, the king may not remove the high priest except for egregious crimes." He paused for effect. "I do believe that no matter how much *some* of us may not like the process, it is the law."

"When I said that I thought the king could have appointed someone a, ah, better qualified," Meurig hastened to interject, "I didn't necessarily mean that our new high priest isn't suitable."

Cattwg looked at the others with incredulous disbelief. "You would let this upstart stranger take what rightfully belongs to us?"

"It's not a question of 'what rightfully belongs to us,' as you put it," Konrud retorted gazing directly at him. "We all know your aspirations Cattwg. Unfortunately this new high priest may outlive you."

Cattwg's eyes flashed anger. "And just what are you insinuating?"

Instead of answering, Konrud turned to the rest of the group. "Unless anyone here knows of a legitimate reason why we should go against the king, I suggest we all get some sleep and determine how we can best serve our new high priest."

The pause was momentary before Tearlach moved toward the doors. "I agree. Good night." That was all that was necessary before the remaining members joined him. As they filed out, Cattwg, Tomos, and Garbhan remained.

"This isn't over," Cattwg brooded. "I *will* be high priest."

Tomos looked doubtful. "And how do you propose to do that?"

Cattwg spun around and stormed up the steps to the high priest dais. Deliberately seating himself, he leaned forward, stretching his arms out and placing his hands on the desktop. "Give me time," he said malevolently. "And when the high priest goes, that sanctimonious bastard Konrud will be right behind him."

Duncan awoke to bright sunlight exploding into his bedroom as Darroch instructed the acolytes to open the curtains. His hands instinctively went to his eyes to block the intense light. Blinking, he was temporarily unsure of his surroundings as he looked around at the unfamiliar room. It was when he focused on the smiling Darroch that he remembered.

"Good morning Eminence," the Steward greeted him cheerfully. "It's a beautiful day, and if I might add, a very busy day." As Duncan sat up in bed, bare-chested, Darroch couldn't help but notice the well-defined and taut muscles. "Um... if I might offer an observation?"

"Sure," he answered, still groggy.

"Most Holy Father, you'll find it is the rare priest who practices the martial skills of the warrior."

"Um... OK?" Somewhat puzzled, he squinted looking up at him.

"It's just that I can't help but notice that you like to take some exercise now and again. If you wish, I can arrange your schedule to accommodate your exercise."

Duncan blinked several more times before it dawned on him what he was hinting at. "That would be good. I need to maintain a sound mind in a sound body."

The Steward pondered the response. "A sound mind in a sound body... I like that," he nodded, then chuckled. "I'm not so sure too many others will." He continued to bustle around the room, opening curtains, opening wardrobe doors, and airing out the room.

Duncan looked over to the now empty chair where he had tossed his clothes before climbing into bed so early this morning. "Where are my clothes?"

The Steward stopped. "I took the liberty of removing them. Begging your pardon Eminence, but you *are* the high priest now, and you must dress like one." He held up a multicolored robe of royal blues, emerald greens, scarlet reds, and deep golds in long vertical stripes. "We may have to let this out a bit, but it should do for now."

Duncan gazed with furrowed brows at the brightly colored robe. "Do I have to wear that all the time?"

"I'm afraid so."

"I do hope I have more than one," he opined, wide-eyed.

Darroch grinned. "You have plenty, Eminence. While your predecessor tended to spend a bit too much time in just one, you have all you need. I'll be sure to get them adjusted to fit you." He walked to a tall door to the left of the bed. "May I suggest a bath this morning? I took the liberty of drawing your water for you."

Duncan threw the covers back and stood up. Wide-eyed, Darroch jerked himself around so that his back was facing Duncan.

"Most Holy Father, you can't do that!"

"Do what?"

"You're naked."

"So what?"

"No one is supposed to see you in your natural state."

Duncan sighed. "Oh good grief. OK... how about getting me a towel or something?"

Darroch ran into the bath chamber and quickly emerged with a large plush towel, all the while averting his gaze. Duncan calmly took the towel and wrapped it round himself.

"OK. You can look now."

He opened his eyes. "I beg your forgiveness Most Holy Father. I should have informed you of the protocol before I took such liberties."

"Forget it. You can bring me up to speed when I get out of the bath." Duncan walked to the doorway. "By the way, what's for breakfast?"

"Whatever you wish."

Smiling, he shrugged. "Surprise me."

The bath water had been hot and splendid, with a hint of sandalwood for aroma. Duncan had wanted to simply soak, to be slowly pulled from an indolent reverie to come to breakfast. But he knew he didn't have the luxury. *Time to build my base; find out who the enemy is. Time to establish myself.* He stirred the water with an index finger. *I need to be careful... build the base first... find out who I can trust... who's really going to be on my side... a little politics won't hurt here... I need to schmooze... gain the love and adoration of the crowds, the common man...* He smiled as he remembered the 'miracle' and the long walk to the Temple. He had walked with Lucan and Konrud and the other priests back up the road to Mull. Along the way, they had mixed with the crowds who were likewise returning. Upon seeing Duncan, the crowds had divided to allow him to pass. So many of them had stopped and bowed, smiling as Duncan waved in acknowledgement, the flickering light from the hand torches flittering across their faces. A great number of them had called out "Safti bless you." *Yes, I need to get them to love me.*

Looking around the large bathroom, he liked its opulence. The walls and floors were of polished marble. There were two tall windows on one wall. The other walls had either tapestries draped from ceiling to floor, or furnishings filling the space. The bathtub stood near the middle of the room, a bit closer to the windows. There was a large wardrobe of blond wood in one corner, with a chair next to it. On the chair were a towel and an article of clothing.

Emerging from the bath, he walked to the chair, leaving wet foot prints on the floor. The towel was thick and plush and he quickly dried himself, while examining the article of clothing. It seemed to be a long smock of extremely fine threads, for it had the touch of silk. It was a simple cream color. *Hmmm. I suppose I'd better put this on, but I'll be damned if I'm going to wear a dress the rest of my life.*

He emerged from the bathroom to find Darroch waiting for him, holding up the multi-colored robe. "Ah, Most Holy Father," he smiled. "That shift will have to work for now until we can get some that fit you more comfortably. I'll be sure to send up the seamers and menders to make you new ones. If you are ready to put this on, you can then attend to your breakfast."

Stepping forward, he slipped on the robe, while the Steward fastened the gold clasps that lined the left side of the robe. The sleeves were of uniform size that widened toward the wrist and ended in a tighter cuff. He waited for Darroch to finish and then held up his arms to look at the result.

"Is there a mirror?"

"Yes, Eminence. Right here." He opened one of the wardrobe doors to reveal a mirror on the back of one of the doors.

Duncan walked in front of the mirror and examined himself. He lightly ran his hands down along the vertical stripes. "Does this make me look fat?" he smiled mischievously, turning to face his Steward.

Darroch barked a laugh and walked up to the grinning High Priest. "Most Holy Father, you are going to be a refreshing change." He motioned towards the door, his eyes still in amusement. "Please, your breakfast awaits."

"Excellent," he replied as they walked out into the hallway. "I had asked Father Lucan and Father Konrud to come by this morning." He looked at the slanting light coming through the windows. "It is still morning isn't it?"

"Yes, Most Holy Father, but not for much longer. When would you like to see them?"

"As soon as I've finished my breakfast." He abruptly stopped, and put a hand on Darroch's arm. "Brother Darroch, what is the custom concerning my meals. I noticed there was only one chair at the dining table." He raised an eyebrow. "Seems an awfully big table for one diner."

Darroch surreptitiously glanced at the High Priest's hand on his arm, a sign of both intimacy and confidence. He warmed to the trust. "It wasn't always like this. Your predecessor liked his solitude. From what I understand his father liked company during meals."

"Good. Do you know if Father Lucan and Father Konrud have eaten yet? If not, I'd like for them to share the meal with me. Sort of kill two birds with one stone."

"Kill two birds with one stone..." he slowly repeated. "Another interesting expression. Hopefully it's not to be taken seriously."

Duncan was about to explain until he looked at Darroch who had the faintness of a smile curling the corners of his lips. "You know what I mean," he smirked, then grew solemn. "Brother Darroch, I will be depending on you for quite a bit. If you see me about to make a mistake, whether protocol or otherwise, I expect you to correct me... gently."

The Steward stared at the new High Priest. He was so unlike Vix, whose arrogance and vice permeated the entire Temple. This man, this High

294

Priest, had a subtle strength and self-assuredness that seemed to give confidence. Even after all the years he had served Vix, Vix had never expressed as much as this man had in less than a day.

"Most Holy Father, I am here to serve you. I will take care of you to the best of my ability. I will let no one harm you." Darroch bowed.

Duncan clapped him on the back. "I believe you." He rubbed his hands together. "Now, if you don't mind, if you would please find out if Fathers Konrud and Lucan have eaten, because I'm starving." With that, he walked into the living room as Darroch headed out the main doors.

Although both Lucan and Konrud had eaten, waiting for him to awaken, they were pleased to be at the High Priest's table. Darroch had retrieved several dining room chairs and they sat across from Duncan while he ate. He then stood off to the side, directing the acolytes who served and waited on the High Priest.

"My apologies for not thinking of inviting you sooner," Duncan said between bites. "But I'll do better. This is delicious," he held up a fork pronged with a morsel of meat. "Please tell the cook he's a master chef. No, wait, I'll tell him myself." He looked over to Darroch. "Brother Darroch, would you please arrange for me to go down to the kitchen and thank those wonderful people."

"With pleasure Eminence," he nodded with delight. Lucan and Konrud looked at each other with surprised satisfaction.

"Holy Father – " Konrud began.

"Stop." Duncan held up his hand. "My name is Duncan. When it is just the three of us, I would prefer it if you used my name. Other times and other venues, you can call me Holy Father, Eminence, or whatever." He turned to Darroch. "It's probably not protocol, but that's how I want it."

His Steward said nothing, but merely smiled and nodded, knowing that the rumors would begin to make their rounds as soon as the serving acolytes left. It would be up to him to control them as best he could.

Duncan pushed aside the plate and focused his attention on Konrud. "Father Konrud, before you begin, know that Lucan and I are friends. I trust him with my very essence. I would have your friendship and trust as well."

Konrud looked to Lucan and saw the face of contentment. Turning back to the High Priest, he realized that something new, something different was happening in Gambria. He thought for a moment and knew he had to take that leap of faith. "I would be honored to be your friend."

"Good. Would you mind coming around the table so that I might tell you something meant only for you?"

Konrud looked again at Lucan who gave a brief nod of encouragement. Pushing himself away from the table, he walked around to where Duncan sat, and leaned in for Duncan to whisper,

"I know the meaning of your name."

Konrud's knees began to tremble, and he felt his temperature rising.

"It's an appropriate name for you. It means 'honest advisor.'"

Konrud dropped to the floor in spasms. Darroch started to move to his aid but Lucan raised a hand and motioned him to stop. Duncan scooted his chair back and stooped down to help Konrud up.

A visibly shaken Konrud stood up, his right hand holding his chest, feeling the palpitations of his heart. He struggled to get his labored breathing under control. Still wobbly, he leaned heavily on Duncan's shoulder. He looked at the faces around the room. Fear was evident in the wide eyes of the acolytes, while Darroch appeared more concerned than afraid. Only Duncan and Lucan seemed undisturbed.

Duncan waited until it appeared that Konrud was recovering enough before leaning over and whispering, "My name means 'brown warrior.'"

Konrud jerked a step back, his jaw dropping simultaneously. "But... but...?"

Duncan calmly sat back down and motioned Konrud back to his seat. "There is much that I know, about each of you," his gaze included Darroch. He then watched as Konrud worked his way back to his chair, supporting himself by holding onto the table. "For instance, Father Konrud is wondering why I chose to exchange this information with him."

Konrud paused his slow journey and leaned on the table. Still catching his breath, he stared at him, a mixture of confusion and apprehension. "Yes... yes, why?"

"As I said, Father Konrud, I would have your trust and friendship. And as I understand those terms, it means that my life is in your hands. Do you accept this responsibility?"

"I... I," Konrud sputtered.

Duncan focused his eyes at Konrud. "Think about what you say and agree to. Do you accept this responsibility because I am High Priest, or because I am a man worthy of your trust?"

His brow furrowed in concentration, Konrud blinked several times as he sifted Duncan's statement. Yes, change is happening, he thought. What is it about this man that he couldn't help but like? Was he willing to again take that leap of faith? And in that moment, he decided where his future lay. He motioned for the Steward and acolytes to leave the room.

Waiting until they were alone, he quietly, yet doggedly, pointed out, "It is a crime, punishable by death, to reveal the meaning of another's name. It doesn't matter who you are. There is no greater evil, for to do so steals a man's very essence."

"Is it a crime to tell another the meaning of one's own name?"

"Why would anyone do that? It gives a power which cannot be challenged."

"Yet I willingly told you the meaning of my name. Why would I do that?"

Konrud took a deep slow breath, shaking his head. "You're crazy?"

Smirking at the response, he leaned forward. "Do you really believe that?"

"No," came the quick reply, "but I still don't understand."

"You two," Duncan motioned at them with his right hand, "are my foundation. I trust you, and will depend on you to help me do what is right. Thus, I take a step of faith that my trust is well founded. Will you do the same?

Konrud continued staring at the new high priest, unsure of the implications. This was all so sudden. Why would anyone willingly give control to another? It didn't make any sense. Yet the man seated before him revealed that most sacred thing about a man, as though he had nothing to fear. Why would the High Priest trust him so, when he didn't even know him? Yet at the heart of it all was this man's faith in him, his trust. What he demanded in return was equal faith and trust.

Deciding he would take that step of faith, Konrud quietly answered, "I will."

Duncan grinned in satisfaction. With Lucan and Konrud as allies, his tenure as High Priest would be both long and pleasurable.

"Excellent. OK then, let's get down to business. I want to know the structure of the religious orders, including the Temple organization, the pecking order of authority, and whom do I need to be especially watchful of?"

Several hours later, Duncan, Lucan, and Konrud were still at the table. Breakfast had been replaced by lunch, and the empty plates collected. Lucan had asked that the platter of roasted Roan be left behind to nibble on. Duncan was surrounded by stacks of papers, most with voluminous notes scribbled on them. Konrud leaned back in his chair.

"Friend Duncan, this has been a most enlightening three hours."

Duncan looked up, as if aware of his surroundings. "Has it been that long? My apologies Konrud. Good company has a way of making the time go quickly."

Konrud chuckled. "It has gone by rather quickly, hasn't it?"

Duncan turned to Lucan. "So, in all the time your brother was High Priest, he never left Mull?"

Lucan shook his head. "He never felt it was necessary. Of course, he didn't' really like to travel."

"And it would've taken him away from the center of power," Konrud added.

"But he was the High Priest. Why would he need to be concerned about being away?" Duncan picked at a piece of meat.

Konrud stood up and stretched. "I think it had more to do with not being in the know. If one's too far away from the center of power, things can happen beyond one's control. Far better to remain here and have one's hands in all that goes on."

Duncan nodded. "You mean like Cattwg and Tomos? Or Garbhan?"

Konrud and Lucan exchanged looks, before Lucan answered. "Yes, like Cattwg and Tomos, *and* Garbhan."

"I understand." He returned to the stack of papers. "I believe I have enough reading material for a while. Is there anything I am forgetting?"

"Yes, Eminence," Darroch interrupted. "Although the king has made you High Priest, there is still the Synod Conclave and coronation."

"My goodness," Lucan smacked his forehead with his hand, "with all that has happened, I completely forgot."

"OK? What's a Synod Conclave?" Duncan leaned back.

"Now that the King has made you High Priest," Konrud sat back down, "the choice needs to be confirmed.

"So how does that happen?" Duncan pulled out a fresh piece of paper.

"It's mostly for show," Konrud said. "The Synod of Fathers meets to either confirm or refuse the King's appointment."

Duncan's ears perked. "So there's a possibility that I could be removed as High Priest?"

"Not really," Konrud pondered for a moment. "Well, now that I think about it, I suppose there is always that possibility, but it takes a unanimous decision by the Synod to refuse the King. And even then, the King can always over-ride the refusal."

Duncan relaxed a bit. "Then what?"

"The Synod must meet three days after the King has made his choice. They have between sunrise and sunset to make a decision. If no decision is made by sunset, it is assumed the Synod accepts the King's choice. An envoy is sent from the Synod to the King to announce the decision. Not too long after the announcement, the High Priest is installed with a coronation ceremony.

Raising an eyebrow, Duncan sifted this new information. "What does the High Priest do during the three days before the Synod?"

Both Konrud and Lucan shrugged. "Bide his time," Konrud answered.

"Looks like I have a few days to get acquainted with folks. I assume the coronation ceremony has either a manual or someone who can tell me what to expect?"

"Yes, Eminence." Darroch spoke. "Father Frang is in charge of the Temple Sacrament and Ceremony."

"Good. Set up a time for us to meet sometime tomorrow." Duncan stood up and twisted to get out the stiffness. "So, assuming last night was the official appointment, is it three days from yesterday or today?"

No one spoke for a moment as they recalled the previous evening's events. Darroch broke the silence. "If I recall correctly, Eminence, it was after midnight when the King appointed you, so it would be three days from today."

Grinning good-naturedly, he shrugged. "I tried."

Lucan smirked in response. "Is there anything else you would like from us, Friend Duncan?"

Duncan watched Konrud stifle a yawn. "No, not now. I thank you both for spending so much of your time with me today." He stretched his arms back. "I think I'll take Brother Darroch and see what sort of mischief we can get into down in the kitchen." He leaned back and winked at his Steward.

Although smiling, Konrud's eyes spoke something else. "Friend Duncan, if I may offer some advice?"

"Of course Konrud. I value your wisdom."

Hesitantly placing a hand on Duncan's arm, he watched to see if he had breached the bounds between friendship and High Priest. When Duncan continued to stare at him, awaiting his advice, he relaxed.

"Change can sometimes be difficult for many to accept. Grown too accustomed to how it has always been, makes many resistant to change. It is who we are. I like the change you bring. It feels... right." He hesitated as he searched for words.

Duncan turned to face him, placing his hands on Konrud's shoulders. "Go ahead, my brother, just say it."

Konrud lifted his head, his eyes misting at the word 'brother.' Never before had someone bared his soul like this man had. The awareness of responsibility settled on him like a thick mantle, heavy yet comforting.

"Most Holy Father... High Priest... and now, my friend... I am both thrilled and afraid. I am thrilled at the change you bring: the freshness, the reawakening of what it means to be a priest again, a shepherd of the people." Here he grew somber. "But I am afraid of the future. I'm afraid that we have been who we are for so long, that some may not be so accommodating to change." He gazed intently at him. "You are still a stranger here. You will have to gain the trust of both the people and their... our, leaders. I fear you must walk a fine line between change and routine, between new and comfortable. Do you understand?"

Duncan grinned self-assuredly. "Absolutely. You don't want me acting like a tarrac in the vase aisle."

Konrud smirked. "I see you're already picking up Gambri slang."

While he was speaking, an acolyte hurried to Darroch to quietly deliver a message. Darroch nodded his understanding and directed the man to another acolyte.

"Most Holy Father, the Queen has come to pay her respects and wishes to know if you will see her."

"The Queen?" Konrud's eyes revealed his pleasure.

The response was not unnoticed as Duncan turned to his Steward. "But of course," he answered. "Is there any protocol I should know about here?"

"No, Eminence. Just be yourself," he grinned as he went to the door. In a moment, he returned, escorting Guina through the center arch of the dining room. Duncan greeted her as she entered.

"Welcome Lady Guina. Please sit." Duncan motioned to the chair Konrud had previously occupied and had now pulled out for her. He watched the exchange between them, and recognized the not so subtle signs of familiarity. "Have you eaten m'Lady? Would you care for something?"

Looking around the room and realizing there were no adversaries, Guina relaxed. "I've already dined," she paused and smiled prettily as she then emphasized, "Holy Father." Arranging her gown, she sat in the offered chair.

An acolyte entered with another chair for Konrud, which Darroch directed to be placed next to Guina. Duncan looked quickly at Darroch and gave a short nod of approval, then sat back down, as did Lucan. Konrud remained standing for a moment and then deliberately sat down, inching his chair a bit closer to the Queen.

"This is an unexpected and pleasant surprise," Duncan grinned good-naturedly. "Are you here to continue our discussion of theological proofs?" he teased.

"Not today, Holy Father," Guina answered good-humoredly. "I merely came to pay my respects. I won't take much of your time, as I know you're very busy."

"Not at all," Duncan responded. "We needed a break right now and you've conveniently given us an excuse to stop. I'm afraid that I've kept these two away from their responsibilities far too long today." He saw Konrud's subtle movement toward protest and quickly cut him off. "But I ask their continued indulgence to sit here a while longer." Smiling to himself, he leaned back as he watched Konrud's body language. *Don't know what you two have going on, but I'm going to exploit whatever it is.*

"Have you heard any news of the battle, m'Lady?" Konrud leaned in towards her.

Guina shook her head. "No Father Konrud. But it has been long enough since they left. We should be hearing news any day now."

As Guina was speaking, a door acolyte approached Darroch. Darroch bent his head forward to hear the information. He leaned back up with a bemused smile.

"My pardons, your Eminence, but Tarrac-Master Menec is here to express his respects."

"Menec! Excellent. Please show him in." Duncan turned back to the other three. "Amazing what a title change does for one. Yesterday I was a mere wizard, and few would give me the time of day. Now I'm the High Priest and I have royalty visiting." He smirked. "I'm just teasing m'Lady," he said when he saw Guina's reaction. "I'm sure if your schedule and other obligations had allowed, you would've stopped by to continue our discussions. I merely point out the obvious."

He turned to look up as Menec walked in. "Menec, *old* friend, I'm glad to see you."

Menec abruptly stopped when he realized that Duncan had other visitors. "My apologies Eminence. I didn't mean to intrude. I can come back another time."

"Nonsense. Grab a seat. In fact, here, take my chair." He stood up and happened to look at the wide-eyed Darroch who was already directing another chair be brought. "OK, take another chair instead."

Menec laughed. "It is good to see you too." He then directed his attention to the other three. "And I see you are in exceedingly good company. M'Lady, it is always good to see you, especially when you're smiling." He inclined a brief bow.

"And you too, friend Menec. How nice of you to arrive while I was still here." She offered her hand. He gave it a gentle squeeze.

"And my two favorite Fathers." He walked over and placed a hand on shoulder each, "Father Konrud, Father Lucan."

"And our favorite Tarrac-master," Lucan rejoined.

"But I'm the only Tarrac-master," Menec affably replied.

Lucan leaned in towards Guina and Konrud and stage-whispered, "Makes it all the easier."

Amidst the laughter, Menec sat down and playfully poked Lucan. "And to think, I was going to tell our new High Priest what a blessing he had in you."

The banter, interspersed with other discussion, continued as the afternoon waned. A contented Darroch kept a watchful eye over the group, having food brought in or refilling drinks. He couldn't remember this room ever containing this much mirth. Neither could he remember anyone ever coming by just to visit Vix. He liked this change. Already the apartment felt like it was shedding its oppressiveness.

While Darroch kept careful watch, Duncan paid close attention to the dynamics of the others. It was obvious that the four of them had a mutual trust and affection. Their relaxed teasing was done with gentle humor and consideration. At the same time, their body language spoke a bond of friendship that transcended simple acquaintances. He noticed the especial solicitousness of Konrud and Guina for each other. Despite their best efforts pretending to be just friends, it was obvious to Duncan that their affection was more than friendship. He studied both Lucan and Darroch to see if they noticed the same indications, but found them to be either oblivious or deferentially indifferent. He made a mental note to ask Darroch later.

As the dinner hour approached, Duncan announced that he wanted to visit the kitchen and would welcome anyone wishing to join him. Both Guina and Menec made their excuses and had departed. Lucan readily accepted, while Konrud stood in indecision.

"Friend Duncan, this has been one of the most enjoyable days I have had in a very long time. I would not burden you with too much of my company."

"You have some place better to go?" he joked.

Konrud thought for a moment, and shrugged. "Not really. I just need to stretch my legs, perhaps clean up a bit."

"I understand." He reached up and squeezed his shoulder. "Might I impose on you to share dinner with us?" He looked at Lucan for affirmation. Lucan's beatific smile was answer enough.

Konrud nodded affably. "With pleasure. Just send for me when you're ready."

"Excellent." While Konrud took his leave, Duncan looked back over his shoulder to where Darroch was fussing over the exchange of tapestries, furniture, and other furnishings. "Brother Darroch, would you be terribly upset if I left you here and had Father Lucan show me around a bit?"

"Not at all Eminence. Hopefully I can have more of this," he pointed to the mild disarray of moved furniture, "organized before you get back. At what hour would your Eminence prefer the evening meal?"

Duncan looked around the apartment for a timepiece, and found none. "What time is it now?"

Darroch looked to the opposite wall, near the main doors. Duncan followed his gaze and saw the clock embedded in the wall, much like the one in Alexis' home.

"It's about seven-sixty-five, Eminence."

Duncan did a quick mental calculation, factoring the time exchange. "Let's make it around eight-fifteen."

Darroch nodded in acknowledgement as Duncan followed Lucan out of the apartment into the hallway. It was wide and stretched to the right. Couches and chairs sat along the sides, and gilded pictures hung on the walls. Light descended through the glass ceiling giving the hallway a comfortable and cozy glow. As they walked down the hallway, Lucan explained the layout.

"My apartment, as you'll remember, is down the hallway. There are only two apartments in this section. The door there is to a council room and other reading rooms." He pointed to a door down the hall on the right. "And here we are," he said as they turned left into an extremely large cavernous room with a high vaulted ceiling, "the Petitionary."

Duncan remembered the room from the first visit with Lucan, seemingly so long ago. Then, he had been viewed with overt suspicion and animosity. The room was alive with a hum of frenzied activity. Towards the center of the room was a large ornate desk, behind which sat a cleric who seemed to have little time, or patience, for those to whom he issued orders. Acolytes, clerics, priests, tradesmen, and supplicants either reacted to orders, or waited patiently for attention.

As the High Priest stepped into the room, the activity jittered to a halt. Silence descended so suddenly that the cleric behind the desk looked up to see what had happened. It wasn't until he looked behind him that he realized who was there. Noticing Duncan standing there, he turned back to his work.

Mostyn's snub was not lost on Duncan, who took another step forward to survey the room. "Brother Mostyn, would you mind coming here for a moment please." His voice echoed in the room.

Without looking up, Mostyn continued writing before replying, "I'm a bit busy right this moment." There was a faint unison of inhaled breath as the crowd waited for Duncan to react.

A faint smile began on Duncan's lips. *Two can play this game.* "Yes, I can see that." He looked for a suitable acolyte and found a tall lad with bright eyes. In a loud voice, he pointed to the acolyte and commanded, "You. Fetch Father Garbhan. Now."

The acolyte's eyes jolted wide as he jumped to respond. As the acolyte ran out, Mostyn realized what was happening and moved to diffuse the potential problem. Putting down his pen, he turned around in his chair. "Yes? How may I help you?"

"Ah, it is I, instead, who will actually help you." He smiled malevolently.

Mostyn raised an eyebrow. "And how will you help me?"

"I see that you are a priest of some importance here. It must be quite difficult balancing all these," he waved a hand at the room's occupants, "competing demands, all these people vying for your attention."

Not sure where the questioning was going, Mostyn shrugged, "I manage."

At that moment, Father Garbhan came tumbling in, his robes swirling behind him, the acolyte in tow. He saw Duncan and hurried over, catching his breath.

"Father Garbhan,," Duncan smiled with the air of authority, "so good of you to come so quickly. Hopefully I haven't taken you away from anything important." He feigned concern.

"Nothing that can't wait, Eminence," he gulped.

"Excellent." He looked over towards Mostyn. "It has come to my attention that Brother Mostyn is over-worked," he said loudly enough for all to hear. "I want him to take a vacation, starting now." Duncan looked evenly at Garbhan.

"But I don't need a vacation," Mostyn protested, standing up.

Ignoring him, he continued. "Father Garbhan, I want a recommendation for his replacement within the hour." Duncan could feel the crowd's mixture of pleasure and concern at this turn of events. "High Chancellor Lucan and I are headed to the kitchen. If you don't find us there, come to my chambers. Do you understand?" He waited and watched as Garbhan was momentarily caught in indecision.

"Of course Most Holy Father. As you wish." He turned to Mostyn. "Brother Mostyn, would you mind meeting with me in my chambers?"

Mostyn stiffened, his eyes glaring at Duncan. He stood rooted to glistening marble floor, debating his choices. After a few moments of weighing consequences, he gritted his teeth and answered, "Yes Father." Collecting his paperwork, he stormed to the far hallway entrance.

Once gone, the crowd began to erupt with demands and pleas. Duncan held up his hands waiting for order. When none came, he shouted "Silence!" The effect was immediate. He slowly examined the group. He saw an older man, stooped from hard work. "You," he pointed at him. "Why are you here?"

The man's eyes widened in fear. "I... I... I'm but a poor man, Most Holy Father," he whined. "I have a wife, and a small parcel of land. Times have been hard."

"Come to the point, good sir; otherwise we shall all miss dinner," Duncan said playfully.

Amidst the scattering of laughter, the man stood a bit straighter. "I come here because my sow has been killed while still in pup."

The High Priest blinked in confusion, then a voice sang out, "He means pregnant." Smiling in acknowledgement, he asked, "And what do you expect the church to do for you?"

The man was momentarily caught off guard. "I... I... came to ask for alms, Most Holy Father," he replied with a tinge of embarrassment

Duncan mused this bit of information. "And how will alms help you?"

The man's discomfit was evident. "It will help us survive, Most Holy Father."

"I understand," he said. "Yet alms will only be a temporary salve. It does little to improve your condition." He watched as the man's shoulders slumped, thinking that the church was going to turn him away.

He turned to Garbhan. "Father Garbhan, I believe the church has a sow, don't we?"

"We have many of them, Eminence," Garbhan responded, the answer

305

too obvious."

"Do we have one, um… in pup?" he smiled.

"I'm sure we do Eminence."

"Excellent. I'm sure we can spare one for this gentleman here." Both the man's and Garbhan's eyes widened, one in joy, one in consternation.

"You… you want us to just give it to him?" Garbhan sputtered.

"Of course." He turned back to the man. "But there is a cost. When this sow gives birth to her litter, you will give the church one of the litter. If the litter has more than one female, then you will give us a female. Is that understood?"

Instead of answering, the man ran up and kneeled before him, reaching up and grabbing his hand. "Yes, Most Holy Father, Yes!"

Placing a hand under the man's chin, he lifted his head to meet his eyes. "As the church has been forthright with you, I expect you to be forthright with her." He raised the man up while turning to Garbhan. "I want him to have a sow that's ready to deliver." Looking back to the man, he asked, "Does your land produce?"

"We have enough to eat, but no more, Most Holy Father."

"Give him thirty days worth of grain for the sow," he directed to Garbhan.

Garbhan inhaled sharply. "Thirty days, Eminence?" Instead of answering, Duncan simply stared at him. Garbhan fidgeted under the stare. "As you wish, Eminence."

As the remaining supplicants watched the bounty to the man unfold, their expectations rose, and they clamored for their various needs. Duncan raised his hands again and this time the crowd settled.

"Father Garbhan will attend to each of your needs. But you must be patient, and orderly. He will need time to hear all of your concerns." He turned to the several acolytes acting as guards to the room. "Allow no more to enter today."

Addressing the crowd again, his voice echoed in the room. "You have come here today to ask the church to help you. And she will, as best she can. What she asks in return is that you give her your loyalty, your love, your devotion, your trust. Remember who we are; we are all followers of Safti." With that, he headed for the stairs with Lucan in tow, leaving Garbhan to pacify the crowd.

Once they had descended the stairs and Duncan had allowed Lucan to lead, he asked, "What did you think of that?"

Lucan walked a bit more before answering. "I'm not quite sure of it all,

Eminence. Part of it feels right, while another part says 'too soon.'"

"What do you mean?"

"It felt right to give that man the sow. He had needs, and we have plenty. Yet the church can't afford to support all the poor in Gambria. We still have to provide for our own priests."

"Quite true," Duncan replied. "But if I do the math correctly, if we give a sow and get a sow, do we not break even?"

Lucan chuckled. "It's not that simple, Eminence."

He lightly touched Lucan's arm. "I know Father Lucan. I will trust you and others to help me in these matters. Yet, it seems to me that there is something else on your mind."

He smiled wryly. "Do you know me so well already?"

"Not well enough, my friend," he confided. "So tell me. What is it?"

"Well, to begin with, you must know that you've made an enemy with Brother Mostyn."

"Yes, I know. But it was necessary."

"Oh, I agree. He was being disrespectful. The problem is that he has allies in Cattwg and Tomos, as well as Garbhan."

Duncan absorbed this piece of information. "I understand. Thanks for the insight."

Lucan continued leading the way down stairs and hallways. "I must confess that I am not disappointed that he is gone."

"Mostyn?"

"Yes."

"And why is that?"

"Cattwg's influence persuaded my brother to promote Mostyn and, with Garbhan's support, he was placed as the Secretary General to the High Priest and Council."

Duncan nodded. "I assume he replaced someone?"

"Yes, Most Holy Father, he did."

"And who was that?"

"You're about to meet him." Lucan pushed open the doors to the kitchen.

The aroma of spices and cooking meat immediately assaulted them. The room was expansive, with a fireplace at the far end so large that a man could walk through. A low fire was giving heat to a large cauldron hung on a toothed rack. An acolyte occasionally stirred the contents. Hanging on the walls on both sides of the fireplace were various spoons, skimmers, scoops, pokers, pincers, skewers, and long-handled forks. Two pairs of half doors on both sides of the fireplace completed the wall. Duncan could see through the fireplace into the large dining hall where priests and acolytes set tables.

As Lucan led the way in, Duncan felt the immediate rise in temperature. A series of wood stoves and ovens lined the wall on the right. The walls above were blackened with the grime from incessant smoke. On the opposite wall was the storage for both food-stuffs and utensils. Just below head level was a long shelf containing spices. In the middle were a series of preparation tables around which half-a-dozen acolytes prepared the evening meal under the watchful eye, and occasional grouse, of a more senior priest. He stopped and smiled broadly when he saw Lucan, and then looked more pensive when he saw Duncan.

"Welcome Holy Fathers," he bowed slightly. "What brings the two highest clerics in the nation to my humble kitchen?"

"I came to compliment the cook who has been making my meals," Duncan answered. "They've been superb."

The priest gave a faint smile of pride. "You can thank that young man over there." He pointed to a medium height young acolyte with thinning hair and focused eyes. "He's a wonder in the kitchen. Everything he touches turns into the finest dining in all of Gambria. The brothers have not so gently reminded me of that." He laughed. "Daimhin," he called several times to the young man who was so absorbed in his preparation that he only awoke to his surroundings when one of the other acolytes nudged him.

Upon seeing who was there, Daimhin reddened and immediately stopped his chopping, and hurried up to them. "Most Holy Father," he knelt, touching Duncan's hand, then stood back up.

"I understand that you are the genius who has prepared my menu," Duncan complimented.

"Brother Drubal has been an inspiration Most Holy Father. He has allowed me to try some different approaches to meal preparation. I am glad that you like it." He kept his eyes downcast as he spoke with Duncan.

"Like it? It's the best I've had in all of Gambria, the King's table included." He watched the smile of satisfaction spread across the man's face. The young man lifted his eyes and the once serious demeanor was replaced with a subtle exuberance. "Now, if you don't mind, I'm going to borrow Brother Drubal for a few minutes."

"Yes Holy Father. Thank you." He turned and hurried back to his preparation table, a bounce in his step.

Drubal lightly placed a hand on Duncan's arm. "Thank you Eminence.

You've made his day," he said with quiet appreciation. A fleeting twinge of guilt passed as he remembered he had tried to kill this man. But he consoled himself with the thought that he had simply done what he had been ordered to do.

"I call 'em like I see 'em," Duncan grinned. "Now, I believe Father Lucan here has just told me that you had some administration experience."

"I told the Most Holy Father about your previous position," Lucan explained.

Drubal said nothing, but warily eyed the two. He had just realized that in the entire time he had been exiled here, not only had Vix never come, the few times he did need something, he sent someone else, and it was either for poison or to complain about the food. What hold Cattwg had on Vix was beyond him. The banishment had been a bitter pill. That was, what… ten, eleven years ago? He had resignedly accepted his demotion, and learned what he could about kitchens and cooking. Thank Safti that Daimhin had shown up last year.

"Am I to understand that you were once the General Secretary to the High Priest and Council before Brother Mostyn?"

"Yes, Eminence." he answered without emotion.

Duncan pursed his lips and nodded. "Good. Report to Father Garbhan and tell him that I have appointed you to replace Mostyn." Before Drubal could answer, he looked over Drubal's shoulder, and called, "Brother Daimhin, might I bother you once more?"

This time Daimhin was more attentive and stopped his slicing, laid down the knife and again hurried over.

"Yes Most Holy Father?"

"Brother Daimhin, how would you like to run this kitchen?"

"Holy Father?" His eyes split wide. "But… but Brother Drubal is in charge of the kitchen?"

"Yes, I know. But I have need of him elsewhere. Brother Drubal, you don't mind do you?"

Drubal was still caught off guard. "I… uh… no, Eminence. No, of course not. When would you like me to begin?"

Duncan clapped him on the back. "Now. Go upstairs and help poor Garbhan out of the mess I left him in, while I let the new Chief Cook show me around the kitchen." He watched the reaction of both the brothers, quite pleased with himself.

Untying the kitchen apron, Drubal tossed it onto a nearby butcher block. "I should probably change into something less, um, piquant," he smiled, lifting his robe at the sides.

"Do so, but please hurry. I fear poor Garbhan will never forgive me," Duncan winked as Drubal hurried off. "Now, Brother Daimhin, perhaps you would show me how a gourmet kitchen works."

Daimhin bowed and chuckled. "Not yet gourmet Most Holy Father, but I will do my best to please you."

It was eight-forty, and laughter filled the dining room of the High Priest's chambers. Duncan was gently teasing Lucan, while the reappointed General Secretary Drubal and Konrud added to the banter. Darroch stood to the side in quiet, yet happy satisfaction, directing the acolytes in serving the meal. The difference between Vix and Duncan transcended more than dining styles. He had listened to the chatter of the other priests in the Temple, and he too could feel it. The oppressiveness had been replaced by a cautious optimism. While a few priests quietly grumbled at the perceived change, many more seemed to breathe more freely.

Darroch leaned back to look when he heard the knock at the door. One of the acolytes opened it to another priest who had a commoner with him. The acolyte's expression told him he needed to find out the news.

He returned to Duncan who in turn noticed his change of demeanor. "What news, Brother Darroch?"

"My apologies, Eminence, but the news is for Father Lucan. It concerns his brother."

Lucan paused mid-bite and put down his fork. Pursing his lips, he slowly inhaled. "What's happened?"

Darroch motioned the commoner into the room. His apprehension was obvious as he nervously wrung his hands. He was a middle-aged man with a full beard like that of the wood-folk. His hands were rough from ax handling. He stood mute, until the Steward prodded him, giving him a curt nod to proceed.

The man coughed to clear his throat. "Beggin' yer pardon, Most Holy Father, not meanin' to innerupt yer eatin.'"

"Please, our meal is of little importance at this moment. You have some news for us?"

"Aye, Most Holy Father. T'was early this mornin' when I went out choppin.' Decided to try a new place, I did. Been this way afore, but not since the last moons. Usual I goes up in the hills by the big river so I can cut and float 'em down. But as I were walkin' the road to Old Mullen, right when the it bends sorta to the left by the end of the pasture fence, afore you get to the woods, I seen 'im." He paused, nodding knowingly.

"Saw whom?" Konrud hesitated to ask.

"Why, the high priest, meanin' no offense," he quickly added to Duncan.

Duncan politely smiled. "What was he doing?"

The man looked surprised. "Why, he weren't doin' nuthin.' He was... uh..." he looked at the four clerics, trepidation suddenly flitting across his face.

Duncan saw his discomfit. "Relax man; no one is going to harm you."

"Was he alive?" Lucan's voice was barely audible.

The man slowly hung his head. "I'm sorry Holy Father, but he weren't."

Lucan's shoulders slumped and he took a deep breath. Duncan reached a hand out and gently touched his confidant's shoulder. "I'm sorry my friend. This is not what I intended."

"I know," he somberly answered. His eyes moistened briefly, and then just as quickly dried. He looked up at the woodsman. "Thank you for coming here to tell me."

Relieved that he was not to share the same fate, the man nodded obsequiously. He stood rooted, waiting for someone to dismiss him. Darroch was about to come to his rescue when Lucan asked,

"How did he die?"

At this question, the man's apprehension increased and he began rubbing at the roughness on his hands. "Well, your worship, er... he were...uh..."

Duncan raised his hand. "Please, relax. We know you to be a good man, one of honor. The fact that you came here by your own choice speaks well of your character. Just tell us what you saw."

The man briefly stared at the High Priest as if trying to divine his intent, yet Duncan merely looked back at him, waiting. Uttering a silent prayer, he decided to plow ahead. "He were trussed up 'tween two trees, 'bout a half a span off the ground." He held his hand horizontally below his knee as description. "They done gelded 'im." He stopped when he saw Lucan close his eyes.

Drubal got up and stood behind Lucan, placing both hands on his shoulders. He leaned in to whisper, "You tried your best, my son. We both did. He lived as he chose. We both knew he would reap the whirlwind of his actions. It was only a question of when. Grieve if you must, but remember who you are."

Lucan shuttered slightly, and settled himself. He let out a slow sigh. "He chose his own path. And though I will grieve his choices, I cannot change what has happened." He looked back at the woodsman. "Please continue."

Finally accepting that his own life was not in danger, the man relaxed. "Well, I seen 'im like he were, and I figure I oughta cut 'im down; but then I thinks to myself, he's up there fer a reason. 'bout this time road's beginnin' to fill up with folks and purty soon a crowd's standin' round starin' at 'im. We get to talkin' and all of 'em is glad he's dead – meanin' no harm your worship," he quickly added to Lucan.

"I understand." Lucan motioned for him to continue.

"Well, like I said, we was standin' there and nobody's sure what we should do. Some says we oughta cut 'em down. Some says to leave 'em alone 'cause he deserves what he got – meanin' no offense. So someone says maybe someone oughta tell you. Nobody wants to go 'cause they's afraid somethin' bad'll happen to 'em, like in the past. So I says, I'll go, 'cause we gotta new high priest and he ain't like this old one – no offence your worship."

Lucan rolled his eyes and shook his head. "Come to the point, man. Is he still there?"

The woodsman shrugged. "Last I seen 'im he still were."

Duncan looked over to his Steward. "Brother Darroch, would you mind sending someone to discover the present status of the former high priest? And if he is still there, please cut him down and convey him back here with appropriate dignity."

"Of course, Eminence." He snapped his fingers and relayed the command to one the acolytes who hurried off.

Duncan was again talking with the man. "How long did it take you to get here?"

"T'weren't long, your worship. Once I got back home and dropped off my axe and saws, I headed here. Only took me half a day."

"Have you eaten then?"

"Brought somethin' with me to eat on the way," he answered proudly.

"Very wise," Duncan affably replied. "Brother Darroch, do you suppose Brother Daimhin might spare a loaf of bread and some cheese for this gentleman's return trip."

"I'm sure we can find something suitable for his journey home," Darroch smiled. "However, with your approval Eminence, it is late and probably not wise to send him home at this hour. I believe we have a bed for him in the cooks' rooms. And I do believe they may be willing to share a pint of their best ale."

The man's eyes lit up, and he bobbed his head in gratitude. "Thank you, your worship. Thank you."

Darroch directed one of the acolytes to escort the man to the kitchen, while the other three clerics directed their attention to Lucan.

"I'm quite allright," Lucan reassured them. He stood up. "However, if you will excuse me Most Holy Father. I should be saddened by this news, but strangely, I'm not. I don't know why, but I'm somehow relieved." He shook his head. "Perhaps a little time to ponder this?"

"Of course, my friend. Should you feel the need to talk with someone, you know where we are," Duncan soothed. As Lucan left, he signaled to Darroch to send an acolyte to watch over him.

"How will this play out in Gambria?" Duncan matter-of-factly asked.

"Very well, for the most part," Konrud answered. "Sad to say, the people will be quite happy he's gone."

"And a few others will not be so happy," Drubal added. "And I would be very wary of those few."

"Like Cattwg and Tomos?" Duncan stated the obvious.

"And others," Drubal replied.

"Hmmm… I suppose I haven't made Mostyn very happy, have I?" he grinned.

"Nor Garbhan," Drubal pointed out. "Although I spent my time exiled to the kitchen, I did listen to the gossip, Safti forgive me." He placed both hands over his heart and bowed his head in one quick nod. He then said nothing more.

"And?" Duncan raised an eyebrow.

"Most Holy Father," Drubal demurred, "I hesitate to give too much credence to gossip."

"A wise position. However, gossip may contain snippets of truth."

Konrud furrowed is brows. "You've piqued my interest too."

Drubal thought for a moment, shrugged, and scooted his chair closer as he leaned in. "Rumor had it that he and Mostyn were collecting more than was necessary. It seems that some of the monks in the treasury are also part of their scheme." He leaned back. "With your permission, Most Holy Father, I'd like to have all our books examined, under the guise of an administration change and accounting."

"My goodness of course. If the Church can't be honest, how can we expect anyone else to be?

"You need to be careful, Brother" Konrud warned. "This may spread farther than we know."

"I agree," Duncan said. "However, we must make the Church pure; otherwise, how can we ever have any legitimacy? You have my full authority behind you. Any documents, writs, or whatever you need to make this happen, simply let me know and you will have it."

Drubal examined this new high priest, a man young enough to be his son. He liked what he was hearing. Yet he hesitated. "Thank you Most Holy Father. You willingly give me this authority? Why?"

"Because Lucan trusts you." It was stated as an obvious truth.

"And that is enough for you, that Lucan trusts me?"

"Yes."

Drubal absorbed the implication. "I thank you Most Holy Father. It's been a long time since I've heard that."

"Well get used to it," Duncan chuckled. "Now, I think that I may need to invite Brother Tomos to dinner very soon. What say you?" he winked.

Garbhan stormed into his apartment to a waiting Mostyn. "You fool! Are you purposely trying to destroy us?"

"No," Mostyn answered, taken aback.

"Well then what's your problem?"

"My problem? You mean you're willing to let this... this fakir assume the sacred position of High Priest?"

Garbhan sighed loudly. "Whatever you think of him, he has the King's authority. If this man wants to demote you to the wastelands, he can. Your impertinence may have just cost us everything we've worked so hard for." He began pacing the room, hands on his hips.

A subdued Mostyn watched him pace. "He still has to survive the Conclave."

"That may not be as difficult as you think."

"What?" His eyes widened in horror. "You all would let him do this to us?"

Garbhan whirled around to face him. "You don't get it do you? It takes a unanimous decision to oust him – remember? He's already got Lucan following him around like a dimwitted dorset." He held up his hand and counted on his fingers. "If Lucan goes, then Konrud will follow. There goes any possibility of getting rid of him. Further, the King's already appointed him, so he can't change his mind now. Whether you like it or not, this man will be our High Priest."

The former Secretary General absorbed the implications. "So what do we do?"

Garbhan shook his head in frustration. "I don't know, but the first thing *you* need to do is to go suck up to his soon-to-be eminence – "

"I'll not grovel to that charlatan." His chin jutted forward.

"Oh yes you will," came the quick retort. "You want him digging around? You want him asking questions?"

Mostyn scowled. "There's got to be another way."

"Well there isn't. And further, thanks to your attitude, he's already chosen your replacement."

"What? Already?"

Garbhan looked pointedly at him. "Don't act so surprised. You knew he was going to replace you the moment he brought me upstairs."

"Who is it then?"

"Drubal." It was said with both fear and distaste.

Mostyn's shoulders slumped and he flopped down into a chair. "What do we do? What's to become of me?"

Pursing his lips, he glowered at man. "I don't know what's in store for you, but the first thing we need to do is call the others together and figure out how we can protect ourselves."

There was a long pause before Mostyn spoke. "If we can get rid of this High Priest, we can get rid of Drubal."

Garbhan folded his arms. "That's the second thing we need to do."

The doors to the High Priest's chambers remained open as the messenger had not dared to enter, but chose to stand in the doorway. He had never delivered a message to the High Priest before. He had been told to deliver a message to the one who called himself a wizard. He had initially stopped at Alexis' home, but had been redirected to the Temple by one of the door-servants Without waiting for further explanation, he assumed to find him in the outer court. It was when he asked for Duncan that he learned of the transformation, and of the wizard's powers, embellished by those who had not been at the beach to witness the midnight sky light up.

Duncan was amused at the messenger's discomfit when he had appeared at his chambers, but the smile disappeared when the news had been delivered. "Are you sure?"

"Yes Most Holy Father. High Commander Brenna specifically told me to deliver the news to you." The man's nervousness was obvious. It was also obvious that, try as he might, he could not take his eyes off of the white streak in Duncan's hair. And from his bedraggled looks, it was obvious that he had been traveling non-stop for several days.

"Relax. I'm not going to turn you into a roan." Duncan saw the man's eyes widen in fear. "I was just joking," he reassured. "Relax. Please. Have you eaten?"

"No Holy Father. My mission was to deliver this message – "

"You've been riding for two days and haven't eaten?" he interrupted. He turned to Darroch who had walked in from the office. "Brother Darroch, would you please have some food brought up for this warrior?"

"Of course Eminence," he answered differentially, signaling to one of the door acolytes.

As the acolyte ran off, Duncan put his arm around the man's shoulders. "Come. Sit down and rest. The food should be here shortly."

Despite the man's trepidation, he allowed himself to be guided to the dining table in the front room of the High Priest's chambers, where Duncan seated him in his own chair. He had been briefly caught off guard when the High Priest had called him a warrior, and sought to correct the mistake.

"Holy Father, I am not a warrior."

"Were you there at the battle?"

"Yes Holy Father, but I am just a messenger."

"Have you been trained for combat?"

"Well… yes Holy Father, but I have not been accepted as a warrior yet."

Duncan nodded knowingly. "I see. But answer me this, were the battle to overtake you, would you fight?"

"Of course Holy Father."

"Then that makes you a warrior, at least in my eyes," he smiled. "But enough of that for now. Tell me the message again."

"Yes Holy Father. High Commander Brenna asked me to relay to you that High Commander Alexis was injured in the battle, but it was not serious. They will be returning any day now."

Duncan leaned on the table. "Did you see her fight?"

"Yes Holy Father, I did." His eyes lit up in admiration. "She was amazing! Lord Alric had initiated the attack in the center, but she didn't wait for the command to move the right flank forward. Instead, she outran the first attack wave and charged the Rugian right flank all by herself. She had this lance and instead of using it to stab somebody, she jabbed it in the ground and leaped over the front row of Rugians." His hands and arms quickly joined in animation. "I could see the Rugian right flank begin to buckle. Then the rest of our warriors crashed into the Rugians and their right flank and it looked as if their right flank was about to crumble when the Rugian reserves rushed to their aid."

Duncan sat down, both fascinated and enjoying the retelling. "Then what happened?"

"Our warriors began to be pushed back, but by then it was too late. Our left flank had overwhelmed their right flank, and then Lord Alric joined the attack in the center. Their left flank saw the center begin to give and they turned tail and ran back towards the river. As soon as they started to run, the rest of the Rugians followed." The man grew solemn. "It was slaughter after that."

"But I thought you hated the Rugians?" he stated.

"I do. But that does not mean I wish them dishonor."

"So they should have stayed and died?"

"Of course."

His response was so matter-of-fact that it briefly caught Duncan off-guard. He looked at the man's strained eyes, the haggard and drawn face, the layers of travel on his clothing. Yet it was this man's demeanor that revealed so much about him. He knew this man could conceive of nothing else. He was trained to be a warrior, and if that meant being the last man standing against absurd odds, so be it.

"Of course," Duncan agreed. "So tell me, did you happen to see Alexis' injury?

"No Holy Father. I was sent before High Commander Alexis came off the battlefield." He turned his head as he saw the acolyte bringing in the food.

Duncan saw his eyes light up at the size of the tray piled high with food. "Eat up my friend. You well deserve it."

"Thank you Holy Father," came the grateful reply as the man broke off a chunk of bread. He was in the middle of slathering it with butter when Darroch appeared.

"Begging your pardon, Eminence, but Father Cattwg is here to see you."

Arching an eyebrow in irritation, he said, "Cattwg? About what?"

Darroch rolled his eyes and shrugged.

"I suppose we ought to show him in." As Darroch stepped out to attend Cattwg, Duncan watched as the man ate. "It is good isn't it?"

"Yes Most Holy Father. It is, and I thank you."

They heard his voice before Cattwg entered the dining room. "Why would you replace Mostyn?" He entered and jerked to a halt when he saw Duncan was not alone. "What's the meaning of this?"

317

Both Duncan and the man looked up. Cattwg stood in the doorway, his back arched slightly in haughty arrogance. His robe was a royal blue edged in wide gold piping, the robe of a Prelate.

"What's the meaning of what?" Duncan calmly replied.

"This... this... man." Disdain dripped from his voice. "Why is he eating here, in the High Priest chambers?"

Duncan stood up, his head tilted slightly as if pondering the gravity of the question. "I've met you before... Brother Cattwg, correct?"

"*Father* Cattwg," came the indignant reply.

"Ah yes, *Father* Cattwg," Duncan replied, emphasizing 'father.' "*Father* Cattwg, whose chambers are these?"

"The High Priest's." Cattwg's glare was a mixture of malevolence and condescension.

"And who am I?" Duncan asked, his tone as though he were lecturing a schoolboy.

Cattwg hesitated.

"Was the question too difficult? Even this 'man', as you put it, knows who I am. And I'm sure *Father* Cattwg, one of the more important clerics in Gambria, knows who I am. Isn't that so, *Father* Cattwg?"

"I know who you are," he retorted.

"Ah, now we're getting somewhere." Duncan looked back to the man who was eating a little more slowly as he watched the exchange and then turned back to Cattwg. "But let's return to your original question as to the meaning of all this. I submit that when one is hungry, one eats, just as *this... this... man* is now doing."

"But he's a commoner."

"On the contrary, he's actually a soon-to-be warrior, which is not all that common." Duncan smiled.

"But it is unseemly." Cattwg bristled.

"Unseemly? How?"

Duncan's smugness was too much. "It is just not done! You don't know your place; you don't know who you are. There are rules to follow, protocol, expectations. You know nothing of what it means to be High Priest. You come here –"

"Stop." Duncan held his hand up. "Are you lecturing me?"

Cattwg was nettled. "If that's what you wish to call it."

Darroch had heard the commotion and had hurried to the dining room. Listening to the exchange, he quickly assessed its direction and motioned the man to follow him. Leading him to the front doors, he solicitously explained, "You won't mind finishing your meal elsewhere, would you? That way we can let them discuss their issue in private." They stepped out together.

"Of course not Brother. I'm pretty well finished anyway, and I need to report in."

Darroch nodded approvingly. "Go with Safti then." He turned and hurried back in, closing the door behind him. As he walked to the dining room, he could hear Duncan speaking.

"Father Cattwg, you don't like me being High Priest, do you?"

Cattwg saw no reason to hide his feelings. "No, I don't."

Duncan nodded. "I appreciate your honesty." He moved from around the table. "By the way, if I recall correctly, you serve at my pleasure," his gaze bore into him. "Don't you?"

Cattwg went white, taking a step back.

"I'm sorry; I didn't hear your reply?" He cocked his ear towards him.

"Yes," Cattwg hissed, barely a whisper.

"Tell me priest," his voice suddenly hardened as he took another step toward Cattwg, "did you lecture Vix when he sacrificed all those children? Did you stand here in the doorway and lecture him on rules, protocol, and expectations? Did you?"

"I... I... it was not my place," Cattwg sputtered, jerking two steps back. Darroch hastened to open the front doors.

"Neither is it your place now." Duncan moved to the doorway, and with each step closer, Cattwg took a step back until Duncan was in the doorway and Cattwg stood an arm's length outside. "Well thanks for stopping by. I'll be sure to keep in mind all that we discussed." He smiled cheerfully. With a hand on each door-edge, he stepped back and closed the doors, leaving an increasingly agitated Cattwg glaring at the opaque and solid wood in front of him.

"Lose another debate did you?" a voice jibed.

Cattwg jerked his head to the left to watch Father Gerallt approach. "What are you doing here?"

"The High Priest asked me to stop by before Council Conclave. Something about my domains."

Cattwg's eyes snapped wide in anger. "Don't you even think about it! I will not let that happen to me; you understand me?"

Gerallt was taken aback. "What are you talking about?"

"Don't play coy with me. You know damn well what I mean."

"Watch your tongue, Father Cattwg," he admonished. "What has you all excited?"

"Go ahead, play the game. But don't think for a moment I'm going to sit still." Cattwg spun on his heels and stomped down the hallway.

Gerallt stood immobile, his eyes blinking in confusion. He then looked at the door acolytes. "My apologies for Father Cattwg's behavior. I'm sure he has a lot on his mind. Now, would you please let the High Priest know I am here," he said, nodding towards the doors.

A little while later, Gerallt emerged, suppressing a broad smile. He had not known what to expect when he had been summoned to the High Priest chambers, but the discussions had proven most interesting. Tomorrow was the Conclave, and he was quite sure how he was going to vote.

As dawn surrendered to brightening day, sixteen Prelates, dressed in formal vestments of royal blue robes edged in gold piping, sat quietly in the Council Chambers, waiting for the guard to close the doors. When he finally pressed them together, he ceremoniously wrapped the handles together in a scarlet cloth, then turned around and stood before the doors, a spear in one hand, and the other resting on his sword.

Lucan sat in the High Priest's chair. To his lower right, a priestly scribe, dressed in robes of forest green edged in silver, sat behind a small heavily carved table, an ornately decorated quill pen in hand to record the proceedings. Eight Prelates sat on one side of the chamber room, and seven on the other. Lucan waited for the nod from the guard before beginning. Picking up a heavy and worn tome, he carefully opened it, and began to read aloud.

"This Synod Conclave has been established to determine and decide the worthiness of the supplicant called Duncan to be anointed as the Most High representative of the Most Holy Safti, to be the guardian of the morality of this nation, and all that is holy, to have the wisdom to decide between the sacred and the profane, to render judgment in all matters spiritual, to continue in the tradition of those who names appear here and now from time immemorial, to add his name to this sacred book, to teach us to remember who we are."

He paused and looked up to the other Prelates. He then nodded to the guard who stamped his spear on the floor and loudly announced, "By decree of King Diad, ruler of the nation of Gambria and defender of the faith, who presents now to this most sacred Synod, the person known as Duncan, both by right of challenge and by choice, to be hereinafter and forever known as High Priest of Gambria."

Lucan leaned forward, peering over the open book. "Is there anyone here who would stand for this supplicant called Duncan?

There was a moment of silence before Konrud stood up. "Yes Holy Father. I stand for Duncan." He remained standing as Lucan continued.

"Is there anyone here who will stand against this supplicant called Duncan?" Before the last words escaped his lips, Cattwg jumped up.

"Yes. I stand against him." He glared as he spat the words.

Lucan let silence settle for a moment before he continued. "Father Konrud has spoken in favor of supplicant Duncan. Father Cattwg has spoken against supplicant Duncan. As tradition has been set down before us, Father Cattwg will now remove himself to the left hand side of the Chamber."

Cattwg stepped down from his place and crossed the floor to the Council seats on Lucan's left side. He stood before the seat closest to Lucan.

"Father Konrud," Lucan stated, "would you please assume the place to my right."

Konrud shuffled down several places and stood before the seat closest to Lucan.

"We see the choices made, and those who stand. It is now time for each of us to choose. By this book and by our heritage, and in the wisdom of Safti, I adjure you to choose wisely. Once made, a choice may not be revoked. I thereby caution you to deliberate before you choose." Lucan spoke slowly, deliberately. "We will now, therefore, choose. I remind you that you may choose to refrain for this moment only. If there is sufficient number to warrant no choice, we will deliberate and choose again. Is that understood?" There was a general acknowledgement as they waited for Lucan to proceed.

"By law and by tradition set down for generations, this Council need not be unanimous in its decision. By simple majority, the supplicant may be either accepted or rejected. If the supplicant is accepted, no further deliberation will occur and a messenger will be sent to the King affirming his choice. If the supplicant is rejected by majority vote, deliberations will continue, upon which another vote will occur. Deliberations will continue until the supplicant is accepted, or unanimity is achieved rejecting the supplicant, or sunset occurs. Should sunset occur prior to a reaching a decision, the majority choice at the time of sunset will be the final decision.

Likewise, the High Chancellor may not cast a vote except in cases where a tie does occur." Lucan paused to make sure all understood the procedure. He looked at Cattwg whose edginess contrasted so obviously with Konrud's serenity.

Taking a deep breath, he pushed on. "Those who stand for Duncan will stand to my right. Those who stand against Duncan will stand to my left. Those who have not yet decided will stand in the middle. Is that understood?" Lucan waited before announcing, "Please stand where you will."

Except for Konrud and Cattwg, the remaining Prelates stood up and began moving to their chosen spots. By the time it was finished, Cattwg, Tomos, and Garbhan stood on the left side. Pewlin and Meurig stood in the middle, and the rest stood with Konrud.

Cattwg had followed the shifting Prelates, and as the number of Prelates to Lucan's right grew, so too did his anger. He glowered at each of those opposite him. And each one returned his stare with equal strength of defiance.

Lucan was inwardly thrilled at the outcome. As was the tradition for the High Chancellor, he had purposely refrained from swaying or canvassing the other Council members, and had been truly concerned at the outcome, afraid that Cattwg had already influenced the outcome. He relaxed, knowing that he could now proceed with closing the synod.

"The choices have been made. Let the record show that Fathers Cattwg, Tomos, and Garbhan have stood against the supplicant; that Fathers Pewlin and Meurig have made no choice; and that Fathers Konrud, Eachann, Keefe, Gerallt, Morvyn, Kinnell, Oran, Frang, Tearlach, Gwern have stood for the supplicant. Let the record also show that while it was not necessary for the High Chancellor to vote, he stands for the supplicant. Thus, let the record show the summation as ten for the supplicant, two not choosing, three opposing the supplicant."

Lucan took a breath, then announced in a loud voice, "By vote of affirmation, the supplicant called Duncan is chosen as High Priest. Let the scribe now enter his name into the annals of Gambria." The scribe stood up and mounted the stairs to stand beside Lucan. Lucan turned the ancient book from which he read so that the scribe could now write Duncan's name below that of Vix. The scribe slowly added the year to end Vix's tenure, and entered the same year for Duncan's accession. He then stood up and placed the quill across the book.

Lucan turned his attention to the guard. "Please send the messenger to the King announcing the elevation of supplicant Duncan as High Priest of Gambria."

The guard formally bowed and turned around to undo the scarlet cord. He opened the doors to where a single acolyte waited. "Announce to the King that the Council has assented to his choice, and His Most Holy Father Duncan is now High Priest of Gambria."

As the acolyte sped off to relay the news, the guard turned around to face Lucan. He tapped his spear on the floor three times. "Holy Father and High Chancellor, the messenger has departed."

Lucan nodded in acceptance and the formality of the information. He then addressed the group. "Holy Fathers of the one true religion of Safti, our choice has been made, and the King informed. By the power vested in me by the Church, I declare this synod closed." He closed the book, and stood up.

There was a general exhale as the members visibly relaxed and talked among themselves as they made their way down from their seats. All except Cattwg, who, as soon as Lucan had declared the meeting closed, had stormed out of the chambers, Tomos and Garbhan following awkwardly behind him.

Meurig and Pewlin remained where they were, feeling self-conscious in their indecision. Konrud walked up to them.

"Are you still undecided?" He smiled.

Pewlin sniffed a smile. "Not anymore. The choice has been made."

"Come," Konrud leaned in. "Let's see what's in the buttery to toast our new High Priest."

Pewlin laughed. "I like the way you think."

Konrud turned to Lucan. "Are you ready?"

Lucan nodded, and descended the steps from the platform. Except for the three who had abruptly left, the rest of the Council had remained. As was custom, the entire Council was to inform the supplicant of their choice. The group parted as Lucan made his way to the front.

"Let's go tell the High Priest the good news," he happily stated, and then left the Council Chambers.

Chapter 20

Wanting life to return to normal as quickly as possible, King Diad ordered Duncan's elevation liturgy to occur as quickly as possible. It was while he was preparing for the ceremony that he heard the sudden roar, the shouts, the jubilation as the noise spilled over the windowsills and filled the room. Puzzled, he motioned one of the servants to the window.

"What's happening out there?" he gruffly demanded.

The Steward of the Privy Chamber, a precise man of little humor, stopped the servant mid-way. "You sir, please attend to the King. We have little enough time as it is. I shall determine the cause of this distraction." His back stiffened as he slowly marched his way to the open window. However, he had temporarily forgotten the height of the King's bedroom tower, and involuntarily sucked in his breath as his first vision was the Sea beyond the city walls. Sidling closer to the window, his view shifted downward to the long and wide, neatly manicured park that stretched from Kinghall to the row of large homes edging the far end of the park. Forming a large rectangle, a wide street trimmed in hardwood trees formed a crisp border between the park and the surrounding homes.

Normally the park was a venue for gamboling children, expectant mothers sharing wisdom, lovers taking their time walking the neatly trimmed paths, and the evening stroll for the burghers and other businessmen at the end of their busy day. Yet today, the park was covered with the swarming mass of Gambria's citizens. Although much of the crowd was from Mull, a significant number had traveled from the other parts of the country to witness this event.

He watched the crowd surge like a flock of birds towards the far right corner. Squinting, he focused on some movement to where the crowd was giving its attention. "My god!" His hand went to his mouth as he stepped back.

"What is it man?"

"The High Priest is already making his way here."

"Now? It's too soon. Get away from me." Diad pushed away the fawning attention of the wardrobe attendants and stalked over to the window. Vainly trying to focus on the activity, he turned to the Steward in frustration. "There's too much confusion. You tell me what goes on." He pointed to the commotion.

The Steward hesitated briefly, then bowed. "As you wish m'Lord," Gazing back out the window he stared in wonder. "The lawn is completely filled with people. So are the streets. I've never seen so many at one time."

"I can see that," the King growled, standing next to him.

"Beg pardon, m'Lord," flustered, he placed both hands on his chest, "of course you can. I was merely pointing out the size of the crowds."

"Get on with it man. I don't need you telling me the obvious. If that's the High Priest," he pointed, "he's not moving very quickly."

The man refocused his attention. "That's probably because of the crowds, m'Lord... no, no wait... I don't believe it!"

"What, what? Out with it dammit."

"There sire," he pointed. "You can see the coronation carriage with the four white uchen. But the High Priest isn't on the carriage... He's walking in front of it!"

"Walking?" Diad furrowed his brows. "He's not supposed to be walking," he said to no one. He continued to watch as the procession made its way forward. By now he could see the acolyte priests out front, vainly holding back the crowds. Duncan, his dazzling robe swirling around him, was in their midst happily working the crowds as he went from one side to the other, touching hands and waving. Occasionally he paused to lift a baby from outstretched hands, gently kiss it on the forehead and pass it back to a radiant mother who held the child aloft as evidence of favored recognition.

Diad watched the crowd pour out its adoration. "How is this possible?" Dumbfounded, he mumbled to himself. "He's been here less than seven days... what has he done to warrant this?"

"Perhaps it's more to do with his predecessor, m'Lord." his steward offered

"But this?" He swept his hand at the churning multitude. "This... this is unseemly. You'd think they'd never had a new High Priest before." He watched with growing distracted irritation, remembering his own coronation, and even that of Vix. What crowds there were for Vix had been subdued, mute spectators lining the streets watching with trepidation as Vix assumed supreme command of the state church, his reputation having preceded him. Diad's coronation had been much better. He remembered getting dressed in this same chamber and looking out the window to see crowds waiting for him to ascend the throne. Having only Vix to compare to, his coronation seemed exuberant.

But not with this… He spun around and started for the door. "I'll put a stop to this. He doesn't know his place."

"Is that wise, m'Lord?" the Steward hurriedly intercepted the King.

"And why not?" Diad stuttered to a halt.

"M'Lord, I fear you would accomplish little except to earn the disdain of this worshipping fodder. If it please, sire, I suggest this display has more to do with his decree of an end to child sacrifice than to adulation."

"He's not High Priest yet," Diad glared. "He can't issue decrees."

"You are right of course, m'Lord, but he has made it known that he will do so upon his ascension. Please, your Highness, let us finish getting you dressed, and let them enjoy this moment. They will calm down soon enough and forget this novelty, and life will return to normal."

Diad pondered momentarily, snarled loudly, then allowed himself to be led back to the dressing area where the wardrobe attendants resumed their fastidious attention. While they worked, his frustration increased with the crescendo of noise as Duncan grew closer.

Sitting on his throne atop the royal dais in front of Kinghall, Diad grimly watched Duncan's approach, the crowd swarming euphorically behind him. It was already past the appointed time and Diad's irritation grew with each passing second.

Next to him, the Steward of Ceremony fidgeted slightly, the weight of the jewel-studded triple tiara growing uncomfortably heavy in his hands. Little beads of sweat began to form on his forehead and temples, and he forcibly suppressed the urge to wipe them away.

Down on the street, on a raised platform off to the king's left, stood the assembled nobility and gentry of Gambria, their attire attesting to either their wealth or position. The ladies fanned themselves with delicate lace and porcelain fans, while the men simply brushed away the offending sweat.

Duncan's entourage was at last approaching the final turn to the right where the barricades would hold back the fawning masses from the actual ceremony. Kissing one last baby, he waved to the crowd and turned his attention to his future. Looking up to the awaiting king, he urged his group to move on.

The sun was high overhead as the new High Priest finally stood on the street below the King and waited. Somewhere in the crowd, someone began chanting "Dun-can, Dun-can, Dun-can." And it quickly spread until the entire assembly gave one loud voice.

"Dun-can, Dun-can, Dun-can."

The King stood up and raised his hands for silence.

"Dun-can, Dun-can, Dun-can." It grew louder.

He shook his hands several times to repeat his command for silence.

"Dun-can, Dun-can, Dun-can."

Controlling his growing vexation, Diad dropped his hands and folded his arms to wait for the noise to diminish. Yet there were no signs of it stopping.

Blithely unaware of the king's annoyance, Duncan waited, enjoying the adoration. It wasn't until he looked up to the Steward of Ceremony whose tight lips, furrowed brow, and slight jerk of the head telling him to ascend that he stirred.

The noise grew with each step as he climbed up the wide polished stone steps. One step down and to his right, Lucan happily marched up with him. Opposite him to the left was Konrud, also quite pleased with the day's events. In descending order and to the right and left of Lucan and Konrud, the remaining Fathers solemnly marched up to their assigned place on the step, the effect like that of a peacock spreading his fan.

As Duncan ascended the next to the last step, he knelt down on both knees before the king. Diad stood silently, waiting for the ripple of understanding in the crowd that nothing would proceed until the noise subdued. Fortunately, the crowd was beginning to grow hoarse and ready to get on with it so they could go celebrate in the many pubs and alehouses nearby. As the noise subsided, Diad raised his hands and in a loud commanding voice, began the ceremony.

"In accordance with the traditions handed down to us by those whose lives and wisdom we have come to love and cherish, we proceed this day in declaring a new leader of the nation's spiritual kingdom. We declare this day that by covenant of King and Council, the chosen one of Safti now kneels before us. By this act of submission, this priest called Duncan yields his obedience to God and state, promising to serve them both though it mean his life. By the authority vested in us as the rightful king and defender of Gambria, I declare this priest Duncan, the forty-fourth Patriarch and High Priest of the Church of Gambria."

The people erupted into boisterous cheers as the Steward turned and handed the tiara to the King who dramatically paused, before lifting it high and then slowly lowering it onto Duncan's head. The weight caught Duncan

327

momentarily off guard, but he quickly recovered and remembered to kiss the King's hand.

Pushing himself up to standing, he turned to face the crowd, one step below Diad so that the King became virtually invisible behind the towering tiara.   What the crowd could see was his hands resting on Duncan's shoulders, a symbol of submission of the church to the state.

"Make it short," Diad growled in a low voice only Duncan could hear.

Duncan raised his hands. "Good people of Gambria," he started, but the noise drowned him out. "Good people of Gambria," he repeated, and kept repeating it until the clamor died down.

"Good people of Gambria. By my oath do I solemnly swear to uphold the laws of this land while leading a nation in obedience to the laws of Safti. Today is a day like many other days, when we experience a transition from what has gone before and now face a new path.   While we can no longer change what has occurred, we can learn from the roads we've traveled, and use this wisdom to forge a better way.   As the Prophet himself said, 'obedience is better than sacrifice.'   What Safti needs is prayers and obedience," he paused for effect as he felt the energy of the crowd, then exclaimed "not sacrifice."   A murmur of excited anticipation rippled throughout the crowd, awaiting the promised edict.   He felt it and drank in the intensity, feeling it flush throughout him and emanate from his fingertips.

"I say again, what Safti needs is prayers and obedience," he paused to look out over the vast audience before loudly emphasizing, "not children."

The effect was electric as though the floodgates had burst.   The crowd roared and surged, and it was with great difficulty that the guards held them back. Several managed to make it through and dashed their way towards Duncan. Armed acolytes moved to intercept them when Duncan intervened.

"Stop! Let them be."

There were five of them, four men and a woman, common trade folk by the look of them, suddenly aware that everyone was staring at them as they stood at the bottom of the stairs, well below Duncan.   And just as quickly as the crowd erupted, it stilled as it waited to see what was to happen to these few who, despite their joy, now found themselves in violation of both expected behavior and laws.

Looking down, Duncan benignly smiled. "And what is it I can do for you friends?"

At first, they were mute, frightened by their own transgression. But one man, a tanner by the lingering smell of him, gathered up enough courage to answer.

"Most Holy Father, we didn't mean ter bust through like this. It were just the moment, but I ain't ashamed of it fer my part. I come to tell yer that yer what we been waitin' an prayin' fer. An God bless yer, and that's all I got ta say." Tears began slipping down his cheeks.

Sensing the affront to tradition, an epiphany hit Duncan as to how to make this work out for the better. "Come, all of you. Come kneel before me."

Amidst the not too subtle quiet consternation of the assembled nobles and religious leaders, the five slowly made their way up and dropped to their knees before him, the woman in the center. Duncan placed a hand on the heads of the woman and the man next to her, and then addressed the crowd.

"As you would have the church be faithful you, I ask that you be faithful to her. So that you know the church will be faithful to you, from this day forward, I decree that never again will our children, nor any other human creature, ever be used as sacrifice to Safti."

The crowd finally had the answer it came for, and the joyous tumult rose to spill over the very walls of the city. Duncan knew it was time, and he motioned the five kneeling commoners to rise and precede him down the stairs. As he descended, the clerical leadership fell in behind him to the street below where the commoners were hustled off to the side so the procession could retrace its steps back to the far corner of the park, and back to the Temple.

Watching the tiara descend before him, Diad tightened his lips in frustrated displeasure. He had read the faces of Gambria's upper class sitting off to his left. Some were plainly disturbed by the display, a few seemed a bit baffled, but most were simply indifferent. They had already moved on, chatting amongst themselves, waiting for the event to end so they could return to their daily lives.

Diad frowned. Were these people so obtuse not to see what was happening? There was something about this new High Priest that wasn't right.

Down on the stage, Bradwr watched his brother. He leaned over to Emer. "Your father seems a bit put out today."

"He ought to be," Emer retorted. "The inept masses here are far more infatuated with this new High Priest than with dear old dad."

"It won't last."

"That's not the point."

"What are you two jabbering about?" Raefgot interrupted, leaning in.

"None of your business. Why don't you just settle back into your drunken stupor and leave the important affairs of state to your betters," Emer sneered.

"Now, now, let's give it a rest for one day, shall we?" Bradwr shook his head at Emer. He turned to Raefgot who was still feeling the sting, searching his muddled mind for a clever rejoinder. "We were discussing why your Father seems to be put out so much today."

A little mollified by his uncle's support, he ventured, "Maybe it's the crowd?"

Emer rolled his eyes. "Do try to keep up. We're past the obvious. But come, my besotted step-brother," he mocked, "tell us of your insight as to the day's events."

Raefgot frowned, blinking. "I don't know what you mean."

"Of course not. And there's obvious reason for that. But that's a topic for another day." He leaned back and pretended to appraise his younger brother. "Why weren't you in today's ceremony?"

"I'm not a priest," he knit his brow, replying to the obvious.

"And that's what I want to know. Why didn't Father put you into the priesthood?"

"We've been through this before," Bradwr calmly interrupted. "The priesthood is not a suitable avocation for a young man of Raefgot's…um…talents."

"Really?" Emer shook his head and stared at his youngest brother. "You may have fooled Father into allowing you to spend your life a wastrel, but when I'm king, you're going to become a priest."

"The hell I will," Raefgot spat.

Emer smiled malevolently. "That's right – the hell you *will*."

Raefgot glared at him, his eyes revealing his hatred. "We can only hope Father outlives you, because god help us if you ever become king." He stormed off the stage and blended into crowds heading for the alehouses.

"Was that wise nephew?"

"He's an idiot."

"Even idiots have their uses," his uncle wisely replied.

"Not him. If you'll excuse me uncle, I think I'll go look to see where my wife made off to." Emer bowed slightly and walked off.

Bradwr watched him go, noticing that instead of looking for Pavia, he walked with a purpose elsewhere. He knew where he was headed. *You can't rule a kingdom hiding away in Buckom*, he sighed. Looking up, he watched Diad's frown evolve to a leer as a buxom lady-in-waiting helped escort him off the throne. He pondered his own future. It no longer was a question of if, but when. He was about to step off the stage when he felt a hand on his elbow.

"A word Cousin."

He recognized the voice before turning to a slender man with a neatly trimmed beard and moustache. "Hello Bradach. What did you think of the ceremony?"

Bradach paused as though deliberating. "He seems too young to be high priest."

"His predecessor was even younger," he pointed out.

"That may be so, Cousin, but Vix was one of us. Who knows anything about this man?"

"The king seems content with him."

"Really? So that sour look of his was just his way of saying how pleased he was with this public display?" Bradach bent his head forward and lowered his voice. "M'Lord Cousin, while you bide your time, others are making their own plans. I fear you wait much longer and your kingdom will be snatched from you like ripe fruit."

"I know about Rhun," he snapped, a tinge of frustration edging his outward calmness. Deeming their elevated position on the platform too public, he smiled as if in response to a jest. "Come, let's walk."

Leading the way down the steps, he glanced over to his right where a corpulent, richly dressed man surrounded by several personal guards was studiously observing him. Catching his eye, he gave him an overly wide smile and affable nod that was answered with a thin smile and curt nod. He inwardly chuckled. Subtlety was not one of Rhun's qualities. He wore his anger like a mantle. That he was once a king's son ruled his personal universe. He could see nothing else. Bradwr briefly mused what it must be like to be so close to being king, only to have one's father give it away... or, he sighed, to be the second child.

As they made their way through the crowds, Bradwr smiled benevolently and nodded at many of the multitude, who respectfully bowed. His own complement of personal guards moved with him, a discrete distance away, pushing their way through the hubbub, constantly monitoring his movements.

"Have you sounded out your father yet?"

"The topic was broached," Bradach replied, "but he is noncommittal. While he is wary of the present, he prefers to stay home, away from all the intrigue. He sees himself as above all this," he stated simply, inclining his head at the dwindling crowd. "Says the future of the kingdom is all he cares about."

"The question is," Bradwr pursed his lips, looking over and around the crowd, "can we depend on him?" His eyes settled on a man leaning against the outside wall of a tavern, yawning. When their eyes met, Bradwr gave a quick nod and the man immediately blended into the crowd and was gone.

Bradach had followed the exchange. "You trust him?"

"Probably more than I trust you," he smiled, "Cousin."

"M'Lord Bradwr," he placed both hands on his chest in feigned offense, "I am your own man, your greatest defender."

"I'm sure you are," Bradwr snorted. At that moment, he caught glimpse of Raefgot blithely unaware as he pushed his way into a tavern.

"What do we do with him?" Bradach wondered aloud.

"Leave him. He may prove useful yet."

Rhun had watched with overt disdain as Bradwr and Bradach made their way into the dwindling crowd. Dabbing a bead of sweat from his forehead, he tugged at the collar of his finely woven shirt, absently thinking that his choice of darker colors wasn't such a smart idea. Yet his eyes followed Bradwr and he watched the fawning reaction of the common folk, those cattle. How could they not see through his sham. The man was too obvious, pretending to be one of the people, unaffected by the crowds, while his own guards hovered within striking distance. Look at him, that fake smile, that benign nod... oh, that was a good one, the touch on the arm, as though he cared... great Safti what pure sow dung.

His thick hand reached out and grabbed the arm of the closest attendant. "You," he grunted. "Follow them and report back to me."

He watched as the man jolted down the steps and hustled to catch up to the dwindling quarry. By now, the crowd had become disinterested in the remaining gentry and he suddenly became acutely aware that none of this rabble had come to pay their respects, to grovel appropriately to one of his position and place. While one or two had caught his eye and nodded politely, none had seen fit to do anything more. This set him on edge. Silently grimacing, he vowed they would be reminded of their place when he became king.

"Nephew," he said, turning to a younger man who stood to his left, "tell Shenayr Kylar we come to come to pay our respects." Handing him several coins, he added, "Don't arrive empty-handed. Find a nice cut of meat or a flagon of a wine – a good wine."

"Yes Uncle," he nodded, accepting the coins. "Will you be long?"

"It will be fine if we arrive before you do," he answered, a tinge of paternal kindness in his eyes. "Off with you now."

The man smiled warmly at him, "I'll be there before you."

Rhun laughed good-naturedly, the irritation of the day momentarily forgotten. Watching him hasten off to his task, he smiled to himself. Vonn was a fine young man. He would make an excellent son-in-law... pliant and obedient. Now all he had to do was to get that silly girl of his to spend more time with him.

He turned to his chamberlain, a thin man of plain tastes. "Where's Heledd?"

"I believe she's gone off with Lady Pavia."

"Find her," he sighed in exasperation. "I want her with us at Kylar's."

"Yes m'Lord." With a flick of his wrist, he sent another attendant racing off to find the wayward daughter.

Rhun stood a moment longer. Damn it was hot. Then an idea suddenly arose. Why hadn't he thought of it sooner? Bradach was yet unmarried... Perhaps Heledd could prove useful. He wiped the sweat from his chin. Yes... tempt him just enough to pry him from Bradwr.

Pleased with himself, and with as much grace as he could pretend, he urged his podgy body forward and descended the several steps, perspiration dampening the edges of his shirt and trousers.

Kylar sat comfortably enough, though the cushions on his chairs these days seemed either too soft or too hard. He fidgeted slightly, his joints aching. 'Must be a change in the weather coming,' he thought to himself. He was ready to get out of this damned city, back to his own home, nestled on the cliffs of the southeastern shores of the Starn Sea. Why he ever decided to keep a place here in Mull was beginning to make less and less sense. It wasn't like he spent much time here. In fact, he avoided Mull as much as possible... too crowded and too hurried. If it wasn't for Bradach, he'd be happy enough to sell the damned place.

Looking out the window, he gazed inattentively at a seagull floating on the warm air above the trees lining the edges of park. Bradach... why wasn't that boy married? He could understand waiting for the right one, or even the right arrangement. But damn, how long is long enough? It wasn't like he couldn't 'scatter his seed' after he was married...

Kylar reached up and pushed his jaw and head to the right, cracking his neck. He'd spent enough on the house and that boy's allowance to build a damned castle back home. Still, he supposed he was useful enough, keeping up with the latest webs and deceits. Besides, what would he do with him if he were home? It wasn't time yet to bring him back. But then, maybe he should give him that cantref on the south. Start giving him some experience. They've been getting uppity lately. Some discipline would do them good. Teach them to remember who they are. Kylar shifted again in his chair, looking back as a young willowy woman walked in

"M'Lord, your grandson Vonn is here to see you."

Sighing heavily, he simply nodded.

"Good afternoon Shenayr," the young man walked in smiling, as if he were genuinely happy to be there. He carried a medium sized glass amphora-shaped wine bottle in his hands. "Uncle Rhun asked me to deliver this to you."

Kylar pursed his lips, raising an eyebrow as he accepted the bottle. Slowly twisting the cork stopper, he lifted it to inhale the bouquet. "Hmm... good fragrance," he nodded appreciatively. "Here," he commanded handing the bottle to Vonn, "pour us a glass."

As Vonn turned to look for glasses, the young woman walked in again. "Your nephew, Lord Rhun, is here to pay his respects, m'Lord."

"No doubt," he flatly answered. "Well don't just stand there, show him in."

But Rhun was already walking in, casting an admiring eye on the young woman as she passed. "Greetings Uncle," he grinned, dabbing at his perspiring forehead. "You're looking well these days."

"Nephew," he acknowledged. "I understand I have you to thank for this," he stated, accepting the filled glass from Vonn. Inhaling the bouquet again, he sipped a small amount, savoring the flavor. "Very nice... very smooth." Settling back, he placed a boney elbow on the arm of the chair, resting his jaw on his knuckles. "Now why would you want to send over such a fine gift?" he asked, slowly swirling the wine in his glass.

Rhun lumbered over to the couch and plopped down, fluttering his damp clothes away from his corpulent chest. "Uncle, you are here so infrequently these days, it seemed only fitting to bring along a little libation to say how pleased we are to see you again." He smiled paternally at Vonn as he accepted a glass. Mimicking Kylar, he tasted the wine, raising his eyebrows in approval. "You've a discerning palate, nephew. Very good."

Vonn nodded demurely, pleased with himself, and settled in a chair enough away to be respectful, yet close enough to participate should he be asked.

"So," Kylar intoned, "what else besides wine brings you here?"

"I didn't see you at the coronation today. I was concerned."

"Too damn hot. Besides, I can see all I need to from here."

"True on both accounts. So what did you think of the ceremony?"

"Took him too damn long to get there, but once there it was thankfully short enough. Don't like all the circus that passes for simply telling everyone we got some new official or another." He finished the wine and held his glass out, shaking it slightly, telling Vonn he wanted more.

"I agree with you Uncle. It all can be rather tedious." Rhun held his glass up to likewise be refilled. "But this new high priest, what do you think of him?"

"Don't give a damn one way or another. As long as he keeps himself out of my business, we'll get along fine."

"But Uncle, don't you think it strange we know so little about him?"

"Just how much do you want to know?" he retorted.

Rhun immediately understood, remembering Vix's perverted penchants. "Perhaps you're right. Though I think Diad might have chosen one of our own – "

"Vix *was* one of our own," he interrupted.

"Alright, you win," he held his thick hands up, laughing good-naturedly. "How long will you be staying?"

"Leaving first thing in the morning," he answered testily.

"Already? Nephew," he turned to Vonn, "I think Shenayr Kylar needs to have his glass refilled."

Kylar lifted his glass again, watching Vonn's deliberate actions. "So," he held his hand up signaling the glass was full enough, "now that we have the pleasantries finished, how about you tell me why you're really here?"

"Cut to the chase, eh? I've always liked that about you," Rhun smiled thinly.

Rolling his eyes, Kylar leaned forward. "Get to the point, Nephew."

"Uncle," he answered, settling back deep into the couch, "what are you going to do about my cousin?"

"So we're back to this again? I don't see that I need to do anything about him," came the gruff reply.

335

"But Uncle, you can't be happy with the way his attention seems to be so readily diverted these days. He seems to get distracted far too easily and far too frequently. Wouldn't you agree?"

"Whether I agree or not, he is still the king."

"But wouldn't you agree, Uncle?" Rhun calmly answered.

"I wouldn't know," he snapped, "don't spend much time here."

"I don't blame you Uncle. If I had your beautiful home across the sea, I probably wouldn't come here either. But living apart doesn't mean you don't know what going on. Surely Bradach has told you what's been happening," he innocently inquired.

A flicker of a smile edged Kylar's mouth. "Yes, as any father's son would do."

"Of course. But doesn't it trouble you that Diad seems to be so easily persuaded? Take this new High Priest for example. How could a king allow this to happen?"

"Seems to me Vix did it to himself. Damned foolishness to begin with."

"Oh, I agree, Uncle," Kylar appeased. "I find it curious that the Council failed to defend him."

"Who'd want to defend that perverted bastard. I'm glad he's gone," Kylar spat.

"But he was still our high priest," Rhun countered.

Kylar glared at him for a moment, then relaxed slightly. "Point taken."

"And what about my sister," Rhun pressed. "You certainly can't be happy with the way he continues to treat her. It's an embarrassment to the family."

"Your sister needs to get a damned backbone," he snarled. "It's an embarrassment because she won't stand up to him. Besides," he swallowed the last bit of wine, "perhaps the embarrassment comes from all the time she spends with Konrud." He quickly held up his hand to stop Rhun's response. "Not that I blame her. What's fair is fair. Still, don't think his wife's none too happy about it."

"Oh?" Rhun's ears pricked up, eager for any sort of gossip. "What've you heard?"

"Small wonder the man stays away," he stated. "The damned woman's a nag, shrill and ill-tempered, with a bit of the dramatic thrown in for good measure."

"So I've been told. But have you heard something else?"

Kylar quietly studied the fat man on the couch in front of him. This man who wanted to be king was far too interested in idle gossip. Diad and he were of the same fabric. Where Diad's weakness was women, his was food and mindless natter. Neither was fit to be king... Bradwr? Ah, Bradwr... the ambition of a younger brother... at least he kept his vices in check.

"What I've heard is just the usual... threatened to come here, denounce them both, she wants a divorce, she wants him home, she forgives him... pick a day, pick a mood." He shrugged, bored with the topic.

Before Rhun could reply, the willowy servant came in holding a small package. Unmindful of the obvious lust in Rhun's demeanor, she gracefully walked up to Kylar.

"M'Lord, Lord Bradwr sends his greetings and asks if you would dine with him tonight. He also sends this gift, saying he thought it would look good on the shelf to the right of the uppermost balcony of your home in Glanon."

Feigning curious indifference, Rhun seethed internally as he watched the obvious pleasure of the old man as he unwrapped the gift.

Kylar let the wrapping slip to his lap, and then the floor, while holding up a small tarrac exquisitely carved from shimmering onyx. The servant bent down to retrieve the wrapping.

"M'Lord, there's a note included," she effortlessly opened the envelope and passed him the folded over card.

"Age is best in three things:" he read aloud, "old wine to drink, old friends to laugh with, and old roads leading one home." Nodding appreciatively, he held up another slip of paper that had been tucked inside the card. "This finely crafted tarrac is certified genuine, dating from the Neued period." Somehow the cushion seemed a bit more comfortable as he nestled in his chair. "Damned fine gift. Now there's someone who appreciates quality." Remembering Rhun, he quickly added, "And I appreciate your gift too, Nephew. An excellent wine." Turning back to admire the small tarrac, he addressed his servant. "Tell him I look forward to dinner. You take care of the specifics, and see that I'm ready in time."

"Yes m'Lord." Bowing, she breezed out.

Turning the object about in his hands, he felt the smooth coldness of the stone. "What were we talking about nephew?"

"Nothing of consequence," he easily answered. "Tell me uncle, how long does it take you to sail home."

"With fair winds, two days."

"Two days," Rhun mused. "Don't you ever get bored? I don't think I could last on a ship with nothing to look at but the sea. At least on land the scenery changes."

Kylar raised an eyebrow. "Bored? I'll tell you what's boring. Listening to all the jabber that passes for intelligent conversation around here, sitting on one's ass all day confined within the walls of this City, and acting as though your life is somehow of greater significance because you know some scrap of gossip." He shook his head in disgust. "At least on the sea I'm moving, I'm free... especially of this place. Nah," he snarled, "you can keep all this damn intrigue and pomp and ceremony. Give me the sea and my home far away from here."

He pulled himself up to standing, looking at them both. "And with that, good day to you nephew, and you too grandson, whichever one you are. Think I'll pack before I have dinner with Bradwr. Thanks for stopping by. Good to see you. Siubhan, show these gentlemen out."

Rhun stood outside as the door closed behind him, feeling as though he just got tossed out of a tavern. His frustration growing, he cursed Bradwr for the subtle upstaging. And he cursed Kylar for being such a crotchety old man who wielded far too much influence, especially for one who lived so far away. Yet he cursed himself for not anticipating. He should have known, he should have anticipated. Then just as suddenly, he calmed himself. He still had time. Kylar being far enough away may be more of an advantage than he had first thought. Besides, he felt his stomach grumbling. There were other more immediate needs.

"Come Nephew, let's find Heledd, and then some dinner. Or perhaps dinner first and she can find us," he grinned. Offering a heavy arm out for Vonn to help him down the steps, he casually commented, "So, what do you think of my daughter?"

Duncan leaned back into the over-stuffed chair, arms dangling over the sides, savoring the peace and quiet away from the screaming adoration of Gambria's common folk. Closing his eyes, he pressed his head back into the cushion, thankful to be free of the tiara. That thing had been heavier than he thought and having to wear it the entire way back to the Temple was an experience he was only too glad to do but once. Reaching up, he placed a palm under his jaw and twisted his head until he felt a pop.

"It certainly has been a very busy day, your Grace."

He opened one eye to see Darroch smiling at him. "I could use a hot bath and a massage."

"And you certainly deserve both, Eminence, but I'm afraid they will have to wait."

Sighing, he opened both eyes. "Now what?"

"You have visitors."

"Already? I just got back," he moaned resignedly. "Well, who is it?"

"Lord Cedrych and his daughter Morna."

Darroch watched Duncan's puzzlement for a moment. "He's one of the King's cousins, Eminence."

"Another cousin? Great Safti that man has family."

"That he does," the Steward chuckled. "Cedrych has a rather large domain on the north eastern boundaries, somewhat sparsely populated, part of Father Kinnell's ecclesiastical province. Brother Fearghus is the Deacon for that diocese."

"And they're here because?"

"Eminence, you must realize that you have just become the most eligible bachelor in the kingdom."

"Pardon?" he sputtered.

Darroch turned to one of the door acolytes. "Tell them he'll be with them in a moment." Turning back, he moved closer. "Most Holy Father, it is expected the High Priest be married –"

"Married!"

"Yes Eminence. Surely you didn't expect to be celibate the entire time you are High Priest?"

"Well, no, but I was hoping for a little time at least to get used to being High Priest."

"You can have all the time you need," Darroch laughed. "But you must understand that you are going to be feted by every father who has an eligible daughter."

Duncan mused for a moment. "Vix wasn't married."

"That was true, Eminence," he answered solemnly. "Your predecessor was not viewed with the same, um, enthusiasm as you are. Fathers were not so willing to parade their daughters before him."

"I understand," he shifted in his chair. "What if I'm sort of interested in someone already."

"Eminence, Tene is a wonderful woman, and I'm sure she will remain a faithful daughter of the church," Darroch gravely said, "but you must put her out of your mind."

Duncan's jaw slacked. "You know about Tene?"

"Of course Eminence. Part of my job is to protect you."

Blinking several times before closing his mouth, he furrowed his brows. "Why not Tene?"

"Most Holy Father, Tene is a servant; you are the High Priest. You must marry someone–"

"– of a more appropriate class." he finished.

Darroch nodded. "We must remember who we are." He watched him silently absorb the choices. "Eminence, there is always the possibility," he ventured, "of enjoying Tene's favors until you do find the right woman."

Duncan said nothing for moment, then slowly shook his head. "I don't see how that could work," he said quietly. "It's not fair to either of us. Besides, she's not that kind of a woman, and I wouldn't do that to her. And again, it wouldn't look good for the church."

"A wise answer, your Grace," he calmly replied, his admiration growing. He let Duncan ponder for a while longer then suggested, "Perhaps it's best to drop the matter for the moment and meet your guests."

Taking a breath, Duncan stood up. "Well, let's get on with it."

The Steward nodded to one of the waiting acolytes. He faintly heard a gruff 'It's about time' as the door opened and Lord Cedrych and daughter were ushered in.

"So you're the new High Priest. I was at your coronation today. Wonderful event. A little hot for my tastes. I prefer the cool mountains of my own domain. Nice place you have here. I've never been in the High Priest's lodgings before."

Duncan listened as the man blustered on, occasionally nodding or grunting an assent. Cedrych was certainly a talker, one who obviously liked the sound of his own voice. A bit shorter than Duncan, but much more rotund, he had a quirky habit of brushing his nose with his right hand when he wanted to make a point. As the man chattered on, Duncan turned his attention to the daughter. While her father spoke nonstop, she had been busy taking in the apartment, as though measuring for drapes and where to place the furniture.

Morna wore a finely woven, off the shoulder azure gown, with a tight bodice that gathered at the waist and descended towards the floor, stopping above her ankles. The attached sleeves were a thin gossamer material that clung to her arms and ended wrapped around the middle finger of each hand. Her auburn hair was gathered up so that her face and neck were clearly displayed. An arrangement that might have been enchanting in another was used less cleverly here. Instead of hiding her faults, it was as though she sought to emphasize her flaws. Though young, she had the beginnings of the corpulence of her father, and the tightness of her gown made it appear a size or two too small.

"And this is my daughter Morna," Cedrych placed a firm hand on her shoulder and pushed her forward.

Quickly recovering herself, she dipped a quick curtsey and flatly answered, "Your Grace," as though already bored with the whole charade.

"Lady Morna. How nice of you to visit." He waited for a response, but she simply looked at him, oblivious to the awkward silence. Silently sighing, he addressed her father.

"How far is it to your domain?"

"About three days journey, in fair weather."

"Excellent. I'll be there in four."

"Four?!" Cedrych sputtered.

"Yes. I need to make a visit to each of my dioceses and I'm going to start with Brother Fearghus. I would be delighted to call upon you and your... lovely daughter."

Cedrych was momentarily speechless as he rapidly tallied up the trip and home preparations. "Yes, certainly, of course. Well it certainly has been a privilege meeting you. Come daughter. We've taken enough of the High Priest's time today. Say goodbye."

Morna repeated the same flat "your Grace" and curtsey before her father turned her and propelled her to the door.

"I look forward to seeing you in four days," he called over his shoulder as he followed her out.

The High Priest and his Steward stood watching them depart, letting the quiet settle. After savoring the peace a bit more, Duncan turned to him.

"That was painful."

"My apologies, Eminence. I didn't have time to properly prepare you."

He nodded, pursing hips lips. "You will, of course, ensure I am appropriately busy here four days from now."

"Of course, Eminence," Darroch mimicked Morna's curtsey.

He snickered and relaxed. "What else do we have for today?"

"There is nothing more today, Eminence, although it is possible you may have more visitors like Lord Cedrych."

"No more visitors today. I just want to relax and do some reading before dinner." He then pointed to a stack of thick tomes on the small table by the chair. "I've finished all but one of these. Would you please have the next six brought up?"

"But Eminence," he frowned, "I just brought those yesterday."

"Yes, I know," he smiled. "I've read them."

Darroch's mouth gaped wide, "but that's impossible."

"You doubt me?" Duncan feigned disappointment.

"Of course not Eminence," he shook his head slowly. "But your Grace, the amount of reading there would take days, if not weeks to wade through."

"Really?" He pulled the book from the top of the stack. "I haven't read this one yet." He plopped back down and settled the book on his lap. Darroch watched with growing doubt as he flipped each page faster and faster until each seemed a blur. In a few short moments, he closed the book and handed it to him.

"Here open it anywhere you like."

Darroch awkwardly stood with the book in his hands, hesitant, not wanting to embarrass him. "But your Grace, you merely flipped the pages without reading anything."

"Go ahead. Open it." he answered with amused assurance.

With an inward sigh, Darroch flipped open the book, about halfway.

"Now begin reading anywhere on the page."

Scanning the page and began reading, "If summoned to a trial by –"

"Competent authority," Duncan continued, "the believer shall have the right to be judged according to the prescripts of the law applied without regard to position or privilege. Neither shall the accused be denied counsel nor access to such counsel, as maybe deemed appropriate and essential. No believer shall be summarily punished without due recourse, except upon conviction of such egregious transgressions as warrant imposition of immediate penalty, and these only in time of national peril. No punishment shall be deemed cruel and unusual."

Darroch's jaw dropped as he looked up from the text, his eyes wide in wonder. "How is this possible? You can repeat each of these texts, word for word, Eminence?" He nodded at the remaining five stacked on the table.

"Yes," he shrugged. "It's a gift, although sometimes I'm not so sure."

"Why is that, Eminence?" he asked, closing the book, his awe still evident.

Duncan settled back into the chair. "I have all this knowledge up here," he tapped his head, "What do I do with it? It's one thing to know so much; it's another to make it useful."

"A wise answer, your Grace," he quietly replied. "It reminds me of our own scholars, sequestered away in Buckom."

He smiled. "I suppose it does. Well, enough of that for now. For dinner tonight, please invite Father Lucan and Father Konrud, Brother Drubal... and I think it's time to invite Father Tomos."

"An excellent idea, Eminence," he answered as he collected the books. "Oh, your Grace, I should have asked you first, but I've taken the liberty of selecting a rector for you."

"A rector? What's he supposed to do?"

"He serves a dual role. He's both a bodyguard and enforcer."

"Bodyguard I understand, though I don't see why I need one, but what's an Enforcer?"

"He's sort of a diplomat with a heavy fist," Darroch stood before him, books piled in his hands front of him. "When you require something or someone, he's available to ensure your wishes are neither delayed nor questioned."

"Interesting. Did Vix have an enforcer?"

"Yes, your Grace," he propped the books against his side. "In fact he had a number of them. Unfortunately for them, with his departure, they have been discredited. No one trusts them. I'm not sure what you'll want to do with them, but they will need to be dealt with."

"Agreed. And who is this new replacement?"

"His name is Hagan, and he comes from a good family. He will serve you well."

Duncan reflected on Darroch's news. "Do I understand that he is a friend of yours?"

"Yes, your Grace."

"And he could have been an enforcer before, but you did not propose him?"

"Yes, your Grace."

"Yet now you do so?"

"Yes, your Grace," he quietly answered.

He was quiet for a moment, slowly nodding his head. "I will do my best to ensure your faith and trust are not misguided."

Darroch shifted the books to his front, and straightened up. He let out a slow exhale. "You already have."

The Lord Purveyor looked up from his desk as the man walked in. "Well?"

Opening his long thin outer coat, the man carefully untied a number of small bags, filled with coins, from around his waist and carefully placed them on the desk. "He was quite happy to invest. After I paid him his profits, he was all too willing to continue his position."

"And no problem with wanting it in coin?"

The man laughed. "Hardly, especially when I reminded him that our arrangement allowed him to avoid taxes."

"Ach, Athdar, some fools are too easy. Pour yourself a drink." He grinned, pointing to a wine pitcher on the table by the window.

"There is one problem though," he said as he poured the cup of wine. "He wants to be there when the ship sets sail."

Slowly stroking his chin, the Lord Purveyor pondered the answer. "When did you tell him it would sail?"

"I didn't."

"Good. That gives us time. What name did you give?"

"The Swift Promise," he shrugged. "It was all I could think of at the time." He swallowed a long draught.

Hefting one of the coin bags as if weighing it, while fondly gazing at the other nine bags in front of him, the Lord Purveyor queried, "How much is here?"

"One thousand."

Opening the bag, he poured the clinking contents on top of the papers spread across his desk. Selecting one, he held it up by the edges, letting the light play across the surface. The gold luster was still bright as though having just been hammered. The design was a profile of a crowned King Diad with the reverse that of a tarrac. The coin-smith had done an excellent job on this coin, as the edges were uniformly round and the imprint finely detailed.

Turning the coin over in his fingers, the Lord Purveyor delighted in the texture and weight. Gold had that allure, that quality, that elusiveness… one could never have enough gold. As though waking from a reverie, he remembered his visitor.

"Tell Kaine. We'll do the usual. Make it sometime next week."

Refilling his cup, Athdar frowned. "My Lord Purveyor, this will be the fifth time we've loaded and lost this same cargo. Someone is bound to talk."

"I agree," he answered, reluctantly setting the coin down. "I do believe Kaine has outlived his usefulness." He tossed two of the bags to him. "You know what to do."

Athdar inhaled slightly as he caught both bags. This was far more than his usual take. He looked inquisitively at his benefactor.

"You deserve it," was the smiling response. "Besides, you'll need the extra to get back home." Then the eyes hardened into coldness. "I don't want anyone alive. No one. You hear me?"

"It will be as you wish." He set the half-full cup back on the table and pulled back his robe to secure the coin-bag. "With fair winds, I should be back within a week or two."

"Good," the Lord Purveyor smiled broadly. "By then, we should have a few more investors for another venture." Tilting his head to the side, he mused aloud, "I wonder what it should be this time?"

Athdar smiled wryly. "M'Lord, what's the trick? We've lost four boats, yet there are always more waiting in line."

"The trick is," he smugly smiled, "never ask for too much at first. Reap a profit, then ask for more. A few will be content with what they have, but most want more. Then, when our ship is buffeted by storms, and all is lost, I'll break the news. In my most groveling and apologetic manner, I will take the blame and offer him one-tenth of his investment, carefully reminding him that I have lost far more – yet, because he is an honorable man and I feel so guilty, I want to make up for part of his loss." He snorted a laugh and leaned back. "I have yet to pay the one-tenth."

"That's it?" Athdar looked doubtful.

"Hardly. The other part is never go to the well too often. Make them come to you. See," he warmed to the charade and his brilliant execution, "the next time I see him, I'll be ever so respectful and grateful, perhaps even buy him a drink. And the next few times I see him, I'll just make conversation. Then, after a while, the next time I see him, I'll let on that one of my investments paid off handsomely. And each time after that, I'll say how well things are going, never asking," he shook his finger, "for so much as a single coin. After a while, he'll want to know if he can get in on the next venture. Of course," he placed both palms on his chest, "I'll tell him that I really couldn't accept his money, especially after our last arrangement had failed." He then smiled wickedly. "Then I'll string him along until he's begging me to take his money.

Athdar shook his head in wry amusement. "I admire your patience."

"Good things come to those who can wait," he slyly answered. "But enough of that for now. It's time to make your arrangements." He gave a curt nod of dismissal and waited until Athdar had closed the door behind him.

Waiting a few minutes more, he listened carefully before scooting his chair back to get up to secure the door. Standing with his ear against the wooden panels, he listened a while more. When it was satisfactorily quiet, he went back to the desk and pulled his chair back. Bending stiffly, he knelt down into the opening below the desktop. Pushing aside the thin carpet, he lifted the small trap door on the floor. Then, in a series of quick movements, he retrieved the remaining coin bags and placed them on top of the growing pile below. Casting one quick loving look at his hoard, he quickly closed the door and replaced the carpet.

Seating himself back at the desk, he resumed his work. There would be plenty of time later to count the contents of his new bounty. Besides, he had financial statements to prepare, and properties to buy, subordinates to manage, and a kingdom's finances to oversee. He smiled contentedly. It was just a matter of timing before he owned the berserker's place. He had always liked that house. Perhaps he might even keep the servants... especially Tene... Now there was a fine looking woman... he would enjoy making full use of her talents...

Tomos stood pensively outside the doors. Why would the High Priest invite him to dinner and not Cattwg? While pleased to be singled out, he had sorted through all the possibilities, and none made sense. The merry atmosphere of the High Priest's meal times was already well known in the Temple, and to be invited to dine was a sign of favor. Since the morning's festivities, the push to be invited was in full strength as clerics and other notables dropped subtle and not so subtle hints to the attendant acolytes, cooks, clerks, and anyone else who might know someone who might know someone.

But Tomos was above all that, and politely refused such requests knowing there was little chance that even he would be invited. Thus, he had been both surprised and immensely pleased when Darroch himself had sought him out and proffered the much demanded invitation. Yet, he had been taken aback by Cattwg's reaction when he told him.

"What?! He's invited you to dinner? And you don't know why? You fool! Why do you think?" Cattwg stormed around the room.

Tomos stepped out of the way. "I give up," he hesitated. "Why?"

The senior cleric stopped and stared at him, as though looking at a child. "I can't believe I have to explain this to you. He's trying to drive a wedge between us."

"I'd already thought of that," he retorted. "He has to know that we voted against him. He also has to know that we are united against him. How could inviting me to dinner change that?"

"I don't know," he fumed, somewhat mollified by his protégé's answer. "But I don't like it."

"Look at it this way," Tomos offered. "He invites me to dinner... he thinks that he can trust me..." He smiled, shrugged, and spread his hands in answer.

"And what makes you think he would trust you? You just said he has to know we voted against him." He glared at him, his frustration telling Tomos his reasoning was that of a simpleton.

"I don't know why you're so angry. Here's an opportunity to get close to the enemy, find out what he's thinking. If he thinks he can trust me, so much the better." Tomos did his best to conceal his irritation at his benefactor's overt condescension.

Cattwg blinked several times, pondering the possibilities. "Who knows... perhaps you're right." He paced a bit more around the room. "Still, be careful. He's a clever one. Report back to me when you're finished there." Tomos had stiffened in silent indignation at the command, but said nothing. He nodded curtly and had walked out and down the long hallway to where he now stood.

Standing there, he still smarted from the implication that he was merely Cattwg's lackey. He would show him that he could hold his own. Motioning to the acolyte to announce him, he was ushered into the dining room with Duncan, Lucan, Konrud, and Drubal, and in what seemed but moments, was laughing along with the group, quite at ease with the banter.

As the evening wore on, he became more garrulous in proportion to the wine he consumed. He soon found himself telling jokes on himself which caused the others to roar with laughter. He beamed appreciatively, liking their responses that were so unlike Cattwg who scoffed at his attempts at humor.

Duncan carefully watched his guest, measuring the appropriate time. He wanted him tipsy, yet coherent enough to understand. "Father Tomos, I am so glad you consented to join us for dinner. We haven't had this much fun in a while. You are quite the comic."

Tomos glowed at the compliment. "Thank you, Most Holy Father."

The High Priest inwardly smiled. Tomos, so resistant to calling him by his title in the beginning, was now following suit with the others, who had been careful to call Duncan by his title the entire time.

"Father Tomos, I have a proposition for you," he smiled warmly.

Although pleasingly tipsy, Tomos was immediately on guard. "Yes, your Grace?" He answered warily.

"I have been examining the positions within the Church, and am about to make some changes"

Tomos wasn't sure he was going to like what he was about to hear. This had all the markings of a set-up. He put down his chalice and focused his fuzzy attention on the High Priest.

"With the recommendation of both Father Lucan and Father Konrud, I am elevating you to the number two position in the Church, behind Father Konrud."

"Number two?" Tomos numbly repeated, then epiphany flooded through him. "Number two!" he repeated, flabbergasted.

"Yes, number two. We all agree that you are what the Church leadership needs. You seem to have more of the true concern for the people," Duncan crooned.

"Number two?" He leaned back, quickly analyzing the ramifications. "What about Father Cattwg?"

"I'm sure I can find another position for him somewhere in the Temple."

The implication was suddenly obvious. Duncan was removing Cattwg as a possible threat to himself, and at the same time actually helping Tomos. With Cattwg demoted well below those with domains, he was purposely creating obstacles for any attempt by Cattwg to regain power. Why, he could even demote him as a Father back down to a mere monk.

Tomos' possibilities suddenly emerged. He was younger than both Konrud and Lucan, and visions of both Chancellorship and Konrud's domains rapidly played on the edges of his consciousness. Here, finally, was his opportunity. He could get out from under Cattwg's thumb, and blame the High Priest for any repercussions. He withdrew from his quick reverie to hear Duncan asking,

"You will accept, won't you?"

"Of course, Most Holy Father," Tomos readily agreed.

"Excellent. Of course I expect you to be available on a regular basis, for meetings such as these," Duncan smiled and gestured to the table full of food and ale, "and at other times when I will look to you for counsel."

"As you wish, Most Holy Father," Tomos replied, finding himself uncomfortably disarmed. He had been so caught up in Cattwg's designs, that he had subordinated his own desires, had harnessed his tarrac to

Cattwg's wagon. Now, without any help from Cattwg, he was the number two priest in the nation. Perhaps it was time to unhook his tarrac...

He leaned back and sipped his wine, half listening to the others. He looked at Konrud and admitted that he had never really disliked the man. In fact, he trusted Konrud far more than Cattwg. And Lucan... actually, he had always liked the big oaf. He was harmless, a priest more interested in peace and harmony, and good food, than power struggles. Why, with a little luck, he could become Chancellor.

The thought pleased him, for he knew that if appointed Chancellor, it would be for life, and he would never have to worry about domains, maneuvering for position, or demotions... like Drubal. He looked at the older priest, happily restored to his position as General Secretary. He had always wondered why Vix had demoted him. Tomos was yet a monk in training when it happened. He smiled to himself, remembering the plain olive-drab robe he had worn as a novice. He had been so focused then. He had worked hard and had been noticed. For some reason, Cattwg had taken to him and caused him to be elevated ahead of his peers.

Cattwg... he had much to thank him for... yet, he demanded much in return. Tomos sifted the memories and saw the years flicker by, wondering where the passion of the novice years had gone. In a subtle epiphany, he realized that it had been replaced by Cattwg and his scheming. Had his life really been reduced to helping another plot to become high priest?

He gazed at the others who were still laughing and joking – the High Priest, the High Chancellor, the Senior Cleric, and the General Secretary. He knew without a doubt that they were a team, a united effort. And what did Cattwg have to offer? He smirked to himself, the answer too obvious.

Yes, it was time to unhook his tarrac.

Cattwg's face said it all. His mouth hung open, but no sound came out. It was his eyes that spoke the loudest – shock, dismay, disbelief all quickly replaced by overt hatred and anger.

"You?! You're going to take over my domain?"

Tomos pretended to be tired, although in truth, he was mentally exhausted, sorting out all the possible consequences of his appointment. It had been a late night and him showing up first thing in the morning did not help. "Yes. What else could I do?"

"You could have said NO!" Cattwg exploded.

"Oh really?" he sneered. "And what would've been my excuse to tell the High Priest, 'I appreciate the thought, but no thank you, because Cattwg would be upset?'"

"That sounds like a damn good reason to me."

"And it would." He poked a finger at him. "You just don't get it do you? You spent all these years ingratiating yourself into the hierarchy, working your way to the top, and when a new high priest is appointed, you suddenly blow the battle horns against him."

Curling his lip, Cattwg glared at him. "Now that you're number two, you suddenly get a set of testicles? You seem to forget that I'm the one who made you. I'm the one who got you here."

Tomos stood to full height. "I make no false claims. I readily admit that you have been instrumental in my success. For that I thank you. My position here is because of your influence."

"Damn right. I'm the one who got you here." He leaned forward, jabbing a finger at him, "And I'm the one who can bring you down."

"So this is the real Cattwg," he calmly replied, "the one who speaks of loyalty, of friendship?"

"You speak to me of loyalty? Where was your loyalty when this interloper who calls himself the high priest made this offer, knowing that he was doing it only to split us apart."

Tomos bristled at Cattwg's tone. "There. You reinforce what I have been saying. This *interloper*, as you continue to call him, is the legally appointed high priest." He held up a hand as Cattwg was about to interrupt. "Let me finish. The legally appointed high priest has the trust and loyalty of," he held up a finger for each name, "the High Chancellor, the Senior Cleric, the General Secretary, the King, and many other senior clerics. It seems to me, Father Cattwg, that you are fighting against odds that are not in your favor."

Cattwg's chin jutted forward. "That's never stopped me before." For a moment, he simply glared at Tomos, then asked, "By the way, did he mention what would happen with me?"

Tomos paused for a moment before answering. "No he did not."

Cattwg saw the hesitation. "You're a liar."

"Father Cattwg," he tersely intoned, "I am not privy to what the High Priest has in mind for you other than him saying that he would find something suitable for you."

"Suitable? And what does that mean?"

"How would I know? I'm not the high priest!" He felt his bile rising.

"You could've asked."

"That's not my place," he retorted.

"No. Your place is now some pet of his, coming whenever he snaps his fingers," Cattwg sneered.

"You mean like I did with you?"

There was a knock at the door, and a tall, powerfully built, young rector entered. He seemed relieved upon seeing Cattwg. "Father Cattwg, I've been looking all over for you. The Most Holy Father wishes to see you immediately."

Fuming at Tomos, he turned disdainfully to the young man. "Who are you?"

"I am Brother Hagan, his Eminence's rector."

Cattwg sized up the man, giving a begrudging admiration to the High Priest's choice. But he was not going to be bullied by the pretender's enforcer, no matter his size. "It's rather late," he dismissively said. "Tell him I'll stop by when I get a chance."

"Begging your pardon, Father, but my instructions were to bring you now." It was said courteously, but insistently.

"I heard you. And *I* said that I will call on when I get the chance," he answered through clenched teeth.

"Yes, Father, that is what I heard you say. However, I must insist that you accompany me."

"What's your name?" Cattwg menacingly asked.

"Brother Hagan, Father."

"And who do you think you are that you, a rector, come here to threaten me?"

Hagan straightened to his full height, towering above both Cattwg and Tomos. "I am rector to the Chosen One of Safti," he firmly stated, "the High Priest of the nation of Gambria, the man and vicar chosen and acclaimed by both King and people. I have been chosen by the High Priest himself, to serve him, to protect him, to enforce his will, should it be necessary. I threaten no one unless he chooses to defy the demands of the Most Holy Father." His eyes turned cold and penetrating. "Now, Father Cattwg, will you come with me?"

Cattwg stood momentarily immobile, caught between further bluff or retribution. "Let's get this over with," he snarled, and stormed out.

Hagan looked quickly at Tomos, shook his head and shrugged. Then, in but a few long strides, he caught up to Cattwg storming down the hall.

In too short a time, Cattwg returned to what would no longer be his parlor. Tomos would now be the lord of these chambers, while he, Cattwg, would descend to one of the lower levels of lodgings in the temple, among the lesser priests and clerics. Venom permeated every cavity of his soul. The meeting with Duncan had turned out far worse than he expected, for not only had he lost his position and domains, he had been demoted for the time being to assisting Father Frang in the Office of Sacraments.

"Until I can find a suitable position for a man of your talents," Duncan had said.

Cattwg had stood immobile as the edict was announced, flames of hatred consuming the last vestiges of any empathy that might have existed for this interloper. Fathers Lucan and Konrud sat in attendance, nodding wisely at the decision. Instead of meekly accepting his fate, Cattwg had spun around and stormed out of the High Priest's quarters, pushing the acolytes out of the way as he left.

He now brooded silently, and paced. *Sacraments... Father Frang, that doddering fool, actually enjoys all the parchments and books and edicts... Why put me there? He's where he belongs. By why me? Why there?* Then the implications of his fall from power suddenly exploded and he was confronted with his future. He flopped into the closet chair and buried his face in his hands.

Yet there were no tears. He rubbed his face and pondered his past. He had overcome adversity before, and he would do so again, now. Cattwg slowly sat back up, and calmed himself to cold hardness. His lip curled into a snarl. *Two can play this game, wizard. You may have won the battle, but this war's not over. Your fall will be far greater than mine, and you will take Lucan and Konrud... and Tomos,* he spat as he thought the name, *with you. And in that day, I will sit in your place and rejoice.*

He stood up, pursed his lips, and began packing.

Chapter 21

The door yawned open and the startled servant gaped at the entourage standing before him. Surrounded by close to a dozen Temple guards and attendant acolytes, the High Priest stood serenely smiling. A small crowd, a mixture of inquisitive children, curious gossips, and passersby, had followed the group and were now milling around the edges. The servant simply stood and stared until one of the acolytes stirred him to action.

"The Most Holy Father has come to pay a call on High Commander Alexis," he loudly announced.

Jittering awake, the servant pulled the door wide open, yet not taking his eyes away from Duncan as if expecting to see something mystical in his transformation, but somewhat disappointed that he didn't look any different. He still looked like the same cocky man who had been sleeping with Tene, except now he wore the robe of the High Priest.

"Please come in... your Grace," he said, with a hint of veiled amusement.

Duncan nodded benevolently at the servant, remembering the man's indifference and occasional surly attitude when Duncan had been merely the guest in this house. The last time he had been here was what... four, five days ago? Had it been that long? What a strange and interesting day that had been, the day of the battle with Vix. Tene had been so afraid for him. Unwilling to let him wander outside the house, she had distracted him with questions and stories, and her marvelous body. Remembering the wild intensity of their love-making, Duncan felt himself aroused and he quickly refocused to the present.

Leaving two guards outside, the rest of the group swept into the hallway just as Tene came hurrying around the corner. Working to disguise her pleasure is seeing him, she bowed submissively.

"Welcome, your Grace. High Commander Alexis awaits you in her private chambers. High Commander Brenna is with her."

"I'm not surprised," he quietly intoned. Turning to his retainers, he commanded, "You all can wait here." Seeing their consternation, he added, "I'll be fine. I'll be with the berserker and one of the Twelve. You," he pointed to the startled servant by the door. "So concerned with my welfare, my friends here have neglected their own comfort and care. I would be appreciative of you finding something for them eat, and perhaps something to drink?"

"Of course, your Grace." He motioned for them to follow him into the large dining hall, while Duncan marched off to see Alexis, Tene by his side. As the two turned the corner and away from prying eye, Duncan reached out and gave her hand a squeeze.

"It's good to see you. I've missed you," he smiled, slowing his pace.

Tene wrapped her hands around his. "And I have truly missed you, your Grace."

Abruptly stopping, he gently turned her to face him. For the moment, he simply stared at her. Reaching up, he tenderly brushed away an errant hair and then let his hand slowly trace the smoothness of her cheek. "I will always be just Duncan to you."

Her eyes spoke her heart, as his did to her. In one motion they came together, wrapping their arms around each other, kissing deeply.

"So now that you're high priest you can molest my servants?"

Jolted as though hit by lightning they jumped apart only to see Alexis standing at the end of the hallway, hands on her hips, impishly smiling.

Duncan started laughing. "It's good to see you too."

"Well don't just stand there like guilty teenagers, c'mon in."

Making their way up to her bedroom, Alexis turned to lead the way and he immediately noticed a bandage covering part of her back.

"What happened to you?"

"It's nothing really. I got hit in the back with something, hard enough to knock me down. Took the wind out of me for a bit. This is just a poultice to reduce the swelling."

"I understand you were quite the warrior," he said admiringly.

"I'm not really sure how many I killed," she replied, warming to the topic. "Brenna said something like twenty-five or thirty. I don't remember. What I do remember is the thrill of it all." She pushed open the door to the room.

Sitting on a large divan near the window, her legs tucked under her, Brenna grinned as the trio entered. "Hullo Wizard. Looks like you've done quite well for yourself."

"It's nice to see some things never change," he smirked.

She gazed at him for a moment. "But I forget myself and my place." She stood up and walked over to Duncan and dropped to one knee before him. "It is good to see you, your Grace."

"Now you're scaring me," he laughed. "Get up. I like the old sarcastic Brenna better."

"As you wish, your Grace." She stood, a respectful smile curling the edges of her lips.

Raising an eyebrow, Alexis looked at her. "What was that all about?"

"Alexis, dear friend," she answered, sitting back down, "our Duncan is now one of the most powerful men in the entire kingdom. Whether or not we understand how it happened, it is what it is."

"Yeah," Alexis looked quizzically at her guest, "how did you manage to pull this off? Especially the lightening and sound... We didn't know what had happened until we were almost to Mull and found out you were to blame."

He thought for a moment, remembering all the events that combined to bring him to where he was today, then simply stated, "It's complicated."

She studied him for a bit, then shook her head. "You're always full of surprises Duncan Stuart." Movement at the corner of her eyes caused her to remember Tene, still standing by the door. She smiled at her. "Come Tene. Please sit and join us."

Tene hesitated, warmed by the personal invitation, yet unsure of her place. She remained rooted in indecision.

"Tene, you might as well stay," Alexis said, then turned to Duncan. "So when is she going to move to the Temple with you?"

Abruptly stiffening, Tene awkwardly mumbled. "I'd better check on your attendants, your Grace." With that, she fled out the door.

"What's wrong with her?" Alexis tilted her head to the left.

"Tene won't be coming to the Temple," he quietly replied.

"Why not?"

"Because she is a servant," Brenna answered for him.

"So what?" Alexis looked at them both, her irritation rising as she surmised the answer.

"When the High Priest marries, it will be to a lady of his status."

"You mean one of those fat things who whine and eat and flaunt themselves in public?"

"If he so chooses," Brenna chuckled.

"Good god, what's wrong with you people? Why can't Tene just stop being a servant and choose something different?"

There was a heavy silence until Brenna quietly stated, "It doesn't work that way."

Audibly sighed, the Berserker scowled. "It doesn't make any sense."

"We are who we are," Duncan softly answered, his voice a low resonance as a sudden awareness of his role began to settle in his core.

Brenna looked askance at him, abruptly realizing that he was transforming, becoming a part of the soul of Gambria. Yet somehow this new insight didn't quite surprise her. In time, he would probably be more Gambrian than one born here, even his accent had disappeared. She briefly scrutinized him. Was he as dangerous as Lord Ronell surmised? What does he really want?

She then turned to study Alexis, this beautiful berserker, this strange combination of grace and death. Strange as it seemed, Alexis was so simple compared to Duncan. There was no pretense, no language games, no hiding behind veiled suggestion. If one wanted to know what Alexis thought, one simply asked.

Yet for all that, Alexis was still a novelty: accepted, but at arm's length. Where Duncan had managed to submerse himself into the essential character of Gambria, Alexis remained aloof, distant. In fact, Brenna wondered if she really knew Alexis, if she would ever know Alexis. They had become close, even intimate, but did that truly mean anything?

Brenna drifted to the first time. What began with a slow kiss swiftly transformed and she found herself on her back on the floor, Alexis straddling her hips, bending down to devour her.

And then suddenly she saw Alexis standing beside her, before the battle, detached and remote, the wind teasing a wisp of her hair. She spoke not a word, but stood firm, immoveable, alone within herself. Brenna remembered looking at her eyes, seeing only a void and coldness. And then the battle spread over her reverie and the cries of wounded and dying mixed with the heavy clang of sword upon sword. The swirling melee and cacophony of pain, anger, grunts and screams became a blur.

And just as the fray rose to crescendo, the image changed to Alexis and Stracaim. Brenna blinked as she remembered this part of Alexis, the caring compassionate piece, and wondered if she would ever share this side of her.

Hearing Duncan's voice as he and Alexis merrily chatted reminded her of the last encounter with Lord Ronell. She began to understand his reasons for wanting her to gain his trust. Alexis was a warrior, nothing more. While her personality spoke layers of complication, to use Duncan's word, her aspirations were satisfied by battle. Yet here was Duncan. In the time between their departure and return from battle, he had not only risen to become High Priest, he was already winning the love of the people, and earning enemies at the same time.

She slowly nodded as she sorted the implications. Alexis was no threat to Gambrian life. Her success in battle was good for Gambria. If she died in battle, another would take her place. Duncan, however, was now immersed in the dangerous game of power. His success or failure could possibly throw Gambria into chaos. Maybe that's why Lord Ronell wanted him protected...

She smiled to herself in sudden epiphany – that's why he wanted her to get involved with Safti and all that other religious nonsense. Amazement settled within her. How could Lord Ronell have known this about Duncan?

Refocusing her attention, she studied Duncan as though for the first time. He certainly wasn't unattractive. In fact, he was rather handsome, although his skin still seemed a bit too white for her tastes. She thought about her first visit here. She had been teaching Alexis some simple phrases when they had heard voices outside in the gardens. They had gone to the window to see Tene turn her back as Duncan undressed.

"Nice butt," Brenna chuckled, further admiring the rest of him.

"Nice butt?" Alexis repeated the unfamiliar words.

Brenna rubbed a hand on Alexis' rear end. "Butt."

"Butt," she smiled in response.

Brenna nodded 'yes' as the two voyeurs watched Duncan quickly descend into the pool. They stayed at the window and watched Tene nonchalantly undress.

"Nice..." Alexis ran her hands over her breasts and down stomach to her hips.

"Body," Brenna answered.

"Body," she repeated.

"Yes."

They watched until Tene likewise descended, and then giggling like teenagers sharing a secret, returned to their lessons.

With that image still in her mind, Brenna silently watched him before her now. The streak in his hair combined with the multi-colored robe, and his perpetual suppressed energy gave him an aura of one whose intensity would overwhelm and dominate. She found it strangely sexual and shook her head at the thought.

Yet she found herself distracted by an awareness that she was actually attracted to him. And just as quickly, she remembered that he was eligible and would soon find a wife. What would it be like to be the wife of the High Priest? Would she have to move into the Temple? Would she have to give up being a warrior? She was one of the Twelve; why couldn't she be both? The combination would be powerful, he as head of the church, and she as head of the military.

Brenna smiled to herself. It could work. It would be one of the most commanding combinations in Gambrian history. And, as one of the Twelve, she was of his rank. She looked over to watch Alexis playfully poke Duncan. What about Alexis? Well... what about Alexis? Brenna blinked in the realization that she and Alexis would never be more than anything but friends, best friends perhaps, battle companions, but just friends nonetheless.

The thought surprised her somewhat as she hadn't much thought about her future. Sure, she had always set aside a good portion of her earnings to invest; after all, she didn't need much to live on right now. Besides, the Lord Purveyor provided her with a monthly record of her investments and she was doing rather well. But the more she envisioned the future, the more she realized something was missing.

Brenna thought about what it meant to no longer be fit for battle. She and Alexis had even talked about it on the way to Gefnyn's domain. Yet she had given it little thought then, instead laughing at Alexis' telling. But in truth, if she followed the path of most other aging warriors, she'd be running a tavern somewhere. The image of drunken commoners and tavern wenches suddenly materialized and she shuddered. There was more to life... to the future, than growing fat in some seedy dung hole somewhere. And while she liked Alexis' motto of living for the here and now, one still needed to plan for the future.

And then the words of Lord Ronell echoed inside her; *Who we are, where we came from, and where we are going are the concerns of us all, and the triumph or failure of us all. We cannot separate kings and priests and warriors – faith and the future belong to us all.* At that moment, Brenna knew she did not want to be a mere observer of Gambria's future.

Gazing at Duncan for a bit, she studied his movements, his demeanor. He certainly was attractive. Perhaps being wife to the High Priest may not be such a bad idea after all.

"You've been awfully quiet," Duncan smiled at her.

"Just watching you two. You're funny. You act like you're related, like brother and sister."

"Interesting analogy," he smirked, remembering the several encounters with Alexis on the ship. "Perhaps best friends might be a better correlation."

Alexis grinned sheepishly and sat next to Brenna. "He's right. You have been awfully quiet. You OK?"

"Absolutely. I'm just enjoying myself watching you two." Turning to him, she asked, "So what's life like in the Temple?"

Duncan considered for a moment, searching for a word. "Frenetic."

"Pardon?"

"It seems everyone is in a hurry. There's purpose without direction."

"I don't understand," she frowned.

"I'm not sure I understand myself," he smiled in response. "It's as though everything runs on its own, sort of like doing the same thing for so long that one no longer thinks about what's being done. It's automatic."

"Is that bad?"

Duncan shrugged. "Not necessarily, I suppose. But then again, if life is merely a series of repetitions, what's the point? If the church is supposed to be looking out for the welfare of Gambria, then it ought to come down off its sanctimonious pedestal and live among the people."

"Ooh. I sense frustration. And to think, you've only been High Priest for two days," she said playfully. "But I think you're right. It always struck me that the church seemed more interested in wealth than actually helping anybody."

"What's this?" he grinned mischievously. "Are you questioning the church? Do I detect some heretical tendency?"

Brenna laughed aloud and plopped back. "To tell you the truth, Most Holy Father, I never was much into this god thing."

Smiling impishly, Duncan leaned in and whispered, "Me neither."

Startled, Brenna scrutinized his face, waiting for the other part of the joke. Instead, he simply continued smiling, locking her eyes with his. She had the peculiar feeling that he was peering deep inside her, and an uncomfortable vulnerability unexpectedly emerged.

As though releasing her, Duncan straightened and turned to Alexis. "Well, I'm glad you two are safe and the battle won. I suppose I ought to go collect my entourage before they eat you out of house and home."

"Is it always like this?" Alexis asked.

Sighing lightly, he shrugged. "I'm afraid so. And I wonder why no one ever invites me over for dinner," he smirked.

Alexis snorted in return. "You're always welcome here."

"From what I've heard, we ought to be begging to have dinner with you," Brenna interjected. "I understand it's quite a festive affair."

Duncan gazed at Brenna, sensing something different in the tone of her words. Perhaps it was just his imagination, but she seemed less edged, less of the battle-hardened warrior. With her legs tucked up underneath her, her dark hair cascading about her shoulders, and her dark eyes focused expectantly on him, he saw her for the beautiful woman she was. The dichotomy puzzled him momentarily, but he brushed it aside.

"You two don't need an invitation. In fact, if you two don't start showing up real soon, I'll send this entourage," he jerked his thumb over his shoulder, "to track you down."

"Deal," Alexis answered, her smile fading. There was a silence for an awkward moment. "But what *are* you going to do about Tene?"

"I don't know," he shrugged.

"You could keep her as a lover," Brenna suggested without a hint of hesitation.

Duncan pursed his lips. "Someone else said the same thing. But I don't see how that could work."

"Many do it," she simply stated.

Shaking his head, he frowned. "I know. But how can a husband, or a wife, tell his mate that he loves her and then sleep with someone else?"

"So a person can't love more than one other person?"

"That's not what I mean, and you know it," he responded, his eyes half-lidded. "Where's the confidence, the trust? If I'm hiding something, that's the same as lying."

"Suppose all know, and agree to the arrangement?" she said, with a slight curl of a smile.

He rolled his eyes, yet smiled. "I suppose then it could work, but that's not how I am."

"Duncan," Brenna softly said, "things are not always so black and white as you would have them."

He blinked, not listening as she continued, for he realized that was the first time she had not called him 'wizard.' He found that he liked the way she said his name. *What's going on here? Why does she seem so different today?* He continued looking at her until he realized that she had stopped speaking and was staring back at him, her eyes full of amusement.

"You haven't heard a word I said," she teased.

"Sure I... haven't..." Duncan hung his head in mock submission. "Sorry. I was distracted."

"Am I that boring?" Brenna joked.

"Hardly. In fact, I was thinking you two ought to come for dinner tonight. A few others will be there and it would be great fun to have a change of topic. I really would like to hear more about the battle."

Brenna glanced over to Alexis. "Should we check our appointments calendar to see if we're free?"

Alexis held up an imaginary pad and pen. "I think we can fit him in if we cancel this appointment here," she scratched the air. "There. All done."

Smirking, he adjusted his robe. "Good. C'mon around seven. You can tell me all about how you two single-handedly won the battle."

Brenna's head tilted to the left as she amusedly pondered aloud. "How can two people do something single-handedly?"

"Are you questioning the High Priest again?" Duncan intoned with mock severity. "Sounds to me like you need a little inquisition."

"Ooh," Brenna purred, "sounds like fun."

Flashing a smile, he shook his head in delight. "Tonight's gonna be a treat. Well, I really do need to go." He held up a hand to stop Brenna who was about to stand. "I truly am glad you both are safe." His voice was warm, genuine. With that, he gave a little wave and swirled out of the room.

As he made his way down the hall, he could hear the contentment in their laughter.

Chapter 22

"You wished to see me my Lord?" Cattwg asked in his most obsequious voice.

Diad lounged luxuriously in a high-backed chair, one leg propped up on a foot stool, an arm resting on the knee. With a flick of the hand, he dismissed the servants and waited until the room was almost empty, the guards at the doors silently remaining.

"You don't like the High Priest, do you?" he loftily asked.

Cattwg stiffened. "No m'Lord, I don't."

"And why is that?"

Hesitating, he studied the King, looking for indications of purpose. Yet the mask remained and he decided to gamble. "We know nothing about him. He shows up here, conjures some trick, and suddenly he's high priest."

"You question my decision?" Diad tightly demanded, leaning forward.

Instead of backing down, Cattwg took a deep breath and pressed forward, choosing his words carefully. "Yes, Sire. Quite frankly, I do question the choice."

Diad glared at him for a brief moment, and then just as suddenly flopped back into the chair. "What could I do?" he complained. "That fool Vix did it to himself. And then the rest of you fell in behind him. I had little choice in the matter."

"Not all of us fell in behind him, Sire," Cattwg quietly answered. And then, unexpectedly, he sensed an opportunity. "But that's neither here nor there. What's done is done. I believe the real question is what to do now?"

The King cocked an eyebrow. "Oh? Is there something we need to do?"

"Sire, you've seen this... this cult of personality that seems to be growing around him. Unchecked, does he not pose a threat to your own authority?"

"Really? He seems to me more akin to Emer than Alric," he observed. "So the people have taken to him. What of it?"

"You are testing me, m'Lord," Cattwg smiled and bowed respectfully. "I would argue that being more akin to Emer makes him more dangerous. He has the craft of subtlety, which is always more dangerous."

The King thinly smiled. "You hit the mark, priest," he nodded. "I understand that you have, um, assumed other responsibilities."

Stung by the remark, he barely hid his anger. "Yes, m'Lord."

"You are still at the Temple?"

"Yes, Sire."

"Good. I want you to keep watch for me. I want to know all that he does."

"Sire," Cattwg ventured, "surely there are plenty of others who could provide you this information better than I. He and I hardly get along."

Diad leaned forward. "Remember your place, priest," he intoned. "If I wanted someone else I would've asked someone else. I need someone who knows the Temple, someone who can read and understand the signs, the moods."

Cattwg bowed in acknowledgement. "My apologies, m'Lord. My point was merely to illustrate that I am not part of his privileged circle. However, I do still have friends who can provide us with what you ask."

"Good." He leaned back into the chair. "I understand his meals are quite festive affairs."

Cattwg discerned a hint of jealousy in the statement. "So I have heard."

"And what else have you heard?"

"About his meals?" he answered, pretending to be puzzled.

"Dammit man, of course about his meals. What goes on there?" Diad peevishly snapped.

"From what I understand," he stalled, rapidly determining his best approach, "they are rather raucous outlandish occasions where they gossip about everyone."

"Oh?" He narrowed his eyes.

"M'Lord," he feigned surprise, "surely you've heard his comments about you." He smiled to himself as he watched the King's nostrils flare.

"Go on," he quietly growled.

"Sire, really, it would be unseemly to repeat such tripe, especially about our own King."

"Dammit, priest, stop this infernal waffling and answer what I asked. If you know what was said, then say it."

"As you wish, m'Lord." Cattwg fairly glowed inside himself. This was too easy. "From what I've heard, he believes you to be, um, shall we say, less than competent. Again, from what I've heard, he believes you spend too much time," he tread carefully here, knowing that sometimes the messenger gets the blame, "um, distracted from your responsibilities."

"Distracted how?" he coldly demanded.

"Sire, I will be direct. Again, from what I have heard –"

"Great Safti man! Again with the 'from what I've heard.' Get to the point."

"As you wish." Cattwg quietly and slowly inhaled. "He believes you spend too much time neglecting your wife and your kingdom, that your attention is easily diverted by any young immodest creature who happens to walk by."

Diad's lips tightened. "He said that?"

Cattwg simply and solemnly nodded. There was an uncomfortable silence as Diad looked fiercely at him.

"And what do you say... priest?"

"Sire, the man mistakes passion for purpose. He knows nothing about the responsibilities of the kingdom. Governing a temple is not the same as ruling a nation. The fact that you seek to, how shall I put this, *relax* by enjoying the favors of willing ladies is really no different than so, so many others."

"And you don't see a problem with this?" Diad looked askance at him.

Cattwg could barely conceal his exuberance. It would only be a matter of time before he was back on top and those bastards got what they deserved, especially that traitor Tomos. "Sire, with as much time as the Queen spends at the Temple with Father Konrud, it seems to me that you are merely satisfying the urges of any virile man in his prime."

"Damn right," he agreed. A heavy silence then ensued as he seemed to ponder Cattwg's comments. "She does seem to spend quite a bit of time there, doesn't she? Wonder why she spends so much time with Konrud? Just how much damned religion can one take?" He looked quickly to Cattwg. "No offense, priest."

"None taken, m'Lord," he smiled.

"Still," he sniffed, "with the way his wife looks, I can see why he spends so little time at home. Is it true he has all girls?"

"I'm afraid so, m'Lord," Cattwg choked his glee.

"Damned pity," He seemed to be studying the wall beyond Cattwg's shoulder. "Doesn't seem likely he'll have a son... at least not with her." He snorted a quick laugh. "Sort of rules him out as high priest, doesn't it?"

"It looks that way, m'Lord," he studiously agreed.

"Of course, something would have to happen to our present high priest for him to even think about it." He stared intently at Cattwg.

"And our high priest is rather young, m'Lord." Cattwg pricked his ears. Did he hear the king correctly?

"Still," the king mused, "it does make for interesting discussion. Who would be the best choice? Who would be best qualified?"

"I'm sure if that were to happen, the King would make a wise choice," he smoothly answered.

Diad leaned forward and focused carefully on the priest standing in front of him. "The next time, it *will* be a wise decision."

Cattwg bowed deferentially, his insides in riotous exuberance. He understood his king quite clearly. "My Lord, It will be a pleasure to do as you have asked."

"Good." His gaze was steady and firm. "I thank you for your time, Father Cattwg."

Bowing reverentially, Cattwg passed through the doors, benignly nodding to the guards. Walking down the hall, his step lively with anticipation, he thought to himself that one of those guards looked familiar. Yet with a self-satisfied shrug, he dismissed the man as unimportant enough to interfere with this glorious day.

The doors closed in a dull heavy thump. One guard removed his ornamental helmet, scratching his head in several places as he walked up to Diad.

"These things are uncomfortable."

"Perhaps you should have found one that fit," he amusedly replied.

Menec chuckled. "I didn't have time."

Diad came directly to the point. "So, what do you think?"

"It's obvious he wants to be high priest."

"And everyone in Gambria doesn't already know that?"

"M'Lord King," Menec frowned, "what is it you wish to accomplish? Why did you want me here today?"

"You heard him," Diad huffily stated. "This high priest of yours gossips about me, spreading discord in my kingdom."

Menec unbuckled the shoulder straps to the brightly polished breastplate, laying both halves on a table close by. "If you remember, sire, I have been a guest at his table. I never heard or saw anything this priest claims. And since when have you been bothered by gossip?"

"Since I saw the way the people fawn over him," Diad tartly admitted. "They adore him. And that," he slowly intoned, "bodes ill for a king."

"Only if the king is unsure of his own throne," he answered, placing the double-edged halberd next to the breastplate.

"A king is always unsure of his throne."

Menec bowed in acknowledgement. "My apologies, m'Lord. I forget the obvious to focus on the question. Yet, I would argue that Duncan is no threat to you. He will have his hands full with the intrigue and jealousies in the Temple for decades to come."

"That may be," Diad stood and carefully studied Menec. "But he is young, the people follow him. Who knows who will sway his attentions? I cannot take that gamble."

Sighing softly, Menec untied the leather straps of the two vambraces, placing one on top of the other. "Is that why Cattwg was here? To find a way to have him removed?"

"It is always better to have someone else do your dirty work, is it not?" The King smiled.

Menec flushed briefly. "Must he also die?"

"Can you give me reason for his safety?"

"He is no threat to you," he reaffirmed.

"I've already addressed that point," Diad stiffly replied.

Menec inhaled deeply, then let his breath out slowly. "He is my friend."

"You are the King's Friend," he acidly answered.

"And no other friendship do I treasure greater," he solemnly stated. "But I fear you err on this account. I do not see anything good coming of this." He shook his head.

"Do you propose to stand in my way?"

"Of course not m'Lord," he reassured him. "I could do nothing to harm my King, my friend. Your safety and welfare are my first concern. You know that... you have always known that."

The hardened eyes softened slightly. "Do not oppose me in this and I will see to it that he is not harmed."

"Thank you, m'Lord." Menec sighed resignedly.

"Well then, there it is. Come. I need some wine, and you can tell me what you've found out."

"It's not much, m'Lord," Menec frowned as they walked out through the doors. "Cu followed him to Curney's, a tavern out toward Gefnyn. He escaped before Cu had a chance at him."

"I know that already. And you are sure he was Rugian?"

"Yes, m'Lord."

Diad frowned in disgust. "What else?"

"There is little else," he quietly replied. "He's stayed the night on occasion at Curney's, kept to himself, paid up front – in Gambri coin. He was always up early and walked where he went. Other than that, we're still asking."

"Do it quickly," he insisted, "I fear our time may be running out."

"You have a visitor, Eminence," Darroch smiled knowingly, motioning for the woman to come in. She was very attractive, her strawberry blond hair cascading below her shoulders. She wore the smock of a servant, yet the cut and fabric spoke wealth. Instead of the simple fold-over, side stitched design of drab monotone brown, hers was a soft light blue, seamless, tucked and formed to accentuate her figure, the front V dropping just enough to show the valley between her breasts. The bottom hem was cut horizontally, almost immodestly at the middle of her thighs, as though purposely displaying the symmetry and beauty of her legs.

Duncan looked up from his reading, involuntarily inhaling, his face quickly transforming to obvious pleasure. "Tene!" He bounded up from the chair, quickly crossing to where she shyly stood.

"Your Grace," she dipped a short courtesy, her faced flushed in self-conscious awkwardness.

Duncan stood happily gawking, then remembered they were not alone. "How did you manage to escape that evil berserker?"

Her eyes widened. "She's not e –" She stopped as she saw his wry smile and laughing eyes. "That's not fair."

"I know," he grinned, yet finding it difficult to take his eyes off her. "It's good to see you."

"And you too, your Grace. High Commander Brenna asked me to bring you this gift." She opened a small finely carved box that contained a goblet, marvelously wrought with tarracs and warriors hunting strange beasts. The rim was gold as was the inside of the bowl. It was supported on the outside by four bands that wound down to the bottom of the bowl, and then winding together down the stem to fill out the base. It was highly polished with a smooth white surface.

Duncan laughed aloud when he recognized the bowl's material. "And who is this?"

"It is the cup of Iomar," she instructed. "High Commander Brenna said she would be happy to tell you the story."

"You may tell her that I look forward to it." He took the box and handed it to Darroch, who reverently accepted it and walked off to find a suitable spot to display such a fine gift.

Tene watched him walk off and then leaned in, lowering her voice. "She also sent another present."

"Oh?" He looked at her hands yet saw nothing more.

"Me."

"Pardon?"

"Me." she smiled mischievously. "I'm your other present. But you have to give me back."

Blinking several times, he was at once aroused yet wary. At that moment, Darroch noisily returned.

"Begging your pardon, Eminence, but I'm not quite satisfied with where I've placed High Commander Brenna's gracious gift. Would you mind if I absent myself for a while to see if I can find something more suitable to use as a display, perhaps a small table or cabinet of some sort?"

"Uh, no, not at all. Take your time."

"In the meantime, would you like me to send up any refreshments?"

Duncan looked at Tene who politely shook her head. "No, I think we're fine."

Darroch bowed and breezed through the doors, deliberately closing them behind him. Turning to the guards, he stared purposefully at both of them. "No one is to disturb the High Priest until I return. Understand? No one. What goes on in there is of grave consequence, and I do not want him disturbed. Understand?" Nodding their understanding, they watched him disappear down the hall.

"Grave consequences, eh?" one snickered. "Looks to me like our high priest is human after all."

"Did you see her?" The other leered. "Wish I was high priest right now."

Tene and Duncan waited as Darroch closed the doors before turning to gaze at each other.

"Brenna sent you as a gift? Don't you have a choice? And why is Brenna sending you? I thought you worked for Alexis?" Despite his concern, he edged closer to her.

"It was Lady Brenna's idea, and Lady Alexis liked it. Are you not happy to see me?" She feigned a demure pout.

"Good god, of course I am," He pulled her to him and kissed her deeply, feeling her glorious body press hard against him, her arms wrapping tightly around his back. Passion quickly enveloped him and he swept her up, lifting her in his arms.

"Goodness," she purred, her arms around his neck. "Now what do we do?"

"How about I show you my home?" he casually replied.

"So where do we start?" she sweetly replied.

"The bedroom."

Duncan lay on his back, his strength dissipated in magnificent contentment. Tene lay beside him, her head resting on his shoulder, a hand gently stroking his chest. It was wonderful to feel her marvelous nakedness again. How he had missed her touch, her care, her concern.

"You never did finish telling me about Brenna and Alexis using you as a gift." His voice was a soft low resonating hum.

"You didn't give me a chance," she said playfully.

"I had other things in mind," he smiled. "So whose idea was it?"

Tene shifted to snuggle closer. "Lady Brenna's."

"I don't understand. Why her? Why didn't you just come on your own?"

"My darling High Priest," she softly stroked his cheek. "It's not that simple. You should know that by now."

He breathed a slow sigh. "What does being a servant have to do with coming to visit me?"

"So, do I just walk in, stand in front of Brother Drubal and say 'Hi, I'm Tene, the High Priest's lover, and I'm here for my lessons?'"

"Well," he grinned, "maybe not like that."

"No, not like that. Dearest Duncan, your Grace, my wonderful Eminence, despite all, I'm a servant. I belong to Lady Alexis, to serve her. In order for me to be here, it must be with her consent."

A somber silence descended and spilled over the edges of the bed. Duncan stared absently at the beams in the ceiling.

"So the only time I can see you is if I visit Alexis, or she sends you here?"

Tene lifted her head to look at him, resting her chin on his chest. "When you lived with Lady Alexis, you were just a man, the 'wizard of sorts.' That was then. Now you are the High Priest, one of the most powerful men in the kingdom." She turned her head and laid it on his chest. "But I am still a servant."

"Suppose I wasn't High Priest?"

"You can't undo what's been done," she said. "Besides, it's no longer just about you." He looked askance at her as she continued. "Have you missed how the people look at you?"

"I just figured they were happy to be rid of Vix."

"That's only part of it. Your reputation is growing. I've heard what you are doing here, and so have the people. They sense a change, a good change." She twisted her head to look at him. "They are happy for this change." She paused for a moment. "Are you happy, Duncan Stuart?"

"That's the first time you've called me that," he mused, then quietly added, "I'd be happier if you were here."

"That cannot be."

"I know that," he let out a frustrated sigh. "But what's to become of us?"

"Us? We are here, now. This is us." She slowly kissed his chest several times.

"So we're reduced to making love on the rare occasion when Alexis, or Brenna, send you here or I go there?"

"So it seems."

"And you're OK with this?"

"Why shouldn't I be?" Her answer was simple, as though stating the obvious.

"Well... but... suppose you wanted to marry?"

"That's always possible. You will marry too. It is expected."

"So I've heard. But what happens if you're married, if we're both married?"

She furrowed her brows. "I don't understand what you mean."

"I mean," he said, in rising exasperation, "what happens to us, if we both are married?"

Tene shifted to sit up facing him, her legs tucked beneath her. "Who knows what will happen?" She shrugged. "Maybe we will find mates who understand how we feel, who won't mind."

"You really believe that?" Duncan's gaze lingered on the erotic visage kneeling beside him.

"Why not?"

"Why not? How can one be married and then sleep with someone else?"

370

"Many do," she countered.

"I know that," he sighed with mild exasperation. "But how can you tell someone you love him, or her, and then sleep with another?"

"So a person can't love more than one person?"

"Geez, not you too," he lamented, rolling his eyes.

"Pardon?"

"Brenna said the same thing."

"A very wise woman," she smiled impishly.

"And then the argument goes something along the lines of 'what if everyone agrees?'" He smiled despite himself.

"See? You do understand." She stretched out beside him again. "You like Brenna, don't you?"

He looked quizzically at her. "You're changing the subject."

"Brenna sent me to please you," she continued. "She knows, and approves, of us being together."

"So? She knows how we feel about each other. A good friend would do that."

After a moment's silence, Tene softly replied, "Suppose I wanted you and Brenna to become more than friends."

Duncan's head snapped back to look at her. "What?"

Tene raised her head up to gaze back at him. "Suppose I said that I would be fine, that I would like for you and Brenna to be lovers."

Stunned, his mouth gaped open, yet no sound emerged as he stared incredulously at her.

"Duncan, my dearest High Priest," she explained. "Can you and I marry?"

"No," he answered, his voice throaty. "But what does Brenna have to do with it?"

"Can you and Brenna marry?"

"I… I suppose so," his response tentative, not liking the direction she was going.

She pushed herself back onto her knees to gaze directly at him. Her eyes were warm, as she reached out to touch his arm. "If you and Brenna are together, then she can get me reassigned to her, and…" she smiled slyly.

"And we can be one big happy family," he testily replied. "Did Brenna put you up to this?"

"No," she brightened, "I just thought of it." She watched his face. "Why does this upset you?"

Duncan sat up on the edge of the bed, his legs over the side. "Why shouldn't I be upset? How can you tell me you love me and then want me to take another lover?"

Tene sidled closer to him, close enough to press her body against him. "It is because I do not love you enough that I ask you to do so. If I loved you more, I would let you go. I cannot do that," she said with a tinge of sadness. "I do not want to do that."

"Nor do I," he huskily replied.

Tenderly turning his face to hers, she held his eyes with hers. "If I can't have all of you, I'm happy to have whatever part I can."

Duncan reached up to gently brush a stray hair from her face. Looking into her eyes, he shook his head in silent resignation. "Looks like I've messed this up. I so wanted to be somebody that I've lost who we were."

Tene shook her head. "You cannot change what was meant to be. It is now up to us to make the best of it."

"You sound like a stoic," he smiled at her.

"A what?"

"A stoic, a philosopher."

"You mean I sound like you?" she teased, pushing him back on the bed. "We can make better use of our time than talking about philosophy, don't you think?" Straddling him, she leaned down to kiss him, firmly, passionately.

They were dressed, sitting in the front room when Darroch returned. As soon as the door began to slowly open, Tene jumped up from sitting next to him and dashed to sit across from him, tugging her smock down and settling herself as best she could. By the time the door had noisily opened and Darroch walked in, she was sitting comfortably, her legs demurely crossed.

"My apologies Eminence, but I just can't seem to find what I'm looking for. Nothing quite fits the uniqueness of the gift." He smiled at them both, relieved that they were not still in the bedroom. "I trust you had a good visit."

Tene stood up. "I've taken too much of your time, your Grace. I really should be going."

"So soon?" he sighed, not ready for her to leave. Duncan suddenly felt awkward, unwilling to lose this past bit of enchantment, yet knowing she must depart. As he walked with her to the door, he felt an aching hollowness. Restraining the urge to hold her once more and kiss her, he simply opened the door for her. "Please be sure to thank Brenna for her gifts," he softly smiled at her.

"I will, your Grace," she replied, dipping a quick curtsey.

As the door closed, she turned and slowly made her way down the hallway, brushing away the tears as she walked.

Watching the door close, Duncan turned to Darroch. "Thank you. That was very considerate of you."

"Eminence?" Darroch stared blankly at him.

"You know… for being gone for as long as you were."

"I do apologize for being gone so long, your Grace, and I ask your pardon. But it was as I said; I couldn't find what I was looking for."

Duncan momentarily gawked at his chief steward, who returned his gaze with calm composure. Then, in quick epiphany, he smiled appreciatively. "No problem. Perhaps we can find something suitable in the markets."

Bradwr poured the wine himself. Motioning for the woman to sit, he slyly studied this very attractive creature. Pity she was only a servant. Still, she had her uses. Handing her the cup, he sat down opposite her.

"So, tell me what you've learned."

"M'Lord," she shrugged, taking a small sip, "I'm not sure what to say. Ever since he left, things are pretty much routine. I go about my daily tasks as before."

"Does she spend the night often?"

"Lady Brenna, you mean?"

"Yes, or course, dear girl. Does she spend the night there?"

"Well," she blinked, thinking. "They really go back and forth, although, of late she seems to spend less time there."

"Oh?" he leaned back. "And why is that?"

"Lady Alexis spends most of her time down at the tarrac barns."

"Tarrac barns?" Bradwr half-lidded his eyes in concentration. "With Menec?"

"I suppose so," she replied, holding the cup in both hands.

Raising an eyebrow, he wryly mused, "Now there's an interesting conjecture, sleeping with father and daughter." He smirked, shaking his head at the thought.

"Oh no, m'Lord," her eyes widened in shock. "It's nothing like that. She spends all her time with the tarracs, out in the pastures."

"In the pastures?" It was his turn to be shocked. "She's out in the pastures? Alone?"

"It's true, m'Lord," she nodded solemnly. "Menec says he's never seen anything like it."

Bradwr decided that he would have to see for himself, later. There were other issues at hand. "I understand you paid a visit to the High Priest today."

"Yes, m'Lord. I brought a gift from Lady Brenna for the High Priest."

"A gift?"

"Yes m'Lord."

"Interesting," he answered, slowly stroking his chin. "And what sort of gift did Brenna offer our new High Priest?"

"The cup of Iomar, m'Lord."

Raising an eyebrow, he swirled the contents of his cup. "An expensive gift indeed." Cocking his head to the side, he studied her. Having been intercepted on her way back from the Temple, Tene still wore the smock that had done so little to hide her alluring assets. Now she sat before him in awkward self-consciousness, vainly trying to lessen her sexual presence. Despite her appeal, Bradwr found himself working through her comments.

Why would Brenna give such a gift to the High Priest? One did not give such presents without expectations. Menec and this new High Priest were friends... Menec was the King's man, and daughter would follow father. The Twelve would also follow my dear brother... Ach! How could he concentrate were her sitting there?

Shifting in his chair, he asked, "Was your visit with the High Priest rewarding?"

Blushing, Tene lowered her eyes. "Yes, m'Lord."

Bradwr smiled in mild amusement. Of course it was. He felt a subtle envy at Duncan's good fortune. Tene was a marvelous lover. He had made sure of that. Her father had been overjoyed when Bradwr had approached him with an offer of assignment to the royal household. The family had been servicing wealthy merchants for generations, and her father leaped at the chance to improve their status.

She had been thirteen when she first came to work for him, not too long after Toreth died. Perhaps it was because she reminded him of Toreth that he chosen her. She had her hair, many of the same mannerisms, that same shy innocence. He soon found himself recreating her. Toreth had been an incredible lover, and Tene was sent to the courtesans to learn the ways of pleasure. In between the lessons and her reaching womanhood, he had her taught how to read and write. She had a surprising quickness and gift for learning. She would have made an excellent scholar had not fate reminded him that she was destined to always be a servant.

The trouble started not too long after she came to live with him. He had forgotten that there was room for only one 'only child.' He had not counted on the overt animosity of Pavia. His attentions to Tene slowly began the rift between father and daughter. He found himself siding with Tene more often than not. That only caused more turmoil. Finally, in the urge to rescue his broken family, repair his relationship with Pavia, he had Tene reassigned, never having had the chance to taste the pleasures for which he had paid these many years.

Unwilling to exile her to some remote province of Gambria, he had managed to have her reassigned to Brenna, who was only too happy to have her own servant, now that she was one of the Twelve. He remembered Tene's face when he had told her. She had stood framed in the doorway to the gardens, a mixture of disappointment and relief flitting across her eyes. Then, in quiet submission, she walked to her room and began packing.

Ach, he sighed to himself. He should have waited. It wasn't too long after she had gone to live with Brenna that arrangements were finalized and Pavia discovered she was to be married to Emer. It was as though something snapped. Instead of her usual rage and fury, she simply grew cold. He had actually been glad when she moved out. Now she was Emer's problem.

Emer… Why in Safti's damned name didn't he have a son yet? Not that it mattered at this moment. In fact, it was better there was no future heir. It could make it far more difficult to make his claim. Emer could be a problem though. He looked at Tene who was patiently sipping her wine and waiting for his attention.

"Is there anything about the High Priest I should know?" he abruptly asked.

Blinking several times as she pondered her response, she slowly shook her head. "I think he is concerned about fixing the church, m'Lord."

"That should take a lifetime," he distractedly replied. Realizing that there was little more to be gained from her at the moment, he stood. "Thank you for stopping by. You're doing excellent work. Be sure to let me know if anything else interesting arises."

Standing, Tene placed the cup on the table. "Of course, m'Lord." She bowed and quickly left.

Watching her leave, Bradwr was again distracted by her thinly covered sexuality and decided that when he was king, she would return to his employ. That, he smiled to himself, would be his first command.

Brenna laughed to herself thinking she should've known better. Arriving at Alexis' house not twenty minutes ago, she had been informed that the High Commander was not at home. No, the door servant didn't know where she was, and no, he didn't know when she would return. Brenna noted that either the man was being insolent, or he hadn't quite woken up yet. Her first reaction was to inform him of his place. Thinking the better of it, and reminding herself that he was Alexis' servant, and that she could take care of his attitude problem later on, she politely informed him to let the High Commander know that she had been here.

She had started to walk back home when it dawned on her that there was one place where Alexis might be. Brenna pushed out through the city gates amidst the vibrant bustle of the morning's visiting merchants and slow moving wagons flowing into the city making their ways to the Merchant's Quarter. By mid-morning, most of these sellers and guild members from the outer districts would have sold, bartered, traded, consigned, or transferred ownership of their wares, returning back through the gate that afternoon either with wagons full of goods for trading back home, or paper receipts denoting significant deposits.

Finally making her way onto the main road that led out of the city, Brenna turned left at the first intersection a short way from the gates, leaving the steady stream of traffic behind her. Pausing for a moment, she deeply inhaled the morning's clean air, the flavor of the sea lingering in the wind. She gazed out over the undulating fields to the sea beyond. Along the coast to the north were the fishmongers, whose wharves and homes spilled out onto the water. Farther up the coast, well beyond the fishmongers' domain were the tanners, whose pungent craft was carefully regulated, and separated from the rest of the city.

Gambri law did not allow anyone to build a dwelling within 5000 spans of the city walls of Mull. Only the cattle and livestock were allowed within that distance, all owned by the King, except for the large fields and pastures allotted to the maintenance and training of Gambria's tarrac. It was toward the tarrac barns that Brenna now walked.

As she got closer, she could see Menec in one of the riding rings directing several riders.

"Morning, Da," she called out.

Menec turned to see who called, and broke into a wide smile and walked over to the fence. "Good morning, my favorite daughter."

"I'm your only daughter," Brenna laughed.

"And still my favorite." Menec grinned. He jerked his head towards his left shoulder. "She's out in the far pasture with her tarrac."

Brenna looked to where he had directed and saw Alexis off in the distance, slowly walking along a low hill line, Stracaim loyally following, his massive head next to hers.

"I've never seen the like," Menec leaned back against the rail and watched Alexis and her tarrac. "It's rare enough to have a woman warrior, let alone a woman berserker. But I've never seen an animal so devoted." He slowly shook his head in wonder.

They stood silently for the moment, watching Alexis and Stracaim walk. Occasionally, she would stop, reach around his head and draw him next to her, her head resting against his. Stracaim simply nuzzled into her, his tail swishing.

"Oswiu never was any good with him," Menec opined. "His method was brute force, bend the animal to his will, make him submit." He shook his head in disgust. "Any fool could see that never works. It was no wonder he fought on foot." He turned back to Brenna. "Pay attention to what she does, daughter. She has the gift of the bonded warrior. It is what I try to instill in these oafs who call themselves riders. Unfortunately, they view this magnificent creature as simply a means of transport and occasional fighting." He sighed loudly.

"I'm getting better," Brenna said defensively.

"I didn't mean to offend you," he chuckled. "And yes, you are getting better, but you need to be down here more, spending more time with your tarrac."

"Like her?"

They heard laughter in the distance and turned to see Alexis chasing Stracaim across the fields, the big animal prancing and dodging just out of her reach. Menec and Brenna watched in fascination as Stracaim would slow down for Alexis to catch up, then run off again.

At one point, Alexis dropped to her knees and leaned back a bit, spreading her hands, and called to him. Stracaim ground to a halt, turned, and slowly made his way back to her to stand directly in front of her. Then, to Menec's and Brenna's amazement, he stretched his right leg out, bent the left leg at the knee and tucked his chin to his belly. Laughing, Alexis jumped up and quickly mounted, bareback. It was then that she saw Menec and Brenna. Alexis waved and with a simple voice command, cantered Stracaim to where the two stood.

Brenna watched Alexis as she came closer, the joy obvious in the experience of this animal. "How long have you been here?" she called out.

Alexis shrugged happily. "Don't know," she called back. "What time is it?"

"Time for breakfast," Brenna laughed in response, as Alexis and Stracaim sauntered up.

She deeply inhaled the mixture of barn smells and morning air. "What a glorious day."

"When are you going to start teaching my other riders how to do that?" Menec asked.

"Do what?"

"That little trick with the bow?"

Alexis jumped down. "I'll leave that to your expertise, Master Menec," she responded deferentially. "I'm not going to pretend I actually know what I'm doing." Stracaim gently bumped her. She turned and quietly appraised him. She reached up and lovingly stroked his cheek and forehead. "OK, go get something to eat then," she said, half growling, half speaking. He bobbed his head and walked off to the barn.

Brenna's jaw dropped. "How do you do that?"

She shook her head, ready to change the topic. "I don't know. We just seem to understand each other."

Menec nodded approvingly. "High Commander, I could only wish the rest of Gambria's riders had your gift."

"Master Menec, I would consider it a favor if you would just call me Alexis." Her eyes spoke her respect.

He tilted his head to study her for a moment. "Alexis it is then."

"Thank you." Turning to Brenna she added, "I need to brush Stracaim, then we can get some breakfast."

"C'mon, I'll help only because I'm hungry," she grinned in return.

Menec watched the two warriors walk to the barn where Stracaim contentedly munched on grain. It was strange, he thought, Duncan was the one who could supposedly talk to animals. Yet this berserker, this new-comer not only fit effortlessly into the Gambri warrior-rider role, she had the gift. He slowly shook his head. He had become Tarrac-Master after years of apprenticeship and more years of study and practice. And while he understood the tarrac, at least more than more than most, he did not love them, not like she seemed to. Still, he had learned to enjoy his role, or at least accept it.

Menec looked back to the riding ring, remembering the first day he had come here. He had been only five summers old. It was the last time ever saw his father. His father had knelt down in front of him, gently grasping his shoulders.

"You listen to this man now, you hear? You're his apprentice. You work hard and you learn. I'll be back very soon." He stood back up and faced another man, a gruff and hard man. "You take good care of him."

"Don't worry man; he'll be like my own son."

What Menec remembered now was the shadow and silhouette of his father walking away, without turning back. Life after that became a blur of harsh discipline and daily toil of mucking stables, hauling hay, cutting meat, cleaning tack, mending fences, and little else. He learned early on to keep his opinions to himself, and react immediately to this new man's whims. Failure to do so meant either a beating, or sleeping in the barn with the tarracs. Menec remembered the beatings, as well as the many cold night in the barn wrapped in warming blankets, huddled among the massive beasts, trying to stay warm. Outside, the snow covered the ground, and the damp bitter winds coming off the sea pushed their way through the gaps in the barn boards.

As he grew older, he chaffed at the discipline, yet submitted, waiting for his father to return. Tarrac-Master Kern begrudgingly taught him the skills of a being a tarrac-master, as well as the skills of the warrior. Menec excelled at both, yet he preferred the role of the warrior. The cold nights of sleeping in the barn, the callous discipline, and daily labor had toughened him, and as his body matured, he developed into a robust and strong warrior.

As often as he could, and as often as he could sway Kern, he would join a warring party and prove his prowess against the Rugians. The numerous crisscrossed scars attested to his mettle. It wasn't long before his skill and abilities as both warrior and leader were recognized and his participation in battle skirmishes increased. With each successful battle, Kern's own jealousy grew. Not only had Menec exceeded his warrior skills, he had surpassed Kern's tarrac-master knowledge. Day after day, Kern watched as warriors sought out Menec for their training.

Kern's resentment festered until one day he took insult when a warrior ignored him and asked for Menec's tutoring. It happened that Menec walked in at that same moment.

"What? I'm not good enough for you, is it?" Kern bellowed, gripping the straps of the bridle he had been untangling.

"That's not what I meant, Master Kern," the warrior said defensively. But then he sealed his fate when he unthinkingly added, "It's just that Menec seems to have a better grasp of the tarracs' moods."

"Tarrac's moods, does he?" Kern whirled around to Menec. "You think you're better than me?"

Menec furrowed his brows, sizing up Kern's mood. In a calm epiphany, he recognized that it was time. "Yes," he serenely replied, "I am better than you."

Kern stood momentarily dumb-founded as the words sunk in. Then he exploded. Swinging the bridle over his head, he struck at Menec, who deftly stepped aside, caught the passing attached reins and pulled Kern off-balance, wrapping the reins around his neck. Menec tightened the reins as Kern wildly struggled to pull them away from his throat. As Kern's struggling weakened, and he sank to his knees, Menec felt a hand on his arm.

"Menec. You've made your point." Menec looked up to see Prince Diad slowly reach down and put his hands on Menec's. "Let's not kill the old man. It sets a bad precedent." He smiled as Menec relaxed and Kern tumbled to the ground gasping for breath.

"My apologies, m'Lord. My temper seems to have gotten the better of me." Menec nodded deferentially.

"No need to apologize. I've often thought of strangling him myself sometimes," Diad chuckled. "Get up Tarrac-Master," Diad poked him with his foot. "Get up and get your things out of the Master's house. I want you gone by the time the sun sets."

The older man pushed himself to standing. "You can't do that. Only the King can release me." He stood gasping, yet insolent.

Rolling his eyes, Diad sighed dramatically, then leaned in, and in an audible whisper said, "You seem to forget who I am... and who you are. If I so choose, I can have you staked and quartered by four tarrac out on that scenic field close to the sea, the one you seem to love so much. And I'd leave you there for the carrion birds to devour."

Kern's eyes widened in shock. "You... you wouldn't dare." Yet he realized that Diad did indeed have the power.

"By sunset." he commanded, staring malevolently at him.

He took a step back, looking at the Prince, and then snarled at Menec. "Your father was a tavern piss pot, a drunkard and a liar. The only reason you're here was to pay off his debts so he could drink more," he snarled. "Your mother was a common tavern wench." He took another step back.

Menec lurched forward, but Diad put a hand out and stopped him. "Let him continue," he calmly suggested.

"You know why he never came back?" he said scornfully. "Because he puked his guts out in the gutter. He died in his own vomit." He spat on the ground.

Unruffled, Diad slowly and deliberately reached down to withdraw a throwing knife from his boot. He flipped it in the air several times, catching it by the handle each time. "I think it's about time you told him the truth about his father." He flipped the knife some more. "In fact, I'm disappointed that you've known all this time and haven't bothered to tell him."

Kern watched the spinning motion of the knife in the air, knowing he dare not turn his back. "I don't know what you mean?"

Diad caught the knife in mid-air, the blade pointing ominously at Kern. "You're a liar."

Kern gritted his teeth. He sensed the other warrior positioning himself behind him to block his retreat. Refusing to back down, he stood there, silent and defiant.

Diad recognized the attitude and knew that Kern would rather die than admit any sort of defeat. After all, he had been a warrior... once. He shook his head and sighed loudly.

"Let him pass Cullan." His gaze burned into Kern. "Get your things and be gone from these stables by sunset, or your life is forfeit." Deliberately turning his back to the older man in dismissive condescension, he spoke to Menec. "Since this worm has not told you about your father, I will. Come, walk with me for a moment." He guided Menec outside to the adjoining paddock.

Kern's jaw muscles tightened as he stood there and pondered his future. To defy the Prince was reckless; even he knew that. It was only by good fortune that he had set aside enough for such a time as this. He turned around to see Cullan still standing there.

"You can go follow your master, you little puppet," he scowled.

Cullan simply smiled, and looked out through the barn doors. "I certainly hope you've not many things to collect, former Tarrac-Master. The day does seem to be slipping away rather quickly."

Kern grimaced and stormed past him. "You won't get away with this," he sneered.

Cullan paid him no mind, but watched Diad and Menec slowly walk along the fence line. He then pulled a bridle off the wall and walked outside to look for his own tarrac in the far pasture. He passed close enough to hear Diad speaking.

"My father trusted your father, friend Menec. That was why he had asked him to take that journey."

"Do you know what happened, m'Lord?"

The Prince looked out over the sea to the far away mountains. "There had been rumors of a visitor coming through the mountains. Such rumors had happened before, and each one proved false. But this time, there was a body. Father sent Kellen to investigate."

"A body?"

He nodded, pensively.

"But why my father?"

"Because Father needed someone he could trust, as well as be discrete. You may not know this, and from the looks of things here, you don't. But your father was the King's Friend. He was someone my Father trusted more than anyone. If the rumor was true, the resulting panic would be difficult to subdue with everyone thinking the Rugians had penetrated our mountain borders. If it was false, then nothing further need be said."

Menec shook his head in confusion. "I still don't understand what happened. Why didn't he come back?"

Diad put his hand on Menec's shoulder in a gesture of compassion. "Kellen brought the body back, under very strict security," he chuckled, "packed in snow. It was apparent that he was not Rugian. It was also apparent that he had been dead for some time. Father decided that the mountains needed further examination, and asked Kellen to take responsibility."

As he paused to consider how to better phrase the next statement, Menec interjected, "They never came back, did they?"

He looked at Menec and shrugged. "For all we know, he could still be up there. The truth is, we just don't know what has happened. The mountains have been our walls for so long, we sometimes forget there are other sides to them."

Menec chewed his lip for a moment, absorbing the story. Exhaling a deep breath, he turned to the Prince and very matter-of-factly said, "Thank you m'Lord, for telling me. I will pray for his soul, wherever it may be."

The King's son appraised the man for a moment, admiring this warrior, and the code of his class. "Well said, friend Menec, that is, Tarrac-Master Menec."

Menec smiled and briefly bowed his head. "I thank you for this honor–"

"Nonsense," he cut him off. "It was far past time we made the change. And speaking of change, with Father's consent, I have decided to make you the King's Friend."

Menec's eyed jolted wide open. "Me?"

"Don't look so surprised," he smiled. "Father trusted Kellen with his life."

"My father, yes," he frowned, "but he doesn't even know me."

Diad leaned in and whispered, "You'd be surprised at how much my father knows. There has not been a King's Friend ever since Kellen left." Diad turned to face Menec. "Father waited for you to come of age out of respect to Kellen. Your Father was my Father's confidant and friend, someone he could trust not just with his life, but with his inner most secrets. Are you willing to do the same?"

A bewildered Menec stood there, trying to absorb the sudden changes in his fortune. "M'Lord, of course I would," he firmly stated. "But... are you sure I'm the one he wants?"

Diad smugly smiled. "Actually, you are the one *I* want." He saw confusion flit across Menec's face. "Friend Menec, although my father is growing old, he still has his wits about him. He chose Kellen for a reason, and was rewarded with complete loyalty. Soon, I will be King. I need someone I can trust. I have decided that you are that man. Are you willing to be as your father once was, a trusted friend and counselor?"

The new Tarrac Master slowly inhaled. Then, in one smooth motion, he dropped to one knee and lowered his head. "I would be honored, m'Lord. I am your man... to the death."

"Let's hope it doesn't come to that," he grinned, both satisfied and pleased. "Stand up then, Tarrac-Master Menec, and now King's Friend. You will have lodgings both here and at the castle. While I don't know what remuneration accompanies both positions, it will certainly be more than you are making now. In fact," Diad grinned, "I believe you can afford to buy me a drink this evening when we celebrate your new position at the Crowing Cockerel."

Menec was brought back to the present by the sound of laughter. He looked over to see Alexis and Brenna chatting happily as they picked Stracaim's hooves or brushed his sides, back, and withers. For a fleeting moment, Menec remembered Brenna as a child, strong willed and precocious, begging to help the tarrac warriors brush their mounts. Unable to tell her no, she garnered more than her fair share of grooming time. In jest, they also taught her how to handle various weapons. Little did they realize her determination. Before she was yet a teenager, her martial skills were evident. By the time she was fifteen, few could best her. At sixteen, she succeeded to warrior status. Four years later, she fought her way into the Twelve.

Menec sadly shook his head. While he was immensely proud of her achievements, he was also deeply worried with the fear of a parent whose child chose battle as a way of life. Despite his stoicism, he was unwilling to grow old alone. Then Catriona's face crystallized before him, bright-eyed and beautiful, her auburn locks tumbling over her shoulders. A wistful pain twisted in his heart. How often he had tried to push her memory away. The practical side of him said there was little sense remembering the dead. Yet every time he saw Brenna, his only daughter, he saw Catriona, heard her laughter, felt her touch.

Menec frowned at himself and shook the thoughts from his mind, the practical side taking control. One cannot go backward, he reflected, one must always move forward. He knew he needed an assistant, one who actually understood tarracs. The two oafs he had now were inept at anything more that mucking stalls. He studied Alexis and wondered what it would be like to have a berserker as a Tarrac-Master.

Shading his eyes to the rising sun, he watched in shock as a warrior-rider smacked his tarrac on the head for not obeying a command.

"You! You imbecile. How dare you treat one of my beauties like that." He grabbed a long lunge whip and headed out to get the warrior's attention.

Duncan looked up from his reading as Darroch approached. "Yes?"

"You have visitors, your Grace. A delegation from what used to be Father Oran's archdiocese. If you remember, it falls within Lord Harun's domain. I believe they're here to complain about a lack of a prelate."

"What happened to Oran?"

"Eminence," he gently chided, "When you demoted Cattwg, the remaining prelates traditionally move up."

Leaning his head back, he let out a short grunt. "How could I forget. So, who is next in line to take his place?"

"Father Garbhan."

"Garbhan?! I will *not* promote Garbhan. I'm not going to inflict that kind of punishment on those poor folk." He closed the book and placed it on the cushion next to him. "I do have other options, don't I?"

"Yes, most certainly, your Grace. But I fear none of them are quite satisfactory."

Pursing his lips, he slowly inhaled. "OK?"

"There are five prelates here serving the Temple. Each expects at some time to get his own archdiocese. Well, except for Father Frang perhaps. He actually prefers the clutter of scrolls, books, and sacramental research. But the other four expect to be rewarded for their service here.

Father Garbhan, by seniority, is the first in line."

"Who's next?"

"Father Meurig."

"Meurig?! Great Safti, he's just as bad as Garbhan. Who's after him?"

"Well, Father Frang, but as I said, he doesn't want to move. After him is Father Tearlach."

"Tearlach. That's better. Go on."

"You certainly may appoint Father Tearlach, but you will earn the further enmity of Fathers Garbhan and Meurig."

"As if I don't have enough of it already?" he replied, raising an eyebrow.

"True enough, Eminence," he smiled. "But you are still fighting with tradition. Regardless of whom you promote, you'll need to promote another to fill the vacant spot here at the Temple. Again, tradition dictates that this person come from the archdiocese of the vacancy. I believe today's group will offer you a recommendation."

Duncan chuckled. "And might you know who this person is?"

"Eluned."

"Is he here?"

"No, your Grace. That would be bad form. The others will speak for him."

"Do you know anything about him?"

"I do not know him personally, Eminence, but I have heard good things about him."

The High Priest mused a moment, his head tilted to the right. "The five serving at the Temple, is there a pecking order?"

"Pecking order?"

"A seniority system."

"Not really, Eminence. You are free to move them as you see fit."

Sighing, Duncan shook his head. "I don't see many options. Moving Garbhan to logistics is like putting a drunk in charge of the ale."

"Quite true, your Grace," he snickered. "A rather interesting analogy."

"So," he thought aloud as he plopped back against the cushion of the couch, "by the look of things, I'm going to make both Garbhan and Meurig unhappy, and possibly others for messing with tradition."

"I'm afraid so, Eminence."

"Well then," he shrugged, "if that's the worst that can happen, let's talk to our visitors and get things moving."

There were five of them, their nervousness apparent as each one kneeled in turn before the High Priest, taking Duncan's right hand and pressing it gently to the forehead. Once standing again, they introduced themselves and then stood respectfully silent.

"Welcome friends," he benignly smiled. "Let me begin by offering my apologies for neglecting my responsibilities. It seems I have made you travel all this way to seek remedy for something that should have been taken care of already. But I'll address that in a minute." Turning to Darroch, he motioned towards the dining room. "Brother Darroch, would you please tell Daimhin that I have guests for lunch."

"Of course Eminence," he bowed, then looked pointedly at one of the attending acolytes who hurried off to relay the request.

Seeing their obvious pride and pleasure at his lunch invitation, Duncan inwardly smiled. "Come, let's get settled in the dining room where we can relax and talk. Brother Thestor, why don't you sit in the middle."

His eyes widening in self-conscious apprehension, a slender fair-skinned man with short, curly hair gingerly bowed reverently. "As you wish, your Grace."

"Father Lucan has spoken highly of you. I understand you are the spokesperson for the group?" He asked as he seated himself. The others sat opposite, carefully scooting the chairs out.

"Yes, your Grace."

"Fine. I understand that you are here on behalf of Eluned?"

The five exchanged quick looks of surprise as Thestor answered. "Yes, your Grace."

"I accept your recommendation," he said simply. "Please convey to him my pleasure and that I look forward to having him here with me."

Their initial reaction was one of blinking doubt as to the alacrity of their success, replaced almost immediately with overwhelming relief. At that moment, several acolytes burst in carrying trays laden with steaming meats and vegetables, and thick loaves of bread. Several others carried pitchers of ale.

"From what I understand," Duncan began as they poured the drink, "you all make some of the finest ale in all of Gambria, a sort of double bock that is quite delicious… when I can find it here. You'll find this a poor substitute," he lifted his mug, a finely crafted porcelain stein with the Temple crest engraved on the side.

"We'd be happy to keep you supplied, Eminence," the priest to Thestor's left responded.

Smiling at him, he quietly appraised the severely thin man, watching as he lifted his mug in salute. "Your offer is much appreciated, Brother Rhodri, and I just might take you up on it. For now though, let's enjoy the meal. Please, help yourselves." No one moved, waiting for him to begin.

"Here, let me help." Standing up, he jabbed a two pronged fork into a large chunk of meat and plunked it on Rhodri's plate. "Brother Rhodri, I don't know what they're doing to you out there, but it looks to me as though they may be stealing your food!" Laughing good naturedly, he stood there, serving fork and knife in hand.

Stunned to inaction, they sat there as he continued serving the others until the priest to his far right stood up. "Most Holy Father, might I take over for you?"

"That would be most kind of you, Brother Penrhyn," he answered, nodding his appreciation, while handing him the utensils. "Now where were we?"

"We were talking about beer, your Grace," Rhodri offered, still amazed that the High Priest had actually served him.

"That we were," he jovially replied, holding up his mug. "But I believe we have more important things to discuss. You are still missing a prelate. I've decided that Father Tearlach will assume Father Oran's responsibilities. I hope that meets with your approval." He watched their responses. Again there was a sense of relief.

"We thank you, Most Holy Father. Father Tearlach will be a blessing to us." Thestor answered for the group.

"Good. Well then, let's move on, shall we?" With that, he proceeded to ask questions about the archdiocese, personal questions, questions about the province and its proximity next to Rugia, and the occasional border skirmishes. He watched as they warmed to displaying their knowledge, and their reserved dispositions transition from guarded to not quite fully relaxed, but certainly happy enough. As the meal progressed, Duncan's demeanor disarmed them. Even the severe looking Sulhidir, to his far left, seemed to allow himself to let down some of his guard.

Duncan quietly appraised each of the clerics. Of the five, only Sulhidir remained remote, as if uncomfortable in the sumptuous surroundings. Duncan smiled at him. *Let's see what's really going on.*

"Brother Sulhidir, you've said very little. Surely you have something to contribute." Duncan focused on him.

Caught off guard, Sulhidir's mouth opened, but no sound emerged. Instead he simply blinked.

"You will have to forgive Brother Sulhidir, your Grace. He spends most of his time at Abbey Bennau, and is not quite used to our garrulous ways," Penrhyn said.

"I see. So you are one who prefers meditation to the sometimes idle gossip that passes for conversation?"

"It's not that, your Grace," he answered, his voice a low mellow baritone. "I get easily distracted."

"He's a singer, Eminence, and writes music too," Thestor proudly stated.

"Really? How interesting. Would it be too inconsiderate to ask for a sample... here... now?"

Sulhidir nearly dropped his mug. Caught between wanting to display his talent and not measuring up, he merely stammered, "I... uh... I..."

"Go ahead Sulhi," Penrhyn soothingly encouraged. "Let the Holy Father hear your voice."

Quickly looking at the others, he realized he had no other choice. Inhaling deeply, he pushed his chair back, quickly surveyed the room, and moved to corner opposite the arched doorway to the dining room. Clearing his throat, he settled himself and began singing,

> *Let not the time of strife hold firm.*
> *Its strength is not what we should fear.*
> *Instead be strong and stay the course.*
> *For in the end we'll persevere.*

His voice was rich and mellifluous, the melody a haunting refrain, nuanced with delicate trills and vibrato. Duncan found himself enveloped in a warm peace, as though, despite the lyrics, all was well in the world. He closed his eyes and allowed the music to fill him, to settle like a soft mantle over him. He drifted back to blissful memories and for a span of time, allowed himself to relax.

It was the polite cough that nudged him back to the present, and upon opening his eyes, he realized they were expectantly waiting on him. Sulhidir had long finished and was yet standing in the corner, waiting for judgment.

Duncan sighed contentedly. "That was more than exquisite. That was, by far, the sweetest music I have ever heard. You have the voice of angels." He watched Sulhidir's embarrassed pleasure and knew he hit the mark. Turning to Thestor, he continued, "My first inclination is to steal him away from you, but that would be completely selfish of me. Instead," he glanced back up to Darroch, "I want him in charge of the Temple's music."

Anticipating their questions, he leaned back confidently. "Now that doesn't mean he has to stay here. However, I want a suitable place for him to begin this work. It needs to be far enough away from the Abbey so he is not disturbed when he needs solace." Leaning forward, he explained, "Genius, such as his, needs room to create. Brother Thestor, I will need your guidance in this."

"As you wish, your Grace." Thestor was almost as thrilled as Suihidir. This was far more than he had expected. The rumors that this man was different were better than true. Visions of his own prospects suddenly emerged and he felt a mixture of guilt and pleasure. Yet Duncan was still talking, and he shook himself to awareness.

"I want every monk, cleric, acolyte, or any other Temple worker, who is gifted in music to have opportunity to excel." He looked back to the still standing Sulhidir. "Come and sit, Brother. I need you to fully understand what I want."

As the radiant Sulhidir returned to his seat, Duncan explained to the seated Brothers, "I want you to provide me with a plan to make this happen. Effective immediately, Brother Sulhidir is the Temple's Music Master. I need to know where you want to establish the Music Center, and how it should be organized. Brother Thestor, I charge you with the administration of this enterprise, as Brother Sulhidir should have enough freedom to create and direct the music. Is that agreeable?"

Closing his slacked mouth, the enormity of the venture sinking in, Thestor could barely contain his excitement. His future looked bright indeed. "Yes, Eminence, that would be most agreeable."

"Brother Sulhidir?" Duncan stared intently at the man, who still seemed in shock.

"I... uh... I,"

"I'll take that as a yes. Good." Remembering the other three, he turned his attention to them. "Now as for the three of you, while Brothers Thestor and Sulhidir are occupied, I will need you three to assume both their responsibilities and assist Father Tearlach in his transition. Is that amenable to you?"

They nodded in happy unison, each quickly realizing his own sphere of influence had just increased.

"Good. I will visit you in two weeks. That should be enough time to determine our future course. Now, in return," he leaned back, grinning impishly, "let's talk about that beer of yours."

Chapter 23

"Excuse me, but I am here to see Father Konrud."

Drubal looked up to see the Queen primly standing before him. He jumped up and came around the desk. "Queen Guina," he said with pleasure. "What a joy to see you." He took both her hands in his.

Squeezing his hands in return, she smiled warmly. "And it is truly good to see you too Brother Drubal," she looked pointedly at the desk behind him, "here, where you belong."

The hubbub of activity still churned as before, but there seemed to be less of the oppressive ambiance she remembered.

"Father Konrud is expecting you?" It was said politely, deferentially.

"Yes," she answered, releasing his hands. She glanced around the great hall. "I sense a change here, for the better."

Drubal nodded in agreement. "Much better. His Holiness is making quite an impact here. There is a much greater sense of purpose." At that moment they saw Garbhan cross the hall in the far end. "Of course, some still prefer the way it used to be."

Guina patted his arm. "Let's hope they don't cause too much trouble."

"They already have," he grimly replied.

"What do you mean?" Her eyes widened.

Drubal was about to answer, but the more he thought of how to respond, the more complicated it became. "Perhaps Father Konrud can better explain. May I escort you to his quarters?"

Her curiosity piqued, she decided to wait. "You are too kind, but that won't be necessary. You have far too much to do here, and I do know the way."

"As you wish," he bowed respectfully.

As she was about to leave, she looked intently at him. "I am so glad you are here."

"Me too," he winked as he sat down and settled into the day's work.

Konrud's pleasure was barely suppressed as the doors closed behind the Queen. "M'Lady, how good of you to remember your appointment," he said a little too loudly. "What questions might you have for me today?"

To his delight, she took his hand and led him to the table by the window. "We have much to talk about." Standing by the table, she reached a hand up to his face and leaned in to give him a tender kiss on the cheek, before sitting down.

Startled, Konrud remained rooted in giddy joy. Then collecting himself, he sat opposite her, relishing the attention.

"It was so good getting to spend so much time with you the other day," she chatted. "And Duncan is such a blessed change. What a wonderful few hours it was."

"It was fun wasn't it? The time went much too quickly."

"Is it always like that?"

"Always," he rolled his eyes, but grinned. "I confess that I now look forward to meals. Hopefully I won't be reduced to gluttony."

"I don't see that as a problem for you," she answered, tenderly touching his hand. "Do you think he knows?"

His joy suddenly became guarded. "Do you think he knows what?"

"Come now dearest Konrud, how long have I been coming here for counseling? I'd be surprised if the entire Temple didn't suspect."

Konrud blanched. "But... but, we've done nothing wrong."

She lowered her head slightly. "Can we really say that? You haven't seen your wife in months, and I spend more time here than I do at home."

"We both know the reasons for that," he flatly stated. "Can't two friends spend time together without everyone thinking the worst?"

"Are we just two friends?" she asked softly.

Konrud's breathing became labored as he wrestled between passion and responsibility. Did he dare tell her he loved her, adored her, wanted her? What right did he have to make any claim on this woman, his Queen? Did she feel the same? What a fool he would appear if she felt nothing more than friendship. Besides, what was the point... they were both married... not that that meant much to so many others... but she was still the Queen. She may be willing to ignore Diad's numerous dalliances, but he doubted the King would be so forgiving at being cuckolded.

Though his mind told him to be responsible, his heart pushed forward, with trepidation. "For my part," his voice was husky, hesitant, "I would have you more than friend." Anticipating her reply, he steeled himself for rejection.

Her hand slowly slipped across the table and rested again on his arm. "For my part, too."

Gaping at her, he blinked numerous times, silently repeating what she said, comprehending it, and then joy flooded throughout him. And just as suddenly, he felt a heaviness lifted from him as though he no longer had to hide a great secret. Yet shouting joy from the rooftops was one thing. Being in love with the King's wife was another.

He took her hands in his and tenderly kissed them, and placed them against his cheeks. Yet for all his giddiness, reality was just as quickly working to smother his elation.

"So what do we do?" he sighed.

"For now isn't it enough that we know, that we admit what we feel?"

He held her gaze in his. "What is it we feel?" He wanted to hear her say it.

Instead, her body settled slightly, as though resigning herself to being responsible. "What good does it do to say what I feel? What good does it do to want to act? We are who we are. Nothing can change that."

Konrud sighed heavily, "For just once, I'd like to be irresponsible."

"We're too old for that," she smiled at him, squeezing his hands. "Besides, you would have far more to lose than I should we give freedom to our desires. And I will not allow that to happen."

Silence filled the space between them. Though their hands held them together, the table separating them seemed an obstacle too firm to wish away. For the moment, they were content to simply stare at each other, the touch of their hands illuminated by the dust motes of the day's sunlight slanting in through the window.

Sensing his inner turmoil, Guina sought to distract him. "Drubal says there's trouble in the Temple."

"I know what you're doing," he said, laughing lightly. "And for now, perhaps you are right to change the topic." He leaned back in his chair, releasing one of her hands, yet keeping the other firmly in his left hand. "Drubal seems to have uncovered some accounting inconsistencies."

"Brother Mostyn?"

"You're quick," he nodded in response. "Unfortunately, I wish it were him alone."

"Let me guess," she leaned forward. "Father Garbhan?"

"Too easy." He cocked his head awaiting her to continue.

Guina pondered momentarily. "I don't know who else."

"That's just it. How can Mostyn and Garbhan be involved if Meurig's in charge of the treasury?"

Considering the implications, she gave his hand a quick squeeze. "What are you going to do?"

"For now, nothing," he shrugged in response. "Duncan told Drubal to be thorough, which may take a while. However, when the dust settles, I have little doubt the guilty will be removed from the church – no matter who they are."

Guina quickly analyzed Konrud's implication. "If the guilty already know their fate, wouldn't this make Drubal's work difficult?"

He simply nodded, "And dangerous."

The loud knocking at the door startled them both and their hands jolted apart as though hit by lightning. Catching his breath, Konrud hurried to the door, irritation rising within him for the interruption. Why couldn't they leave him alone for just one hour.

Flinging the door open, he was surprised to see Drubal. "Yes?"

"My apologies for disturbing you Father Konrud, but I need you to come with me. There has been a," he paused looking at Guina, "situation. I'm sorry m'Lady, but I'm afraid that I need to borrow Father Konrud for a while."

Guina was already up and moving towards them. "I understand. I probably should go anyway. But I'll be back soon," she responded to Konrud's pained expression. Patting his arm as she slipped between them, she smiled warmly at them both.

Watching her walk away, Konrud was again struck by her beauty, and felt his desire rise within him. But he quickly remembered Drubal next to him.

"What's going on?"

"It's started," he quietly answered as they hurried down the hallway. "The Holy Father is visiting the berserker," he whispered through the corner of his mouth, "and I've already sent someone to fetch him."

"Where are we going?" He queried.

"Buttery," he simply replied as he led the way.

There was a crowd already milling around the open doors to the buttery. Two acolytes stood guard as the others peered over and around them to look inside. Upon seeing Konrud and Drubal arrive, they immediately settled, bowed reverentially, and stepped aside.

Drubal glared at the group. "You all attend to your duties. There's nothing more for you to see here." Disappointed, yet respectful, they separated and shortly the outer room was empty save for Drubal, Konrud and the two acolytes.

"He's in here," Drubal intoned and he passed through the doors.

At the far end of the long room, lined on both sides with barrels of wine and beer, Konrud could see the man, a priest, propped against a barrel, his legs splayed wide in front of him. His head was bent to his chest, and his hands seemed to be holding something. As they grew closer, he saw he was holding a small paper sign. The word 'Sinner' was neatly printed on it.

"Who is it?" he asked as they stopped in front of the man. The front of his cassock was stained a dull purple just below his head and down to the sign.

"Brother Eideard," Drubal answered, shaking his head. "His throat's been slit."

Konrud sighed in pained exasperation. "What has he done to deserve this?"

Drubal looked directly at him. "He was working for me. This," he pointed to the dead priest, "is a warning."

Konrud's lips tightened, and he gravely nodding as he sorted out the implications. Looking back the way they came and then following the floor to where they now stood, he analyzed the scene. "Looks like he was probably killed here. There's no trail of blood. Still, I'm no expert in matters like this. We'd better send for the Inquisitor."

Surprised, Drubal furrowed his brows. "Do you really think that's necessary?"

"We don't have much of a choice. I'm sure the word is already spreading throughout the Temple."

"As well as the message." Drubal turned to call one of the acolytes guarding the entrance. "You," he pointed, "Fetch Brother Daegan." As the young man ran off, Drubal looked back to Konrud. "I'll wait here, if you like, and you can go wait for our Holy Father."

"Yes," Konrud nodded pensively. "Bring Daegan with you when he's finished here." Glancing back at the priest on the floor, his eyes moistened as he softly spoke. "I know his parents... good people. They trusted the church to take care of their son. And this is how we reward them."

She was adjusting the single flower in a small slender vase on the table when Duncan walked in. She smiled warmly at him as the door closed behind him, and the footsteps outside faded away.

"Your Grace," she dipped a slight curtsy, her eyes filled with impish humor. "I'm glad you could come."

"How could I possibly refuse?" *And why would I want to refuse?* He found himself gawking despite himself. Brenna stood next to the table, her hand resting on top of a high-back chair. She wore a loose sleeveless, off-white blouse of gossamer silk that buttoned up to a wingless collar. The material had a diaphanous sheen to it, scintillating the fabric as she breathed. Instead of drawing his attention to her well-defined shoulders and arms, he found himself focusing on the way the smooth silk cascaded over her breasts, as if emphasizing each one.

Forcing himself to take in the rest of her, he paid little attention to the delicate and supple leather pants that seemed to be a part of her. Instead, he visually traced the dips and lines of the muscles in her thighs. Looking up, he was abruptly aware that she was still smiling at him.

"Um... where's Alexis?" He looked around.

"Probably at her house, or most likely the tarrac barns."

"Is she coming?"

"Not that I know of," she gave a slight shrug. "You don't mind, do you?"

"Of course not," he replied, almost too quickly.

"Good," she laughed. "I only had enough prepared for two. You sit here." She pulled the chair out for him.

Duncan suddenly realized that there was food already on the table, as the aroma of roasted meat finally invaded his senses. As he made his way to the table, he watched her walk to the other side in a slow sensual rhythm.

"This smells good," he awkwardly offered. "Thanks for the invite."

"I needed to do something to make up for our previous missed engagement." She motioned for him to begin, while she poured the wine.

"Sorry," he sheepishly replied. "My time is not always my own these days."

"I understand." She passed him the goblet. "But that's what you get for wanting to be High Priest," she teased.

Smirking, he held up the wine cup. "And before I forget, thank you for your gift. It was very generous."

"I'm glad you liked them," she grinned knowingly.

Duncan flushed, yet smiled. "Yes... yes, I did."

"So," she said, selecting several small pieces of meat and putting them on his plate, "I believe we left off our conversation the last time with you offering to conduct a little inquisition on me." She puckishly eyed him.

"Ah yes," he templed his hands, fingertips tapping lightly together. "If I remember right, you were questioning the High Priest. Rather audacious don't you think?"

"Depends," she answered, slowly sipping her wine. "Will you beat me?" Leaning forward, her eyes sparkling in overt daring, she whispered, "I might like that."

The sun's dimming reflection rippled on the waves of the sea. Shielding his eyes as he leaned against a fence, Menec looked out above the tree line edging the tarrac pastures, and briefly watched the returning fishing boats in the distance, their sails taut with wind. Deeply inhaling the mixture of hay, tarracs, and wind-borne sea, he let the smell settle through him, soothing him like fragrant incense. Looking to his left, he sized up the city walls and all they held within, shaking his head and asking himself why he had ever wanted to live within the madness of those walls in the first place.

He had been much younger then, newly appointed as the King's Friend to then Prince Diad. At first it had been fun, a nice change. But eventually the banality of carousing, late nights, and vapid sycophants left him with a sour taste for the City and the nobility who controlled it. By the time Diad became king, Menec was where he belonged, here at the tarrac barns, away from the perpetual intrigue, shifting alliances, and thin veneer of supposed friends.

Out here, he had peace. If only Brenna were here with him, he would truly be content. Smiling wistfully, he reminded himself that she was still young, and the City was far more exciting than tarrac barns. Like him, she had grown up here. And like him, she had fled to the City at first chance. Perhaps, like him, she would return... Even as he thought it, he knew it would not be. He would have to find another to take his place. Brenna's future lay within those walls.

Straightening up, he noticed movement in the far paddock closest to the perimeter road that separated it from the tree line at the water's edge. Focusing as best he could in the fading light, he made out far too many of the familiar shapes of those majestic beasts. 'My god,' he thought to himself, 'what fool had left enough gates open to allow that many beasts to gather.' A fear settled in the pit of his stomach as he thought of the disaster that was about to occur. Yet there was something different in their movement, something odd in the way they were acting. He could hear the occasional growl, yet no anger was in the sound.

Menec hoisted himself up and over the fence and began a slow jog along the fence line to the right. Tarracs were both territorial and dangerous, even to a Tarrac Master, and he needed to have an easy escape avenue available. He had seen what carelessness could do. Every so often, some young warrior, thinking himself too busy to take precaution, would heedlessly plunge into a paddock and be ripped apart before he realized his error. The last time was two years ago. By the time he and others were able to get to the man, there was little left, other than bits of broken bones and chunks of flesh.

Turning left at the first junction, he increased his pace slightly. It was after he had zigzagged along the fence line a few more times that he came closer to the paddock. Slowly and quietly approaching the fence separating him from the growing noise and movement, he could clearly make out at least twenty of the huge animals, some pawing the ground, others jabbing their massive heads up and down, and still others in an almost skittish exuberance. A thin cloud of dust had been kicked up, surrounding them, creating a surreal image. Then one of them noticed him and for the first time in his life, he knew he was a dead man.

With an explosive angry growl, the group turned as one and charged towards him. Menec instinctively turned to flee and had already taken several strides, when he heard a loud commanding "No!"

The charging mass skidded to a halt. His breath fast and labored, he stopped and turned. Just a few spans from the fence, their nostrils flared, snorting in a cacophony of anger and indecision, they waited.

Moments later, a silhouetted apparition emerged from the middle of the pack, gently pushing the massive beasts out of its way.

"Alexis?" Menec gaped.

"Master Menec. What brings you here?" she calmly replied as she walked to up to the fence, several tarrac tagging alongside her. Menec instinctively took a step back.

"What are you doing?" His mind raced. While it was not unusual to have several tarracs in the same paddock, one made sure each was securely hitched to some immoveable object.

"We're just getting acquainted." She reached up under the neck of the tarrac to her right and brought its head closer to her. The one to her left placed its head on her opposite shoulder. "Looks like Stracaim here is the dominant." She patted the tarrac's cheek to her right. "And while I don't know her name yet, this beautiful lady here to my left and he seem to have a thing for each other."

Menec could hear the humor in her voice, but it did little to inspire confidence. "You are playing a dangerous game," he nervously warned.

A low growl emerged from Stracaim and after shaking his head several times, he gave a few slight upward jerks as if trying to push him away.

"Master Menec," she observed, "I believe it would be best if you went back to the barns. I can meet you back there if you like, after I'm finished here."

He stood immobile, briefly caught in indecision. "Yes, I suppose that would be best." Backing away, he watched her place a hand on Stracaim's withers and leap up and onto his back. Leaning down, she whispered into his ear. Bobbing his head in a nod, he turned and slowly plodded off, the entire group moving with him.

In moments, Menec was alone. He could hear an occasional growl in the darkening night as the group moved farther away. Turning, he fled back along the fence line. It wasn't until he was at the barns that he breathed a sigh of relief.

There was lightness in Duncan's step as he walked back to the Temple, his entourage drowsily following. Though late, the streets were still alive with revelers meandering their way home. He looked back at his faithful plodding along, reminding himself there were too many with him. Why he needed anyone tagging with him everywhere he went seemed silly. These poor souls should be back at the Temple, happily asleep.

He quickly shook his head when the thought of sneaking out on his own flitted by. That might be interesting, but once word got out, and it would, it wouldn't look good. *I need to be different... better.*

Many of those wandering home were alert enough to recognize the High Priest. Standing aside, the men either doffed their hats or lifted their right hand, lightly pressing a knuckle to their foreheads in recognition and respect. The women curtsied, slightly bowing their heads, their eyes following him as he passed. In return, he smiled warmly and gave a friendly wave of acknowledgement, as though genuinely happy to see them. He saw the pleasure in their faces, the subtle surprise that the High Priest would notice them. And he heard the delight in their voices as they resumed their way home, reminding themselves to tell others the High Priest had smiled and waved at them.

Duncan inhaled the night air, savoring the flavor of the mixture of scents. Though the spice tables had long been put away, their aromas had a way of lingering, as though the surrounding walls and houses had absorbed their fragrances and were now releasing them into the night. It was strongest here in the Merchant's Quarter, yet he remembered the faint whiffs even at Alexis' home by the City wall overlooking the sea. When the wind swept down from the mountains, pushing the piquant fragrance out over the walls, the aroma permeated almost half the City. Yet it was a delicious smell, reminding one of succulent meats, warm breads, and pleasant wines. Small wonder the merchants fought any demands to control and contain the heady scent. That would be bad for business.

And just as quickly, the bouquet reminded him of his time tonight with Brenna. It had been a rather interesting evening. The meal had been full of light-hearted banter, and they had happily laughed and chatted as if old friends. Still, he had been guarded, surprised at her knowledge of Safti, and even more surprised that she was actually interested. Yet throughout the evening, interspersed amongst the chitchat and religious discourse was the occasional sexual intimation, more than a tease, yet not quite an offer. It had initially unsettled him, but he then simply attributed it to nothing more than playful teasing.

That was until the end of the evening, when he had stood and had thanked her for a wonderful evening. Before he realized it, she had moved closer to him and, pressing against him, held his face in her hands and gave him a firm kiss on the lips, then stepped back and quietly stated, "We'll have to do this again. Very soon." He had remained rooted there, staring into her inviting eyes, indecisive as to whether he should cast all caution out the window, when he felt a gentle touch on his arm and her servant say, "This way, your Grace."

Now, as he walked home in the late evening, he could still feel her body pressed against him, and he found himself wishing he was still back there. And suddenly, Tene invaded his thoughts, and just as quickly, a twinge of guilt passed through him. Yet, wasn't it Tene who suggested Brenna as a lover? Could he have both? *What am I saying?*

Frowning, he sifted his thoughts. *What am I saying?* As he walked, he could still hear Brenna's voice, "Duncan, things are not always so black and white as you would have them." He had replayed her statement many times since that evening at Alexis'. Why was such a simple observation so complicated? And then a slow discernment began to emerge. *Perhaps she's right. Maybe I'm making this more complicated than it needs to be. And anyway, it's not like I have to choose.*

Blinking at the strange epiphany, he smiled to himself. *I could have worse dilemmas.* Chuckling lightly, he breathed deeply the night's fragrance, a serene contentment settling over him as he pondered his future.

Flickering torch light spilled out of the open barn doors. Off to the side, in the shadows, Menec sat on a stool, leaning back against the weathered boards, looking out into the darkness. Partially hidden by drifting clouds, the twin moons gave little light to the night's sky. Hearing the gate close, he knew she was close by.

"You are still in one piece?"

"Of course," she answered, walking up to stand before him.

There was a heavy silence as Menec weighed this evenings' discovery. Shaking his head, he let out a slow sigh. "I'm not really sure what to say. By all the laws of nature, we should be looking for a new berserker. Instead, perhaps we should be looking for a new Tarrac Master."

"I don't know what you mean," she calmly answered, moving to his side, then resting back against the barn, her hands behind her backside acting as cushions.

"Alexis," he spoke, "what you are doing with these animals is beyond my understanding. Until tonight, I thought myself a more than capable Tarrac Master, one who knew these beasts better than any man alive. I have spent my life learning their moods, their mannerisms, their quirks. I have trained hundreds of warriors to be tarrac riders, preparing them for battle… tarrac and warrior, a molded team capable of killing our enemies." He paused, the sounds of the nights filling the void. "I have seen what a tarrac can do to a man. What magic do you hold over them?"

"I don't know that I'd call it magic." She shifted the weight at her hands. "I can't explain it, but I feel a sort of oneness with them, a bond, as though we are connected… more than simply rider and tarrac…." She snorted a laugh. "And that sounds so stupid."

Menec chuckled. "At the surface, I suppose it might. Yet, I know what I saw." Remembering his first encounter with these two newcomers, he smiled despite himself at Duncan's mischievous response about being able to talk to King's Companions. "And here I thought that only our High Priest could talk to animals."

Alexis was about to say 'it's true,' but thought better of it. "I wouldn't put King's Companions and tarracs in the same class," she joked. "And I seriously doubt he would want to spend much time here trying."

"Like you do?" He looked up at her.

401

"Like I do," she shrugged. "I'm happy here. I feel at peace. I'm not a bother being here am I," she suddenly worried.

"Hardly," he somberly replied. "It's actually a pleasure to have someone here who cares about them more than I do. Though with as much time as you spend here," he teased, "you may want to find a place closer."

"I'll just move in with you," she flippantly replied. Realizing what she had just intimated, she suddenly felt both awkward and embarrassed.

Menec sat quietly for a bit, simply nodding his head as though working through a decision. "I think that's an excellent idea," he stated as he stood up.

"It's not like I spend a lot of time at home," she added, as though justifying her comment.

"I can see that." He turned to face her, the light from the barn just edging his left side. "I have a proposition for you."

"OK?"

"By now, I should already have another tarrac master in training, someone ready to take my place should I die in battle or have grown too old. I have spent these past many years looking for him, but none have measured up... until now." He shook his head and sighed. "What's odd is that instead of being the master, I have become the student."

"Are you saying that you want me to become the next tarrac master?" She asked, a hint of excitement in her voice.

"Exactly. But hear me out. This has never been done before, berserker and tarrac master in one. You have already pushed our world off balance when you became our berserker. I hesitate to think what would happen if they saw what I saw."

Alexis reflected a moment. "Then why do you want me to be the tarrac master?"

"Because it is the right thing to do," he answered simply. He took a slow deep breath, then slowly exhaled. "The winds of change are blowing across this land. I felt them before you two showed up. But they seem to be blowing stronger now." He looked beyond her shoulder out over the pastures to the sea beyond, quietly saying, "Who knows what part we all will play."

She stood quietly, letting him ruminate. She could hear the occasional growl off in the distant paddocks, and she felt the desire to be back with her beasts, her tarracs.

"Well," Menec returned to the moment, "what do you think?"

"I would like that very much."

"Good. We will need to have the King's consent, but I don't think it good to approach him quite yet. You will still have your lodgings in the City, but you will also have your place here, which, I'm afraid to say, is nothing like what you have in the City." He smiled.

"I'm not all that excited about that place to begin with," she answered. "I don't need all that space and all those people hanging around. I ought to sell it or something."

"That would not be a good idea right now. And those people hanging around are servants, good folks doing what they were trained to do," he gently chided.

"You are right, of course," she nodded, accepting her reproof. "I was merely stating that I prefer much simpler affairs."

"That's good," he laughed, "because living here is definitely a much simpler affair. Oh," he added, as though just remembering another concern, "I have one more proposition for you."

"Yes?"

He stood before her, his arms folded. "Alexis, I have one daughter, but I would like to have two."

"Pardon?" She furrowed her brows in confusion.

"I said I would like two daughters."

"OK?" She hesitated, analyzing his statement. "Are you saying you want to get married again?"

"That's always possible. But I want another daughter now." There was a tinge of mischief in his response.

"And how do you plan on doing that?"

"I want you to be my daughter."

"Me?" She stood straight up.

"Yes, you."

"You mean like, adopting me?" She felt her heart flutter, a strange sensation she had not felt for some time.

"Yes."

"And you would be my father?"

"Yes. If you would have me."

She stood there before him, sudden images of her own father rising within her, quickly culminating in the last vision of him on screen telling her goodbye. And then a heavy sadness tried to push its way in and she felt her anger rise as she fought against it, struggling to overcome this weakness. Her father was dead. Nothing could bring him back. Now this man standing before her wanted to take his place, an impossible likelihood. But

403

then, Menec probably already knew that. What was he offering her? A father's love? Could he do that? Was she willing to let him?

Feeling the leaden silence grow, a somewhat discomfited Menec was about to tell her to think about it, when she spoke.

"I would like that," she softly answered. "Yes, I would like that."

By the time Duncan had returned, he was already apprised of the news. The scowl on his face acted as a shield causing all to step aside as he purposely strode back to his apartment. In tow, Konrud and Lucan hurried to keep pace. When the doors firmly closed behind them, Duncan turned to his confidants.

"Someone explain to me what's going on."

"Duncan," Lucan quietly replied, "what did you expect? You've made some people quite nervous."

"Are you saying that I'm responsible for his death?"

"The one who killed him is responsible for his death," he answered. "What I'm saying is that the road ahead for us will be difficult."

The knock on the door momentarily startled them, but they quickly settled as Drubal and Daegan, walked in. Daegan was an austere man, who placed great importance on his place in the Temple. Yet for all his vanity, he was content with his place, his ambition tempered by the acceptance of his abilities.

"So?" Duncan asked.

"He was killed somewhere else, Most Holy Father," Daegan bowed respectfully, "most likely sometime yesterday."

"Where?"

Daegan placed the fingertips of his hands together. "Most Holy Father, it will take me some time to discover that, if at all. Whoever killed him didn't leave much in the way of clues. With the size of the young man, my guess is that at least two individuals carried him here."

"You said 'individuals.' Why not say priests? Who else could have done this?" Duncan asked, studying the man.

"I have given that great consideration, Eminence," he began, enjoying the attention. "It *is* possible that someone, or others, besides priests might be involved."

"That's impossible," Drubal interrupted. "Anyone other than a priest in the Temple would immediately draw suspicion."

Raising an eyebrow, Daegan paused. "What about... assassins?"

"But that would take money," Konrud countered. "That would take..." He stopped mid-sentence as the epiphany hit him. "Good god, he's right," he stammered. "Why not take some of the money skimmed from the Temple and pay an assassin to do your dirty work?" He looked from Daegan to Drubal for support.

"I don't buy it." Duncan shook his head. "Why would an assassin leave a sign saying 'sinner'? That's hardly discreet."

Daegan smiled as he nodded in agreement. "I absolutely agree, your Grace. It was not the work of assassins."

"Then why suggest they did?" he demanded through pursed lips.

"My apologies, Eminence. It didn't make sense to me either, but I needed to make sure we were all in agreement."

Staring at the man, he wasn't sure whether he liked him or not. "What do you need to proceed?"

"Just your authority, Eminence."

"You have it."

Bowing obsequiously, Daegan placed both palms to his chest. "Then I will leave you all." With that, he hurried out.

Duncan watched him as the doors closed behind him. "What a strange man."

"He is," Lucan agreed, "but he's good at what he does." There was a long silence as each thought about what to do next. Duncan broke the spell.

He walked to the door and opened it, poking his head out, addressing one of the acolytes. "Tell Father Garbhan I wish to see him, now." Using his back to close the doors behind him, he addressed the three clerics. "We continue as planned. Father Garbhan will now become part of the investigation." He looked pointedly at Drubal. "Give him several of your most trusted workers to help him. Let's have him begin by examining Meurig's department."

Drubal's jaw dropped. "But Eminence, both of them are the very ones we're investigating."

"Yes, I know," he grinned slyly. "As the saying goes, keep your friends close, and your enemies closer. I also want you to quietly let on to Meurig that Garbhan asked for this assignment. Let's see how long it takes before they stop getting along."

Drubal flashed a smile, as understanding crept in. "As you wish, Eminence."

"He's losing control, m'Lord." Cattwg smugly announced as he was ushered into the King's private chamber.

Diad pushed the young woman off his lap and smacked her bottom. "Fetch us more wine." Ignoring her playful pout, he flipped his hand dismissing her, then watched lasciviously as she sauntered away. Looking back to Cattwg, he blinked as if seeing him for the first time. "What's this?"

"He's losing control, m'Lord. He spends too much of his time away from the Temple with the berserker or bedding some servant girl."

Diad stared at the man, suddenly aware of his own indifference to the Temple affairs. "That's it?"

Cattwg leaned in, whispering conspiratorially "There's been a murder."

Leaning back, he abstractedly scratched his cheek. "Go on."

"One of the acolytes has been murdered."

Studying him, the King was all too aware that this obsequious sycophant was the man he needed as his high priest. This man would be pliable and obedient, and a useful ally. Vix had been difficult, too haughty for his own good, expecting more in return than he delivered. And this Duncan character... too in love with the people, and they with him... never a good combination for a secure throne... thank Safti no one liked Vix. A few religious fanatics fanned to mystical delirium would be enough to shake the foundations of this kingdom.

Cracking his neck, he flopped a leg over the arm of the chair. "What happened?"

"Brother Eideard had his throat slit." he answered almost gleefully, his part in the deed conveniently neglected.

"Why would someone want to slit the poor fool's throat?"

"Oh," Cattwg replied nonchalantly, "he was investigating the Temple finances."

Diad exploded in loud exasperation. "Damn it priest. The fool gets killed because he's investigating the internal affairs of the Temple. Do you really believe I'm so daft as to think that the people will suddenly blame the High Priest for this?"

Cattwg's humor evaporated as he sought to recover. "But... but, it's all part of a bigger picture. What about all this time he spends with the berserker or the servant girl?"

"Listen you damn fool," Diad growled, leaning forward. "This man's a saint compared to that pervert before him. Yet the people did nothing when Vix was High Priest, even when he took their children." He snarled as he flipped his hand in disgust. "They're like fattened dorsets, following anyone who touches their vanity. Yet provoked enough, even dorsets will charge. Look at what finally happened to Vix." He placed his hand between his own legs as emphasis.

The door opened and the King's lovely distraction slipped in holding a jar of wine. She said nothing but stood at the door, her head bent slightly as she looked coquettishly at her lover.

Diad held his hand out to her, and without looking at Cattwg dismissed him with, "Give me what I want, priest. Or I'll find another who can."

Garbhan whistled softly as he left the High Priest's chambers. He wasn't sure whether the man was incredibly stupid, or this was some sort of ploy. Appointing him to investigate Temple finances was too good to be true. Sure there were some of Drubal's lackeys to deal with, but he could drag this thing out for months, maybe even years… and by that time, those fools would be in the thick of it just like the others.

He chuckled with bitter satisfaction. He still smarted from Tearlach's elevation to a prelate that was rightfully his. This High Priest thinks he's so smart. He'd show him. He'd have his revenge.

Entering the Petitionary, he saw Drubal hard at work. Briskly crossing the room to the hallway leading to his own rooms, he turned and noticed Drubal studying him. Giving a quick wave and a weak smile, Garbhan retreated into the long corridor, reminding himself that he could use Mostyn's help in his investigation. That would certainly make an impression.

Chapter 24

As Lucan opened the door, a look of terrible fear flitted across his face. The look did not go unnoticed by the four women standing before him.

"Well," Pavia sweetly chided, "are you going to let us in?" Lucan stood immobile and mute. Not waiting for an answer, she pushed past him with the other three in tow. "I have such exciting news, and I wanted you to be the first to know. Well, maybe not the first... these three here already know," she smiled sweetly. "But I wanted you to be among the first to know. Come, sit here with me." She patted the chair next to her as she sat down at the table.

Lucan obediently came over to her, but remained standing.

"Does he have any wine?" Meinwen whispered to Pavia.

"Father Lucan, dearest, could we trouble you for something to drink? We decided to walk over here and it was such a long way."

Lucan shook himself awake. "Yes, yes of course." Walking over to a rather large cabinet, he pulled out four finely wrought silver goblets. Warily regarding his visitors, he grabbed a large porcelain carafe of wine on the way back.

"Lady Pavia," his voice betrayed his fears as he poured the first glass, "what do you wish to share with me." There was a slight tremble in his hands.

"I really ought to wait for all the wine to be poured, but this news is just too exciting."

He poured the second glass and handed it to Siani. He reached for the third glass just as Pavia announced, "I'm going to have a child!"

The shattering of the wine pitcher reverberated in the room and Lucan backed away in terror.

"Oh dear," Pavia stood up. "You look terrible. Are you sick?" Lucan stood next to the table, trembling. "You poor dear."

The door jerked open and an acolyte peeked in. Seeing the broken shards and puddle of wine, he hurried in. "Is everything OK Father?" Grabbing several cloth napkins, he dropped to his knees and began dabbing at the wine while collecting the shards.

"It slipped out of his hands," Meinwen explained.

Lucan stood silent, slack-jawed, his eyes still wide with anguish.

"Perhaps we've come at a bad time," Pavia cooed soothingly. "I'm sure he's very busy. We'll just see ourselves out. Come ladies," she winked. "We'll let the Holy Father get back to his work."

Midway down the corridor, Heledd turned to the other ladies. "Did you see him? There's no doubt from me." She turned to Pavia. "When do you want us to start?"

With a light bounce to her step, Pavia turned to the three. "When we made our bet, it was with the understanding that you would become my servants for a week. But that is not fitting for ladies such as you. I will allow a substitute for each one of you." She saw the visible relief in their eyes. "So is it agreed?"

"Yes, of course," all three replied together.

"Good. I'll meet you back at Heledd's."

Pavia watched them as they made their way down the hall then through the main doors, chatting cattily amongst themselves. "Yes, go home my little birds. I win again." Grinning arrogantly, she followed a safe distance behind them as they descended to the city.

Soon lost in her own thoughts, Pavia stuttered to an abrupt halt when Raefgot fell out onto the street in front of her. "Why am I not surprised?" She looked disdainfully at the unkempt prince and then back to the tavern from which he had just been ejected.

Raefgot sat on the road, his legs splayed before him, and squinted up at his comely sister-in-law. "Well if it isn't the royal trollop."

"Now, now," she sniffed as she reached down to help him up, "such a strong word for so feeble a mind. Did one of your child whores teach you that?"

He slapped her hand away. "One of these days you'll all be sorry."

"We already are sorry," she taunted. "You really should take better care. Don't you ever think of who you are?"

"All the time," he answered quietly.

"Then you should know better than to let yourself be thrown out of some tavern like a low commoner."

"Yeah, well I won't be down here forever. And then you'll be sorry."

"As I just said, I already am sorry, and bored with you. Perhaps one of these days you could pull your head out of the place you're sitting on and become a man." With that, she left him searching for some clever repartee that finally came faintly on the wind.

"Your time will come."

His hands clasped behind him, Duncan stood before the open window absently gazing out over the far walls of Mull. It was a dreary morning with dark thick clouds hiding the sun. He could hear the occasional clink of plates as the breakfast meal was cleared. He felt strangely off balance. Neither Konrud nor Lucan had appeared at the meal, as was custom. Instead, Daegan had come by to state that he had nothing to report. Other than the fact that he was assisting Drubal in the financial probe, no one seemed to know anything more. Offering a resigned shrug, he opined, "I remind you Eminence that it will take some time."

An acolyte had come later to relay that Lucan had left early that morning to visit his father's grave. At first he had felt excluded, but quickly assumed that Lucan needed alone time. It was as he was justifying Lucan's absence that Darroch ushered in another acolyte.

"Begging your pardon, Eminence, but Parthlan has some news concerning Father Konrud."

Duncan turned to face a young man with narrow shoulders, and a face equally pinched. He blinked frequently as though stifling pent up energy. Duncan wasn't sure what Konrud saw in him to be his steward, but he apparently did his work well. He stood silently, waiting to be acknowledged.

"Well?"

"I was there, your Grace. A messenger brought news for Father Konrud as he was getting ready for sleep last evening. It was Sawdm, and he had come all the way from Brecknot. He brought news that Lady Berthog had died."

"My god," he muttered aloud. "What happened?"

Parthlan took a breath and shrugged his thin shoulders. "Sawdm said that it happened a couple of days ago. She threatened to kill herself. She'd said that plenty of times before, so no one paid her any mind. He said that made her angry, so she stood on a chair to tie a rope to the beam at the top of the stairs, the entire time yelling how unfaithful Father Konrud was, and her death would serve him right. It was when she threw the rope over the beam that the chair broke."

Duncan bit his lip to suppress a smile, the imagery too ironic. "I understand she was a, um, large woman."

"Very, your Grace," he answered matter-of-factly.

"What happened?"

"Well, she fell backwards," Parthlan mimicked with his hands, "and broke through the railing and balusters, all the while holding onto the rope which wasn't yet attached. She landed on the stone floor below, her neck broken."

Duncan cleared his throat. "I understand. When did he leave?"

"Last night, Most Holy Father."

"How long will it take him to get home?"

"Tomorrow morning."

"Forgive the interruption, Eminence," Darroch broached, "but Parthlan really ought to be on his way. I'm sure Father Konrud is expecting him in Brecknot."

Duncan softly scratched his left cheek. "Of course. Please convey to Father Konrud my deepest sympathy. Tell him to take all the time he needs."

He watched as Darroch ushered him out before returning to gaze out the window again. Besides feeling a dismal emptiness, Konrud's absence reminded him that he needed to expand his coterie of confidants. Perhaps he should get away from Mull for a while. He really needed to visit the different patriarchies. While he had met the ten Patriarchs during his coronation, except for Konrud, Cattwg, and Tomos, the rest had departed back to their respective ecclesiastic domains immediately after the ceremony. *Maybe I'll start in the west and work my way back to Mull. Leave Lucan in charge... I doubt too much could go wrong while I'm gone.*

Dull morning light drifted through the windows casting edgeless shadows across the room. Standing silently before the divan in front of her bed, her arms folded as though comforting herself, Queen Guina stared at the door where just moments ago, Parthlan had departed after sharing his news.

She wasn't sure what she should feel. While she was glad for Konrud's sake, there lingered a sadness at her own fate. She no longer loved the man who was her husband. Truth be told, she doubted she had ever loved him. Love wasn't a consideration when her marriage was arranged. No... she had never loved him. She was his wife, the stable mate arranged to produce heirs, nothing more.

Wrapping her thin gown more tightly around her naked flesh, she sat down on the divan. She had produced two heirs, but that wasn't enough for him. She had even given her love to the third, a bastard of his own making.

And for that he had never forgiven her. Instead of banishing Raefgot to some distant nursemaid in the outer reaches of Gambria, she had kept him in the castle, a constant reminder of Diad's weakness and failings. She had done it out of compassion for the child. Yet the King saw it as a not so subtle provocation.

But what did it matter… really? She was the queen. She was who she was. Sadly, she had known Diad for who he was before they were married. She had tried talking father out of the arrangement, but didn't understand the consequences of his choices until after her marriage. It was then that he exposed his love for Mair, deserting her mother for someone he truly loved. Shortly thereafter, he stepped down, and his brother Bowyn became king, which made Diad the heir apparent.

At first she was angry. How could he do this to her? How could he desert mother? How could he deprive his own son the kingdom of Gambria. How could he forget who he was? Later, as the years slipped away, she began to understand. Like her, her mother was a brood mare, a means to produce sons. She had no more loved her husband than Guina did Diad. Her father knew this. Perhaps that was why he had allowed himself to fall in love. He had fallen deeply in love, and nothing else mattered. She had witnessed his happiness and an emulative yearning grew inside her, especially as she compared it to her own troubled marriage. And then she saw what her brother was truly like. In her heart, she knew. Had he become king, her fate would have ended long before the bearing of children.

But was that enough to forget, forget who he was, forget who she was? She smiled bitterly at the recollection. She had been trained too well. Even in the midst of disappointment, she was always conscious of who she was.

She stood up and walked to stand in front of the gilded oblong mirror on the wall by her wardrobe. In its reflection, she wasn't sure what she felt about what she saw. She stared at herself staring back. Her light blue eyes studied the copper blond hair that cascaded over her shoulders, the smoothness of her cheeks, the lines beginning to form at the corners of her eyes. Lifting her hands, she traced the dips and valleys of her face, then down along her jaw and throat, floating down, down curving over her breasts, pausing to cup each one. She continued down to her stomach and then her slender hips.

Was she too thin? Though her breasts were still full and firm, the rest of her seemed sallow. Perhaps Diad was right… she needed more fat on her. Sighing resignedly, she walked over and sat at the edge of the bed. What did it matter what he wanted? She loved another. And now he was free.

But she wasn't.

She stood back up and began pacing. Who was she? Was she really condemned to spend the rest of her life cast aside, a pathetic voyeur of her husband's conquests? If two played this game, what would be the consequences? She deliberated the possibilities, envisioning fleeting happiness, yet always returning here... to the darkness of this room. She was still the Queen, the mother of the future king. She could not change who she was.

Standing in the middle of the room, surrounded by opulence and wealth, she felt even more alone. Yet she knew. A terrible sadness enveloped her. Lifting her head towards the ceiling, her eyes closed, the image of Konrud's beatific face smiling at her, she mouthed the words.

I must let you go.

His cassock pulled down to his waste, Lucan lay outstretched, his face buried in the wind bent grass that covered the cairn. Scattered raindrops splattered upon his back mixing with the blood that oozed from the in crisscrossed stripes, a contrast of crimson and pallid flesh. The flagellation whip lay neatly beside him. A few feet from his extended hands, a heavy simple stone with veins of amethyst and gold rose skyward. No tool had trimmed its shape nor compressed its form, yet it rose like a spike, half a head taller than a man. Where the side opposite Lucan was rough and coarse, the side that now looked down upon him glimmered in it smoothness. A single name had been painstakingly etched into the face – Shan. No date, no eulogy, just a name. And it was to this name that Lucan now opened his soul.

Deliberately and heavily, he pushed himself to his knees and wiped the rain from his red eyes. He sighed deeply, his shoulders slumping in anguish. Slowly he raised his head to look at the name.

"How was I to know she would do this?" He shook his head. "Why me?" His eyes clouded again and his lips tightened. "What am I to do father?" he pleaded. "Great Safti I am ruined." He looked off into the distance at the gulls beating the wind. Dark clouds mixed with dark thoughts of Vix and that night on the beach spilled into his memory, when he saw the heresy of his own brother. "Is this also my punishment? Am I to add his apostasy to my sins? What have I done to deserve this? I did all you asked," his voice became stronger. "I denied myself, just as you wanted... and this is my reward?"

He sat back on his haunches, his robe draping to the ground. Rain and traces of blood fell in rivulets down his back. Yet it still stung and he grimaced as he moved.

Quietly, he heard it... that word... expiation... expiation. Frowning, he looked up at the etched name, yet heard the word... expiation. Images of her melded with visions of that night on the beach when his own twinge of doubt had breathed life. Yet still he heard the word – expiation. Then, like a rushing epiphany, its meaning flooded though him.

Lucan mimicked the stone before him, mute and immobile, yet allowing the revelation to run its course. In place of his anguish, a serene resignation settled. He understood what he must do. Yet even more, he understood why he must do it. Lifting his eyes, he gazed out over the fields to the great castle of Mull. The rain was steady now as the storm moved toward the sea. Breathing deeply, he inhaled the wet fullness of the day. A pang of sadness edged his new found resolution. He would miss all of this, the storms, the parting clouds, the bustle of living.

Yet his resolution grew firmer. Pulling up the top of his robe, he stuffed his arms through the sleeves. As best he could, he folded the two split edges of his rent cassock from where he had grabbed the front of the cowl and ripped apart the thin fabric down to his thick stomach. He stood up and breathed the sigh of internal peace.

"I tell you this though father, the prophet of Safti has come. I know he is true. He is a name holder. He told me my name and I nearly gave up the essence right there and then. And then he told me his name. Can you imagine? As easy as you please: no conditions, no fear. He wanted to do it. It was so odd, almost child-like." Lucan smiled at the memory. "Our devotion, our prayers, all have been answered. Yet there are many set against him, just as it was written. He will need my help... and so my fate is the easier to accept."

Lucan reached up and fingered the name in the stone. "I will see you soon." Grimly smiling, he turned to plod home, the rain soaked wind flapping his cassock behind him.

His arms folded, Bradwr stood gazing out the window at the waves whipped up to froth by the stiff wind. Storm clouds rolled heavily across the morning sky. Fishermen were hastily lashing down their boats and pulling down the nets left to dry from the previous day. Out on the streets, shutters were slamming closed and pedestrians hurried inside various shops and taverns, thankful for an excuse to stay inside.

"And you say that you could not see his face?" he questioned without turning from the window. The wind ruffled the long heavy window drapes. He brushed his hair out of his face.

"No m'Lord. The room was too dark."

"But you did see some other folk there."

"Yes m'Lord."

"And besides Cu, did you recognize anyone else?"

"Yes sire, but no one of real consequence."

"And how many were there?"

"About a dozen, sire."

"And you don't know where you were?"

"No m'Lord. We were blindfolded and led to the meeting place."

Bradwr pondered this latest bit of news, and it did not sit well with him. "And why did Cu bring you to this man?"

"To become a follower. Cu said that this man would restore the rightful kingdom back to Gambria, one not endowed to the sons of a lecherous –" He quickly glanced up. "Begging your pardon m'Lord."

He merely waved a hand. "I understand… and I agree. What else did he say?"

"Well m'Lord," the man continued hesitantly, "Cu said that it was only a matter of time before the uprising, and for us to be ready."

He turned to face his guest. "And what promises did he offer? What words did he use to charm enough people to want to throw off the very nature of Gambria?"

"Actually, m'Lord, he spoke of honor and trust, and how Vix and others had poisoned Gambria with all these sacrifices; how not so long ago, Gambria wasn't so divided."

"Enough." Bradwr held up a hand. He had seen the faint glow of desire in his guest's voice, the subtle acceptance. "Are you dissatisfied? But of course not," he answered his own question. "Otherwise you would not be here sharing this with me. You are to be commended for seeing through his charade. These types of charlatans are dangerous to Gambria, for they stir up trouble and needlessly agitate the ignorant masses. They preach about perceived slights with half-truths and soon innocent Gambrians are caught up in the middle of a rebellion that has no foundation and which they don't understand, and too many get hurt. We will have to root them out, but ever so carefully." He narrowed his eyes and held the man's attention. "Will you help me?"

"Of course m'Lord." The man humbly bowed.

"Good. I want you to continue in this secret society. Learn as much as you can about it and report everything to me. But you must be especially careful. Secret societies have a way of knowing what you do."

The man blinked at the sudden realization that he might be putting his life in danger. "M'Lord, I'm just a humble man, a poor fisherman who can barely feed his family."

Without saying a word, Bradwr crossed over to his large desk and opened a small chest on top. Reaching in, he pulled out a small bag of coins and carefully handed them to the man. "I understand. You put yourself in grave danger for the good of Gambria. When this is all behind us, I will ensure the scholars give you the credit you deserve." He saw avariciousness flick across the man's eyes. "This should help when the catch is poor."

The man obsequiously bowed while at the same time trying to see the amount of coins in the chest. Pleased with what he thought he saw, he carefully accepted the coins. "Thank you m'Lord, thank you. I will be only too happy to serve you."

Bradwr smiled, closing the lid. "I'm sure you will. Now, I believe you should find your way home by a different route."

The man recognized his dismissal and bowed before turning and hurrying out door. As the door closed behind him, the curtains rustled to the side of the window through which Bradwr had just been gazing, and Emer stepped out.

"Well Uncle, it seems we may have a problem."

"I know lad, I know."

"Of course, we don't really know just how many we're talking about. For all we know, this may be an isolated incident and this fakir he's following may only have a small following."

"I'm not so sure. I've heard rumors of an individual quietly building a following." Holding his nephew's gaze with his own, he said, "You still think it wise to keep this from your father?"

Emer rolled his eyes with disdain. "Uncle Bradwr, you know what will happen. The man's paranoid as it is. Any hint of something real would just set him off, causing him to destroy all of our careful work. It is better that I, that we, find this group and eliminate it, with all the possible fanfare at the right time."

Bradwr nodded in wise agreement, smiling to himself, amazed that someone supposedly so smart could not see he was being manipulated. Deciding to change tack, he smiled broadly and clapped Emer on the back, "I understand that congratulations are in order!"

"They are?"

"Don't tease me boy. I pray your first will be a son," Bradwr walked over to a large chest, spread open the doors, and selected two golden goblets and a decanter of wine. "This calls for a drink."

Emer remained rooted next to the desk, his face an empty slate of ignorance.

As he placed the goblets on the desk, Bradwr looked up at him and understood. "You haven't a clue of what I'm talking about, do you?" he smirked.

Emer shook his head 'no.'

"Why is it the women in this family never tell the husbands anything? It was the same with you and Alric. Diad never knew a thing until she was three months along - both times. Raefgot... well, let's just say that he was unexpected."

"Let's just call it what it is – not wanted," he scornfully added.

Bradwr raised a hand. "Have it your way. Let's drink to the future kings of Gambria - you and your son."

"I don't have a son?" he said, the answer obvious.

"You soon will." Slowly sipping his wine, he continued to watch him. "How?"

"The same way it's been done for centuries – Pavia's pregnant."

"How'd that happen?" He said it before he thought about it. Bradwr snorted a laugh and Emer blushed. "That's not what I meant, Uncle."

"I know, I know," he smiled, though having second thoughts. "It's always the same. The husband never finds out until everyone else does."

"Did Pavia tell you this?" He grew suddenly cautious.

"No, no. I overheard that twittering friend of hers, Heledd. I overheard her talking to Pavia's other friends... something about a bet and Pavia's pregnancy. I'm sure you'll find out soon enough. Don't worry, I won't tell anyone else until Pavia tells you."

"Thank you Uncle." Emer said it slowly, coldly, before deliberately setting the goblet down and nodding his goodbye.

As Bradwr watched him leave, understanding swept through him. It was another of her bets... another game. More than likely, she was not pregnant... which was good. The last thing he needed now was a grandson.

Pavia sighed contentedly as she pushed open the doors to her bedchamber. She crossed to the window and deeply inhaled the moistening air.

"So who is it? The stable boy or the sailor from Mull?"

Startled, Pavia turned to see Emer lounging on a thick chair against the wall. "Wouldn't you like to know?" she sneered.

"As a matter of fact, I would," he calmly replied. "If a supposed child of mine is to assume the throne after me, it'd be nice to know who the father is."

"Don't worry, when that time comes, you'll know," she smirked.

"Now that's interesting. The way I heard it, the time had already come." He viewed her through cold hardened eyes.

"What are you talking about?" She momentarily stiffened.

He saw it and a slight smile began to form. "You're not pregnant, are you."

"Of course not. What a stupid idea. Where did you come up with that one?" She awkwardly turned back to look out the window.

He slowly stood up. "Your father told me."

Pavia whirled around. "My father?"

Emer was grinning broadly now. "I do believe I'm going to enjoy this. Yes, your father."

"Where'd he get such an idea?" she asked, hesitantly.

Emer crossed over to the window where Pavia was standing, his exuded confidence like a shield causing her to move out of his way. He savored the air and the whipping winds. "Apparently he overheard it in one of the bazaars. You know how news of the mighty spreads so quickly. And of course, simply everyone wants to know news of Lady Pavia, the jewel of Gambria, especially when it concerns a future king." He glanced over to a pale Pavia. "My, my, no quick repartee? No sneering attack? Have you lost your fangs?"

Pavia chewed her lower lip, completely ignoring him. She began to pace around the room.

"Got yourself in a dilemma you can't fix with just batting your eyes, or with your honeyed words?" he teased malevolently. "Teach you not to gamble so much."

"What? What did you say?" She abruptly stopped.

"I said it appears that you've got yourself in a dilemma that you can't seem to get out of. I wonder why your friends would be spreading rumors about you being pregnant. Now what would cause them to do such a thing?" He paused, smug, relishing her disconcertion.

"I don't know what you're talking about," she defensively replied.

"This sounds to me like another one of your games, your bets. The last time was Heledd seducing some cousin. Unfortunately, he was killed at Twin Forks. The Rugians almost managed to keep his body."

"How... how did you know about that?" Pavia's jaw dropped.

"Look at you. I've actually caught you by surprise. Do you think that you're the only one around here with spies?" Emer stretched his legs. "So, what is it this time?"

Pavia warily appraised her husband, wondering if he could be trusted. "Do you really want to know?"

"Why not. I'll find out sooner or later."

Inhaling, she let her breath out slowly. "I bet that I could seduce Lucan."

Emer's eyes snapped wide. "You slept with Lucan?"

"Of course not! How repulsive. I got him drunk and he fell asleep. I left signs around his chambers as though he and I had been intimate."

Emer envisioned the scene. He had been to Lucan's chambers often enough when he was younger. "And you don't think he would say something about it?"

"Him? Never. The man's terrified of women." She paced around the room, a netted bird.

"So how does being pregnant fit in?"

"I had to somehow convince Heledd and the others."

"The inseparable triumvirate," Emer smirked.

Pavia gave him a weak smile. "I suppose. I told them that since Lucan would never admit to a relationship that I would tell him I was pregnant and they could see his reaction."

"So what happened?"

"The poor man feinted," she chuckled. Emer almost seemed to be like the Emer of their childhood, when they were friends. She began to warm to the memory.

He grinned in spite of himself. "That, I would've liked to have seen."

"It was rather funny," she laughed. "He dropped the wine pitcher he was so frightened." Still grinning, he nodded his amused respect for the prank. Pavia studied his face and hesitantly ventured, "So you'll help me then... keep to the story?"

Emer stood up. "Are you serious? I wouldn't touch this with a two-length tarrac rod. You've made your bed with more than one lover – now you can sleep in it." With that he swaggered to the door. "I'm going to enjoy this game. I think I'll call it, 'How long can Pavia pretend she's pregnant before someone finds out she's a liar?'" He sneered a laugh as he pushed out through the door.

Pavia stood in the middle of the floor, caught off-guard by his refusal. The tiny warmth that she felt beginning to reemerge within, the warmth from the early years of their marriage, suddenly blackened and dropped with finality into cold, dead ashes. Her jaw tightened as she squared her shoulders.

"Laugh while you can, you bastard. One day I will rule this kingdom – with, or without you."

Outside, the rains began to pour and the winds swirled inside the room. Turning, she hurried to close the drapes. And in that moment of shutting out the storm, she grew surprisingly calm. The decision was too obvious; it was more a question of how. Yet she knew what she must do, after all… it was about time.

Studying herself in the mirror, Pavia was pleased with what she saw. A wry smile curled the corners of her mouth as she contemplated her next game. Two ladies-in-waiting stood behind her mistakenly thinking the smile was for them and they returned her smile with a mixture of relief and satisfaction. Pavia allowed them their unfounded pleasure, too absorbed in her own thoughts.

This new game would be far more difficult than any she'd ever done before… and the consequences far more complicated. But that's what made this one more exciting. Yet she would win. She always did.

Leaning closer to her reflection, her eyes sparkling with pent up anticipation, she whispered, "Time to begin."

Bradwr leaned on the balcony railing watching the storm sweep up over the western hills. Sniffing lightly, he could smell the rain. He enjoyed moments like this, when the weather gave excuse to stay inside. On a day like this, there was nothing better than a good book and a glass of wine, a sort of enforced idleness. Smiling at the reverie, he chuckled. That would have to wait.

Bradach pushed open the doors to the balcony. "Good evening Cousin. Looks like we're in for some rain," he added as he walked up beside him.

"Shouldn't last long. You can see the breaks in the clouds over there." He nodded to the far west where the clouds were less ominous. "That should make the trip less miserable."

"You're leaving?"

Standing up, Bradwr turned to face him. "It's time I returned home."

"And how long will it take you to get back to Aberhond?"

"About the same amount of time it will take you to sail to Glanon," he stated as Bradach raised his eyebrows in understanding. "Tell your father I will send word within the week. All he need do is remain home. A package will arrive a few days from now. He can deal with it when he is sure."

Bradach eyed him curiously. "May I ask why the sudden change in plans?"

"It seems my son-in-law is about to have an heir," he commented. "I need to move before news spreads."

"I didn't think they cared for each other."

"They don't. But I can't take that chance," he turned to watch the storm, "even if it isn't true."

The storm had quickly passed, and the ominous darkness was shifting out over the sea, whipping up the waves and imperiling any fisherman foolish enough to remain out gathering his daily catch. As the storm moved on, black clouds had been replaced with scattered white billows that occasionally blocked the sun and sent shadows racing along the ground. The air had a cleanness to it that caused one to stop and drink deeply the fullness of the day

In Mull, the wet cobblestone streets became quickly crowded with normalcy. Merchants returned their ware carts to the roadside, their hawking voices adding to the growing din of loaded wagons, shoppers, and busy workers.

In the castle, Alric sat on a chair in the great dining hall, inspecting and polishing his chest plate. Shafts of daylight burst through the tall windows, illuminating the entire side of the hall. Alric had positioned his chair next to an open window, and seemed at peace, tasting the day's freshness while rotating his armor to inspect the markings and brightness.

Normally a valet would perform this mundane task, but Alric had always preferred cleaning his own weapons and armor. There was a cathartic pleasure in the repetitive motions of polishing and sharpening. The actions required no expense of thought or debate. One simply cleaned, sharpened, and repaired as necessary. And the process could be accomplished in the presence of other warriors, immersed in the banter of retelling the battle, or, as Alric often did, in the comfort of solitude, left alone in his thoughts.

Immersed in his ponderings, he did not hear the far door open. It wasn't until he heard the footsteps approaching that he looked up. His initial irritation at being disturbed was quickly swept aside when he saw who it was.

"Lady Pavia. What a pleasant surprise." His voice was warm and open.

"And just how bright did you plan on polishing that?" She moved close to him, almost touching his left shoulder.

He involuntarily looked at the mirrored surface and then back to her. His eyes were momentarily level with her breasts, and in that quick glance he took in the clinging silk fabric that accentuated her body: the small waist, the flat stomach, the round firmness of her breasts.

Pavia had chosen an azure-colored silken blouse with a 'V' cut in front, not too deep, the cut and the color just enough to draw attention to her cleavage. As she bent over to gently touch the armor, the fabric pulled away slightly, a teasing reminder of what lay beneath.

"How do you get it so shiny?" She remained bent over, and placed a hand on his shoulder for balance. She slowly turned her head to gaze at him.

Alric willed his eyes away from her chest and looked up. Her eyes spoke her desire. They had played this game before, but had always stopped with simply teasing each other of promised delight. Yet he sensed something different this time, a difference that was not necessarily unwelcomed.

"I take my time," he coyly replied.

"Taking your time… I like that," she purred.

His eyes danced in mischievous challenge. "I find that going slowly and paying attention produces the best results, don't you think?"

"I think," she stood up, "you've spent enough time on this piece of metal." She took the armor from his hands and set it on the closest dining table. She turned to face him, measuring his temperament, smiling as she read his desire. Here he was, this handsome virulent man, this captain warrior, wanting her. While she knew why she had been given to the bookish Emer in marriage, she also knew he was no king. The real king sat before her. It was just a matter of time before he accepted it.

She walked over and stood in front of him. Hiking up her dress, she straddled his lap.

"I think it's about time you and I stop teasing each other." she commanded. She felt his strong hands along her sides.

"What about the servants?" he huskily queried.

"I told them we were not to be disturbed," she softly answered as she pressed his head into the valley between her breasts.

The bedroom window curtains were open wide, and the afternoon sunlight spilled quietly over the ledge. The door had been bolted shut. On the bed, Alric lay on his side, his head propped up on his hand. Pavia lay on her back next to him, her eyes closed in contentment.

Alric gently traced the curves and bends of her prefect naked body. He had had beautiful women before, but none like her. All the times of teasing had finally been fulfilled, and the event exceeded anticipation. There was an almost reckless wildness to her, a bursting intensity that matched his own – pity that she was his brother's wife. A brief twinge of guilt flitted for an instant and then was gone. Emer didn't deserve her. He studied her faultless flesh, the soft exterior of a determined woman. Yes, Emer did not deserve her. She needed someone to tame her, to control her, someone to be her tarrac master.

He leaned over and kissed her on the forehead. "Now wasn't this a much more enjoyable place than the dining hall?"

She languidly opened her eyes. "Much better."

Alric studied her face. "I am curious though. Why now?"

She reached up and caressed his check. "Like I said, it's about time,"

He sniffed a laugh. "I thought it was about time a while ago."

She smiled coyly in return, "Me too." She then sighed. "But there is more." Her hand stopped and held his face. "I won't pretend that I've been a saint, especially when it comes to being faithful to Emer."

"OK?" Alric hesitated, an eyebrow raised.

She saw his expression and stroked his chin. "It's not what you think. You asked, 'Why now?' Truth is, I'm tired of searching for satisfaction, for someone my equal. I'm tired of being unfulfilled at home. I'm tired of his cold touch, his passionless attempts at love-making. I've always known you were the one. I just couldn't bring myself to put you in this position,"

Alric visibly relaxed. "I always knew Emer didn't deserve you."

Pavia pulled his head to hers and kissed him deeply. "But you do."

Alric smirked. "Yes I do." He pulled away slightly. "The problem is, no matter how much I deserve you, unless something were to happen to brother Emer, he will be king... and you his queen."

"Emer doesn't deserve to be king," she stated matter-of-factly. Her fingers began tracing the outlines of various scars on Alric's chest.

"So, not only does he not deserve you, he doesn't deserve to be king?" he chuckled

"Stop it. You know very well what I mean." She rolled onto her side facing him, noticing his obvious approval of what he saw. "Let's be realistic about this. Emer is a scholar. I grant him his knowledge." She pushed him onto his back and began kissing his chest. "So tell me, Lord Alric," she said softly, "what scholar has ever lasted as king?"

Despite the distraction of Pavia's attention, Alric tried to think about her question. However, her attention too easily interrupted his concentration and he huskily answered, "None that I can remember."

Pavia raised her head. "Exactly my point."

Frowning, he studied her. "What are you suggesting?"

"About Emer?" she playfully shrugged. "Nothing." She pushed herself up and straddled him. "About us? I suggest we continue where we left off." Grinning wickedly, she bent down and kissed him.

Chapter 25

Raefgot perked up when she sauntered by again, her hips bumping patrons out of the way as she carried steaming plates of roasted game to the several boisterous tables close by. Each time their eyes met and she gave him a smile, different, not like all the others; it was warm, genuine. Her eyes smiled along with her lips, as if she really did like what she saw.

She was young, yet old enough to serve ale in a place like this, old enough to handle the drunken grabbing libertines who called out bawdy suggestions. He watched her deftly avoid the wayward hands while threading the gauntlet of crowded tables, all the while full of good-natured banter. They cheered lustfully each time she passed.

One time he saw her talking briefly with the pub owner, both of them looking at him. The owner cupped his hand to his mouth as he bent closer to talk into her ear. She seemed to like what he said, because she smiled and looked at Raefgot.

A flicker of irritation passed as he thought of all the other times he had seen the same interaction. He knew what they discussed. He could recite the words without effort. 'He's the king's son.' 'He's a cheap drunk.' 'Throw him out when he runs out of money.' 'He'll come back. He always does.' He always does... Lost in his own rising bitterness, he didn't realize she was standing there looking at him.

"Don't go," she entreated, "I'm free as soon as Caela arrives," she looked up, "which is now." A short, well-built woman with thick black hair cut horizontally at her shoulders burst through the doors. A cheer erupted as she entered and stood in the doorway, hands on her hips.

Surveying the room with saucy aplomb, she loudly announced, "Don't cross me tonight boys, or you might get spanked!"

The room burst with laughter and cat-calls, some standing up and bending over, volunteering to be first. Taking a small cleaning towel from one of the dirty tables close by, she twisted it up and snapped at the volunteers as she made her way back to the kitchen.

"I'll be right back," the girl announced, undoing her apron.

Raefgot watched her walk away as the din of the room subsided to merely being loud. In moments she had returned and sat down opposite him.

"My name's Tegan," she stated. "I don't remember seeing you here before."

"I've been here before, sometimes," he guardedly answered. He knew the routine. 'Buy me a drink,' and then more drinks, coming in smaller and smaller sizes, yet costing the same each time. His money spent twice as fast, he would be thrown out that much sooner. Before he could tell her to move on, Caela showed up, smiling mischievously.

"What'll you have?" she said to Tegan.

"Just a small mug of the darker ale, and another whatever-he's-drinking for him. Put it on my account."

"Sure sweetie," she winked at them both and sashayed away.

Raefgot warily eyed his guest. This was a first, not that no one had ever bought him a drink before, but it was always the precursor to him spending far more. Yet he begrudgingly accepted the gesture. "Thank you."

"Are you really the king's youngest son?" she pertly asked, scooting her chair in a bit more.

"Yes." Despite his guardedness, he liked what he saw. She was a little taller and more slender than Caela. Her ash brown hair was cut short above her shoulders, framing her face. In contrast to Caela's brash sexuality, Tegan seemed more demure.

"What do you do?"

"Pardon?"

"What do you do? I know your older brother, the one next in line to be king, is a supposed to be a scholar. The other is a warrior. What do you do?"

"I drink," he answered testily, holding up his tankard.

"No," she laughed at his wit. "Really, what do you do?"

He slowly lowered the tankard, resting it carefully on the table. "As I said, I drink." He held her eyes with his.

She blinked only for a moment, as understanding crept in. "That must get boring after a while," she stated matter-of-factly. "What would you like to do?"

He tilted his head to the right to study her. What a curious woman… She seemed so unaffected by what he was or who he was. "No one has ever asked me that before."

"That's too bad," she sympathized.

Caela moseyed up and gently set their drinks down. "I see you've staked out a claim tonight," she glanced at Tegan then gave Raefgot the once over. "He's pretty," she said playfully before strutting off to attend another table.

Raefgot flushed in awkwardness. Everything was upside down. Why were they being so nice to him? Yet he liked what he was feeling, the attention, the respect. He held the new tankard up in thanks.

Sipping quickly, she placed her mug closer to his tankard. "I've heard about your brothers. The oldest, what's his name? Edner, Eman?"

"Emer."

"Yes, Emer. He's quite the scholar."

"And he wastes no opportunity to make sure you know it," he sourly retorted.

Leaning forward, she lowered her voice to just above the din. "Would you be offended if I told you something?"

"Uh… I suppose not," he cautiously replied.

"I don't think anyone likes your brother Emer. They say he should keep to studying books and things and leave the kingdom to someone else."

"Tell me something I don't already know," he sniffed.

"Well, there you go. You can become king." She smiled prettily.

His head jerked back slightly at the suggestion. "Interesting. There's the little problem of older brother Alric, father's pet."

"But he's a warrior isn't he? So, he could be the head of all the warriors. Emer could be the head of the book learning and scholar stuff, and you then could be the king."

Raefgot rolled his eyes. "If only it were that easy. You know nothing about me, yet you're ready to make me king. Why is that?"

Tegan looked around the room filled with rowdy patrons. "Your brothers… they're never here. They don't really know who we are, the common folk. You, you have no problem being one of us. I think you would make a good king."

There was a logic to her words, though the reality was far too impossible. Still, the thought had some merit. Maybe he ought to look at his options, especially if Emer were to become king. But that could wait. She was smiling at him, waiting for him to say something.

"An interesting thought, but I doubt it will happen, though I appreciate your vote of confidence." He took a deep swallow, the lager tasting particularly good at the moment.

"Prince Raefgot, I hope you didn't mind that I asked you to stay," her eyelids fluttered charmingly.

"Of course not," he quickly replied. He liked the way she said his name, *Prince* Raefgot. Usually it was just 'm'Lord', a sort of non-descript appellation to hang his personality on. But the way she said it, it had meaning to it.

"Dear Prince, I'm finished for the night and I need to go and attend to my parents."

"I'll walk you home."

"Not tonight, Prince Raefgot. I just met you. What would my parents say?" She stood up and reached down to touch his hand. Smiling alluringly she added, "But I'll let you walk me home tomorrow night."

Smiling contentedly, he watched her walk to the back. Turning, she gave a quick wave before disappearing thorough the doors leading into the kitchen. Settling back, he slowly sipped his lager. This was a refreshing change.

The pub owner was waiting for her as Tegan pushed through the kitchen doors. "Well?" He queried.

"No problem. He'll be here again tomorrow."

Grinning, he flipped her a small bag of coins. "I'll let her know."

Tegan tossed the bag in her hand. "How long am I supposed to do this?"

"She didn't say. But you're getting paid good money for it, so be thankful."

"Oh, I don't mind. Just curious, that's all." Tossing the bag once more in her hands, she giggled, "Guess I better go check on my parents, wherever they are."

The door before them was firmly locked. Duncan gently fingered the gold push plate and then slid his fingers over the curves and curls of the marvelously carved walnut colored wood, the shallow grooves spreading into ornate designs of flowers and mythic animals.

"I've wondered what was this door was for," he said, turning to Lucan.

"I apologize for not informing you sooner, Holy Father," he humbly bowed, fidgeting in his cassock pockets.

"Holy father? What's got into you? I appreciate your reverence towards me, but you're starting to call me 'holy father' more often lately. What happened to just Duncan? Something bothering you?"

Lucan blanched but shook his head. "No Holy Fa ... uh ... Duncan."

He withdrew the large key to the door from his pocket. "I'm sorry. I've been preoccupied and have failed in my responsibilities to you. I am truly sorry." He tenderly touched Duncan's arm.

Knitting his brows, he stared at his friend. "There is something bothering you. Have I done something to upset you?"

"God no! It's not you." He caught himself and stopped.

"But it is something." He put his hand on Lucan's shoulder. "You are my friend as I am yours. Your pain is mine also. If you are troubled about something, tell must me. You know I will do everything and anything I can to help you." He leaned in slightly. "Whether you realize it or not, you are my teacher here in Gambria. Your council and patience, and friendship, have been my saving grace. I expect to accomplish great things here, but I need you to do it."

His shoulders sagged and despite the grateful smile, his eyes began to well up. "I too need you," he said huskily. He then straightened himself up, brushing the wetness from his eyes. "Yes it is something, but it will be corrected soon. Come," he turned to unlock the door. "It is time for you to understand the essence of my naming." Pulling the door open wide, he tugged his friend with him, stepped into the room, before closing the door and leaving them in total blackness.

Duncan could feel the thickness of the carpet beneath his boots. "Am I supposed to see something?"

"In a moment," Lucan patiently urged, his voice somewhere in the darkness. "This is my favorite part."

At first, he could see nothing, but then a faint glimmer began in what soon became a ceiling. The room slowly filled with light and he could make out the shapes of chairs along the wall and a single table in the middle. The room continued to fill with light and he searched for the source, but the entire ceiling was aglow in brightness. "Interesting. How'd you do it?" he asked as he looked around for a switch mechanism.

"I didn't do anything," he shrugged. "It does this anytime someone enters the room. It's as though the room senses life."

Duncan nodded. *Probably some sort of heat detector.* The room itself wasn't exceptionally large, probably about half the size of his sleeping chamber here in the temple. Except for the ceiling, the room was layered in heavy tapestries, intricately woven in forest greens, brilliant vermilion, golds, and vibrant hues of azure blue. Several thick, short-backed chairs nestled against the walls. He looked at the small round table in the center of the room. It was a simple design and a small hand stitched geometric-patterned cloth partially covered the top. Resting in the center of the table was a large stone, a clear crystal, irregularly shaped, lying length wise.

"That's a beautiful stone. What is it?" He watched as the light danced along the edges of the crystal, and then swirled inside the stone itself, giving it almost a living quality.

"Come stand by it with me and I'll explain it to you." Leading the way, he positioned the High Priest on the opposite side of the table. "This is both a naming stone and an essence stone," he said. Reverently, he picked it up and handed it to him.

Duncan was not prepared for its lightness and almost dropped it. "Whoa! Amazing. What material is this?" He brought it closer to his face, examining the fissures and crystalline streaks and looked up to see him frowning. "Sorry," he said sheepishly, placing the stone back on the table. "Sometimes my curiosity gets the better of me. Perhaps you'd better explain."

Lucan sighed, smiled thinly. "That is my family's stone. All of my lineage have used this stone for each naming and passing. The stone is passed only through the eldest male. Each extended family in Gambria has a single stone, so that brothers and sisters, cousins, uncles, and all related through the male heir use the same stone."

"So Vix received this stone from your father."

"Yes. What do you use in your family?"

"Nothing I can think of," he shrugged.

Lucan's eyes widened. "Nothing? How is this possible? How can you conceive new life without a stone?"

"Most folks just use a bed."

"You, ah ... you use a bed?" he blinked.

"Sometimes, I suppose. It really all depends where it happens. Sometimes one can't wait and the living room works just as well," he winked. Seeing his friend's look of incredulity he added, "Um, perhaps you ought to explain more." He pointed to the crystal "If I understand this right, there has to be a male heir in order to keep passing the stone. Suppose there is no male heir?"

Curiously eying Duncan, he continued. "If there is no direct male heir, the stone then passes to the male closest to the direct lineage of the stone possessor."

"So this stone is now yours."

"Yes," he answered solemnly. "It knows that Vix is no more. I am now the heir. It was the stone upon which I was both conceived and named."

Duncan leaned forward. "Now we get to the crux here. Explain the naming and especially the essence thing."

Lucan smiled. "I will do my best." He paused to take a breath. "I believe you already understand the naming part. You saw the results when you told me the meaning of my name."

"I remember," he replied, the vision of a weakening Lucan still vivid.

"Then you understand that every child conceived in Gambria is given a name that is uniquely its own. And in that name is the essence of both the child and its heritage."

"That I understand; the child is a result of the intermarriage of preceding generations. Yet I think there is more to this essence thing than just the name." He stared at the fissures in the crystal.

Lucan smiled slightly. "That is true, for there can be no children without sacrifice."

Duncan stiffened, remembering the trial at the edge of the sea, and the death of the little girl. "I'm not sure I'm going to like where this is going."

Seeing his reaction, he quickly explained, "It's not what you think. Yes, there must be a sacrifice, but it is not as you think."

"Go on."

"There must be bloodshed in order for the stone to pass along the essence of the lineage. While a man's blood is possible, the result is final. That's why we use another sacrifice."

Duncan scrunched up his face in confusion. "I don't understand."

Nodding thoughtfully, his High Chancellor continued. "Perhaps this will help. You've seen the animals we call roans?"

"Yes," he smiled. "Delicious."

Lucan chuckled. "Yes they are. But they are more than food. They are what keeps Gambria alive." He grew solemn. "What happens is that when a husband and wife decide it is time to have children, they find a young roan, and take the roan to the family's naming chamber."

"Every family has a naming chamber?" he interrupted.

"Most do, although a chamber is not really necessary. It merely affords privacy. Some of the poorer families simply find a secluded place outside. What is important is that no one else knows your name's essence, its meaning."

Duncan pondered a moment before asking, "So where does the roan fit in?"

"I'm coming to that Holy...um, friend Duncan." He inhaled deeply. "The roan is brought into the naming chamber and its throat is cut, allowing its blood to flow." He held up a hand to stop Duncan from asking another question. "The man and wife dip their hands in the flowing blood and then place their hands on the naming stone. At that moment, the power of the stone, the blood of the roan, and the lineage of the two families are united and the woman is made fertile."

Duncan nodded knowingly as comprehension settled within. "I think I understand. The sacrificial roan..." He thought for a moment and then asked, "I have two questions. First, does the woman always become fertile? Will she always become pregnant?"

Lucan thought for a moment. "No, not always. But a woman can become fertile no other way."

"So the only way a woman can become pregnant is via the roan and the naming stone?"

"Yes."

"Do they have to be married?"

Lucan blanched. "Uh... uh, um... I ... I suppose not."

"Are you OK?" he asked, noticing the sudden change.

Lucan looked away. "Yes," he whispered. "I am fine." He turned back to face him. "Do you have another question?"

"Yes." He focused his attention on Lucan. "You said that a man's blood is possible, but the result was final. What do you mean?"

Blinking several times, he sighed quietly. "A man may use his blood instead of a roan, but in doing so, he forfeits his life."

"He dies?"

"Yes."

"Why?"

Lucan shrugged. "As the roan dies, so must the man. The life of the roan is taken so that another life may begin. If a man chooses to do so, he must understand the consequences." He lifted his head slightly, looking at the far wall. "There is no turning back," he quietly answered.

Positioning himself on one side of the table, he directed Duncan to the other side. "Come. We must proceed with your learning. Here," he pointed to the crystal. "Place your hands here." He showed him where there were softer edges to the crystal from the repeated warmth and pressure of so many previous hands. "Now I place my hands here." He placed his hands opposite Duncan's, but with his fingers just touching Duncan's fingertips.

"Now what?"

"Close your eyes, say nothing, and listen intently." Duncan closed his eyes and concentrated. "The stone is the conduit of my heritage," Lucan intoned. "It is the root stone of my essence and the pinnacle of my leaving."

"Leaving?" Duncan whispered.

"Shhh. I must finish, and then you will understand."

Duncan felt a warmth emanating from Lucan's fingers, and he felt his own hands warming. He cracked his eyelids to see what was happening, but there was only Lucan across from him, intoning some sort of ritual monologue. He closed his eyes again to concentrate and listen to the musical voice

"I am the rightful heir, the only male, the legitimate one, having passed to me through Vix. The stone knows his passing and knows me now. I claim my right as heir to this lineage to thus pass it on, here and now, freely of my own volition, to this man called Duncan. It is in him and through him that I now pass on our heritage."

In one rapid motion, Lucan withdrew a small knife from the folds of his robe and deftly slit the skin across his right wrist. Placing his hands on the stone, he let the blood flow down his wrist and hand and onto the stone.

Duncan felt the strangeness of fluid on his hands, and just as he opened his eyes to look, he felt surges of energy engulf his body, peaking in a rage of pain and he cried out. He tried letting go, but the stone held him fast. Images crammed themselves in layers; a kaleidoscope of scenes and people loomed large and then vanished. Here was Vix as high priest and then just as suddenly it was Vix and Lucan as children gamboling in the fields outside of Mull. A severe looking man stood close by in obvious paternal pleasure. Then it was the severe man as a child in his bedroom gazing out over the Starn Sea.

Duncan writhed in pain and still the stone held him. His head jerked back and he let out a loud howl. And the scenes continued in rapid staccato, rolling back in time. Every now and then, he saw his own father beckoning him, his sad eyes pleading for him to help. And then his father's head exploded, the body dissolving into the crumbled mass of human flesh just outside his apartment door on the ship. He tried reaching for him, but his hands wouldn't leave the stone. He frantically tried prying them away but the stone would not let him go. And then visions filled his mind and he saw vast deserts changing into large armies colliding in loud impact. He saw grand ships hovering above the sea, streams of people flowing out and down into the water. Then suddenly emptiness filled his soul, but it was the emptiness of great loss and it racked him and then the pain began again, growing like the pain before Talane had found him.

Then the stone released him and he swung about wildly, careening against the table, sending the stone in a twirling spin in a low arc down to the floor where it shattered into thousands of shards. Duncan continued raging about the room, furiously holding his head, trying to force the pain out. Chairs tumbled out of his path, and tapestries jerked down. The emptiness grew with the pain. His legs began to quiver, and just as he collapsed, Spikey's tow-headed wide-eyed face appeared, smiling benevolently.

"I think I heard something." Garbhan whispered.

"They've been in there far too long," Cattwg mused. He then scanned the long dark corridor, ensuring they were alone.

"I agree," Mostyn nodded, his face tight in consternation. "I think we ought to see what they're up to." He stood looking dumbly at the other two.

Cattwg waited for Mostyn to act, but he stood immobile. "Well why don't you knock?" Cattwg sighed.

Mostyn hesitated, but then politely, yet firmly, knocked on the door, and leaned in to listen.

Cattwg scanned the empty hallways.

"I don't hear anything now," Garbhan whispered. "Are you sure they're in there?"

"We followed them here and saw them go in," Mostyn frowned at him. "Our high priest seemed quite taken with himself while he waited for Brother Lucan to unlock the door."

"Lucan's been acting fully strange of late. He's not his usual fat jolly I-see-nothing self. I don't like it." Garbhan shook his head.

"Nor I." Cattwg straightened. "He's been even more attentive to the high priest. Something's obviously up." He turned back to the door. "I don't hear anything. Knock again!" Mostyn hesitated and Cattwg pushed him aside. He tried the door and found it unlocked. Gently, he pried it open.

The lights were still on in the room. Duncan lay in a crumbled heap on the floor.

The room was a shambles. Tapestries were torn and partially ripped from the walls, revealing the cold gray of the stone walls behind. Chairs were scattered as if carelessly tossed into the room. Cattwg strode over to him and reached down to feel Duncan's neck. "He's alive." Cattwg looked up to see Garbhan standing wide-eyed next to Lucan's empty cassock, the up-ended table, and the shattered stone. Lucan was nowhere to be found.

"My god, you don't think –?" Mostyn shook his head in disbelief.

Cattwg stood up. "That's exactly what I think," he said through pursed lips. "No wonder Lucan's been acting so strangely."

"But the stone," Mostyn pointed. "He can't use it anymore."

"Of course not you fool. Have you forgotten your scriptures so soon? *And when the blessed one comes the stones will yield their secrets and be no more.*"

"You... you think he's the one?" Garbhan stammered, his eyes wide.

"Of course not, you fool," Cattwg answered. "There's too much strange about him to be the promised one."

"I don't like it," Mostyn worried. "We'd better leave before someone finds us."

"Not so fast," Cattwg commanded.

Mostyn cocked his head at Cattwg. "What're you going to do?"

Cattwg glanced at him through half-lidded eyes. "Not me... We." He crossed over to where Garbhan was and scooped up Lucan's cassock. "We may need this." He turned back to the prostrate Duncan. "Give me a hand here." He walked over and stood at Duncan's head.

The other two obediently grabbed hold of one of Duncan's legs. "Where're we going?" Garbhan demanded.

"Let's take him to the holding room off the granary." He tossed the cassock on Duncan's limp body.

"What if somebody sees us?" Mostyn fretted.

"We can say he's drunk," Cattwg snapped. "Let's go before someone *does* see us!" With that, Cattwg and Mostyn struggled to carry Duncan down the long corridor.

They were halfway down the hall when the attackers leapt out from the shadows. So startled were the priests that they dropped Duncan on the floor. Unwittingly, Cattwg grabbed Lucan's cassock in the melee and fled back the way they came, the other two close behind.

Menec kneeled before the enthroned figure. Behind him, four assassins, cloaked in black, likewise bowed. The scent of rose petals hung heavily in the air and candles flickered thick shadows within the room. Duncan lay prostrate, an unmoving occupant in the quiet of this room. No one spoke for some time, but watched his chest as it rose and fell with each breath.

Lord Ronell moved ever so slightly. "You say that the three priests were carrying him?"

"Yes m'Lord." Menec answered.

435

"And you had no trouble?"

"'No m'Lord," Menec suppressed a snicker. "They were no trouble at all."

"We must wait until he awakens. Please come forward friend Menec." Menec rose and moved quickly to the figure's side. Lord Ronell leaned forward and whispered, "Please convey to Rulf my deepest gratitude. His loyalty is a great treasure. But you my friend, you must be very careful. There are many eyes watching you. You had better leave by the east wall drains."

Menec bowed and reverently reached up and grasped the gloved hand. He felt the pressure of a return squeeze and quickly let go. "As you command m'Lord." He turned to the still bowed group. "Let's go."

Cattwg leaned against the door to, his chest heaving. A breathless Garbhan stood a little to the side, holding up a small torch while scanning the room. Mostyn stood close to him.

"Are we safe?" Mostyn gasped.

Pushing himself upright, Cattwg, walked to the table in the center, his flickering shadow preceding him. "For now." Leaning on the edges, he pushed Lucan's robe to the center. "Did you see them?"

"Assassins," Mostyn whispered.

Cattwg inhaled deeply to settle himself. "Why didn't they kill us?"

"What?" Garbhan squeaked.

Cattwg walked to the other side of the table, staring at the robe. "Assassins don't leave witnesses. Why leave us alive?"

"Perhaps because of who we are?" Mostyn wondered aloud.

"And just who are we? Are we that important to still be alive? Assassins work for the highest bidder. It's that simple."

"Maybe because you two are prelates," Mostyn responded unconvincingly.

Shaking his head, Cattwg poked at the robe absentmindedly. "Perhaps it was to send a message?"

"Like what?"

"I don't know," Cattwg slowly responded. "Whoever sent them knew we were there." He looked up to the ceiling, shaking his head. "This doesn't make sense." He turned to where Garbhan had stood rooted next to the door. "Quit standing there and make use of that thing and light the rest of the candles. I need to think, and I need some light."

Regaining his composure, Garbhan walked along the edges of the room, lighting the wall sconces. In short time, the room was filled with light. He extinguished the torch in the barrel by the door and walked over to Cattwg, reaching down to touch the garment.

"What should we do with this?" Furrowing his brows, he looked up at Cattwg. "Can he have really given up his essence to... to him?"

"Apparently so," Cattwg sneered. "The question is; what are we going to do about it?" He began to slowly pace about the room. "What are we going to do?"

"Lucan actually p...passed on his essence to this interloper high priest," Mostyn stammered, the incredulity of the act still astounding him.

"We've determined that already," Cattwg snapped. "Stop whimpering like a child and get a hold of yourself. Lucan's gone. Get over it. Let me think!" He stopped and leaned forward on the table. "Why did assassins take him from us? It's almost as though someone is protecting him?" He mused quietly for several minutes, lost in thought when suddenly he jerked back upright. "I'll be damned. That bastard."

"Who?" a startled Mostyn asked.

Cattwg resumed his pacing, only quicker now, shaking his head in galled epiphany. "Don't you see? It takes money to hire assassins. It takes even more money to hire them to protect someone." He stopped and glared at them. "And who has money to do that?"

Mostyn and Garbhan stared blankly at each other, then shrugged. Mostyn spoke for the two of them. "Lots of people have money."

"You idiots," Cattwg barked in frustration. "Are you both so clueless to what goes on in the kingdom?"

"Perhaps if you spoke plainly we could understand," Garbhan retorted.

Audibly sighing, he stopped pacing. "Pay attention, because your future depends on it. Think. Why would someone want the High Priest protected?"

"Damn it, how should I know?" Garbhan angrily replied. "You've made an assumption and have obviously reached a conclusion. Why not just tell us?"

Cattwg folded his arms, and calmly answered, "Bradwr."

"Bradwr? But I thought he disliked the High Priest?" Mostyn shot back.

"So did I," Cattwg said sourly. "But who has the most to gain by keeping him safe?"

"I still don't see how Bradwr benefits from keeping Duncan safe. I thought you and he had an understanding," Garbhan frowned.

"He's playing both sides. I doubt he planned on Lucan's demise, but that plays into his hands even better. Let's face it; Bradwr was backing the successful tarrac. My future seemed to be fading. With Lucan gone, Bradwr can let on that he was protecting Duncan. And now he'll own him."

Mostyn still looked doubtful. "I suppose it could be a lot easier to be king when the church is behind you."

Cattwg nodded and spread his hands. "Two can play this game."

Garbhan thought for a moment. "But we'd still have Konrud to deal with."

Cattwg shook his finger. "Konrud's far enough away to be of no concern. We can take care of him when he returns. We need to get rid of Duncan first." He resumed pacing and had gone only a few steps when a slow malevolent grin spread upon his lips. His shoulders hunched, he looked back over his shoulder and chuckled. "I believe I have an answer to our problem."

Menec stood in the shadows watching the four assassins dissolve into the night, at one point becoming one with the teeming crowds and the next moment invisible. He smiled to himself as he covertly noticed one assassin hide the clothes of his trade in a loose stone near a rain down spout. Moments later, the same assassin emerged on unsteady feet, feigning a drunken stupor. Passersby laughed at him and gave him wide berth until another drunk stumbled out of one of the taverns and the two suddenly fell together like great friends. The assassin allowed himself to be coaxed into another drink, and the two lurched back into the flickering lights of the tavern.

Menec leaned against the house wall, gazing carefully up the full length of Merchants Walk. Lights shimmered through the windows in the taverns and upper storied living chambers. Pedestrians ambled along, some hailing friends, others engrossed in their own conversations. Lovers drifted upon the newness of the night, wrapped in each other, impervious to crowd or noise. The pulse of life overflowed this part of Mull.

Menec glanced once more at the bustling night activity and emerged from the dark alley, adjusting the front of his trousers as if having just relieved himself.

"Tarrac Master Menec! I'm surprised to find you here."

Menec turned to find Llwyd, still in his scholar's robes, in the company of several friends. "Master Llwyd. To what honor do these simple folks in Merchant's Quarter owe that they should have a scholar of the second rank mixing here among the common folk?"

Llwyd preened at the praise. "Oh my, you are too kind Master Menec."

"Hardly Master Scholar Llwyd." Menec turned to address the scholar's companions. "Did you know that your friend here has written one of the finest treatises in the kingdom on ancient Gambrian pottery?"

Llwyd seemed momentarily stunned. "You ... you know about that?"

"I've read it," he replied with smug satisfaction.

"You, you actually read it?" His stammer belied his deep appreciation.

"Word for word. Ancient pottery happens to be an interest of mine. Come walk with me for a bit and explain how you determined that the bi-chromatic urns in lsar were related to the bi-chromatic vases in Solway."

There were a few groans, but Llwyd did not hear them as he joyously explained his premise to the attentive Menec. And soon, Menec's presence in the night crowds of Merchant's Walk was perfectly normal.

Alexis struggled to coherence, as she was shaken awake from a deep sleep. As her eyes focused, Brenna's comely face looked down on her

"Hey," Alexis blinked several times. "What's up?"

"I need your help. I have a problem that only you can help with."

"Huh?" She sat up and rubbed her face. "What?"

She sat on the bed next to her. "I'll explain as we go. But first, I need you to understand something and for you to trust me."

"I already trust you," Alexis yawned.

Brenna examined her closely and decided to take a chance. "You know I serve the king and the kingdom of Gambria."

"Of course. That's obvious."

"Yet there is another I serve, to whom I give allegiance beyond and above that of the king."

Alexis wasn't sure she wanted to hear more, but knew her well enough to know that she was not prone to excessive drama. She gently touched her on the arm. "Whatever it is, I trust you and will help you. You are my covenant sister warrior. My bond to you is unbreakable."

Brenna visibly relaxed and she smiled. "Good."

"So what's the problem?"

"It seems our High Priest needs our help?"

Alexis rolled her eyes. "Duncan? Now what?"

"Come with me. I'll explain as we go."

Alexis and Brenna stood in the rose scented room. Candles flickered dimly. Duncan lay on the floor in front of them, his eyes closed, but his face revealing his lingering pain. Alexis looked around the vacant room.

"Were we supposed to meet someone here?"

"No. I was instructed to bring you here to help me with him."

Kneeling next to him, she studied the pained face. "What's wrong with him?" Her voice gave away her concern.

Brenna shook her head. "All I know is that it had something to do with Lucan. I don't think it will last long. Lord Ronell had him brought here and told me to get you."

"Me? What am I supposed to do?"

"We need a safe place for him until he recovers. Since he had been with you before, it would not seem unusual if he were with you again." She bent down opposite her.

"But he's the high priest. Why not just take him back to his own chambers?" she suggested.

Brenna placed a hand on Alexis' hand. "Because it is unsafe at the Temple. While he may be high priest, there are those who seek his death from among his own."

"Other priests?"

"Yes."

"Who?" Her eyes hardened. "And why?"

"You spend so much time at the tarrac barns that you're missing what's going on around you," Brenna gently chided. "Duncan is a stranger who has disrupted centuries of tradition." She sat back on her haunches. "The Book of Safti teaches about a man like him, a sort of returning messiah, one who disrupts the status quo. There have been one or two pretenders long ago, and every now and then someone says he's the one. But it always ends the same. Once the high priest gets hold of him, he's never seen again." She looked up and around the room. "This is the first time that the high priest himself was challenged... and lost. Not everyone is happy with the sudden change, especially some in the Temple."

Alexis shook her head. "All this religion stuff is boring. I understand jealousy and power, and that's what this is all about."

Brenna chuckled. "You are right, yet it changes nothing." She bent down and put her hands under his shoulders. "Come, let's get him moved."

"Whoa. How do you propose we do that without drawing attention?" She moved to his feet.

"There's more than one way back home. I'll show you."

440

Together, they hoisted him up and carried him down the long narrow corridors.

It was mid-morning when Tene distractedly moved through the market stalls. The sounds and smells that once made her thrill to the hustle and bustle of the market now left her with a queasiness. Before coming to the market to gather up the day's meals for the Berserker, she had spent a bit of the morning in the lavatory cleaning up where she had been sick. She thought perhaps it might have been a passing bug, but the sickness seemed to come with each morning for the past week. Likewise, certain smells would cause her to gag.

Stopping before a melon merchant, she thumped the outer shell of a golden brown one. She absentmindedly looked over the other melons in the large basket.

"Ah Tene, good to see you again. These are fresh this morning," the portly merchant pointed to the full basket in front of her. "I also have some more coming in this afternoon." He was about to continue when he saw her haggard look. "My goodness, you don't look well. Is everything OK?"

Tene inhaled slowly. "I'm just tired."

"You look more than tired." He peered closely at her. "Have you seen a physician?"

"A physician? What for?"

The merchant pursed his lips. "Wait here for a moment. I'd like the missus to look at you."

Tene smiled weakly. "I didn't know she was a physician."

The merchant sniffed a laugh. "She's not. But she's been a mother seven times over. And I've been a father to each one of them. And I think I know what I'm seeing."

Cocking her head to the side, she stared at him in confusion. "Huh?"

"Guard the fruit," he ordered and went to the back of the stall. He returned with a pleasant-faced middle aged woman behind him. She had the look of contentment with her lot in life.

"Here she is," he stated matter-of-factly. Neither of the women was sure which one he meant, and stood there awkwardly for a moment. Ignoring the discomfort, he barged ahead, addressing his wife. "Take a look at her and tell me if my suspicions are right."

The woman benignly smiled. "Pay no attention to him. Apparently he's forgotten his manners. My name is Mabli."

"Her name is Tene," he interjected.

"Yes, I know who you are." The woman's manner was caring, almost maternal.

"You do?" Tene was caught off guard.

"Well yes. You're here often enough and little happens in Merchant's Walk without everyone else knowing. So how is our lady berserker?" she said amiably.

Tene relaxed a bit. "She's well thank you."

Mabli studied Tene, looking at her face and eyes. "How many mornings have you been sick?"

"Just this past week," Tene responded, somewhat involuntarily. "Why?"

"Well my dear, looks like you're pregnant."

Tene's eyes widened as she stepped back and bumped against a fruit basket.

"Whoa, careful there." The merchant caught the basket and settled it back in place. "Why are you surprised? It's not as if you didn't plan it. I didn't realize that you were married."

"I'm not... and I didn't..." Tene's hand went to her mouth.

"Beg pardon?"

"I... I..." Tene started backing away.

Mabli turned to her husband. "Gervin, dear husband, why don't you go back to hawking our produce and let this young one and I talk?"

"Suits me," he grinned, but with a hint of curiosity added, "that's all women's talk anyway." He moved around them and was soon proffering fruit to passersby.

"Come with me child, and let's see what's happened here." She took Tene by the elbow and maneuvered her to the back of the stall. "Do I understand that you're not married?

"No. No I'm not," Tene replied as she sat down on a large over-stuffed cushion. Mabli sat on another cushion next to her.

"Well child, it's obvious you've been intimate with someone."

Tene hesitated, "Well... uhh... I... I have... but how can I be pregnant? We've done no sacrifice."

Mabli grew pensive as she studied Tene. "May I be so bold as to ask who this gentleman is?"

Tene fidgeted, and tears began to form.

"Now, now child, it can't be as bad as all that," she soothed. "I'm sure there's a reasonable explanation. Do you love this man?"

Tene hung her head and nodded, the tears now descending freely.

442

"And does he love you?"

Again Tene nodded.

Mabli leaned forward. "Well then, as long as he's not married, there shouldn't be a problem. He's not married, right?"

Tene said nothing but simply shook her head no.

"Good." Mabli chewed her lower lip a bit. "Did I hear you right, you've done no sacrifice?"

Tene looked up, her tear-filled eyes wide in anguish. "No," she mutely replied.

"That's impossible," Mabli answered matter-of-factly. "Come child, tell me who the father is and perhaps we can make sense of all this."

Through the tears, Tene mouthed 'Duncan.'

"Pardon?"

"Duncan," Tene said a little louder.

"Duncan?" Mabli raised an eyebrow, "as in the high priest Duncan?"

"Yes." Tene meekly replied.

Mabli sat back. "Oh my."

"Gone? When?" Diad barked as the messenger struggled to keep pace as they walked into the great hall.

Several servants stiffened to attention as they entered. One pulled out the king's chair as another sliced bite-sized pieces of roasted roan and carefully arranged them on a plate. Still another filled the chalice with a fortified wine.

"Yesterday, m'Lord." The messenger crossed to the other side of the table.

"Damn it," he snarled, sitting down. "Why wasn't I notified sooner? I didn't give him permission to leave."

"He said to tell you that he sends his regrets," came the nervous reply, "but that urgent business required his immediate attention, and that he couldn't w–"

"Couldn't' wait?" Slapping the table, Diad's voice grew louder. "He couldn't wait? What? Is that what you said?"

Trembling, the messenger weakly nodded. "M'Lord, that's all he told me. He –"

"Get out," he roared, "before I skewer you myself. In fact," he stood up simultaneously glaring at both a sword hung on the wall and the closest servant, "give me that sword and I'll do it this instant."

Wide eyed, the man turned and fled.

Diad's lips tightened and he sat back down. Despite the urge to throw something, he willed himself to simply drum his fingers on the table.

"You," he glowered at the servant closest to the door. "Find Menec. Now."

"Really?" Rhun leaned back, deliberately placing the wine goblet on the table. Dabbing at the edges of his lips with an embroidered napkin, he held the man's eyes with a stern gaze. "Yesterday. And I'm just finding out about this now?"

"He left in secret m'Lord," the man explained. "I were watchin' the back gate, like ya asked. Only time I were gone was I had ta get somethin' ta eat."

Rhun studied the pathetic creature groveling before him, his distaste evident at having to personally deal with such human dross. He had selected the man for his supposed ability to blend in. A flaw in the man's character, an unfortunate trait amongst the low bred, contributed to his failure.

Smiling in empathetic understanding, Rhun asked, "Did you ever try that little alehouse just down the road a bit? I think it's called 'Two Forks'?"

The man's eyes brightened. "Aye m'Lord."

"I've been told the food is quite excellent there. Oh, I also understand a winsome flirt named Cadi works there... evenings... midweek only I think. I hear she's quite something." He winked.

"That she is, m'Lord. But she works there every night."

"Every night? Humpf. That's not what I was told."

"Aye it's true m'Lord. I know."

"And the food? Is it good?"

"The best. And at a fair price." The man beamed with knowledge.

"And you're able to eat there every night? Am I paying you enough to have something left over? I certainly don't want you to have to expend all your funds on food."

"I thank you m'Lord. I've enough."

"Good. That's good. Yet it must get boring eating at the same place all the time."

"Oh, I don't eat there all the time m'Lord. Sometimes I go 'round to another place just 'round the corner."

Rhun nodded in understanding. "Excellent. Well, thank you for bringing me the news. Good work. Be sure to stop by the kitchen on the way out to refresh yourself." He held up a bit of roasted game on his fork. "My cooks are among the best in Gambria."

Bowing in gratitude, the man whistled happily as he left.

Rhun watched him leave. "Besides, a man's last meal ought to be something memorable." Turning, he beckoned a burly man lounging in the shadows. "I want it to be particularly ugly, a reminder to all. Then find me somebody who will do what I ask."

Chapter 26

When Duncan awoke, his whole body hurt, especially his head. Opening his eyes, he focused on a somber Alexis staring down at him.

"Where am I?" He twisted his head to look.

"My place," Alexis answered.

"How'd I get here? Where's Lucan?" He sat up, recognizing Tene's bedroom. "What's going on?"

"I'm not sure, but apparently you're becoming quite a problem."

Duncan eased himself up, groaning. "My head feels like it's exploding inside. How long have I been here?"

She sat on the bed next to him. "Three days. What happened back there in the Temple with you and Lucan?"

"I'm… not entirely sure," he wearily replied. "We went to his naming chamber. I remember putting my hands on his naming crystal, and the next thing I know is I wake up here."

"What's a naming chamber?"

Duncan's head began to slowly clear as he recalled Lucan's instructions. He softly laughed. "I just realized this whole pregnancy thing."

"S'cuse me?" Alexis raised an eyebrow.

"Pregnancy. Apparently a woman can only get pregnant on purpose."

Alexis frowned. "As opposed to getting pregnant not on purpose? What are you talking about? And what does this have to do with this naming chamber?"

Duncan looked up in epiphany. "It's the roan. The blood must act as a sort of electrical conduit for the two, with the stone functioning as a generator." He looked to Alexis for support.

"I haven't the faintest idea what you're talking about," she blankly responded.

He pressed on. "It's why these folks have sex without consequences. The only way a woman can get pregnant is predetermined."

She stood up, sighing audibly. "You're making no sense. What's this have to do with Lucan?"

"I'm getting to that," Duncan was about to continue when Brenna barged in, Tene in tow.

"We have a problem," she announced, looking at Duncan.

"Now what?" Alexis mumbled.

"Tell him." Brenna pushed Tene in front of her.

Tene stood there trembling.   Duncan took hold of her hand and soothingly said, "Whatever it is, I'll fix it."

Tene looked into his eyes and knew he meant it. "I... I'm... pregnant."

There was an extended pause as the bit of information sank in.   He blinked his eyes several times before replying, "Pregnant?   How's that possible?"

"Do I need to draw you a picture?" Alexis muttered, shaking her head.

Brenna snickered despite herself.   Then turning somber, she looked at Alexis. "Yet he does ask the right question."   She looked back to where he sat, still holding Tene's hand. "She tells me that there was no naming stone, no sacrificial roan.   How is it possible that she is now pregnant?"

Duncan reflected a moment. "Is it possible she is wrong?"

"Oh no Duncan," Tene interjected. "Mabli told me I was."

"Who is Mabli?" he asked.

"A merchant's wife," Brenna answered.   "She's also a midwife and knowledgeable about these things."

"Now that's interesting," he mused. "How is it possible for a woman of Gambria to get pregnant without a roan and naming stone?"   Tugging on his chin, he looked at the three of them. "It seems that I don't need a roan or a naming stone."

Brenna stepped back in guarded apprehension. "This is not the time for humor, Duncan."

He shrugged.   "I'm not trying to be funny.   Do you have another suggestion?"

She looked to Alexis for help, only to realize that Alexis hadn't a clue of the gravity of what had happened. "I see no good coming of this," she pointedly stated. "Besides, Lucan is gone.   No one has seen him since you and he were last together.   There are already rumors."

"Rumors?"   Duncan's head still ached, but he sifted through what he could recall.   Then suddenly the naming chamber emerged and he was standing there with Lucan before the table, their hands touching on the stone.   And he heard the words once more: *A man may use his blood instead of a roan, but in doing so, he forfeits his life. He dies... He dies... He dies.*

His strength evaporated as he sank to the floor. "O god no... please no... not like this... O god."

Tene moved quickly to his side as the other two kneeled next to him. "What's happened?" she coaxed, her heart trembling.

Duncan leaned forward on his hands. "He's gone," he said looking up at her. "He's gone."

Brenna stretched out a hand to gently touch his shoulder. "What happened?"

Duncan remained where he was, his chest heaving heavily. His head hurt immeasurably now, and he sat back, shaking his head in disbelief, his hands pressed hard against his head trying to force the pain away. Finally, as the pain weakened, he looked up. "Lucan has given me his essence."

Brenna jumped back as though bitten. "What?"

"He told me he needed to show me one more thing so that I would understand what it meant to be high priest. He took me to his naming chamber."

Her mouth gaped wide. She knew what he was about to say, yet did not want to believe it. "Why?"

"I don't know why," he responded in bewilderment. "It doesn't make any sense."

"Will someone please explain to me what's going on?" Alexis stood up.

"It's complicated. Simply put, Lucan has given up his essence to Duncan."

"I don't know what that means," she peevishly answered.

"It means that Lucan is dead and his spirit is now inside Duncan," Brenna replied with finality.

Shaking her head in confusion, Alexis was about to speak when the door servant, standing by the open bedroom door, politely coughed to get attention.

"Yes?" Alexis demanded.

"Begging your pardon High Commander, but there are several priests downstairs again asking to know if you have seen the high priest."

Alexis quickly looked to Brenna. "Now what?"

Brenna hesitated, unsure of what was to unfold. "Stall. Make up something."

"Why not tell them I'm here?" Duncan interjected quietly, his headache lessening. "In fact," he slowly inhaled as he shakily stood up, "I'll tell them myself."

Taking a step towards the door, Brenna moved to stand in his way. "Wait Duncan. I'm not sure that's such a good idea." She stopped short of blocking his exit.

Duncan slowed to a halt. "You may be right," he intoned, his body still feeling heavy. "But we are who we are… and I am still the high priest."

"That's not the point." She hesitated, unsure of what to do. "We were told to bring you here."

"By whom?" The ache in his head was subsiding, only to be replaced with a sort of fatalistic resignation.

Brenna didn't answer, but looked to Alexis for support. Yet Alexis stood rooted where she stood, both unaware and unsure of the real reason for him being here.

"Listen," he answered. "It is me they want. Protect yourselves." With that, he walked out of the room, Tene right behind him.

"Duncan, maybe Brenna's right. Maybe she knows something you don't," she pleaded, reaching up to touch his arm.

He turned to face her, and held her by the shoulders. "You're sure you're pregnant?"

Lowering her head, she softly answered, "Yes."

"Then whatever happens, be sure our child knows who he is."

Tene raised her head, her eyes moist with a mixture of fear, and confusion. "But how can this be? We did nothing that would allow for a child."

"You forget who I am," he said, somewhat doubtfully. "Remember, who I am." He repeated as if to reassure himself.

She stared into his eyes, loving him, but also afraid of him. "But who are you, really?" she whispered.

"I'm the promised one," he answered. "And it's time everyone accepts it." Squaring his shoulders, he turned and walked down the stairs to the awaiting priests.

The two priests were in muted discussion when Duncan descended into view. They both looked up simultaneously, a mixture of apprehension and nervousness.

"Good morning to you both," Duncan greeted them affably. "I understand you were looking for me."

"Yes Holy Father." The taller of the two, a severely thin man, bowed deferentially. "King Diad asks that you attend him immediately,"

"Anything I should know about?" He walked up to where they stood just inside the door. Tene had hung back at the top of the stairs, watching.

The two exchanged uneasy looks. The other priest, a middle aged man with a weak chin, fumbled with his hands before replying, "Um… we're not

449

sure Holy Father... we think it might be something about Father Lucan."

"What about Father Lucan?" Duncan's confidence was momentarily rattled.

"Um... we're not really sure," the older priest hesitated. "We were just sent to find you."

"Well, you've found me." He motioned for them to move. "Let's not keep the king waiting."

Tomos stood next to Drubal's desk, tapping his fingers on the top. The lull in the activity in the Petitionary merely accentuated the strangeness of the day.

"Something's going on. I can feel it." Tomos continued tapping.

Frowning, Drubal carefully placed his quill next to the writing pad. "Something's been going on for these past three days. Where's Duncan?"

"And where's Lucan? You've looked?"

"Everywhere. It's not like them to miss even a meal."

"I know," Tomos scowled. "They would've said something if they were going to be gone."

"Maybe it's time to ask some of my friends for their help," he quietly offered.

Remembering Drubal's past, Tomos stopped tapping. "Do you think that wise?"

"I don't know what else to do," he shrugged. "I fear we delay any longer, we may be too late."

Tomos placed a hand on his shoulder. "Do what you need to do."

Walking down the tapestry covered corridor, Menec mused the interaction he just had with the King, and he didn't like it. Something wasn't right. Instead of loud exclamations and verbal abuse as was his usual fashion, Diad seemed preoccupied, distracted. Even news that Bradwr was gathering men didn't seem to bother the King. Yet when Menec mentioned the whereabouts of the High Priest, Diad wouldn't meet his eyes. Instead, he charged him to sound out Kylar, and do it quickly.

That meant going by ship. That meant he would be gone for at least four days, provided fair winds. It was as if Diad was getting rid of him for a while. In fact, the King seemed impatient for him to leave. What was so important that he had to leave now? What more would he find out that he didn't already know now.

Lost in his thoughts, he nearly bumped into Garbhan who was hurrying past him towards the rooms Menec just left. "My apologies Bro- er, Father Garbhan," he said, raising an eyebrow.

Ignoring him, Garbhan breezed past him, several other clerics racing to keep up. The last one nodded benignly at him and caught up to the rest. When they assembled at the door, Garbhan paused to catch his breath and settle himself. Deciding he was ready, he gave a curt nod to a younger cleric who knocked on the door.

Despite the overwhelming curiosity to follow them back in, Menec knew it was not his place. Besides, he needed to tell Alexis to look after the stables while he was gone. He watched the door open to accept the priests, waiting until the last one bowed respectfully and entered, the door closing silently behind them.

Letting out a frustrated sigh, he decided he'd better get to the tarrac barns before heading out to book passage on whatever ship would take him to Glanon. At one hall junction, he paused to think of the fastest way out of the castle. Turning right he hurried down the hall, deciding that the fastest way was through the gardens. Had he paused a little longer, he might have watched as Duncan was escorted to the King's chambers.

Diad lounged on a high back chair intently staring at his wine glass, his nonchalance belying a pent up excitement. He glanced up when Duncan was ushered in.

"If it isn't our high priest." Diad settled himself back into the chair. "I see you've been busy of late."

Duncan took a quick survey of the room. For the king's privy chambers, it seemed a strange mixture of occupants. Garbhan, Mostyn, and three other priests he didn't recognize stood on either side of Diad. "M'Lord?" Duncan moved forward, an apprehension growing that he might not have many friends here. He stopped in front of the king and gave a curt bow.

The King leaned forward "There seems to be some concern of Lucan's whereabouts."

Sensing the direction of this new inquisition, Duncan raised an eyebrow. "M'Lord, am I to understand that you've called me here to ask where Lucan is?"

"Have you seen him?" He tilted his head to the left.

"It's been a few days."

At that moment, Cattwg breathlessly barged in. "My apologies m'Lord."

"Father Cattwg here," Diad intoned as Cattwg made his way to stand next to the king, "seems to think foul play has occurred."

Duncan looked to Cattwg, and saw the malice in his eyes. "And what might that be Sire?" he asked, still focused on Cattwg.

"Perhaps Father Cattwg ought to inform us of his accusation." The King sat back, a pensive air about him as if he were solving a puzzle.

"M'Lord," Cattwg coughed to clear his throat. "Sire. No one has seen Father Lucan these past three days. The last time was when he and the high priest here," he nodded somewhat disdainfully at Duncan, "were seen together."

"So?" Duncan challenged.

"So?" Cattwg spat. "Then there is this." He proffered the robe to the King, who took it and began examining it.

"And this is?" the King asked, a bit louder than necessary.

"That is Father Lucan's robe, M'Lord. You'll notice the large number of bloodstains on it." Cattwg pointed deferentially.

"Do you know anything about this?" Diad slowly queried, gazing directly at Duncan.

"Of course not. What I remember is that we were in his naming chamber – " he heard an audible gasp, and he immediately knew his cause was lost. Gathering himself, he stood erect. "M'Lord, if you, or anyone" he slowly looked around the room, "think that I might have done ill to Father Lucan, you are wrong. I would never harm him, or any of my other priests."

"Your other priests," Cattwg sneered. He turned to King Diad, his energy rising. "M'Lord, here are the facts. No one has seen Father Lucan since he and the high priest were together. We know they went to Father Lucan's naming chamber – the high priest here admits as much."

"What of it?" Duncan demanded.

"You'll get your turn," Cattwg retorted. "He doesn't remember anything except being in Father Lucan's naming chamber." He paused for effect, and looked pointedly around the room. He looked at the king, but pointed to the High Priest. "What he really means to do is convince us that Father Lucan sacrificed himself by passing on his essence to him." There was a sudden and heavy quiet that pervaded the room as the gravity and implication settled on each one of them. He turned back to Duncan. "Why would Father Lucan do that?"

"I haven't the faintest idea. Why would Father Lucan do that?" Duncan said evenly.

Cattwg ignored him and continued. "M'Lord, yesterday, when we couldn't find Father Lucan, I organized a search. Two lay brothers found the naming chamber open and investigated." He turned around to motion a priest forward. Duncan recognized the tall thin priest who had escorted him here. "Tell us what you found, brother."

The priest bowed respectfully. "We found nothing m'Lord."

"That's evidence?" Duncan shook his head.

"He's not finished," Cattwg interjected.

"What I mean to say," the priest spoke calmly, "is that while the room was neat and clean, there was no naming stone in the room."

"So?" Duncan demanded. He slowly glanced at the others. Their feigned self-righteousness and obvious disdain told him that nothing he said mattered.

King Diad sighed audibly. "Let's cut to the chase, priest. What is it exactly you are accusing the high priest of?"

"Patience please, Sire. I have one more point to make." He turned to face the entrance doors and raised his hand. The doors opened and two priests escorted a young woman in.

"Tene?" Duncan involuntarily reacted.

Her nervousness was obvious as she was escorted to stand next to him. He took her hand when she came close.

"They came for me just after you left," she said quietly.

"It'll be OK," he firmly replied, although not quite as sure of himself as he had been back at Alexis'.

"Sire, you ask me to cut to the chase, and here it is," Cattwg smugly continued. He watched Diad's reaction to her physical attractiveness. "This young woman is a servant for the berserker. She and the high priest have been lovers since he came here."

Diad smiled in mild amusement and asked her, "Is this true?"

Tene bowed her head, then meekly replied, "Yes m'Lord."

"Yet there is more Sire." He confronted Tene. "Tell the King your latest news."

As Tene stood there silently, her shoulders sagged. She struggled to answer.

"Well?" The king demanded.

After a moment more of indecision, she softly answered, "I'm pregnant."

"You're what? Speak up child. You're what?"

"Pregnant," Cattwg loudly answered for her. "The woman is pregnant. But there's more, much more. Tell them how you got pregnant without a naming stone, without a sacrificial roan." There was a subtle murmur of incredulity as Cattwg awaited her response.

"Well?" King Diad was now curious. "Answer child. Is what this priest says true? You claim that you became pregnant without a naming stone?"

"Yes," she sighed quietly, refusing to look up.

"That's impossible!" The king plopped back, his hands firmly holding the arms of the throne. "Are you mocking us girl? What you claim is impossible." He focused back to Cattwg. "So, what is it that you are claiming here, priest?"

"M'Lord, there is still another point."

"Well out with it man," Diad barked. "What else is there to know?"

"M'Lord, despite the young lady's attempt at convincing us of immaculate conception, we went to her own naming chamber. Tell me young lady," he demanded sanctimoniously, "when was the last time your naming chamber was used?"

Tene remained silent.

"What? Have you forgotten already? The last time it was used was when you were born. Isn't that right?"

"Yes." Her response was barely audible.

"What?"

"Yes," she replied louder.

"Yet when we went there yesterday, there was blood all over your room. Your naming stone was clean, but we did find these," he reached for a small bag from another priest and carefully, yet deliberately, spilled the contents on the floor in front of the king. "These are the broken shards of Father Lucan's naming stone." He selected a long sliver of stone and held it up. "The blood is not roan's blood." He inhaled slowly. "It is human blood. It is Lucan's blood."

The room erupted. Shouts of 'murderer' and 'harlot' rose above the din. Diad sat momentarily stunned until he realized he needed to regain control.

"Silence!" he roared, "silence!" The room slowly settled down. "Are you accusing the high priest of murder?" He confronted Cattwg.

"Yes Sire. That is exactly what I am accusing him of." Cattwg exuded arrogant confidence. "I accuse the high priest of consorting with his mistress to kill Father Lucan and use his blood in order to produce a child."

"But why would I do that." Duncan cried above the din. "To what benefit would killing Lucan do me? Why not just use a sacrificial roan and produce a baby that way?"

"Because you needed Lucan's essence in order to pass the high priest heritage."

"But why kill him? Why not simply ask him to help?"

Cattwg shook his head in condescension. "You know nothing of us Wizard. You come here assuming some sort of right to our laws and our land, yet you know nothing. It was impossible for Lucan to help you," he paused, "because he was celibate." He turned and announced to the entire crowd, "Lucan couldn't have fathered a child because he was celibate. Remember? He had taken the vow of celibacy when he was a teenager. Everyone knew that – except for this one who calls himself the high priest." He turned back to face Duncan. "You forget who you are, Wizard. And you forget who we are."

Cattwg walked over to the side of the throne. "Sire, it is obvious that this one who calls himself Duncan, has murdered Father Lucan. I ask that the laws of the land of Gambria be applied to both him and his consort."

Duncan stood there immobile, disbelief permeating his soul. His hand tightly held Tene's hand. He could feel her slight trembling. He searched for a way out, but felt more and more helpless as he realized that not only was he no longer going to be the high priest, there was a good chance that both he and Tene would be put to death. And so he stood there, waiting for the next shoe to fall.

"Do you have anything to say?" King Diad stared at Duncan.

"What can I say that would have you believe otherwise? You are wrong. Yet if your justice is so blind to condemn me, then so be it. But let this innocent woman go free."

"Then you admit your guilt?" Cattwg eagerly demanded.

"I do no such thing," Duncan snapped. "You accuse me of murder, yet have no body. There is blood on a robe, a robe supposedly belonging to Father Lucan. Yet how do you know it is Father Lucan's blood and not another's?"

Cattwg was momentarily caught off guard.

"Is not the woman with you pregnant?" A voice called out from the group. Cattwg relaxed when he saw Garbhan move forward.

"Yes she is pregnant." Duncan affirmed.

"Did you use a naming stone and a roan?" The question was specific, direct.

Duncan thought quickly, but knew no escape. If he lied, it would implicate Tene. "No, we used neither."

Garbhan shrugged and spread his hands. "While myths of immaculate conception are fun for fairy tales, they have no reality in Gambria. All evidence seems to point to only one thing... murder."

The low murmuring began again as Diad pondered the step. "We have much to consider here. I will decide shortly. Until I do, high priest, you are confined to your present chambers. This woman is likewise confined to the berserker's care for now." He looked over the group and was satisfied. "Well, there it is. Take them away."

As they turned to leave, Duncan squeezed Tene's hand and whispered, "It's not over yet." He turned to face the king. "Sire, if I recall correctly, Gambri law states that the believer shall have the right to be judged according to the prescripts of the law applied without regard to position or privilege. Neither shall the accused be denied counsel nor access to such counsel, as maybe deemed appropriate and essential. No believer shall be summarily punished without due recourse, except upon conviction of such egregious transgressions as warrant imposition of immediate penalty, and these only in time of national peril. As Father Cattwg has accused me of an egregious crime, I demand the right of both trial and council."

Silence fell upon the room as his accusers suddenly realized they might have just been out maneuvered. One of the priests spoke up.

"He is right m'Lord."

Cattwg glared at the man, making mental note of his transgression. "Yes, yes, we know all that. Nobody questions that." Asserting his new found authority, he pointed at the transgressor. "You. The King has given a command. See to it."

As the priest hurried out, Cattwg moved to stand at the left of the king's chair. Folding his arms in contemptuous satisfaction as he watched Duncan's smug cockiness evaporate, he mused that this just might be the second best day of his life. The first was yet to come.

Coming Fall 2014

Wolf 359:
Queen to Play

Volume 2 of the Wolf 359 Saga

Caught between a jealous king and a prelate angry at being denied the High Priesthood, Duncan is condemned to die in the wastelands in the hope that the desert sands eradicate any memory of the former wizard. His pregnant lover at his side, Duncan faces his greatest challenge, and must now trust his knowledge and luck if he is to save their lives. Left to fend for herself, Alexis is suddenly caught up in the maelstrom of power struggles as the king's own brother assembles his armies to take the throne.